# THE DECAMERON

# THE
# DECAMERON
## OF
# GIOVANNI
# BOCCACCIO

TRANSLATED
FROM THE ITALIAN
BY FRANCES WINWAR

THE MODERN LIBRARY *New York*

*Random House* IS THE PUBLISHER OF *The Modern Library*

BENNETT A. CERF · DONALD S. KLOPFER · ROBERT K. HAAS

Manufactured in the United States of America

by H. Wolff, New York

*

# TRANSLATOR'S NOTE

TRANSLATIONS OF WORKS WHICH, LIKE "THE DECAMERON," ARE apt to be associated in the vulgar mind with a certain hint of the not quite proper, suffer alike from the sin of omission as of commission. Omission, by arbitrarily excising what might give offense to Boccaccio's own "virtuous, sainted spinsters," robs Peter, the author, but does not pay Paul, the reader. Commission, on the other hand, by covert implication and elaborate euphemism defames the one, by making a vice of what was only robust fun, and frustrates the other by leaving him mentally prurient, whereas he would have been the healthier for an honest laugh. *Turpiloquium,* in the sense of common indecency, does not exist in Boccaccio, and his delightful rogueries, quaint conceits and penetrating allegories need not even his dictum—that a corrupt mind has never given any word a pure meaning—to defend them from the unhealthily hypocritical.

The aim of the present translator has been neither to omit nor to commit, but to reproduce in our common, understandable idiom the hundred tales as they are, through their kaleidoscopic shiftings, from rollicking, every-day fun to high, pure morality—for as Boccaccio's Florentines were great fun-makers, livers and lovers, they were also great moralists. Everything, therefore, has been given in this translation, nothing has been omitted, and nothing added that was not implicit. Where a literal rendering gives the author's intent, literal translation is employed. Where, for the understanding of some delicious roguery, the original *double entente* may be obtained only by an imaginative transliteration, as in the word *priemere* (Day I: Story 4), instead of the dead *press,* or the figurative *mortify,* the synonymous *lie heavily* is given, thereby making a witty tale hang where, in previous translations, no tale hung before.

Again, lifeless renderings of words no longer in dictionaries are eschewed by consulting the ever-living and ever-current book of common speech. There is the word *galle,* for instance (Day VIII: Story 6), which one translator renders *boluses* and another, faithfully following the wrong cue, *pills.* Boccaccio describes these boluses or pills as *belle galle*—and where, except perhaps in a catalogue of pharmacopeia, were such medicinal treats ever qualified as fine, or delicious? Again, these ginger-boluses are bought by the pound, to be distributed, with wine, to a group of men. Even in those days of Gargantuan gullets, it would have been a generous dose to buy a pound of pills at the *speziale's,* the druggist's, or spice-dealer's. It was this gentleman's calling that led the former translators astray, as though then, as well as now, one could not get at the *speziale's, belle galle,* which would not be pills. In a recent visit to Florence, this translator also went to a *speziale's* and also bought delicious *gallette,* but they were nothing more nor less than little cakes, with or without frosting, the culinary descendants, perhaps, of Boccaccio's own. Again, to convince the scholarly that Bruno performed his ordeal with cakes and not with boluses, which according to the story were not gulped down but masticated, the dictionary to-day has the word *galletta,* a biscuit. A long instance for such a trifling point, perhaps, but it is typical in little of what Boccaccio has suffered at large, and which the present translator has sought to remedy.

F. W.

# ✻

# CONTENTS

# 1

# THE FIRST DAY

# 2

## THE SECOND DAY

# 3

# THE THIRD DAY

All's Well...

Sonnet 144?

# 4

## THE FOURTH DAY

# 5

## THE FIFTH DAY

# 6

# THE SIXTH DAY

# 7

## THE SEVENTH DAY

# 8

## THE EIGHTH DAY

# 9

## THE NINTH DAY

# 10

## THE TENTH DAY

# THE DECAMERON

### * * *

## PREFACE TO THE

## LADIES

WHENEVER I REFLECT HOW FULL OF PITY YOU ARE BY NATURE, I accordingly realize what a heavy and irksome beginning this present work must have, reminding you as it immediately does of the recent plague, harmful alike to all who witnessed it or knew of it. But I do not want this to prevent you from reading further, or think you are expected to sigh and weep all the way through.

Let this gruesome beginning be like a steep and jagged mountain which wayfarers must surmount before they reach the pleasant, delightful plain beyond. Then the greater the difficulty of the climb and descent, the keener the pleasure in the end; for, as the extreme of happiness is never without its pain, so is suffering ended by supervening joy. Following this brief tedium—I say brief because it will be over in a few pages—will come the sweetness and delight I promised you before, which perhaps you might not have expected from such a beginning if I had not prepared you beforehand.

Indeed, had I been able to lead you to my purpose by a less rugged path than this, I should willingly have done so, but since I could not have shown you the source of what follows without this reference to the past, I am constrained by necessity to write it.

In the year of Our Lord 1348 the deadly plague broke out in the great city of Florence, most beautiful of Italian cities. Whether through the operation of the heavenly bodies or because of our own iniquities which the just wrath of God sought to correct, the plague had arisen in the East some years before, causing the death of countless human beings. It spread without stop from one place to another, until, unfortunately, it swept over the West. Neither knowledge nor human foresight availed against it, though the city was cleansed of much filth by chosen officers in charge and sick persons were forbidden to enter it, while advice was broadcast for the preservation of health. Nor did humble supplications serve. Not once but many times they were ordained in the form of processions and other ways for the propitiation of God by the faithful, but, in spite of everything, toward the spring of the year the plague began to show its ravages in a way short of miraculous.

It did not manifest itself as in the East, where if a man bled at the nose he had certain warning of inevitable death. At the onset of the disease both men and women were afflicted by a sort of swelling in the groin or under the armpits which sometimes attained the size of a common apple or egg. Some of these swellings were larger and some smaller, and all were commonly called boils. From these two starting points the boils began in a little while to spread and appear generally all over the body. Afterwards, the manifestation of the disease changed into black or livid spots on the arms, thighs and the whole person. In many these blotches were large and far apart, in others small and closely clustered. Like the boils, which had been and continued to be a certain indication of coming death, these blotches had the same meaning for everyone on whom they appeared.

Neither the advice of physicians nor the virtue of any medicine seemed to help or avail in the cure of these diseases. Indeed, whether the nature of the malady did not suffer it, or whether the ignorance of the physicians could not determine the source and therefore could take no preventive measures against it, the fact was that not only did few recover, but on the contrary almost everyone died within three days of the appearance of the signs—some sooner, some later, and the majority without fever or other ill. Moreover, besides the qualified medical men, a vast number of quacks, both men and women, who had never studied medicine, joined the ranks and practiced cures. The virulence of the plague was all the greater in that it was communicated by the sick to the well by contact, not unlike fire when dry or fatty things are brought near it. But the evil was still worse. Not only did conversation and familiarity with the diseased spread the malady and even cause death, but the mere touch of the clothes or any other object the sick had touched or used, seemed to spread the pestilence.

What I am going to relate is indeed a strange thing to hear —a thing that I should hardly have dared believe and much less write about, though I had heard it from a trustworthy witness, had I not seen it with my own eyes, and in the presence of many others. So active, I say, was the virulence of the plague in communicating itself from one person to another, that not only did it affect human beings, but, what is more strange, it very often proceeded in an extraordinary way. If an article belonging to one sick of the plague or who had died of it was touched by an animal outside of the human species, the creature was not only infected, but in a very short time it died of the disease—a fact which among others I observed one day with my own eyes, as I said before. The rags of a poor fellow who had died of the plague, had been thrown into the public street. Two hogs came across them and, according to their habit, first they went for them with their snouts and then, taking them in their teeth, began shaking them about their jaws. A little while later, after rolling round and round as though they had swallowed poison, both of them fell down dead upon the rags they had found to their misfortune.

Because of such happenings and many others of a like sort, various fears and superstitions arose among the survivors, almost all of which tended toward one end—to flee from the sick and whatever had belonged to them. In this way each man thought to be safeguarding his own health. Some among them were of the opinion that by living temperately and guarding against excess of all kinds, they could do much toward avoiding the danger; and forming a band they lived away from the rest of the world. Gathering in those houses where no one had been ill and living was more comfortable, they shut themselves in. They ate moderately of the best that could be had and drank excellent wines, avoiding all luxuriousness. With music and whatever other delights they could have, they lived together in this fashion, allowing no one to speak to them and avoiding news either of death or sickness from the outer world.

Others, arriving at a contrary conclusion, held that plenty of drinking and enjoyment, singing and free living and the gratification of the appetite in every possible way, letting the devil take the hindmost, was the best preventative of such a malady; and as far as they could, they suited the action to the word. Day and night they went from one tavern to another drinking and carousing unrestrainedly. At the least inkling of something that suited them, they ran wild in other people's houses, and there was no one to prevent them, for everyone had abandoned all responsibility for his belongings as well as for himself, considering his days numbered. Consequently most of the houses had become common property and strangers would make use of them at will whenever they came upon them even as the rightful owners might have done. Following this uncharitable way of thinking, they did their best to run away from the infected.

Meanwhile, in the midst of the affliction and misery that had befallen the city, even the reverend authority of divine and human law had almost crumbled and fallen into decay, for its ministers and executors, like other men, had either died or sickened, or had been left so entirely without assistants that they were unable to attend to their duties. As a result everyone had leave to do as he saw fit.

Many others followed a middle course, neither restricting themselves in their diet like the first, nor giving themselves free rein in lewdness and debauchery like the second, but using everything to sufficience, according to their appetites. They did not shut themselves in, but went about, some carrying flowers in their hands, some fragrant herbs, and others divers kinds of spices which they frequently smelled, thinking it good to comfort the brain with such odors, especially since the air was oppressive and full of the stench of corruption, sickness and medicines.

Still others, of a pitiless though perhaps more prudent frame of mind, maintained that no remedy against plagues was better than to leave them miles behind. Men and women without number, encouraged by this way of thinking and caring for nobody but themselves, abandoned the city, their houses and estates, their own flesh and blood even, and their effects, in search of a country place—it made no difference whether it were their own or their neighbor's. It was as if God's wrath in seeking to punish the iniquity of men by means of the plague could not find them out wherever they were, but limited itself to doom only those who happened to be found within the walls of the city. They reasoned as though its last hour had struck, and therefore no one ought to be there.

Although the members of these different factions did not all perish, neither did they all escape. On the contrary, many in each group sickened everywhere, and since they themselves had set the example to those who had been spared, they were abandoned to their lot and perished altogether.

Let alone the fact that one man shunned the other and that nobody had any thought for his neighbor; even relatives visited their folks little or never, and when they did, they communicated from a distance. The calamity had instilled such horror into the hearts of men and women that brother abandoned brother, uncles, sisters and wives left their dear ones to perish and, what is more serious and almost incredible, parents avoided visiting or nursing their very children, as though these were not their own flesh.

As a result, the only help that remained to the many men and women who sickened was either the mercy of friends, who were rare, or the covetousness of servants who agreed to nurse them at the prospect of ridiculously exorbitant wages. Even at that, however, these servants were scarce and of the run of coarse-grained men and women, unused ,to such services and whose chief duty was perhaps to reach the patients whatever they called for, or to watch them die. Often their occupation brought them to perdition, together with their profits. From this neglect of the sick by neighbors, relatives and friends, and from the scarcity of servants, an almost unprecedented custom arose. Once sick, no woman, however charming, beautiful or well-born, hesitated to engage a man in her service, no matter whether he was young or old, high-born or low, or to reveal any part of her naked body to him if the disease required it, as if he had been of her own sex—all of which later resulted in immodesty in those who were cured. It followed also that many who might perhaps have lived if they had been tended, perished of this neglect. So great was the multitude of those who died in the city night and day, what with lack of proper care and the virulence of the plague, that it was terrible to hear of, and worse still to see. Out of sheer necessity, therefore, quite different customs arose among the survivors from the original laws of the townspeople.

It used to be common, as it is still, for women, friends and neighbors of a dead man, to gather in his house and mourn there with his people, while his men friends and many other citizens collected with his nearest of kin outside the door. Then came the clergy, according to the standing of the departed, and with funereal pomp of tapers and singing he was carried on the shoulders of his peers to the church he had elected before death. Now, as the plague gained in violence, these customs were either modified or laid aside altogether, and new ones were instituted in their place, so that, far from dying among a crowd of women mourners, many passed away without the benefit of a single witness. Indeed, few were those who received the piteous wails and bitter tears of friends and relatives, for often, instead of mourning, laughter, jest and carousal accompanied the dead—usages which even naturally compassionate women had learned to perfection for their health's sake. It was a rare occurrence for a corpse to be followed to church by more than ten or twelve mourners—not the usual respectable citizens, but a class of vulgar grave-diggers who called themselves "sextons" and did these services for a price. They crept under the bier and shouldered it, and then with hasty steps rushed it, not to the church the deceased had designated before death, but oftener than not to the nearest one. Usually they walked behind five or six members of the clergy, with little light and sometimes with none at all. Then, with the help of these "sextons" the priests, without exhausting themselves with too long or too solemn a service, lowered the dead into the first unoccupied grave they came across.

More wretched still were the circumstances of the common people and, for a great part, of the middle class, for, confined to their homes either by hope of safety or by poverty, and restricted to their own sections, they fell sick daily by thousands. There, devoid of help or care, they died almost without redemption. A great many breathed their last in the public streets, day and night; a large number perished in their homes, and it was only by the stench of their decaying bodies that they proclaimed their death to their neighbors. Everywhere the city was teeming with corpses. A general course was now adopted by the people, more out of fear of contagion than of any charity they felt toward the dead. Alone, or with the assistance of whatever bearers they could muster, they would drag the corpses out of their homes and pile them in front of the doors, where often, of a morning, countless bodies might be seen. Biers were sent for. When none was to be had, the dead were laid upon ordinary boards, two or three at once. It was not infrequent to see a single bier carrying husband and wife, two or three brothers, father and son, and others besides.

Times without number when a couple of priests were walking, carrying a cross before a corpse, they were soon followed by two or three sets of porters with their respective biers. And, where the holy men had thought to be burying one man, they found seven or eight on their hands, sometimes more. Nor were these dead shown the respect of candles, tears or mourners. Death had become so common that no more attention was given to human lives than would be given to goats brought to slaughter nowadays. It clearly proved that the wisdom which a natural course of events, with its trivial and infrequent trials, had not been able to impress upon men of understanding —that is, to bear evil patiently—had become an open book to the most unthinking by the very magnitude of their miseries, causing them to expect and accept them for what they were worth.

So many bodies were brought to the churches every day that the consecrated ground did not suffice to hold them, particularly according to the ancient custom of giving each corpse its individual place. Huge trenches were dug in the crowded churchyards and the new dead were piled in them, layer upon layer, like merchandise in the hold of a ship. A little earth covered the corpses of each row, and the procedure continued until the trench was filled to the top.

But I shall not linger over the details of our city's past afflictions, for while such bitter times were upon it, the country round about was not spared. In the castles which were as miniature cities compared to the large towns, through the scattered hamlets and in the fields the wretched, poverty-stricken peasants and their families died helpless and untended. On the wayside, in the tilled fields, about their houses, indifferently by day or night they fell dead, more like animals than human beings; whereupon those who remained, growing lax in their habits like the city folk, and careless of their duties, lived as though every day were their last. Perversely they did their best, not to help improve the products of their beasts and of the soil over which they had sweated, but to consume whatever was within their reach. The animals, oxen, asses, sheep, goats, pigs, fowls—all of them ran wild. The very dogs, known for their faithfulness, were driven from their houses, and went straying as they pleased through the fields, where the neglected wheat crop drooped, ungarnered and uncut. Sometimes the undisciplined beasts went back to their homes at night like rational creatures, for they had had enough food all day, and returned well-satisfied.

To go back to the city—what more can be said? Such was the cruelty of heaven and to a great degree of man, that between March and the following July it is estimated more than a hundred thousand human beings lost their lives within the walls of Florence, what with the ravages attendant on the plague and the barbarity of the survivors toward the sick. Who would have thought before the plague that the city had held so many inhabitants?

What vast palaces, what beautiful houses and noble dwellings once full of lords and ladies remained deserted to the least servant! Alas! How many memorable families, how many vast heritages, how many notable fortunes were left without a lawful heir! What brave men and lovely ladies, what charming youths whom Galen himself and Hippocrates and Aesculapius would have pronounced in the soundest health dined in the morning with their relatives, only to sup that very night with their dead in the other world!

But I am weary of dwelling on such miseries. . . . Let me pass over as many of them as I can. Now, while our city was in the throes of this tragedy, and nearly empty of inhabitants, it chanced that seven young women were gathered in the venerable church of Santa Maria Novella, as I have been informed by trustworthy persons. It was on a Tuesday morning, when there was hardly anyone else present. They were attending the divine service in deep mourning, the proper garb for such unfortunate times, and one could see they were bound by ties of friendship, acquaintance and blood. Not one of them had passed her twenty-eighth year, and the youngest was hardly less than eighteen years old. Each was of noble birth, and wise, lovely of body, well-mannered and of honest charm.

I would willingly give the true names of these ladies, if I were not prevented by a just scruple—simply that I should not want a single one of them to be offended in the future by the things that follow, which they are said to have told and listened to. Nowadays the laws of pleasure are somewhat more strict than they used to be, for the reasons I have already shown, though at the time I speak of they were lax not only for persons of their years but for their elders. Besides, I am not anxious to give the envious occasion for running down the virtue of these worthy ladies by insinuation, knowing as I do how eager such creatures are to snap at every praiseworthy life. Nevertheless, to avoid confusing what they are going to say and the better to enable you to understand, I shall call each one by a name that will more or less describe her qualities. The first and the eldest, we shall name Pampinea, the second Fiammetta, the third Filomena and Emilia the fourth; then the fifth we shall call Lauretta, Neifile the sixth, and the last Elisa, not without good reason.

Now these young women, who had met rather by chance than by appointment in a corner of the church, sat down in a circle and, heaving frequent sighs, ceased their devotions and began discussing the times in which they lived. After a while, when the others were silent, Pampinea spoke.

"Dear girls," she said, "you must have heard often enough, as well as I, that a person who uses his just rights legitimately injures nobody. It is the natural right of everyone born to help, preserve and defend his life as best he can. In fact, this is taken so much for granted that it is sometimes done at the expense of another's innocent blood. Now if this is conceded by laws that are supposed to look to the welfare and safety of every mortal, how much more justified we ought to be, or others like us, in taking every possible means to preserve our lives—of course, without harming others! Whenever I consider what we did this morning, and many mornings past, and call to mind the things that form the subject of our conversation, I am convinced that each one of us is in mortal terror for herself. I'm sure all of you feel the same way. And it's no great wonder! But I certainly *do* wonder that, clever though we are, we take no measures to prevent what we have so much reason to dread.

"We all look, for all I know, as though we were waiting to see just how many bodies are brought in for burial. Or are we keeping tab on these poor friars whose chapter has almost dwindled to nothing? Or listening to find out whether they chant their offices at the proper hours? Are we perhaps making a show of our multiple afflictions by the clothes we wear, for the benefit of the chance passer-by? Whenever we leave this place we see nothing but corpses or the bodies of sick persons being dragged about. Or we see evil-doers whom the law has banished, swarming the place, indulging in crime as if they laughed at authority—for do you suppose they do not realize that those who enforced the laws are either sick or dead? Then there are the dregs of the city population, those creatures who call themselves *sextons*. Battening on our blood they mock our sorrows, ramp everywhere and overrun the streets, throwing up our griefs to us with indecent song. We hear nothing but *So-and-So is dead* and *So-and-So is about to die*. If there were any left to weep, we'd hear nothing but wailing everywhere.

"When we return to our homes—I don't know whether it is the same with you as with me—what do we see? Of my large household I, for one, find not a soul at home, only my servant, and I am terrified! I feel every hair of my body standing on end! No matter where I go, wherever I may be about the house, the shades of the dead are always before my eyes, not with the same faces they once had, but ghastly, horrible! God only knows how they came to look that way . . . and I am scared out of my wits!

"Consequently, whether at home or not, I am uneasy, for I do not think there is a single person left besides us, who has strength enough to go about. Yet even if there are others remaining, for there must be, as I have been told, they have lost all sense of right and wrong. Let their appetites prick them and they give in to them, whether alone or in company, by day or night, it makes no difference. And it's not only of the common run of folk that this holds true. Even monks and nuns shut up in monasteries break the laws of obedience, thinking what's sauce for the goose is also sauce for the gander, and give themselves up to all kinds of debauchery like the worst of them, fancying the while they're escaping from peril!

"Now if things are as they are—and you can surely see for yourselves—what are we doing here? What are we waiting for? Why are we moping? Why are we less solicitous for our welfare than the rest of the people? Do we hold ourselves more cheap than everybody else? Or do we imagine our lives are linked to our bodies by a stronger chain, so that we don't have to worry that anything will hurt them? We are mistaken. We deceive ourselves. What fools we are if we believe all that! If we'd only take the trouble to think of the many young men and women who have been carried off by this cruel plague, we'd need no other proof!

"I don't know whether you're of the same opinion, but for my part I think it would be a mighty good thing if we all left this town, that through stubbornness or nonchalance we may not fall into a mess we could avoid if we cared. Of course we'd shun the bad example of others like death itself. We would go quietly to our own country places, which all of us have a-plenty and there, without in the least overstepping reasonable restraint, we would take what innocent pleasure and enjoyment we could find.

"There we'll hear the little birds sing, and see the green of the hills and the plains, and watch the fields full of wheat rising and falling like the waves of the sea. A thousand kinds of trees will rustle there, and the sky will reveal itself more open overhead. Even if it should frown it could not deny us its eternal beauty, far more pleasing to the eye than the desolate walls of our city! Besides, the air is more refreshing, and we would have plenty of everything we needed, with fewer worries to trouble us. It's true the peasants die there, as the townspeople do here, but the sorrows are less, for the houses and dwellers are fewer.

"On the other hand, here we abandon nobody, unless I'm mistaken. I might more truly say we are the forsaken ones, for our folks, whether dying or fleeing from death, have left us alone in this great suffering as if we were nothing to them. What could we be blamed for if we followed my advice? Nothing. But sorrow and trouble and even death, perhaps, might come upon us if we did not.

"So then, let's take our servants whenever you please, and let them follow us with whatever we need. We'll stay here to-day and there to-morrow, and get as much fun and enjoyment out of it as these evil times allow. Surely, I think it would be the best thing to do. Besides we'll be able to see what end heaven has in view in all this—unless death should intervene. To begin with, I want you to bear in mind that it is no more forbidden us to go away honorably, than it is to many other women to remain in dishonor."

When the rest of the ladies had heard Pampinea they not only approved of her advice but, eager to follow it, they had already entered into the details of carrying it through, as though the moment they got up they were to set out on their way. But Filomena, who was a very prudent young lady, said: "My friends, although Pampinea was right in all she said, it does not mean you should rush into things, as you seem to desire. Remember, we are all women, and none of us is so young that she doesn't know what foolish things we would do without the help of some man. By nature fickle, we are all stubborn, suspicious, cowardly and timorous, which fine qualities, I am sure, would cause us to break up our company sooner than we expected, and with little honor to ourselves, unless we had someone else to guide us. It wouldn't be a bad idea to provide ourselves before we begin."

"As a matter of fact," Elisa rejoined, "men are the betters of women, and seldom does anything we undertake succeed well without their help. But how can we get these men? We all know that most of our men-folk are dead, and those that have been spared are scattered far and wide with various groups, goodness only knows where, running away from the very thing we're trying to escape. It wouldn't be proper, on the other hand, to invite strangers. The only way to avoid trouble and scandal, then, if we want to look out for ourselves, is to decide upon some rule to follow, wherever we may wander, for rest or pleasure."

While the women were debating among themselves three young men entered the church, the youngest of whom was about twenty-five. They were brisk lads, the fire of whose love neither evil times, the loss of friends and kin nor fear for themselves had been able to quench, much less to cool. The first of them was called Pamfilo, the second Filostrato, and the last Dioneo—all three very agreeable and well-bred gentlemen. As it was, they had come to look for their mistresses, their only source of cheer in these troublous times. It happened that the three women they were seeking were among the seven gathred there, and of the others some were related to either one or another of them.

No sooner had they espied the ladies than they themselves were seen, and Pampinea began, smiling: "Fortune certainly is favorable to our undertaking, for here she has sent us these fine young gentlemen, who would gladly serve and guide us if we only took the trouble to ask them."

But Neifile exclaimed, blushing, for she was the mistress of one of the youths: "For goodness' sake, Pampinea, guard your tongue! I know nothing but good could be said of any one of them, and I think them capable of undertaking a far greater responsibility than this. Not only that, but they could certainly be trusted in the company of far lovelier gentlewomen than we, and still retain their honor. But you see, they're in love with some of us here, and I'm afraid that, without any fault of ours or theirs, for that matter, we might stir up scandal if we took them with us."

"That doesn't mean a thing," said Filomena. "If I live in honesty and there's nothing to bother my conscience, let people say what they will. God and truth will take up arms for me. If only those young men were willing to join us we might really say with Pampinea that Fortune favors us."

Hearing the decisiveness of her tone the other women not only did not protest, but agreed to call the youths and inform them of what was required of them in the proposed expedition. Pampinea, who was related to one of them, got up and walked toward the three gentlemen, who were standing there

observing the women. Cheerfully she greeted them, told them
her errand and entreated them on behalf of her friends to
keep them company in pure fraternal friendship. At first the
men thought she was making fun of them, but when they saw
she was in earnest they answered gaily that they were ready, and
gave orders then and there for the necessary preparations.

Their servants they dispatched in advance to the place they
intended visiting and bade them make everything ready for
their arrival. Toward daybreak the following morning, that is,
Wednesday, they left the city and started on their way, the
women with a number of their servants and the three men with
three of their domestics. They had hardly left the city two short
miles behind when they came to the place they had set out for.

It was a charming spot on a little hill, removed on every side
from the roads, full of different shrubs and plants, and lush with
green foliage that was a delight to the eye. On the summit
there rose a palace with a lovely spacious court in its midst,
and halls, parlors and chambers, each perfect in itself and decorated with gay and costly paintings. Lawns surrounded it, and
marvelous gardens; there were wells of cool water and vaults of
rare wines, more suitable to carousers than to sober and virtuous ladies. The whole place had been swept clean; the beds
were made in the chambers, and everywhere, to their delight,
the happy group found the season's wealth of flowers and green
rushes strewn about.

They sat down at the first opportunity and Dioneo, who was
the handsomest youth of the three, and full of fun, began:
"Ladies, it was your cleverness rather than our prevision that
led us here. I don't know what you intend doing with your
worries . . . I, for one, left them inside the city gate the moment I quit it to follow you. Now either you make up your
minds to have a good time and laugh and sing with me—of
course, in all propriety—or you give me leave to go back to my
cares and remain in the city of sorrow."

Pampinea, as carefree as though she herself had checked all
her troubles, lightly answered him: "Very well said, Dioneo!
We're here to have a jolly good time, for no other reason
prompted us to flee our sorrows. But, since extremes can't last
very long, I who started the argument which brought this fine
band together, should like to have us continue in our joy.
Therefore I think it necessary for us to choose someone whom
we must honor and obey as leader, and whose every thought

must be to keep us entertained. But that all of us may feel the
weight of responsibility as well as the fun of leadership, I propose that each should be granted the burden and the honor for a
day. And that there may be no jealousy and nobody be overlooked, the leader must be chosen in turn from among the
men and the women. Let the first be elected by us all, and as
for the others, let them be chosen toward evening by whichever
one has had the leadership for the day, when he may select this
man or that woman as he pleases. Then each new ruler will
dictate where or how we are to pass our time, according to his
pleasure, all through the period of his sovereignty."

Pampinea's words met with great favor, and unanimously
she was elected queen for the first day. Filomena, running to a
laurel tree whose leaves she had often heard spoken of as
worthy of honor and as conferring honor upon anyone wearing
them, broke off some branches and twined a beautiful wreath.
This she placed upon Pampinea's head, and from that day on,
while their band lasted, it became the symbol of royal office
and leadership.

Pampinea, now queen, requested them all to be silent and,
calling together the servants of the three youths and the maids,
who were four in number, she said: "To set you the first example by which our group may ever prosper and continue
happy, orderly and virtuous as long as we see fit, I appoint first
of all Parmeno, Dioneo's servant, to be my steward. To him I
commit the care and management of our family in everything
that concerns the house and banquet-hall. Sirisco, Pamfilo's servant, I choose to be our treasurer and purveyor, under the direction of Parmeno. Tindaro will be in Filostrato's and the other
two gentlemen's employ, taking care of their rooms whenever
the others are prevented by different business. My maid Misia,
and Licisca, Filomena's, will remain in the kitchen and diligently prepare whatever meals Parmeno orders. Lauretta's Chi-
mera and Fiammetta's maid Stratilia I delegate to the care of
the women's rooms and the keeping of the places where we
shall be. I further request and command each and every one of
you, at the cost of my friendship, to beware of bringing any but
good news from the outside world, no matter where you roam,
or what you may hear and see."

These orders summarily given and approved, she rose briskly
to her feet. "Here are gardens," she said. "Here are lawns and
many other pleasant places where you may go wandering to

your hearts' content. By three o'clock I want you all back here, that we may dine when the day is cooler."

The gay company was now at liberty, whereupon the young men and women went walking easily in the garden, chatting of pleasant things, weaving themselves garlands of different leaves and singing love-ditties. When they had whiled away the time the queen had designated, they returned to the palace, where they found that Parmeno had made a skilful beginning at his office. The tables in one of the lower halls were laid with snow-white cloths and glasses that shone like silver, and blossoms of the broom were scattered everywhere. At the queen's pleasure they washed their hands and then took their places according to Parmeno's arrangement.

Dishes exquisitely concocted were brought, and delicate wines, and the three serving men waited quietly at the tables. Cheer rose high, inspired by meat and drink and the merry-making and pleasant talk that seasoned them. Finally the tables were cleared. All of them, both men and women, were graceful dancers, and some excelled in playing and singing. Knowing this, the queen commanded the instruments to be brought and at her bidding Dioneo took a lute and Fiammetta a viol. Softly, and in unison, they struck up a dance-measure. Meanwhile the servants were sent away to their meal in the kitchen, and the queen, with the rest of the women and the two youths, commenced a round. With slow, graceful steps the dancing was begun, and no sooner did it come to a close than charming, lightsome ditties were gaily sung. So for a long time they amused themselves, until the queen decided it was time to retire and dismissed them all. The three young men withdrew to their chambers, removed from those of the women. The beds were beautifully decked, and many flowers were strewn about as in the hall. Undressing, they went to sleep; and the women in their apartments followed suit.

The morning hour had hardly struck when the queen rose and bade the rest follow her example, the three men as well as the women, for she maintained it was injurious to the health to sleep late into the day. They went to a meadow, full of tall, green grass. There the sun could not penetrate, and a delicious little breeze stirred. Following the queen's wish they sat down in a circle upon the green, and she addressed them.

"As you see," she said, "the sun is high, and the heat intense, and we hear nothing but the cricket in the olive-trees. It would be utter foolishness to go anywhere at this time. Here it is cool and pleasant, and see, we are provided with tables and chess-boards for our amusement if we should be so minded. But if you want my opinion, I'd rather we did not play—for in chess the mind of one of the players must necessarily be uneasy about the moves, which is no fun, either for the other player or for those who look on. Let us rather tell stories to while away these sultry hours of the day, for when one tells a story the whole company derives pleasure listening. You'll hardly have finished telling your stories when the sun will have gone down and the hottest part of the day be over. Then we'll be free to go wherever we choose for our diversion. If you're pleased with my idea—for mind, I'm here to follow your pleasure—let's begin. If not—well, let each one do as he pleases until evening."

Everyone, however, acclaimed the idea of telling stories.

"Well, then," said the queen, "since this suits you, I'll leave each one free this first day to choose whatever subject he pleases."

She turned to Pamfilo, who was seated on her right, and cheerfully asked him to begin the story-telling with some tale of his. They listened to him, as he readily complied with the queen's bidding.

# 1

# THE FIRST DAY

\*

## THE FIRST STORY

*Master Ciappelletto dupes a holy friar with a trumped up confession and dies; and though he had been a very wicked man in life,*
*, in death he was deemed a saint and called Saint Ciappelletto.*

IT IS ONLY PROPER, DEAREST LADIES, THAT WHATEVER WE DO should be rooted in the great and holy name of Him who is the Creator of all things. Therefore, since I must be the first in our story-telling, I shall start with one of His wonders, so that once heard we may rest our faith in Him, the Immutable— may His name be forever praised!

It is evident that, as all worldly things are transient and mortal, they are also replete with trouble, pain and toil within and without, and subject to those infinite dangers which both enmesh and form part of our being and which we could neither endure nor ward off if God's special grace did not lend us strength and foresight. But we must not flatter ourselves that this grace descends upon us through any merit of our own, for it is motivated by His goodness and obtained for us by the intercession of those who were once mortal like ourselves but who have now become eternal with Him, and blessed, by following His commandments while alive. We, who are not bold enough to address our entreaties to the Mighty Presence, petition these saints instead for the things we need, knowing our advocates to be informed of our shortcomings by their own past experience. There is this besides. Though it sometimes happens that out of ignorance of true values we may choose as our intercessor before the Lord one who has been banished from the Presence to eternal exile—for what human sight can penetrate the mystery of the divine mind?—God, from whom nothing is hidden and who abounds in merciful liberality toward us, considers the innocence and not the ignorance of the suppliant. He disregards the graceless state of the banished saint and gives ear to those who entreat him, as though he were still blessed in His Presence . . . all of which will clearly appear from the story I wish to relate—I say clearly, according to man's poor judgment, not God's.

When Musciatto Franzesi had risen from the condition of a rich and prominent merchant to the rank of knight, he was obliged to go to Tuscany with Charles Lackland, brother to the king of France, at Pope Boniface's bidding. As often happens to men engaged in business, he found his affairs in a hopeless tangle somehow or other, and since he could not easily set them to rights in the short time he had at his disposal, he decided to entrust them to the hands of various persons. He found a way for every difficulty except in the matter of some loans he had made to certain Burgundians, and he could think of no one sufficiently capable to recover them. He had reason to worry, for he knew the Burgundians to be quarrelsome, mean, disloyal fellows, and no matter how he strove he could hit on nobody perverse enough to be a match for their wickedness. After long consideration he suddenly called to mind a certain Ciapperello da Prato who was a frequent visitor at his Paris home. He was a little fellow, very meticulous in his dress, whom the French used to call by the diminutive Ciappelletto, not knowing the meaning of Cepparello and taking it to be *chaplet* or *garland* in their vernacular. As Ciappelletto, therefore, he was known everywhere, and very few knew him by his true name.

Now this Ciappelletto was a very peculiar person. He was a notary by profession, and whenever one of the very few deeds he drew up was discovered to be other than false, he suffered deep humiliation. Counterfeit deeds, however, he would have issued to his heart's content, more willingly and without charge, than would anybody else for a considerable sum. He would

bear false witness with the greatest relish in the world whether
anyone asked him or not; and since at that time in France the
utmost faith was placed in oaths, he used to win crookedly whatever suits he was called upon to swear to on his honor. He was
inordinately fond of creating ill-feeling among friends and relatives, and went out of his way to stir up scandal among them;
then the greater the evil consequences, the more delighted
he was. Never would he refuse to take part in murders and
other horrible mischief—indeed, he always accepted such offers
with alacrity. Many a time he had been known to wound and
murder willingly with his own hands. He was a notorious
blasphemer of God and His saints, and had a temper that would
burst into fury at the slightest provocation. Never would he
enter a church, and with most abominable words he railed at
the holy sacraments as things to be despised. On the other hand
he was an assiduous and willing frequenter of taverns and other
indecent places. As for women, he was as lickerish of them as a
dog is of a stick, for he took greater pleasure in the opposite sex
than any other depraved rogue alive. He would have sacked and
robbed with the conscience of a pious man making an offering
to God, and he was so immoderate a glutton and a guzzler that
sometimes he fell as shamefully sick as a dog. He was a terrible
gambler besides, and a caster of trick dice . . . but why enlarge in so many words? In short, he was perhaps the worst
man ever born.

For a long time Musciatto's influence had stood Cepparello's
wickedness in good stead. More than once he had shielded him
from private persons he had gulled, and from the law as well,
which he was forever violating. However, no sooner did this
Cepparello come to the mind of Musciatto, who was fully acquainted with his mode of living, than he was convinced he
had found the one to cope with the Burgundians' viciousness,
so he had the man summoned.

"Ciappelletto," he said, "as you know, I am about to retire
from here altogether. But among other things I have some business with Burgundians, crafty rascals, and full of mischief. I
can't think of anyone better suited than yourself to get out of
them what belongs to me, especially since you're out of a job
at present. But I want you to understand you'll gain something
out of this, too, for I intend to give you what's coming to you
of what you recover, and earn you the favor of the court into
the bargain."

It did not take Ciappelletto very long to come to a decision. Indeed, finding himself unemployed and unprovided with the goods of the world and with the prospect, besides, of losing the man who had been his mainstay and support for so long a time, he was almost compelled to say he accepted. They soon came to an agreement. Ciappelletto received the procuration and letters of recommendation from the king, and Musciatto once gone, set out for Burgundy where he was almost unknown. There, contrary to his nature, he began with gentleness and benignity to do what he had to do toward the recovery of the loans, reserving the expedient of violence for the last.

In the meantime, he took lodging in the home of two brothers, Florentines, who used to lend money at interest. For Musciatto's sake they held him in great esteem, when suddenly he fell sick. The two brothers immediately sent for physicians and servants to care for him, and did all in their power to nurse him back to health, but every help was of no avail, for the scoundrel, an old man by now, had moreover burned his candle at both ends and was going from bad to worse. According to the doctors he was suffering from a mortal illness, which caused the brothers no little concern. One day, next to the room where Ciappelletto was lying ill, they began considering the state of affairs.

"What shall we do with the fellow?" said one to the other. "We have the worst of it with him here, for if we were to pack him out of our house while he is so sick, it would stir up reproach against us and adverse criticism for our small wisdom. What would people say, seeing that first we took him in and had him nursed carefully, and then, without his doing anything that could offend us, we suddenly turned him out, sick unto death besides? On the other hand he has been such a bad customer that he won't hear of confessing or taking any sacrament of the church, and if he should die unshriven no holy place would receive his body—he'd be thrown into a ditch like a dog. Then again, even if he did confess, his sins are so many and so dreadful that the result will be the same—there's neither friar nor priest who would or could absolve him. So dying unabsolved, again he'd be flung into a ditch. As it is, the people of this city are always speaking ill of us, what with the sort of business we carry on, which they consider scandalous, and what with their itch to rob us. If what we fear should happen they will raise a rumpus and shout, 'We'll not put up any longer

with these damned Lombard dogs—even the church refuses to
receive them!' On top of that, they'll run to our houses and
they'll not only plunder our goods but even take our lives. Either way we'll have the worst of it if this fellow dies."

Master Ciappelletto who, as we said, was lying near the place
where the two were talking things over, had a pretty sharp ear,
like most invalids, and could not help hearing what they said
of him. Sending for them, he spoke: "I don't want you to have
any doubt of my good intentions, nor do I want you to be
afraid of coming to harm through me. I heard what you were
saying, and I'm positive things would happen as you say if what
you discussed comes to pass. But the matter will have quite a
different issue, leave it to me. I've played so many dirty tricks
during my life on the Lord God that it'd be but a drop in the
bucket if I played Him another now that I'm about to die. Look
here, I'd like you to go about getting me a good and worthy
friar—the best and holiest you can find. Then leave the rest to
me and I'll settle your affairs and mine in such a way that all
will be well and you'll have every reason to be satisfied."

Although the two brothers had little faith in what he said,
they went to a monastery and asked for a wise and holy man
to take the last confession of a Lombard who was lying ill at
their house. An aged friar of good and sinless life was given
them. He was, moreover, learned in Scripture and a very venerable man, for whom all the city folks had very deep and special
reverence. The two brothers took him along.

Reaching the room where Ciappelletto was lying ill, the friar
sat down beside him, first comforting him with kindly words
and then asking him how long it was since he had last confessed.

"Father," answered Ciappelletto, who had not once gone to
confession, "it has always been my custom to confess at least
once a week, and sometimes much more often. It's true that
since I've been ill these last eight days I have not been able to
do my holy duty, such is the trouble my sickness has caused
me."

"My son," comforted the friar, "you have done well, may you
so continue in the future. I can see that I'll have an easy time
questioning and listening to you, considering you confess so
often."

"Ah, don't say that," said Ciappelletto, "don't say that, good
friar! I've never confessed so often or so frequently that I should

not make a general confession of all the sins I can remember, from the day I was born to the day I last confessed. Please, then, dear father, question me as particularly in everything as if I had never confessed before. And do not spare me because I am ill. I had much rather punish my body than out of half-heartedness cause the perdition of my soul which my Saviour redeemed with His own precious blood!"

These words were very gratifying to the holy man, who found in them the proof of a well-intentioned mind. Then, after he had lavished much praise on Ciappelletto for his habits, he began to ask whether he had ever sinned in lechery with any woman.

With a sigh Ciappelletto answered: "Ah, my father, I'm afraid to tell you the truth about this, for I might fall into the sin of vainglory."

"Speak in all security," encouraged the friar, "for truth, whether in confession or elsewhere, has never been the cause of sin."

"Well," said Ciappelletto, "since I have your assurance, I'll tell you. I'm still as much a virgin as the day I came out of my mother's body."

"May God bless you!" cried the friar. "How well you have done! And how much more deserving of praise you are, for if you had only wished, you could have had more liberty to do the contrary than we, or all others who are restrained by any rule."

After this he asked if he had ever offended God in the sin of gluttony. Again, with a deep sigh, Ciappelletto said that he had, and many times. For, besides the Lenten fasts that are held yearly by the faithful, he was accustomed to have only bread and water at least three days out of every seven, and he had drunk the water with such avidity and relish, especially on those occasions when he had been weary through prayer and pilgrimages, that no wine-bibber could have equalled him. Often he had even coveted those dainty vegetable salads that women prepare when they go to the country. While eating, too, he had had more enjoyment of it than one should feel who fasted out of devotion, as he did.

"My son," said the friar, "such sins are only natural and slight, and I would not have you burden your conscience with them more than is needful. No matter how holy the man, it often happens that after a long fast he finds pleasure in eating, and also in drinking, after toil."

"Oh, father!" cried Ciappelletto. "Don't tell me this to comfort me! You must know I am conscious that whatever is done in the service of God should be done with a pure and spotless soul. Whoever does otherwise is guilty of sin."

The friar was very much pleased. "I am very glad you believe that in your heart of hearts," he said, "and I also admire your clear and wholesome conscience. But tell me, have you ever been guilty of the sin of avarice, wanting more than your share or keeping what you should not have kept?"

Ciappelletto replied, "My father, I shouldn't want you to have strange notions because I happen to be in the house of these moneylenders. I have nothing to do with such business. Indeed, I came here to rebuke and punish them, and to rescue them from this abominable way of making money. I even think I might have succeeded if God had not visited me with sickness. You must know that my father left me in excellent circumstances, but most of my wealth I gave away after his death, in the service of God. Then, for my livelihood, and also to help Christ's poor, I became a merchant in a small way and hoped to make some profit. But I always went half and half on my gains with God's poor, using my share for my needs and giving them the other. So well has my Maker helped me in this, that I have always succeeded in bettering my condition."

"You have done well," said the friar. "But have you often fallen into wrath?"

"Oh," moaned Ciappelletto. "I must admit I have, very often. But who could help it, to see men doing improper things the livelong day, observing neither God's commandments, nor fearing His judgment? Many times in the course of a day I have wished myself rather dead, than alive to see young men seeking after vanity, cursing and swearing, going to the taverns and neglecting the churches, and sooner following the ways of the world than God's."

Then said the friar: "My son, yours is a righteous wrath, and for my part I could not find it in me to impose a penance on you. But tell me, did wrath, by any chance, ever impel you to commit murder, or speak ill to any one or do any other wicked deed?"

"Alas, sir," answered Ciappelletto, "and here I've been thinking you a godly man! How can you even speak such words? Why, even if I had had the tiniest little thought of doing any one of the things you mention, do you think I can believe God would have tolerated me so long? Such things only outlaws and wicked men could think of doing, and I have never had occasion to see one without saying, 'Go, may God convert you!' "

"Now tell me, my son," continued the friar, "may God bless you! Did you ever bear false witness, or speak ill of your neighbor, or help yourself to another's property against his will?"

"Never, sir! Yet . . . Yes . . . ," answered Ciappelletto. "I have been guilty of speaking ill. Once I had a neighbor who would do nothing but beat his wife for no good reason in the world, and to such an extent that I once spoke ill of him to the wife's relatives . . . I felt so sorry for the miserable little wretch whom he used to trounce as only God can tell you—and that, whenever he'd had too much of the bottle."

"You say you have been a merchant," said the friar. "Tell me, did you ever cheat anybody the way merchants do?"

"By my faith, sir, now I think of it, yes," said Ciappelletto, "but I can't tell you exactly except that a fellow once brought me some money he owed me for cloth I had sold him. I put the money into a chest without counting it, and a whole month later I found there were four farthings more than there should have been. So because I never saw the man again I gave them away in charity after I had kept them a year for him."

"That's a trifle," said the friar, "and you were right in doing what you did." Then he asked him many other questions, all of which Ciappelletto answered in the same vein. He was already proceeding to offer him absolution when Ciappelletto interrupted: "Sir, I have still a few other sins I have not confessed."

The friar asked him what they were and he said, "I remember that on a Saturday after dusk I made a servant of mine sweep the house, neglecting to observe the holy Sabbath as I should have."

"Oh, that is a little thing, my son!" the friar comforted.

"Not at all," answered Ciappelletto. "Don't say it is a little thing! The Sabbath is greatly to be honored, for on that day our Lord rose from death to life!"

"Well, now, have you been guilty of anything else?" asked the friar.

"Alas, sir, yes," answered Ciappelletto, "for once I spat unintentionally in the house of God."

The friar smiled and said, "That's nothing to worry about, my son. We, who are pious brothers—why, we spit in it all day long."

"And you do a villainous thing," reproved Ciappelletto. "No place should be kept cleaner than the holy temple, where we offer up sacrifice to God."

In short, Ciappelletto filled his head with many such things. Then, he began to sigh and at last to sob aloud, as he knew very well how, when he chose.

"Why, what's the matter, my son?" asked the holy friar.

"Woe!" groaned Ciappelletto. "There is still a sin that I've never confessed—I was too much ashamed to speak of it . . . and whenever I think of it I fall to weeping as you see. I'm almost certain God will never show me mercy . . ."

"Come, come, my son," said the friar. "What are you saying? If all the sins committed by mankind, or that will be committed while the world lasts—if all these sins, I say, were lodged in one man and he were as repentant and contrite as I see you, so great is God's mercy that if he confessed God would freely forgive him all. So speak in all confidence."

Still weeping bitterly, Ciappelletto said: "Alas, father, mine is a great sin. I can hardly believe God will ever forgive it in me without the help of your prayers."

"Speak with security," the friar urged him, "and I promise to pray God for you."

Ciappelletto still wept and said nothing, while the friar kept on comforting him to speak. But after he had held him in suspense with his weeping for a very long while, he heaved a deep sigh. "Father," he said, "since you promise to pray God for me, I'll tell you. Know, then, that when I was a little boy I once cursed my mother," and having spoken, he sobbed aloud again.

"Oh, my son, and does this seem to you such a dreadful sin?" asked the friar. "Why, men go on cursing God the livelong day, and yet He willingly forgives those who repent. Don't you suppose He will forgive you this? Don't weep, my son! Cheer up! Indeed, even if you had been one of those who nailed Him to the cross, God would forgive you for the contrition you show."

"Woe is me! What are you saying?" cried Ciappelletto. "Too great a sin it is, and too terrible . . . To think I was wicked enough to curse my sweet mother, after she carried me nine months in her body, day and night, and held me about her neck a hundred times or more! Surely this sin will not be forgiven unless you entreat God for me."

Seeing Ciappelletto had nothing more to say, the friar gave

him absolution and his blessing, taking him for a very holy man, and firmly believing everything he said was true. And who would not have believed, hearing a man speak that way, at the point of death? Finally the friar said: "Ciappelletto, with the help of God you will soon be well. Yet if God should be disposed to call your good and blessed soul to Himself, would you wish your body to be buried in our locality?"

"Indeed, sir, yes," replied Ciappelletto. "As a matter of fact I should not want it to be buried anywhere else after you promised to pray God for me. What's more, I've always had a special respect for your order. I pray you, then, when you reach your monastery, please see to it that I get the true body of God which you consecrate on the altar in the morning. For with your permission, I should like to take it, even though I am unworthy. After that, let me have extreme unction, so that even if I have lived a sinner, I may at least die a good Christian."

The holy man said he would gladly do as he wished and commended him for his sentiments. Moreover he promised he himself would see that the consecrated wafer should be brought to him soon.

The two brothers who had been very much afraid Ciappelletto might be deceiving them, had posted themselves near a wooden partition that divided the room where he lay from an adjoining one. As they listened they easily heard and understood what Ciappelletto was telling the friar. Sometimes they were so tempted to laugh on hearing his confession that they almost burst, and they would say to one another: "What a man this must be if neither old age nor sickness, nor fear of death that is staring him in the face, nor even God Himself before whose judgment he expects to be—what a man, if not all these things can serve to turn him from his wickedness or prevent him from dying as great a rogue as he lived!"

Once they had heard him contrive to be accepted in the church for burial, they had no care for anything else. Some time later Ciappelletto received the sacrament, and as he grew worse and worse, was given extreme unction. A little after vespers, the very day he had made his wonderful confession, he gave up the ghost.

The two brothers, commissioning a respectable funeral from his own money, notified the monastery, asking the friars to come that night to keep vigil, according to the custom, and to take the body the following morning. When the good friar who had confessed Ciappelletto heard of his death, he went with the prior of the monastery, had the chapter rung, and convening the brothers, told them what a holy man, to judge by his confession, the deceased had been. Then, with the hope that God might show many miracles through Ciappelletto, he persuaded the brothers to receive the body with the utmost reverence and devotion. The prior and the other credulous friars agreed to it. That evening they gathered in the place where the body was lying and kept a long and solemn vigil over it. Next morning, setting out in their copes and albs, with books in their hands and crosses before them, they went singing to get the body, and amid rejoicing and pomp they bore it to their church, followed by the city population, men and women together.

As soon as the body was deposited in the church the pious friar climbed up into the pulpit and delivered a fine preachment about Ciappelletto's virtues—his life, his fasts, his chastity, his simplicity, innocence and holiness, saying many other marvelous things besides. Among them he mentioned what the weeping Ciappelletto had confessed to him as his greatest sin, and how he, the friar, had hardly been able to make him understand that God would forgive it. From this he turned to rebuke his listeners. "And you, accursed of God," he said, "blaspheme Him and His Mother and all the court of heaven for every little straw you stumble over."

These and other things he said of his loyalty and purity. In short, he managed with his words, listened to with entire faith by the townspeople, to place Ciappelletto so high in their devotion, that the moment the service was over they swarmed to kiss the body's hands and feet. All the clothes were torn from his back, and the man who managed to have a shred of them thought himself fortunate indeed. It was necessary, even, to leave Ciappelletto lying there all day, that everyone might have the chance to visit and see him.

The following night he was buried with great ceremony in a marble vault in one of the chapels. As early as next day people began going to him, lighting tapers and adoring him, making vows, even, and hanging up wax images as a fulfilment of their promises. So widespread was the fame of his sanctity and so great the devotion of the people, that there wasn't a soul in adversity who did not make vows to him rather than to any other saint. They dubbed him Saint Ciappelletto, and so he is known to this day. They even affirm God has revealed many miracles through him, and still does so to favor whatever man commends himself to his graces with devotion.

So lived and died Cepparello da Prato and became a saint, as you have heard. I do not deny it possible for him to be beatified in the presence of God, for although his life was so wicked and evil, he may have shown such contrition in the end that God may have had mercy and received him into His kingdom. But since this is hidden from us I should judge from what we do know, that he ought rather to be in the hands of the devil, in perdition, than in heaven. If it should be that way, we may appreciate the goodness of God toward us in regarding the purity of our faith and not our error whenever we make an intermediary of His enemy, thinking him a friend. And so He grants us our prayer, as if we had indeed resorted to a true saint to plead for us. Therefore that our merry little band may remain safe and sound by His grace in these adversities, let us praise His name, under which we united, and commend ourselves to Him in our needs, in the assurance of being heard.

Here he was silent.

## THE SECOND STORY

*Abraham the Jew, urged by Jehannot de Chevigny, visits the court of Rome, and witnessing the loose life of the clergy becomes a Christian.*

PAMFILO'S STORY ROUSED LAUGHTER IN PART AND WON THE UNdivided approval of the women, who had listened to it attentively to the end. Then the queen asked Neifile who was sitting beside Pamfilo to take up the thread of the diversion by telling a story of her own. Neifile, as charming and courteous as she was beautiful, willingly acquiesced and began:

Pamfilo has shown us in his story how the lovingkindness of God overlooks our faults when they proceed from causes of which we have no knowledge. In mine I intend to show how this same lovingkindness—suffering patiently the faults of those who should bear true witness of it both by word and deed, yet practice the contrary—gives us a veritable proof of itself, to help us pursue our belief with even firmer strength of mind.

I have heard tell, gracious ladies, of a wealthy merchant who lived in Paris—a fine fellow, loyal and upright, whose name was Jehannot de Chevigny. He carried on an extensive business in cloth and stuffs, and he was a friend, strangely enough, of a very rich Jew called Abraham, a merchant, like himself, and like him, too, an honest and upright man. Observing Abraham's fine qualities, Jehannot began to be very much concerned that the soul of such a splendid fellow should be damned for his mistaken faith, so out of friendship he constantly urged him to forsake the errors of the Jewish creed and embrace Christian verity, which, he argued, Abraham could see prospering and growing for its holiness and good, while his own, on the contrary, was ever waning and coming to nothing. At that the Jew would reply he believed no faith but the Jewish to be either good or holy. Besides, he argued, he had been born into it, and in it he wanted to live and die. There was nothing that could ever move him from his resolve.

Nevertheless Jehannot was not deterred from returning to the argument a few days later with similar words, trying to prove to Abraham in his blunt, simple, business-like way why his religion was better than the Jewish. Now the Jew was a learned master in the Hebraic law, but whether Jehannot's wholehearted friendship touched him, or whether the words which the Holy Ghost put into the uncultured fellow's mouth worked the miracle, the Jew soon began to take pleasure in Jehannot's arguments. Still, holding firmly to his faith, he would not allow himself to be shaken. The more obdurate he remained, the more insistent grew Jehannot's importunities. Finally, conquered by so continued an attack, the Jew said:

"Now, listen, Jehannot. You insist that I become a Christian. I am willing to do so, but first I want to go to Rome and see the man who, you say, is God's vicar on earth, that I may consider his ways and habits and those of his brother cardinals. If they seem to me such that between them and your arguments I can convince myself your faith is better than mine, as you have gone out of your way to show me,—why, I'll do what I said. If not, I'll keep on being the Jew I am."

Jehannot was exceedingly troubled to hear this, and said to himself: "I've wasted my efforts, which I thought so well-employed, when I imagined I was converting Abraham. If he should go to the court of Rome and see the filthy life of the clergy, far from being converted from Jew to Christian, he would most assuredly turn Jew again were he the most devout

Christian in the world!" But turning to Abraham he said: "Now look, my friend, why should you want to go to the trouble and expense of traveling from here to Rome, especially when you consider that for a man of your wealth a trip by land or sea is full of danger? Are you afraid you'll not find the man here to baptize you? If you should still have some doubts concerning the faith I've preached to you—where could you find greater teachers and more learned men than here, to explain whatever questions you'd like to ask? In my opinion your trip is unnecessary, taking all in all. Just realize that the prelates there are no different from ours here—they're only better for being nearer the chief Shepherd. So follow my advice and reserve this trouble for some other occasion when you may wish to attend a jubilee. Perhaps then I'll even keep you company."

"I am sure, Jehannot," answered the Jew, "that everything is as you say. But to make a long story short, if you want me to do what you've asked me so often, I insist upon going on my trip. If not, I wash my hands of the whole matter."

Jehannot saw Abraham was determined. "Well, go and good luck to you," he said, though he was certain Abraham would never become a Christian when he saw the court of Rome. But then, reflecting that he himself was losing nothing, he refrained from further action.

The Jew took horse and without losing time went to the court of Rome, where he was welcomed with all due honor by his fellow Jews on his arrival. Then, remaining in Rome without telling anyone the purpose of his visit, he began prudently studying the habits of the Pope, the cardinals and other prelates, as well as all the members of the papal court. Between what he himself gathered, for he was a very perceptive man, and what he heard from others, he found that all, from the highest of rank, to the meanest, were shamefully guilty of the sin of lechery. Not only did they indulge in normal lust, but without the least restraint of remorse or shame, even in sodomy, and to such an extent that the influence of whores and minions was of no little importance in currying favor. Various other attributes he found them to possess besides lechery. They were gluttons, swillers, guzzlers in general, and devoted to their bellies like brute beasts. Investigating further he saw they were all avaricious and greedy for money. Human blood, indeed, Christian and sacred things pertaining to the sacrifice, they used to barter for money, making a bigger business of them and employing more agents than the people of Paris had for their stuffs and merchandise. Blatant simony they called *procuration* and gluttony *sustentation,* as if God did not know either the meaning of the words or the intention of those evil minds, and allowed Himself to be gulled like His creatures by the mere names of things.

These, and many other enormities that were better passed over in silence, offended the Jew, who was a sober and humble man, and thinking he had witnessed enough, he decided to go back to Paris.

When Jehannot heard of his return the last thing he hoped for was that Abraham should have become a Christian. He went to see him, nevertheless, and they greeted each other joyfully. Then, when Abraham had rested a day or so, Jehannot asked him what he thought of the Holy Father, the cardinals and others of the papal court.

"I think they are rotten," the Jew readily replied. "God punish the whole brood of them! I tell you—unless I did not see things straight—I found no holiness, no devotion, no good work or example or anything else in a single man of the clergy. On the contrary, lust, gluttony, avarice and worse things, if there could be anything worse—all were in such high favor, I would have taken it all for a mill of devilish works, not holy! For all I can judge it seems to me your Shepherd and consequently everyone else with him do their utmost, exercise every care, wit and art at their disposal to ruin the Christian faith entirely and ban it altogether from the world, instead of striving to be its foundation and mainstay. Yet when I notice their aim is not fulfilled, but that your religion continually grows and becomes more bright and clear, it seems to me very evident that the Holy Spirit is its foundation and support, so it must be the truest and holiest of all faiths. Therefore in spite of my obduracy in rejecting your pleas for my conversion, I tell you frankly that nothing in the world could deter me from becoming a Christian. Come, let's go to the church, then, where I may be baptized according to the proper custom of your holy faith."

Jehannot, who had expected quite the contrary conclusion, was the happiest man alive when he heard his friend express himself in this fashion. He went with him to the church of Notre-Dame in Paris, and asked the clergy to baptize Abraham. When they heard Abraham himself make the request, they granted it readily. Jehannot then raised him from the sacred font and named him Jean. In after-days Jean had himself duly instructed by famous men in all matters pertaining to our faith, which he learned without trouble, and he became a much respected man, renowned for holy living.

✳

## THE THIRD STORY

*Melchizedek the Jew avoids a trap set for him by Saladin, by a parable about three rings.*

WITH NEIFILE'S STORY OVER AND GENERALLY ACCLAIMED, THE queen indicated it was her pleasure to hear Filomena, who spoke as follows:

The story Neifile just told reminds me of the scrape a Jew once got into. Though we have been hearing many fine things about God and our faith, we must not be prevented from coming down to the actions and vicissitudes of men from now on. I will now tell you a story which I think will make you more cautious in answering questions that are put to you.

You must know, dear friends, that as stupidity often drags a man to misery from a happy state, good sense may rescue a wise man from grave dangers and lift him up to a place of high security. We see how true it is that stupidity leads some from happiness to wretchedness, from many examples which we do not even have to bother mentioning. They are always thrusting themselves upon us, and by means of a brief story I shall show you, as I promised, how good sense is the source of comfort.

Saladin, who was so powerful that he rose from an ordinary man to the rank of Sultan of Babylon and won countless victories over Saracen and Christian rulers, found that he had exhausted all his wealth, both in war and in the exercise of his extraordinary munificence. Now, by some chance, he felt the need of money, and a lot of it, too, and not knowing where he could get it as quickly as he wished, he thought of a rich Jew called Melchizedek who was a moneylender in Alexandria. This usurer, he was certain, had money enough to help him, but he was also aware the man was so miserly that he would never do so of his own free will. Violence Saladin did not care to use. However, urged by his need, and thinking over ways and means of making the Jew serve him, he decided to use a show of force, colored by some plausible reason. Summoning the Jew, he received him cordially, bidding him sit at his side, and then spoke:

"I have heard from all quarters, sir, how learned you are, and how far in advance of all other men in the knowledge of godly things. I'd be very glad to learn from you which of the three laws you consider the true one—the Hebrew, the Saracen or the Christian?"

The Jew, who was truly a man of understanding, was only too confident that Saladin was trying to trip him up in some statement, and so have grounds to start a suit against him. He realized he could not praise any one of these three without giving Saladin his pretext; therefore he sharpened his wits, as he had good reason to, and sought an answer that would save him from the snare. A thought occurred to him at once.

"Sire," he said, "the question you have set me is a difficult one, and the better to express my opinion concerning it I will have to tell you a story which I beg you to heed.

"If I remember aright, I've heard tell many times of a rich and powerful man who had among his treasures a rare and valuable ring that he prized above everything else. Because it was so precious and beautiful, he wished to treat it with the honor it deserved, and leave it to his descendants. He decreed, thereupon, that whichever of his sons found he had inherited the ring, after his death, should be looked upon as the chosen heir, and be esteemed and respected by the rest, as the head of the family.

"The man to whom the ring was left by his father had the same understanding with his sons, and did as his predecessor had done. To be brief, this ring passed from hand to hand many times, until at last it reached a man who had three handsome, virtuous sons, obedient to all his wishes, because of which he loved each one with an equal love. Now the three youths knew the tradition connected with the ring, and as each was anxious for priority over his brothers, he pleaded with his father, who was now of a ripe old age, to leave it to him when he died.

"The worthy man was in a predicament, for he loved the three equally, and could not decide to which he would rather bequeath the ring. Since he had promised it to the three of them, he decided to satisfy them all. In the utmost secrecy he ordered a skilful goldsmith to make him two other rings, and they were so much like the first that he himself, who had ordered them, scarcely knew which was the original. Then, when his time came to die, he gave each son one of the rings in secret. However, after his death they all wanted to occupy the place of honor and receive the inheritance; this one refused to yield it up, and that one denied it to the rest. Finally, each produced his ring, to prove he was in the right. On examination they were found so similar that the true one could not be detected. Thus the question as to which one was the true heir of the father was unsolved, and remains so to this day.

"And so I say to you, sire, of the three laws given to the three peoples by God the Father, and about which you propounded your question. Each race believes it possesses the inheritance and the true law of the Father and fulfils His commandments. But which one it is that is the true possessor still remains a question to be solved, as with the rings."

Saladin had to admit that the Jew had ably extricated himself from the snare laid at his feet. He concluded therefore to speak openly to him about his needs, and find out whether the man was willing to help him. He did as he proposed, confessing what he had secretly hatched in his heart if the man had not answered him so prudently, whereupon the Jew freely gave Saladin all he required and Saladin afterwards paid him back in full. Moreover, the Sultan made him many fine gifts and always looked upon him as a friend, keeping him at his court in a high and honorable position.

## THE  FOURTH  STORY

*A monk who had fallen into a sin deserving of severe punishment, cleverly reproached that same fault in his abbot and so avoided its penalty.*

FILOMENA, HER STORY FINISHED, WAS NOW SILENT WHEN DiONEC who was sitting beside her, knowing by the regular order established that it was his turn to go on, began to speak as follows without waiting for the queen's bidding:

If I have rightly understood you, gentle ladies, we are here to amuse ourselves by telling stories, and provided one does not go against the agreement, it is permitted each one of us to tell what he considers the most diverting tale—at least that is what

I gathered from our queen a little while ago. We have already heard how Abraham saved his soul by the good advice of Jehannot de Chevigny, and how Melchizedek by his wisdom guarded his riches from Saladin's schemes. Now, if you will allow me, I'll tell you a short tale of how a monk saved his body from unpleasant punishment through his own adroitness.

Not very far from here in the country of Lunigiana, there is a monastery more crammed with monks and holiness than any I know of to-day. Among others there was a young spark of a monk whose lustiness nothing could dam, neither vigils nor fasts.

One fine day, toward noon, when the other monks were taking their midday nap, he was strolling by himself about the church, which was situated in a secluded spot, when he caught sight of a very pretty girl, the daughter, probably, of some peasant of the countryside. She was going about the fields gathering herbs, and no sooner did our monk spy her than he was fiercely assailed by the prickings of the flesh. He walked up and began to engage her in conversation. One thing led to another; he soon came to an understanding with her and brought her to his cell, no one being any the wiser.

Now he was so carried away by his desire that he sported with her less cautiously than was wise. It happened just then that the abbot, risen from his nap and gliding softly by the monk's door, could not help hearing the noises the two were making. Stealthily approaching the door, the better to hear and recognize the voices, he discovered there was certainly a woman within. At first he was tempted to have the door opened, but he thought it better to follow another course. Returning to his room he waited for the monk to go out.

However, though the young blade was engrossed in fine sport and delight with the girl, he could not help keeping on his guard. Presently he was almost sure he heard the shuffling of feet in the dormitory. Peeping through a tiny crack he saw the abbot, clear as day, standing there, eavesdropping. Too well he realized the old man was aware of the woman in his cell, which worried him not a little, knowing that dire punishment was in store for him.

Yet, concealing his chagrin from the wench, he briskly turned over many things in his mind, wondering whether he could not find some wholesome solution. Suddenly he hit upon a novel scheme that went to the very bull's eve.

"I must look around for a way to get you out of here without your being seen," he said to the girl, pretending he had already remained long enough with her. "So stay here quietly until I come back."

Once out, and the door of his cell locked on her with the key, he went directly to the abbot's room and handed it to him, according to the custom of each monk on going out. Then, "Sir," he said, with the face of innocence, "I wasn't able to have all the faggots I cut this morning brought here. With your permission I'd like to go now to the wood and have them fetched."

The abbot, thinking the monk unaware of having been caught, was more than delighted to seize the opportunity of finding out further details of the offense the youth had committed. Willingly he took the key, and as willingly gave him leave to go.

The monk once out of the monastery, the abbot fell to wondering which was the better course to follow—whether he should open the scapegrace's cell in the presence of all the other monks, expose his sin and so afford them no ground for murmuring against him when he gave the rogue his punishment, or whether he should hear from the girl's own lips how the business had taken place. Besides, reflecting that the girl might happen to be the wife or daughter of some man he knew, and therefore whom he did not wish to shame by exhibiting her publicly to the friars, he decided to see first who she was, and then to arrive at some conclusion. Accordingly, going quietly to the cell, he opened it, entered and locked the door again behind him.

When the girl saw the abbot approaching, she was horrified with shame and dread, and immediately began to cry. But our abbot, casting his eyes upon her and finding her fresh and luscious, old though he was, suddenly began to feel the urge of the flesh no less violently than his young monk before him. And he began debating in his mind: "Truly, why shouldn't I take my pleasure when I can? Sorrow and annoyance for that matter are always ready, whether I want them or not. Here's a fine wench, right at hand, and nobody knows a thing about it. Now if I can get her to do my pleasure, why shouldn't I have it? Who will be any the wiser? No one! And a sin that is hidden is half shriven. This opportunity may not come to me again, and it is the best sort of wisdom to take advantage of a bounty when the Lord God sees fit to send it."

So saying, and with a purpose entirely different from the one he had set out with, the abbot went up to the girl and began gently consoling her, entreating her to dry her tears. Then from one word going to another, he succeeded in making his desire known to her. The girl was neither iron nor adamant. Obligingly enough she lent herself to the abbot's pleasures. Kissing and embracing her many times he clambered into the monk's little bed. Then, perhaps, out of regard to the grave burden of his dignity and the girl's tender age, or fearful of hurting her with his considerable weight, instead of mounting upon her breast he laid her on his own. And so for a long time he frolicked with her.

The monk, meanwhile, who had only made a show of going to the woods, had concealed himself in the dormitory. When he saw the abbot enter his cell alone, he felt assured that his scheme would take effect; and when he saw the abbot lock the door from within, he had not the least doubt of it. Coming out of his hiding-place, he proceeded softly to a crack, and through it he both heard and saw everything the abbot said or did.

The abbot, feeling he had disported himself long enough with the girl, locked her in the cell and returned to his room. After a while he heard the monk about, and thinking that the youth had come back from the woods, he made up his mind to give him a sound scolding and lock him up, that he himself might have full possession of the fine quarry he had acquired.

He had the monk brought before him. Severely, and with a very forbidding face, he reproved him and ordered him put in prison, but with great alacrity the monk spoke up: "Sir, forgive me! I have not been a member of Saint Benedict's order long enough to know every detail of it. Besides, you had not yet shown me that women should lie as heavily on men as fasts and vigils. But now that you have shown me, forgive me, and I promise never to sin that way again. Indeed, I will always do as I have seen you do!"

The abbot was no fool, and it did not take him long to understand that the young monk not only knew more than himself, but had also seen what he had done. His conscience stung by his own guilt, he was ashamed to inflict upon the monk the very punishment he himself deserved. Seeing no other way, he forgave him, and making him promise to say no word of what he had seen, they put the girl out decently—but you may be sure they let her in again, many a time thereafter.

✳

# THE FIFTH STORY

*The Marquise of Monferrato checks the mad passion of the King of France by means of a dinner of hens and certain pretty words.*

AT FIRST DIONEO'S STORY MOVED THE WOMEN TO SHAME, WHICH outwardly manifested itself in modest blushes, but then, as they looked slyly at one another, hardly able to contain their laughter, they listened to the rest, smiling archly. Once ended, they chided him prettily, pretending such naughty stories were not the sort to tell in the presence of women, and the queen, turning to Fiammetta who was sitting next to him on the grass, requested her to continue. With sweet grace and a blithe face she began:

Since we're on the subject of showing the power of apt and ready answers, it occurs to me, lovely ladies, to tell you the story of how a noble lady retained her virtue by word and deed, and kept a man from violating it. We all know that a man shows great good sense by placing his affections in a woman of higher station than himself. We also know it shows remarkable discretion in a woman to keep herself from yielding to the passion of a man above her in rank. Here is the story it is my turn to tell.

The Marquis of Monferrato, a man of rare courage and a standard-bearer of the Church, had gone across the seas in an armed crusade of the Christians. It so happened that at the court of King Philip le Borgne, who was preparing to set out from France on the same crusade, a knight stated that there wasn't a single couple under heaven fit to compare with the Marquis of Monferrato and his lady. For as the marquis was famed among his knights as a man of rare virtues, his wife was held among the women as incomparable for beauty and worth.

These words so struck the king's fancy that although he had never seen the lady he immediately fell deeply in love with her, and determined to sail for the crusade from no other port than Genoa, so that by journeying as far as that city by land, he might have a plausible pretext for stopping to see the marquise on the way. He thought, you see, that since the marquis was away, he might contrive to give vent to his desire.

The plan had no sooner entered his mind than he began to

put it into effect. He sent all his men ahead, keeping only a small retinue of nobles about him, and set out on his journey. Then, when he was but a day's distance from the marquise's territory, he sent word to inform the lady that he would be pleased to dine with her the following morning. The marquise was a shrewd and discreet woman. Smiling, she replied she deemed the king's visit the highest possible favor, and that she would be delighted to welcome him. But privately she could not help wondering why on earth the king, of all people, should come to visit her while her husband was away. Nor was she wrong when she concluded that her beauty must have lured him there.

Nevertheless, like the gentlewoman she was, she made up her mind to receive him with due honor, and calling to her whatever men had remained behind, she managed with their help to make all the necessary preparations. The dinner alone, and the meats, she chose to decide upon for herself. As quickly as might be, she ordered all the hens the countryside contained to be brought, and commissioned her cooks to make a variety of dishes, but of such fowl only.

At last, on the day established, the king arrived, and with great honor and festivity the lady received him. He was even more impressed with her actual beauty, virtue and courtesy than he had been on hearing the knight's words, and he marveled greatly. He did nothing but shower her with praise and grew more and more inflamed with desire, the more he realized how far the woman exceeded his former conception of her.

First he rested a while in the beautifully decorated rooms that had been made ready with everything suitable to receive so great a king, and when dinnertime came, both he and the marquise took their places at table. The rest of the guests, according to their quality, were entertained at other tables.

One after another, many dishes were served the king, and wonderful, costly wines, all of which pleased him immensely, yet not so much as the delight he experienced whenever he gazed upon the ravishing marquise. And yet, as course followed course, the king could not help feeling puzzled, for in spite of the variety of the dishes, he perceived that they were all concocted of hens. Now he knew very well that the neighborhood must have abounded in all kinds of venison and game. Moreover, he had given the lady ample notice of his coming, for her to have had the leisure to send the men hunting.

Nevertheless, although it caused him much wonder, he had

no wish to take exception to anything but the omnipresent hens. Turning to her merrily, he said: "Tell me, madam, are only hens born in this place, and not a single cock?"

The marquise understood his question only too well. Reflecting that God had at last offered her the opportunity she desired for speaking out her mind, she turned to the king.

"No, sire," she answered boldly. "But although females may differ in garb and dignity, they are all made the same here, as anywhere else."

On hearing these words the king was not slow to understand the reason for the dinner of hens, nor did he fail to appreciate the virtue hidden in her answer. He knew that words would be useless with such a lady, and that violence was out of place. Therefore, since he had unwisely flared up with passion for her, he could follow no other course for his honor's sake, than wisely to quench his ill-conceived ardor. Without uttering another word for fear of her retorts, he continued eating hopelessly. With the dinner over, he thought it best to take his leave as soon as possible, to cover his dishonorable visit. Thanking her for the honor she had done him and she, in turn, commending him to God, he set out for Genoa.

❋

# THE SIXTH STORY

*With a witty saying an honest man confounds the wicked hypocrisy of religious orders.*

EMILIA WAS SITTING NEXT TO FIAMMETTA, AND AFTER THE DARING of the marquise had been applauded, as well as the pretty rebuke she had flung at the King of France, she began, at the queen's pleasure, to speak boldly:

I, too, won't refrain from telling you of the dig that an honest layman gave a miserly monk, by making a witty remark which is as funny as it is laudable.

Not so very long ago, dear girls, there lived in our city a friar Minor, who served as inquisitor in cases of heresy. Like most of his kind, although he went out of his way to give the impression of being a pious and tender lover of the Christian faith, he was no less assiduous in finding out what man had a well-filled purse, than in discovering which one was lacking in

religion. Thanks to his solicitude, he happened to fall upon
an honest fellow, more endowed with money than sense, who,
speaking lightly perhaps in the heat of merriment and super-
abundant gaiety, rather than out of any lack of faith, was said to
have remarked one day among his boon companions, "I have
such marvelous wine, that Christ himself might drink it."

These words were reported to the inquisitor. Learning that
the man's property was large and his purse well-stocked, he
proceeded with all speed, *cum gladiis et fustibus,* to concoct a
jolly suit against him, looking forward not so much to a spiritual amelioration in the culprit, as to a fine overflow of florins
into his own hands, if things proceeded according to his hope,
which they did.

He had the good man summoned, and asked him whether
what had been said were true. The poor fellow said yes, and
tried to explain to him the way it had happened. But the very
holy inquisitor, a faithful follower of Saint John-of-the-
Goldenbeard, said:

"What! Did you dare to make Christ a guzzler and a lover
of heavy wines, as though he were Cinciglione himself, or God
knows what other of your drunkards and tavern rats? Now with
your soft talk you'd like to make me believe it's a mere trifle.
But it's not as you think! If we were to give you your just
deserts, it's into the fire you'd go, I tell you!"

With similar words and many others he addressed him, scowling menacingly the while, as though the poor wretch had been
Epicurus himself, denying the immortality of the soul. In short,
he gave him such a mighty scare that the simple fellow managed to have the inquisitor's palm oiled through certain gobetweens, with a goodly quantity of Saint John Goldenmouth's
balm, a sovereign remedy for the pestilential disease of covetousness in the clergy, and especially in brothers Minor who
dare not touch money. This way he hoped his judge would be
merciful toward him.

The balm, which is very effective in spite of the fact that
Galen does not mention it in any one of his medical writings,
worked so extremely well, that the fire he had been threatened
with was, out of grace, commuted to the wearing of a cross.
And that it might provide him a handsomer banner in case he
went crusading across the sea, the inquisitor specified it should
be a yellow cross on a dark ground. Besides this, after he had
already pocketed his money, he kept the man with him several

days, making him work out a penance by hearing a mass every morning at the church of Santa Croce, and then reporting to him at dinner time. The rest of the day he was at liberty to spend as he chose.

Diligently the man fulfilled his duties. One day at mass he heard a Gospel, in which the following words were chanted: "For every one ye shall receive a hundred, and shall possess eternal life." This sentence he learned by heart, and then went as usual to present himself before the inquisitor, whom he found at his meal.

"Did you hear mass this morning?" asked the man.

"Yes, sir," he answered promptly.

"Did you hear anything," continued the inquisitor, "that you are in doubt about, and concerning which you'd like to ask a question?"

"Most assuredly I have no doubt of anything I heard," replied the honest fellow. "Why, on the contrary, I firmly believe everything to be true. But there was one thing that made me feel very sorry for you and the rest of your brothers—to think of what a pickle you'll be in, over there, in your next life."

"And what was this," asked the inquisitor, "that moved you to such pity for us?"

The good man answered: "Sir, it was the verse in the Gospel that says, *For every one ye shall receive a hundred.*"

"That's excellent," said the inquisitor. "But why did this particular verse strike you?"

"Sir," he replied, "I'll tell you why. Ever since my stay here I've noticed that you dole out to a lot of poor folks, sometimes one and sometimes two great big caldrons of broth a day—you know, the broth that's left over after you and the other brothers here have had your fill. Now if for each one of these caldrons you were to receive a hundred over there, you'd have so much that you'd all surely drown in it!"

Everyone at the inquisitor's table burst out laughing; but he felt the sting of the imputed brothy hypocrisy and was quite perturbed. Had he not received blame enough for what he had already done, he would have clapped another lawsuit on the fellow for insulting him and his worthless brethren by that funny thrust. As it was, he had to bid him go his own way from then on, and never come before him again.

✳

# THE SEVENTH STORY

*Bergamino frankly condemns a strange miserliness that had come over Can della Scala, by telling him about Primasso and the Abbot of Cluny.*

EMILIA'S CHARMING WAYS AND THE STORY SHE TOLD MADE THEM all laugh and applaud the novel emblem of the crusade, but when the laughter had subsided and everyone was quiet, Filostrato, whose turn it was, began:

It is a mighty fine thing, noble ladies, to hit a fixed target, but it is almost miraculous when some unusual thing crops up suddenly, and is pierced directly by the archer. The vicious and filthy life of the clergy by its almost constant indication of evil, easily offers the occasion for the gossip, spite and criticism of anyone who has a mind to them. Therefore, even more laudable than the simple fellow who rebuked the inquisitor for the hypocritical charity of the friars, who give away what is even unfit for hogs or refuse—more laudable than that fellow, I say, is the man I intend to tell you about. It was the preceding story that called this one to my mind—the story of a gentleman who reproved the magnificent Can della Scala for an unusual fit of miserliness that had sprung up in him, and rid him of it by means of a clever tale, in which he had another person go through the events that concerned themselves.

The fame of Can della Scala has resounded all over the world. Fortune smiled upon him in many things, and he became one of the most famous and magnificent lords Italy had ever known, since the time of Emperor Frederick the Second. Once upon a time he proposed to arrange a marvelous celebration in the city of Verona, inviting many people from all parts of the world, and especially distinguished men of every profession. Suddenly, for no reason that one could perceive, he called everything off, provided in a small way for the guests who had already arrived, and dismissed them all.

One man only, Bergamino by name, he retained. This Bergamino was a fluent, well-spoken man, whose golden speech no one could imagine unless he heard it. Since he was neither rewarded nor sent away, Bergamino remained behind in the hope that his stay might not prove without profit. But Can della

Scala had taken it into his head that anything he might give him would be wasted even more than if he were to throw it into the fire; but he displayed no inkling of his private opinion, either by word or deed.

After loitering about the court a few days, Bergamino began to worry. He had not been called upon to do anything pertaining to his art, and in the meantime, besides being compelled to waste his time in idleness, he was squandering his money at the inn, providing for his horses and his servants. Nevertheless he continued waiting and hoping, convincing himself he would not be doing the proper thing if he left.

He happened to have brought with him three rich and handsome garments which other lords had given him that he might cut a fine figure at the celebration. But his host demanded money, and in lieu of it, the first suit was surrendered to him. Still Bergamino lingered, and since he wanted to keep on good terms with his host he was obliged out of decency to give him his other suit. Soon the third began to provide for his bare necessities, whereupon Bergamino decided to see what would happen while it lasted and then leave the city.

At this juncture he found himself one day before Can della Scala, who was having his dinner. Bergamino looked very woeful, whereupon Can said, more to hurt him than to derive any pleasure from his speech: "Why, Bergamino, what's the matter? How woebegone you look! Come, tell us about it!"

Then, without pausing for thought, as though he had racked his brain beforehand, Bergamino began to tell this story, *à propos* of his own predicament:

"My lord, no doubt you know what a learned man Primasso was, and without an equal for clever improvisations in verse. Indeed, he became so famous for his talents that, although he might not have been known by sight, he was certainly renowned the world over, at least by name and repute.

"Once in Paris he found himself in pretty bad straits, which was not unusual with him considering what little value is put on learning by those very men who could do so much to further it. Anyhow, while in these circumstances he chanced to hear of the Abbot of Cluny, who was said to be the richest man, for his income, that the Church of God possesses, not excepting the Pope. He heard marvelously extraordinary tales of this prelate, among them, that he always held open court, and that any man who ever went to see him was never refused meat and drink provided he made his request known while the abbot was at table. Primasso no sooner heard of it than he made up his mind to go and see the magnificence of this lord for himself, for he delighted in the company of nobles and gentlemen. Accordingly, he asked how near Paris the abbot was then living, and was told only about six miles away, at one of his estates. Primasso reflected that if he were to set out bright and early in the morning, he might manage to arrive there toward dinnertime.

"As he found no one to accompany him, he had the way pointed out, and for fear that by some mischance he might lose it and find himself where he might not easily get something to eat, he thought of taking along three rolls against possible hunger. Water, he reflected (for he was not overly fond of it), he would surely find anywhere. He put the rolls in the bosom of his coat and went on his way, making such good time that he arrived at the abbot's place before the dinner-hour. He went in, examining everything. Seeing the vast number of tables laid and the great to-do in the kitchen and many other things being prepared for the dinner, he said to himself: 'Truly, he is as magnificent as people say.'

"For awhile he took note of these things. Then the abbot's steward ordered water to be brought for the ablutions and mealtime approached. Their hands washed, the guests were given their places at table, and by some chance Primasso was made to sit exactly opposite the door of the chamber out of which the abbot had to pass to reach the dining-hall.

"It was the custom of that court that neither wine nor bread nor other food and drink were ever to be set upon the tables, before the lord of the place had taken his seat. After everything was ready, the steward had the abbot notified that dinner would be served at his pleasure. The door was opened admitting him into the hall. On the threshold he looked before him, and as luck would have it, the first man his eyes fell upon was Primasso, in a shabby, sorry state. The abbot did not know him by sight, and the moment he saw him an unworthy thought entered his mind, such as had never harbored there before. 'Look at the kind of creatures I feed,' he said to himself.

"Turning back at once, he had the door shut and asked the people about him whether anyone knew who the ruffian was, sitting at the table opposite his chamber-door. No one could tell him.

"Now Primasso, who was much inclined to eat, having had sufficient exercise and being, moreover, unaccustomed to fasts, waited a considerable while, but seeing that the abbot did not make his appearance, he took one of the three rolls out of his coat and began munching it. Some time later the abbot asked one of his servants to look and see whether the fellow had gone away.

" 'No, my lord,' answered the man. 'On the contrary he's eating some bread that he must have brought with him.'

" 'Let him go on eating his own bread, then, if he has it,' said the abbot, 'for he'll be tasting none of ours to-day.'

"It was his wish to have the fellow go away of his own accord, thinking it would not be right of him to send him packing. However, Primasso had disposed of a roll, and seeing that the abbot still did not make his appearance, he started on the second. This was likewise reported to the abbot who had sent to see if he had not yet gone. At last, the host still not coming, Primasso began eating the third roll, for the second was gone. Once again it was told the abbot, who wondered within himself, and said: 'What on earth is this strange bee in my bonnet to-day? What kind of stinginess is this? What sort of spite? And against whom? For many years I have made free of my table to anyone who wished to come, without distinction—highborn or low, rich or poor, merchant or peddler. With my own eyes I have seen my substance wasted by a multitude of rapscallions, and never for a moment did I think of anything approaching what that poor wretch brought into my head. Certainly this fit of avarice couldn't have seized me for a no-account scamp. There must be something in it, for although the fellow looks to me nothing more than a ruffian, he has succeeded in bowing my spirit to honor him.'

"At that the abbot wanted to know who he was, and learning it was Primasso whom he had long known by repute as a distinguished man, and that he had come to see whether his magnificence were as great as it was trumped up to be, he was mortified. Eager to make amends he went out of his way to honor him. After dinner he had Primasso clad in as fine a suit as befitted his state, and giving him money and a horse besides, left it to him whether to go or stay. Primasso was very well pleased. He thanked the abbot with all his heart and returned on horseback to Paris, which he had left on Shanks's mare."

Can della Scala, a quick-witted man, understood perfectly

well what Bergamino meant without need of further explanation. Smiling he said to him: "Bergamino, you have very eloquently displayed both your wrongs and your worthiness, as contrasted to my own miserliness, as well as what you want of me. Believe me, I had never in my life known avarice until now, when I felt it regarding you. But I shall cudgel it out with the very stick you yourself contrived." He had Bergamino's host paid. Then clothing the worthy magnificently in one of his own suits and giving him money and a horse besides, he left it to him, for the time being, whether to go or stay.

## THE EIGHTH STORY

*Guglielmo Borsiere chastises the stinginess of Erminio de' Grimaldi with some choice words.*

WHEN LAURETTA, WHO WAS SITTING NEXT TO FILOSTRATO, SAW Bergamino's cleverness meet with appreciation, she felt it was her turn to say something, and without waiting to be bidden, she graciously began:

The preceding story, dear friends, inspires me to tell you how a noble courtier jabbed at the niggardliness of a very wealthy merchant in much the same way, and not without profit to himself. It must not be deprecated, however, because it somewhat resembles the last, considering that good came of it in the end.

Well, then, a long time ago there lived in Genoa a man of good family, called Erminio de' Grimaldi. As rumor went, he was far above every other extremely wealthy Italian citizen both in the extent of his lands and in the amount of his actual riches. But as he surpassed all other Italians in his wealth, so did he far outdo in avarice and sordidness, the worst miser and penny-squeezing old crank that ever lived. He not only pulled his purse-strings tight against entertaining people, but even in the care of his own person he suffered the greatest privations, rather than spend his money—a very unusual thing in a gentleman of Genoa, whose citizens are all known to be fine dressers. He was likewise stingy in his food and drink, so that his last name Grimaldi was deservedly dropped by everyone who knew him, and he was known only as Erminio Avarice.

While this old crank was increasing his goods by saving his money, there arrived in Genoa a courtly, well-bred, well-spoken minstrel, whose name was Guglielmo Borsiere, not at all like the sort of scoundrels we know to-day. The minstrels of to-day, indeed!—These fellows—be it said to the shame of the corrupt and dishonorable customs of those who wish to be thought gentlemen and lords—these fellows, I say, who ought rather to be called asses, nurtured as they are in all the ugliness and lewd living of the scum of mankind! How different from those of the kingly courts! Once it was the minstrel's duty and the purpose of his endeavors, to negotiate peace where feuds and misunderstandings had arisen among gentlemen. He transacted marriages, alliances and friendships. With fine and pleasant words, it was his pleasure to soothe the minds of the weary and solace the courts of kings. Or with sternness, like a father, he took it upon himself to chasten the faults of the unruly. And all this for very meager recompense. To-day the minstrel wastes his time in bearing tales and sowing trouble, in backbiting and gossip. What is worse, no matter who is present, he accuses his fellows of all kinds of mischief, loose-living and depravity—whether justifiably or not, God only knows! With deceitful lures he coaxes good men to vile and shameful deeds . . . Indeed, the worse a minstrel's speech, nowadays, and the more abominable his actions, the better he is loved and honored and welcomed and rewarded by our rude and wretched nobles! What a shameful indictment against our modern world! How evident that all virtues have left us, abandoning us poor mortals to the very dregs of vice!

But, to come back to my story—it was a just scorn that made me digress a little more than I had intended . . . As I was saying, this Guglielmo was held in high favor by all the gentlemen of Genoa, and was gladly received wherever he went. He remained in the city a number of days, and hearing much talk of Erminio's meanness and avarice, he was anxious to see him.

Erminio had already heard what a fine man this Guglielmo Borsiere was. In spite of his sordidness he still had in his breast a little spark of courtesy, so he received the minstrel with a bright face and friendly words and conversed with him on many different topics. Still talking, he led him and a few other Genoese gentlemen to a new house of his that he had had built as beautifully as possible, and after showing it off from cellar to garret, he said: "Well, now, Messer Guglielmo, you who have seen and heard so many things . . . Could you show me, perhaps, something that's never been seen, so that I might have it painted in the reception room of this house of mine?"

Guglielmo, at this arrogant speech, replied: "Sir, I'm afraid it would not be possible for me to show you anything that's never been seen—unless you mean sneezes, and such things. And yet, if you wish, I suppose I could show you something that I think you've never seen."

"Well, well, come, tell me what it is," urged Erminio, expecting no such answer as the minstrel had in store for him.

"Have Generosity painted there," he answered, readily.

The moment Erminio heard the word he was overwhelmed with such sudden shame, that it immediately transformed him into an entirely different man. "Guglielmo," he said, "I shall have it painted in such a way that neither you, nor anyone else will ever have just cause to say I have never seen or known it."

The virtue of Guglielmo's words was so great that from then on Erminio was the most generous and gracious of gentlemen, entertaining more strangers and townspeople than any other man of his time in Genoa.

✳

## THE NINTH STORY

*The King of Cyprus, reprimanded by a Gascon lady, turns from a craven to a man of character.*

THE QUEEN'S LAST INVITATION WAS TO BE FOR ELISA, WHO SPOKE, all smiles, without waiting to be told:

We all know that, what a variety of rebukes and punishments have often not availed to accomplish in a man, a chance word thrown in at the proper moment has done with success. Lauretta's story showed this perfectly, and I'd like to prove it further with another very short one. Good examples are always useful, dear ladies, and should be listened to with a wide-awake mind, no matter who tells them.

Now, then—in the days of the first king of Cyprus, after the conquest of the Holy Land by Godfrey of Bouillon, a noble lady of Gascony undertook a pilgrimage to the Holy Sepulchre. On her way back she had just reached Cyprus when she was criminally attacked by some mean scoundrels. She complained bitterly, but without avail, and at last she thought of applying to the king for satisfaction of her wrongs. She was told, however, that she would be wasting her efforts, for the king was so cowardly and lackadaisical that he not only failed to exercise his justice in avenging the wrongs of others, but even tolerated with shameful poltroonery countless insults to himself. Indeed, whoever bore him a grudge used to vent his feelings by doing him some wrong or shameful spite.

When the woman heard this, she gave up all hope of being avenged, and yet, if only to get some slight compensation for her suffering, she thought it might be worth her while to appear before the king and sting him to the quick.

"Sire," she said, coming before him in tears, "I am not here to seek vengeance for the indignity done me, but I beg you, as a sort of satisfaction, to show me how you are able to bear the wrongs I hear you put up with, that I may learn from you how to shoulder my own with patience. God knows, I would willingly transfer them to you if it were only possible—so well you seem to bear them!"

The king, who up to that time had been slow and torpid, awoke as if from sleep. Beginning with the outrage done to the woman, which he severely punished, he set about being an unflinching prosecutor of anyone who dared commit anything to tarnish the honor of his crown.

# THE TENTH STORY

*Master Alberto of Bologna courteously turns tables on a woman who had sought to shame him for being in love with her.*

NOW THAT ELISA HAD CEASED SPEAKING, THE FINAL STORY REmained for the queen to tell, and she began it with great feminine charm:

Gracious ladies, just as on a clear night the stars are the adornment of heaven, and in the spring, the flowers of the green meadows, so, too, are witty conceits the embroideries of fine manners and pleasing speech, especially when they are wittily brief, for then they are more becoming to women than to men. Long and abundant speech has always been more prejudicial to women than to men, especially when it can be dispensed with, so that nowadays there's hardly a woman left who can catch a clever sally or make a fine rejoinder—even if she chanced to understand it. Shame on us, and on all women alive! To-day the wit that once adorned the minds of women long dead, is being expended on the embellishment of the body. Now the woman on whose back you see the most extravagant glory of color, and gauds, and stripes and fringes, imagines herself far more deserving of respect and honor than anybody else—not realizing that if only there were a man to do it, an ass' rump and shoulders could be laden with much more finery than any living woman could bear, which simply means she's no more to be honored than an ass.

I hate to confess it—for there's nothing I can say against others that does not reflect upon myself. But really, just think of these women, all trimmed and painted and bedecked, who either stand dumb and senseless like marble statues at the least question, or answer in such a way that it would have been far better for them to keep silent! They give you to believe, too, that their deficiency of conversation with women or intelligent men, proceeds from the purity of their minds, and upon their stupidity they bestow the name of virtue! As if no woman were virtuous but the one who can only speak to her servants, her washerwoman or the pastry-cook! They'd convince you, besides, that if nature had intended, she'd have given them quite another manner of chattering. The truth is, that in this as in other things, one must consider the time and place and the person to whom one is talking. Otherwise it sometimes happens that those who hope to raise a blush with some bit of charming cleverness, fail to measure forces with their opponents, and so the embarrassment they wanted to throw on others, falls back upon themselves. Now then, in order that you may know how to look after yourselves, and what's more, that you may not give grounds for the proverb which says women always get the bitter end of things, I'd like you to take to heart this closing story, which remains for me to tell. And as you are distinguished from the rest of our sex by the loftiness of your minds, I want you also to reveal yourselves in a class apart, by the perfection of your behavior.

Not so very long ago, there lived in Bologna—and for all I know may be living to this day—a famous physician, renowned the world over, whose name was Master Alberto. He was seventy at the time, and although well-nigh all the natural heat had left his body, such was his youthfulness of spirit that he did not disdain to welcome the flames of love. At a party, noticing a beautiful widow called, as some say, Malgherida de' Ghisolieri, he was so immensely taken with her that he exposed himself like the merest boy to the fire of passion, and was so burnt that he would toss sleepless on his bed all night unless he had gazed upon the lady's lovely face the day before. Pricked by his longing he formed the habit of passing by her house, either on foot or on horseback as the whim seized him, until finally both the lady and many of her friends grew cognizant of the reason for his assiduous promenades. Very often they enjoyed themselves greatly, at the thought of a learned graybeard like Master Alberto in the throes of passion, as though the sweet rapture of love could only dwell and thrive in the witless minds of youth, and nowhere else.

Now while he continued his promenading, the widow and a number of other women who were sitting with her in front of the door on a certain holiday, caught sight of him at a distance, bound towards them on his usual errand. Together they hit upon a plan to welcome him and do him honor, in order to tease him later about this flame of his. No sooner said than done. They rose at his approach and inviting him to enter, led him to a cool courtyard where they ordered the choicest wines and dainties to be brought. At length they began with many pretty words to ask him how he could be so rash as to fall in love with the fair lady, considering how many fine, handsome, brisk young men languished for her. The doctor felt their padded sting, and answered without twitching a muscle:

"Madam, the fact that I'm in love should not astonish a person of sense, and you least of all, for you are worthy of my love. It's true that in the natural course of things old men are deprived of the vigor necessary to amorous bouts; nevertheless they are not deprived of the will to love, nor of the good taste to know what ought to be loved. On the contrary, it is appreciated by them all the more, because of the advantage of their experience over youth. The hope that moves me, an old man, to have a passion for you who are adored by so many young blades is simply this—I have often been in places where I have been able to watch women eating lupins and leeks. Now in the leek very little is good except the head, which is less disagreeable and perhaps a little pleasanter to the taste than the rest of it. But you women, what do you do? Depraved in your appetite, you generally hold the head in your hands and chew at the leaves, which are not only worthless but nasty to the taste. How should I know, my dear lady, that you don't do the same thing in choosing your lovers? If that's your practice, I ought to be the chosen one, and the others sent packing."

The gentle lady and her friends were put to the blush. "Sir," she said, "you have very justly punished us, in your mannerly way, for our boldness. I want you to know I appreciate your love, as all love should be, that comes from a wise and virtuous man. Everything I have, saving my honor is at your disposal, to do with as you like best."

The doctor rose with his companions and thanked the lady. Then, laughing gaily, he took leave of her and went home. This way the woman, who did not realize whom she was trying to abash, was herself put to shame—which you will all take care to guard yourselves against, if you are wise.

The sun was already sinking toward dusk, and the heat had greatly subsided when the day's stories came to an end.

"From now on," the queen pleasantly addressed her court of men and women, "little more is left in my power to do except to give you a new queen whose task it will be to arrange her life and ours for the future with all thought to our legitimate pleasure, according to her judgment. Though the day may be said to continue from now until nightfall, it seems to me we cannot very well provide for what is to come, unless we take advantage of a little time beforehand. Therefore I think all subsequent days should start at this hour, so that the new queen may have a chance to plan what she thinks suitable for the day after. In reverence to Him, then, through whose grace all things have life, and for our delight, I choose Filomena to rule our kingdom for to-morrow, in her wisdom and discretion."

When she had spoken she rose to her feet and taking the laurel wreath from her own head, she laid it respectfully on Filomena's. She was the first to salute her as queen, and after her the young people together, who gladly submitted themselves to the new rule.

Filomena blushed slightly to see herself crowned with the symbol of power, but bethinking herself of what Pampinea had said a little while since, she had no wish to appear foolish and quickly regained her confidence. To begin with, she confirmed all the offices established by her predecessor and gave orders for the night's supper, as well as for the next day's preparations. Meantime they remained where they were and Filomena addressed them:

"Dearest friends, although Pampinea has made me your queen, more out of her innate courtesy than because of my ability, I am still not disposed to follow my judgment alone in arranging for our continued habitation, but I'd appreciate your opinion as well. To make myself clear, I'd like to tell you in a few words what I want you to do, and then you may improve upon my plan to make whatever suggestions you see fit. To-day I studied Pampinea's procedure very closely, and I found it both pleasant and laudable. I should not want it to be altered in any way, that is, not unless it should bore us either through too long usage, or for any other reason. Well, then, abiding by what we have begun, let's get up and walk about a little for our diversion. Later, in the evening freshness, we'll have supper by the light of the setting sun, and sing and dance and amuse ourselves a while. Then it would be sensible for us to retire. To-morrow we'll get up in the cool of the morning, and again we'll pass the time somewhere amusing ourselves according to our individual desires, after which we shall have our meal at the proper hour, as we did to-day. Dancing will follow that, and then, rising from our nap, we'll come back here to resume our story-telling which seems to be as profitable as it is delightful.

"There's still another thing I'd like to introduce which Pampinea was unable to do in her rather late election to power. It's simply to limit the theme of our story-telling and give you the subject beforehand, so that you may have ample time to think of some interesting story to tell *à propos*. If my plan pleases you, here's the theme: inasmuch as men have always been tossed about by the various tricks of chance since the very beginning of time, and doubtless will continue at their mercy to the end of time, let each of you tell *of someone who after being tormented by various misfortunes achieves at last a happier result than he had hoped for*."

All of them approved of the new order and agreed to abide by it. Dioneo alone had something to say after the others had quieted down. "I'm quite in accord with what my companions have said," he pronounced, "and think the order you have given is highly pleasant and much to be praised. But as a special grace I beg a privilege which I hope you will grant me, as long as our band stays together. Don't let me be bound by this rule to tell a story on a set theme, if I don't feel like it—rather, leave me free to tell whatever I please. But to avoid the misconception that I'm begging this privilege, simply because I'm the sort of fellow who hasn't plenty of stories at hand, I'm quite content to be the last to speak, from now on."

The queen knew him to be a merry, spirited rogue, and was perfectly well aware he made the request simply to cheer the company with some prankish story when they were all tired of their diversion. With the others' consent, she gladly acquiesced to his request.

They rose when all was settled and wended their way slowly to a stream of crystal-clear water, that coursed down a little hill to a valley shady with many trees, where it continued among vivid mossy rocks and fresh green grasses. They waded in the water, their arms and legs bare, and played many little games among themselves. Toward supper-time they returned to the palace and ate with good will. Afterwards the queen called for the instruments and asked for a dance to be led by Lauretta while Emilia sang a song to the accompaniment of Dioneo's lute. Obediently Lauretta took up a round without need of coaxing, and conducted it while Emilia amorously sang:

"So stricken am I by my beauty's might
That in all other love
I'll never burn nor ever find delight.

In my own beauty when I hold the glass
I see that good which overjoys the mind.
No newer fortunes or old thoughts that pass
Can take from me the sweetness there I find.
What object of more pleasurable kind
Could I then see to love,
Or stir within my heart a new delight?

It never flees from me whenever I
Would gaze upon it for my own content;
Indeed, it gently comes my pleasure nigh
With such sweet grace, that never mortal bent
To speak it fair could know its whole intent
Unless he also love
And be inflamed with similar delight.

And I with every hour more fiercely burn
The more my gaze upon it I arrest,
All of me yield to it, myself I turn
To its dominion . . . Now the joys I wrest
That it had promised, and await the best
The sweetest joy of love
That never yet was equalled for delight."

The ballad over, in which all had joyfully taken part, though a few were not a little puzzled by the words, a number of other dances were performed. By this time a good part of the all too short night was past, and the queen thought it best to call a halt, and the torches were lighted. Dismissing her little company, she sent the men and women to rest in their separate apartments until morning.

# 2

## THE SECOND DAY

✻

ALREADY THE LIGHT OF THE SUN HAD SPREAD ABROAD THE NEW day, and the little birds, trilling their gleeful carols among the green branches, announced it to the ear. The women and the three youths rose with the bright day and all went into the garden together, treading the dew-wet grass and wandering about as they pleased, twining lovely garlands for themselves and romping for a long while.

Once more they did as they had the day before, lunching during the cool hours, dancing, and then away for a rest. They got up from their nap after the heat of noon had abated, and gathering in the fresh meadow at the queen's pleasure, they sat in a circle about her. Then Filomena, who was a shapely girl, and even lovelier than ever wearing her laurel wreath, gazed around at her little band and after a moment's reflection asked Neifile to begin the day's stories. She obeyed without demur, and began most graciously:

✻

## THE FIRST STORY

*Martellino, pretending to be a cripple, makes believe he is healed over the body of Saint Heinrich. His trumpery is discovered and he is beaten; then captured, and in danger of being hanged by the neck, he eventually escapes.*

IT IS OFTEN THE CASE, DEAR LADIES, THAT A MAN WHO GOES OUT of his way to make fun of other men and particularly of things that ought to be respected, often finds himself alone with his jibes, and sometimes is himself the goat. Well, in obedience to the queen's command, I shall usher in the given theme with one of my stories, and tell you of the extraordinary adventures that befell a fellow-townsman, who fortunately got out of them in the end, none the worse for the experience.

Not so long ago there lived a German at Trevigi, whose name was Heinrich. He was a poor devil of a fellow who used to carry burdens for anyone who paid him, but was highly thought of as a man of good and holy living. When the time came for him to die, the people of Trevigi insisted that the bells of the great cathedral had begun to ring mightily when he drew his last breath, and the wonder of it was that no hand had been there to ring them. Looking upon this as a miracle, they began spreading the rumor that Heinrich was a saint. Soon all the people of the city, gathering at the house where his body lay, took it and bore it, with the pomp befitting a saint, to the cathedral. What is more, they led with them the lame, the paralyzed and the blind, and many other wretches stricken by all kinds of sickness and deformity, expecting all of them to get well again simply by touching the body.

In the midst of all this hubbub and running of people, fate would have it that three of our townsmen arrived at Trevigi, of whom one was called Stecchi, the other Martellino, and the third Marchese. They were actor-folk who used to visit the courts of great lords and delight their audiences by mimicking and counterfeiting any given man, with many a comical trick and gesture. Since they had never been in that city before, they were amazed at seeing everybody running about, and hearing the reason for the commotion, they were all agog to see things for themselves. They deposited their baggage at an inn, and Marchese said: "It's all well and good for us to want to go and look at this saint, but I can't see how we'll be able to manage it. The square is full of Germans, and soldiers that the prince has stationed to prevent mischief. Besides, from what I hear, the church is so full of people that there's hardly room for a fly."

Then Martellino, who was itching to see what was to be seen, cried: "Don't let that discourage you! I'll see about finding a way of getting to the holy body." "Yes? And how?" asked Marchese.

"I'll tell you," answered Martellino. "I'll make believe I am a cripple. You on one side, and Stecchi on the other, will hold me up as though I couldn't walk by myself, and you must pretend that you want to lead me to the saint, for him to make me well again. There won't be a single man Jack of them that won't make room to let us pass, the moment he lays eyes on poor me!"

The trick tickled the fancy of Stecchi and Marchese. They left the inn without delay, and when all three had reached an unfrequented place, Martellino fell to twisting his hands, his fingers, and his arms and legs. Even his mouth, eyes, and his whole face he screwed up in such a way that he was a fright to see. There wasn't a man who wouldn't have sworn he was really the wreck of a human body, to look at him. Taking him up in this shape, Marchese and Stecchi then directed their steps toward the church, pulling very long, pious faces, and humbly beseeching everyone to make way for them, for the love of God. No one could withstand them. In short, they were the cynosure of all eyes, and so terrible a sight that almost everyone shouted, "Make room! Make room!" until at last they reached the place where the good saint's body was lying. Helped by some gentlemen who stood around, Martellino was quickly lifted up and laid upon the body, that by its virtues he might regain the blessing of health.

While the people were craning their necks to see what would happen to him, Martellino, after waiting a moment, began feigning in a manner of which he was a master. First he stretched out a finger, and then his whole hand, and later an arm, little by little straightening himself out altogether. When the people saw the wonder, they set up such a tumult in praise of Saint Heinrich, that God's own thunder couldn't have been heard above it.

As luck would have it, a Florentine was near by who knew Martellino very well. He had not recognized him at first—for who would have, seeing him led up in such shape?—but now that he saw him straight, he knew him immediately. Spontaneously, he broke into a laugh, saying: "The devil take him! Who wouldn't have believed him really a cripple, to see him in that fix?"

These words were overheard by some people of Trevigi, who questioned him at once: "How? What? Wasn't this fellow crippled?"

"Of course not, so help me God!" replied the Florentine. "He's always been as straight as either you or I. But he's a clever rogue, who knows better than anyone else, as you saw for yourselves, the art of playing these tricks and changing himself into any shape he wishes."

They needed nothing further. Pushing forward by main force, they began shouting: "Seize the traitor! Catch this mocker of God and his saints! Get hold of him who was no cripple and came here only to jeer at us and scoff at our saint!"

So saying, they seized him and pulled him down from where he was, and taking him by the hair ripped all the clothes off his back, and set to giving him a sound hiding. There wasn't a man among them who didn't run to have his share of the fun. "Mercy, for God's sake!" roared Martellino, defending himself as best he could. It was in vain, and the crowd at his back grew larger with every passing minute.

Seeing the state of affairs, Stecchi and Marchese reflected that things were getting too hot for their comfort, and fearing for their own hides, they did not dare come to his aid. Indeed, with the rest of them they cried, "Kill him! Kill him!" though inwardly they planned how best to get him out of the mob's hands. Undoubtedly he would have been killed if Marchese had not done some quick thinking. He knew that the retainers of the gentlefolk were outside. As fast as his legs could carry him, he went to a man who was acting for the provost, and said: "Help, for God's sake! There's an ugly ruffian inside who's cut my purse with a good hundred gold florins in it. Catch him, good sir, I beg you, and let me get back what belongs to me!"

Immediately soldiers a dozen strong ran to the place where Martellino was being torn to shreds, and breaking through the mob with the greatest pains in the world, rescued him, all broken and bruised as he was. Away to the palace they led him, followed by a multitude of men who somehow considered themselves personally offended by him. Hearing that Martellino had been taken for a cutpurse, and considering they could have no better pretext to lead him a merry dance, they all began saying they had had their purses stolen by him. The rumors reached the ears of the judge, a harsh and bitter man. He promptly took Martellino aside and began asking him questions. But Martellino answered smartly, as though making a jest of his capture, at which the judge was so incensed that, ordering poor Martellino to be trussed up, he had him given a good trouncing to make him confess what he was charged with, so that later he might be strung up by the neck.

When he was released again, and the judge asked whether the things the people reported against him were true, Martellino, having learned the better part of valor, said: "Your honor, I am ready to confess the truth. But first, let each of my accusers say when and where I stole his purse. Then I'll tell you what I did do, and what I did not do."

"That suits me," said the judge, and caused a number of the accusers to be brought before him. One said Martellino had stolen his purse eight days ago, still another, four, and some even said that very day.

"Your honor, they all lie in their throats!" cried Martellino. "I can prove to you that I am telling the truth. Believe me, I got here only a couple of hours ago, would to God I had never come at all! The moment I arrived, I went, God help me, for a peep at that holy body in the church, where I was mauled as you can see with your own eyes. The Prince's officer, who is in charge of arrivals, his registry-book and my landlord, too, can prove that what I say is true. So if you find things to be as I tell you, for mercy's sake don't torture me, or put me to death at the instigation of these wicked men!"

While things were at this pass, Marchese and Stecchi who had learned that the provost's judge was shaking the devil out of Martellino, and had already given him a good trouncing, were very much frightened, saying to themselves: "A fine job we've made of it, taking the poor wretch out of the frying pan, only to throw him into the fire!"

With all the haste they could muster, they went in search of their landlord, and when they had found him, related how the matter stood. He laughed loud and long to hear it, and then introduced them to a certain Sandro Agolanti, who lived in Trevigi and enjoyed great favor with the Prince. Telling him everything exactly as it had happened, the landlord, supported by the two friends, pleaded with him to interest himself in Martellino's case. Accordingly, after many a laugh, Sandro went to the Prince and begged him to send for Martellino.

The men who went to fetch him, found Martellino still in his shirt, completely bewildered and very much afraid, because the judge seemed to have made up his mind not to listen to reason. Indeed, cherishing some grudge, as it happened, against Florentines in general, he was in love with the idea of hanging

Martellino by the neck, and by no means would he surrender his victim to the Prince, until he was virtually compelled to yield him, much against his wishes. At last, in the presence of the Prince, Martellino related everything in due order, pleading that as a special grace he should be allowed to go away, for as long as he was out of Florence he felt the air was not good for his health, and he couldn't get rid of the notion that the halter was around his neck.

The Prince laughed very heartily at Martellino's misadventures, and ordered a fine suit of clothes to be given to each of the three friends who, delivered beyond all their expectations from so great a peril, at last returned home, safe and sound.

✳

## THE SECOND STORY

*After falling into the hands of robbers, Rinaldo d'Asti finds his way to the town of Guglielmo, where he is taken in by a widow. He gets back all his goods and returns home none the worse for his adventure.*

CHOKING WITH LAUGHTER OVER THE PREDICAMENT INTO WHICH Martellino had got, the women attested to their delight in Neifile's story. Since Filostrato, sitting next to Neifile, seemed especially amused, the queen bade him take his turn with a story, and he began without delay:

Lovely ladies, I am inspired to tell you a tale of Catholic things, partly mingled with mishaps and matters of love, which, I'm sure, will do you no harm to hear,—particularly those of you who have traveled through the dubious lands of love, where even he who has said Saint Julian's Paternoster, is often ill-housed, though he may have a good bed.

Once upon a time in the days of the Marquis Azzo da Ferrara, there lived a merchant called Rinaldo d'Asti who had come to Bologna on certain business. Having attended to it, he was making his way homeward when, on the road between Ferrara and Verona, he came across some men who looked like respectable merchants, but were in reality robbers and men of low life and rank. Very foolishly, he stopped to talk with them, and joined their company.

As it was, they were aware he was a merchant, and suspected

he must have money on his person, which made them decide among themselves to fall upon him the first chance they got. They did not want to rouse his suspicions, however, so like decent folk they told him all kinds of fairy-tales about honesty, loyalty and so-forth and so-on, doing everything in their power to make him think them very humble and well-disposed toward him. They so cajoled him, that he soon believed himself very lucky to have met them, for he was traveling along, with only one servant, on horseback. As they rode on and on together, they got to talking about one thing and another, as is always the way in such cases, and finally came on the subject of prayer. One of the bandits, who were three in number, addressing himself to Rinaldo, said: "I say, my good man, what prayers are you accustomed to say when you travel?"

"To tell the truth," answered Rinaldo, "I'm a plain, simple man, unlearned in these things, and I've only a couple of prayers at my command. Mine is the old-fashioned way of living, with my philosophy that six of one are as good as half a dozen of the other. But anyhow, it has always been my custom when I'm on the road, to say a *Paternoster* and an *Ave* for the souls of St. Julian's father and mother, the moment I leave the inn. Afterwards, I pray directly to God and the good saint himself, to send me proper shelter for the coming night. It's often happened in my day that I've been in many a hole in the course of my travels, but I've always managed to escape danger, and at night I've even found myself in a safe and well-sheltered place. That's why I firmly believe that St. Julian—all honor to him!—has always won me this grace of God. Why, I've got so that I'm convinced I couldn't have a good journey during the day, or reach a lodging-place at night, unless I had said my prayers in the morning."

Then the man who had questioned him said again: "And did you say them this morning?"

"I should think so," replied Rinaldo.

Then the rogue, who knew how things were going to be, said to himself: "May they do you much good, then, for if nothing comes to spoil our plans, you're likely to have mighty poor lodging, to my way of thinking." Aloud he said: "I too have traveled a lot, but I've never said this prayer to St. Julian, though I've heard many people recommend it. Yet in spite of that, it's never happened that I have found anything but good lodging. Perhaps to-night we'll be able to test which one of us is going to be better housed—you with your prayer, or I, without it. It's true, though, that I say others instead, like the *Dirupisti,* or the *Intemerata,* or the *De profundis,* all prayers of remarkable power, to believe an old grandmother of mine."

As they journeyed on, talking of different things, and biding the propitious time and place for their evil purpose, they came towards evening to a spot some distance from the town of Guglielmo, at the fording of a stream. Seeing that it was late, and the locality deserted and lonely, they fell upon Rinaldo, robbed him of everything he had, and left him bare-footed, with only his shirt on his back.

"Now go and find out," they said, "if your precious St. Julian will give you as fine a lodging as our saint gives us."

Fording the stream, they galloped away.

Rinaldo's servant, seeing his master attacked, did not raise a finger to help him, like the coward he was, but turning his horse away from the fray, goaded it on and did not stop riding until he had reached the town of Guglielmo. It was night by this time, and without bothering his head about anything further, he went in and found shelter for the night.

It was bitter cold and the snow was falling heavily. Poor Rinaldo, abandoned to his fate, bare-footed and with only a shirt to cover him, did not know what to do when he saw night already approaching. His body shivering and his teeth chattering pretty music, he looked about him in the hope of finding some hole where he might pass the night and not freeze to death, but there was nothing to be seen. Only a little while past, a war had broken out in that part of the country and everything had been razed to the ground. But the cold urged him on, and running as fast as he could, he went toward Guglielmo, not knowing whether his servant had fled to that town or elsewhere, but trusting anyhow that God would send him help, if only he could succeed in entering its gates.

The darkness of night overtook him about a mile from the town, and he reached it so late that as the gates were closed and the drawbridges lifted, he was unable to gain entrance. Who can say how sad and forlorn he was, and how he wept as he looked about him for a shelter where at least it wouldn't be snowing on his back? Fortunately, he was able to perceive a house that projected somewhat beyond the town walls, and under that protection he decided to wait until morning. When he crawled under, he found a door against the wall, locked fast, so heaping up a mound of straw that happened to be strewn about, he made himself a bed at the foot of it and settled down in a woeful state, complaining to St. Julian that he certainly deserved better treatment than this, for the great faith he bore him. But St. Julian had indeed a sincere regard for his petitioner, and readily set about to find him proper lodging.

In this town there chanced to be living a widowed lady, as handsome a one as you could ever hope to see, whom the Marquis of Azzo loved as his own life. There he had put her up for his pleasure, and as it happened, in the very house under whose projection Rinaldo had settled down. Only the day before, the marquis had come to Guglielmo in order to go to bed with her, and had secretly ordered a bath to be prepared at her home, and an excellent supper. Everything was ready and nothing was lacking but the arrival of the lover, when a messenger came to the town-gate bringing the marquis news that obliged him to take to horse and ride away post-haste; thus he notified the lady not to expect him, and went quickly away. The lady was quite disappointed and didn't know what to do. She resolved therefore, to go into the bath prepared for the marquis, and then to have supper and go to bed. Without more ado she entered the bath.

As it happened, the bathroom was situated near the door against which the miserable Rinaldo had huddled up, on the other side of the town-wall, so that as she bathed she could not help hearing the music and dance kept up by the poor fellow as he wept and shivered. Indeed, he seemed to have become a regular stork.

The lady summoned her maid. "Go up," she said, "and look down over the wall at the foot of this door. See who it is, and what sort of man, and find out what on earth he's doing there."

The maid went, and in the limpid atmosphere she was able to discern the unfortunate creature, barelegged and in his shirt, all huddled up and trembling violently.

"Who are you?" she called.

Rinaldo could hardly form the words, he shivered so miserably; but as briefly as he could, he told her who he was and what had brought him there. Then most piteously he entreated her not to leave him to freeze to death during the night, but to shelter him if she could.

The maid was moved to pity at his predicament and returned to her mistress, telling her all she had learned. The lady, too, was sorry for him. Suddenly she remembered she had the key to the door which was sometimes used by the marquis on his secret visits.

"Go," she said, "and let him in very discreetly. There's all this supper here and no one to eat it, and we've no lack of room to put him up."

The maid praised her for such humanity and went to admit Rinaldo. The lady, seeing him almost frozen stiff, invited him: "Quick, poor thing, get into that bath! It's still warm."

He needed no coaxing, and did as he was told. Soon he was so soothed by the pleasant warmth that he fancied himself brought back from death to life.

Meanwhile the lady had some clothes prepared for him, that had belonged to her recently departed husband, and no sooner did Rinaldo put them on, than it seemed as though they had been cut to his figure. As he waited for the woman's further bidding, he thanked God and St. Julian for delivering him from the horrible night he had expected, and bringing him to the wonderful lodging the place seemed to promise.

Rinaldo once dressed, the widow, who was by this time somewhat rested from her bath, had a cheery fire made in her drawing-room, and inquired how things were going with the poor fellow.

"Madam, he's all dressed," said the maid, "and he's a good-looking man, too. Besides, he has a well-bred way about him, as though he amounted to something."

"Go and call him, then," said her mistress, "and tell him to come by the fire and eat, for I'm sure he must be starved."

Rinaldo entered the room, and seeing the woman, who looked to him like a person of rank, he greeted her courteously and thanked her in his best manner, for the kindness she had done him. She, too, on seeing him and hearing him talk, found him to be as her maid had described him. Cheerfully she greeted him, and invited him to sit with her familiarly by the fire, and then asked him what misadventure had brought him there in that predicament. One by one, Rinaldo told her the events as they had occurred.

It happened that she had heard rumors of the affair when Rinaldo's man had arrived at the town, so that she had to make no effort to believe all he said. She told him, besides, what she knew of his servant, and advised him how he could locate him the following day, without much trouble. Then the table was laid and according to her wishes, both washed their hands together and sat down to supper.

A tall, well-set man was Rinaldo, with a handsome, pleasing countenance and charming, ingratiating ways. He was young, too, and in the prime of life. More than once the lady had allowed her eyes to steal a look at him, and inwardly she had passed very favorable judgment on what they saw. As her flesh was already stirred by anticipation of the marquis, who was to have lain with her, she found no difficulty in taking a fancy to Rinaldo.

After supper they rose from the table, and privately the woman asked her maid's advice. Wasn't it right, since the marquis had left her in the lurch, that she should take advantage of the boon which luck had brought her? The maid knew what her mistress was aiming at, and encouraged her to do as she wished. At that the lady returned to the fireside, where she had left Rinaldo by himself, and gazed at him with love in her eyes.

"Come, come, Rinaldo," she said. "Why are you so sad? Don't you think you can be compensated for the loss of a horse and a few clothes? Cheer up! Be gay! You're at home here. Listen, I'll whisper something else! When I saw you in those clothes that used to belong to my late husband—dear soul!—I thought you were he, and really, more than a hundred times to-night, I felt like throwing my arms around your neck and kissing you! If I hadn't been afraid of making you angry, I'd have done it, I swear!"

On hearing this pretty speech and seeing the flashing of the woman's eyes, Rinaldo who was no fool, went toward her with open arms.

"Madam," he said, "considering that I owe my very life to you, and realizing what a predicament you helped me out of, I'd be an ill-bred lout if I didn't do my best to please you in every possible way. Come to me, and for the present hug and kiss me to your heart's content. As for me, I'll not have to be begged to do the same for you, dear lady."

No other words were needed. The widow, who was burning with desire, flung herself quickly into his arms, and after she had pressed him close with yearning and kissed him a thousand times, receiving as many kisses in return, she left the room with him and both went to her chamber. They got to bed immediately, and many times before daybreak, they fulfilled their desires to the utmost.

But when dawn began to filter in, they rose at her suggestion, to avoid the shadow of suspicion. She gave him some shabby clothes and a purse full of money, told him how to go about finding his servant in the town, and let him out through the little door by which he had entered, begging him not to reveal their little secret.

The town gates were opened in broad daylight. Rinaldo, pretending he came from a much greater distance, made his way in and located his man. Changing into the clothes he found in his saddlebag, he was about to mount his servant's horse when, as by divine providence, the three malefactors who had despoiled him the night before, and had just been caught for some new mischief, were being led to town. On the strength of their confession, Rinaldo's horse was restored to him, as well as his clothes and money, and he found himself short of only a pair of garters, the loss of which the robbers could not explain.

Proffering his thanks to God and St. Julian for their mercies, Rinaldo mounted his horse and returned home safe and sound. As for the three robbers, the following day they danced a jig at the end of a rope.

✳

## THE THIRD STORY

*Three young men are facing poverty, having squandered their inheritance, when a nephew of theirs, journeying home in great discouragement, meets a young abbot and finds him to be the King of England's daughter in disguise. She marries him and restores all his uncles' losses, setting them up in plenty once more.*

THE WOMEN HAD LISTENED WITH WONDER TO THE ADVENTURES OF Rinaldo d'Asti, and his devotion pleased them so much that they gave thanks to God and St. Julian for having come to his rescue in his sorest need. Nor did they think the woman foolish for taking advantage of the bounty God had let fall in her very house though, of course, such things were said secretly among themselves. While they were mischievously commenting on the wonderful night the widow must have enjoyed, Pampinea, who was sitting beside Filostrato, and knew her turn would come next, as indeed it did, took her opportunity to think over what she was going to say. Then, at the queen's command, she began with as much spirit as gaiety:

The more we speak of Fortune's ways, noble ladies, the more we find to talk about, in all justice to her. And it's not to be wondered at, when we seriously consider how everything we foolishly call our own, is really in her hands, shifted from one to the other and back again, in a way that we cannot even understand. Even though this fact is fully demonstrated every single day, in every possible thing, and though it has been proved in some of the previous stories, I'll add one of my own, which may be of some service to you, since our queen wishes us to abide by the theme she set us. I hope you will like it, as I think you will.

There was once in our city a nobleman by the name of Tedaldo, who some claimed was descended from the Lamberti stock, and others from the Agolanti, basing this, perhaps, more on the business which his sons later carried on, than on anything else—a business which the Agolanti have always been known to be engaged in, and follow to this day. But that is beside the point. Well, as I was saying, he was a nobleman in his time, and very rich. He had three sons, besides, the eldest of whom was called Lamberto, the second Tedaldo, and the third Agolante. All of them were fine, strapping youths, but when the wealthy Tedaldo came to die, the eldest was barely eighteen years old. However, all his worldly goods, both movable and immovable, fell to them as his legitimate heirs.

When the young men found themselves in the possession of such tremendous wealth, both in money and lands, and with no restraint upon their own sweet will, they began to squander money recklessly. They maintained a huge household, kept many fine horses, hounds and hawks, and continual open house. They gave generously, arranged all kinds of feats of arms, and not only led the sort of life gentlemen are supposed to lead, but did whatever pleased their youthful appetites as well.

They had not been carrying on in this fashion very long, when the wealth their father had left them began to dwindle. Their income alone was no longer enough for their current expenses, and soon they had to sell or mortgage their lands. Disposing of one to-day and another to-morrow, they discovered they had almost nothing left of their patrimony, and now poverty took the scales from the eyes which prosperity had blinded.

One day Lamberto called his two brothers to him, and made

them understand how vast their father's wealth had been, how considerable their own riches, and how abject, also, was the poverty to which they had sunk through their inordinate profligacy. Then he urged them, before their poverty became notorious, to sell what little was still left them and leave the country. They thought it well to act on his advice. Without any leavetaking or further ceremony, they left Florence and did not cease traveling until they came to England. There they took a modest house in the city of London, and living very economically, set up as moneylenders. So generously did Fortune smile on their enterprise, that in a few years they accumulated such enormous wealth that one by one they returned to Florence, bought back a great part of their former possessions, as well as other people's property, settled down and married. In the meantime they still carried on their money-lending in England, sending a nephew of theirs, Alessandro by name, to take charge of their affairs while they remained in Florence. However, in spite of the responsibilities of their married state, and unmindful, too, of what their former profligacy had once made them suffer, they continued to waste money more recklessly than ever. They became indebted for vast sums of money, to the merchants who trusted them for any amount, however exorbitant; but to a certain extent their expenses were eked out for several years by the income Alessandro used to send them. The youth had set up in business for himself, lending money at interest to barons, on their castles and other holdings, and finding it exceedingly profitable.

Soon, however, while the three brothers were squandering their money with such a free hand and borrowing as freely and still putting their trust in England, an unexpected war broke out between the English king and his son, which divided the whole island into two factions, some siding with the one and some with the other. All the castles Alessandro held from the barons were confiscated, and he was left without any source of income whatsoever. Day in and day out he hoped for peace between father and son, with the consequent restoration of his goods, both interest and capital, and on the basis of that vain hope, he refused to leave the island. In Florence, meanwhile, the three brothers did not limit their reckless expenditures one jot, but went on borrowing more and more each day. At last, when several years had elapsed and their hopes bore no fruit, they not only lost their credit, but their liberty to boot; for when their creditors had clamored to be paid and the brothers' property did not suffice to cover their debts, they were clapped into prison for the remainder.

Their wives and little children were separated and scattered. Some took refuge in the country, some here, some there, in the worst of circumstances, and with no expectation but poverty as long as they lived.

As time went on, Alessandro, who had been waiting in England for a peace that did not come, began to reflect that he was not only wasting his time in vain, but also placing his life in jeopardy. He determined, therefore, to go back to Italy, and accordingly, one day he set out, all by himself. Just as he was leaving Bruges, he perceived that an abbot in a white gown was starting out at the same time, accompanied by many monks, a large retinue, and with imposing equipage in the fore. Two elderly knights followed behind, who were related to the king. Alessandro greeted them as old acquaintances, and he was admitted to their company, without further ceremony.

While he pursued his way with them, he quietly asked who all those monks were, that were traveling before them with such an escort, and where they were bound for.

"The young man who is riding ahead," said one of the gentlemen, "is a young kinsman of ours who has recently been appointed abbot of one of the largest abbeys in England. He's much younger than the age-limit such dignity demands, so we're going to Rome with him to urge the Holy Father to give him a dispensation for his youth, and confirm him in his office. But people mustn't know of it."

The new abbot was traveling, now in front and now behind his retinue, as is often the case with a party on a journey, when suddenly he chanced to see Alessandro near him on the road. Now Alessandro was a very personable young man, both of body and features, and as courtly, genteel and agreeable as any young gentleman you'd ever wish to see. From the very first, the abbot liked him so wonderfully well that nothing had ever pleased him more! He called Alessandro to his side, and engaged him pleasantly in conversation, asking him who he was, where he came from, and whither he was going, to which the youth answered frankly, leaving no question unsatisfied. What's more, he offered the abbot his services, in what little he could do for him.

Hearing Alessandro speak with such gentlemanly poise, and

studying his behavior more closely, the abbot concluded he must be well-born in spite of his mean trade, and began to like him even more than before. As it was, his sympathy had already been aroused by the young man's misfortunes. In all friendship, he consoled him and told him to be of good hope, for if he bore up like a brave man, God would set him high again in the place from which Fortune had flung him—indeed, He would give him an even higher pedestal. He begged him besides, that since he was bound for Tuscany, he join his company, for he, the abbot, was also on his way there. Alessandro thanked him for his encouragement and replied that he was ready to serve him in every wish.

Together they proceeded on their way, the abbot feeling all kinds of novel sensations in his breast, in the presence of Alessandro. A few days later they chanced to come upon a village that was rather lacking in hostelries. Since the abbot expressed a desire to stop there overnight, Alessandro had him dismount at the house of an innkeeper whom he happened to know pretty well, and had a bedroom prepared for him in the least uncomfortable part of the inn. By this time Alessandro had become a sort of steward to the young abbot, because of his competence, and in the present circumstance, he contrived to the best of his ability to find lodging here and there in the village, for all the retinue.

The abbot had his supper; it was already quite late and everyone had gone to bed. Alessandro approached his host and asked where he himself was going to sleep.

"To tell you the truth, I don't know myself," replied the host. "Every place is full, as you see, and my own family is sleeping on the benches. But now I think of it, there are some sacks full of grain in the abbot's room. I can take you there and fix you up a sort of bed. You can make the best of it and lie there for to-night, if you like."

"But how can I go into the abbot's room," objected Alessandro, "when you know it's so very small and narrow that not even a single one of his monks was able to lie there with him? If I'd only thought of it before his bed-curtains were drawn, I might have had some of his monks sleep on the bags, and then I could have stayed where they are now."

"Well," said the host, "this is how things stand. It's all up to you. If you'd only wish, you could be the most comfortable man in the world. The abbot's asleep and the curtains are drawn. I'll spread a mattress there on the sly, and you can go and sleep."

Alessandro saw it could be managed without disturbing the abbot, and agreed. Then as quietly as he could, he slipped in and settled down.

The abbot was far from asleep, thinking as he was, of the new desires that tormented him. He had heard what Alessandro and the innkeeper had discussed, and had also noticed where the young man had gone to lie, which made him rejoice exceedingly.

"God has ordained the proper time for my desires," he said to himself. "If I let the opportunity slip, it may not offer itself again for a long, long time."

He made up his mind to take it. Everything seemed hushed at the inn. In a low voice he called Alessandro, and invited him to lie beside him. The youth protested a good deal at first, but then undressed and lay where he was told. Immediately the abbot placed his hand on his chest and began to caress it in the manner amorous young girls use with the men they love. Alessandro was very much taken aback, and had his suspicions that the abbot was perhaps stricken with unnatural lust, feeling him all over, as he was. Somehow, whether intuitively, or through some unguarded motion of Alessandro's, the abbot immediately guessed his misgiving and smiled. Then, with a quick gesture removing the shirt he was wearing, he took Alessandro's hand and laid it on his own breast, saying: "Get rid of your foolish notions, Alessandro. Look here, and you will discover what I have been hiding."

Beneath his hand Alessandro found on the abbot's bosom two dainty little breasts, round and firm as though they had been made of ivory. No sooner was he aware that the abbot was a woman, than he needed no more urging but embraced her at once and would have kissed her, when she said: "No, listen to what I have to tell you before you come closer, Alessandro. As you see, I am a woman, not a man. I left my home a virgin, and I was on my way to the Pope, to be given away in marriage. Whether it is your luck or my misfortune I can't say, but when I saw you the other day I fell so ardently in love with you, that I'm sure no woman has ever loved a man as I love you. That's why I have determined to have you before any other man in the world. But, Alessandro, if you do not want me for your wife, go from me now, and return to your land."

Although Alessandro had no notion of who she might be, he thought of her large following and considered she must surely be nobly born, and rich. Moreover, he saw how beautiful she was. It did not take much reflection for him to reply that if this pleased her, he was more than eager to do as she wished.

At that she sat up in bed. Then, before a picture of Our Lord, she put a ring into his hand and had him perform the marriage. After the ceremony, they embraced each other, and all the remainder of the night they sported together, much to their mutual delight.

The new day rose. Together they arranged how best to settle their affairs, and getting up, Alessandro left the room the way he had come, nobody suspecting where he had slept that night. He was overflowing with joy when at last he started out again with the abbot and his following. Many days later they reached Rome. There they rested some days longer and the abbot, Alessandro and the two knights, with no one else accompanying them, gained entrance to the Pope's audience chamber. With due reverence the abbot saluted him and began:

"Holy Father, you must know better than anyone else that a person who wishes to live a good and honest life must avoid, as much as possible, everything that might lead him to live to the contrary. It was because I wished to live virtuously, to the best of my ability, that I fled secretly in the disguise you see, with a great part of the treasures of the King of England, my father. I am a young girl, but my father wanted to marry me to the King of Scotland, who is a very old gentleman. So I set out to Your Holiness, that you might give me away in marriage. It was not so much the age of the Scotch king that made me run away, as the fear I had of the weakness of my youth.

"I was terrified that if I had married the old king, I might have done something contrary to divine law and the honor of my father's royal blood. But the good Lord alone knows what is best for everyone. As I was on my way here with the intention I expressed, the Lord—out of His own loving kindness, I am sure—placed before my eyes the man He had chosen to be my husband, this very youth—" and she pointed to Alessandro, "whom you see beside me. Believe me, Holy Father, his manner and his merit are worthy of any noble lady, even though his blood may not run as pure as that of royalty. I have taken him, and I will have him, and no other man, whatever my father or anyone else may think. So much for the principal reason that brought me here. I have also wished my journey to be complete, that I might visit the holy and venerable places of this city, and you too, Holy Father. Now I trust that, through your grace, I may reveal to you, and so to the whole world, the marriage between Alessandro and me that was contracted in the presence of God alone. I humbly trust, Holy Father, that what has pleased both the Lord and me, may please you too, and I pray you, give us your blessing, that we may be assured of the grace of God, whose vicar you are. So in God's honor and yours, we shall live, and when our time comes, die together."

Alessandro was astonished and secretly overjoyed, to learn that his wife was the King of England's daughter. But much more astonished than he, were the two old knights, who were so furious that they would certainly have done him, and perhaps even the girl, some injury if they had been anywhere else but in the presence of the Pope. As for His Holiness, he also marveled greatly, both at the girl's clothes and the choice she had made. However, he realized that what was done could not be undone, and agreed to grant her prayer.

First he pacified the two knights, whom he knew to be angry, and made them come to terms of friendship with the lady and Alessandro. Then he issued the necessary orders.

The appointed day came. In the presence of the cardinals and many other mighty gentlemen, who had come to attend the wonderful feast at his invitation, the Pope brought in the lady, clothed in regal garments, and looking so beautiful and winning that she was deservedly acclaimed by everyone. Likewise Alessandro was introduced, also magnificently attired. Both in bearing and appearance, he looked nothing like a man who had once been a money-lender, but rather like a veritable prince of the blood, honorably escorted as he was by the two knights. With great solemnity, the Pope had the marriage celebrated once again, and after the sumptuous wedding feast, he dismissed them with his blessing.

It was Alessandro's wish, and also his wife's, upon leaving Rome, to go directly to Florence, where the news had already been spread of his marriage. There they were both welcomed with the utmost honor by the citizens, and the lady had the three brothers set free, after each creditor had received his due. Moreover, she reinstated them and their wives in their possessions, and with the unanimous approval of the people for what had been done, she and her husband left Florence, taking Agolante with them. In Paris they enjoyed the hospitality of the king.

Meanwhile, the two knights left for England, where they employed such persuasion with the king, that he granted his daughter and her husband grace and welcomed them with great festivity, later conferring a title upon Alessandro, together with the Earldom of Cornwall. The new earl soon proved himself a man of such capability in all his undertakings, that he succeeded in bringing about a truce between father and son, which proved so great a blessing to the island that he won the single-hearted love and favor of the people. As for Agolante, he recovered everything that was owing him and his brothers, and returned to Florence in the possession of phenomenal riches, having been made a knight by Alessandro.

Long and gloriously, the earl lived with his wife. Indeed, as some say, what with his wisdom, prowess, and the influence of his father-in-law, he even conquered Scotland, and was later crowned its king.

✳

## THE FOURTH STORY

*Landolfo Ruffolo is impoverished, and becomes a corsair. He is captured by the Genoese, shipwrecked, and saves himself by floating on a chest full of precious jewels. At Corfu he is rescued by a woman, and then returns home rich.*

LAURETTA, WHO WAS SITTING BESIDE PAMPINEA, HEARING HER reach the triumphal end of her story, spoke without more ado:

In my opinion, most gracious ladies, Fortune could not better reveal herself, than in raising a man from abject misery to royal state, as in the case of Pampinea's Alessandro. Since we must keep to our theme henceforth, I'll make bold to tell you a story which will not have such a splendid climax, though it recounts even worse misfortunes. I know you will listen to it with less interest, because of that, but since I can do no better, I hope I'll be forgiven.

Some people say that the coast from Reggio to Gaeta is the most delightful part of Italy. Along those shores, very near Salerno, there is a promontory overlooking the sea which the inhabitants call the Amalfi coast, a place full of little towns, gardens and fountains, and wealthy men as bustling in commerce, as any in the world. Among these little towns, Ravello has even nowadays many rich men, but years ago there was one called Landolfo Ruffolo by name, who was extremely wealthy. Nevertheless, he was not content with his riches, and in his effort to double them he almost lost them all and put his own life in jeopardy.

One day, Landolfo Ruffolo made a reckoning, as merchants do, bought an immense ship, freighted it with all the merchandise his money could buy, and set out with it to Cyprus. But alas! when he got there he found many other ships had come with cargoes of the very same merchandise, so that not only did he have to dispose of his goods for next to nothing, but he was also obliged to throw a good part of them away. Consequently, he came near ruin.

He was worried to death over his misfortune, and did not know what to do, seeing himself on the verge of poverty, while a short time before he had been so rich. At last he made up his mind either to die, or retrieve his fortunes by plunder, for he could not return a pauper to the town he had left as a rich man. He succeeded in finding a buyer for his great ship. With the proceeds, and whatever else he had received for his cargo, he purchased a light bark, suitable for piracy, and fitted it out for the purpose in the very best style, with all the necessary arms and trappings. That done, he plied his trade, appropriating the goods of others, of Turks especially, the while Fortune showed herself more benevolent in this, than she had in his legitimate trade. In hardly a year's time he had captured and pillaged so many Turkish ships that he calculated he had not only retrieved what he had lost in commerce, but more than doubled it.

By this time, chastened by the shock of his first experience, he thought it wiser not to fall twice into the same hole; therefore resolving to be content with what he had, and not to crave more, he decided to return home. He had had enough of commerce to be shy of it, so he did not bother to invest his money, but simply plying his oars, he set out on the same little bark with which he had earned it.

He had just entered the Archipelago, when a mighty wind rushed up from the south-east, which was not only unfavorable to his course, but churned up such terrible waves that his tiny vessel could not weather them. He pulled into a gulf made by the projection of a small island, and there, protected from the wind, resigned himself to await more propitious weather. Not long afterwards, however, two large Genoese galleys coming from Constantinople, made their way arduously to the little haven, escaping from the very thing Landolfo had avoided. As soon as the captains caught sight of the little vessel and learned it belonged to Landolfo whom they knew to be so wealthy, they made ready to seize it, in their desire for rapine and gain. Accordingly, they blocked his escape, landed part of their armored men, wielding crossbows, and stationed them in such a way that it was impossible for anyone to leave the bark without being shot. The rest of the crew got out in small crafts and with the help of the current, neared Landolfo's ship. It cost them little time and trouble to seize it, crew and all, to the last man. As for Landolfo, they took him aboard one of their galleys, leaving him nothing but a worn coat. They despoiled his bark of everything, and then sunk her in the sea.

The following morning the two ships got under weigh in a favorable wind, and all day they sailed prosperously. Towards nightfall, however, a gust sprang up, which raising a mountainous sea, parted the two galleys. So boisterous did the wind become, that the ship on which the unfortunate Landolfo happened to be, struck a shoal and crashing violently against the island of Cephalonia, split and shattered like a piece of glass dashed against a wall. Chests, bales of cargo and planks, soon floated everywhere in the deep blackness of night. As always happens in cases of shipwreck, the poor wretches who had been on board swam if they knew how, though the waves were swollen to hills, and groped about for some stray wreckage to cling to. With the rest, Landolfo who had called upon death many times the day before, choosing it rather than the prospect of returning home in poverty, was mightily afraid of it when he saw it so close, and like the others, the moment a board fell within his reach, he clutched it with all his might and main. If he postponed drowning a while, he reasoned, God might ultimately send him a means of escape. Accordingly, he clambered astride the plank which was tossed hither and thither at the mercy of sea and wind, and kept afloat until daylight, when looking around he could see nothing but clouds and water and a chest floating on the waves. Now and then it was hurled nearer to him, much to his horror, for it might dash against him and make him sink. Whenever it came within his reach, he pushed it with his hand as far from him as he could, using the little strength he had. But suddenly a blast of wind came out of the sky, whipping up the sea, striking the chest and driving it so violently against Landolfo's plank that it overturned and spilled him into the waves. He rose again, buoyed up more by his terror than his strength, only to find the plank far out of reach. He despaired of getting hold of it again, and made for the chest, which was close by. Laying himself flat on the lid of it he guided it as well as he could, and thus he was tossed about by the waves, eating nothing, for there was nothing to eat, and drinking much more than he had stomach for. All of that day and the coming night he remained in that predicament, ignorant of where he was, and with no sight but the sea about him.

It may have been God's will, or a gust of wind that did it, but however it was, he was borne the following day to the coast of Corfu, dripping like a sponge and clutching with both hands the rims of the chest in a way peculiar to drowning folk. A poor woman happened to be busy at the moment, scouring and polishing her pots and pans with sand and salt-water, and when she saw this thing devoid of human shape approaching, she drew back with a terrified shriek. Poor Landolfo had no voice left, and could scarcely manage to see, so he said nothing. But soon, however, as the sea pushed him toward the island, the woman was able to make out the chest, and on closer inspection she saw the arms stretched out over it. Then she caught sight of the face and knew directly what it all meant.

Pity overcame her. She waded a few steps into the sea, that was now calm, and pulling him by the hair of his head, she dragged him to shore, together with the chest. It was with much trouble that she was finally able to disengage his hands from the coffer, which she laid on the head of her little girl who was with her, and she herself carried the man ashore, as though he were a child. On reaching her hut she put him into a tub and so rubbed and washed him with warm water, that the departed heat returned to his body and he regained a little of his strength. When she thought it was time, she took him out of the bath, brought him to with strong wine and cakes, and arranged to lodge him with her a few days, until he recovered and had some consciousness of where he was. "Now," thought the good woman, "I'd better give him back his chest, and tell him to go on his way."

As it was, Landolfo had not the least notion of any chest belonging to him. Nevertheless, when the woman presented it to him, he took it, considering it might at least be worth enough to pay his way for a few days. He found it very light on lifting it, and his hopes sank. Anyhow, when the good woman was out of the house, he forced open the lid, to see what it contained, and found a quantity of precious stones, both set and loose. He was an expert in such articles, and realized their great value; and praising God, who had not forsaken him in his straits, he was altogether cheered.

Twice in a very short time, however, had Fortune cruelly harassed him. A third stroke might be expected, whereupon he reflected it was best to proceed cautiously if he wanted to bring his treasures safely home with him. He wrapped them up carefully in some rags, and told the woman he had no further need of the coffer—would she be so good as to give him a sack and keep the chest for herself? The good woman readily agreed. He thanked her with all his heart for the kindness he had received at her hands, and flinging his sack upon his shoulders, bade her good-bye.

He took a ship as far as Brindisi, and thence sailing coastwise, reached Trani at last. There he came across some fellow citizens of his, who were cloth merchants in town, and after he had told them the many vicissitudes he had undergone, keeping only the finding of the chest to himself, they clothed him in the spirit of charity. Moreover, they loaned him a horse and sent him with a body-guard as far as Ravello, at his request.

He was safe at last. Thanking the Lord, who had so far been his guide, he opened his bag, and examining its contents more carefully, discovered he possessed so many precious stones, and of such rarity, that if he were to sell them at a reasonable price, or even for less, he would still be twice as rich as he had been on starting out.

In a short time he found means of disposing of his jewels, after which he sent a considerable sum of money to the good woman of Corfu, as a reward for the service she had rendered in rescuing him from the sea. An equal sum he sent to Trani, to the men who had clothed him in his need. The remainder he kept for himself, without investing any of it in commerce, and so he lived honorably to the end of his days.

❋

# THE FIFTH STORY

*Andreuccio of Perugia, coming to Naples to purchase horses, has a number of serious mishaps in the course of one night, but finally escapes them all and returns home with a ruby.*

THE JEWELS LANDOLFO FOUND, SAID FIAMMETTA, WHOSE TURN IT was, remind me of a story as full of adventures as the one Lauretta just told. But it's rather different, for although Landolfo's overtook him in the space of some few years, my hero's happened all in a single night, as you shall hear.

There once lived in Perugia, as I've heard tell, a young man whose name was Andreuccio di Pietro, a horse-dealer by trade. He happened to hear that horses could be bought at a bargain in Naples, so stocking his purse with five-hundred gold florins, he left home for the first time in his life and went there, with other dealers. It was Sunday, towards vesper-time, when he arrived in Naples, and asking his host all the necessary information, he set out next morning for the market. There was no dearth of horses, and fine ones at that, which suited him perfectly. However, by dint of bargaining about this one and that, he was unable to come to a decision.

Now Andreuccio was a simple lout and a greenhorn, and to show that he was there on the important business of buying horses, he would pull out his purseful of florins, and wave it before the nose of any inconsequential rascal who passed by. He was engaged in showing it off, when a good-looking young Sicilian woman passed by, unnoticed by him, and caught sight of the handsome purse. She was one of those fair ladies who are not averse to doing any man's pleasure for a trifle, and immediately she said to herself: "Who could make better use of that money than myself, if I only had it?" And she went her way.

An old woman, a Sicilian, too, was with her at the time, who, the moment she spied Andreuccio, let her companion go ahead and fell on his neck most affectionately. The young woman observed the scene with keen attention, and without saying a word stepped aside and waited. Andreuccio, turning around and recognizing the old woman, made a fuss over her, and let her go only when she promised to visit him at the inn. Then he went back to his bargaining at the horse-market, but that day he made no purchase. The girl, meanwhile, had made her own mental notes, first of Andreuccio's purse, and then of the old woman's friendship with him. All the money, or even part of it, would have been quite acceptable to her, so to gain her end she began asking her companion all kinds of questions, very warily. Who was the fellow? Where did he come from? What was he doing there? And how did it happen that she knew him? In a very short time, the old woman had given her such particulars of Andreuccio's life, that he himself couldn't have done better. She told of how she herself had once lived with Andreuccio's father, first in Sicily and then in Perugia, and then informed the young woman of where he was lodging, and what had brought him to Naples. With such complete details about his parentage, and the names of his relatives up her sleeve, the girl laid her plans to gain what she desired by some cunning trick. Returning home, she kept the old woman busy all day long, so that she wouldn't have a chance to visit Andreuccio as she had promised. Calling a little maid of hers whom she had schooled for such services, she sent her toward evening to Andreuccio's inn. As it was, the girl found him alone at the door, and told him whom she had come for. He answered that he was the man she wanted.

"Sir," she said, drawing him aside, "a nice young woman of this town would like to have a word with you, any time you're ready."

On hearing her words, Andreuccio took stock of himself. "I'm a mighty fine spark," he thought, and was certain the woman must be madly in love with him, as though there were no one as handsome as himself to be found in all of Naples. Without a moment's hesitation he said he was at her service, and wanted to know when and where this nice young lady wished to speak with him.

"Sir, any time you're ready," answered the maid. "She's waiting for you in her own house."

"All right, go ahead," said Andreuccio promptly. "Lead the way, and I'll follow you." And he went, without leaving word at his inn.

The girl conducted him to the woman's house, situated in a section called Illdive, the very name of which describes the sort of honest quarter it was. But Andreuccio neither knew nor suspected it, for that matter, thinking he was bound for a respectable place to see a lady of some consequence. Boldly he entered the house on the heels of the little maid, who had gone somewhat ahead of him, calling to her mistress: "Here's Andreuccio," and as he went up the stairs he saw the lady herself at the landing, waiting to welcome him.

She was quite young, and tall, with an attractive face and rich, lavish clothes and adornments. As soon as he was near enough, she ran down three steps to meet him with open arms, and clinging about his neck, was speechless for a while, overwhelmed, perhaps, by her extreme tenderness. Weeping, she kissed his forehead and with a voice breaking with emotion, "Oh, my Andreuccio!" she exclaimed. "Welcome, welcome here!"

He was dumfounded by all these affectionate caresses, and stammered in embarrassment: "You . . . are well-met, dear lady."

Presently, she took him by the hand and led him to her parlor; thence, without another word, she brought him into her bedroom, all fragrant with roses, and orange-blossoms and other perfumes. An imposing curtained bed furnished it, and a number of dresses hanging from pegs, together with other beautiful, costly gew-gaws, according to the custom of that city. He was green in worldly matters, and all this array firmly convinced him she must be a noble lady, at the very least. Making room for him beside her on a chest at the foot of her bed, she said: "I'm sure you must be terribly surprised to see me pet you and cry over you this way, Andreuccio, for maybe you don't know me and you may never have even heard of me. But you'll soon be hearing something that will astonish you much more, yes . . . and it's just this—I am your sister, Andreuccio! Ah, now that God has done me the grace of letting me look on one of my brothers before I die—my dear brothers, whom I'd love to see, every single one of them—now, I tell you, I'll not die unhappy when my time comes! Maybe you've never heard a word of this, but I'm going to tell you, Andreuccio.

"Pietro, your father and mine, once lived for many years in Palermo, as you must know, where he was loved, and still is, by everyone who knew him, for his goodness and wonderful disposition. But of all who adored him there was one who loved him most, and that was my mother, a lady of noble birth, who was a widow at that time. She cherished him so, that she had no fear of her father and brothers, or for her honor, and she lived with him in such a way that I was born, and came to be just as you see me now.

"The time arrived, though, when Pietro had to quit Palermo and go back to Perugia, and he left me, a little child, with my mother. Then, for all I ever heard, he forgot all about us. Really, if he hadn't been my father, I'd have paid him well for his behavior—to *think* of how ungratefully he behaved toward my mother—not to mention me, whom he should have loved. Me, his own daughter, born of no servant-girl or loose woman, I'll have you know! Ah, my poor darling mother! And after she loved him so faithfully as to turn over all her possessions to him, her own body, even! But what's the use! Things that happened so long ago are better blamed than remedied. But anyhow, that is how it happened.

"Well, as I was saying, he left me a little child in Palermo, where I grew up as you see me now. My mother was rich, so she married me off to a fine gentleman of Girgenti, who thought so much of me and her, that he came over and made his home in Palermo. He was a powerful Guelph in politics, and he made a lot of treaties with our King Charles. But alas! King Frederick learned of them, and before anything could be done, we were obliged to flee Sicily, at the very time I expected to become the finest peeress the island had ever known! We took with us the few things we could lay hands on—I say few in comparison with all the wonderful things we had—and leaving our lands and palaces, we came to this city for safety. Here we found King Charles so gracious to us, that besides giving us back everything we had lost for his sake, he even made us gifts of other houses and estates. He is always giving things to my dear husband—your brother-in-law, to be sure—as you can see for yourself. So that is how I happen to be here, where, thanks to God and not to you, darling brother, I am able to lay my eyes on you at last!"

She fell to hugging him again after her speech, and weeping with deep feeling, kissed him on the brow. When Andreuccio heard the story so cunningly contrived by this woman, whose words flowed unfalteringly from a glib tongue, he recalled that his father had really been in Palermo; and knowing by personal experience how young men generally behave in matters of love, catching fire at the least straw, and witnessing the tender tears and hugs and sisterly kisses she gave him, he more than believed everything she said. He answered, upon her silence:

"You must not wonder that I am surprised, dear lady, but the truth is, that I never heard of you, as though you'd never been born. However it might be, my father either never said a word about you and your mother, or if he did, it never reached my ears. But I'm all the happier to find a dear sister here, most of all because I'm alone in this city, and I was far from expecting anything of the kind. I mean it!—And I can't think of any man, no matter how great he is, who wouldn't be glad to love you, not to speak of myself, who am only a humble horse-dealer. But please explain one thing to me. How did you come to know I was here?"

"Why," she replied, "a poor woman told me about it this morning. She comes to see me quite often, because, as she says, she lived with our father a long time, both in Palermo and Perugia. If it hadn't been that I thought it more proper for you to come to see me in my home, than for me to visit you at a stranger's, I'd have sought you out earlier."

So saying, she asked politely after all his relatives by name, one by one, and he told her about them all, swallowing whole the very things he should not have believed. The talk had been long and the heat intense. She called for Greek wine and cakes and offered Andreuccio a drink. He would have taken leave after the refreshments, for it was supper-time, but she would not hear of it, and pretending she was terribly hurt, put her arms around his neck.

"Ah, poor me!" she cried. "I see clearly how little I mean to you! Here you are with a sister of yours whom you've never seen—you're in her own house, where you should have lodged as soon as you got here—and you're dying to leave it for a measly supper at an inn. Do say you'll stay and have supper with me, like a good sport. Even though my husband is not here—more's the pity—I'll know well enough how to entertain you, as well as any woman."

"I love you as much as a sister ought to be loved," replied Andreuccio, who did not know what else to say. "But if I don't go they'll wait up for me all evening at the inn, and hold supper, and that wouldn't be a nice thing to do."

"Glory to God," she cried, "as though I had nobody in the house to send over, to tell them not to expect you—though the proper thing, your duty, I should say, would be to send for all your friends and have them sup here. Then, if you really insisted on leaving, you could all go together in a party."

Andreuccio answered he wanted none of his friends that night, and that he was willing to have her do with him as she wished. At that she made a pretense of sending word to the inn, not to expect him for supper, and after much talk they sat down to their meal. Many delicious courses were served, and very cleverly she contrived to linger at table until night had fallen, when they got up and Andreuccio displayed a desire to go. She would not allow it, she said, for Naples was not the sort of city to wander in at night, particularly for a stranger. Moreover, when she had sent word that he was not to be expected to supper at the inn, she had also let them know he was not going to sleep there that night, either. Fooled by false testimony into believing her, and delighting in her company, he remained.

For a long time after supper they talked about many different things, not without a purpose. A good part of the night was past, so leaving Andreuccio to sleep in her own room, with a little boy to help him in case he should want anything, she retired to another chamber with her women.

The heat was unbearable, and the moment he was alone, Andreuccio stripped himself of everything but his waistcoat, pulled off his hose, and laid them at the head of the bed. However, he soon had a natural urge to rid himself of the superfluous burden in his belly, and asked the youngster where this might be accomplished. The boy showed him a door in a corner of the room. "Go in there," he said.

Confidently, Andreuccio went in and when, inadvertently, he put his foot on a board that had broken loose from a beam at the other end, down he went, board and all. God protected him, however, for he was unhurt from his fall, though he had gone down a considerable distance. But he could not avoid being daubed all over with the filth that filled the place.

I shall describe the place, so that you may better understand what is to follow. Over a narrow space, like those one often sees between two houses, a couple of beams had been set up from one building to the other. A few boards had been nailed over them, and the seat placed on top. It had been one of these boards that had fallen away with Andreuccio.

As soon as he found himself down in the narrow alley, he was very much put out, and set up a howl for the boy. The lad, however, had quickly run to inform his mistress when he had heard Andreuccio fall, and she in turn, hurrying to his room, looked about excitedly to see if his clothes were there. She

found them, together with the money, which he always foolishly carried about his person, in mistrust of his neighbors.
Now that this lady, who had pretended she came from Palermo,
but was the sister of a Perugian, had laid her hands on what she
had set her trap to catch, she forgot all about her victim and
quickly locked the door he had gone out of as he fell.

Andreuccio called and called, and getting no reply from the
boy, began to bawl still louder, but in vain. Too late he suspected he must have been made the butt of some trick, and
climbing upon a low wall that shut off the alley from the street,
he clambered down into the road and went up to the door of
the house which he had every reason to be acquainted with.
Long and vainly he called, knocking at the door and shaking it
violently. And he wept and bewailed his misfortunes, which he
now saw all too clearly.

"Alas, poor wretch that I am," he moaned. "Who would have
thought I could have lost five-hundred florins and a sister in
such a short time!"

Once more, after many further lamentations, he fell to
pounding at the door and shouting. He kept up such a racket
that many of the neighbors, startled out of their sleep and jumping out of their skins for the noise, got up to see what was the
matter. One of the woman's servants, coming to the window as
though she were still half asleep, called, with the voice of a
scold: "Who's knocking down there?"

"What do you mean?" said Andreuccio. "Don't you know
me? I'm Andreuccio, Mistress Fiordaliso's brother."

"You must have had too much to drink, my poor fellow,"
she said. "Go away now, sleep it off and come back tomorrow
morning. I don't know what Andreuccio you're talking about,
or what stories you're telling me. Go away in peace and let us
sleep, if you don't mind."

"What!" exclaimed Andreuccio. "Do you mean you don't know
what I'm talking about? Indeed you do! But if Sicilian relations are made and forgotten at such short notice, give me back
the clothes, at least, that I left with you, and I'll gladly go away."

Then laughing, she answered: "I'm afraid you're dreaming,
my good man." And as she spoke, she went in and shut the
window.

By this time Andreuccio had no further doubt of his loss,
and because of the misery he felt, his uncontrolled fury was
nearing the verge of madness. Determining to regain by ill

means what his words had not availed to recover, he took up a large stone and fell again to battering the door with more violent blows than ever.

This new procedure brought to the windows many of the neighbors who, vexed at his continual pounding, had already awakened and got up out of their beds. Thinking him some scoundrelly nuisance, who had made up this story to provoke Mistress Fiordaliso, they cried and shouted at him like a pack of familiar hounds barking at a strange dog: "It's a damnable shame for the likes of you, coming at this hour to a respectable woman's house and talking all this rot. Go, get out of here, for heaven's sake, you, and let us sleep, if you've no objection. Come back to-morrow if you've business with her, but spare us this plague to-night."

Perhaps encouraged by these words, a man who was in the house and was the fine lady's pimp, whom Andreuccio had neither seen nor heard, looked out of the window, and in a great, gruff, ugly, thundering voice asked: "Who the devil is that down there?"

Andreuccio, raising his head at that roaring, perceived someone who, for all he could make out, seemed to be a tough bully of a fellow, with a thick black beard covering his face, yawning and rubbing his eyes as though he had just got out of bed from heavy sleep.

"I—I'm a brother of that woman in there," he answered, not without trepidation.

The bully did not wait for him to finish speaking, and called, even more threateningly than before: "I don't know what's holding me from coming down and beating you to a pulp, you pesky, drunken ass, keeping us up all night," and stepping back into the room, he banged the window shut.

Some of the neighbors, who were better acquainted with the pimp's temper, spoke persuasively to Andreuccio. "Go away, for God's sake, poor soul," they said, "if you don't want to lose your skin in this. Go, go, for your own good."

Terrified by the voice and looks of the bully, and won over by the advice of those good people who seemed to be speaking out of compassion for him, Andreuccio took the road along which he had followed the little maid, and set out for the inn, though unconscious of where he was going, despairing of ever getting back his money, and as miserable as could be.

On the way he was disgusted with the aroma that emanated

from him, and anxious to reach the sea to wash himself off, he turned to the right and followed a street called Ruga Catalana. As he proceeded toward the upper part of town, he saw two men coming toward him with a lantern in their hands. Fearing they might be members of the police-force or other gentlemen, bent on mischief, he tried to avoid them by stealing quietly into an old shack that was close by. But the men proceeded to the very same place, as though they had been bound for it, and slipped in. Presently one of them laid down a number of iron tools he had been carrying on his shoulder, and both examined them, discussing them the while. Suddenly one exclaimed: "Hell, what do you suppose this is? I've never smelled such a stink in my life!" So saying, he lifted his lantern, and seeing the pathetic figure of Andreuccio, both he and his companion exclaimed in astonishment: "And who the devil are you?"

Andreuccio shut up like a clam, but they drew up with their light, asking him what he was doing in that mess. He told them all that had happened to him, while they wondered where he could possibly have got into such a scrape, saying to themselves: "It must have been in the house of Scarabone Buttafuoco."

"Well, friend," said one, turning to him, "though you've lost your gold, you've every reason to thank your stars you had the good luck to fall down, and couldn't get back into the house. If you hadn't had that fall, you may be sure the moment you were asleep you'd have been clubbed to death, and lost your hide as well as your money. But what's the sense of wailing? You might as well be crying for the stars in heaven, as to have your money back. What's more, you might be killed if the fellow ever heard you say a word about it."

Talking the matter over a while together, they said to him: "See here, comrade, we're sorry for you, so listen. If you're willing to join us in a little business we have on hand, we're sure your own share in it will more than make up for what you've lost."

Andreuccio, at the end of his rope, said he was ready.

That day Messer Filippo Minutolo, an archbishop of Naples, had been buried, and with him some of his richest ornaments, including a ruby ring on his finger that was alone worth more than five hundred florins in gold. It was these gentlemen's intention to go and rob the archbishop, and they imparted their proposal to Andreuccio, who was more greedy for gain than he was wise. Accordingly, he started out with them. On their way to the cathedral Andreuccio stunk more than they could bear, and one of them suggested: "Can't we manage to have this stink-pot wash himself, somehow, so he won't smell so awful?"

"I guess so," replied the other. "We're near a spot where there's a well, with a rope and pulley and a great big bucket always ready. Let's go there and clean him up in a jiffy."

They got to the well and found the rope, as they had expected, but the bucket had been taken away. They considered what was to be done and decided to tie Andreuccio himself to the rope and lower him into the well to wash himself. Then, after he was good and clean, he was to tug at the rope and they would pull him up.

As fate would have it, they had barely lowered him into the well, when a couple of members of the police, overheated and thirsty from pursuing some mischief-maker, came to the well for a drink. No sooner did the two rascals catch sight of them than they took to their heels, before the policemen could see them.

Andreuccio had already performed his ablutions at the bottom of the well, and tugged at the rope to be hauled up. The officers, who were dying of thirst, putting down their shields, arms and coats, began to pull at it, thinking to find the bucket attached to the other end full of water, and the moment Andreuccio saw himself nearing the brink of the well, he dropped the rope and clutched at the edge with both hands. The policemen were stricken with such dread at the apparition, that they released their grasp without more ado and made off as fast as their legs could carry them.

Andreuccio was agape with astonishment, and but for the fact that he was holding on to the ledge for dear life, he might have fallen to the bottom and crippled or even killed himself. But when he came across such arms as his companions surely had not brought, he was more astonished. He could not get his wits together, and was afraid of falling into another trap, so leaving everything as it was and bemoaning his fate, he thought it best to be off and walked on aimlessly.

He had not gone very far when he stumbled upon his two companions on their way back to haul him out of the well. They were amazed when they recognized him, and asked who had got him out. Andreuccio answered that he was no wiser than they, told them how it had all happened, and described what he had found beside the well. Putting two and two together, they understood, and laughing, told him in turn why they had run away and who had done him the service of drawing him up.

It was midnight by now. Without further words they went to the cathedral, entered it without any trouble, and made for the archbishop's tomb. It was of marble, and very large. They pried open the massive lid with the help of their crowbars, raising it just enough to let a man slip through, and propped it up in place.

"Who's going to get in?" asked one.

"Not me," said the other.

"Nor me, either," answered the first. "Let Andreuccio do it."

"Not on your life," he said.

"What!" cried both of them, turning upon him. "You won't enter? By God, if you don't, we'll play such a tune on your skull that we'll make you fall down dead."

Andreuccio crept in out of fear, but once there, he reflected: "Those two scoundrels want me in here so that they can fleece me. Just as soon as I've handed them everything and I'm struggling to get out, they'll go their sweet way, and I'll be stung!"

He determined, therefore, to secure his own portion beforehand. As soon as he was down in the crypt, he suddenly remembered the valuable ring he had heard them talking about. It was the matter of a moment for him to slip it off the archbishop's finger, and slide it onto his own. Then taking the dead man's crosier, mitre and gloves, and stripping him to the shift, he reached everything over to his partners and said there was nothing more. No, they insisted, the ring must be there; he was not to leave a single spot unsearched. He kept on answering that he could not find it, and making believe he was looking for it everywhere, kept them guessing for a good long while. But they, on their side, were no less cunning than himself. They continued urging him to look, and at last, taking advantage of the delay, pulled out the prop that supported the lid, and took to their heels, leaving Andreuccio shut up in the tomb.

What his sensations were on finding himself closed in with the dead, you may imagine. Again and again he attempted to raise the lid, by dint of working with his head and shoulders, but it was all lost labor. At last, overcome by despair, he fainted and fell upon the body of the archbishop. Had anybody seen both of them together, he would have found it difficult to determine which was more of a corpse, the archbishop or Andreuccio.

Some time later, when he regained his senses, he broke into a desperate fit of weeping at his certain doom to one of two fates. If nobody came to let him out, either he must die of hunger and the stench of corruption, among the worms of the body, or if anyone did come and discover him there, he must be strung up for a thief on the gallows. While entertaining himself with such thoughts in the agony of his deep chagrin, he heard footsteps in the church and the voices of many people, who, as he was soon aware, were coming on the very errand he and his comrades had already accomplished. His terror knew no bounds.

As soon as the new visitors had pried open the tomb and propped up the lid, a dispute arose among them as to which of them should enter. Nobody was willing.

"What are you afraid of?" cried one of the priests, after a long debate. "Do you think he'll eat you up? The dead don't eat the living. I'll go in myself."

No sooner had he spoken, than he lay flat on his stomach at the edge of the tomb, turned his head toward the outside and thrust his legs down, ready to let himself drop to the bottom.

Andreuccio at this opportunity jumped up, seized the priest by a leg and made believe he wanted to pull him in. At that the man let out a yell fit to bring down the heavens, and leapt madly out of the tomb, putting the others into such a panic that leaving the lid propped up as it was, they all fled as though a hundred thousand devils were hot upon their trail.

Now that the way was clear, Andreuccio immediately clambered out of the crypt, happier than he had ever hoped to be, and retraced his steps out of the church. Dawn was breaking. Aimlessly, he walked through the streets, wearing the ring on his finger.

At last, coming to the seashore, he was able to find his way back to the inn, where his friends and the host had waited up all night, wondering what could have happened to him. After he had related his many adventures, the host offered the opinion that Naples was not a healthy place for Andreuccio, and said he'd better leave it, and the sooner, the better. And Andreuccio did, readily enough, returning to Perugia, after having invested his money in a ring, when he had set out to buy horses.

*

# THE SIXTH STORY

*Lady Beritola, after losing both her sons, is discovered on a desert island with two kids, and is taken to Lunigiana. There, one of her sons, in service with the lord of the land, is caught lying with his daughter and is clapped into prison. In the meantime, Sicily rebels under the rule of King Charles. Lady Beritola recognizes her son, who marries his lord's daughter; then his brother is found, and all are restored to their former prestige.*

EVERYONE HAD ENJOYED A GOOD LAUGH OVER ANDREUCCIO'S MIS-adventures, as Fiammetta related them, and Emilia, realizing the story was over, began, at the queen's request:

The devious ways of Fortune are indeed great and ponderable. It's wise, then, while we discuss them, to prod our minds into wakefulness, for they are too prone to fall asleep, lulled by her deceitful dreams. We should never tire of listening to examples, whether we're happy or miserable, for the happy are made wary, and the miserable, comforted. So then, in spite of the many wonderful things that have preceded, I am going to tell you a story that is no less true than pathetic, on our given theme. I warn you it's a sad one, so sad, that although it has a happy ending, the bitterness was so protracted I can hardly believe it could have been sweetened by any happiness that came thereafter.

You must know, dearest ladies, that after the death of Emperor Frederick the Second, Manfred was crowned King of Sicily. Occupying a lofty position in his court, there lived a Neapolitan nobleman called Arrighetto Capece, who had to wife a beautiful, virtuous lady, whose name was Beritola Caracciola, of Naples also. While Arrighetto was acting as governor over the island, he heard that King Charles the First had conquered and slain Manfred at Benevento, and the whole kingdom had risen in revolt against the victor. He had little assurance in the fickle faith of the Sicilians, and as he did not relish the idea of becoming a subject of his king's enemy, he made preparations for flight. But the Sicilians discovered his purpose, and soon Arrighetto and many other friends and servants of King

Manfred, were given over to Charles as prisoners. The surrender of the island followed shortly after.

Lady Beritola was lost in all this turmoil. She did not know what had become of Arrighetto, yet in an agony of foreboding, she abandoned all her possessions, and for fear of further dishonor went aboard a little boat and fled to Lipari with a small son, Giusfredi, of some eight years of age. There, poor and pregnant, she gave birth to another son, whom she called the Outcast, and taking a nurse, embarked with her and the two children for Naples, where her family lived.

But Fate willed otherwise. At the mercy of a boisterous wind, the ship that should have sailed for Naples was driven to the island of Ponzo, where, sheltered in a tiny harbor, they awaited more propitious weather for their journey. While there, they went ashore on the island, Lady Beritola with the rest, and finding a place of seclusion, she withdrew from her company to mourn for Arrighetto. Day by day she went alone in this manner; but once, as she was engaged in her solitary lamentation, a corsairs' galley stole up, unobserved by the lady's sailors or any one else, made them all prisoners, and sailed away. On her return to the shore to see her children, according to her habit, she found the place deserted. At first she was puzzled, but then, suspecting what must have happened, she peered out across the sea in time to perceive the galley, not so very far away, towing the little ship behind it. Too well she knew that she had now lost both her children and her husband. The blow was more than she could bear. Alone, poor and forsaken, despairing of ever finding any of them again, she fell upon the sand unconscious, calling upon her dear ones. Not a living soul was about to restore her wandering senses, by the aid of cold water or other means, and they strayed leisurely, at their sweet will. Finally, her lost powers returned to her body, and with them tears and wailing. Long she called upon her children and searched for them in every crag and cranny, but at last she resigned herself. It was all in vain. Night was coming on. Still hoping, she did not know for what, she began to feel some concern for herself, and leaving the shore, went inland to the cave where she was accustomed to weep and mourn.

That night was spent in terror and immeasurable sorrow. The next day came. It was already past nine o'clock, and as she had not eaten the previous evening, and pangs of hunger were beginning to make themselves felt, she fed on herbs. Making the

best of what she could find, she gave herself up to thoughts of
the future, and wept. In the midst of her reflections, she caught
sight of a goat going into a nearby cavern. It remained there a
little while, and then went off to the woods. She rose in surprise
and entered the cave which the she-goat had left, and there
found two tiny kids, born the same day, perhaps, which she
thought the sweetest, loveliest things in the world. Her milk
had not yet dried after her recent child-bearing, so she took up
the young things tenderly, and gave them the breast. They did
not turn away, but nursed at her bosom as though she were
their dam, and from then on they chose impartially between her
and their mother. Now that she had found company in that
desert place, the good lady resigned herself to live and die there,
in the friendship of the mother-goat and the two kids. She ate
grass with them, and drank the same clear water, and wept
whenever she called to mind her husband and children, and her
former state.

During this state of affairs, when Beritola had become a creature of the wilds, a Pisan ship stopped a few months later in
the very harbor whence she had been driven by the wind, and
there it lay for a few days. A nobleman by the name of Currado, belonging to the Malespini family, happened to be on
board with his wife, a good, pious lady, on the way home from a
pilgrimage to the holy places of the Apulian kingdom.

One day, to while away the time, Currado and his wife with
a few servants and hounds, left the ship, to roam about the island. Suddenly, not far from Beritola's cave, the hounds began
chasing the two kids that had now grown large enough to go
pasturing by themselves, and the little creatures, finding themselves pursued, sought refuge where Beritola was hiding. The
moment she saw what was taking place, she started up, and laying hold of a stick, frightened the dogs away. Currado and his
wife, who had followed the hounds close, marveled when they
came upon this brown, lean, disheveled woman, and even more
than they, Beritola was astonished at their presence. However,
after Currado had called back his hounds at her entreaties, he
and his lady succeeded, after much coaxing, in persuading her
to tell them who she was and what she was doing there. She related frankly all they wanted to know, confessing her state, and
what she had gone through, affirming besides that she was determined to remain alone in that desert place.

Currado, it seemed, had known Arrighetto Capece, and hearing Beritola's story he wept with compassion. He tried to shake her from her wild resolve with many sound arguments, offering to conduct her to her own home or keep her with him honorably as his sister, until God should send her happier days. But when she did not consent to his proposals, Currado left his wife behind, asked her to have food brought, and clothes of her own for the woman, who was all in tatters, and urged her to do everything in her power to bring her away. Alone with Beritola, the kind lady mourned with her for a long while over the misfortunes she had suffered; then, sending for food and clothes, she made her dress herself, after much trouble, and then eat. At last, by dint of prayers and entreaties, the while Beritola insisted she would never set foot where anybody knew her, Currado's wife induced her to accompany her to Lunigiana, with the two kids and the mother-goat, which had come back in the meantime, greeting their mistress with such affection that the noble lady wondered greatly.

As soon as fair weather permitted, Beritola with Currado and his wife embarked on their ship, taking with her the kids and the goat, because of which, since her own name remained a secret, she was known everywhere as Cavriuola. They hoisted sail in a favorable wind, and in time reached the source of the Magra, where they went ashore and mounted to Currado's castle town. There Beritola lived in widow's weeds as one of her lady's companions, in all honesty, humbleness and obedience. Nor did she ever fail to love her kids and nourish them tenderly.

In the meantime, the pirates who had captured the ship that had carried Beritola to Ponzo, and left her behind, unseen, set forth for Genoa with everyone on board. The booty was divided among the captains of the galley, and Beritola's nurse with the two children fell to the lot of a certain Guasparrino d'Oria, who sent them off to one of his estates, as slaves in the service of the household.

Long did the nurse weep and wail for the loss of her lady, and for the wretched state to which she herself had been reduced, with the boys. But alas! tears were of no avail to remedy their lot, as she knew, for she was a wise and discreet woman, though poor. Therefore, she made the best of the situation, and realizing where they had been cast by Fate, she considered that if the children were recognized, they might surely be made to suffer. Moreover, there was still the hope that fortune might change at some time or other; if death spared them, they might

even get back their lost estate. She resolved, therefore, to breathe
no word to anyone of their identity, until the proper occasion
offered, and in the meantime passed them off as her sons. The
elder of the two she no longer called Giusfredi but Giannotto
di Procida, and the younger's name she left as it was. Then, with
the utmost patience, she explained to Giusfredi why she had
changed his name, and tried to impress upon his childish mind
the dangers he might run if he were discovered. Not once but
many times she repeated her lesson, and as the boy was naturally
intelligent, he followed her advice in every detail.

For several years the two boys and their nurse lived together,
poorly clothed and worse shod, and bore everything patiently in
the household of Guasparrino, where they did the most menial
tasks. Giannotto had attained by this time to the age of sixteen,
and with more pluck than is usually found in a servant's nature,
he rebelled against the humiliation of his slavish state, and
ran away from Guasparrino's service by getting aboard one of a
fleet of galleys bound for Alexandria. Hither and thither he
wandered, traveling to many places, but without managing to
better his condition. Finally, three or four years after his flight
from Guasparrino, and already grown a tall, handsome lad, he
heard that his father, whom he had thought dead, was still alive,
but alas! kept in prison by King Charles. He went from place
to place, despairing of Fortune, almost a vagabond, when by
some trick of fate he arrived at Lunigiana and found employ
with Currado Malespina. Excellently well he served him, and
entirely to his master's satisfaction. Now and then, he would
come face to face with his mother, in the company of Currado's lady, but not once did he recognize her, nor she, him, so
much had time altered their features, from what they had been
when they had last seen each other.

During the time Giannotto was in Currado's service, a daughter of his master's, by the name of Spina, was left a widow by
her husband, Niccolo da Grignano, and returned to her father's
hearth. She was a handsome, pleasant lass, hardly over sixteen.
One day, she allowed her eyes to linger on Giannotto and his
on her, and both fell passionately in love with each other. Their
passion was not long without fulfilment, and months passed before anyone even suspected it. Gaining boldness, as a result,
they were less cautious than they should have been, and one day,
as they were passing through a beautiful, thickly-wooded forest,
Spina and Giannotto together, they broke away from the rest of

the company and went on before. They thought they had gone far ahead of the others, so they lay down in a delightful enclosure, full of sweet grass and flowers, with trees forming a border, and began to take love's pleasure of each other. For a long while they lay together, but the sweetness of their joy lent wings to time, making it seem very short. Thus as they were embracing, they were discovered first by the girl's mother, and then by Currado himself.

The father was exceedingly grieved at the sight. He caused them to be taken by three of his men, and without saying a word in extenuation, had them carried off in chains to one of his castles. Wrath and a passion for revenge seethed in him, and he resolved to make them both suffer a shameful death. The girl's mother, on the other hand, troubled though she was, and convinced that her daughter deserved the severest punishment for her sin, got an inkling of Currado's purpose toward the culprits. It was too much for her. She ran to her husband with prayers and entreaties, and pleaded with him. He must not act rashly in his old age, making himself his own daughter's murderer and staining his hands with the blood of his menial. He must find other ways to satisfy his ire—he might put them in prison, there to pine and bemoan the sin they had committed. So long did the good lady plead with him, and so many arguments did she advance, that she succeeded in making him change his mind about killing them. Instead, he commanded them to be imprisoned in separate places, under close watch, with meager food and many discomforts, until he should decide upon further action. His command was executed.

What their life in prison must have been, with tears aplenty and longer fasts than were good for them, you may imagine for yourselves. They had been in their sad plight about a year, forgotten entirely by Currado, when King Pedro of Arragon stirred up a rebellion on the island of Sicily, by an understanding with John of Procida, and took the kingdom away from Charles. Currado, a Ghibelline in politics, was the happiest man in the world when it happened. Rumors of the event reached Giannotto, through one of his guards, and he drew a deep sigh. "Poor miserable me!" he said. "For fourteen years I have been tramping about the world, hoping for no other thing than this! And now that it has come, leaving me no more hope of fortune, here I am in this prison, which I may never leave until I die!"

"What's that?" asked the prison keeper. "What are the doings of mighty kings to you? And what have you to do with Sicily?"

"My heart nearly breaks," answered Giannotto, "when I consider what my father once had to do with it! I was only a child when I ran away from there, and yet I remember seeing him a mighty lord, when King Manfred was alive."

"And who was your father?" asked the keeper.

"Who my father was I may safely tell you," proceeded Giannotto, "now that I'm in the very peril I had hoped to avoid by keeping his name a secret. He was called—he is called, if he still lives—Arrighetto Capece. My own name is not Giannotto but Giusfredi, and I'm sure that if I were free and returned to Sicily, a very high station there would still be mine."

The worthy keeper said no more, but the first chance he got, reported everything to Currado. The lord made a show of taking his words lightly, but going to Beritola he asked her in an offhand way whether she had ever had a son called Giusfredi by her husband Arrighetto. She answered, weeping, that if the elder of her two sons were still living he would be bearing that name, and he would be about twenty-two years of age. Currado had no doubt when he heard, that the youth must be Beritola's son, and mused that since such was the case, he might now perform a merciful deed, and clear both his daughter's shame and his own dishonor, by giving her to him in marriage. Secretly he called Giannotto to him and examined him closely on his past life, discovering by obvious signs that the youth was truly Giusfredi, the son of Arrighetto Capece.

"Giannotto," he addressed him, "you realize how great is the extent of the evil you have done me in the person of my daughter. I always treated you well, almost like a friend, and as a worthy servant you should have labored for the welfare of my property and my honor. Many a man in my place would have had you die a shameful death, for less than what you did to me. But my compassion would not permit it. Now if it is really true that you are, as you say, the son of noble parents, I should like to put an end to your trials, if you are willing, taking you from your wretchedness and captivity and re-establishing at the same time both your honor and my own. You know that Spina— whom you loved in a manner unworthy of both you and her— is a widow, with a considerable dowry. You know, besides, what sort of girl she is, and you are acquainted with her father and mother. Now, if you consent, I am disposed to make her, who was once unlawfully your mistress, your own wedded wife, and you may live here as my own son, as long as you wish."

Imprisonment had wasted Giannotto's flesh, but it had not diminished the generous spirit that was his own birthright, nor the single-hearted love he had for his mistress. Although he fervently desired what Currado proposed, and knew himself still to be in his power, not a word did he spare of what his lofty spirit impelled him to say.

"Currado," he answered, "neither ambition for power, nor lust for riches, nor any other motive made me spread snares treacherously against your life and possessions. I loved your daughter, I still love her, and shall love her forever because I deem her deserving of my love. If, according to common opinion, I acted dishonorably toward her, the sin I was guilty of is in the blood of youth, and you must eradicate youth itself if you want to be rid of it. Oh, if only the old would bear in mind that they once were young! If they would only judge the sins of others by their own, and vice versa, our sin would not seem as heinous as you, or others, make it. Besides, it was as a friend, not as an enemy that I committed it. The thing you offer me now I have always desired, and if I had imagined you would have granted it, I should have begged it of you long ago. But now it will be all the dearer to me for all the vain hope I placed upon it in the past. I pray you, if your words belie your true intent, don't feed me with false hopes. Send me back to prison and torture me as you wish. As long as I continue loving Spina, I shall love her for her own sake . . . No matter what you do to me, I shall still respect you."

Currado was amazed at this speech, and deemed him great of soul and of fervent affections, which qualities made him hold the youth dear. He stood up, embraced and kissed him, and without a moment's delay had Spina summoned.

Imprisonment had made her thin and pale and weak, and she looked as different from her former self, as Giannotto from the strapping lad he had been. In Currado's presence the two young people were bound in marriage, by common consent, following our tradition. After some days had elapsed, while everyone was in ignorance of what had happened and the bride and groom had been provided with everything necessary and agreeable to them, Currado thought the time had come to make their mothers happy. He called his wife and Beritola to him and addressed them.

"What would you say, Beritola," he asked, "if I brought you back your elder son as the husband of one of my daughters?"

"What should I say, sir?" she answered. "If it were possible for me to be more grateful to you than I am, I should be even a thousand times more so, for you would be restoring to me the dearest thing I have in all the world. For if you brought him to me as you say, you would be giving me back a little of the hope I had lost."

Weeping, she was silent.

"And what would you think?" asked Currado, turning to his lady, "if I were to give you such a son-in-law?"

And she answered: "Even a vulgar servant would please me if you chose him, my lord, not to speak of such a youth, who is of noble birth."

"I hope to grant you both your hearts' desire before long," he said to them.

By this time the newly-married pair had regained their former beauty. Currado had them clothed magnificently, and then asked Giusfredi: "Would you not be even happier than you are now, if you were to see your mother again?"

"Alas!" he replied, "I hardly think grief and misfortune have spared her life so long. But if it were only possible, it would be the greatest happiness in the world to me, all the more so, because I am sure through her advice I might even regain a great part of my estate in Sicily."

Currado sent for the two women. Both of them rejoiced in the newly-wedded bride, and made much of her, wondering what inspiration could have brought Currado to a mood of such extreme benignity, as to marry her to Giannotto. Recalling the words Currado had uttered, Beritola studied Giannotto's face for a long time. A vague memory of her son's boyish features awoke in her, in some occult manner, and without waiting for further proof, she ran to him with open arms and flung herself about his neck. Not a word could she say, so much had excess of emotion and maternal joy overwhelmed her; indeed, so did they dam her senses, that she fell into her son's arms like one dead. Giannotto was seized with wonder, recalling how often he had seen her about the castle without knowing who she was; but instantly he felt the maternal aura, and blaming himself for his former carelessness, he took her in his arms and tenderly kissed her, tears brimming in his eyes. Currado's wife and Spina gently soothed Beritola with cold water and other means, until her distracted senses were recalled. Once more she fell upon her son, with many tears and words of endearment, and kissed him a thousand times with maternal tenderness, as he gazed on her reverently and comforted her. Then, when their simple, joyous greeting had been many times exchanged, while the others looked on happily, they related to each other their various vicissitudes. In the meantime Currado had informed his friends of the new kinship he had made, to the utmost satisfaction of them all, and had already given orders for a sumptuous feast.

"Currado," Giusfredi addressed him, "you have given me happiness in many things—among others, in that you have treated my mother with honor for many years in your household. But now you must leave nothing incomplete. I beg you, then, rejoice my mother and me, and make the gathering at my bridal feast even happier for the presence of my brother, who is kept in slavery by Guasparrino d'Oria. I have already told you how the lad and I were captured by him in one of his voyages. After that, sir, send someone to Sicily, and let him find out fully about the state and the condition of the country. Let him discover what has become of Arrighetto, my father. Is he alive, or dead? If he is still alive, what are his circumstances? Let the messenger inform himself of every particular, and then come back to us."

Currado favored Giusfredi's request and sent trustworthy men without delay both to Genoa and Sicily. The Genoese envoy sought out Guasparrino and diligently entreated him on Currado's part, to send him the Outcast and his nurse, telling him consecutively, all that his master had done for Giusfredi and his mother. Guasparrino could not get over his astonishment at the news.

"It's true I'd do anything in my power for Currado," he said. "He has only to ask it. And it's also a fact that I've had in my house for the past fourteen years, the boy you request, and a kind of foster-mother of his. I'll gladly send them both to him. But don't fail to tell Currado on my part, to beware of being too gullible, and not to believe the fairy tales of Giannotto, who now styles himself Giusfredi. He's a far more cunning rascal than Currado imagines."

Guasparrino had the gentleman looked after, and sending for the nurse secretly, examined her on the subject very craftily. News of the Sicilian rebellion had reached her ears, and also that Arrighetto was still alive. Dismissing her former fears. she told him everything, in sequence, and revealed the reasons that had compelled her to behave as she had. Finding her narrative to coincide in all respects with the envoy's, Guasparrino had faith in her words. He was a very clever man. Using all possible artifice, he considered the matter from all angles, and the more he examined it the more facts he discovered to strengthen his belief. Ashamed of the way he had treated the boy, and anxious to make amends for it, now that he knew what his father's position had been and still was, he gave the Outcast in marriage to a pretty eleven-year-old daughter of his, with a substantial dowry. A splendid feast was celebrated for the nuptials, after which he embarked on a well-equipped galley, together with the youth and his daughter, Currado's messenger and the nurse, and sailed away to Lerici. Currado came to receive him, and conducted him and his entire party to one of his castles, which was a short distance away. There a splendid banquet awaited him.

Who can express the delight of the mother upon beholding her son again? And who, the joy of the brothers in each other, and of all three in the faithful nurse? And the cheer given by everyone to Guasparrino and his daughter, and by them to everyone else? Who can describe it, or the reciprocal rejoicing of them all, with Currado and his wife and his children and his friends? No, I leave it all to your imagination, dear ladies.

God, who when He wills is the unstinting All-giver, wished the festivity to be even more complete, and added the glad tidings of Arrighetto Capece's certain life and prosperity. The feast was at its gladdest, and the guests, both men and women, had just sat down to their first course, when the messenger from Sicily arrived. He told, among other things, that while Arrighetto was still being held in confinement by King Charles and the rebellion had broken out against the ruler throughout the land, the people dashed madly to the prison, and putting the guards to death, released him as King Charles' chief enemy. Then, appointing Arrighetto their leader, they followed him to rout and kill the French. His deeds won him the high favor of King Pedro, who set him up again in the estate and honor he had formerly enjoyed, and now Arrighetto was in the best of circumstances. Moreover, added the envoy, he himself had been received with all possible courtesy, and had witnessed with what inexpressible joy Arrighetto had welcomed the news of his wife and son, whom he had not heard of since his imprisonment. He was sending a mighty ship to fetch them with a company of the finest gentlemen aboard who would arrive at any moment.

The envoy and his tidings were greeted with a frenzy of delight, and shortly after he had told his news, Currado with a number of his friends, set out to meet the escort that was coming for Beritola and her son.

Gladly he welcomed them, and led them into the banquet-hall, where the lady and Giusfredi as well as the rest of the company showed such happiness at the sight, that the like has never been seen. The gentlemen saluted Currado and his lady, on the part of Arrighetto, before sitting down to the feast, and thanked them with all courtliness for the honor they had shown the wife and son of their master, who was at their service in whatever they might require. Then, turning to Guasparrino, whose favor had been unexpected, they declared themselves confident that Arrighetto would proffer him like thanks, and even greater, the moment he learned what that gentleman had done for the Outcast. Their speeches over, they joyfully sat down to the nuptial feast of the two brides and grooms, and partook of it heartily. Nor were the celebrations over that day, for Currado entertained his son-in-law many days more, with his friends and kin together.

Once the festivities were at a lull, Beritola, Giusfredi and others thought it was time for them to take their leave. Weeping copiously, they bade Currado and his lady farewell, and getting aboard the brigantine, they got under weigh, taking Spina along. The wind favored their voyage, and in a short time the shores of Sicily were reached.

Arrighetto welcomed his sons and daughters-in-law, and all his dear ones alike, in the city of Palermo, and their exuberance could never be described. It is believed they lived happily together for a long, long time, in worship and gratitude to God for all His mercies.

✳

# THE SEVENTH STORY

*The Sultan of Babylon sends one of his daughters to be married to the King of Algarve. Within the space of four years she comes, through strange incidents, into the hands of nine different men in various places. Finally she is brought back to her father a virgin, and goes to marry the King of Algarve, as she had set out to do in the first place.*

IF EMILIA'S STORY HAD CONTINUED MUCH LONGER, THE PITY which the young women felt for Lady Beritola in her misfortunes would surely have made them burst into tears. Once it was ended, however, the queen was pleased to let Pamfilo continue with a story, and he, a very obedient youth, began:

It is not always easy, adorable ladies, for us to know what is proper for our good. We have often observed how many have imagined they could live safe and free from care, if they were only possessed of riches. Not only have we seen them praying to God for wealth, but we have watched them sparing no pains or danger, in their indefatigable quest. But alas! no sooner had they attained their end, than they, who had been so much in love with life before becoming rich, found some wretch, covetous of their vast inheritance, to murder them.

Others, who have risen from lowly stations to the heights of power, steeped in the blood of brother and friend, through a thousand perilous battles—these, I say, who have thought to find their supremest happiness in a kingdom free of the endless cares and fears they found it actually to abound in, have discovered, at the expense of their lives, that poison may be drunk from golden goblets at royal tables.

Still others have hungered ardently after strength of body, beauty, and other physical accomplishments, not realizing they had misplaced their desires, until those very things became the cause of death or a life of pain.

But why should I catalogue all these human yearnings? Let me say briefly, that there's not one that can be chosen with complete confidence by us mortals, which would be entirely exempt from the pranks of Fortune. If we want to do the right thing, let us then simply resign ourselves to accept and make the best of what God has granted us, for He alone knows our needs, and can bestow them upon us.

Now, while men sin in wishing for different things, you, charming ladies, are chiefly guilty in one particular—the desire to be beautiful. So much so, in fact, that not content with the charms nature has given you, you seek to enhance them still more with marvelous art. I shall be glad to tell you how unfortunate a Saracen lady was, through her very beauty, and of how she happened to marry nine different times within scarcely four years.

Quite a long time ago, there was a sultan in Babylon by the name of Beminedab, whom Fortune seemed to favor in his day. Among his numerous progeny, male and female, he had a daughter called Alatiel, who was considered by all who set eyes on her, the most beautiful woman of her time. During a mighty victory which he had won over a horde of Arabs who had fallen upon him, he had been extremely well aided by the King of Algarve, and at his request he had bestowed her upon him in marriage, as a mark of special favor. With a considerable company of men and women and a quantity of splendid furnishings, he had set her upon a ship, well-armed and equipped, and sent her off to her husband, commending her to God.

Encountering favorable wind and weather, the sailors hoisted sail, and leaving the port of Alexandria journeyed uneventfully for a few days. Sardinia had been passed, and the end of their voyage seemed near, when suddenly contrary winds arose one day, each one more tempestuous than the other, and so violently did they toil and moil about the ship which held the lady and her sailors, that more than once they gave themselves up for lost. They were courageous men, however, and doing all in their power and experience, held out two days longer against a raging sea. Already the gloom of the third night appeared, but the tempest showed no signs of subsiding. Indeed, as it increased in violence with every moment, the sailors, who had no idea of where they were—so difficult it was to determine anything by nautical computations, or to distinguish the sky through the murk of clouds and night—suddenly felt the ship rip open beneath them, a little off Majorca. They saw no other way of escape but to shift for themselves, and leave the rest to the devil. Accordingly, a safety-boat was lowered into the sea, and trusting it, rather than the sundered ship, the officers piled into it, followed by the rest of the crew. The first men who had taken possession of the little boat defended it, knife in hand, from the incursion of the others, but in vain. Everyone crowded into it, and in seeking to escape death, they ran to meet it, for the bark, too frail to hold so many or withstand the raging elements, went under, drowning each and every one of them.

Not a soul remained on the vessel but Alatiel and her women, lying about the deck in the throes of terror and despair, at the sight of the wrathful sea. A tempestuous wind drove the ship onward at a terrific speed, even though it was now almost filled with water, through the yawning gap in its body, and finally dashed it against the shore of Majorca. So forceful was the shock, that almost a stone's throw from the waves, the unfortunate ship was half buried in the sand. All night long it lay there, tormented by the sea and the wind, which had no power to release it.

The new day dawned clear and the tempest had somewhat subsided. Feebly, the princess, who was nearly dead with terror, raised her head and vainly called the members of her crew. They were too far away to hear. At first she wondered when no one answered her summons, and then she began to be filled with mortal dread. Struggling to her feet, Alatiel saw her companions and the rest of the women lying prostrate. She called them by name, time and time again, now this one, now that, and receiving no reply, discovered there was scarcely one of them conscious. The greater part had perished, what with sea-sickness and fright, and her own terror increased with the knowledge. But it was no time to weaken. Compelled by necessity, and the thought that she was all alone, and without the least inkling of where she might be, she nursed those who had still some life in them, until they managed to stand upon their feet. When she found, however, that they had no notion of what had become of the men, and saw furthermore that the vessel was half-buried and entirely water-logged, she wept with them in an access of despair.

It was past noon before they saw any sign of a human being about the island, to whom they might turn for help; but as it was, a gentleman by the name of Pericon da Visalgo was returning that way from one of his country-places, with a few followers on horseback. On seeing the ship, he immediately surmised what must have happened, and without delay, sending one of his men to climb on board as best he could, he ordered him to report what he found. Arduously, the man made his way on deck, and discovered the princess huddled timidly under the bow with the few women she had left. The moment they saw him, they tearfully implored his mercy again and again, but perceiving he did not understand them, and that they themselves could not make out what he was saying, they endeavored to explain their plight by means of signs.

The servant took stock of what he found, and told Pericon all that he had discovered on board. Soon the gentleman had the ladies brought down to the shore, together with whatever valuables could be rescued from the ship, and took them to one of his castles, where he restored them with food and rest. From the magnificence of her clothes, Pericon concluded that the woman he had found must be of noble birth, and was all the more convinced, when he saw what respect her companions showed her and her alone. In spite of her pallor, and the disorder in which her clothes were, due to the stress of her sufferings upon the sea, Pericon could not help being struck by the unusual beauty of her features. He decided, on the spur of the moment, that if she had no husband he would supply the need, and if she could not be his wife, why, then, he would endeavor to win her graces.

Pericon was a lusty man, and of imposing figure. He had Alatiel attended with exceeding care for some days, and when she was herself again and he saw how incomparably beautiful she was, he regretted that he could not understand her, nor make himself understood, so that he might find out who she was. Despite this lack, he was roused beyond measure by her beauty, and with many a show of love and tenderness tried to induce her to yield to his pleasure without a struggle; but to no purpose. She repulsed all his blandishments, and the more she rejected them, the more passionate he became.

Alatiel lived with Pericon a few days, and in the course of that time, saw by the customs of the people about her, that she must be among Christians and in a land where it would do her no good to make herself known, even if she were able. Besides, she was conscious that in the long run she would have to surrender herself, willy nilly, to Pericon's pleasure. With great loftiness of spirit, she resolved to rise above her wretched fortune, and made her three remaining women promise never to divulge her identity to a living soul, unless they should happen to be where they might expect certain aid in regaining their freedom. More than that, she was eloquent in urging them carefully to guard their maidenheads, for so far as she was concerned, she had sworn that no one but her lawful husband would enjoy her own. They admired her point of view, and swore that they would take her advice to heart, as far as it lay within their power.

Meanwhile, Pericon grew more and more importunate every day, and his ardor increased when he saw the desired object so near, and yet so unattainable. Away with supplication, he de-

cided, since it had brought him no good. It was now time for
cunning and adroitness, with force reserved for the last. He had
noticed that the lady was lickerish of wine, which was something new to her, since her religion forbade it, and thought
there could be no better way to obtain her, than by using it as
an advocate for Venus. From then on, he pretended he did not
care a brass farthing for the thing she insisted on withholding,
and one evening, as a special treat, he prepared a fine supper,
which the lady attended. Many things enlivened the feast, and
among them various kinds of mixed wines, which he had ordered the man serving her to pour in generous proportion. The
fellow did his master's bidding punctiliously, and thus Alatiel,
who had no suspicion of the trick, was more tickled with the
deliciousness of the wine than her modesty should have permitted. Gradually she flung her troubles to the winds, and
when she saw some women dance in the mode of Majorca, she
outdid them in the fashion of Alexandria. Pericon watched, and
saw his bird almost in hand. More and more lavishly, he supplied the feast with meat and drink, until far into the night.

At last, when the guests had left, he went with Alatiel alone,
into her bedroom. The heat of the wine in her was not at all
tempered by shyness, and taking no more notice of Pericon than
if he had been one of her women, she undressed before him
without the least blush and slipped into bed. Pericon was not
long in following her. Extinguishing all the lights, he nimbly
lay beside her, and clasping her unresisting body in his arms,
he began some amorous pastime with her. No sooner did she
feel it—for she had never known before with what sort of uni-
corn men did their butting—than she suffered a change of heart,
almost regretting that she had not surrendered sooner to Pericon's advances. From that night on, she did not wait for an invitation to the fun, but very often offered herself of her own
accord, not with words, by which she could not express herself,
but with deeds.

However, while she and Pericon were enjoying such good
times together, Fortune, not content with humbling her from
the rank of a King's prospective bride, to the mistress of a country squire, was preparing a still crueller alliance for her.

Pericon had a younger brother of twenty-five, fresh and fair
as a rose, whose name was Marato. He had seen Alatiel and
liked her enormously, all the more because, as he interpreted
her actions, she was not averse to him. Accordingly, he thought

there was nothing to prevent the consummation of his desire, except the strict watch Pericon kept over her, and an evil plan came to him, which was soon followed by its villainous performance.

At about that time a ship was lying in the harbor of the town, freighted with merchandise and waiting to set sail for Chiarenza in Roumelia, under the command of two young Genoese shipmasters. Already, the shrouds had been lifted, and only a fair wind was lacking for the start. Marato had an interview with the shipmasters, and arranged with them to receive him and a lady on board, the following night. Then, with some trusty friends to whom he had imparted his plans and whose help he had secured, he went secretly and under cover of darkness concealed himself in the house of Pericon, who had implicit faith in him. Part of the night elapsed. Softly, he let his friends in and accompanied them to the room where Pericon slept with Alatiel. They opened the door without a sound, and murdering Pericon in his sleep, seized the woman, who was now awake and weeping, threatening to kill her if she cried for help. Carrying away a large part of Pericon's most valuable possessions, they sped to the sea-shore, unobserved. Marato led Alatiel on board, without losing a moment's time, and the accomplices returned to their homes. A good, fresh wind sprung up; and the sailors sent the ship full-sail upon its voyage.

Bitterly, Alatiel bewailed the fate that had willed her first, and then her new misfortune, but Marato, brandishing that blessed Saint Increase, which God bestowed upon us men, offered her such consolation that she was soon at home with him, and forgot all about Pericon. A certain comfortable quietude seemed to have settled upon her, when Fortune, not content with her past sorrows, prepared her a new trial. She was extraordinarily beautiful, as we have said repeatedly, and very attractive in her ways, whereupon the two young shipmasters fell so madly in love with her that, forgetting everything else, they exerted themselves to wait on her and win her favor, taking care, however, not to let Marato in on their secret. But they could not hide their passion from each other. Talking the matter over confidentially, they came to terms, agreeing to take the lady for their mutual enjoyment, as though love could stand such treatment, like vulgar business or profit.

Marato kept the strictest watch over her, and for some time they could not put their plan into execution. But one day, as the ship was headed full tilt into a gusty wind, and Marato was standing unsuspectingly on the poop, looking out over the water, they both went up to him and grasping him quickly from behind, pitched him overboard. The ship had proceeded more than a mile before anyone was even aware that Marato had fallen into the sea. When the unfortunate princess learned of it, and saw there was no way of getting him back, she commenced her lamentations anew.

The two lovers were not slow in comforting her with honeyed words and extravagant promises to allay her suffering, though little enough of it reached her understanding, engaged as she was in bewailing her merciless destiny, even more than the loss of her husband. Long and often they continued expostulating with her, until at length they thought she was sufficiently comforted, when they began arguing with each other, as to which was to be the first to take her to bed. Each was more eager for the privilege than the other, and there seemed to be no way of arranging it amicably. Word followed word in a fiery quarrel which was soon kindled to fury. Laying hold of their knives, they lunged at each other so madly that before they could be parted by the passengers, they had stabbed each other again and again. One of them died then and there of the wounds. The other still breathed, though his body was pierced through and through.

Alatiel was in deep distress, alone as she was, and with no one to advise her in her trouble. Besides, she was in mortal terror that the relatives and friends of the two shipmasters might vent their wrath upon her for what had happened. The entreaties of the wounded youth, however, and the early arrival of the ship at Chiarenza, delivered her from all peril of death.

She landed in the new country with the wounded man, and took up her residence with him at an inn. Presently the fame of her marvelous beauty spread through the city and reached the ears of the Prince of Morea, who was stopping at Chiarenza at the time. He insisted upon seeing her, but hardly had he done so than he found her to be even more ravishing than people had said, and fell so immediately and violently in love with her, that he had no mind for anything else. Somehow he learned how she had come to be there, and thought he could succeed in gaining possession of her. He was in the midst of considering ways and means, when the wounded man's folks heard of the prince's pleasure. They shipped her off to him, bag and baggage, without more ado, which delighted the prince more than words can tell, and Alatiel equally, who felt as though she had been rescued from the teeth of danger. As he studied her, and found that besides being beautiful, Alatiel was as well-bred as a king's daughter, he knew by that, as by no other token, that she must surely be of noble parentage, and his love for her redoubled. Accordingly, he treated her with the greatest honor, befitting not only a mistress, but a lawful wife.

Alatiel, bearing in mind her past tribulations, considered the present a most fortunate state and was entirely contented. She grew happy again and her charms flourished so splendidly, that all of Roumelia, it seemed, could find nothing else to talk about.

In no long while the fame of her beauty reached a friend and cousin of the prince, the Duke of Athens, a young, handsome, healthy gentleman of fine physique. He was dying to see her, and pretending to come on one of his usual visits to the prince, he arrived at Chiarenza with a numerous company, and was entertained with all due worship and rejoicing. A few days went by. Once, when the two were talking of the woman's beauty, the duke asked if she were indeed as wonderful a creature as people claimed.

"Much more," answered the prince, "but I don't want you to simply take my word for it. You must see her with your own eyes."

At the duke's request, they went together to Alatiel's apartment. She had already heard of their coming, and received them with cheer and rare courtesy. They invited her to sit between them, but they could not have the pleasure of conversing with her, for she knew little or nothing of their language. As a result, they were content to gaze upon her, as on one of the wonders of the world, especially the duke, who could hardly convince himself that she was a creature of flesh and blood. As he gazed and gazed, thinking to appease his desire with the sight of her, he was unconsciously drinking in the poisonous potion of her fascination, and yielding himself implacably to her spell, by the ardent passion he felt for her. Later, when he had left with his host, and had the leisure to collect his wits, he was sure the prince must be the happiest man in the world, to have so glorious a being at the disposal of his pleasure. On further and more varied reflection, he determined, on the spur of his fiery love, which had more weight with him than his sense of honor, to rob the prince of his happiness and procure his own.

He could not await the fulfilment of his wish, therefore putting aside all reason and justice, he abandoned his mind entirely to a treacherous plan. One day, yielding to his wicked purpose, he secretly got his horses and baggage ready for his departure, with the help of Curiaci, one of the prince's most trusted valets, and the following night he was stealthily admitted by the same fellow into the prince's chamber with a friend, both of them fully armed. It was a hot night, and the duke saw that while Alatiel slept, the prince was standing naked by a window facing the sea, enjoying the breeze that rose from the water. He had already primed his accomplice, so stealing through the room without a sound, he went to the window and stabbed the prince through the small of his back until the blade showed on the other side. Lifting him up quickly, he flung him out of the window.

The palace hung high over the sea, and the window at which the prince had been standing, overlooked certain dilapidated houses that had crumbled down from the beating of the waves. Seldom, indeed, hardly ever, did anyone pass that way, so, as the duke had foreseen, the fall of the corpse could neither have been witnessed nor heard. Once the duke's accomplice saw this part of the work done, he took out a noose he had brought for the purpose, and pretending to strike Curiaci with it in jest, slipped it cunningly around his neck and tightened it, so that the wretch could not utter a sound. The duke then came up. Together they strangled Curiaci and sent his body to follow the prince's, below.

The deed accomplished, the duke, confident that neither Alatiel nor anyone else had seen, took a lamp in his hand and carried it to the bedside. Gently he uncovered her from head to foot. She was sleeping soundly, and he took his fill of gazing at her loveliness in awed admiration, conscious that though she had pleased him clothed, she thrilled him beyond belief as she lay there, naked. Hotter desire inflamed him. Undaunted by the crime he had recently committed, and with hands still bloody, he lay down at her side and took his joy of her, as she responded, half asleep, believing him to be the prince.

He remained with her for some time in the keenest pleasure, and then got up and called in a number of his companions. They laid hold of Alatiel at his bidding, so that she could not

cry for help, carried her through the secret door by which he
had entered, and setting her on a horse, all of them made their
way toward Athens as stealthily as they could.

The duke was already married, hence he did not take Alatiel
directly to Athens, but to one of his handsomest country seats,
situated at some distance from the city, and facing the sea.
There he kept that most unfortunate of women, in the utmost
secrecy, providing her with everything her heart desired.

Next morning the prince's courtiers waited till noon for him
to arise. There was no stir. They pushed open the doors of his
rooms, which were not locked, and finding no one, decided he
must have taken a few days' vacation with his fair companion.
At that they worried no more about it. However, the following
day, an idiot wandering among the ruins where the bodies of
the prince and Curiaci were lying, pulled the servant out by the
rope around his neck and went trailing him along after him.
The body was recognized, to the utmost consternation of the
people, who by dint of coaxing and cajoling, managed to make
him conduct them to the place from which he had dragged it.
There the body of the prince was brought to light, and amid the
mourning of the whole city, was given honorable burial. When
they investigated, in order to discover the authors of the abominable murder, they found that the Duke of Athens was nowhere to be seen, but had furtively stolen away. They concluded
that he must have committed the crime and carried off the lady,
which indeed was the case.

Immediately, a brother of the murdered prince was placed
in authority, and the people goaded him to vengeance, while
other indications were not wanting to convince him that matters were as his subjects suspected. Summoning his friends, kin
and vassals from their various dominions, he soon collected a
large, competent, and powerful army and prepared to make war
upon the Duke of Athens. On his side, the duke concentrated
his forces for defense, upon hearing the rumor of the prince's
intentions, and at his summons, many lords came to his aid,
among whom the Emperor of Constantinople sent his son Constantine, and his nephew Manuel with a large body of soldiery.
They were gladly received by the duke, and even more gladly
by his wife, who was their sister-in-law.

Day by day, war was drawing to a head. Biding her time, the
duchess called for the two youths at the first opportunity, and
in the privacy of her room unburdened herself with free-flowing

tears and words aplenty, and told them the true reasons for the war, including the insult the duke inflicted upon her by keeping a mistress behind her back, as everybody knew. Very bitterly she complained of it, and implored them to do their best to set the matter straight, both for the sake of the duke's honor and her own peace of mind. The two young men were already acquainted with the state of affairs. They asked few questions and pacified her with such consolation as they could offer, filling her with hopes for the best. Then they found out from her where Alatiel was to be found, and went away. Many a time they had heard praise of the woman's wondrous beauty, and yearned for a sight of her, for which they pleaded with the duke. He had long forgotten what had happened to the prince who had shown her to him, and promised to grant them their desire.

In Alatiel's house there was a lovely garden, where the duke had tables set for a splendid luncheon and invited the two youths, with certain other friends, to be her guests. As it happened, Constantine, who was sitting beside her, began to gaze at her with wonder in his eyes, admitting to himself never to have beheld a mortal creature to equal her. The duke certainly ought to be condoned, he reflected, or any other man who attempted any wicked or treacherous deed in order to gain possession of such a prize. Again and again he turned to look at her, and when everyone else fell to praising her, the very thing was suddenly confirmed in him, which had been true of the duke. He went away very much enamored of her. Every thought of the war escaped his mind, and he gave himself up to devising means of wresting her from the duke, while keeping his love a secret.

As he consumed himself in the fire of his passion, the time arrived when the army had to meet the prince who was approaching the duke's domains. Orders were issued and the duke, Constantine and the rest of the army went off to defend certain frontiers from the prince's advance. For several days they remained there. Now Constantine, whose every thought reverted to Alatiel, imagining that since the duke was not with her, he could succeed in putting his plan into effect, feigned severe illness for the purpose of returning to Athens. He gave all his troops over to Manuel, and with the duke's permission returned to his sister-in-law, in the city. A few days went by. Somehow, he drew the duchess into a conversation on the subject of the insult the duke offered her through the mistress he was keeping, and suggested that he might be of great service if she were willing, by abducting Alatiel. The poor woman thought he made the offer for her own sake, not for Alatiel's, and readily consented, on condition her husband should never know that she had ever had a hand in it. He promised her faithfully, and she gave him her permission to do as he saw fit.

At that, Constantine had a small, fleet vessel secretly armed and brought one evening to the shore near the garden where Alatiel lived. He left instructions with certain of his men on board, and in the company of other friends, repaired to the lady's home. He was made welcome by the servants, and by Alatiel herself, who strolled with him in the garden at his suggestion, followed both by her retinue and his companions. Then he withdrew alone with her, as though he had something to communicate on the part of the duke, and led her to the recess of a gate that led out to the sea. One of his men had already opened it. At a given signal the ship was brought nearer, Alatiel captured in the twinkling of an eye and carried off on board.

"Let no one move or make a sound, if he values his life!" cried Constantine, turning to Alatiel's servants. "What I have done does not mean that I am stealing the duke's harlot, but am removing the reproach he inflicts upon my sister's honor."

Nobody dared answer. Constantine went aboard with his men, and approaching Alatiel, ordered his sailors to ply their oars and start off. They did not row, they flew, and toward morning of the next day they reached the shores of Egina. Here they landed and rested a while, and Constantine had his pleasure of Alatiel, who had every reason to curse her ill-starred beauty. Once more they embarked, and arrived at Chios in the space of a few days. Now Constantine was afraid his father might rebuke him, and perhaps take the stolen woman away from him, whereupon he thought it wiser to remain at Chios, as the safest place. Many days the lovely Alatiel bewailed her lot, but at Constantine's consolations, she was restored as she had been many times before, and made the best of what Fortune had set in store for her.

In the meantime Osbech, King of the Turks, who was always waging some war or other on the emperor, came to Smyrna. When he heard that Constantine was leading a care-free, dissolute life with a whore he had abducted, and took no defensive precautions whatsoever, he sallied forth one night, with a small fleet of light-armed vessels, and treacherously invading the city with his soldiers, surprised many of the inhabitants in their beds, before they could realize the enemy was upon them. Others, who had run to arms at the alarm, they put to the sword, and then, setting fire to the whole city, returned to Smyrna, their ships laden with booty and prisoners. On looking over his captives Osbech, who was a young man, came upon the beautiful woman whom he recognized, to his great delight, as the very one he had seized while she lay sleeping with Constantine. He made her his wife without wasting time, celebrated the nuptials, and bedded her happily, for many months.

Prior to these events, the emperor had entered into a treaty with Bassano, King of Cappadocia, by which the king was to fall upon Osbech from one side with his troops, while he himself attacked him on the other. However, he had not yet reached a satisfactory agreement, refusing to consent to certain matters which Bassano insisted on, but which he thought inconvenient. However, when he heard what a scrape his son had got into, he was saddened to the heart, and without losing a moment's time, did everything the King of Cappadocia demanded, urging him to fall upon Osbech while, on the other hand, he made preparations to attack him from the opposite direction. Osbech heard of the plan. Mustering his army he took the initiative, rather than be crushed between two such powerful rulers, and went to meet the King of Cappadocia, leaving Alatiel at Smyrna in the care of a faithful servant and friend. Waging battle with Bassano some time later, he entered the fray and was slain, and his army routed and scattered. The victorious Bassano marched toward Smyrna, and in his path all the people subjected themselves to his rule, as conqueror.

When Osbech's servant, Antiochus, a man fairly advanced in years, saw the marvelous beauty of the lady who had been left in his care, he forgot all promises of his lord and friend and fell in love with her. He was able to speak her language, which made her very happy, since for many years she had been obliged to live like a deaf mute, understanding no one, and never making herself understood. Pricked by love, therefore, Antiochus was soon so familiar with her, that before many days had passed they both lost all consideration for their lord, who was fighting on the battlefield, and made their acquaintance not only friendly but amorous, taking great delight in each other between the sheets. But when news reached them that Osbech had been discomfited and slain, and that Bassano was advancing, taking everything on his way, they thought it the better part of valor not to wait for him. Making a bundle of Osbech's most precious belongings, they stole away together and went to Rhodes. Hardly had they settled there, when Antiochus fell mortally ill. In the course of his flight he had come across a Cyprian merchant who had been a close friend of his, and whom he dearly loved. Feeling the hand of death upon him, he decided to bequeath his possessions and his dear lady to him, so calling them both to his bedside he said:

"I feel my life gradually but surely ebbing away, and it grieves me considerably, for I never found it more pleasant to live, than now. There's one thing that compensates me for my death, and that is that though I must die, it shall be in the arms of the two I love best in the whole world—yours, my dearest friend, and this woman's, whom I have loved more than my very self, from the moment I knew her. It is true that I am grieved at the thought of leaving her here a stranger, without help or counsel, once I'm gone. It would grieve me still more if I did not know you here, for I am sure you will be even more solicitous of her for my sake, than you would have been of me. I beg you then, take care of her and of my possessions, and dispose of them both in the way you think would be of most comfort to my soul. As for you, dearest lady, ah, don't forget me after my death, for in the other life I desire the pleasure of boasting that I am loved on earth by the most beautiful woman nature ever created. If you will only assure me of these two things I shall leave life behind, entirely happy."

Antiochus' friend and Alatiel burst into tears on hearing these words, and the moment he was silent they comforted him, promising on their oaths to do everything he asked, if he should die. Not long after, he breathed his last and they gave him honorable burial.

Some days later, the Cyprian merchant settled all his business in Rhodes, and planned to return to Cyprus on a Catalan galley that was lying in harbor. He asked Alatiel what she proposed to do, as he had to go back to his country, and she replied that she would willingly join him, if he wished, and hoped he would treat her in everything as a sister, for the sake of Antiochus. The merchant agreed. Therefore, to guard her from possible insult on the way to Cyprus, he informed everyone that she was his wife. They embarked, and on board the galley they were given a snug cabin on the poop, where, that his deeds might not

contradict his words, he was obliged to lie with her in a very
tiny bed. Then a thing happened which neither had bargained
for on leaving Rhodes. It was dark in the cabin. The snugness
and warmth of the bed, strong temptations in themselves, soon
goaded them on, and all love and respect for the late Antiochus
were thrown overboard when a mutual desire drew them together. They began pretty games with each other, and even before they touched the shores of Baffa, the Cyprian's birthplace,
they had forged a close bond of intimacy.

Once at Baffa, Alatiel took up her lodgings with the merchant, and lived with him for some time. It so happened that a
certain gentleman by the name of Antigonus, great in years,
yet still greater in wisdom, had come to Baffa on business, about
that time. He had scarcely a cent to his name, for luck had been
against him in the service of the King of Cyprus, in whose affairs he had been involved. Now one day, as he was passing the
house where Alatiel lived with the merchant, who had left for
Armenia to dispose of some goods, he caught sight of her
standing at a window. Her beauty attracted him and he stared
at her fixedly, little by little becoming possessed of the notion
that he must have seen her somewhere before, though where he
could not recall. Alatiel herself, who had been the plaything of
Fortune so long, but who was drawing toward the end of her
trials, scarcely set her eyes on him than she recalled having met
him in her father's house at Alexandria, where he filled an important post. Instantly, she was seized with sudden hope that
perhaps by the old man's advice she might still regain her royal
station. Her merchant could not hear, for he was far away, so
calling the man to her immediately, she asked him prettily
whether she was right in supposing him to be Antigonus of
Famagosta.

"I am he," replied Antigonus, "and it seems to me that I must
know you, lady. For the life of me I can't recall where I met
you, and if I'm not asking too much I'd like you to refresh my
memory about yourself."

As soon as Alatiel heard he was indeed Antigonus, she fell
weeping upon his neck, to his great astonishment, and after a
while she asked him if he recollected ever having seen her at
Alexandria. In a twinkling, he recognized her to be Alatiel, the
Sultan's daughter, whom everyone believed lost at sea. He would
have knelt to her as her rank demanded, but she prevented
him and begged him to sit with her a while. He acquiesced, and

reverently asked what circumstances had brought her there, when all Egypt was certain she had perished at sea many years before.

"Ah, if only I had been drowned," sighed Alatiel, "instead of leading the miserable life I have! Even my own father would wish the same, if he ever came to know the truth."

Very bitterly, she wept anew, though Antigonus comforted her. "Don't despair before there's need for it," he said. "If you don't mind, tell me what you've gone through and what sort of life you've led. Perhaps things are not so bad that we can't turn them to good account, by the aid of God."

"Antigonus," said the lovely Alatiel, "when I laid eyes on you, I thought I was seeing my own father, and it was the very love and tenderness I have for him, that made me reveal myself to you, though I could easily have kept my secret. There aren't very many persons the sight of whom would have rejoiced me more. As to a father, Antigonus, I'll confide to you what I've been keeping a dead secret in my misfortune. If you think there's any way of restoring me to my former station, after what I tell you, why, then, please do. If not, never tell a living soul that you have seen or heard anything of me, I implore you."

Still in tears she told him all that had happened to her from the time her ship struck Majorca to that very moment, and the story moved him to weep with compassion. After pondering a while, "Princess," he said, "since you have kept your true rank a secret throughout your misfortunes, I'm sure I can make your father love you more than ever, when I bring you back to him, and the King of Algarve, too, whose wife you will be."

She asked how that could possibly be accomplished, and he showed her, point by point, how the matter might be handled. He would suffer no impediment to spoil the plan, and without letting a moment slip by, he returned to Famagosta and went before the king.

"Sire," he said, "if it's agreeable to you, it's in your power to do much honor to yourself, at little expense, and a signal service to me, who became impoverished in your service."

"In what manner?" asked the king.

Antigonus replied: "The Sultan's beautiful young daughter, whom we have long thought drowned, has just come to Baffa. She has gone through bitter suffering these many years, to protect her honor. Now she is in wretched circumstances, and wishes to return to her father. If you would only send her to him, in my charge, it would result in your glory and my great advantage, and I can assure you that the Sultan would not easily let such a service slip his mind."

The king, moved by regal generosity, spontaneously replied that he would do as Antigonus suggested. He sent for the princess, in fitting fashion, and had her conveyed to Famagosta, where she was entertained by him and the queen with indescribable honor and magnificence. When they asked her of her adventures, she told them everything according to the teachings of Antigonus. Some days later, at her request, the king sent her to the Sultan, under Antigonus' wing and with a noble retinue of men and women. How can I describe with what joy she was gathered into her father's arms, or what festivities greeted her escort, Antigonus and all her company?

When she had somewhat rested from the fatigue of the journey, the Sultan wanted to know how it happened that she was still alive, and where she could have been so long, without sending him word of her circumstances. Alatiel had proved more than apt to the instructions of her mentor, so keeping them well in mind, when her father was silent she said:

"It must have been some twenty days after I left you, father dear, that a terrible storm struck our vessel, tore it in half, and cast it ashore one night near a place in the west called Aguamorta. What happened to all the men who had been on board I never knew, and I don't know to this day. I only remember that when day came and I woke up—it was as if I had risen from death to life—I noticed that the battered ship had already been found by the country-folk of that place, who ran from every side to plunder it. While they did their pillaging, they set me and two of my women, ashore. Suddenly some young men seized the poor girls, and ran away with them in different directions. That's the last I saw of them, because at the same time two scoundrels fell upon me and dragged me around by the hair, unmindful of my loud lamentations and the efforts I made to defend myself. Then, while they were trailing me along a road that led to a terrible forest, four men on horseback chanced to be passing by, and no sooner did the two young ruffians spy them coming, than they let me go and took to their heels. The four mounted gentlemen, who looked very respectable, hurried over when they saw this, and asked me many questions. I spoke at length to them, too, but alas! we couldn't make out what we were saying, for I didn't understand them, nor they, me. However, after much deliberation among themselves, they put me on one of their horses, and took me to a place where there were many women who were vowed to religion, according to their faith—a convent, I think it was. Whatever the four gentlemen told them, I can't say, but anyhow those ladies took me in most kindly, and always treated me with consideration. Later, following their example, I learned to serve with much devotion, one Saint Increase-in-the-Hollow, a worthy whom the women of that country hold in great affection. When I had been living with them for some time and had learned a little of their language, they asked me about myself. Now, realizing where I was, I feared they would chase me away, as an enemy of their faith were I to tell the truth, so I said I was the daughter of a Cyprian gentleman who had sent me to be married in Crete, but that unfortunately the vessel I was on, had struck their shores and been wrecked. In many ways and in many things, I observed their customs out of self-defense, until one day the chief of those women, the abbess, they called her, asked me if I should like to go back to Cyprus. I answered that no other thing was nearer my heart. But she was very careful of my virtue, and wouldn't think of putting me in charge of anyone going to Cyprus, until about two months ago. At that time certain French gentlemen arrived with their wives, among whom was a lady related to the abbess. When she learned that they were all bound for Jerusalem, where the Man they worship as God was buried, after the Jews had slain Him, the abbess commended me to the care of these pilgrims, and begged them to present me to my father in Cyprus.

"It would take too long to tell you how well these gentlemen treated me, and how gladly they admitted me to the circle of their women. Well, we all took ship, and after sailing a few days, arrived at Baffa, where once there, I didn't know a soul. I racked my brains for some credible excuse to offer the gentlemen, who were anxious to take me to my father, following the recommendation of the venerable abbess. But, by the grace of God, who must have taken pity on me, whom should I discover on the landing-place at Baffa the moment we disembarked, but Antigonus himself! I called him to me quickly, and in our own tongue, so that those gentlemen and their wives might not understand, I asked him to welcome me as his daughter. He understood perfectly, and made a deal of fuss over me, treating my companions with as much generosity as his poor means would allow. Later, he took me to the King of Cyprus, who entertained me royally, and then sent me to you with such courtesy, that I can scarcely find words to express myself. If there is anything I have left out, Antigonus will supply it, for he has heard the story of my adventures from my lips, time and time again."

At that Antigonus began, addressing himself to the Sultan: "Sire, that is exactly how things happened, as I have heard many times from Alatiel herself, and from those worthy gentlemen and ladies who accompanied her. There's one thing she has neglected to tell you. I think perhaps she considers it unbecoming to mention it herself. It is simply this—how highly those good pilgrims praised the chaste, virtuous life she had led with the holy women, how well they spoke of her laudable manners, and with what tears and wailing those gentlemen and ladies took leave of her, after they had consigned her to my care. Indeed, if I were to begin relating all they said to me, not only this whole day but the coming night would not suffice. It is enough to say that, as their words fully proved, and as my observations further certified, you may well boast of having the most beautiful, modest and most virtuous daughter of any king now wearing a crown."

The Sultan was exceedingly delighted, and offered up many prayers to God, for the grace adequately to compensate everyone who had been kind to his daughter, particularly the King of Cyprus, through whom she had been conveyed to him. A few days later he had many splendid gifts made ready for Antigonus, and gave him permission to return to Cyprus. Then by letters and special ambassadors, he proffered his heartfelt thanks to the king, for all the courtesies he had shown his daughter.

Anxious to put a fitting end to what had been begun, that is, to marry off Alatiel to the King of Algarve, the Sultan informed him of what had occurred, writing him besides that if he wanted her, he should send for her. The king was happy beyond measure at the news, and sending for her in sumptuous style, gave her a rousing welcome. As for Alatiel, who had lain perhaps ten-thousand times with eight different men—why, she went to bed with him—a virgin, and made him believe it, too. She lived with him for a long while as his queen, and it was of her it was said,

"A mouth crushed with kisses loses no boon,
But ever reflourishes, as does the moon."

✳

# THE EIGHTH STORY

*The Count of Antwerp, falsely accused, goes into exile and leaves his two children in different parts of England. On returning incognito, he finds them in good circumstances. Then, enlisting as groom in the army of the King of France, he is proved innocent and restored to his former dignity.*

THE LADIES HEAVED MANY SIGHS OVER THE ADVENTURES OF THE lovely Alatiel, but who can tell what inspired them? It may be some sighed as much out of yearning for such frequent nuptials, as out of pity for the princess. But enough of that, for the present. They laughed a little at Pamfilo's last words, and when the queen saw his tale had come to an end, she turned to Elisa and requested her to continue with a story. Blithely Elisa obeyed.

It's a wide field we're wandering in to-day, she began, and there is not one of us who couldn't run a race in it, even ten, considering how ample Fortune has made it with her extraordinary and unhappy accidents. Of all her infinite varieties, I am going to choose a single one to tell you.

When the Holy Roman Empire was transferred from the French to the Germans, there sprang up a bitter enmity between the two nations, and a raging continuous state of warfare. As a result, the King of France and one of his sons mustered up a tremendous army from the backbone of the kingdom, and with the aid of as many friends and kindred as they could collect they started out against the enemy, in the defense of their realm and to the offense of their opponents. However, not wishing to leave the kingdom without a ruler, they appointed Gautier, Count of Antwerp, in their place, as vice-regent over the whole of France, and went their way, knowing Gautier to be a wise, noble man, a faithful friend and servant, and moreover, better suited to handling delicate situations than warfare, though he was well-trained in things martial.

Wisely and discreetly, Gautier gave himself up to the office in his trust, always consulting both the queen and her daughter-in-law in every matter under his jurisdiction; for although they, too, had been committed to his custody, he never failed to look upon them as his superiors, and honor them accordingly.

Now Gautier was a man of very handsome presence, nearing

his forties, and as pleasant and courtly a gentleman as one might wish to find. He was, besides, the most charming, best-dressed, exquisite gallant of his day, and a widower besides, for his wife had died, leaving him two little children—a boy and a girl.

It so happened that while the King of France and his son were away at the war, Gautier frequented the court of their wives discussing the business of the realm, and the bride of the king's son fixing her eyes on him, was smitten with great affection at the sight of his beauty and courtliness, and secretly burned with passionate love for him. Reflecting on her own youth and freshness and on his wifeless state, she had no doubt but that she could easily gratify her desire. Her modesty alone could prove a stumbling-block, but that she resolved to dispense with, by making a clean breast of her sentiments, to him personally. She found herself alone one day, and the time seeming ripe, she sent for him, on the pretext of a desire to discuss different matters. The count was far from suspecting what way the wind blew, and going to her room without a moment's thought, sat down on a couch beside her at her invitation. There was no one else in the room. Twice the count asked why she had sent for him, and twice she had answered with silence. At last, prompted by her love, she began, blushing with shame, tearful and trembling, and her voice breaking.

"Dear sweet friend and master, as a wise man you ought easily to realize how weak we naturally are—all of us, men and women—and some much more than others, for different reasons. Before a fair-minded judge, even the same sin should not deserve the same punishment, depending on the kinds and qualities of people who commit it. Who will deny that the poor man or woman who ought to be sweating for the bare necessities of life, but goes chasing after love instead, ought to be more severely blamed, than the idle rich woman who has nothing between herself and her desires? Nobody, I'm sure. So I think wealth and enforced idleness ought, in a sense, exonerate the woman who suffers through them, once she lets herself stumble into love. As for the rest, she ought to be given credit if she chooses a wise and discreet lover. Now I am in both these predicaments, not to mention others that lead me to temptation—my youth, for instance, and my husband's absence. Everything should cry out in my defense, then, for the burning love I feel at the sight of you. If all my agonies can prevail upon you—in-

deed, they would convince the very sages—please, please give
me the help and counsel I ask of you! I confess I've been powerless to conquer the stings of desire in my husband's absence,
and the temptation of love. Why, even the strongest men have
been overcome by their power. Every day we see them falling
victims to their might! What shall we say of weak, tender
women? I am no different. You see me lolling in comfort and
idleness. Is it any wonder I have let myself go in quest of love's
pleasures, and allowed myself to succumb? I grant you such a
passion would be immoral, if the world ever knew of it, but
since it's hidden—why, it's moral enough, to my way of thinking. Besides, Cupid has shown himself so kind in my behalf,
that not only has he not deprived me of proper judgment in se-
lecting a lover, but he has even seconded it, proving you entirely worthy of receiving the love of a woman of my quality.
For—if my senses don't deceive me—you are the handsomest,
finest, and most accomplished cavalier to be found in all France.
What's more, just as I might say you have no wife, I also have
no husband. Come, then, and for my ardent love's sake, don't refuse me yours. Have pity on my youth that—God help me!—
melts before you like ice before fire."

Her words were followed by such a flood of tears, that her
speech was cut short, though she would still have offered further
entreaties. Thus, lowering her face, at the end of her forces, she
wept and let herself droop until her head was on the count's
bosom. But he was too loyal a gentleman. With grave reproaches, he repressed her mad passion, pushing her from him
as she would have thrown herself upon his neck, and swearing
many a solemn oath, saying he would sooner be drawn and quartered than permit so grave an affront to his lord's honor,
whether through himself or anyone else. Immediately, the woman's love was forgotten, and kindling into a violent frenzy,
"What!" she cried. "Do you imagine I'll let you trample on my
passion like this, you villain? Since you'd rather let me die—
God forbid!—I'll see to it that you're put to death instead, or
hunted out of the world!"

Clutching at her hair with her hands, she tore and disheveled
it, and then rending her clothes from her breast, screamed
with all her might: "Help! Help! The Count of Antwerp is
trying to force me!"

At that the count, more afraid of the courtiers' envy than of
his own conscience, and worried that the woman's malice would

be credited sooner than his own innocence, rose quickly to his feet, left the palace and fled to his house. There, he put his children on horseback without further thought, and mounting after them, made the sparks fly as he galloped in the direction of Calais.

In the interim a crowd had gathered at the woman's shrieks, and when the people saw her all disheveled and heard the account she gave of what had made her scream, they not only believed her implicitly, but added that the count's courtliness and gallantry had long been his means to attaining his ends. In a moment, there was a rush to arrest him at his quarters, but when he could not be found, his house was plundered and then burned to the ground. The news in its distorted form was not long in reaching the ears of the king and his son. They were mad with rage, and condemned the count and his descendants after him to perpetual exile, promising besides, a considerable reward to anyone who delivered him up, dead or alive.

Gautier, grieved that he had converted his innocence to guilt by running away, at last reached Calais with his children, undiscovered and unrecognized. From there, he quickly crossed over to England, and dressing himself very shabbily, went on toward London. Before he entered the city, however, he instructed his children in two particulars: first of all, they must patiently bear the poverty to which Fortune and himself had reduced them, though God knows, through no fault of his own, and secondly, if they valued their lives, they must cleverly avoid telling anyone where they came from, or whose children they were. Both Louis, the nine-year-old boy, and Violante, the little girl, who was perhaps seven, understood their father's instructions as well as their tender years might grasp them, and showed it afterwards by their actions. For greater safety, the count thought it advisable to change their names, calling the boy Pierrot and the girl Jeannette. Then the three entered London, dressed very poorly, and went begging alms, as we have seen many a French vagrant doing.

One day, while they were standing in front of a church, a lady, the wife of one of the King of England's chief officers, happened to be coming out, and seeing the count and his two children with their hands held out, asked him who he was, and whether the little ones were his. He replied that he came from Picardy, and that he had been obliged to leave the country with these, his two little children, because of a crime committed by a ne'er-do-well elder son. The lady was tender-hearted by nature, and when she looked at the little girl she was very much taken with her, because of the charm, grace and nobility of her manner.

"Listen, good fellow," she said, "if you are willing to leave this little girl of yours with me, I'll gladly take care of her, for she looks promising. Then, if she grows up to be an honest woman, I'll give her a good husband when the time comes, so that she will be well provided for."

The count was overjoyed with this proposal, and readily acquiesced. Then, giving Jeannette over to the lady, he urged her, with tears in his eyes, to look after her well.

Now that his daughter had been placed with a person of appreciable position, he thought he had remained in London long enough, and begging his way across the island came with Pierrot to Wales, but not without intense agony, for he was not accustomed to journeying on foot. Another of the king's important officers, it happened, lived there in great luxury with a large household of attendants, and frequently Gautier and his son used to go to his court for food. Here the lord's sons and other little boys belonging to gentlemen of the court, were accustomed to try their prowess in various games, such as running and leaping, and Pierrot began to mingle with them, performing the feats as skilfully as the rest, and even outdoing them. The lord of the house noticed him on certain occasions, and liking the child's manner and behavior, asked who he might be. He was informed that Pierrot was the son of a poor man, who sometimes came to the court for alms, whereupon the gentleman sent word to Gautier asking whether he would consent to let him have the boy. The count, who had been praying God for nothing better, freely gave up Pierrot to him, although it greatly pained him to part with the lad.

Now that Gautier had found a home for both his son and daughter, he thought he had lived long enough in England, and made the best of his way to Ireland. In the town of Stamord, he went into service with an earl's knight of that country, performing all those tasks that fall to the lot of a groom or lackey. Nobody ever knew who he was, and for many years he lived there in the midst of discomfort and arduous toil.

Meanwhile Violante, or rather, Jeannette, was living in London with the noble lady who had adopted her, increasing in years and body and comeliness as time went on. She had so suc-

ceeded in winning the hearts of her foster parents, and of everyone else who came in contact with her, that it was wonderful
to see. Indeed, no one who ever remarked her behavior, failed
to say she was worthy of the best, so that the noble lady
who had received her at the hands of her father, without knowing a thing about her except what he himself had said, was
now thinking of marrying her off honorably, in keeping with
her supposed station. But God, who is an accurate judge of one's
merits, knowing Jeannette was of noble birth and innocently
suffering under the weight of another's sin, willed otherwise. In
fact, we are compelled to believe He must have permitted what
came to pass through His own goodness, that the gentle girl
might not fall into the hands of some unworthy lout.

Jeannette's foster parents had an only son whom they loved as
the apple of their eye, both because he was their own flesh and
blood, and because he deserved their love for his many excellent
qualities of mind and body. He was perhaps some six years
older than Jeannette, and observing how lovely and gracious she
was, he fell so desperately in love with her, that he had eyes for
nobody else. Yet because he imagined she was of lowly stock,
he not only did not dare to ask his parents for her hand, but
fearing rebuke for loving so unworthily, he did his best to
conceal his passion, which kept him in a hotter furnace than
if he had given vent to it. Consequently, his frame was shattered
for the suffering it could not bear.

A number of physicians were called in consultation, who examined one symptom and another, but were unable to diagnose
the disease. They despaired of his recovery, which made his
parents suffer agonies of sorrow so intense, that greater could
not have been borne. Time and time again they urged him
with pitiful entreaties to reveal the cause of his illness, but he
either sighed or answered he felt himself utterly consuming.

One day, by a strange coincidence, while a young but learned
doctor was sitting beside the patient holding him by the wrist,
Jeannette, who nursed him tenderly, out of regard for his
mother, entered the room on some errand or other. No sooner
did the boy see her than without the outward indication of a
word or motion, he felt the force of his passion surging more
fiercely in his heart, causing his pulse to beat more violently
than ever. The doctor perceived it immediately and wondered
at it, but stood motionless to see how long the excitement would
last. The moment Jeannette was out of the room, the beating

subsided, which led the doctor to believe he had come to the root of the malady. He waited a while, still holding the patient by the arm, and sent for Jeannette on another pretext. She came without delay, and had hardly crossed the threshold when the youth's pulse began its galloping, calming down the moment she was out of the room. The doctor thought he had proof enough. Rising from his seat, he drew the lad's parents aside and spoke to them.

"Your son's recovery," he said, "is beyond the help of doctors, but lies entirely in the hands of Jeannette. He's head over heels in love with her, as I discovered by sure signs, though the girl is unaware of it, for all that I can see. It's up to you to know what to do, if you treasure his life."

They were glad to hear what the doctor had to say, for at least there seemed to be a way of saving their son, though it was the very remedy they had fearfully anticipated—that is, giving him Jeannette to wife. Once the doctor was gone, they went directly to the boy.

"Son," said his mother, "I'd never have thought it possible for you to keep any desire of yours from me, and what is worse, pine away for lack of it. You ought to have known, indeed, you ought to know, that there is nothing I might do for you, even beyond the bounds of honesty, that I would not venture, as for my very self. Yet though you have behaved this way, God Almighty has been more merciful toward you than you yourself, and opened my eyes to the cause of your illness, that you may not die. It is nothing more or less than a deep love you are feeling for some young girl—I don't know who. But really, you shouldn't have been so squeamish about speaking out, because it's all due to your youth, and if you weren't in love I'd think there was something lacking. There now, don't keep anything from me, my child, but open your heart, in all confidence. Get rid of the worry and melancholy that prey upon your mind, and bring about this illness. Cheer up, and rest assured that there's nothing you can ask me to do to please you, that I'll not turn the world upside down to accomplish, loving you as I do, more than my life. Away with shame and fear! Tell me if I can help you in this little affair of yours. Then, if you find I am not diligent or if I don't show you results—call me the meanest mother that ever bore a son!"

At first, during this speech, the boy was ashamed, but then, conscious that no one could further his pleasure more easily than his mother, he forgot his shyness and replied: "What made me hide my passion, mother, was only the fact that when people are old, they usually hate to remember they were once young. At least, that's how I feel. But since you have been so sensible about it, I'll not deny what you said you noticed. It's true, and what is more, I'll even tell you who it is, provided you adhere to your promise of helping me as much as you are able. That is the only way you'll ever have me well again."

Over-confident, in an issue that was not to be as she expected, the fond mother urged him to speak frankly of his desires, promising she would interest herself in obtaining him his pleasure without delay.

"Mother," continued the young lad, "it was our dear Jeannette's beauty and sweet ways that made me fall in love with her. Then, because I could not declare my love, much less move her to pity, or even dare to reveal it to a living soul—all these things combined, brought me to this. If what you promised does not come true, somehow or other, you may rest assured I'll not be long among the living."

The lady forced a smile, knowing comforting words were more suitable to his case than a scolding, and said: "Ah, my poor child, and it is for this you let yourself pine away? Come, be of good cheer, and as soon as you are yourself once more, leave things to me."

Buoyed up by his hope, the youth rapidly showed signs of improvement, which so gladdened his mother that she contrived a way of attaining what she had promised him. One day, calling Jeannette, she asked, in what seemed a goodnatured jest, whether she had a lover. The girl was rosy with blushes.

"Madam," she answered, "a poor girl like me, who has been banished from her own hearth and home and has to tend to the business of others, cannot properly think of love, nor is it expected of her."

"Well, then," said the lady, "since you have no lover, we'll provide you with one, who will give you all the joys of life and let you make the most of your beauty. It's foolish for a girl as good-looking as you, to remain without a lover."

"Madam," replied Jeannette, "you took me out of my father's poverty, bringing me up as your own daughter. For this alone I ought to obey you in everything. But I can never do what you say, and I think I'm in the right. If you intend to give me a husband, I promise to love him, but never another man. I may have only my virtue from my ancestors, but I mean to keep it unpolluted as long as there's life in me."

This answer was quite contrary to what the lady had thought to evoke on behalf of her son, and though, like the prudent woman she was, she inwardly admired the stand the girl took, she said: "What do you mean, Jeannette! Supposing our lord the king, who is as handsome a young gallant as you are a lovely girl—supposing he asked you for some love-delight, would you deny him?"

Promptly the girl replied: "Our lord the king might perhaps succeed in taking what he wished by force, but of my own free will, he could get nothing but what is in keeping with my honor."

The woman, seeing which way the wind blew, said no more and determined to put her to the test. Going to her son, she told him that as soon as he recovered his health, she would try to leave Jeannette alone in a room with him, when it would be up to him to get what he wanted. As for herself—she thought it rather indecent to be pandering for him like a go-between, to obtain the favors of her maid. The boy was not at all pleased with the turn things were taking, and grew suddenly worse, which, when the mother saw, made her face the facts boldly and speak openly to Jeannette. But the girl was adamant. There was nothing left for the lady to do but to go to her husband and tell him all she had attempted. Together they held counsel and finally decided to let their son marry Jeannette, reasoning it was far better to have him alive, even with a wife of lower rank, than dead without any wife at all. And so it was done, after much commotion.

Jeannette was exceedingly happy at the outcome, and fervently thanked God for keeping her in mind. However, even at the time she was married, she divulged nothing of her parentage except that she was the daughter of a man from Picardy. In the meantime, the sick youth regained his health. Happier than any man alive, he celebrated his wedding and did not fail to regale himself with his wife.

In Wales, Pierrot who had been left in charge of the King of England's officer of state, grew in the estimation of his lord, and became as handsome and doughty a lad as any on the island. Neither in tourneys, jousts or any feat of arms whatever, was there a man of the country who could measure up to him. His fame spread all over the land and he was known everywhere as

Pierrot the Picard. In the course of years, just as God had not forgotten Jeannette, He also showed that He kept the youth in mind. It chanced at the time, that a fatal plague swept the country, wiping out half the population. Of the survivors, a great part fled in fear to other countries, and what with the dead and the fleeing, the whole land was deserted. Among others, Pierrot's master and his wife and son had lost their lives, and many more of the family—brothers, nephews, relatives. All of them perished, until of the great lord's household no one was left but a girl, old enough to be married, and Pierrot, with several other servants. The raging pestilence slowly died out. Then the young woman, acting upon the advice and approval of the few gentlemen whom the plague had spared, took Pierrot as her husband, for his courage and bravery, and made him master of everything she had inherited.

Not very long afterwards, when the King of England learned that his officer was dead, and was acquainted with the merit of Pierrot the Picard, he appointed him marshal in place of the deceased lord, and so were settled the fortunes of the two children whom the Count of Antwerp had abandoned for lost.

It was now eighteen years since Gautier had fled Paris, and he was still living in Ireland. Life had spared him none of its hardships in his servitude; old age, too, had come upon him, and he was filled with a desire to learn, if possible, what had become of his children. Altered as he was in appearance from the man he had been, and more resisting in body, through his arduous exercise, than in his idle youth, he left his master and set out for England with a lean pocket and mean clothes. There he appeared at the place he had left Pierrot, and found him a marshal and a healthy, vigorous, handsome, powerful man, which gladdened his old heart to bursting. However, he would not reveal himself until he had discovered how Jeannette had fared.

Proceeding on his way, he did not stop until he reached London, where, making cautious investigations concerning the lady with whom he had left his daughter, and inquiring after her lot, he found that Jeannette had become the wife of her only son. The old man could not have been happier, and deemed his past suffering insignificant in the face of his children's prosperity. A wish to see Jeannette obsessed him. From that day on he went back and forth in the vicinity of her home, like a beggar. Once, Jacques Lamiens, Jeannette's husband, came upon him, and moved to pity at his poverty and age, ordered one of his men to take him in, and give him food out of charity, which the man did, readily enough.

In the course of time Jeannette had borne Jacques several children, the eldest of whom was perhaps eight years old, and all of them the loveliest youngsters in the world. When they saw the stranger at table, they flocked about him one and all, and petted and made much of him, as though, guided by some secret intuition, they had discovered him to be their grandfather. He knew very well they were his grandchildren, and showed them so much love and tenderness, that they refused to leave his side, although their teacher clamored for them. Jeannette, roused by the noise, came out of an adjoining room, and entering the count's, threatened to spank them if they did not do as their master bade them. The little ones cried and pleaded, saying they wanted to remain with that nice old gentleman who loved them more than their teacher did, which made Jeannette and the count laugh. He had risen, not like a father but like a beggar, to greet his daughter with the respect due to a lady, and a keen joy had pierced his heart at the sight of her. But she did not recognize him, either then, or later, so greatly had he changed. Old, gray and shaggy he was, and lean and brown, looking more like a stranger than the debonair count of the past. Jeannette, seeing the children were loth to leave him and cried whenever any effort was made to tear them away, asked their teacher to let them indulge their whim. Just at that time, while the little ones were with the old man, Jacques' father returned home and learned from their teacher what had taken place. Now he had always felt a certain scorn for Jeannette, and cried: "Leave them alone, plague take them! They're only showing where they spring from. Their mother's a vagrant's brat, and it's not astonishing that they should prefer the company of vagrants!"

The count heard the words, and a sharp pain smote him, but he shrugged his shoulders patiently, swallowing that insult as he had done many others before.

Meanwhile Jacques, learning what a reception the children had given the old man, was uneasy about it. However, he loved them so dearly, that rather than let them cry, he suggested that if the poor fellow was willing to work for him in any capacity, he would take him into his service without further question. The count said he would gladly stay with him, but that the only thing in which he was skilled, was the tending of horses, which he had been accustomed to all his life. A horse was given over to his care, and after his work was done, he used to play with the children.

While Fortune was amusing herself with the count and his children in this manner, the King of France died, having made many treaties with the Germans, and in his place that son whose wife had been the cause of Gautier's banishment was crowned. The last truce with the enemy was ended, and on the basis of that fact, the new monarch started another even fiercer war, aided by the King of England, who sent him a large body of soldiers for the new kinship's sake. Pierrot, his marshal, was in command, and Jacques Lamiens, son of the other marshal. With them also went the count, who remained for a long time in disguise, serving the army as a menial, but in his own quality doing much more than was required of him, through good advice and faithful service.

The war was in full swing when the Queen of France was taken seriously ill. She knew intuitively that death was near at hand, and repenting of her sins, she made open confession to the holy Archbishop of Rouen, who was everywhere celebrated for his goodness. She told him many things, among them the grievous wrong the Count of Antwerp had suffered at her hands. Not satisfied with telling the archbishop alone about it, she narrated everything as it had come to pass, before an assembly of worthy gentlemen, imploring them to prevail upon the king to re-establish the count in his former eminence, if death had spared him, or if not, at least one of his children. Hardly had she spoken, when she died. She was buried with due pomp, and her confession was communicated to the king. He sighed deeply at the wrongs the noble man had undeservedly suffered, and issued a proclamation through the army and the land that whoever gave him any information about the Count of Antwerp or his children, would receive magnificent rewards for each one, as the queen had cleared Gautier of the guilt for which he had been banished, and he, the king, intended to raise him to his former state—or even higher honor.

The tidings, ringing with the tenor of truth, reached Gautier's ears. In the wink of an eye he went to Jacques, and begged him to go with him in search of Pierrot, for he wished to show them the very man the king was looking for, he said. When the three were together, the count, resolved to reveal himself, addressed his son.

"Pierrot," he said, "Jacques here has married your sister. He never received a dowry with her, and that no one may say she went to him a pauper, he and nobody else should receive the great benefits the king promises. Go then, and declare yourself the son of Gautier, Count of Antwerp, whose sister Violante is Jacques' wife, and whose father, the Count of Antwerp—I am!"

At these words, Pierrot, gazing at him steadily, recognized him, and falling at his feet embraced him crying: "Dear father, you are most welcome!"

Jacques was filled with such wonder and joy, first at the count's words and then at Pierrot's greeting, that he hardly knew what to do. He was soon aware that it was no dream, and heartily ashamed of the rudeness he had sometimes been guilty of toward the stable-boy count, he humbly begged his pardon on his knees. The old man, raising him up, magnanimously granted it. For some time they talked of their mutual adventures, weeping and laughing by turns, and then Pierrot and Jacques suggested dressing the count in proper garments. He would not hear of it. On the contrary, he insisted that after Jacques had made sure of the promised reward, he would present him to the king, just as he was, in his groom's clothes. Thus the king would be made to feel all the more ashamed.

Acting upon their purpose, Jacques and Gautier, followed by Pierrot, came before the king, offering to produce both the count and his children provided the reward were forthcoming according to proclamation. Then and there, the king had the marvelous triple guerdon dangled before Jacques' eyes, telling him, moreover, that he was free to take it away with him, on condition he really showed him the count and his children, as he promised. Jacques turned around. Placing the count, his groom, before him, together with Pierrot, "Sire," he said, "here, before your eyes, are the father and the son. The daughter, my wife, who is not here, you shall soon behold, God willing!"

The king looked steadfastly at the count, when Jacques had spoken, and though the old man had changed greatly, he recalled him after a moment. Tears almost started from his eyes as he raised the kneeling count, and then kissed him and clasped him in his arms. In friendship, too, he greeted Pierrot, and then ordered the count to be given clothes, retinue, horses and all necessary trappings—everything his noble rank required. His commands were promptly executed. As for Jacques, the

king treated him with the utmost courtesy, and asked to be informed about his fortunes. Then, as the young gentleman was
about to take his magnificent reward, the count turned to him
and said: "Take this bounty of our sire, the king, and don't
forget to tell your father that your children, his grandsons and
mine, are not the offspring of a vagrant brat."

Jacques took his gifts and summoned both his mother and his
wife to Paris, where Pierrot's lady also joined them. Great was
their rejoicing over the count, whom the king had re-established
in all his former estate, making it even vaster than it had been
before. Then, with Gautier's sanction, all returned to their
homes, and he himself remained in Paris, living in more glory
and renown than ever.

✳

# THE NINTH STORY

*Bernabo of Genoa, tricked by Ambrogiuolo, loses his wager and
orders his guiltless wife to be slain. She escapes, and disguised
as a man, goes into service with the Sultan. Here she meets the
trickster and brings her husband to Alexandria where the scoundrel is punished. Then, in her own clothes, she returns to Genoa
with her husband and much wealth.*

ELISA HAD FULFILLED HER DUTY WITH HER PATHETIC STORY, WHEN
Filomena, the queen, a tall, handsome girl with the loveliest,
cheerfullest face in the world, took it upon herself to speak:

We must keep our promise with Dioneo, she said, so since he
and I are the only ones left, I'll tell my story first and leave him
for the last, as he requested. Then she began:

There's a popular saw often quoted to the purpose, that the
deceiver lies in the end at the feet of the deceived. The truth of
it is best shown in the actual events about us, and so, while
keeping to the set theme, dear ladies, I also mean to prove this
to you. I hope you won't find my story disagreeable, either, for
it should teach you to be wary of deceivers.

At a certain Parisian inn, a number of important Italian merchants had come together, for one thing or another, as is their
way, and one night, after a hearty dinner, they began to talk
about various things. From one trifle the conversation led to an-

other, until the topic turned to their wives, whom they had left at home.

"I don't know how my wife carries on," said one of them in jest, "but I know one thing. Just let a pleasing wench fall to my hand, and I say good-bye to my love of my wife, making the best of what I find."

"And so do I," rejoined another. "Whether I believe my good woman to keep an honest bed or not, she's sure to do as she pleases, so what's sauce for the goose is sauce for the gander. Besides, an ass gets as good as he gives."

A third capped them both in their own strain. In short, it looked as though they would all agree in saying that the women they left behind lost no time in making hay in their husbands' absence. Only one man among them, Bernabo Lomellin of Genoa, defended the fair sex, saying that by some special grace of God he had married a lady who was a paragon of all the virtues women should possess. Women, did he say? Why, she was accomplished in all the qualities of a knight, or a gentleman, for that matter. Not all of Italy could boast her equal. She was beautiful, quick and agile of body. Moreover, she was skilled in silk embroidery, and in everything else a woman should do, outshining every mother's daughter of them at their tasks. There was no servant or butler who could serve better, or more expertly at his master's table than she, so well mannered was she, and clever, and discreet. What's more, he did not even stop at vaunting her skill with horses and hawks, reading and writing and arithmetic—she might have been a merchant, the way she handled figures. Finally, arriving at the matter under dispute, after many more compliments to the lady, he swore a solemn oath they could find no woman more virtuous and chaste the world over. "Why," he affirmed, "if I were to be away from home ten years, or even the rest of my life, she would not so much as think of such nonsense with any other man."

Among this company there happened to be a young merchant called Ambrogiuolo of Piacenza, who burst into a roar of laughter at Bernabo's closing words. What, he asked him scoffing, and had the emperor granted him that privilege over all other men? Stung to the quick, Bernabo said no, but that God, something more powerful than the emperor, had bestowed that boon upon him.

"I haven't the least doubt you think you're right, Bernabo," said Ambrogiuolo. "But it strikes me you've not looked deeply into the nature of things. If you had, I'm sure you're not so stupid that you couldn't have learned some facts which might curb your tongue. Don't think because we've gossiped about our wives that we imagine them different from yours or made of other stuff. It was simply out of a natural shrewdness about such things; and to prove the point, I'd like to have a little talk with you.

"I've always heard it said that man is the noblest of mortal creatures God has made, and after man comes woman. But as we generally believe and observe from our own experience, man is more perfect. Being more perfect, he must undeniably possess more stability and constancy, since women are universally weaker, for reasons I could show you by natural arguments galore. But I'll not speak of them for the present. To go back— if a man with all his firmness cannot help himself not only against the woman who angles for him, but will be lusting for any wench that strikes his fancy; if besides lusting, he goes out of his way to be with her, all this occurring not once a month but a thousand times a day, how do you expect naturally flighty woman to resist the importunities, flatteries, gifts and the thousand other tricks a clever fellow has up his sleeve to obtain the love he wants? Do you imagine she can be firm? Of course, even though you may say so, I don't think you believe it in your heart of hearts. You yourself admit your wife is a woman of flesh and blood like the rest. In that case she must be subject to the same appetites as other women, and her powers to overcome them must be identical. It's more than likely, then, that she does what the rest of them do, however virtuous she may be. A thing that's in the range of possibility shouldn't be so dogmatically denied, my friend, nor the contrary affirmed, the way you do."

"I'm a simple merchant, and not a philosopher," replied Bernabo, "and I'll answer like a merchant. I grant you what you say can happen to foolish hussies who don't know the meaning of shame. But prudent women are so careful of their honor, that they become stronger than men when they're called on to defend it, which is more than our sex would ever think of doing. Now my wife is one of these women."

"Well, well," said Ambrogiuolo, "if a horn were to sprout on their foreheads as a mark of each little trick they indulged in, I suppose few women would be inclined to frisk. But far from sprouting horns, clever women show neither trace nor spot of any indiscretion. It's only in discovery that you'll find shame and dishonor. When they can do a thing in secret—why, they do it. If not, they're simply fools. Rest assured there's only one sort of virtuous woman—the one who was never coaxed, or the one who coaxed but was rejected. Believe me, I know what I'm talking about, and not only because it's bound to be so, for obvious natural causes. I wouldn't be speaking so positively, if I hadn't made my tests lots of times, and with lots of women. I'll go so far as to assert that if I were near this holy paragon of a wife of yours, I'd soon bring her to the point of doing what many others have done for me."

Bernabo was annoyed, and answered: "It's easy enough to bandy words till doomsday. You'd have your say and I mine, and in the end it would all amount to nothing. Since you insist women are all so weak and your genius so strong, I'm willing to let you try my wife's honesty for yourself. I lay my head against a thousand gold florins, you'll not succeed in making her do anything to gratify you."

Ambrogiuolo, who had warmed up to the argument, rejoined: "I don't know what earthly good your blood would do me if I won the bet. But if you're willing to put the thing to the test, lay down five-thousand florins in gold—less dear to you than your head, I hope—against the thousand that I'll stake. What's more, since you set no time limit, I'll pledge myself to go to Genoa, and within three months from the day I leave, I wager your wife will have done as I please. Besides, I'll even bring you some precious trinkets of hers, and prove it to you by so many indications, that you'll be obliged to admit the truth of it. But you must bind yourself upon your oath, not to set foot in Genoa within that time, or to write to her about it."

Bernabo consented readily, and although the other merchants did their best to upset the wager, aware that great harm might come of it, the two participants were so wrought up that they put their agreement in writing and signed it with their hands, in spite of the dissuasions of the rest. The pledge signed, Bernabo remained behind and Ambrogiuolo went to Genoa at the earliest opportunity.

Once in Genoa, he spent a few days craftily investigating where the woman lived and what sort of reputation she had. Bernabo's praise was corroborated and surpassed, until Ambrogiuolo was almost convinced he had set out on a fool's errand.

However, he struck up a friendship with a poor woman who frequented the lady's house and enjoyed her kindly generosity. By hook or crook he got her into his confidence with bribes of money, and at last contrived to get himself brought inside a trunk made according to his specifications, not only into Mistress Ginevra's house, but into her bedroom. There the woman left it at Ambrogiuolo's suggestion, in the lady's care for a few days, on the pretext that she was going somewhere. During the night, when Ambrogiuolo thought Ginevra must be asleep, he opened the chest by means of some mechanism, and slipped stealthily out into the room. A light was burning. Taking advantage of it he examined the arrangement of the room, the paintings and everything unusual in it, carefully taking stock of what he saw. Then he approached the bedside. Ginevra was lying with a little girl, and from their breathing he perceived that they were sleeping soundly. Gently he uncovered her from head to toe. She was as beautiful in her nakedness as in her clothes, and as he gazed he could see no significant spot that he could identify her by except for a tiny mole under her left breast, on which clustered a number of delicate golden hairs. Softly he laid the blanket over her again, although, seeing her so beautiful, he was lickerish to lie down beside her, even at the risk of his life. But he had heard enough of her unapproachableness, and did not dare. He loitered about the room for the greater part of the night; then taking a purse, a dressing-gown from her chest, and some rings and girdles, he put them all into his trunk, got in himself, and locked it up as before. Two nights in succession he continued so without arousing Ginevra's suspicion.

The third day, the woman called for the trunk, as they had agreed, and had it brought back to its original place. There Ambrogiuolo got out, gave the woman the reward he had promised, and returned post-haste to Paris with his trophies, before the time agreed. Calling together the merchants who had been present at the discussion and the wager, he said before Bernabo that he had won the bet, by fulfilling all he had boasted of. To prove his words true, first he described the room and the paintings in it, and then produced the trifles he had brought, saying he had received them from Ginevra. Bernabo admitted the room was as he said, and granted the gown and girdles were indeed his wife's, but protested some servant might have told him about the room, and as for the tokens—he might easily have obtained

them from the same quarter. No, unless Ambrogiuolo had something better to offer, he did not think this was enough to proclaim him the winner.

"In all fairness it ought to be sufficient," said Ambrogiuolo,
"but since you insist on having me say more, listen to this. Your
wife Ginevra has a good-sized mole under her left breast,
around which are about six little hairs, yellow as gold."

When Bernabo heard his last remark, it was as though he had
been stabbed through the heart, so keen was the pain he felt.
Not a word did he say, but his face was so altered, that it
was confession enough of the truth of Ambrogiuolo's statement.
After a while he found sufficient strength to say: "Gentlemen,
what Ambrogiuolo says is true. He has won. Let him come and
get his money whenever it suits him."

The following day, Ambrogiuolo received every cent of the
wager, while Bernabo left Paris and started out for Genoa, his
spirit raging vindictively against his wife. He was approaching
the city when he chose not to enter it, proposing rather to stop
off at an estate of his some twenty miles away. From there he
sent a trusted servant to Genoa with two horses and letters to
Ginevra, telling her that he had returned, and that she was to
meet him with the bearer. As for the fellow, he ordered him in
close confidence to accompany her, and when he had reached a
conveniently lonely place, to kill her without mercy and then
come back to him.

At Genoa, the man did his errand and delivered the letter,
receiving a fine reception from Ginevra. Next morning she
took horse with him and both started on their way to the estate.
Conversing about all kinds of things, to the pace of their horses,
they came to a deep, solitary valley, shut in by tall caves and
trees. This, thought the servant, would be the ideal spot in
which to accomplish his master's command in all safety.

"Lady," he said, unsheathing his knife and taking her by the
arm, "commend your soul to God, for now you must die."

Ginevra was terrified at the sight of the knife, and hearing
his words cried: "Mercy, for God's sake! Tell me, before you
kill me, how have I offended you, that you must take my life?"

"Lady, you've not offended me in anything," he said. "I don't
know how you have offended your husband, but I do know that
he asked me to kill you in this lonely place. 'Without mercy,
too,' he said, and besides, that he'd string me up by the neck if
I didn't obey him. You know how much I am beholden to him,

and that I can't refuse anything he asks me. God knows I'm sorry for you, but there's nothing I can do."

"For God's sweet sake, mercy," she pleaded, weeping. "Don't be the murderer of an innocent woman, to do another's bidding. The Lord is my witness, from Whom nothing is hidden, that I was never guilty of anything to deserve this from my husband. But we shall not speak of that. Listen, if you only wished, you could serve God, your master and me at the same time. Take my clothes, and give me only your jacket and a hood. Bring my things to your master and tell him you've killed me, and I swear by the life I'll owe to you, that I shall vanish to some place from which neither he nor you will ever hear of me again."

The man was unwilling to slay her, and easily felt the tenderness of compassion. He took her clothes and giving her in exchange a jacket of his that had seen much service, and a hood, allowed her to keep whatever money she had. Then, entreating her to disappear from the country, he left her in the valley without a horse to carry her and presented himself before his master. Not only had he fulfilled his commission, he told him, but he had left the woman's body at the mercy of a pack of wolves.

Some time later, Bernabo returned to Genoa, where the story spread and he was severely criticised.

Ginevra, meanwhile, forsaken and disconsolate, awaited the coming of night, and disguising herself as well as she could, found her way to a neighboring hamlet. She obtained some necessary materials from an old woman of the place, and skilfully she adjusted the jacket to fit her, shortened it, and sewed herself a pair of breeches from her smock. Then clipping her hair short, and disguising herself completely as a sailor, she went to the docks. A Catalan gentleman, called Senor Encararch, happened just then to leave his ship, anchored nearby, and came down to Alba to cool himself at a fountain. Ginevra engaged him in conversation. Before long she arranged to enter his service, and went aboard with him calling herself Sicurano da Finale. New clothes were provided by the gentleman, and she attended him so skilfully and so well, that she found a high place in his esteem.

As time went on, the Catalan merchant had to make a voyage to Alexandria, with a ship full of cargo, and on the trip took along with him some peregrine falcons as a gift to the Sultan. Several times the Sultan invited him to dinner, during which he had occasion more than once to notice the fine breeding of Sicurano who always waited on his master. He took a sudden fancy to him, and asked the merchant to let him have the youth. Much against his will the Catalan complied. It was not long before Sicurano had won the grace and love of the Sultan as he had won his former master's.

In the course of time, the season of the year drew on when a gathering of merchants, both Christian and Saracen, was to be convened in Acre under the dominion of the Sultan. It was his custom to send one of his foremost men, together with other officials and a company of troops, for the safeguarding of the merchandise, so that the merchants might have nothing to worry about, and on this occasion, he chose to commission Sicurano, who was already proficient in the language. With his governorship and captain's authority, Sicurano arrived at Acre to watch over the merchants and their goods, and while he went about his task, doing it efficiently and well, he met merchants from all parts of the world, among them Sicilians, Pisans, Genoese, Venetians and many other Italians. The memory of his country spurred him on to associate with them. One day, as he happened to stop, as often before, in front of the warehouse of some Venetian merchants, his eye fell on a purse and girdle, among other things which, to his great astonishment, he immediately recognized as having belonged to him in the past. He gave no outward sign, however, but simply asked whom they belonged to, and whether they were for sale. Ambrogiuolo da Piacenza, as it was, had come there on a Venetian ship, with a quantity of merchandise, and when he heard the captain of the guard asking about the trinkets, he came out.

"Sir, those objects are mine," he said, laughing, "and they're not for sale. But if you like them, I'll gladly make you a present of them."

Sicurano was afraid, from the fellow's laugh, that by some gesture of his he had betrayed his disguise. Nevertheless, he said, without flicking a lash:

"Are you amused perhaps, to see a soldier like me interested in such womanish trifles?"

"Not at all, sir," Ambrogiuolo replied. "I'm not laughing at that, but at the way I got them."

"Good luck to you, then," said Sicurano, "and if it's not too personal, tell us how you came by them."

"Sir," said Ambrogiuolo, "they were given to me among other

things by a Genoese lady called Ginevra, wife of Bernabo Lomellin, after I had slept with her one night, and she begged me to accept them as a keepsake. I laughed just now thinking of that silly Bernabo, who was fool enough to lay down five-thousand florins against a thousand, that I couldn't induce her to yield to my pleasure. I did, and so I won the bet. But Bernabo, who should have been punished himself for his simplicity, returned from Paris to Genoa and had her murdered, from what I gathered, for doing what all other women do."

As he listened to the man, Sicurano was quick to understand the motive that had impelled Bernabo's wrath against the wife he would have slain, and was convinced this was the scoundrel who had been at the bottom of all her misfortunes. He swore inwardly that the man would not go scot free. Outwardly, he pretended huge amusement at the story, and made an artful show of friendship. He was so successful, that by the time the fair was over, Ambrogiuolo packed up bag and baggage at his persuasions, and went to Alexandria. There Sicurano opened up a shop for him and invested much of his own money with him. The future seemed very bright for Ambrogiuolo, and he needed no coaxing to remain.

Sicurano, however, anxious to prove his innocence before Bernabo, could not find a moment's peace, until he had brought him on a credible pretext to Alexandria, with the help of some powerful Genoese merchants. The poor man could hardly have been called prosperous on his arrival, but Sicurano had him lodged with a friend, and left him there until the time was propitious for him to do what he intended. Meanwhile, he had already had Ambrogiuolo tell his story for the Sultan's diversion. But when he saw that Bernabo was at hand, and that it was not worthwhile to drag the matter further, he seized a favorable opportunity and begged the Sultan to summon Bernabo and Ambrogiuolo, so that in the presence of the wronged husband, the trickster might be made to confess even by force, if need be, the whole truth of his boasting about Ginevra.

The two men were called. Before a multitude of people, the Sultan sternly commanded Ambrogiuolo to confess what means he had really employed to win his five-thousand florin wager from Bernabo. Ambrogiuolo turned to Sicurano in whom lay all his hopes. He saw he could expect nothing from that quarter, for Sicurano's even more forbidding countenance threatened the direst punishment if the truth were not told. He was clearly between the devil and the deep sea. Seeing no way out, and confident that at the very worst he would be made to give back the five-thousand florins and the stolen articles, he made a clean breast of everything before Bernabo and the assembled people. When he had spoken, Sicurano, as the Sultan's attorney, turned to Bernabo. "What did you do to your wife for this lie?" he asked.

Bernabo answered: "Wrath at the loss of my money, and shame at the dishonor I thought my wife had done me, got the upper hand, and I had her put to death by one of my men. From what he said, she was soon eaten up by a pack of wolves."

The Sultan listened to everything that went on in his presence, wondering what purpose could have moved Sicurano to request all this, when the latter addressed him.

"Sire," he said, "you can clearly see how much that poor woman had to boast of, both in her lover and her husband. Her lover robbed her of honor, and blotted her fair name with lies, cheating her husband at the same time, while the husband, poor fool, basing more on the treachery of others than on the truth he ought to have known by long experience, had her murdered and devoured by wolves. What's even more extraordinary, the husband and the lover dote on her so, that although they've been living with her a long time, neither of them knows her. However, I want you, sire, to have a clear conception of what these two deserve, and if you will punish the cheat and forgive the victim by your special grace, I will have the woman appear here before you all."

The Sultan had nothing but Sicurano's pleasure at heart, and willingly assented, asking him to bring the woman before them. In his astonishment, Bernabo did not know what to think, for he was positive Ginevra was dead. As for Ambrogiuolo, he began to realize the full extent of his peril, and that there might be worse in store for him than the refunding of the wagered money. Not knowing whether to hope for the best, or dread the worst in the coming of the lady, he waited for her with a feeling of awe.

As soon as the Sultan granted his request, Sicurano fell on his knees before the throne and wept, and dropping at the same time both his assumed voice and masculine appearance, said: "Sire, I am none other than that most unfortunate of women, roaming the world for six long years in man's clothes. I am Ginevra, falsely and vilely slandered by this traitor Ambrogiuolo, and delivered by that other cruel, merciless wretch, to be murdered by a menial and devoured by wolves."

She tore her clothes from her, and revealing her breasts convinced the Sultan and everyone else of her womanhood. Then she turned to Ambrogiuolo, her eyes flashing with indignation. Let him dare repeat he had ever lain with her, as he had boasted! But now that he knew her, he was dumb with shame and answered nothing.

The Sultan, who had always taken her for a man, was so bewildered when he saw and heard all that was going on, that more than once he thought it all a dream. When he got his wits back, and was aware of the truth of it all, he was eloquent in his praise of the life and virtue and constancy of Ginevra whom he had always known as Sicurano. He ordered the richest gowns to be brought her, and a number of ladies-in-waiting, and at her prayer forgave Bernabo and pardoned him the death he had deserved. The poor dupe, who knew her to be indeed Ginevra, threw himself at her feet, begging her forgiveness with sobs and tears. Graciously she raised him to his feet, forgiving him, although he was unworthy, and accepting him again as her husband, in a tender embrace.

After peace had been made between them, the Sultan commanded Ambrogiuolo to be carried immediately to some eminence in the city, bound to a stake, and his naked body anointed with honey. There, exposed to the burning sun, he was to be left, never to be removed until his bones fell under him. The sentence was put into execution. This done, he ordered all Ambrogiuolo's worldly possessions to be turned over to Ginevra, which amounted to the goodly sum of almost ten thousand ducats, and then, making a sumptuous banquet, he honored Bernabo as Ginevra's husband, and her as a most virtuous lady. In the course of the entertainment, he gave her gifts in plate, gold and silver and money, that amounted to at least ten thousand ducats more. A ship was furnished for them when the celebration was over, and he gave them sanction to return to Genoa whenever they pleased.

They arrived at their native town, rich in happiness and wealth, and received a worshipful welcome, especially Ginevra who had long been thought dead. To the end of her days, she enjoyed her reputation of exceeding virtue.

As for Ambrogiuolo, the selfsame day he was impaled and his body covered with honey, he not only died in excruciating agony, because of the flies, wasps and hornets abounding in that country, but was cleaned to the very bones. White and awful, they were left hanging by the sinews, a token to all who saw them, of Ambrogiuolo's wickedness. And so it was that in the end, the deceiver lay at the feet of the deceived.

✳

## THE TENTH STORY

*Paganino of Monaco kidnaps the wife of Ricciardo da Chinzica who, on learning where she is, makes friends with Paganino and asks to have her back. Paganino consents, if the woman is willing; but she refuses to go home, and when Ricciardo dies, she becomes the wife of Paganino.*

EVERYONE IN THE PLEASANT COMPANY WAS LAVISH WITH PRAISE of the queen's story, especially Dioneo, the only one still left to speak for that day.

Ladies, he began, after many compliments, something in the queen's tale made me change my mind, and I've decided to tell you another story instead of the one I had intended. I'm referring to Bernabo's simplemindedness (which, after all, stood him in good stead) and the stupidity of all men who think the way he did, fancying that while they go about the world having a good time with this wench and that, their wives remain at home with their hands in their laps. As if we, who are born and brought up in those laps, had no idea what they're always hankering after! The object of my story is to show you how foolish such people are, and how much more so those who imagine themselves stronger than nature herself, when they think that by virtue of fairy tales they can accomplish wonders, and convert others to their own deficiencies, in spite of their victims' make-up.

There was once a judge in Pisa blessed with more brains than vigor, whose name was Ricciardo da Chinzica. Taking it into his head that he could satisfy a wife with the same qualities he employed in his studies, and having money to burn, he went about eagerly searching for a mate who was to be both good-looking and young—two things he should have fled from, if he had taken the advice he gave others. He was not long in gaining his desire, for Lotto Gualandi gave him one of his daughters in marriage. Bartolomea was her name, and she was one of the best-looking, most attractive girls in Pisa, though to tell the truth, that is not saying much, considering there are few among them who can boast of better looks than a lizard.

Rejoicing at his luck, the judge took her home. His wedding was splendid, the feast magnificent. The first night he strove vigorously to accomplish one bout which would consummate the marriage, and it was by a hair's breadth that even that one didn't turn out a failure. But alas! he was so lean and wasted and spiritless the morning after, that he had to resort to old wine, tonic comfits and many another remedy to coax him back to normal.

Now that the worthy judge was better able to gauge his power than before, he began to teach his wife a pretty calendar like one of those made in Ravenna for good little children who are learning their *abc's*. There was not a day, he showed her, that was not devoted to some saint—indeed, to a host of saints, in whose honor men and women had to abstain from such sins as intercourse. As if those sainted days were not enough, he piled on fast-days and ember-days, vigils in honor of the apostles and a thousand other holy worthies, Good Fridays and Saturdays, the lunar phases and exceptions without number, thinking perhaps, it was as proper to take numerous vacations from women in bed as he took while pleading his cases in court.

This state of things continued for a good long time, to the extreme vexation of Bartolomea, whose lot it was to get her enjoyment once a month, perhaps, sometimes hardly as often as that, while he guarded her jealously, in mortal terror someone might come to teach her the workdays as he had taught her the Lenten.

The season of the year drew on when the weather was insufferably hot, and Master Ricciardo, fancying a few days' holiday at a delightful country place of his near Monte Nero, went there to enjoy the air, and brought his handsome wife along with him. During the vacation, he thought he would give her some sort of amusement, and arranging a fishing party, sailed out in two little skiffs, one manned by himself and the fishermen, and the other containing Bartolomea and the rest of the ladies. The pastime fascinated them, and before they knew it, they had drifted several miles out to sea. The sport was still engrossing their attention, when suddenly, a galley belonging to Paganino da Mare, a notorious pirate, rose on the horizon, and spying the two small boats, made straight for them. Immediately, they plied their oars, but Paganino was faster. Before long he came upon the craft containing the women, and catching sight of the handsome Bartolomea, he seized her, disdaining the rest, and put her aboard his galley under the very nose of Master Ricciardo, who was watching from the shore, and away he sailed.

It's useless to ask how the judge felt about it, poor wretch, who was so jealous that he mistrusted the air he breathed! Everywhere, in Pisa, and away from Pisa, he poured out his heart against the wicked practice of piracy, but in vain. He could neither discover who had abducted his wife, nor where she had been taken. Paganino, however, seeing what a beauty he had captured, thought himself in luck, and as he had no wife, decided to keep her for himself. She wept bitterly. Gently, sweetly, he tried to cheer her up. But when night came, and his calendar slipped from his belt and every fast- and feast-day was swept out of his mind, he resorted to deeds to comfort her, seeing of what little avail words had been. Indeed, he cheered her up so capably, that by the time they had reached Monaco, the judge and his regulations were completely forgotten, and she began leading the gayest life in the world with Paganino. But that was not all. Besides the cheer he gave her both day and night, he cherished and honored her as his wife.

Some time went by, and Master Ricciardo learned where his wife was to be found. He was overcome with a fiery desire to have her again, but he could trust no one to handle the situation —oh, no!—he must go himself to get her back, even if it took a mint of money for her ransom. His mind made up, he embarked and went to Monaco, where he caught sight of Bartolomea and she of him. That evening she reported it to Paganino, and told him also what she intended to do.

Next morning Ricciardo went up to Paganino and greeted him familiarly, quickly working up a close friendship. The pirate remained silent, pretending he did not know the gentleman, and waited to see what would follow. Soon Master Ricciardo seized the opportunity and told him in the most appropriate terms what had brought him there, imploring him finally to take whatever else he wished, but to give him back his wife.

"You're welcome here, sir," said Paganino, smiling pleasantly, "and to make a long story short, this is the state of affairs. I have a young woman at home, it's true, but whether she's your wife or someone else's I can't say, first of all because I don't know you from Adam, and second, because I know nothing of her except that she's been living with me for some time. If you're her husband, as you say, I'll take you to her, for you look like a gentleman, and I'm sure in that case she'll recognize you. If she says things are as you state, and she's willing to go away with you, why, sir, give me whatever you wish as her ransom, for politeness' sake. But if it shouldn't be so, you'd be playing me a scurvy game to rob me of her. I'm young and lusty, and I can take care of a woman as well as any other man, especially a fine girl like her, who's the jolliest I've ever seen!"

"I'm certain she's my wife," said Ricciardo, "and if you take me to her you'll see for yourself the way she'll be throwing her arms around my neck! Come, I'm willing to settle the matter exactly as you say."

"Well, then," said Paganino, "let's be on our way."

They walked together to Paganino's home, where he asked her to be summoned, while they waited for her in the parlor. She came out of a neighboring room, all dressed and adorned, and appeared before them, taking no more notice of Ricciardo than if he had been any other stranger visiting Paganino. The judge, who had expected to be received with the utmost joy, was much surprised, and reflected: "Maybe the melancholy and protracted agony I've suffered since I lost her, have changed me so much that she does not know me any more."

Aloud he said: "It was an expensive trip, taking you fishing, dear wife, for I've been racked with such pain since I lost you, that no man alive has ever felt the like. And now you don't recognize me—you don't even give me a word! Can't you see I'm your own Ricciardo? Can't you understand I've come to pay whatever this gentleman might demand, in whose house we are together, to take you back with me? See, he's kind enough to let me have you again, at my own price!"

"Are you talking to me, sir?" she turned to him with a sly little smile. "I'm afraid you're mistaking your party, for so far as I know, I don't remember ever seeing you before in my life."

"Watch out!" cried Master Ricciardo. "Be careful what you say! Look closely at me. There, if you make an effort, you'll see I'm your own Ricciardo da Chinzica."

"You must forgive me, sir," she said, "but it doesn't strike me as quite the proper thing to be staring at you, as you imagine. But I've already seen enough of you to know I've never cast eyes on you in my life, before this moment."

It occurred to Ricciardo that his wife was giving him no sign of recognition out of fear of Paganino, and begged him to grant him leave to talk alone with her in a room. Paganino found no objection except to warn him not to kiss her against her will, and addressing Bartolomea, requested her to follow Ricciardo to a room apart, listen to what he had to say, and answer him as she saw fit.

Once alone with her, and comfortably seated, Ricciardo began: "O heart of hearts, my sweet soul, dearest hope of mine, is it possible you don't know your own Ricciardo who loves you more than himself? How can it be? Have I changed so much? Look at me, apple of my eye, gaze on me just a little!"

Bartolomea burst out laughing at this rigmarole, and did not let him go farther. "You know I'm not such a scatterbrain," she said, "that I don't recognize you, Master Ricciardo da Chinzica, my husband. But as for you, how little you knew me all the time I lived with you! If you were the clever man you'd have people think you are, you should have realized I was young and fresh and full of life—yes, you ought to have known what it is that young women demand, besides food and clothing, though they're too shy to say so. How did you acquit yourself in that respect? Oh, you know well enough! You shouldn't have married, if the practice of law was more agreeable to you than keeping a wife, though to tell you the truth, I'd hardly have taken you for a judge. A walking church-calendar was what you were, I swear, so well you knew your fast-days and vigils and sacraments and Lord knows what! Really, if you had given as many holidays to the farmers who till your fields, as to the man who had the working of my one little plot, you'd never have harvested a single kernel! But the Lord had pity on my youth, and put me in the way of this fine fellow here. Yes, this is the room we stay in, and we don't so much as know the meaning of a day of worship—the kind you used to keep with such zeal, devoted as you were more to the service of God than that of women. There's never a Good Friday or Saturday coming in that door, nor vigil, nor ember-day, nor Lent, that's so awfully long. Oh no, sir! Here we go laboring day and night and thwack our mattress vigorously. Why, last night, once he started ringing the matin-bell, I can tell you it went at a pretty speed, from the first strike on! So I mean to stay and work with him while I'm young, and reserve the days of worship and absolution and fast for my old age. Go, then, as fast as you can, and good luck to you, and celebrate as many saints' days as you wish—but not with me!"

Ricciardo was beside himself with chagrin at these words, and exclaimed, as soon as she was silent: "O my sweet soul, what things are you saying! Have you no concern for your honor and your family's? Do you mean you would rather live here in mortal sin, as this man's strumpet, than in Pisa as my lawful wife? Know then, that once this fellow has had enough of you, he'll turn you out of doors in ignominy, while I'd always cherish you and hold you dear, as the mistress of my house, even if I didn't want to. You will not prejudice your honor for the sake of this sluttish, shameful appetite, and abandon me, who love you more than life itself? Ah no, my darling hope! Don't speak that way again, but come with me! I swear, since I know your desire, I'll force myself to content you from now on. Only change your mind and come with me, my own precious darling, for I haven't had a moment's comfort since the day I was deprived of you!"

"So far as my honor's concerned," she replied, "I don't want anyone to be ticklish about it, now that it's too late. Would to God my folks had thought of it when they gave me to you! But they didn't care at all about my honor then, and I don't intend to worry about theirs now. You say I'm living in *mortal* sin? The devil I care while the pestle is in! So don't you lose any sleep about it. What's more, here I feel like the lawful wife of Paganino, while in Pisa I felt like your punk. There we only succeeded in having a miserable bout by virtue of lunar phases and geometrical squares, and the clashing of planets, while here my darling Paganino holds me all night long in his arms, and hugs and bites me and—God alone can tell you how he handles me! You say you'll force yourself? What for, pray? To try it three times over before you accomplish it once, and beating it up to put it in good fettle? My, my! I had no idea you had grown into such a lusty spark since I saw you last! Go, go, my poor man, and force yourself to live. I swear you seem only to be boarding here, you look so weak and consumptive! Another thing I want to tell you. If Paganino should ever leave me, which doesn't seem at all likely as long as I'm inclined to stay, I'll never come back to you! Why, if I squeezed you from now till doomsday there wouldn't be enough stuff in you to make a wee pot of sauce! I was enough of a fool, living with you once to my own loss and detriment, to know I'd better seek my pittance elsewhere in the future. I repeat, here I know no vigils and saints' days, so here I intend to remain. So go away as fast as you can, for heaven's sake, or I'll cry out that you want to take advantage of me!"

Ricciardo saw he was doomed, and that very moment realized his folly in marrying a young wife while he himself was sapless. Sad and doleful, he left the room and unburdened his soul to Paganino; but all he said was not worth a fig. At last, his labor lost, he returned to Pisa without his wife and fell into a state of such senility out of vexation, that whenever he went through the streets and people greeted or addressed him, he always made the self-same reply: "A bad hole wants no vacation." Not long afterward, he died.

News of his death came to Paganino, who, knowing the love Bartolomea had for him, took her as his lawful wife. Days of worship never existed for them, nor vigils, nor Lent which was so long, and while their legs could carry them they toiled and moiled and had a merry time of it. So you see, my dear ladies, when Bernabo argued with Ambrogiuolo, he only succeeded in riding the nanny-goat down the precipice.

The story had set them all laughing until their jaws ached, and with one accord the ladies said Dioneo was right, and that Bernabo had been a fool. But when the story was over, and the peals of laughter subsided, the queen saw it was getting late. Besides, everyone had spoken and her rule was at an end, according to the stipulated order. Removing the wreath from her head she laid it on Neifile's. "From this moment, dear friend," she said, beaming, "the government of our little band is yours." And she went back to her place.

Neifile flushed at the honor conferred upon her, and looked for all the world like a fresh rose of April's best, or of the month of May at dawning. Her lovely eyes, half-lowered in modesty, shone like the morning star. When her companions' approving murmur at her choice had somewhat calmed down, and she had collected enough boldness to speak, she took a higher seat and said: "Since I am to be your queen, I'll not abandon what my predecessors have done, for all of you have shown yourselves well pleased by obeying, and I'll tell you in a few words what my intention is. If it meets with your approval, we shall follow it. To-morrow is Friday, as you know, and the day after, Saturday, both of them days which some people find annoying because of the special diet that is customary. But Friday should be kept, for He who died on that day for our salvation suffered martyrdom. It is only just and proper, in my opinion, that we spend that day in prayer for God's glory, rather than in story-telling. Now for Saturday. We women usually wash our heads on that day, and cleanse ourselves of the accumulated dust and dirt of the week. There are many, likewise, who keep it sacred to the Virgin Mother of the Son of God, fasting and doing no menial work in honor of the coming Sunday. I think it would be only proper to rest from our story-telling on that day also, since our manner of living will be interrupted anyway. By that time we shall have been here four days, and if we want no intrusions from outsiders, I think it would be sensible to move and go elsewhere. As for the place, I've already thought of it and made arrangements.

"On Sunday, then, after our nap, for we've had plenty of stories for to-day, I think we shall base our theme on another phase of Fortune. I want you to have plenty of time to think about it, and moreover, it will be lots more fun to confine ourselves a little in our narratives. Let's see . . . Our next stories will deal with *people who through their own efforts have obtained something they wanted very badly, or got back what they had lost*. Think of some story that will be useful, or at least amusing to the rest of us—except Dioneo, of course, who is privileged to tell whatever he pleases."

They were all heartily in favor of the queen's suggestion, and agreed to carry it out. Accordingly, Neifile summoned her steward, directed him where to lay the tables for the evening and settled with him about everything she wanted done during the period of her regency. Then, rising to her feet she dismissed the band, and left them all free to spend their time as they pleased.

Together they wended their way to a pleasant little garden, where the men and women played a while until supper-time. The meal progressed amid sport and merrymaking, and when it was over Emilia led the dance at the queen's direction while Pampinea sang this song, of which the rest of the ladies took up the refrain:

"What other woman if not I should sing,
 Fulfilled of all my love in everything?

Then come, O Love, the source of all my gain,
    Of every hope and every sweet delight,
       Let us a while make choir,
Not of the sighs, nor yet the bitter pain
    That now make sweeter still my am'rous plight,
       But only of the ray
       Wherein I burn yet live in cheer and play,
You as my God, O Love, still worshiping.

Before my eyes you did present, O Love,
    Upon that day when to your fire I won,
       A youth of worth so rare,
Of beauty such, and prowess, that above
    None could be found excelling, no, nor one
       Who could with him compare.
What though inflamed by him, I still can bear
To sing with you in unison, my King!

In that my sovereign pleasure lies in this:
    That he adores me as I him adore,
       Yours is the praise, O Love.
Thus in the world I have my treasured bliss,
    And after death, the peace that I implore
       I trust to win above,
         Crown of the faith I bear him, for 'twill move
Almighty God to take us 'neath His wing."

Other ditties followed it, and rounds, and musical selections, until the queen thought it was time to go to bed. The torches were lighted. Behind their flares each one went to his room for the night.

The next two days were spent in piety as the queen had suggested, and in waiting longingly for Sunday to come.

# 3

# THE THIRD DAY

*

WITH THE APPROACH OF THE SUN, THE CRIMSON DAWN WAS AL-
ready taking on a mellower orange. The queen arose, and with
her, all her company. It was Sunday. The steward had long
since sent the necessary supplies to the new abode, as well as a
number of servants to prepare everything, and seeing that the
queen and the whole band were on their way, he broke up
camp, loaded everything that remained, and followed in the rear
with the provisions and the other servants.

The queen set a dignified pace, while the women and the
three young gentlemen followed suit, accompanied by the warbling of some twenty or more nightingales, and other sweet-
throated birds. Westward they went, along a secluded path
overgrown with green grasses, and flowers shyly opening at the
spell of the coming sun. Babbling, jesting, laughing with her
companions, the queen had hardly walked two thousand steps,
when she conducted them to a fine, luxurious palace, which rose
upon a gentle incline, above the plain. It was now scarcely half-
past nine.

They entered the palace without delay, and when they had
seen the reception halls and the spotless chambers, furnished
with elegance, they were all praise, and were sure that the lord
of it must have been a magnificent gentleman.

Then they went down to the court, which was a spacious and
delightful place. Moreover, when they saw the cellars full of

extraordinarily fine wines, and the wells of ice-cold water in great plenty, they were more than ever taken with the palace.

Later, going to a gallery overlooking the court and decked with the flowers and shrubs of the season, they sat down to rest, and were refreshed with choice wines and rare sweets by the tactful steward. They asked to be shown into a walled-in garden, that flanked the palace, and as they entered, they were so struck with the marvelous beauty of the sight, that they went about studying each feature of it. Round about it and radiating from the center, ran spacious alleys, straight as darts, overgrown with grapevines that gave promise of a plentiful vintage before the end of the year. The vines were just then in full bloom, and filled the garden with so sweet a scent, that as it mingled with the fragrance of other growing things, it transported them all to the spice-fields of the Orient. Along the sides, forming a wall of intoxicating shade, twined bushes of red and white roses, and jessamine, so that not only in the morning, but even when the sun was at its noon, one could wander everywhere, without being touched by its rays.

It would be an interminable task to describe the plants that flourished there, or to tell you how they were arranged. If a flower could thrive in our climate, it was sure to be found in that garden, growing in profusion.

But what was more remarkable than all else, was the lawn in the middle of the garden, whose grass was so fine and green, that it almost seemed black. At least a thousand kinds of flowers embroidered it in vivid colors, and sturdy green-leaved orange and citron trees enclosed it on all sides, offering not only pleasant shade to the eye, but soothing pleasure to the senses, with the fragrance of their branches, heavy with blossoms, the old fruit and the new. A fountain of white marble was set in the middle, carved with reliefs that were wonderful to see, and from a figure atop a column, which rose straight from its center, there sprang heavenward a mighty jet of water, from some natural or artificial source. The water fell back musically into the clear fountain, and with such force, that even less would have served to turn a mill-wheel. Then, as it overflowed the basin in abundance, it left the lawn by a secret conduit, and reappeared again along its borders, shimmering in skilfully contrived channels. Similarly, it meandered through the garden, tumbling at last, outside the lovely spot, into a reservoir from which it flowed limpidly toward the plain, not, however, before turning two mills with the power of its flood, to the great profit of the owner.

The young people were so enraptured with the garden and its arrangement of plants, the fountain and the streamlets flowing from it, that they agreed if Paradise were possible on earth, it would not be conceivable except in the shape of this beautiful place, exactly as it was, for they could not have suggested a single improvement. They went walking about it very happily, weaving themselves charming chaplets of leaves, and listening to the melodies of many different kinds of birds, that seemed to be singing in rivalry, when they noticed another charming feature which they had not seen at first. At least a hundred varieties of pretty creatures were to be found: rabbits scampering here, hares there, kids lying in one place, fawns pasturing in another, and many a harmless animal romping and frisking tamely about, all of which they delighted in pointing out to one another, much to their added pleasure.

At last, when they had feasted their eyes on this and that, the queen ordered the tables to be laid, about the lovely fountain. They sang some half-dozen songs and danced a little, and then, at a signal from her, they sat down to a dinner which was served with ease and order. The delicious food heightened their spirits, and when they rose from it, they indulged in more music, songs and dances, until the queen thought it was time for their noonday sleep, since the heat was getting stronger.

Some of them retired, but the others were so fascinated with the charm of the place, that they had no heart to leave it, preferring to remain there and read romances or play chess and gammon, while the others took their nap.

After three, the sleepers arose, washed their faces in cold water and joined the rest on the lawn near the fountain, when, taking their accustomed places beside one another, they waited for the story-telling to begin, in accordance with the queen's chosen subject. Filostrato was called upon first, and began accordingly.

✻

# THE  FIRST  STORY

*Masetto da Lamporecchio pretends dumbness, and is engaged as
gardener for a convent of nuns, who hasten to lie with him.*

LOVELIEST LADIES, THERE ARE MANY PEOPLE FOOLISH ENOUGH TO
believe that, once a girl has a white band tied around her head,
and a black cowl hanging down her back, she is no longer a
woman, with a woman's desires! As though by becoming a nun,
she had turned to stone! If those fools happen to hear anything
contrary to their belief, they fly off the handle as though an execrable, unnatural sin had been committed, unmindful of their
own personal experience—they whom even license cannot satisfy, and disregarding the great temptations of idleness and
brooding. Then, there are also those who believe that a pick
and shovel, wretched food and poverty, rid the day-laborer of
all desire for physical pleasure, besides making him coarse-
witted and dull. But I'd like to show you how greatly they are
mistaken, by means of a little story that is in keeping with the
given theme, and which I shall now tell you, since the queen
has asked me.

There used to be a women's convent in our neighborhood—
in fact, it still is standing—which enjoyed a great reputation for
holiness. No, I'll not mention its name—far be it from me to
detract a jot from its good reputation!

Not so very long ago, when it boasted only eight nuns and
the Mother Abbess, all of whom were quite young, there used
to be a funny little old fellow who tended their magnificent
garden. Somehow, he became dissatisfied with the wages, so settling his accounts with their steward, he went back to Lamporecchio, his home-town. Among others glad to see him was
a sturdy, healthy young laborer, a handsome brute of a peasant
called Masetto. "Where have you been so long?" he asked.

The old simpleton, whose name was Nuto, told him.

"And what was your work at the convent?" asked Masetto.

"I used to tend a fine, big garden of theirs," replied Nuto,
"and I'd also go to the woods sometimes for faggots, and carry
water, and do a lot of odd jobs. But those women gave me
such stingy wages, I couldn't keep myself in shoe-leather. The
worst is, they're all young and full of the devil, and nothing you

do suits them. Sometimes, when I was in the vegetable-garden, this one said, 'Put this here,' and another, 'Put that there,' and a third grabbed the spade out of my hand. 'That's no good,' she'd say, until I was so crazy-mad I'd wish the work to the devil, and fly out of the garden. What with one thing and another, I got sick of it and quit—here I am! Before I left, that fellow of a steward begged me that if I came across someone for the job, I should send him over. I said, 'Sure,' but I'll see him in hell first, before I do!"

While Nuto was speaking, Masetto was taken with such a tormenting ambition to be with those nuns, that he could scarcely bear it, especially when he understood from the man's words that it was not at all impossible. But he knew nothing would come of it if he confided in Nuto, and simply cried: "God, you were certainly right to come back! How is it possible for a man to live with a bunch of women? He'd easier live with devils. Why, nine times out of ten, they themselves don't know what they're after!"

Later, when Masetto had had enough of the conversation, he cudgeled his brains for a way to get to the nuns. He knew well enough that he would not be rejected on the grounds of inexperience, for he was as skilled as Nuto in the tasks he mentioned. But he was young and quite an eyeful—there was the rub! However, after thinking a good long time, he hit upon an idea. "The place is quite a way off," he thought. "Nobody knows me there. Suppose I made believe I was dumb, I'd positively be engaged!"

No sooner said than done. Strapping a hatchet on his shoulder, and without revealing where he was going, he went his way, like a tramp, to the convent where, as luck would have it, he stumbled upon the steward himself in the yard. Immediately, Masetto approached him, and making himself understood like a deaf-mute by means of signs and gestures, conveyed the information that he wanted food, for God's sake, in return for which he was willing to chop wood. The steward gladly gave him something to eat, and then laid some logs in front of him, which Nuto had not been able to chop. Masetto cut them up in no time, strong and vigorous as he was. It happened that the steward had to go to the woods, and taking Masetto along with him, set him to cutting up firewood; then, showing him the donkey, he indicated that Masetto was to lead the beast home with the faggots. The deaf-mute acquitted himself nobly, and the steward kept him for some days, to clear up odds and ends of work that had to be done.

One day the abbess came across him, and asked the steward who the fellow was.

"Madam, he's a poor deaf-mute," he informed her, "who came begging here the other day, so I helped him and gave him a few things to do. If he knows anything about gardening, and is willing to stay here, we could certainly use him to our satisfaction, for he's mighty strong and willing to do anything we set him to. What's more, you wouldn't have to worry about his jollying your lasses."

"You're right, indeed," replied the abbess. "Find out if he knows anything about the garden, and try to keep him here. Give him a pair of clods and an old hood. Flatter him, cajole him, and stuff him with good things to eat."

The steward consented, and Masetto, who was not far off, pretending to be busy sweeping the yard, took it all in. "If you put me in there," he said to himself, "I'll do you such gardening as you've never seen in your born days!"

When the steward had assured himself that Masetto could till, he asked him by means of signs whether he was willing to stay. In the same language Masetto answered that he was ready for anything. Accordingly, the steward engaged him, showed him what he had to do, and set him to work in the garden, leaving him alone while he attended to other duties about the convent.

Day in and day out, Masetto was busy about his gardening, and soon the young nuns began teasing and poking fun at him. They even addressed the wickedest little words to him, the way people often do with deaf-mutes, confident that they were not understood. As for the abbess, she did not worry her head about it, under the impression, perhaps, that he was as devoid of tail as of tongue.

One day, as he was taking a rest after a bit of hard work, two little nuns who were walking about the garden, came up to him, and as he made a feint of being fast asleep, looked him over very closely. At that, one of them, bolder than her friend, said: "If I were sure you could keep a secret, I'd tell you something that's often occurred to me, and I think it might help you, too."

"Cross my heart," said the other. "Out with it. I promise I'll never breathe a word to a soul."

Then the little wanton began: "I don't know whether you've ever considered how strictly we're kept, so much so, that no man dares come near us, unless it's the steward, who's decrepit, or this dumb fellow here. Now I've been told time and time again, by many women who come to see us, that all the pleasures in the world aren't worth a straw, compared with what a woman feels when she lies with a man. I've often thought of that, and I've wanted to try it out on this mute, since it's out of the question to do it with anyone else. He's perfectly ideal for my purpose, because even if he wished to tell on us, he couldn't, and he wouldn't know how. You see what an overgrown simpleton he is, who's developed in body at the expense of his brains. Well, how does it strike you, sister? I'm anxious to hear."

"God help us!" exclaimed her friend. "What are you saying! Have you forgotten that we've pledged our virginity to the Lord?"

"That's nothing," she said. "There are a thousand things promised Him all day long, and He doesn't get a solitary one. What if we've pledged it to Him? He can find another, plenty of others, in fact, who would keep their word."

"Yes, and what if we should become pregnant?" asked the other. "What then, sister?"

"You think of trouble before it comes," she rejoined. "Just let it happen, and then we'll worry our heads about it. There are a thousand ways of doing it, so that nobody will know, provided we don't let the cat out of the bag ourselves."

"How shall we go about it?" asked the other nun, who was now more eager than her friend to find out what sort of hobbyhorse man was.

"Let's see, it's near noon, now," she said, "and I think all of the sisters are taking a nap except us. Come, let's look through the garden to see if anyone's around. If not, what's left for us to do, but to take this fellow by the hand and lead him to the shack where he takes shelter from the rain? One of us can slip in with him, while the other stands guard. He's such a fool, he'll do anything we say."

Masetto listened to their discussion, and willing enough to comply, was only waiting for one of them to take the initiative. In the meantime, they had looked all around the place. Reassured that no one could see them from any side of the garden, the first nun went up to Masetto and woke him up. He rose to his feet directly. Soothing and cajoling him with many gestures, she took him by the hand and led him, grinning inanely, to the shack, where he did not need overmuch prompting to do what she desired; afterwards, with her wish fulfilled, she gave up her place to the other nun, like the staunch friend she was. Masetto, still playing the idiot, did their bidding. They did not leave the shack, until they had made several trials of how the deaf-mute could gallop, and later, when they talked things over by themselves, they admitted it was indeed as sweet a delight as they had heard, and more!

From then on, they took every available moment to go frolicking with the dumb lad. It happened, one day, that a sister, spying on the game from her narrow cell-window, called it to the attention of two others. At first, they were all for reporting the girls to the abbess, but then, suffering a change of mind, they came to an understanding with them, and enjoyed their share of Masetto's prowess. The three remaining nuns joined the ranks at different times, and under other conditions.

Last but not least, while the abbess, as yet unaware of the merry business, was taking a stroll by herself in the garden, she came upon Masetto, stretched under an almond tree, fast asleep, for now even a little work was too much for him, considering the galloping he had to do at night. As he was lying so, the wind blew up the front of his smock, and there he lay, showing his bounties to the world. The abbess gazed, and seeing she was alone, succumbed to the very ardor which had tempted her little nuns. Rousing Masetto, she led him to her cell, where, to the great consternation of the sisters, whose gardener did not show up to work their garden, she kept him several days, tasting over and over again the pleasure she had once condemned in others.

Finally, she released him, and sent him back to his chamber. But she required him so often, and claimed so much more than her own share, that Masetto, the demands for whom were more than he could satisfy, fell to thinking his dumbness might lead to worse mischief, if he kept it up. Accordingly, while he was with the abbess one night, he unloosed his tongue and said: "Madam, I've heard people say one cock is enough for ten hens, but that ten men could hardly toil hard enough to please a single woman. As for me, I've had nine women to work for, and I tell you I can't keep it up for anything in the world. It's come to such a state that, after all my labor, I'm able to accomplish little or nothing. Let me go, then, for God's sake, or try to find some way of setting it to rights again."

The abbess was astounded to hear the dumb man speak, and asked: "What's the meaning of this? I thought you were dumb!"

"Yes, ma'am," said Masetto. "I was indeed dumb, as you say, but not by nature. Sickness took my speech away, and tonight for the first time, it's been given back to me, for which I thank God from the bottom of my heart."

The abbess believed him, and asked what he meant when he said he had nine women to work for. Masetto made himself clear, and she understood from his speech there wasn't a slip of a nun who was not far cannier than herself. She was a prudent woman, however, and without letting him depart, decided to talk the matter over with her nuns, and find some way by which to save her convent's reputation from any gossip in which he might indulge.

At about that time, the steward happened to die, so that after the nuns had made a general confession of their secret doings, they managed, with Masetto's consent, to spread the news among the people of the neighborhood, that he had got back his speech after long dumbness, by virtue of the nuns' prayers and the grace of the convent's patron-saint, and they appointed him steward in the dead man's place.

However, his duties were so apportioned that he could take care of them with ease. Although, in consequence, he fathered monklets aplenty, the matter was carried on so prudently, that none got wind of it until after the abbess' death, when Masetto was no longer young, and thought of returning wealthy to his home-town. When his wish was known, he had no trouble in putting it into effect.

And so it was that Masetto, who had made his youth pay by using his wits, went back rich in both money and children, for whom he had suffered neither a belly-ache nor a farthing's expense, and settled in the town he had left with only a hatchet on his back. He always used to say that that was the way Christ treated those who adorned His cap with horns.

*

# THE SECOND STORY

*A groom lies with the wife of King Agilulf, who, on discovering it, finds the man and cuts off a lock of his hair. The shorn man clips the hair of the rest of the servants, and so escapes punishment.*

AFTER FILOSTRATO HAD FINISHED HIS STORY, WHICH AT TIMES HAD evoked blushes and laughter from the ladies, the queen requested Pampinea to continue, who with a smile still lingering on her face, began:

Some people are so indiscreet in insisting on displaying their knowledge of things they were better ignorant of, that they sometimes think to mitigate their own shame by condemning the hidden faults of others, when, as a matter of fact, they only succeed in making it far greater. That this is a fact, I'll prove by its opposite, when I show you the cunning which a fellow of even less significance than Masetto employed in outwitting a wise and valorous king.

Agilulf, King of the Lombards, established his capital in the city of Pavia in Lombardy, as his predecessors had done before him, and married the widow of Autari, also a Lombard monarch —Teudelinga, a lady endowed with beauty, wisdom and great virtue, but alas! unfortunate in her lover.

The Lombards prospered under the wise and valorous rule of King Agilulf, and the land was enjoying a state of peace. At this time, one of Teudelinga's grooms, a low-born vassal, but as far above his birth and station in all things, as in his handsome body and height, which was equal to the king's, was stricken with an unreasonable love for the queen. He was not so much a vassal, that he did not feel the enormity of such love as his, and being a prudent man, he did not breathe a word of it to a living soul. Not even to the queen did he dare reveal it with his eyes. Though he hadn't the ghost of a chance to win her favor, he lived in the secret glory of his high-flung love, and in the fire of his passion he strove to outdo his fellow-servants in accomplishing all kinds of little services, which might please the queen. As a result, whenever she had to go out riding, she preferred to mount the steed in his charge, rather than any other, which he deemed a mark of supreme favor, and he did not leave her stirrup for a moment, considering it a blessing from heaven, whenever her clothes chanced to brush him.

But as we know so well, crushed hope engenders mightier love, and so it was with our poor equerry, who could scarcely control his secret passion, which continued at that, without a ray of fulfilment. Often, when he saw how impossible it was for him to conquer it, he even thought of death, and upon reflection determined to come upon it in such a way that there should be no doubt he had perished for love of the queen. Thereupon, he decided to tempt Fate in a manner that would grant him the fulfilment of his desires, or at least a taste of that fulfilment. Not a word would he say to the queen, nor would he write of the love he bore her, knowing well that he would be wasting time; but he set all his wits to work to find a way of lying with her. However, there could be no means of accomplishing it except by contriving to get to her in her bedroom, disguised as the king, who, as he knew, was not in the habit of sleeping with his wife all the time. It remained for him to find out how the king went to her, and what he wore on those occasions, and for that purpose he concealed himself several times under cover of night, in a great hall of the palace, between the king's chamber and the queen's.

One night he saw the king come out of his room enveloped in a wide cloak. In one hand he carried a lighted torch, and in the other a slender rod. Then, going to the queen's room he tapped once or twice upon the door with the rod, saying not a word, and immediately it was opened, and the light taken from his hand. The groom observed this procedure, and seeing the king return the way he had come, he decided he would do likewise. He managed to obtain a mantle like the king's, a torch, and a rod. Bathing himself carefully, so that the smell of the stables might not offend the queen's nostrils and cause his trick to be discovered, he went to his usual hiding place in the hall.

The palace was wrapped in sleep, and the time seemed propitious for him either to fulfil his desire, or to meet the yearned-for death, in his lofty daring. Softly, he struck a spark with the flint and steel he had brought, and after lighting his torch, he wound his cloak closely about him and approached the queen's chamber-door. Twice, he tapped with his rod. A sleepy maid opened, took the light and muffled it. Then, without a word, he slid between the curtains, took off his cloak and got into the bed where the queen was sleeping. He knew that the king had a habit of remaining absolutely silent whenever anything was on his mind, and therefore assuming the pose, he took the queen in his arms, filled with deep yearning. Not a word passed between them, the while he tasted the sweetness of her body several times. It was a serious effort for him to leave her at last, but fearing delay might convert his satisfied pleasure into pain, he rose, took his cloak and light and went away, as silently as he had come, going back to his own bed in a twinkling. He had scarcely crept into it, when the king arose and went to the queen's room, which caused her no little amazement. As he joined her in bed, and greeted her cheerfully, she was embold-ened by his good humor.

"What novelty is this, my lord?" she cried. "Why, you scarcely left me tonight, after taking unusual delight of me, and here you are again, so soon! Be careful of yourself!"

The king, hearing what she said, supposed at once that she must have been tricked by someone who resembled him phys-ically, as well as in his ways. With his usual wisdom, when he perceived that neither the queen nor anyone else had been aware of the deceit, he decided to keep her ignorant of it. Many a fool in his place would have used no such discretion, but blurted out: "I wasn't here! What man was with you? How did it happen? or Who came to you?" which would have led to a thousand complications, that might have given the lady food for thought and perhaps awakened a wish to desire again what she had already experienced. Thus, whereas silence brought him no scandal, speech would have resulted in his shame. Accordingly, the king, more troubled inwardly than either his face or his words betrayed, replied: "Don't you consider me man enough, dear lady, to come to you once and return again?"

"Indeed, yes, my lord," she answered. "But still, I wish you would look after your health."

"This time, I'll follow your advice," he said, "and go without troubling you further."

His mind teeming with wrath and vengefulness for the injury wrought him, he took his cloak and went out of the room, de-termined to find the guilty man, who, he was sure, must be of his household, and therefore could not have left the palace. He provided himself with a feeble light in a hand-lantern, and pro-ceeded to a long corridor, built over the palace stables, where all his servants slept in separate beds, concluding that whoever the scoundrel might be who had lain with his queen, his heart and pulse-beats could not have had time to settle down to normal, after his recent agitation. Stealthily, he went from one man to the other, beginning at one end of the corridor, and felt at his chest, for his heart-beat.

Although all the members of the household were sleeping soundly, the groom who had lain with the queen was still wide-awake, and suspecting, when he saw the king, what he was after, he became so terrified, that to the thumping caused by his recent exertions, his heart added the further acceleration of dread —for he was certain that if the king found him out, he would be put to death without a moment's delay. Desperate thoughts occurred to him, thick and fast, but then, seeing the king was entirely unarmed, he decided to feign sleep and so wait and see how he would behave.

The king had examined many men, and not one seemed to be the culprit. Finally, when he came to the groom and perceived the violent pounding of his heart, "Aha! Here's the fellow!" he said to himself.

He had no desire to betray his intentions, and contented himself simply by clipping with a pair of scissors he had brought, a few locks from one side of the man's hair. It was worn quite long in those days, and by that shearing, the king was sure he would know him from the rest the following day. This done, he went away and returned to his room.

The groom was an artful rogue. He had formed his own notions of what had happened, and knew why he had received the signal distinction. He arose, and finding a pair of scissors among those that were usually left about the stalls for the horses' care, he stole quietly through the corridor, from man to man, and clipped the hair of every mother's son of them above the ears. This done, he too returned to sleep, without being caught.

Next morning, the king had no sooner risen than he ordered all his household to appear, before the palace-gates were opened. The men stood bare-headed in his presence, but as he examined them to discover which one he had shorn, he found to his astonishment that most of them had received the same style of haircut.

"The scoundrel may be a base-born knave," he said, "but he's certainly no fool."

Convinced of the impossibility of laying his hands on the culprit without rousing scandal, and none too anxious to bring about his own dishonor, for the sake of a petty vengeance, he was satisfied to rebuke him with a word informing him that he, the king, was well-aware of everything. Turning to the men, he said: "Let him who did it, not dare to do it again. Now go, and God be with you."

In his place, another would have had them racked, whipped, tortured and questioned, and by that process, disclosed what a decent man should have kept secret. Then, the thing once known, his dishonor would have increased a thousand-fold, even before he had gained his revenge, and his wife's reputation would have been ruined.

The king's servants wondered at his words, and for a long time asked one another what they could possibly mean. But no one ever knew, except the man they had been intended for, who wisely kept the knowledge to himself while the king lived, and never again risked his life in similar gambles.

✱

## THE THIRD STORY

*A lady, in love with a gentleman, succeeds in gaining her ends by means of a sanctimonious confession to a solemn friar, who becomes her tool without knowing it.*

PAMPINEA WAS SILENT, AND AFTER THE GROOM'S BOLDNESS AND cunning had been commended by several of them, as well as the king's wisdom, the queen bade Filomena follow, who began graciously to speak:

I intend to tell you of a merry prank that was really played on a solemn friar by a lovely lady, which ought to delight us laymen all the more, because although monkish folks are a foolish, strange, peculiar set, they think themselves better and wiser than everyone else in everything, when, as a matter of fact, they're worse than the rest of us, and not being spunky enough to stand on their own feet, they find refuge, like pigs, where they can stuff themselves. I'm going to tell it to you, sweet ladies, not merely to continue the established sequence, but to inform you that the highly religious men in whom we place such stock in our simplicity, can be made fools of, in a clever way, not only by men, but sometimes even by some of us women.

Not many years ago, in this city of ours, that is fuller of intrigues than of love and trustworthiness, there lived a lady whom nature gifted with more beauty and grace, spirit and subtlety, than many another of her sex. I'm not going to give her name, though I know it, nor the name of any other person in this story, as there are people still living who might take it amiss, when as a matter of fact they ought to allow it to slide by, with a laugh.

When this lady, who was of gentle birth, saw herself married off to a wool-merchant, she could not swallow the indignity of being a mere tradesman's wife, for she maintained that no matter how wealthy, a shopkeeper was never worthy of a gentlewoman. When she saw, besides, that for all his riches, he could never progress beyond manufacturing a plaid, weaving a roll of linen, or discussing yarn with a weaver, sne made up her mind to have none of his embraces, except when she could not very well refuse them. She determined to look around for someone to gratify her who, in her estimation, would be worthier of her than the clothier. She fell in love with a distinguished, middle-aged gentleman, and so desperately, that if a day went by without her seeing him, she spent a most uncomfortable night.

However, the worthy man was ignorant of the whole business, and did not trouble his mind about it. She, on her part, being a canny woman, didn't dare waken him to it, either by sending a message through an obliging woman, or even by letter, dreading the possible mischief that might ensue; but seeing that he was very friendly with a friar, who, though a dull-witted sot of a man, nevertheless enjoyed the reputation of being a wonderful clergyman because of his holy manner of living, she thought he would make an ideal go-between for herself and her lover. Turning over in her mind the best attitude to adopt, she went to his church at a seasonable hour, and sending for him, said she was anxious to confess to him whenever he was at leisure. He looked at her, and seeing she was a lady of some distinction, lent himself willingly.

"Father," she said, after confession, "I'm in such straits, that I must have your help and advice in what I'm going to tell you. You know who my people are, for I've just told you about them, and you know my husband, who dotes on me more than on his life. There's no wish I can express, that he wouldn't grant in a twinkling, for he's a rich man, and money is nothing to him. For both these reasons, I love him more than myself, and if I were even guilty of thinking something prejudicial to his honor and pleasure—doing it is out of the question—I'd be the wickedest woman alive, and nobody would be fitter to burn than myself. Now a certain gentleman has appeared—whose name I've really no notion of—respectable enough in appearance, tall

and handsome and usually dressed in very proper dark clothes—
he's rather friendly with you, if I'm not mistaken. Well, it seems
that this gentleman has no idea what sort of woman I am, and
has virtually laid siege to me. I can scarcely go to a door or window, or lay foot out of my house, without his popping up in
front of me—I wonder he's not here this very moment. I'm awfully put out about it, as you can well imagine, for it's just such
nonsense that makes honest women lose their reputations, without any fault of their own. I had resolved to let my brothers
warn him once for all, but then I reflected that men sometimes
deliver messages in such a way, that hasty answers are bound to
follow, which bring on arguments, and which arguments, in
turn, lead to deeds. So I kept quiet about it, to avoid trouble
and scandal, and thought I'd rather tell you than anyone else,
especially since it seems you're a friend of his. Moreover, it's
part of your holy duty to admonish such behavior, not only in
your friends, but in utter strangers. Please then, for God's own
sake, chide him for it, and beg him not to carry on in that manner any longer. There are plenty of other women, all too ready
for such pastimes, who would be glad enough to be spied on
and flattered by him, but as for me, I haven't the least inclina-
tion to such things, and he only succeeds in being a serious
nuisance."

She bowed her head at that, as though she were on the verge
of tears.

The good friar understood her at once to be talking about the
very man she meant, and praising her virtuous resolve, in his
firm conviction that she was telling the truth, he promised he
would take such care of the matter that she would never be annoyed by that villain again. Knowing her to be rich, he also
spoke highly of the virtues of charity and almsgiving, not forgetting to mention his own needy state.

"I beg you, for God's sake," said the woman, "if he should
claim ignorance, make no bones about telling him that it was I
who told you everything, and complained to you about the
whole affair."

Her confession over and her penance assigned, she bethought
herself of the friar's homilies on almsgiving, and slyly filling his
fist with money, she begged him to say a few masses for the
souls of her dead. Then she rose from her knees before him and
went home.

A little later, the gentleman paid one of his usual visits to the friar, and for a time they conversed together generally, when the holy man, drawing him aside, gave him to understand as politely as possible that it was not seemly for him to be ogling and dogging the lady, as she had let him know. The gentleman was greatly astonished, as he had never laid eyes on her and seldom, if ever, passed in front of her house, and would have denied all guilt; but the friar prevented him.

"Come, now, don't pretend to be surprised," he said, "or waste your breath in denials, because you can't convince me. It wasn't from the neighbors I got my information, but from the lady herself. Yes, she told me about you, complaining very bitterly, too. You're not young any more, and such nonsense is not becoming a man of your age. Besides, I may as well tell you, if, ever there was a woman who despised such foolishness, it's she; so please, for your honor's sake and for your own peace of mind, put an end to it, and leave her alone."

More keen-witted than the holy friar, the gentleman was not slow to grasp the woman's subtlety, and pretending to be rather out of countenance, promised never to show his face to her again. Then bidding his friend good-bye, he made his way to the lady's house. Now she was forever peeping out of a little window, to see if he would pass by, and when she spied him, she greeted him so joyfully and graciously, that he was convinced he had interpreted the friar's words aright.

From that day on, under pretense of other business, he took to promenading back and forth, with the greatest discretion, in her neighborhood, much to his satisfaction and the lady's comfort. When she noticed, after a while, that she was as agreeable to him as he was to her, she was eager to stir his passion, and assure him of her love, and awaiting the fitting time and occasion, she paid the friar another visit. Crouching down at his feet, she burst into tears.

"Why, what's the matter?" he asked, full of sympathy at the sight.

"Ah, father," she said, "the matter concerns none other than that accursed of God, your friend, about whom I complained to you the other day. I do believe he must have been born for my damnation, or to make me do something I'll regret the rest of my days, and cause me to be ashamed ever to kneel at your feet again!"

"What!" cried the friar. "Hasn't he stopped annoying you yet?"

"Lord, no," she answered. "On the contrary, since I spoke about him to you, he seems to have taken it amiss, and now, out of spite, I'm sure, he's become worse than ever, and passes my house at least seven times for each once in the past! Would to God he were satisfied with simply passing by and hounding me! Why, he was bold and brazen enough to send a woman to my house yesterday, with his stuff and nonsense, and as though I hadn't trinkets enough and to spare, he offered me a purse and girdle. I was so offended, and I'm still so upset about it, that really, if I hadn't taken care of not falling into sin, and thought of the regard I have for you, I'd have flown into a tantrum fit to raise the devil. But I calmed down and resolved not to take any steps, until I had told you about it.

"What's more, I had already thrown the purse and girdle at the slut who brought them, for her to give back to him, and I had sent her flying, but then, rather worried that she might keep them for herself and say I had accepted them—such hussies are not above that sort of thing—I called her back and tore them spitefully out of her hand. And here I've brought them to you, that you may give them back to him, and tell him I need none of his gifts, for thanks to God and my husband, I have enough purses and girdles to bury him in. You must forgive me, but I speak to you as to my own father: if this friend of yours does not put a stop to his folly, I swear I'll tell my husband and my brothers too, and then I shall not be answerable for what happens. Frankly, I had much rather he come to grief, if it's inevitable, than for me to be blamed on his account. So that's that!"

Still shedding copious tears, after her speech, she produced a rich, lavish purse from under her coat, and an adorable little girdle, and flung them into the friar's lap. He swallowed everything she told him, and was extremely wrathful at it. Taking up the trinkets, he said: "Daughter, it's no great wonder you should be incensed at this state of affairs, and I can't find it in my heart to blame you. Indeed, I can only praise you for following my advice. I admonished my friend the other day, and he has badly carried out the promise he made me. For the past offense, and for this new one, I'm going to make his ears smart in such a way that he'll not dare provoke you any more. But don't, for mercy's sake—don't be so carried away by your wrath as to breathe a word of this to your people. Terrible mischief might come of it for the wretch. And don't be afraid you'll heap up shame for yourself, for I'll always be a staunch witness to your virtue, before God and man."

The lady made a semblance of being considerably cheered, and changing the subject, she said, fully cognizant of his greed and that of his brother-monks: "Father, these last few nights I've seen the spirits of a number of my dead, and they seem to be in terrible agony. They do nothing but beg me to give alms, especially my mother, who looked so miserable and afflicted, poor thing, that it was a pity to behold her. I'm sure she's tormented, seeing me in all this trouble with that enemy of God, and I wish you would say forty masses of Saint Gregory for all their souls' sakes, and some prayers of your own, that God may release them from the fires of purgatory."

Her speech over, she slipped a florin into his hand. He accepted it very gladly, and confirming her faith with high-sounding words and pious examples, gave her his blessing and sent her home.

She had no sooner gone, than he sent for his friend, never for a moment suspecting that he was being tricked. The gentleman came, and seeing him so moody, knew directly there was news for him from the lady. He waited for the friar to speak. Again, the holy man repeated his earlier rebukes, and sternly addressing him once more, admonished him severely for what, according to the lady, he had done. Still, he did not see what the friar was driving at, and feebly denied having sent the purse and girdle, so that if the lady had really made him believe any such thing, the friar might not be scandalized.

"Do you dare deny it, you wicked man?" cried the friar, flying into a passion. "Look here! See, she herself brought them to me in tears. Examine them, and see if you can't tell they're yours!"

"Yes, yes, I know they're mine," said the gentleman, looking quite crestfallen. "I grant I was entirely in the wrong, and I swear that since she's determined in her behavior, you'll never hear a word on that score again."

A long discussion followed. In the end, the goat of a friar gave the purse and girdle to his friend, filling his head with prayers and admonitions not to meddle with such nonsense, and exacting his promise in return, took his leave of him.

The gallant was delighted, both with the certain pledge he had received of the woman's love, and with the splendid gift, and the moment he left the friar, he went to a convenient place,

whence he showed his lady that he had received both the one
thing and the other. She was overjoyed, particularly when she
saw how well her plan was working toward success. There was
nothing wanting for her to bring it to fulfilment but for her
husband to go on a journey, and as it happened, he was obliged
some time later to leave for Genoa. The morning he took horse
and went away, the lady repaired to the monk.

"Ah, father," she said, weeping, after many wails and lamentations. "I tell you I can't put up with this any longer, but since I
promised you the other day that I wouldn't undertake anything
without first consulting you, I'm here to ask your forgiveness.
You must believe me when I say I have every reason in the
world to weep and eat my heart out with vexation, and I want
to tell you what that friend of yours, that devil from hell, did to
me early this morning. I don't know what ill wind brought him
the news that my husband left yesterday for Genoa. Anyhow
this morning, at the hour I mentioned, he broke into my garden, and climbing a tree to my bedroom window, that overlooks
the green, he had already opened the shutters and would have
come into my room, when I awoke. I leaped up immediately,
and was about to cry out. Indeed, I'd surely have screamed, when
he, who hadn't yet come in, begged me not to for God's sake
and yours, and told me who he was. On hearing what he said, I
remained silent, for your sake, and naked as I was born, ran and
banged the window shut in his face. I guess he must have
gone away—the devil take him—for I didn't hear him after that.
Now tell me if this is the sort of thing one can put up with. I
certainly won't any longer, I tell you frankly. As it is, I've stood
for entirely too much, wholly out of regard for you."

The friar could scarcely contain his anger at this, and found
little to say except to ask her, now and again, whether she was
quite sure she had not been mistaken in her man.

"Good Lord!" she cried, "as though I couldn't tell him from
another, at this stage of the game! I tell you it was he, positively,
and don't you believe him if he denies it."

Then the friar spoke: "Daughter, what can be said, but that
it was a very bold and wicked thing for him to do, and that you
did your duty in sending him about his business? But since God
has preserved you from dishonor, I want to entreat you once
again to follow my advice, as you have done twice before. Just
this once, forbear complaining to any one of your people, and
leave it to me to see if I can check that unchained devil, whom

I thought a saint. If I can raise him from his depravity, so be it. If not, you have my permission and my blessing, from this moment on, to do with him as your conscience dictates."

"Well," said the woman, "I don't want to make you angry or go against your will, just this once. But please see that you prevail upon him not to vex me any more, and I promise I'll never come to you again about this."

Without another word, she left the friar and went angrily away. She had scarcely left the church, when the gallant appeared. The friar sent for him, and drawing him aside, called him a villainous, treacherous, disloyal wretch, using the strongest language ever heard. Twice, the gentleman had already experienced the friar's reproofs; therefore, keeping on his guard, and endeavoring to draw him out with perplexed answers, cried, first of all: "Why all this to-do, friend? Did I crucify Christ?"

"What, shameless wretch!" exclaimed the friar. "Just listen to him! He speaks as though a year or two had gone by, and time had driven his pranks and wickedness clear out of mind! Pray, have you forgotten the way you insulted someone, early this morning? Tell me, where were you a little before sunrise?"

"How should I know?" replied the gentleman. "But wherever I was, you got wind of it pretty quickly."

"Of course I did!" cried the friar. "I guess you imagined that because the lady's husband was away, she'd take you in immediately, with open arms! A pretty state of affairs! A fine specimen you are! A pillar of honor! So! He has become a night-raker, a sneaker into gardens, and a tree climber! Are you crazy enough to believe you can overcome the good lady's virtue with boldness, that you clamber up her windows at night, by the aid of trees? I'll have you understand there's nothing on earth she loathes as much as you, and there you go, taking all those chances! Disregarding the fact that she's shown you time and time again how she feels about it—a fine improvement you've made after all my rebukes! But I want you to know one thing! She's kept quiet so far about all your insults, not through any love she bears you, you may be sure, but out of regard for my prayers. I warn you, she'll stand for your foolishness no longer. I've already given her permission to do as she pleases, in case you vex her again in anything. What would you do if she were to tell her brothers?"

The gallant gentleman, who had a clear notion by this time of what he had to know, pacified the friar as well as he could with many extravagant promises, and took his leave. Near dawn of the following day, he entered his mistress' garden, climbed the tree, and finding the window wide-open, jumped into the room. Then, without wasting time, he slipped into the arms of his fair lady, who had been awaiting him with great longing, and greeted him joyfully saying: "Many thanks to our friend, the friar, who so ably showed you the way here!"

A little later they took joy of each other, chatting and laughing at the stupidity of that simpleton of a friar, making fun of the whole tribe of wool-mongers, carders and combers, and having a jolly time. Besides, they so arranged their affair, that without the further mediation of the friar, they were able to get together many a night thereafter, to their mutual happiness—may God in His great mercy lead me quickly to it, and all other good Christians who are so inclined!

✳

## THE FOURTH STORY

*Felice teaches Brother Puccio how to gain blessedness, by performing the penance he sets him; and while Puccio is busy at it, Felice has a good time with the pious man's wife.*

FILOMENA WAS SILENT AT THE END OF HER STORY, WHICH DIONEO had lavishly praised with ingratiating words, both for the lady's subtle wit and Filomena's final exhortation, when the queen smiled at Pamfilo, saying: "Come, now Pamfilo, take your turn and tell us some pleasant tale for our amusement." He answered readily that he was perfectly willing, and began:

Madam, there are many people, who by their efforts to attain to heaven, unconsciously pave the way for others, as was the case with a neighbor of ours, not so long ago, as you shall hear.

Near San Pancrazio, or so I've heard, there used to live a rich but simple fellow, by the name of Puccio di Rinieri. At some time or other, he became imbued with the holy-spirit, and joining the Franciscan Order as a lay-friar, was generally known as Brother Puccio. He had no family to support, except his wife and a servant, and as he did not have to attend to any kind of business, he would virtually haunt the churches. Now he was a man of common stuff, and a veritable blockhead, and did nothing but tell over his paternosters the livelong day, attend sermons, kneel through the celebration of the mass, and would never miss a single of the *Lauds* sung by the laymen. With all that, he fasted and mortified his flesh, and there was even a rumor that he belonged to the Flagellants.

His wife Isabella, a woman between twenty-eight and thirty years of age, fresh and pretty and round as a country apple, was often obliged to keep longer fasts than she had a mind to, what with her husband's devoutness and his advanced age; and whenever she wanted to go to bed or frisk a little with him, he would invariably quote her the life of Christ, the sermons of Brother Nastagio, the lament of the Magdalen and suchlike pieties.

At about this time, a monk of the monastery of San Pancrazio, by the name of Felice, returned from Paris. He was quite young and personable, besides being sharp-witted and a scholar of parts, and Brother Puccio formed a close intimacy with him. Since this monk used to disentangle all his doubtful problems, to his entire satisfaction, and reveal himself of the loftiest piety (knowing his sanctity), Brother Puccio began inviting him home to dinner or supper, as the case might be. Moreover, for Puccio's sake, Isabella had also become Felice's friend, and entertained him most obligingly. As he became a more and more assiduous visitor at Puccio's house, and observed his fresh and roly-poly wife, he suspected what must be the thing she missed most in her life, and thought that if there were nothing against it, he would supply the lack, and spare Puccio the labor. He began ogling her so consistently and so well, that he succeeded in lighting in her mind, the same lusty spark which was in his, and as soon as he saw his deed accomplished, he took the first opportunity to broach the subject of his desire.

However, though she was well-disposed to bring the matter to fruition, there seemed to be no means of doing it, for nothing would induce her to trust herself anywhere alone with the monk, except in her own house. But that was out of the question, as Brother Puccio never left town, whereupon the monk was vexed beyond words. At last he thought of a way to be with Isabella in her own home, without arousing suspicion, even though Brother Puccio should keep to the house all the time.

"It has often occurred to me, Brother Puccio, that all your desire is centered upon becoming a saint," said Felice, one day, when Puccio had come to see him. "But it strikes me that you're taking the longest road by far, when as a matter of fact, there's a very short one, which the Pope and his other chief churchmen know and take advantage of, though they don't want the knowledge of it to spread abroad. The clergy, who live by charity, would certainly fall into ruin, considering that the people would no longer bother placating them with alms, or such gifts. But since you're such a dear friend of mine, and have treated me so well, I'd gladly show it to you, if I were only sure you'd follow it, and not breathe a word of it to anyone in the world."

Brother Puccio, lusting for this secret, first kept begging Felice to show it to him, then swore away his life that he wouldn't tell a living soul, unless the monk himself desired it, and he finally declared that if it were the sort of way he could follow, he would positively engage himself in it.

"Well, then, since I have your oath," said the monk, "I'll show it to you. You must know, the church fathers maintain that whosoever desires to be beatified, must first do the penance I'm going to tell you about. But understand me clearly! I don't mean that after the penance is over, you'll not be the same sinner you are now. Only this will happen. You will be purified of all the sins that you committed, up to the time of your penance, and because of it they will be forgiven you. Moreover, those you fall into in the future, will not be written down against you for your damnation, but like other venial sins, they will all be washed away with holy-water.

"To begin with, you must make a clean breast of all your peccadilloes, before you start upon this penance. Then, you must initiate a period of fasting and strict abstinence, forty days in all, during which you must not go near any woman whatever, not to mention your own wife. Above and beyond this, you must find a suitable spot in your own home, from which you can see the sky at night. There you're to arrange a fairly wide board, in such a way that as you stand, you may lean the small of your back against it, and while your feet are on the ground, you may stretch out your arms as though you were on a cross. You're allowed to rest them on a peg, if you want to. Now you must go to that room when the final service is over for the day, and in the position I described, you're to watch the sky without winking a lid, until the early hours of the morning. If you were a bookish man, I might tell you some prayers that would be proper under the circumstances, but since you're not, you must say three-hundred Our Fathers and three-hundred Hail Marys out of respect to the Trinity. Besides, while you're looking up at the sky, you must bear in mind that God is the Creator of Heaven and earth, and remember the passion of Christ, as you stand in the position He took as He hung upon the cross.

"As soon as the matin-bells ring, you may leave the room, if you wish, and throw yourself, dressed as you are, upon your bed to snatch a little rest. It's customary, also, to go to church the morning after, to attend at least three masses, and recite fifty Our Fathers and as many Hail Marys. When that's done you may attend to matters of business if you have any, in all humbleness of spirit. Then dine, and go to church again after vespers, to say certain prayers that I'll write out, and which you couldn't do without. Toward the final service, then, you must go back to the penance I described before. There! If you follow faithfully what I've already done myself, I'm confident that before the penance is over, you'll be feeling the wonderful effects of eternal blessedness—that is, provided you put your heart and soul into it."

"It's not such a terribly hard thing," said Brother Puccio, "and it doesn't take so awfully long, either, so there's no reason why it shouldn't be done. I'm going to start it Sunday, in the name of the Lord."

Taking leave of Felice, and with his permission, he went home and told Isabella all about it. She understood very well what the monk was driving at when he ordered Puccio to stand still without moving a lash until morning, and as the idea seemed a good one, she expressed her approval of it, as of every other pious duty her husband performed for the benefit of his soul. Indeed, she was even willing to second him in his fastings, that God might favor the penance, but farther she would not go. So the matter was decided.

When Sunday came, Brother Puccio began his penance, and Sir Monk, having reached an understanding with Isabella, arrived almost every night, when he wouldn't attract notice, bringing with him plenty of good things to eat and drink, for a hearty feast with her. Afterwards, he lay with her until morning, when he would get up and go, while Brother Puccio flung himself upon the bed.

The place Brother Puccio had selected for his penance happened to adjoin the room where Isabella slept, and was divided from it by a very thin partition. One night, as the monk and Isabella were romping together a little too wildly, it seemed to

Puccio that the floor of the house had taken to trembling under him. He had already recited one hundred of his Our Fathers, and calling out to his wife, without budging from his place, he asked her what she was doing.

Isabella, who had a roguish tongue, and was perhaps mounted that very moment upon the beast of Master John Thursday, or perhaps Master Jack Goodfellow, answered: "Well, dear husband, I'm flopping about as much as I can."

Said Puccio: "How, flopping? What's the meaning of this flopping about?"

Isabella, laughing heartily, for she was a jolly wanton, and had, besides, good reason for merriment, replied in jest: "How is it that you don't know what it means? Why, I've heard you say at least a thousand times, *Who fasts all day, no doubt, All night will flop about.*"

At that Brother Puccio believed her fasting was at the bottom of her wakefulness, and caused her to move about in bed, so with simple gravity he said: "Wife, wife! I've told you time and again, *Don't fast!* But since you wouldn't listen to me, don't let your mind dwell on it now and try to rest. You flop about so violently that the whole house shakes, and everything in it."

"Don't worry about that," said Isabella. "I know what I'm doing. Do your best there, so far as you're concerned, and for my part, I'll do as well as I can."

Brother Puccio was silenced, and took up the telling of his Our Fathers once more. As for Isabella and Sir Monk, they saw to it that a bed was set up in another part of the house, in which they had a merry time of it, all through the period of Brother Puccio's penance. The moment the monk went away, Isabella would immediately go back to her own bed, where she was joined a little later by her husband, fresh from his orisons. So while Brother Puccio kept up his striving toward blessedness, Isabella had her fun with the monk, to whom she would say, roguishly:

"You've made Puccio work out a penance, but it has certainly given us our heaven." The good lady found herself in clover. Indeed, she had been made to fast so long by her husband, that she took an inordinate fancy to the monk's victuals, and even before Brother Puccio's term of penance was over, she arranged discreetly to banquet with her lover elsewhere, to her long and continued delight.

Well, then, that my last words may coincide with my first—

you see how it really happened that though Brother Puccio tried to win heaven by means of penance, he paved the way for the monk who had shown him the quickest road, and for his wife, who suffered a sore lack, poor woman, of the very thing which the monk supplied in abundance, from the generosity of his heart.

## THE FIFTH STORY

*Il Zima gives Francesco Vergellesi one of his riding-horses, and, in exchange, gains leave to speak to his wife. As she makes no reply, he speaks for her, and the desired effect follows upon his answers.*

PAMFILO HAD FINISHED HIS STORY OF BROTHER PUCCIO, NOT WITH-out a chorus of laughter from the ladies, when the queen used her feminine prerogative and asked Elisa to continue. She began rather saucily, not out of malice, but of an old habit she had:

There are many people who think that because they're very wise, others know nothing at all, so that often when they are confident that they have the best of someone, they discover in the end that they themselves have been fooled. I think, therefore, it's the height of folly for a man to go out of his way to try another's mental powers. But as many of you may not agree with me, I'm going to tell you, now my turn has come, what happened to a gentleman of Pistoia *à propos* of what I said.

There was once in the noble Vergellesi family of Pistoia, a knight called Francesco, who was extremely rich and wise and sensible in most things, but as covetous as could be. He was elected to go as provost to Milan, and had everything prepared to make his triumphal journey, except for a saddle horse which should be handsome enough to be in keeping with his dignity. As he had not been able to find one to suit him, he was very much put out about it.

At that time, there also lived at Pistoia a young man called Ricciardo, of small family but enormously wealthy, and so stylish and well-dressed that he was commonly nicknamed Il Zima. He had long been in love with Francesco's wife, who was exceedingly beautiful and as virtuous as she was fair, but all his courting had been of no avail. Now Il Zima had one of the finest

riding horses in the whole of Tuscany, which he prized for its
great beauty; and since his love for Francesco's lady was an
open secret, some people began to suggest to Francesco that
if he were to ask for that horse, he would surely get it from
Il Zima, for the sake of his wife.

Covetousness got the best of him, so sending for Il Zima,
Francesco asked him whether he would sell him his horse, expecting the youth to offer it as a gift. Il Zima was not averse
to it.

"Sir," he said to the knight, "if you were to give me everything you had on earth, you couldn't get me to sell my horse
for love of money. As a gift—well, that's another matter. You
could have it that way easily enough, on condition that before
you took it, you would grant me leave to speak a few words to
your wife, in your presence, but sufficiently far away from everyone to be heard by her alone."

The knight, itching to get the handsome beast, and hoping to
outwit the youth, assented and said he was willing to allow him
to speak to his lady as long as he desired. Leaving him in
the reception hall of his palace, he went to his wife's room, and
after he had explained how easily he could obtain the steed, he
ordered her to go below and listen to what Il Zima had to say.
However, she was to beware of making any answer, short or
long. The lady was averse to the whole procedure, but then,
since she had to accede to her husband's wishes, she consented,
and walked behind him into the hall to hear what Il Zima had
to say.

Once more, he sealed the bargain with the knight, and drawing to one side of the hall, far from everyone else, he sat down
with the lady and began: "I know you are too wise, noble lady,
not to have realized long ago how great is the love your beauty
has inspired in me, for indeed, you surpass, by far, any mortal
creature I have ever beheld, not to mention the charms and virtues you possess, which are enough to capture the immortal soul
of any man alive. Well, then, I need not prove with words, that
this love I bear you is the most fervent and passionate that ever
any man felt for woman, and that as long as there is life left in
my body, I shall continue to love you—and beyond, through
all eternity, if one is permitted to love there, as here below. Believe me, there is nothing you call your own, however precious
or mean it may be, nothing that you lay claim to, and count
upon, that you can more surely have than my humble self and

all I am master of. I want you to be convinced of this, dear lady.
Set me a task for your pleasure, and rest assured that besides
looking upon it as a mark of grace, I should not more promptly
obey you, than my people should obey me, if I were lord of the
world. Come, then, since I am as wholly given up to you as
you hear—allow me to dare address my prayers to your sovereignty, which is the source, the only source, from which my
peace, my well-being and my health can spring. As a most humble servant I implore you, O my treasure, my soul's only hope
that feeds upon the fire of love! Let your goodness be moved!
Soften the harshness you have always shown me, who am yours,
body and soul, so that when you have comforted me, I may say
that as your beauty inflamed me to love, your pity re-awoke me
to life! Life! Alas, if your proud soul does not bow down to
my beseeching, I shall surely waste away and die, and you
might then be called my murderer!

"Let's except the fact that my death will have done you no
honor. Yet I am sure that sometime, when you suffer the pangs
of conscience, you will regret that you were guilty of it, and to
yourself you'll say: 'Woe! How cruel of me not to have taken
pity on my poor Zima!' And then, because your repentance will
have come too late, you will suffer all the more. Listen to me
then! Now that there is still help for it, let it not happen. You
have it in your power to save me. Have mercy on my lot,
and be moved to pity before I die, for it rests with you to make
me the happiest or the most wretched of mortals. I have hope
in your grace. I know you will not permit such love as mine to
receive death as a reward. No, for with a sweet and gracious
answer, you will comfort my weary spirit that lies trembling
and awed before you!"

Here he was silent, and the tears dropped from his eyes accompanied by deep-drawn sighs, as he waited for the lady to
speak. What neither the long courting, nor the swordplay, nor
the morning music and other blandishments that Il Zima had
indulged, for love of her, had ever succeeded in doing, the passionate words of the fervent lover accomplished, making her
feel what she had never before experienced—love itself!
Though she said nothing, in obedience to her husband's command, still she could not prevent a little sigh, now and then,
from betraying what she would willingly have shown Il Zima,
had she answered.

He waited a while, and seeing that no reply was forthcoming, wondered what the silence could mean, until the craftiness the knight had used began to dawn upon him. As he gazed into her face, however, and caught the fitful flashing of her eyes, and the way she struggled to keep her sighs from leaving her bosom in all their passionate power, he was filled with renewed hope, and plucking up courage, devised a new plan, answering for her himself, as she listened:

"My own Zima, of course I was aware, long ago, how great and perfect is the love you bear me, and now that I'm even more acquainted with it, from what you tell me, I am happy, as I ought indeed to be. Anyhow, if I have appeared heartless and cruel to you, you must not believe that in my heart of hearts I was what my face seemed to indicate. I have always loved and cherished you above all other men, but I've had to behave that way for fear of another, and also to keep my fair name. Now the time has come when I may clearly show you how much I love you, and reward you for your past affection, and the love you bear me. Be of good cheer, then, and hope, for Francesco will be leaving to be provost of Milan in a few days, as you know very well—for haven't you given him your handsome riding-horse for love of me? As soon as he leaves, I swear upon my honor and the true love I bear you, that within a few days you may come to me, and we shall bring our love to a happy and entire fulfilment.

"Now, that I may not have to speak to you about it again—when you see two napkins hanging from my chamber-window, which fronts the garden, manage to come to me that evening by the garden-gate, and be careful that nobody sees you. You'll find me waiting for you, and together we'll have a world of joy and delight of each other, all through the night."

After Il Zima had voiced the lady's sentiments, he spoke again for himself.

"Dearest lady," he said, "my senses are so ravished with overwhelming happiness at your gracious answer, that I can scarcely find words to thank you as you deserve. If I could only express myself according to my desire, time would not suffice for me to thank you as I should wish, or even as I ought. I leave it to your fine understanding, to conceive of what I cannot put into words, for all my desire. But I tell you this only—I shall do my best to accomplish without fail, what you have commissioned me to do. At that time, then, when I shall perhaps be more certain of the dear gift you have granted, I shall do all in my power to render you my greatest thanks. Nothing more remains to be said for the present, may God give you that joy and felicity you desire above all things, and hold you in His keeping."

Not a syllable had the lady breathed throughout his speech. At last, Il Zima rose and was about to walk toward the knight, who seeing him standing, went to him, saying with a laugh: "So, now! What do you say? Haven't I kept my promise faithfully to you?"

"Not at all, sir," said Il Zima. "You promised to let me speak to your wife, and you had me do all my talking to a graven image."

The knight was quite pleased at that, and whereas he had had a good opinion of his wife, he held a still higher one now.

"Well, then," he said, "now the riding horse is mine that once belonged to you."

"Yes, sir, that it is," answered Il Zima. "But if I'd had any idea that I should obtain such fruits as I received of my request, I'd have given the horse to you without asking a favor at all. Would to God I had done it, for now you have bought my riding horse, while I have not sold it."

The knight laughed loudly at his words, and since he was now provided with a horse, he started on his journey within a few days, to assume his power at Milan.

The lady, left at perfect liberty in her house, reflected on Il Zima's words, his love, and the riding-horse he had given away for her sake, and as she often saw him passing, said to herself: "What am I about? Why do I waste my youth? My husband has gone to Milan and will not be coming back these next six months. When will he ever be able to restore them to me? When I am old? Moreover, when shall I ever find a lover to equal Il Zima? I'm alone, and I've nobody to fear. I don't see why I shouldn't grasp this fine opportunity while I can. I'll not always have as much time at my disposal, as I have now. Nobody will ever learn of it—and what if one should? It's far better to do and repent, than not to do, and repent anyhow."

Advising herself in this fashion, she took two cloths one day, and hung them out at the garden window, as Il Zima had told her. He was overjoyed when he saw them, and at nightfall went cautiously to his mistress' garden gate, which he found open. From there, he proceeded to another door leading into the house, where he found the lady awaiting him. She rose to meet him at his approach, and greeted him with great rejoicing, as he strained her to him and kissed her a hundred-thousand times. Then he followed her up the stairs to her room.

They went to bed without wasting a moment, and soon experienced the very height and fulfilment of love. This first time was not the last, you may be sure, for during the knight's stay at Milan, and even after his return, Il Zima went back to his mistress, time and time again, to the utmost delight of both of them.

\*

## THE SIXTH STORY

*Ricciardo Minutolo, in love with Catella, the wife of Filippello Fighinolfi, works upon her jealousy, and pretending Filippello has an appointment with his own wife at a house of assignation, contrives to get Catella there, who thinks she has been with her husband, but discovers it was Ricciardo.*

ELISA HAD NOTHING MORE TO SAY, WHEREUPON THE QUEEN, PRAISing Il Zima's nimble wit, asked Fiammetta to go on with a story. "Willingly, my lady," she answered merrily, and began:

There's no lack of examples in our city, to illustrate every point, as there is no lack of anything else, and yet I think we should go a little beyond it, like Elisa, and tell of things that have taken place in the outside world. Let's pass on to Naples then, and I'll tell you of how one of these angels who seem to be so terribly afraid of love, was made to taste its fruits by the cleverness of her lover, even before she had known its blossoms —which ought to make you wary in future love-affairs, and amuse you at the same time, with those already past.

In the very ancient city of Naples, which is as pleasant as any in Italy, and perhaps more so, there once lived a blue-blooded young gentleman endowed with great riches, whose name was Ricciardo Minutolo. He had a good-looking and very charming lady to wife, but nevertheless he fell in love with another, to whom all other Neapolitan ladies couldn't hold a candle for beauty. Her name was Catella, and she was married to a young gentleman as high-born as Ricciardo, called Filippello Fighinolfi.

Now Catella was a very virtuous woman, and there was no

one she loved or cherished more than her husband, so that Ricciardo, who was in love with her, and employed all the customary arts for winning the favor of a lady, to no purpose, was almost at his wits' end for despair. Ignorant of how to conquer his passion, or perhaps, finding it beyond his power, he neither knew how to seek peace in death, nor to make life tolerable.

While he was in this predicament, some women of his family advised him to control his passion, since he was only wasting his efforts. Catella could see no farther than her precious Filippello, and was so jealous of him, that no bird was free to fly through the air without her thinking it was after him, ready to snatch him from her. That was enough for Ricciardo, and he instantly set to work, thinking of how he might obtain his desire, by means of her jealousy.

From that moment, he pretended he hoped no more for Catella's love, and therefore made the best of it, consoling himself with another flame. For this new lady's sake, he began to indulge in feats of arms and jousting, and in everything he had formerly done for love of Catella. Before long, everyone in the town, Catella included, was convinced that not she, but this other damsel, was the object of his passion. He kept up his pretense so long that no one had further doubt of it, and even Catella, who had always kept aloof from him for his love of her, now lost her reserve, and greeted him whenever they met, with the same cordiality she felt for the rest of her neighbors.

The hot season arrived, when according to the Neapolitan tradition, many picnic parties of men and women set out to enjoy themselves at the seashore. Ricciardo, knowing Catella had also gone there with her group, followed her, accompanied by some friends. It was only after a great deal of coaxing and urging, that he finally consented to join Catella's company of ladies, and acted as though he had no desire at all to be there with them. Soon they began teasing him about his new love, Catella as well as the rest, and he put on a semblance of such ardent devotion, that he gave them even more food for gossiping.

Little by little the ladies were dispersed, as is always the case in such places, and when Catella remained alone with a few of her companions, Ricciardo let fall a chance word of a certain intrigue her husband Filippello was carrying on. Instantly, her jealousy roused, she burned inwardly to learn what Ricciardo had implied. For a while, she contained herself, but then, at the end of her power, she begged Ricciardo, for the sake of his best-beloved lady, to explain his remark about Filippello.

"You entreat me for the sake of so precious a person, that I cannot refuse you anything you ask," he said. "I am ready to tell you, but first you must give me your promise, never to say a word of it to Filippello or anybody else, until you have seen for yourself the truth of what I am about to tell you. As for that, I'll lead you to it any time you wish."

· Catella had nothing to say against his suggestion, and swore she would never speak of it, being more than ever confident that he was telling the truth. They withdrew to a place where the others might not hear them.

"Catella," began Ricciardo, "if I still loved you as dearly as I once did, I'd never be bold enough to tell you anything that might hurt your feelings. But since that's all over now, I'll have fewer scruples about disclosing the whole truth. I don't know whether Filippello was ever provoked by the love I used to bear you, or whether he had any suspicion about your loving me. However it was, he never gave me the least inkling of his true feelings. But now, it seems to me that after awaiting the timely occasion to find me off my guard, he is anxious to do to me what he fears, perhaps, I had done to him. In short, he'd like to satisfy his pleasure on my wife. From what I've discovered, he's been shrewdly currying her favor by means of various messages, which she has reported to me word for word, and answered according to my advice.

"This very morning, before I came here, I found a woman at home with my wife, talking very intimately with her. I knew her at once for the sort she was, so I called my wife and asked her what the woman wanted. 'That's Filippello's go-between,' she said, 'that you've inflicted upon me with all your encouragements. She says he wants to know definitely what my intentions are, and that if I'd be willing, he'd contrive to let me be admitted secretly to a bagnio in this town. He's such a plague and a nuisance about it, that if you hadn't made me keep up this nonsense with him—Lord knows why!—I'd have got rid of him in such a way, that he'd never so much as dare to raise his eyes to me again!'

"I thought things were going too far, and it was about time to put a stop to it, so I decided I'd tell you, and let you know what returns you receive for that wholehearted faithfulness of yours, that was almost the death of me. Don't imagine these are mere idle words and fabrications, for in order to give you the opportunity of convincing yourself with your own eyes, any time you wished, I made my wife tell the woman that she was willing to be at the house of assignation early tomorrow morning, when folks are asleep. She went away quite pleased with the answer, too. I hope you don't believe for a moment I intend to send my wife there. Yet if I were in your place, I'd work it so that he'd find me instead of the woman he expected, and after I'd been with him a while, I'd let him discover the real state of affairs, and give him the roasting he deserved. Really, if you did this, I'm sure he'd be so put out about it, that the wrong he intends doing you and me would be avenged at one and the same time."

While Catella listened, she took no account of the man who gave her the information, or thought of suspecting any trickery behind it. Like most victims of jealousy, she swallowed his words, bait, hook and sinker, and began applying past events to the present action. Flying into a fury, she said she would certainly do as he said—it wasn't such a hardship, after all—and swore if Filippello showed his face there, she would set such a hornets' nest about his ears to shame him, that he'd never fail to be reminded of it, whenever he looked at a woman again. Ricciardo was satisfied with the result.

Thinking his plan excellent, and progressing toward the desired end, he encouraged Catella in her decision, with many other words, and strengthened her conviction, entreating her, however, never to reveal that she had acquired the information from him. She gave him her word of honor.

The following morning, Ricciardo went to the gossip who kept the house he had spoken of to Catella, told her what he intended doing, and begged her to second him as well as she was able. The woman, who respected him, was perfectly willing, and arranged with him all the details of what she was to do and say. It so happened that in this house there was a room that was extremely dark, because it hadn't a single window communicating with the light. The woman cleaned it up, at Ricciardo's request, and set up a bed in it, as best she could. Into it, Ricciardo settled himself as he had planned, and waited for Catella to come.

Now when Catella had heard Ricciardo's words, placing more faith in them than she should have, she returned home in the evening, bursting with spite. As it was, Filippello, his mind occupied with quite other thoughts, got back at about the same time, and failed to greet her with the affectionate endearments he would have used on ordinary occasions. No sooner did she notice it, than her suspicions redoubled. "Truly," she said to herself, "my fine lord has his mind on that woman with whom he fancies he'll be having a jolly time tomorrow morning. But it certainly won't happen, if I can help it."

All night long she dwelled upon her resolution, and thought over what to tell him when she should be with him.

But what more need I say? At the appointed hour, Catella took her chaperone with her, and went to the house Ricciardo had pointed out, never relaxing in one jot of her resolution. There she found the gossip, and asked her if Filippello had been there that day. The woman had been well-primed by Ricciardo, and said: "Are you the lady who's to come and talk to him?"

"Yes, I am," replied Catella.

"Well, then," said the gossip, "go in there to him."

Catella, who was heading for the very last thing she wished to find, had herself conducted to the room where Ricciardo was waiting, entered with her head covered, and locked herself in. Ricciardo rose up gladly when he saw her come, and gathering her in his arms said, softly, "At last, soul of my life!"

She hugged and kissed him in return, to give the impression she was other than herself, and made a great fuss over him, without uttering a syllable, fearful that if she spoke, she would be known by him. The room was pitch-dark—so dark, indeed, that the eyes did not become accustomed to it even after a lapse of time, which suited both of them perfectly. Ricciardo led her to the bed. There, in utter silence, that their voices might not betray them, they remained a considerable time, to the great delight of one, if not the other.

At last, Catella thought it was about time for her to give vent to her repressed scorn, and flaming with wrath, began: "Ah, poor women that we are! How wretched is our lot, and how ill-placed the love most of us waste on our husbands! Alas, miserable me! For more than eight years I have loved you more than my very life, and here you are, judging from what I hear, wearing yourself to a frazzle for love of another woman! Ugly, perverse creature that you are! Whom do you think you were with, pray, tell me, now? With the woman you've been deceiving so long with all your false wiles, pretending you loved her when all the time your heart was elsewhere! It's Catella I am, not Ricciardo's wife, you deceitful wretch! Listen, and see if you don't recognize my voice! That's who I am, Catella, all right! Why, it'll seem an eternity till we're in broad daylight again, when I can shame you as you deserve, dirty, disreputable cur that you are! Poor me! On whom have I wasted such a wealth of love all these years? On this disloyal dog, who, thinking he had a strange woman in his arms, was more prodigal of caresses and endearments in the short time I was with him, than in all the years I've lived with him put together! You were spunky enough to-day, weren't you, scurvy dog, whereas at home you're usually weak and impotent and without fettle! But thank God, it's your own field you've tilled to-day, and not another man's as you thought to be doing! Is it any great wonder you didn't come near me last night? You were waiting to unload your saddles elsewhere, weren't you, now, and you were for reaching the bout in fine shape, eh? But praise be to God and my foresight, the stream flowed downward, where it should have!

"What, you've no answer, my fine fellow? Why don't you say something? Did you lose your tongue, hearing me speak? The Lord only knows what's keeping me from sticking my hands in your eyes, and plucking them out for you! You were cocksure of deceiving me in all secrecy, weren't you? But by God, I'm as clever as you, and you didn't manage it, eh? I had better hounds at your tail than you thought!"

Ricciardo was inwardly relishing her words, and without answering her at all, embraced and kissed and caressed her more than ever, as she kept up her denunciation.

"Yes, yes," she said. "You think you're taking me in now, with your fine caresses, you troublesome dog, and calming me down, and consoling me! You're greatly mistaken! I'll never have a moment's peace and comfort in this, till I've shamed you before as many of our family and friends and neighbors as we have. Tell me, perverse rake, am I not as good-looking as Ricciardo Minutolo's wife? Am I not of as fine a family? Why don't you answer me, you lousy cur? What's she got that I haven't? Get out of here—don't lay a hand on me. You've broken enough lances for the day. I know well enough that whatever you'd do, now that you realize who I am, you'd be doing against your will! God grant me grace, I'll let you hunger after it, I promise you! I don't know what's preventing me from sending for Ricciardo, who loved me more than his life, and could never even boast he'd had as much as a look from me! I don't see what harm there could be in it, at that! You thought you had his wife here, didn't you? Well, it's as though you had really had her—it wasn't your fault the plan fell through! So you see, if I were to have him here with me, you couldn't be blaming me with any justice!"

Abundant were Catella's words, and sore her chagrin. At last Ricciardo, considering that if he were to let her go away in her misapprehension, serious trouble might result, thought it better to make a clean breast of his ruse and undeceive her.

"Sweet soul of mine," he said, clasping her tight in his arms so that she could not extricate herself, "don't be angry, please. What I couldn't get by simply loving you, Cupid showed me how to obtain through subterfuge. I am none other than your own Ricciardo."

On hearing him, and recognizing him by his voice, to be indeed Ricciardo, she would instantly have jumped out of bed, but she could not. She would have screamed, but he laid his hand over her mouth and prevented her, saying: "Catella, what's been done to-day, couldn't be undone if you were to scream from now till doomsday. Besides, if you cried out and somehow brought it to the knowledge of others, two things might happen. In the first place, you'd lose your good name and reputation— which should make you stop and think—for if you were to say I brought you here under false pretenses, I could deny it, and declare I induced you to come with promises of gifts and money, and simply because they did not come up to your expectations, you were furious and raised all this rumpus. You ought to know how much readier people are to accept evil than good, and so I'd be believed more easily than you. In the second place, your husband and I might get into a deadly feud, and it's quite possible that I'd just as likely kill him as be killed by him, which would certainly deprive you of happiness and peace of mind the rest of your days.

"So, then, heart of my heart, don't ruin your good name, and place your husband and me in danger of a serious quarrel! You're not the first woman who's been tricked, and you'll not be the last. It wasn't to rob you of what was yours, that I deceived you, but out of the great love I bear you, as your most humble slave. Long have I and all my worldly power and possessions been yours, to do with as you pleased. From now on, I want them to be more wholly yours than ever. Come, now, you are wise in all things! I am sure you will also be wise in this."

During all of Ricciardo's speech Catella was weeping bitterly. However, though she was beside herself with wrath, and protested vehemently, her mind lent such conviction to the truth of his words, that she knew things might really occur as he had said.

"Ricciardo," she said, "I don't know how God will give me the fortitude to bear the insult and the trick you subjected me to. I don't want to make any noise here, where I was led by my stupidity and excessive jealousy. But be sure of this—I'll never rest till I've had my revenge, somehow or other, for what you've done to me. Come, now, let me go! Don't hold me any more. You've had what you wanted, and sported with me to your heart's content. It's about time you released me. Please, let me go, now!"

Ricciardo saw she was still very angry, and took it into his head not to set her free until she had forgiven him. With gentle words, he fell to pacifying her, and so spoke, and begged and implored her, that she was finally won over and on good terms with him again. They remained together of their own free will, for a long time after that, to their overwhelming delight.

As for Catella, now that she knew how much tastier than a husband's a lover's kisses could be, all her harshness toward Ricciardo was converted to tender affection, and from that day on she loved him most ardently. Many a time, acting with discretion and wisdom, they culled the sweets of their love. May God give us joy of ours!

# THE SEVENTH STORY

*Tedaldo, after a misunderstanding with his mistress, leaves Florence, whence he returns some time later, disguised as a pilgrim. He talks to her and makes her aware of her error, delivers her husband, who had been condemned to death on the grounds of having murdered him, and makes peace between him and his brothers. Then he prudently enjoys himself with his lady.*

FIAMMETTA HAD CEASED SPEAKING, AMID GENERAL APPLAUSE, when, to save time, the queen bade Emilia continue directly.

I'd like to come back to our city, she began, which the last two ladies departed from, and show you how one of our fellow-citizens retrieved his lost mistress.

Well, then, there once lived in Florence a young gentleman called Tedaldo Elisei, who was desperately in love with a noble lady, Ermellina, the wife of Aldobrandino Palermini. He was entirely worthy of enjoying the fulfilment of his desires, but alas! Fortune, arch-enemy of all happiness, denied him that pleasure.

For a while, the lady had lent herself to Tedaldo's wishes, but all at once, for some reason or other, she would have nothing to do with him, and refused not only to receive any of his messages, but to see him altogether, which threw him into sullen, cruel despair. However, he had kept his love for Ermellina so secret, that no one had the least suspicion that it lay at the bottom of his melancholy.

Many and various attempts did he make to regain the love he had lost through no fault of his that he could discover, but when everything proved fruitless, he thought of vanishing from the world, that at least he might not give the woman who was the cause of his suffering, the satisfaction of seeing him wasting away. Collecting as much money as he could, he left without saying a word to anyone but a comrade who was acquainted with the facts of the case, and reached Ancona, where he allowed himself to be known as Filippo di Sandoleccio. He made friends with a wealthy merchant of that town, and entering his service, embarked with him on one of his ships bound for Cyprus. The man was so taken with his way of doing things, that he not only gave him good wages, but made him his partner, entrusting him as well with a considerable share of his commerce, which he expedited with such care and solicitude, that before many years had passed he also became a rich and well-established merchant of no mean repute.

Often, even in the midst of his transactions, he would think of his cruel lady. Then his love tormented him most fiercely, and he ached to see her again; but so firm was his will, that for seven long years he came victorious out of the struggle. One day in Cyprus, he happened to hear a ditty sung, one that he himself had made long since, in which he told of his love for his lady, of her love for him, and the delight he took of her. No, he thought, she could not have forgotten him; and at the memory, he burned with such intense desire to see her again, that at the very end of his resistance, he determined to return to Florence.

Settling all his business, and taking only his servant with him, he went to Ancona, whence he shipped his effects as soon as they arrived, to Florence, in charge of a friend of his Anconese partner's. As for himself, he followed close upon them secretly, with his servant, and disguised as a pilgrim on his return from the Holy Sepulchre, he took up his quarters in Florence at a modest hostelry kept by two brothers, in the vicinity of his lady's dwelling.

The first thing he did was to pass by, to see if he might catch a glimpse of her, but the windows and doors were barred, and everything else. Fearful that she must either have died or moved away, he hastened in agony of mind to his brothers' house, where he saw the four of them clad in the deepest mourning. He scarcely knew what to think. Knowing, however, that he had changed in appearance and mode of dress from his former self, and that he could not easily be recognized, he went up to a nearby cobbler, and asked why those gentlemen were in mourning.

"Why, they're in black," he said, "because only two weeks ago a brother of theirs was murdered—a young gentleman called Tedaldo, who had been away a long time. I believe they've proved in court that Aldobrandino Palermini, who's in prison, did away with him—thought him enamored of his wife, you know, and come back on the sly, just to be with her."

Tedaldo wondered greatly that anyone could resemble him to the extent of being mistaken for himself, and was sorry for Aldobrandino's misfortune. When he learned that Ermellina was alone and well, he returned to the hostelry, for it was already dark, his mind teeming with a multitude of thoughts. He had supper with his servant, and was put up for the night in the garret. What with the thoughts that tormented him, and the uncomfortable bed, and perhaps also because of his lean supper, half the night had already sped and he had not been able to sleep a wink. Indeed, he was wide-awake when, toward midnight, he had the impression of hearing people clambering down into the house from the roof. A little later, he saw a light coming from below, through the cracks of the door. Very stealthily he crawled up to a chink, and peering through it, saw a good-looking girl holding the light, while three men, evidently descended from the roof, walked in to meet her. They exchanged cordial greetings, and then one of them addressed the girl.

"Thank God, we can rest easy from now on," he said. "We know for a sure thing that the blame for Tedaldo Elisei's murder has been clapped on Aldobrandino by the dead man's brothers. The prisoner has even confessed, and the sentence is written. But mum's the word, for all that. If it ever leaked out that we killed him, we'd be in the situation Aldobrandino is in now."

After speaking with the woman, who seemed quite pleased with the information, they went downstairs to sleep. Tedaldo fell into deep thought at the knowledge, reflecting how subject to error is the human mind. First, there were his brothers, who had mourned and buried a stranger, thinking to be burying him, Tedaldo. Then, there was that innocent man, accused on mistaken evidence, and brought to the verge of death by false witness. And there was the blind severity of laws and lawgivers, who, in the guise of truth-seekers, most often exalt falsehood by their cruelties, calling themselves ministers of God's justice, when they're only the devil's instruments. Finally, turning his thoughts to Aldobrandino's rescue, he decided inwardly what course was best for him to follow.

In the morning he arose, left his servant and started off to his lady's house, at a convenient hour. The door, as it happened, was ajar, and he went in, to find Ermellina crouched on the floor in a small lower room, weeping bitterly. The sight almost brought tears of sympathy to his eyes, and going to her, he said: "Do not despair, lady. Your peace is coming."

She lifted up her head on hearing his voice, and said, still weeping: "You look like a stranger to me, good pilgrim. What can you know of my peace or of my sorrow?"

"Lady, I am from Constantinople," he said, "and I've just come here at God's prompting, to turn your tears to joy and save your husband from death."

"But if you're from Constantinople," said Ermellina, "and you've just arrived, how do you know of me or my husband?"

The pilgrim, beginning at the beginning, repeated to her the whole story of Aldobrandino's tribulation, told her who she was, how long she had been married, and many other facts about her with which he was well acquainted. Ermellina was aghast with amazement, and taking him for a prophet kneeled at his feet, imploring him in the name of God, that if he had really come to deliver Aldobrandino, he get to work immediately, as there was not much time left.

Tedaldo looked his holiest. "Lady," he said, "arise and do not cry, but pay attention to what I have to tell you, and beware of repeating it to a soul. The trouble you're in, I gather from God's revelations, has befallen you because of a sin you committed in the past. God Almighty has chosen this trial, to make you expiate it to a certain extent, and it is His will to have you make up for it altogether, unless you want to bring down a worse calamity upon your head."

"Ah, father, I have many sins on my conscience," she said. "How should I know which one it is God desires me to expiate? Please point it out to me, if you know, and I'll do all I can to make amends."

"Lady, I know perfectly well what sin it is," said the pilgrim. "I'm not asking you because I want to be better informed, but to give you the chance of feeling remorseful by telling it yourself. But to the point. Tell me, do you remember ever having a lover?"

Ermellina drew a deep sigh at the question, and wondered, for she believed nobody ever suspected it. About the time the man was buried who was thought to be Tedaldo, however, a certain rumor had been current, arising from some indiscreet remarks passed by Tedaldo's comrade, who had known everything.

"I can see God reveals our inmost secrets to you," she replied, "and I'll not hide mine. It's true that in my youth I dearly loved the unfortunate gentleman of whose death my husband has been accused. I've mourned it as bitterly as it was agonizing to me, alas! for although I simulated cruelty and harshness before he went away, neither his departure nor his absence, no, nor even his terrible death, have succeeded in tearing him from my heart."

"You never loved the unfortunate wretch who was murdered," said the pilgrim, "but you did love Tedaldo Elisei. Tell me, though, what was the reason for your anger against him? Did he ever offend you in any way?"

"Of course not, never," answered Ermellina. "The words of a scurvy friar were at the root of my spite—a fellow to whom I once confessed. When I had made a clean breast of my love for Tedaldo, and told him of our sweet intimacy, he loosed such thunder about my ears that I am still terrified at the thought of it. I'd land right in the devil's maw, he said, in the deepest hell, and I'd be pitched into devouring flames. Oh, what a scare he gave me! Well, I resolved to give up all friendship with Tedaldo, and I wouldn't accept any more letters or messages from him, for fear of falling into temptation. And yet, I think if he had persisted a little longer, instead of going off in despair, as I believe, my cruel determination would have yielded, I know, seeing him wasting away that way—like snow in the sun—for there was nothing I wanted more than to go back to him."

"Lady, this is the sin you are now expiating," said the pilgrim. "I know for a fact that Tedaldo never forced you. When you fell in love with him, you did it of your own free will, because you liked him. Then, when you were ready, he came to you and enjoyed your intimacy, which, both by your words and actions you seemed to relish so much, that if he loved you before, that love became a thousand times more intense. If it was so—as I know it was—what reason in the world could have made you tear yourself from him so mercilessly? You should have thought of these things beforehand, and if you felt that you would ever have regretted them as wrong, you ought not have acted upon them. When he became yours, you likewise became his. If you no longer wanted him, you could have disposed of him at your pleasure, as of something entirely your own. But when you took yourself from him, against his will, you, his own possession, were guilty of robbery and dishonest behavior.

"You see I'm a friar, and that therefore I am cognizant of every one of their ways. If I speak to you at length about them, for your own good, surely I'll not be blamed, as another man would, in my place. I'd like to tell you about them, that you may know them a little better in the future than you did in the past.

"Once upon a time friars were fine, holy men, but those who call themselves so nowadays, and wish to be reputed pious, have nothing of the order but their habit, which, for that matter, is not a real monk's gown. To begin with, the founder of the brotherhoods said their gowns must be scant and humble, and of rough cloth, displaying the monks' faith—which despised all worldly goods by the fact that they covered their bodies with so poor a garment. Nowadays they make them generous, lined, shiny, and of the best materials. They've developed them to a smart, pontifical style, and are not ashamed to show them off,

like peacocks in the church and market-place—every bit like
common folks, making much of their finery. They are just like
fishermen with nets—for as the fisherman catches many fish at
one sweep, our fine monks, enveloping themselves in the widest
of gowns, do their best to draw in a lot of silly spinsters, wid-
ows and other foolish men and women. That's what they love to
do above everything else. Truly, what they possess is not the
monk's garment, but only its color. Indeed, whereas the friars of
old desired the spritual health of mankind, our contemporaries
want nothing so much as women and wealth.

"They expend all their energy in terrifying the minds of fools
with exhortation and example, showing how sins may be washed
away with almsgiving and masses, to the end that they who have
taken refuge in the monk's habit, not out of devotion, but sluggishness and unwillingness to work—that they, I say, may be
given bread by this one, wine by another, and money by someone else, for the souls of his dead. No doubt, alms and prayer
wipe away sins. Still, if the people who give those alms knew
to whom they entrusted them, or realized what sort of creatures they were, they would sooner keep them for themselves or
throw them before so many hogs. Moreover, the monks, being
aware that the fewer the possessors of wealth, the better they can
enjoy it, every man of them does his best to drive away all others with thunder and nightmares, from the treasure he would
keep for himself alone. They condemn lechery in men. Why?
That when the culprits abstain from women, the moralisers may
take possession of them. They damn usury and ill gains, that
when the money is placed in their hands for restitution, they
may widen their gowns with the very lucre which leads its
possessors to hell, and buy bishoprics and even higher church-
honors.

"What do they answer when they are rebuked for such behavior? *Do as we say and not as we do.* That seems to them to
be the proper discharge of every heavy burden, as if sheep
could be more constant and iron-willed than their shepherds!
Most of them know well enough, how many of the people
to whom they address their answer, understand it differently.
Yes, to-day friars want you to do as they say—stuff their purses
with money, confide your secrets to them, be chaste and patient, forgive all wrongs and avoid evil-speaking—very good
things indeed, and proper, and pious. Ah, but why do they
preach them? Why, simply that they may do what wouldn't

be possible for them, if the common folks did it. Who doesn't
know that sluggishness would be shortlived without money?
If you squander your bounty on your pleasures, how can the
poor friar twirl his thumbs in idleness in the monastery? If
you're chasing after women, how can the monks have their
turn? If you're not patient and forgiving of wrongs, they could
not dare come into your house and ruin your family. But why
should I seize on everything? They themselves are their own accusers, whenever they plead their excuses before the wise. Still,
why don't they stay in their monasteries, if they think it beyond their powers to be chaste and devout? Or else, if they insist on giving themselves up to this manner of living, why don't
they quote that other holy verse of the Gospel, *Christ began to
do and to teach?* Let them act first, and then take it upon themselves to teach others. I, for one, have in the course of my life
seen thousands of them in the rôles of gallants, lovers, and seekers after not only women of the world, but of nuns in convents
—and if you please, among them the very men who make the
loudest noise from their pulpits. Is it for us to follow creatures
of the sort? Let each man do as he sees fit. God alone knows if
he is doing the wisest thing.

"Suppose, now, we granted the truth of what the friar said
to you—that it is a very grave wrong to break the marriage vow.
Isn't it a much worse sin to rob a man? And a still more terrible
one to kill him, or send him wandering, a wretched outcast,
about the world? Why, every one will grant it! When a woman
is intimate with a man, she is only guilty of natural sin. But
when she robs and kills or banishes him—such behavior
springs from wickedness of mind. I have already shown you
how you robbed Tedaldo, by withdrawing yourself from him,
after you had made him the gift of yourself, of your own free
will. Moreover, you killed him, so far as you were concerned,
for it wasn't your fault he didn't commit suicide, the way you
increased in cruelty toward him as time went on. Doesn't the
law say that the person who is the instigator of wrong-doing,
is every bit as guilty as the man who commits the deed? Besides, nobody can deny that you were the cause of his exile and
his seven years' tramping about the world. Whatever way you
look at it, you committed a far greater sin in each one of these
three things, than you did in your love together.

"Now let's investigate. Did Tedaldo, perhaps, deserve to be

treated this way? Not at all! You yourself admitted it, and I know for a fact he loved you more than his life. There's no woman alive who was ever so honored, exalted and praised above another, as you were by him, whenever he had occasion to speak of you without rousing suspicion. He had nothing he could call his own, that he did not lay at your feet—every possession, honor, or liberty. Tell me, wasn't he of high birth? Could he not hold his own for beauty among his fellow-citizens? Wasn't he proficient in all that belongs to the province of youth? Was he not beloved and cherished and esteemed by everyone? You cannot gainsay me! Then how on earth could you take such a cruel decision against him, at the instigation of a stupid, crazy, jealous, insignificant little friar? I can't tell what quirk gets into women, that makes them despise men and think little of them! If they only considered what they are themselves, and reflected with what nobility man has been invested by God above all other living creatures, they ought to take pride in the love of a man and cherish him above everything in the world. Yes, they ought to do all in their power, and employ every care to give him pleasure, that he may never cease to love them. As for you—I don't have to tell you how you behaved at the prating of a mere friar—some brothy, tart-eating clown he must have been, for sure, anxious to smuggle himself into the very place from which he was doing his best to chase another.

"Well, this is the sin that divine justice, which metes out its every deed with an accurate balance, has ordained not to leave unpunished. Just as you did your best unreasonably to deny yourself to Tedaldo now, without reason, your husband is in danger through him, and you yourself have come to grief. The only way you can get out of it is by promising, and what's more important, accomplishing the following. If it should ever happen that Tedaldo came back here from his long wandering, you must give him your grace and love and affection, yes, and yourself, once more, and restore him to the position he occupied, before you foolishly listened to that lunatic of a friar."

The pilgrim was silent, when Ermellina, who had listened to his words with great attention, believing implicitly in his arguments and considering herself suffering punishment as he asserted, for the sin she had committed, said: "Good father, I have no doubt that all you say is true, and now I think I know, thanks largely to your proof, what sort of men these monks are, that I used to look upon as saints until a little while ago. I know, too, that I am greatly to blame for my treatment of Tedaldo, and if it were in my power to make up for it, I'd certainly do it, according to your suggestion. But how can that be? Tedaldo can never come back, for he is dead. I don't see, then, how I can promise you to do what can't be done."

"Tedaldo is by no means dead," rejoined the pilgrim, "judging by what God has shown me. Indeed, he is alive and well, and he would be entirely happy if he only enjoyed your grace."

"Take care what you say," cried Ermellina. "I saw him dead in front of my own door—stabbed through and through with a knife—I gathered him here in my arms and bathed his dear dead face with tears. That's what must have given that fellow the occasion to speak such ungentlemanly things."

Then said the friar: "No matter what you say, lady, I assure you Tedaldo is alive, and if you give me your word that you'll bide by what you promise, I hope you'll be able to see him soon for yourself."

"Most willingly," she said. "Nothing could make me happier than to see my husband at liberty, without a hair of his head coming to harm, and Tedaldo alive."

Tedaldo thought the time had come to make himself known and inspire Ermellina with surer confidence in her husband's safety. "Lady," he said, "in order to comfort you about your husband, I'll have to disclose a secret that you must not reveal to a soul, upon your life."

They were in a secluded part of the house, and alone, for Ermellina had the utmost confidence in the pilgrim's holiness; thereupon Tedaldo produced a ring she had given him the last night they had been together, and which he had treasured with great care. "Do you recognize it?" he said, showing it to her.

The moment Ermellina laid eyes upon it, she knew it and said: "I do indeed, father. I myself gave it to Tedaldo, long ago."

The pilgrim rose to his feet, took off his gown and hat in a trice, and with a Florentine twang, "Do you know who I am?" he asked.

When Ermellina looked at him, she saw he was Tedaldo, and was filled with awe, dreading him as one dreads the spirits of the dead, when they go about in the form of the living. By no means did she fly to greet him as her own lover returned from

Cyprus, but would have fled in terror, as though he were the ghost of Tedaldo, risen from the tomb.

"Have no fear," he reassured her. "I am your own Tedaldo, flesh and blood, and quite unharmed. I did not die. I was not murdered in spite of what you and my brothers think."

She was somewhat reassured by his natural voice, and looking at him a little longer, was convinced he was none other than Tedaldo. Weeping, she put her arms about his neck and kissed him. "My dearest Tedaldo," she said. "Welcome back!"

Tedaldo, after kissing and holding her close, said: "Dearest, now is not the time for more intimate greetings, for I must see about bringing Aldobrandino to you, safe and sound. I hope, before to-morrow evening, that you'll have tidings that will gladden you, unless, as I believe, I may have earlier word of his deliverance, in which case I'd like to come to you to-night, and tell you about it at greater length."

He put on his gown and hat again, and giving her one more kiss, told her to be of good cheer, and went to the prison where Aldobrandino was confined, more occupied with the fear of overshadowing death than with hopes of any future safety. Tedaldo entered with the keeper's permission, and sitting beside the prisoner as a sort of spiritual comforter, began:

"I am a friend of yours, Aldobrandino, sent for your salvation by the Lord, who was moved to compassion by your innocence. If you will grant me a little favor, out of reverence to the Almighty, I am sure that before tomorrow evening when you expect your death sentence, you will hear the words of your deliverance."

"Good man," answered Aldobrandino, "since you have such regard for my salvation, I'm sure you must be a friend of mine, as you say, even though I don't know you or remember ever setting eyes on you before. I can say with a clear conscience, I never committed the crime for which the laws of man condemn me to death. Other sins I am guilty of, it's true, and perhaps those sins have brought this judgment upon me. But this I can assure you of, in reverence to the Lord. If He is moved to pity me, I will not only promise, but faithfully perform any great sacrifice—not to mention a small favor—and most willingly, too. Come, ask whatever you wish, and if it ever really happens that I regain my freedom, I will abide by my promise without fail."

"The only thing I ask," said the pilgrim, "is that you forgive Tedaldo's four brothers, for having caused you all this misery in their belief that you were guilty of his death; and when they ask your forgiveness, take them to your heart again, as friends and brothers."

"Nobody knows how sweet revenge can be," remarked Aldobrandino, "or how ardently it is desired, more than the man who has been wronged. Still, if God looks after me, I'll forgive them with all my heart, yes, from this very moment. Then if I should escape with my life, I'll act in such a way, that you cannot but be pleased."

The pilgrim was satisfied. He did not wish to tell him anything further, but earnestly encouraged him to take heart, saying that before the next day was over, he would receive definite word of his deliverance. Taking leave of him, he went straight to the court of justice, and said confidentially to one of the magistrates: "Sir, it is everyone's duty to strive wholeheartedly to discover the truth of things—particularly such men as you, who occupy a position of such responsibility. It is necessary, first of all, so that the innocent may not suffer punishment for a crime they have not committed, and secondly, that the guilty may be brought to justice. It is for this I have come here before you, and I trust it will result in your honor and the chastisement of those who deserve it. You know you have exercised the limit of the law against Aldobrandino Palermini, in your belief that he was really the murderer of Tedaldo Elisei. Indeed, you are about to sentence him to death. But you are entirely mistaken in your judgment, and I shall give you complete proof of it before midnight, by delivering the true murderers of the youth into your hands."

The judge, as it was, had taken pity on Aldobrandino, and lent a willing ear to what the pilgrim had to offer. He talked the matter over with him at great length, and on his instruction seized the two innkeepers and their servant without a struggle, just as they had fallen asleep that night. He would have put them to torture, to extract a confession of how the murder had taken place, but the men did not require it. Individually and then together, they confessed murdering Tedaldo Elisei without knowing who he was, and when they were interrogated in detail for their reason, said that he had insulted the wife of one of them, when they were away from home, and would have forced her to surrender to his desire.

When the pilgrim heard how the matter stood, he excused himself from the judge, and went secretly to Ermellina's house.

He found her alone, for everyone else was asleep, waiting for him, as anxious to hear good news of her husband as to make up completely with her beloved Tedaldo.

"Dearest love of mine," he said, going up to her with a cheerful face, "take heart, for tomorrow you'll have your husband back again, safe and sound." To reassure her more completely, he told her all he had done. She was as glad as could be, at two such strange and unexpected events—to begin with, that Tedaldo was hers again, alive, when she was certain she had mourned over his corpse; and then, that Aldobrandino had been liberated, though she had expected to be mourning his death before many days were over. In her rejoicing, she clasped and kissed Tedaldo affectionately. Soon they went to bed together, and sealed a gracious and happy peace with good will, deriving intense joy from their mutual converse.

Toward morning Tedaldo rose, after having informed Ermellina of his intentions, and begging her again to keep the matter secret, went out in his pilgrim's clothes to take care of Aldobrandino's case. Later in the day, the magistrates, fully satisfied with the facts, released the prisoner, and had the true murderers' heads chopped off before many days had passed.

Now that Aldobrandino was free, to his great joy and the delight of his wife, friends and kin, he knew he owed it all to the pilgrim's efforts, and therefore gave him the freedom of his house for as long as he desired to remain in the city. Husband and wife never tired of showing him the utmost courtesy and hospitality, especially Ermellina, who knew whom she was entertaining.

A few days later Tedaldo thought it time to reconcile his brothers with Aldobrandino, for he had learned that they were not only suffering humiliation after the prisoner's release, but that they went about armed for fear of mischief. Thereupon, he reminded Aldobrandino of his promise, who answered promptly that he was at his disposal. At that, the pilgrim had him prepare a handsome feast for the following day, requesting him to receive, together with all the members of his family, Tedaldo's four brothers with their respective wives, adding that he himself would go immediately, to extend the invitation on Aldobrandino's behalf, to his friendship and his banquet.

Aldobrandino was pleased with the pilgrim's request, whereupon Tedaldo went directly to the four brothers, addressing them with words appropriate to the occasion. At last he convinced them with irrefutable arguments, of the necessity of being friends with Aldobrandino once again, by asking his forgiveness, and when they had consented, he invited them and their wives to dine with his host the following morning. They freely accepted, in the assurance of the pilgrim's good faith.

Next day, toward dinner time, Tedaldo's four brothers arrived in deep mourning, accompanied by a number of friends, and entered the house of Aldobrandino, who was awaiting them. Before all the people who had been invited to welcome them, they threw their weapons on the ground, and surrendering themselves to Aldobrandino, begged his forgiveness for all the harm they had done him. He received them with tears in his eyes, and kissing them on the mouth, forgave them everything in a few words. The men were followed by their sisters and wives, all in somber clothes, and were graciously welcomed by Ermellina and the other ladies.

They were magnificently served during the feast, and there would have been no jarring note but for the constraint caused by the fresh sorrow of the mourning of Tedaldo's relations. Some of the guests had looked askance at the pilgrim's suggestion of the banquet for that reason, and he had noticed it. Thinking it was about time to dispel the gloom, he rose, as he had planned, while the rest were at their dessert, and said: "Nothing has been wanting to make this a merry feast except for the presence of Tedaldo. But since you have not recognized him, though you've had him continually among you, I want to reveal him to you."

Throwing off his pilgrim's gown and all other appurtenances, he appeared in a green silk tunic, to the great wonder of the company, who stared and stared, not venturing to believe it was indeed he. Tedaldo remarked it, and refreshed their memories by telling them many little events and details of their relations, as well as his own vicissitudes, among other things. At last his brothers and the other men rushed to greet him, the tears of joy starting from their eyes, and later the women followed suit, whether they were related to him, or not. Ermellina was the only exception.

"What's the matter, Ermellina?" asked her husband, noticing her aloofness. "Why aren't you rejoicing over Tedaldo, like the other women?"

"No one would more willingly welcome him than myself," she replied, that all might hear, "considering how much I owe him for restoring you to me. It's only the gossip that circulated when we were lamenting over the man we thought Tedaldo—that's what's restraining me."

"Nonsense!" said Aldobrandino. "Do you think for a moment I believe those scandal mongers? He showed clearly enough that there was no truth in all that by saving my life. What's more, I never thought anything of the sort. Make haste, now, get up. Go and embrace him, too."

Ermellina, who wanted nothing better, was not slow to obey her husband's request, and rising, went to kiss Tedaldo, making much of him, as the other ladies had done. Aldobrandino's open-mindedness was greatly commended by Tedaldo's brothers and the rest of the company, and whatever doubt had existed in the minds of any of them, was quickly dispelled by his attitude.

After everyone had rejoiced over Tedaldo, he tore the mourning clothes from his brothers, sisters and in-laws, and had them send for others. When that was done, the entertainment, with its songs, dances and other amusements, began in good earnest, and the feast which had been ushered in by gloom, ended in a tumult of merrymaking. Later in the day, the guests sallied forth to Tedaldo's house in the height of mirth, and supped there that evening. And so the feast continued some days longer.

It took the Florentines a little while to get over looking at Tedaldo with wonder, as on a man risen from the dead, and many, his brothers among them, still had a certain lingering doubt in their hearts as to whether it was really he. Indeed, they were not fully convinced and perhaps would not have been for a long time, had not a strange incident proved beyond a doubt the identity of the slain man.

One day some liveried servants from Lunigiana were passing by the brothers' house, and on seeing Tedaldo, came toward him, saying: "Hello there, Faziuolo!"

"You're mistaken in your man," answered Tedaldo, while his brothers were by. On hearing his voice, the men were embarrassed and begged his pardon, saying: "Really, sir, you look as like a comrade of ours, as two peas. It's Faziuolo da Pontremoli his name is, and he came here two weeks ago, perhaps more. We never heard what became of him. To tell you the truth, we were surprised at your clothes, for he was only a common soldier, like us."

Tedaldo's eldest brother came forward on hearing this, and

asked specifically how Faziuolo had been dressed. They told
him, and it was exactly as they said, so that what with these
and other details, the murdered man was identified as Faziuolo,
and not Tedaldo, to the ultimate assurance of his brothers, and
others who had still held any doubts.

Thus Tedaldo, who had brought back great wealth on his
return, continued in his love, and had long joy of mutual passion with his lady, who had no more misunderstandings with
him.

May God give us joy of our love!

✳

## THE  EIGHTH  STORY

*Ferondo is buried for dead, after swallowing a certain powder.
He is later taken out of the tomb by the abbot (who in the meantime enjoys his wife), and is held in confinement, believing himself
in purgatory. Then, when he is brought to life again, he brings up
as his own, the child that the abbot had begot on his wife.*

EMILIA'S LONG STORY HAD COME TO AN END, NOT THAT IT HAD
bored any of them—indeed, the ladies thought it could not
have been shorter in the number and variety of incidents it contained—when the queen simply nodded to Lauretta, indicating
her wish.

Dearest ladies, Lauretta began, I have quite a task before me,
in the true story I am going to tell, which seems to hold more
fiction than it really does, and which came to me from what
we have just heard tell of a person who was mourned and buried for another. I'll tell you, on the other hand, of how a
living man was buried for dead, and of how he and many others
later believed that he had really risen from the dead, and not
been alive at all, winning for himself the worship due a saint,
when he ought to have been punished for the trickster he
really was.

Once upon a time, there was an abbey in Tuscany, that is
standing to this day, which was built like many others of its
kind, in a fairly unfrequented spot. Once, a certain monk was
appointed abbot of it, who was as pious and holy a gentleman
as you could hope for, except as far as women were concerned.

In this matter, he was so sly a fox that no one knew of it, much less had the least suspicion, esteemed as he was for his general piety and righteousness.

Now there was a well-to-do farmer, who had struck up a close friendship with the abbot—a simple bumble-head of a fellow, by the name of Ferondo, whose acquaintance the abbot was pleased to encourage, for the fun he sometimes derived at the expense of the man's simplicity. As their friendship grew closer, the abbot discovered that Ferondo had quite a handsome wife, and he fell so hotly in love with her that he could think of nothing else, day and night. However, when he learned that though Ferondo was stupid and crack-brained in everything else, he was certainly efficient in the love and protection he gave his wife, the abbot was almost driven to despair. But he was a cunning man; little by little, he so wheedled Ferondo, that he managed to have him come to the abbey garden now and then with his wife, for a bit of leisure. There, he would modestly entertain them with homilies on the blessedness of life everlasting, and the good works of men and women now dead, until at last the woman took a fancy to confess herself to him, and asked her husband's permission, which was readily granted.

Much to the abbot's delight, she finally came to confess, and sitting at his feet began, before saying anything else: "Father, if the good Lord had only given me the right sort of husband, or none at all, perhaps I might now be really on the road that leads others to life everlasting, as you said, especially with the help of your teachings. But for my part, considering what sort of man Ferondo is, I might call myself a widow, married though I am— worse than that, for while he's alive I can't take another husband. But although he's such a numskull, he's so frightfully jealous, and for no reason at all, that my life with him is a continual hell of misery and wretchedness. I beg you, then, before I make my confession, please, please give me some advice, for if I don't obtain relief now, neither confession nor anything else will do me the least good."

Her disclosure was mightily gratifying to the abbot, who felt luck had certainly paved the way to his heart's desire. Thereupon he said: "Daughter, I can understand what a trial it must be for a lovely, sensitive woman like you, to have a nitwit for a husband. It must be a thousand times worse, to have a jealous one. Since you're blessed with both the one and the other, I can readily believe what you say of your trials. Still, to cut the matter short, I can offer you no advice, or see any way out of it, except to rid Ferondo of this jealousy of his. I know well enough how to concoct the medicine that will cure him —but for that you must be strong, and keep what I'm going to tell you a strict secret."

"Don't worry about that, father," said the woman, "for I'd sooner die than breathe a word to anyone of anything you cautioned me not to tell. But how can you manage what you say?"

"If you want me to cure him," replied the abbot, "he must be made to go to purgatory."

"But how can that be done, while he's alive?" she asked.

"He must first die, and then he'll go there," answered the abbot. "Then, after he's had enough of hell-fire to cure him of his jealousy, we'll offer up certain prayers to the Almighty, to bring him back to this life, and the Lord will do so."

"What do you mean, father," she asked, "am I to become a widow?"

"Exactly," replied the abbot, "but only for a while, during which you must take great care not to get married to another man, for the good Lord would take it amiss. Besides, if you did, you'd have to go back to Ferondo on his return, and he would be more jealous than ever before."

"Well," she said, "if he'll only be cured of this unfortunate trait, which keeps me pent up at home like a prisoner, I'll be grateful enough. So do as you please about it."

"That I will do," he said. "But what will you give me as a reward for such a service?"

"Anything you wish, father," she said, "provided it's in my power, though I don't see what a poor woman like me can do, that would be worthy of a great man like yourself."

At that the abbot replied: "You can do nothing short of what I'm going to accomplish for you, for since I'm disposed to do everything for your welfare and consolation, you may also serve in something, that will be the health and very life of me."

"In that case, I'm at your service," she said.

"Well, then, love me a little," said the abbot, "and grant me joy of your body, for I'm wasting away in a flame of passion for your sweet sake."

The woman replied, all in a flurry, at the sudden declaration: "Mercy, father, what on earth are you asking? And I took you for a saint! Is that the proper behavior for a holy man, I ask you—making such suggestions to a woman who goes to him for advice?"

"Sweet soul of mine," said he, "don't be concerned about it, for holiness is not lessened a jot on that account. You see, holiness resides in the soul, and what I'm asking of you, is only a little sin of the body Anyhow, whatever it is, the power of your beauty is so great and so bewitching, that the love it inspires obliges me to act so. I assure you, you have more reason than any other woman to glory in your loveliness, since it's pleasing to the very saints, who are accustomed to gaze on the wonders of heaven. Besides, even though I'm an abbot, I'm a man like the rest, and not so very old, as you can see. What I require wouldn't be hard for you to do. In fact, you ought to desire it, for while Ferondo is in purgatory, I'll be keeping you company through the night and giving you the consolation he should be offering. Not a hint of it will ever leak out, as everyone believes me to be the sort of man you took me for a little while ago—or even better. Come, don't reject the bounty God is sending your way. Plenty of women are yearning for what may, and will surely be yours, if you'll only be sensible and follow my advice. What's more, I have many lovely jewels of great worth, that I intend for no one but you. Come, then, my darling hope, do for me what I'll gladly do for you."

She remained with head bowed, not knowing how to refuse, yet fearful she would not be doing the right thing by consenting. The abbot, however, seeing that she had listened to him and hesitated about answering, felt he had already half-won her. Thereupon he piled up so many other arguments that, before he had finished, he had already convinced her of the rightness of the deed. Blushing, she replied she was ready to obey him in everything—but not before Ferondo had been consigned to purgatory.

"We'll see to it that he gets there right away," said the abbot, delighted, "but you must try to have him come and stay with me to-morrow, or the day after."

As he spoke, he cautiously slipped a handsome ring into her hand and sent her away. She was quite pleased with the gift. Indeed, she looked forward to others, and as she went back to her companions, marvelous were the things she told of the abbot's holiness. Then she returned home with them.

Some days later Ferondo came to the abbey, and the moment the abbot saw him, he prepared to send him to purgatory.

First of all, he produced a powder of extraordinary virtue, which he had obtained in the Orient from a mighty prince. That was the drug, the prince had said, that was used by the Old Man of the Mountain, whenever he put anyone in a trance in order to send him to paradise, or bring him back again. Depending on the quantity of powder used, the man who swallowed it slept a longer or shorter time, without being in any way injuriously affected by it; but while the effect of the powder lasted, no one could say that there was any life left in the sleeper.

The abbot, accordingly, took enough of the powder to put a man to sleep for three whole days, and mixing it in a glassful of young wine, that had not yet cleared, made the unsuspecting Ferondo drink it in his cell. Presently he led him to the cloisters, and with a number of his monks began to laugh at him and his absurdities. The fun had not long continued, when the powder began to have its effect. Suddenly, Ferondo was overcome by a drowsiness so powerfully deadening, that he fell asleep on his feet, and collapsed.

The abbot, to all appearances, seemed terribly concerned at the accident. He had Ferondo's clothes loosened, called for cold water and sprinkled it on his face—in short, he used all kinds of remedies, as if he were trying to revive him from some stomach-humor, or similar attack. However, when the monks perceived that Ferondo did not come to despite their labors, they felt his pulse, and detecting no sign of life, were certain he must be dead. They sent word to his wife and relations. Soon all of them arrived, and for some time they wept and wailed, his wife no less than the rest. Finally the abbot had him put in a tomb, in the clothes he was wearing.

Thereupon, Ferondo's wife returned home, and telling the world she would never part with a little son she had had by him, kept to her house, taking care of her child and the riches that had belonged to her husband.

That night the abbot arose very cautiously, and accompanied by a Bolognese monk, in whom he had implicit faith, and who had newly arrived, took Ferondo out of the tomb and transported him to a crypt ordinarily used as a place of confinement for monks who deviated from the path of righteousness. Not a ray of light could penetrate it. Removing Ferondo's clothes, they dressed him up as a monk, laid him on a heap of straw, and left him there to regain consciousness. Meanwhile, the Bolognese monk received instructions from the abbot on the procedure he was to adopt, and unknown to the rest of the world, waited patiently for Ferondo to recover his senses.

Next day the abbot and a few of his monks went to pay a pastoral call at the widow's house, and found the lady dressed in black and immersed in sorrow. He comforted her awhile, and then, in a low voice, reminded her of her promise. She was free now, with neither Ferondo nor anyone else in her way; besides, she spied another handsome ring on the abbot's finger. Replying she was ready, she arranged to have him come to her the following night. When it was dark, therefore, the abbot went to her, dressed in Ferondo's clothes, and accompanied by his monk. All night long, until dawn of the next day he lay with her, to his infinite delight, and then retraced his steps to the abbey. He footed the path very frequently from then on, in the performance of that service, and people meeting him coming or going took him for Ferondo's spirit, pacing about the countryside in expiation of some penance. Many fantastic tales sprang up about him among the credulous peasants, and were afterward related to his wife, who knew only too well what it was all about.

Meanwhile, when Ferondo came to and found himself Lord knows where, the Bolognese monk rushed in with a bloodcurdling yell and falling upon him, gave him the thrashing of his life, with a bundle of withes he had in his hand. Ferondo cried and howled, and yelled: "Where am I? Where am I?"

"You are in purgatory," said the monk.

"What!" cried Ferondo. "And am I dead?"

"You're dead all right," replied the monk, whereupon Ferondo set up a mighty keening over himself, his wife and child, saying the most extraordinary things imaginable. When the monk brought him something to eat and drink, "Do you mean to say the dead eat?" he asked in astonishment.

"Certainly," answered the monk. "This food I'm bringing you is what the wife you had in the world of the living sent to church this morning, to order a mass for your soul's good, and Almighty God said it should be brought to you."

"God bless her," said Ferondo. "I was always crazy about her before I came to die. I'd hold her tight in my arms all night long, and I did nothing but kiss her and kiss her—ay, and I did something else, too, when I felt like it."

He had developed a hearty appetite, and began to eat and drink. The wine did not seem the best to him, however.

"The devil take her," he cried. "Why didn't she give the priest the other wine—from the tun against the wall?"

When he had finished eating, the monk took hold of him again and gave him another mighty basting with those same withes, while Ferondo howled himself hoarse and asked: "Say, why are you handling me this way?"

"Because Almighty God ordered you to be thrashed twice a day," the monk informed him.

"And why should I be?" inquired Ferondo.

"Because you were jealous," replied the monk, "even though you had the best wife in the whole neighborhood."

"Alas!" said Ferondo. "You never said a truer word. Yes, the best wife and the gentlest. Why, she was smoother than honey. But I had no notion Almighty God didn't like a man to be jealous. Otherwise I shouldn't have been."

"You should have seen to it when you were on earth," said the monk, "and taken pains to mend yourself. If you should ever go back, bear in mind what I'm doing to you now, and take care you're never jealous again."

"My!" cried Ferondo. "Do you mean the dead go back to earth?"

"Yes," replied the monk, "those whom God wishes."

"Well, well," said Ferondo. "If I ever go back, I'll be a model husband, all right. I'll never beat her, and I'll never say a nasty thing to her—except about the bad wine she sent this morning. She didn't send any candles, either, and I'm obliged to eat in the dark."

"Oh, yes, she did," said the monk, "plenty of them, but they were lighted at the masses."

"Ah, is that so?" asked Ferondo. "Well, I swear if I should ever go back to earth, I'll let her do whatever she wishes. But tell me, who are you, beating me like this?"

"I'm dead, too," said the monk. "And I come from Sardinia. But because I was once too generous in praising my master for being jealous, God has damned me to this punishment. I'll have to give you food and drink, and thrash you soundly until God decides on something else for you and me."

"Isn't there anyone but us two here?" asked Ferondo.

"Why, certainly, thousands of others," replied the monk,

"but just as you can't see or hear them, they can't see or hear you."

"And how far are we from our hometowns?" asked Ferondo.

"Aha!" said the monk. "As for that, we're more miles away from them, than we could ever cover with droppings."

"You don't say! That's certainly far enough," said Ferondo. "For all I can see, we must be well out of the world, since it takes every bit of that!"

For ten whole months, Ferondo was lodged in the crypt, enjoying similar conversations, meals and thrashings, while on earth the abbot paid frequent and happy visits to his fair lady, regaling himself with the best time in the world. Unfortunately, she discovered that she had conceived, and immediately told the abbot about it. The only thing to do, they considered, was to hale Ferondo back from purgatory and have him return to her, that she might foist the paternity upon him. The selfsame night, the abbot had Ferondo summoned in a strange voice. "Be of good cheer, Ferondo," it said. "God wills that you return to earth, where you shall have a son by your wife. Benedict, you shall name him, for it is through the prayers of your pious abbot and your wife, and Saint Benedict's intercession that God grants you this grace."

He was happy indeed to hear this message, and answered: "I've nothing against it, the Lord bless God Almighty and the abbot and Saint Benedict, and my own dear cozy, sweet little sugar wife."

Accordingly, the abbot had him dosed with wine in which enough powder had been mixed to make him sleep about four hours, dressed him in his own clothes, and thrust him secretly again into the tomb in which he had been buried.

Toward dawn the following morning, Ferondo awoke from his trance, and seeing through some crack in the tomb a ray of sunshine which for ten whole months he had been without, he thought he must have come to life.

"Open! Open!" he bellowed, butting so vigorously with his head against the cover of the tomb that he loosened it, for it had no great resistance. He was about to throw it off altogether, when the monks, fresh from their morning prayers, rushed in on recognizing Ferondo's voice, and reached him in time to see him jump out of the grave. They were awed at the strangeness of the scene, and ran off to tell the abbot, who made a pretense of rising from his orisons.

"Don't be afraid, my children," he said. "Take the cross and holy water, follow me and let us see what God in His omnipotence would reveal to us!" And he led the way.

Ferondo had come out of the tomb, looking as pale as a ghost —nothing to wonder at, since he had been deprived of the open air so long. The moment he saw the abbot, he ran to him and fell at his feet. "Ah, father," he said, "it was your prayers that rescued me from purgatory, according to my revelations. Yes, your prayers, and my wife's and Saint Benedict's, have brought me back to earth, may God bless you and give you a good Christmas, now and forever!"

"Praised be the omnipotence of the Lord!" cried the abbot. "Go, my son, since God has sent you back among us, go comfort your wife who has been in a well of tears from the moment you departed this life! And from now on, strive to be a friend and servant of the Lord."

"Ay, father, that's the very thing I've been told. As for my wife, leave her to me. The moment I find her, I'll kiss her with all my might—I'm so crazy about her!"

Alone with the monks, the abbot feigned the utmost wonder at the event, and caused the *Miserere* to be fervently sung.

Ferondo, however, returned to the village, where all the people fled from him as from some preternatural thing; but he called them back, assuring them he had been resurrected from the grave. Even his wife seemed to be terrified at the sight of him. Little by little, the people were somewhat more at ease about him, seeing that he was quite alive, and began plying him with all kinds of questions. He answered them in the most wonderful way, as though he had returned with more wit than before, related them tidings of their dead, and spun the most fantastic yarns about the doings in purgatory. He even went so far as to deliver for their edification, the revelation made him by the mouth of the Rangel Bragiel before his resurrection. As a result, when he returned home to his wife, and regained possession of all his goods, he caused her to conceive by him, as he believed, and at the proper time, according to the opinion of fools who think a woman must be exactly nine months gone with child before she delivers, a boy was born to her, who was named Benedict Ferondi.

The return of Ferondo, whom everyone firmly believed risen from the grave, and the things he said, added inestimably to the abbot's reputation for holiness; and as for Ferondo himself, his breech had been so well-warmed for his jealousy, that he was entirely cured of it from then on, exactly as the abbot had promised his mistress. She was happy enough about it, and went on living with her husband as honestly as ever, except that whenever she could, without much trouble, she would gladly manage to meet the good abbot, who had been a great help and comfort to her in her most urgent need.

*

# THE NINTH STORY

*Gillette of Narbonne cures the King of France of a fistula; she asks as a reward to marry Bertrand of Roussillon, who goes through the ceremony against his will and then leaves for Florence in a scornful temper. There he courts a young woman, and imagining he is with her, lies with his own wife, who bears him two sons. Thereupon, he loves her and restores her to her rightful place.*

IT REMAINED ONLY FOR THE QUEEN TO SPEAK, NOW THAT LAUretta's story was over, unless she cared to infringe upon Dioneo's privilege, so without waiting for her friends to urge her, she began, briskly:

How can any story we can tell sound like anything after Lauretta's? It's a good thing she was not the first, or few of the others would have cut any sort of figure, as I'm afraid will be the case with those still left for to-day. Well, anyhow, I'll tell the first story that comes to my mind.

In the kingdom of France, there once lived a knight called Isnard, Count of Roussillon, who suffered very much from ill-health, and therefore always kept a physician in attendance, whose name was Gerard of Narbonne. The count had an only son, Bertrand, a beautiful, winning child, who was being brought up with other children of his age, among whom was Gillette, the physician's daughter. In spite of her tender years, she bore the boy a more fervent and boundless love than is common with children, so that when the count, Bertrand's father, died, leaving him in the king's charge, and he was obliged to remove to Paris, the young girl was left in the depths of despair. When her own father died, shortly afterwards, she would willingly have gone to Paris, on any suitable pretext, if only to lay eyes on Bertrand, but as she was strictly kept, being all alone, and a wealthy heiress, she saw no respectable way of doing it. By this time she had come to a marriageable age. Nevertheless, since she could not tear the love of Bertrand out of her heart, she rejected many suitors that her guardians proposed to her, without giving any plausible reason, while her love for Bertrand grew more and more ardent, especially when she heard that he had grown up handsomer than ever.

Now, about this time, she happened to learn that the King of France was severely ill. A putrid growth on his breast had been badly healed, and as a result a fistula had developed, which gave him the greatest pain and discomfort. Although many doctors had attempted to cure him, no one had as yet succeeded in bringing about an improvement; on the contrary, they had only made it worse, so that the poor king gave up in despair, and wouldn't hear of more advice or help from anybody. Gillette rejoiced at the news, for now, she mused, she had not only a legitimate excuse for going to Paris, but if the king's disease was what she suspected, she might easily succeed in winning Bertrand for a husband. Profiting by the knowledge she had gained from her father, she prepared a powder of various herbs, beneficial to what she believed to be the king's malady, mounted her horse, and went straight to Paris.

The first thing she did, was to see Bertrand. Then, coming before the king, she begged him as a special favor, to allow her to examine the source of his disease. She was young and attractive. The king could not find it in himself to refuse, and let Gillette look at the sore. The moment she saw it, she was certain she could heal it.

"Sire," she said, "if you will allow me, I hope with God's help, to cure you of your disease before eight days are over, without causing you the least trouble or exertion."

The king refused to take the words seriously, and said to himself: "Really! How can a mere slip of a girl know how to treat what has baffled the greatest doctors in the world, and made them give up in despair?" Aloud, he thanked her for her gracious interest and told her he had made up his mind to consult no other physician.

"Your Majesty," she answered, "you have no faith in my ability because I'm only a young girl. Need I remind you that I don't heal by my art alone, but with the help of God and the learning of Dr. Gerard of Narbonne, my father, who was a famous physician in his lifetime?"

Then the king pondered: "Perhaps this girl has been sent me by God. Why shouldn't I give her a trial, since she promises to cure me in so short a time, without any trouble on my part?" He decided to give her a chance.

"Suppose you don't cure me, my child," he asked, "after I've broken my resolution, what is to be your penalty?"

"Sire," she answered, "let me be strictly guarded. If I don't cure Your Majesty within eight days, let me be burned alive. But if I do, what's to be my reward?"

"I believe you're still unmarried," said the king. "I shall give you a great and noble husband, if you succeed in healing me."

"Your Majesty," replied Gillette, "I am happy you wish to give me a husband, but I want him to be the man I ask of you—excepting your own sons, of course, or princes of royal blood."

The king willingly granted her request, and the girl began her course of healing. Soon, even before the time allotted, she restored him to health, whereupon, feeling he was quite himself again, the king said: "You have well earned a husband, my child."

"Ah," she said, "then I have earned Bertrand of Roussillon, with whom I fell in love when I was still a child, and whom I've always dearly loved above everyone else."

The king thought she was asking too much, but since he had promised and did not want to go back on his word, he called the youth to him and said: "Bertrand, you are now a man, and versed in everything you should know. It is my wish that you return to your country, to assume its government, and take along a young lady whom I've chosen to be your wife."

"Who is the lady, sire?" asked Bertrand.

"The one who brought me back to health by her treatment," the king replied.

Bertrand had seen Gillette and recognized her; still though he found her beautiful, he knew she was not of parentage noble enough to mix with his own blood. "My liege," he said, his voice trembling with disdain, "do you mean you would have me marry a mere she-doctor? God forfend I should ever unite with such a woman!"

"Would you have me go back on my word?" asked the king. "The young woman asked to have you for a husband, and for the sake of my health, I promised. Would you have me fail, now?"

"Sire, you may take from me all I possess," said Bertrand, "and give me away as your servant to whomever you please. But be sure of one thing—I shall never be a willing second to such a marriage."

"Of course you will," said the king, "for the lady is beautiful, and wise, and loves you dearly. I'm sure you will be even happier with her, than with another of nobler rank."

Bertrand remained silent, whereupon the king ordered magnificent preparations for the wedding. The appointed day arrived, and much against his will Bertrand, in the presence of the king, married Gillette, who loved him more than her life.

The ceremony over, Bertrand, who had considered what he was going to do, asked the king's leave to go to his own country, there to consummate the marriage. Once on horseback, however, he did not go there at all, but rode on to Tuscany. As it was, war was raging between the Florentines and the people of Siena. Bertrand decided to take sides with the Florentines, who accepted him readily into their ranks, and made him captain over a company of soldiers. The provisions they afforded him were of the best, and so he remained for a long time in their service.

Meanwhile, the newly-wedded bride was little pleased with this turn of affairs. Nevertheless, she thought that by acting tactfully she might get Bertrand back to his own country, and settled at Roussillon, where she was received by the vassals as their lady and mistress. Everything had gone to rack and ruin, in a land which had been too long without a ruler; but with the wisdom of which she was mistress, Gillette used such diligence and care, that soon everything was restored to order, bringing contentment to her subjects, who loved and esteemed her and blamed the count bitterly for his scorn of her.

When the country was again enjoying a state of prosperity and peace, Gillette notified the count by two knights, imploring him that if she was the only obstacle keeping him from returning to his land, he should let her know, and she would go her way, to please him.

"Let her do as she wishes about it," he answered, harshly. "As for me, I'll go back to her only when she has this ring on her finger, and a son of mine in her arms."

The ring he mentioned was one by which he set great store,

for some quality he had been made to believe resided in it, and
he would never consent to part with it. The knights realized
full well the difficulty of the condition; he had set her two almost impossible demands. But when their words could not avail
to move him from his decision, they returned to their lady and
gave her his answer. Needless to say, she was saddened beyond
words. Still, after long consideration, she determined to find out
whether those two conditions were so impossible, after all, and
planned how and where she might manage to fulfil them and
retrieve her husband.

She laid her plans. Calling together some of her best and
most distinguished subjects, she told them piteously what she
had already done for love of the count, and showed how little
it had served, saying besides that she had no desire to allow
him to remain in perpetual exile, because of her presence there,
but that she intended to spend the rest of her life in pilgrimages and works of charity, for the good of her soul. Then, begging them to take the care and government of the land into
their hands, she requested them to inform the count that she
left him free and undisputed possession of Roussillon, and had
gone away, resolved never to return.

Many a tear did her faithful vassals shed, during the course of
her speech, and many an entreaty did they offer, to make her
change her mind and stay, but all in vain. Commending them
all to God's keeping, she set out on her journey, telling no one
where she was going. A cousin and a maidservant were her sole
escorts, and all three were dressed as pilgrims, but provided
with plenty of money and precious jewels. On and on they traveled, and did not stop until they came to Florence, where Gillette put up at an unpretentious inn kept by a respectable
widow. There she led a quiet, peaceful life, as a poor pilgrim,
awaiting tidings of her husband.

The following morning, by some strange chance, she saw
Bertrand pass the inn on horseback, followed by his retinue, and
though she knew him only too well, she asked the widow who
he might be.

"That's a foreign gentleman," the innkeeper informed her.
"Count Bertrand's his name—a wonderful, agreeable man that's
won the hearts of all the folks of this town. He's crazy about a
neighbor of ours, who's of good family but poor—a very respectable girl. It's only her poverty has kept her from finding
the husband to marry her, and so she's still with her mother who

is the soul of goodness and decency. I'm sure if she hadn't had this mother of hers to look after her, she'd long have done the count's sweet will."

The countess was all attention, and took stock of the woman's words. On closer consideration, she was able to grasp every particular and detail, and forming a clear notion of how the matter stood, she thought out the best plan to follow. One day, after she had obtained the names and address of the woman and her daughter, with whom the count was in love, she set out quietly in her pilgrim's outfit to seek them, and found them both in very modest circumstances indeed. She greeted them and told the mother she had something to communicate to her alone, at her convenience. Then and there, the good woman rose and said she was ready, and as they sat together in a room apart, the countess began:

"It seems to me that Fortune and you are not on friendly terms. Neither am I with her. And yet, if you would only consent, you have it in your power to benefit both yourself and me."

Upon the woman's reply that she desired nothing better than to improve her condition by honest means, Gillette resumed: "But I must have your word of honor, for if I were to place myself in your hands, only to have you go back on your promise, you would be ruining both your chances and mine."

"Speak in all confidence," answered the honest woman, "and tell me everything that's on your mind, for you'll never be betrayed by me."

At that the countess, beginning from the moment she fell in love, made a complete confession, telling the woman who she was, and all she had gone through, up to that day. She told everything in such a convincing way, that the good woman could not help believing her words, especially since she had already indirectly heard something of her story from common report, and was filled with pity.

"So you see, as though my troubles were not enough," the countess added, "what sort of conditions I must fulfil, if I want to regain my husband! There's no one I know who could be of greater help to me in accomplishing them than yourself, if what I hear is true—in short, that the count, my husband, is madly in love with your daughter."

"Madam, I can't be sure whether the count really loves my daughter," replied the woman, "though he certainly behaves as though he did. But what could I do to help you in this case?"

"I shall tell you," said the countess. "But first I'd like to show you what good you would derive from helping me, in case you should decide to. I notice that your daughter is a good looking lass, old enough to be married, and from what I've been able to gather, you're obliged to keep her home, because she hasn't enough of a fortune to get her a husband. It is my intention to reward you for the services you render me, to give her, out of my own money, whatever dowry you think appropriate to marry her off very decently."

The woman, who did not enjoy the best of circumstances, liked the proposal well enough; nevertheless she had a certain pride. "Madam," she said, "tell me what it is you'd like me to do for you. If it is honorable, I shall do it without hesitation, and later you may reward me as you please."

The countess spoke. "What I'd like you to do is simply this," she said. "Inform the count, my husband, by some trusty messenger, that your daughter is ready to yield herself to him, provided she can be sure he loves her as much as he seems to, and which she'll believe only if he sends her the ring she has heard he prizes so, and which he always wears upon his finger. If he should send you that ring, you are to give it to me. Later, you will inform him that your daughter is ready to do his will, whereupon you'll have him come here in great secrecy, and manage without his knowing, to let me be with him, instead of your daughter. Who knows, but God may grant me the grace of conception? And so, if I succeed in having his ring on my finger, and his own son in my arms, I shall win him over to live with me as a husband should live with his wife, and the credit for it will be all yours."

The woman was aghast at the idea, fearful that scandal might come out of it for her daughter. However, when she considered how well it would reflect upon her to restore the count to his wife, and how, after all, she would be working toward an honorable end, she put her trust in the lady's good intentions, and not only gave her word, but before a few days were over, she was able to procure the ring, by following the countess' instructions with secrecy and caution (though the count was loth to part with it) and cunningly put her to bed with him, instead of her daughter.

By God's will, the countess became pregnant of two sons, as her delivery revealed at the proper time, during those first embraces which the count so passionately craved. Not once, but many times did the good woman contrive to satisfy her with her husband's intimacies, and so discreetly did she manage, that no one ever knew of it, not even the count, who was certain he had been with the girl he loved, and not with his own wife. Every morning, before he took leave of her, he would make her a present of elegant, costly jewels, which Gillette very carefully treasured.

However, when she saw she had conceived, she was unwilling to be of further trouble to the woman, and said: "Thanks to the Lord and you, I have obtained what I was after, and I think it's time for me to reward you and take my leave."

"I'm glad of it for your sake," said she, "for I did it without thought of gain. It was my duty, and the right thing to do."

"I appreciate your sentiments," said the countess, "therefore I am not going to give what you ask of me, in compensation for your pains, but simply to do the right thing, also, which I think is only as it should be."

Necessity pinched her, so the good woman asked her shame-facedly for a hundred lire, as her daughter's marriage portion. The countess, appreciating her delicacy, gave her five hundred because of her modest demand, and precious jewels to a like amount, which so pleased the woman that she scarcely knew how to thank her. Then the countess returned to the inn, while the woman, in order to avoid giving Bertrand any further excuse for sending to her house, or coming there personally, moved away and took up her residence in the country with her daughter, at the home of her people. As for Bertrand, when he was notified soon after by his subjects that the countess had disappeared, he returned to Roussillon.

Gillette was happy at the news of his departure from Florence, and his return to his own domain, and remained behind until the time of her delivery, when she gave birth to a pair of boys who were the image of their father. Very tenderly, she had them nurtured, and when she thought the time was ripe, went her way and arrived at Montpellier, without divulging who she was. There she put up for some days. On inquiring about her husband, she learned that on All Souls' Day he was going to hold a great celebration at Roussillon, to which all the knights and ladies were invited, and in her pilgrim's garb as usual, she made her way there.

The lords and ladies were gathered at the count's palace,

ready to take their places at table. With her two little children in her arms, and in her humble gown, Gillette walked into the great hall. From one man to another she went, until at last she found the count, at whose feet she cast herself.

"My lord," she said, weeping, "I am your unfortunate wife, so long an outcast in the world, that you might come back home. I am here to beg you, in God's name, to keep your promise in the tasks you set me, by those two knights I sent you. Look, here in my arms I have not only one son of your blood, but two, and see, here is your ring on my finger. The time has now come, when you must take me to you as your wife, according to your pledge."

The count could not get over his amazement at her words. He knew the ring, and his children, too, who were so like him; still he asked: "How could it have been?"

The countess narrated the whole story, as it had happened, to the astonishment of the count and the whole assembly, and he could not but admit the truth of what she told. Seeing her perseverance and wisdom, and two such handsome boys, out of consideration for his promise and the pleasure of his lords and ladies, who were pleading with him to take her and cherish her as his wife, he raised up the countess and embraced her. Then and there, he acknowledged her his lawful wife, and the two children as his own, had her dressed in rich garments befitting her rank and to the joy of his whole court and the rest of his subjects, he declared a holiday for that day and many another. Thenceforth, he honored her as his wife and loved and cherished her above all else.

✳

## THE TENTH STORY

*Alibech becomes a recluse, and Rustico, a monk, teaches her how to put the devil back in hell. Then, when she is taken away from Thebais, she becomes the wife of Neherbale.*

DIONEO HAD LISTENED ATTENTIVELY TO THE QUEEN'S STORY, AND seeing that it was over and he alone remained, he proceeded with a roguish smile, without waiting to be asked:

Perhaps you've never heard, most gracious ladies, how the devil is put back into hell, so I'm going to tell you, without getting too far from the spirit of to-day's story-telling. Besides, the information may help you save your souls, and also make you realize that, though Love more willingly frequents gay palaces and downy chambers than humble cots, he does not fail, for all that, to assert his power in the recesses of the forests, and the bleak mountains, and solitary caves. Indeed, we might truly conclude that all things are subject to his dominion. To the story, then.

Once upon a time, there lived a very rich man in the city of Capsa, Barbary, who had, among other children, a young, pretty, and very charming daughter whose name was Alibech. Of course, she was not a Christian, but when she heard the praises of the Christian faith from the mouths of many of the gentile inhabitants of the town, and the delight of serving God, she asked one of them how He might best be served with the least trouble. "They best serve God," he answered, "who flee from the things of the world, like those good people who take refuge in the desert solitudes of Thebais."

The girl, who was only fourteen years old or thereabouts, and very ingenuous at that, stole away all alone the following morning, in search of the desert of Thebais, without telling anyone about her intention. It was no reasoned urge that led her on, but a mere childish whim, and pricked onward by it, she reached those lonely places some days later, after great hardship.

At last she spied a little hovel at a distance, and going toward it, found a holy man standing at the threshold. He was astonished to see her there, and asked her what on earth she was seeking. She was inspired by God, she answered him, yearning to be of service to Him, and in search of someone to show her how best to serve Him. The pious worthy saw how young she was, and how pretty, and was seized with fear that if he let her stay, the devil might work him mischief. Praising her good intention, he regaled her with roots, herbs, wild apples and dates and a drink of water. Then, "Daughter," said he, "there's a holy man not so far from here who's a much better teacher for what you require, than I could ever be. Go, my dear, and seek him out." At that, he showed her the way. When she came to the holy gentleman, he received her with the selfsame words, until finally, as she proceeded, she came to the cell of a young sprig of a hermit by the name of Rustico, a devout youth, and the soul of sanctity. Alibech made the same request of him, that she had made of the others.

Now he wished to put his firmness of will to a stringent test, and did not send her away like his brethren, but kept her with him in his cell. At nightfall, he prepared her a little bed of palm leaves and told her to lie on it. She obeyed.

Before long, the surge of temptation began its assault upon his powers of resistance. Alas! it had, by far, the advantage over him! It was hardly worthwhile to keep up the struggle, so turning right about, Rustico yielded himself up, vanquished. Soon he flung pious meditations, prayers and mortifications to the winds and fell mentally to dallying with visions of the girl's youth and loveliness. Moreover, he set about devising ways and means of approaching her, and obtaining what he wanted, without rousing in her mind any suspicion of his lecherous purpose. Paving the way with different questions, he learned that she had never been intimate with a man, and was indeed as innocent as she seemed. Accordingly, he realized that the only way to get to her, was to make her believe she was doing it all in the service of God. To begin with, he showed her very eloquently what a terrible enemy of Almighty God was the devil; later, he gave her to understand that the most pleasing service she could render the Lord, was to put back the devil in the hell to which He had condemned him.

"And how do you do that?" asked the girl.

"You'll know it soon enough," Rustico replied, "but you must do whatever you see me do."

At that, he flung off the few clothes he wore and remained stark naked. Alibech followed his example. Then he fell on his knees, as though he were about to pray, and had her do likewise, facing him. At this juncture, Rustico flared with hotter desire on seeing her so beautiful, and his flesh grew stiff. Alibech stared, full of wonderment at the sight.

"Rustico," she asked, "what is the thing you have there, sticking out like that, which I have not?"

"Ah, daughter," said Rustico, "this is the devil I told you about. Look at him! See? He's giving me so much trouble that I can scarcely bear it!"

"Praise be to God," exclaimed the girl. "I see now how much better off I am! I haven't any such devil!"

"You're right," said Rustico. "but you have something else I haven't, in place of this devil."

"Ooh, really!" said Alibech. "And what can it be?"

"It's hell itself, you have," replied Rustico. "I'm sure God sent you here for the good of my soul, because when this devil here insists on giving me so much trouble, you could be of great comfort to me, if you'd only have pity, and let me put him back into hell. You'll also be doing the Lord a pleasure and a service, if, as you say, you really came to this desert for that purpose."

Very earnestly Alibech answered: "Well, father, since I've this hell, you may as well put him back any time you please."

"God bless you, daughter," said Rustico. "Let's proceed to it immediately, then, and put him in, so that he'll give me some peace."

As he spoke, he led the girl to one of their little pallets, and showed her what position to take in order to lock up that accursed of God. Alibech had never yet put any kind of devil into hell, and for the first time felt a little pain, which made her say: "I'm sure, father, that devil of yours must be a terror and a real enemy of God. Why, even hell itself, not to mention the rest of us, resents it when he's put back in it!"

"Daughter," said Rustico, "it'll not always be like that." Indeed, to prevent its happening, they put the devil back into hell on six occasions before they ventured to leave the bed, until the poor wretch had his pride so thrashed out of his head, that for the time being he was quite willing to remain in peace. Many a time thereafter they returned to the task, and as the girl went on, yielding herself obediently to it, she began to take a liking to the game.

"It's just beginning to dawn on me," she remarked, "what those good men of Capsa meant, when they said it was such a delightful thing to serve God. I can't for the life of me think of anything else I ever did, that gave me as much pleasure and joy as putting the devil back in hell. Do you know, I really think all people are fools, who spend their time at anything but the service of God."

Very often, therefore, she would come to Rustico, saying: "Father, I came here to serve God, not to idle away my time. Come, let's get busy putting the devil back in hell."

Sometimes, while they were engaged in it, she would remark: "Do you know, Rustico, I wonder why the devil ever escapes from hell! If he remained there as gladly as hell welcomes and holds him, he'd never get out of it."

By dint of Alibech's frequent invitations, urging Rustico to the service of God, the stuffings were so knocked out of his jerkin that he shivered with cold whereas another would have sweated; and he would admonish her that the devil was not to be punished or put back into hell, except when he stuck up his head with pride. "We've taken him down such a peg, by the grace of God," he added, "that he does nothing but pray the Lord to be left in peace."

So for a while, he succeeded in silencing Alibech's importunities; but when she saw he did not invite her to put the devil back in hell, she said to him, one day: "Listen, Rustico, if that devil of yours has had the stuffings knocked out of him, this hell of mine doesn't give me a moment's rest. I think it's up to you to help me quiet the fury of my hell, the way I helped you to lower the pride of your devil!"

Rustico's sole nourishment consisted of roots and water, and he could therefore respond but poorly to the demands made upon him. Quite a lot of devils, he told her, were needed to quench hell, but he would do his best to help her, anyhow. Now and then, therefore, he would gratify her, but so infrequently, that it was like throwing a bean into a lion's mouth. Alibech thought she was not doing her duty by the Lord as assiduously as she desired, and complained, oftener than not.

However, while this argument was in progress between Rustico's devil, that could not, and Alibech's hell that would, a fire broke out in Capsa that destroyed Alibech's father in his own house, together with all his children and the rest of his family, leaving her sole heir to all his possessions. A young man, called Neherbale, who had consumed all his goods, burning the candle at both ends, learned somehow that Alibech was alive, and set out to look for her. He found her, just in time to prevent the court from appropriating her father's wealth, according to the law regarding the property of men dying without successor, and to Rustico's great relief, though much against her will, he took her back to Capsa, married her himself, and became joint heir to her father's considerable possessions.

There, when the women asked her, before Neherbale had lain with her, what she did in the desert to serve God, she replied she did His service by putting the devil back into hell, adding that Neherbale had been guilty of a grave sin by taking her away from so holy an occupation.

"Why, how do you put the devil back into hell?" the women asked her. Alibech showed them how it was done, by words and gestures. They laughed loud and long about it, and it's a common joke among them to this day.

"Don't take on about it, dear child," they consoled her. "For that matter, we manage pretty well even here. Neherbale himself will serve the good Lord well enough, with you."

They repeated the story to one another all over the city, until it became a popular saw, to the effect that the most pleasant service one could do the Lord, was to put the devil back in hell. The saying has even reached us across the sea, and is current to this day.

As for you, dear young ladies, who are badly in need of God's grace, learn to put the devil back in hell, since it's highly agreeable to the Lord, and a joy to both parties—besides, much good might come of it.

Time and time again, Dioneo's story had made the blushing ladies break into a laugh, so very droll and amusing did his words appear to them. When he had reached the end, however, the queen knew the close of her day's rule had come, and taking the wreath from her head, laid it on Filostrato's hair, with a gracious gesture.

"We'll soon discover," she said, "whether the wolf will know how to guide the lambs, better than the lambs have guided the wolves."

Laughing, he capped her words with, "if you had followed my way of thinking, the wolves would have shown the lambs how to put the devil in hell, every bit as well as Rustico taught Alibech. So you'd better not call us wolves, for you've been no lambs. Well, anyhow, since the government has been delivered over into my hands, I'll do the best I can."

"Listen, Filostrato," cried Neifile, "maybe you'll learn sense, after you try to teach us, the way Masetto of Lamporecchio learned of the nuns, and get back your speech as he did, only after your bones had learned to play a tune without a master."

Realizing that he received as good as he gave, Filostrato laid jesting aside, and settled down to rule the little kingdom committed to his care. He sent for the steward and made inquiries about the state of things. Then, prudently ordering whatever he thought advisable and most pleasing to the company during the period of his regency, he said, addressing himself to the women:

"Adorable ladies, it's been my misfortune from the time I was able to distinguish good from evil, to fall a slave to the loveliness of some one or other of your sex. Whether I obeyed the promptings of love, showing myself humble and obedient, or whether I followed him in all his ways as well as I was able, nothing did me any good, for I was soon discarded for another. So I have gone from bad to worse, and so I think it will be, to the end of my days. Tomorrow, then, I wish you would tell stories *à propos* of nothing but what is nearest my case, that is, *of those whose loves have ended unhappily,* for I expect mine to have no different end, as time goes on. It wasn't for nothing that the name you know me by was bestowed on me by a certain lady who knew all too well what it meant."

On delivering his speech, he rose and gave them leave to do as they wished until supper-time.

The garden was so lovely and pleasant that not one of them chose to leave it in the hope of finding more delight elsewhere. The sun was much more temperate now, and made it possible for some of the party to chase the kids, rabbits and other tame beasts that ran wild in it, and who had skipped among them a hundred times or more, while they had been engaged in their story-telling.

Dioneo and Fiammetta began to sing the ballad of Guglielmo and the Lady of Vergiu; Filomena and Pamfilo sat down to a game of chess. What with one thing and another, time passed and supper-hour drew nigh. The tables were laid about the handsome fountain, and there the company supped that evening, as delighted as could be. Filostrato had no wish to depart from the precedent set by the two queens before him, and when they had risen from the tables, he requested Lauretta to begin a dance and sing a song.

"Sire," she said, "I know no songs but my own, and not one of them seems appropriate enough to please such a jolly gathering. But if you insist on hearing one of them, I'll gladly sing it."

"Nothing you can do could be other than lovely and charming," said the king. "Sing whatever song you have at your command!"

In a mellow voice, but rather sorrowfully, Lauretta began her song, as her companions took up the refrain:

> "No maid more cause than I
>     Can have to mourn her fate
> And for her love all unrequited sigh!

For He who moves the stars and firmament
   Created me to shine
Pleasing with kindness and delight. He lent
   Me grace and good and loveliness divine
That I His true intent
   Might manifest, and of His work a sign.
But mortal minds decline
   To see His worth in me:
      The work misprized, the worth they do deny.

Once one did come, and dearly did he prize
   The virgin maid that tight
He clasped to him, and in whose ardent eyes
   His mind and body flamed. Then all the flight
Of time in longing sighs
   And tenderness he spent, and it winged light
   The while to his delight
     I yielded me entire.
       But now, alas! lorn of all love am I!

Then one did come who proud before me stood,
   A youth all overbold,
Himself renowning for his hardihood
   And gentle birth. He took me, but behold!
His jealousy I rued!
   Thus now, alas! great are my woes, untold;
   For me one man would hold
     That am decreed to be
      The joy of all . . . but I cannot comply!

Alack, in vain I curse the luckless day
   When but to change my dress
I told him 'Ay,'—so fair in dark array
   I found me, and so gay! But now distress
Courts me in this, alway;
   While some there are, cause me unhappiness
   Deeming my virtue less
     In my resplendent robes.
      Oh, that ere this, my lot had been to die!

O my beloved, that solaced me more
   Than other man a maid,

Now that before God's face you stand, implore
   Of Him who you and me together made,
Pity of one that sore
     Grieves and forgets not. Let it not be said
     The radiant flame is dead
       That kindled you to passion,
          And grant that we may joy in it on high!"

Here Lauretta's song was over. All of them had paid special heed to it, but interpreted it differently, some going so far as to think it meant, according to the Milanese, that a good hog is to be preferred to a jolly lass. Others, however, gave it a more ethereal, better and truer significance, which it is not necessary to mention here.

Later, the king had a number of torches lighted on the flower-studded grass, and requested other songs, until each rising star had begun to set, when, thinking it was time to sleep, he wished them all a good night and sent them off to their respective apartments.

# THE FOURTH DAY

*

DEAREST LADIES, DUE BOTH TO THE WORDS I HEARD OF WISE MEN, and the different things I myself had observed and read, I had labored under the impression that the bitter, blustering wind of envy could only strike the loftiest towers or highflung tree-tops. But I find that I have been wrong in my belief. Whenever I fled the fury of that rabid gust, as I have ever struggled to do, I sought refuge not only on the plains, but in the deepest lowlands, as anyone can see for himself, who takes the trouble to glance through these stories of mine. They are not only written in the common vernacular, in prose, and without my name as the author, but they are also cast in the simplest and quietest possible style. Still, in spite of it all, I have not been able to avoid being furiously tossed about, almost uprooted, and torn to shreds, by the claws of envy. Indeed, too well can I appreciate the truth of the sages' observation, that only misery is without envy here below.

There have been various individuals, prudent ladies, who have observed on reading these stories, that I am much too fond of you, and that it isn't decorous of me to take such delight in pleasing you, and keeping you in good spirits. Some have even inferred worse things, from my praise of your sex. Others besides, anxious to speak with maturer wisdom, have ventured that it is not fitting for a man of my age to rush in pursuit of such nonsense, meaning my preoccupation with women and their en-

tertainment. Still others, pretending great concern for my reputation, have gone so far as to say I'd be wiser to spend my
time with the muses on Parnassus, than to fritter it away among
you, with such trifles. Spite, and not wisdom, has prompted
another group to remark that I'd be showing more common
sense worrying where my next loaf of bread is to come from,
than chasing after these straws and feeding upon air. And still
others go out of their way in quite another fashion, to belittle
my work and say that the events I relate are quite different
from my representation of them.

Alas, noble ladies, it is by such blasts and sharp, cruel fangs
that I am tormented, trying to serve you, yes, agonized and
stabbed to the quick! God knows I listen to them all, and accept
them with an open mind; and although my defense should really
fall to you, I have no intention of sparing myself the trouble.
Indeed without wasting on them the lengthy answer they deserve
to have, I shall hasten to hush their buzzing about my ears
with a pleasantry. For if, at this point, when I have scarcely
reached a third of my work, they are so numerous and so boldly
presumptuous, I'm sure that by the time I have reached the end,
they will have so increased and multiplied, if left scot free, that
their slightest effort might overwhelm me. Then not even your
powers could save me, considerable though they be. Nevertheless, before I make reply to any of my critics, I should like to
tell a story myself—not a complete one, for I don't want to be
accused of thrusting any tale of mine among those of the fine
company I have presented to you. No, I shall tell only part of
one, that its very incompleteness may show, clearly enough, that
it does not belong with the rest.

Well, then, critics of mine—a long time ago there lived in
our city a man by the name of Filippo Balducci, of humble
parentage but rich, skilful and experienced in everything his
circumstances required. He was married to a woman whom he
dearly loved, and who reciprocated his love as fervently, and so
they lived peacefully together, doing their best to give each
other joy in everything.

But as it happened, the good lady died, following the common lot, and left as sole reminder of herself their only child, a
boy perhaps two years of age. Filippo was as griefstricken at the
death of his wife as any man might be, having lost the one thing
he loved best in the world; therefore, when he found himself
deprived of his dearest companion, he thought there was no

longer room for him in this temporal life, and resolved to devote himself to the service of God, together with his little son.

Accordingly, he gave everything away to the poor, and went off as soon as he could to Mount Asinaio, where he found refuge for himself and his son in a tiny cell. For a long time they lived a holy life of fasting and prayer together, Filippo taking care never to make the least mention of any worldly matter to his son, or to show him anything of the world, that nothing might distract him from his pious service. He would always talk to him of the glories of life everlasting, of God and the saints, and taught him nothing but prayers. In this fashion, he brought up the boy for many years, never allowing him to leave his cell or lay eyes upon anyone but himself.

It was the good man's custom, now and again, to visit Florence and get whatever he needed for his simple life, from the friends of God; then he would return to his cell. The boy, by this time, had reached the age of eighteen, and Filippo was already old. One day his son asked him where he was going. Filippo told him.

"You are old now, father," said the boy, "and you can't stand much hard work. Why don't you take me to Florence with you, some time? You can introduce me to those godly friends of yours, and then, since I'm young and can bear fatigue better than you, I can go to Florence for our needs, whenever you say, while you stay at home."

The good man reflected that this son of his was now quite grown up, and so habituated to the service of God that worldly temptation would with difficulty seduce him. "The boy is quite right," he thought, and the next time he had to make the trip, he took him along.

At the sight of the palaces, houses, cathedrals and all the wonderful things a city contains, the youngster was filled with awe, for he could not remember ever having seen anything of the sort. Eagerly, he asked what this was, and what that was called, and when his father told him, he would beam with joy and ask about something else. While this was going on, the lad full of curiosity, and his father answering him, they came across a party of lovely young girls dressed in their Sunday best, on their way home from a wedding.

"And what may those be?" asked the boy.

"Hush! Lower your eyes and don't look at them," cried his father. "They're wickedness itself!"

"And what are they called, this wickedness?" inquired the boy.

The father had no wish to stir up fleshly desire in the youth's susceptible mind, or waken him to an appetite that would do him no good, and instead of saying they were women, he replied: "They're called young geese."

Wonder of wonders! The stripling, who had never before set eyes on a woman, forgot all about the fine palaces, the oxen and horses; he no longer cared a straw for the donkeys, and money, and whatever else he had seen. "Father, father!" he cried, eagerly. "Do see to it, please, that I get one of those young geese."

"Hush, my son," admonished his father. "I tell you they're wickedness itself!"

At that the lad asked, "Oh, is that the way wickedness looks?"

"Yes," said the man; but the boy went on, "I don't know what you're talking about, father, or why you say these things are wickedness. As for me, I've never clapped eyes on anything so pretty, or so wonderful as these creatures. They're ever so much nicer than the painted angels you've shown me so often. Come, father, if you really love me, you must try to carry off one of these young geese for me, and I'll take it home and feed it something in its pretty mouth."

"No, that I will never do," said his father. "You've no idea what mouth it is you have to feed!" However, he had to avow nature was much stronger than his wisdom, and he regretted ever bringing his son to Florence.

So much for the story. Now let me turn to those for whose benefit I related it. Some of my critics say, young ladies, that I am wrong to dedicate myself to such an extent in seeking your pleasure, and claim that I go out of my way trying to win your favor. I make no bones about their charges. Yes, I certainly do love you, and admit I do my best to please you. Is it any wonder, I ask them? Let's discount the delicious kisses I have often enjoyed of you, sweetest ladies, and your tender embraces, and the amorous bliss of our bodies' union. It ought to be enough to have seen, and still be blessed, with your pretty ways, your rapturous loveliness, your charm, and most of all, your womanly perfection—considering that even a youth who had been nurtured and reared on a wild and desert hilltop, between the narrow walls of a tiny cell, with no other human companionship than that of his father, no sooner saw you, than he desired you, demanded nothing other than you, pursued only you, in the promptings of his love. Will they then blame me, stab and tear me to pieces between them, if I, whose body heaven created on purpose to love you, if I, who gave up my soul to you since my boyhood, under the influence of your eyes' gentle light, the mellowness of your sweet words, and the flame arising from your swooning sighs,—will they still blame me if I love you, or do my best to please you, when we consider that you charmed a little hermit-boy, above everything else,—a mere undeveloped stripling, a wild creature, I might say? Of course it can't be denied, that those who do not love you have no desire to be loved in return. But such people, like those who rebuke me, neither feel nor know the sweetness or power of wholesome love. I shall not bother my head about them.

As for those others who inveigh against my age—they simply show their own ignorance of the truism that though the leek has a white head, it has a green tail. To these worthies I say, laying jesting aside, that as long as I live, I shall never think it shameful to ingratiate those beings whom Guido Cavalcanti and Dante Alighieri honored, and whose approval they prized in their old age, yes, and Cino da Pistoja, too, when he was a very reverend old man. If I cared to deviate from the customary rules of argumentation, I could quote plenty of historical facts, full of instances of noble oldsters who did their utmost, in their hoariest years, to win the favor of the ladies. But if my friends the critics are ignorant of them, let them go and learn them for themselves.

That I should remain with the muses on Parnassus, is good enough advice, I must admit. Nevertheless, since we can neither stay with the muses, nor they with us, can a man be blamed for taking leave of them, if he delights in the sight of creatures who resemble them? The muses are members of the fair sex, and although women cannot justly be ranked with them, still, they look like them, at first glance. Therefore, even if I liked women for no other reason, that should be sufficient. There's something else besides: women have been the reason for my writing a thousand verses, where the muses never gave me occasion for writing a single one. They were of great assistance to me, it's true, and showed me how to compose those thousand verses. Perhaps even in the writing of these stories, humble though they be, they may have come, sometimes, to keep me company for the sake of the women, or in appreciation of the resemblance they bear them. It is for that reason that I don't wander as far from Mount Parnassus or the muses, in the stories I weave, as some would have it.

But what shall we say to those who take such pity on my starveling state and advise me to see about obtaining my bread? I have no idea, except that whenever I wonder what their answer would be if I were to ask them for some in my need, they would say, I am sure: "Go and look for it among your fairy tales!"

True enough! Much more did the poets discover among their tales, than many rich men among their treasures. Many of them, following their dreams, made their era flourish, when on the contrary, others who sought after more bread than they needed, died in bitterness. What more can I say? Let these gentlemen cast me off when I ask for bread, though, God be praised, I have no need of it yet. Moreover, if I should ever feel the pinch of necessity, I know, like the Apostle, how to take abundance and how to suffer need: so let no one be more tender of myself than I am.

Now for those who say that these events were not as I represent them: I should be very much obliged to them if they brought me the originals, so that if I found they did not agree with my writings, I might grant the justice of their objection and try to improve. However, while they have nothing but words to show, I shall leave them to their opinion, and pursue my own, repeating to them what they say to me.

I think I shall call a halt in my confutation for the present, and say that, armed with patience, the help of God and your support, in which I rely, I shall go onward with my work, my back to this wind, letting it rage as it will. I know it can only be with me as it is with the motes of dust. A whirlwind cannot move them from the earth, or if it does, it blows them high, often laying them on the heads of men, on the crowns of kings and mighty emperors, and sometimes even on the crests of lofty palaces and soaring towers; then, when they fall again, they can sink no lower than the place from which they were raised.

If I have ever given myself up to please you in anything, I shall now endeavor to do so, more than before. I know that nobody can with justice say anything against it other than that both I, and others like me, who love you, labor only in the way of nature, whose laws it takes superhuman strength to violate. And such violation is very often not only in vain, but injurious to the foolhardy wretch. I have not that strength, let me confess it, nor do I wish to have it, in this respect. Indeed, even if it were mine, I'd sooner lend it to someone else, than employ it myself. Let my backbiters be silent, then, and if they cannot feel the heat of passion, let them live in their lunacy and the enjoyment of their peculiar delights—depraved appetites, I should say—leaving me in peace to enjoy mine in this brief space that is allotted us.

But we must now return, lovely ladies, to the place we set out from, and follow the established order, for we have strayed far and wide indeed.

The sun had already frightened to paleness every star of heaven, and banished the damp shadow of night from the earth, when Filostrato rose and awakened all his company. Together, they went into the pleasant garden and amused themselves until dinner-time, when they enjoyed their meal where they had had their supper the night before. Later, they arose from the nap they had taken when the sun was at its zenith, and resumed their places as usual near the playful fountain.

Then Filostrato signaled Fiammetta, to inaugurate the day's story-telling, and she began with pleasing femininity, without waiting to be told:

✳

## THE FIRST STORY

*Tancred, Prince of Salerno, has his daughter's lover murdered, and sends her his heart in a golden goblet; she pours poisoned water over it, drains it, and dies.*

IT'S A DOLEFUL ENOUGH THEME OUR KING HAS GIVEN US TO DIS-course about. Here we came to have a good time, and we're obliged to tell of other people's woes! The worst of it is, that they can't be told without wringing the heart of the one who tells them, and afflicting those who listen. I suppose he selected the subject to somewhat temper the merriment of the last few days; but whatever the reason that prompted him, it's not for me to go against his pleasure, and I shall therefore tell you a pathetic story—a very unhappy one, to be sure, and worthy of your tears.

A humane ruler, and a naturally merciful man was Tancred,

Prince of Salerno, and he would have enjoyed that reputation to this day, had he not stained his hands with the blood of two lovers in his old age. He had no other child in the course of his long life, than an only daughter—(though it would have been far better if he had had none at all) whom he loved more dearly than any girl has ever been loved by her father. She had long passed the age when a girl should be given a husband, yet Tancred's love was so great, that he could not bear the thought of parting from her, and kept her with him, a spinster. At last, however, he resigned himself to marry her to a son of the Duke of Capua, with whom she scarcely went to live, than she was widowed of him, and returned to her father.

Ghismonda was as beautiful of form and feature as any woman alive. Besides, she was young and frolicsome, and with more wisdom in her head than might be expected of a woman. As she continued living with her doting father, in the midst of such luxury as befitted a lady of her rank, she remarked that, in his selfish love of her, he took little trouble to find her another husband. As for her, she was too sensitive to give him the slightest hint, and therefore resolved that it was up to her to find, if she could, a fine lover, with whom she might take her secret pleasure.

There were many gentlemen, of noble intellect and otherwise, whom she saw about her father's court—the habitués of all princely places, and as she studied their manners and attitudes, she was attracted by a young valet of her sire's, Guiscardo by name. He was humble enough of birth, but so far excelled all other courtiers in obvious merit and gentlemanliness of behaviour, that Ghismonda singled him out for her affection, burning ever secretly with love, the more frequently she saw him, and every day discerning more virtues in him. Guiscardo, sprightly and alert enough, became aware of this passion of hers, and in turn he so enshrined her in his heart and mind, that he had no room for anything else.

So they continued loving each other in secret. Now Ghismonda yearned for nothing in the world so much as to be alone with her lover, but as she did not wish to reveal her secret to anyone in the world, she thought of a novel subterfuge to tell him how it could be done. Writing a letter, in which she gave him complete instructions of what he was to do the following day in order to gain access to her, she slipped it into the hollow of a cane and handed it to him, saying with a laugh: "Here, this will make a good blow-pipe for your servant, when she kindles the fire tonight."

Guiscardo took it, knowing very well she had not given it to him with a little jesting remark for no reason at all, and taking leave of her, he returned home. He turned over the cane and examined it closely; it was split. Opening it, he found her letter, read it over, and taking stock of what he had to do, was as happy as could be. Immediately, he made provisions for going to her, according to her instructions.

Near the prince's palace, there had long been a cave, hewn ages past out of the rock of the mountain-side. No light ever entered it, except for what dim rays could penetrate a tunnel that had been bored through the mountain; but even that tunnel had been closed up by overgrowing thorns and weeds, during the long period the cave had been abandoned. Now there was a way of reaching that hollow, by means of a secret stair, sealed by a massive door in one of the ground floor rooms of Ghismonda's apartment; and so completely had the knowledge of this stair been wiped out of people's minds through its long disuse, that hardly anyone recalled its existence. Yet Love, to whose eyes nothing is so secret but that he finds it out, had brought it back to the lovelorn woman's mind. Many days had she toiled and labored by herself, to avoid arousing suspicion, using whatever tools she could lay her hands on, before she had succeeded in forcing open that door. Then, descending all alone into the cave, she discovered the tunnel. It was through that passageway that she instructed Guiscardo to come to her, and gave him an idea of how high it must be from the outer opening to the cave bottom.

Directly, Guiscardo set about making preparations to reach his love. He provided himself with a rope, knotted and twisted into a ladder suitable for him to go up and down, dressed himself in a leather jacket to protect himself from the thorns and briers, and set out for the tunnel, without giving an inkling of his movements. One end of the ladder he fastened to a massive stump that had grown over the tunnel's orifice, and lowering himself into the cave, he waited for Ghismonda to come.

Next morning, on the pretext that she wanted to sleep, Ghismonda sent away all her companions, locked herself in her apartment, opened the heavy door and went down into the cave, where she found Guiscardo waiting. They greeted each other joyfully, and together mounted to her room, where they remained in the height of happiness a good part of the day. Later, taking prudent measures to keep their love a secret, Guiscardo returned to the cave, while she shut the door upon him and then joined her companions outside. At nightfall, Guiscardo climbed up the ladder of rope, stole out of the aperture by which he had entered, and returned home. But once he had learned the way, he followed it again and again as time went on.

Alas! Fortune was galled at so great and continued a pleasure, and by a tragic misfortune turned the lovers' bliss to bitter weeping!

It was Tancred's custom to come alone, now and then, to Ghismonda's chamber, chat with her a while, and then take his leave. One day, after dinner, he paid one of his customary visits, but as Ghismonda was in one of the garden arbors with all her ladies-in-waiting, he entered her room, unnoticed by anyone, and waited, not to interrupt her pleasure. The windows were closed, and the curtains lowered over her bed. He sat down on a stool at the foot of it, leaning his head against it, and then pulled the curtain over himself. In that position, as though he had studiously contrived it, he fell asleep.

Unfortunately, Ghismonda had sent for Guiscardo to come to her that day, and leaving her maids in the garden, she stole away into her room, shutting herself in, without observing the presence of anybody else. Then, opening the secret door, she admitted Guiscardo, who had been waiting for her, and both got into bed as usual. While they were playing together and taking their delight, Tancred awoke at the sound, and saw what his daughter and Guiscardo were doing. Grief, more cruel than any he had ever experienced, came over him. At first, he would have cried out at them in wrath, but he thought better of it, and decided to remain in his hiding-place, if possible, that he might subsequently carry out with greater secrecy and less dishonor to himself, the vengeful resolution he had already taken.

For a long time, the two lovers remained together, as usual, without discovering Tancred, and when they thought it time to part, left the bed, Guiscardo returning to the cave, and Ghismonda going out of her chamber. Tancred, too, went out, but not by the door. In spite of his age, he let himself down into the garden by one of the windows, and stricken to the heart with bitter grief, slunk to his own room, without being observed. That very night, at about the time of one's first sleep, he ordered Guiscardo to be seized by two men as he was coming out of the tunnel, encumbered by his leathern suit, and had him privately brought before him.

"Ah, Guiscardo," he said, his voice quavering with sorrow when he saw him, "my kindness to you deserved better than the outrage and shame you have inflicted upon me in the thing I hold most dear, as I saw to-day, with these old eyes of mine."

Guiscardo could make no answer but, "Love is more powerful than either you or I."

Tancred commanded him to be imprisoned and guarded in one of the rooms of the castle, and his wish was carried out.

Next day, after dinner, Tancred went on one of his customary visits to his daughter's chamber, his mind teeming with all kinds of plans which he had devised. Sending for her, still in ignorance of the event, he shut himself in with her and said, weeping: "I thought I knew your virtue and honesty, Ghismonda, my daughter, and not for a moment would I have believed you capable of yielding to any man alive, or even of entertaining the thought, unless he were your lawful husband. No, I would not have believed it, even if it had been dinned into my ears. But I have seen it with my own eyes, and the memory will embitter to the last the remaining years which my old age still reserves for me! Oh God! If only you had chosen someone of your own rank, since you had to succumb to such dishonor! Of all my courtiers, you had to choose the meanest, this Guiscardo, a low-born knave whom we brought up from childhood, almost out of charity, I might say! You have wounded me to the soul in this, my child—I scarcely know what to do! I know well enough how to deal with Guiscardo. Yes, I had him seized last night as he was leaving the tunnel—he's now in prison. But as for you, God only knows, for I cannot think! Love pleads for you on the one hand, the love I've always cherished for you, deeper than any father ever bore his daughter. On the other, I am torn by righteous wrath at your unworthy folly. My love begs your forgiveness; my wrath would have me turn cruelly upon you, against every instinct of my being! But before I take another step, I want to hear what you have to say in your defense."

He bowed his head at the last words, and sobbed like an injured child.

While listening to her father, Ghismonda realized that not only had her love been discovered, but that Guiscardo had been captured, and a sorrow so boundless took possession of her, that more than once she would have given vent to her womanly weakness in sobs and tears. But her proud spirit conquered. Controlling her face with remarkable strength of will, rather than plead in her behalf, she inwardly resolved to have done with life, since, as she thought, her lover was dead. It was not as a woman, grieving because she was being punished for her guilt, but with the dry eyes and calm countenance of the recklessly brave, that she answered her father.

"Sir," she said, "it is not my intention either to deny my fault, or to ask to be forgiven. Denial would do me no good, and I will not have your forgiveness. Nothing will persuade me to be beholden to your mercy and affection. I had rather confess the truth, first to defend my honor by revealing the just provocation that led to my love, and then to vindicate it by bravely following the promptings of my soul with deeds. It is true I loved Guiscardo. I still love him, and while I live—which will not be long—I shall continue loving him. Yes, even after death, if there is love beyond the grave, I shall not cease adoring him. It was not my womanly weakness that induced me to love, but your indifference to finding me a mate. But above all, it was Guiscardo's worth. You ought to have known, sir, that since you are a man of flesh and blood, you could only engender a daughter of flesh and blood, not of stone or iron. You ought to have borne in mind, for all your white hairs, how many and varied are the laws of youth, and with what power they assail us. Even though you're a man, and exercised yourself in the hardships of a soldier's career during the best years of your life, you still should not have been ignorant of the temptations idleness and luxury put in the way of all, the old as well as the young.

"I am as you made me, of flesh and blood, and I've lived so little that I am still young. For both these reasons, I am overflowing with desire for love and passion, all the more because through my only marriage, I experienced how sweet is the delight to be found in their fulfilment. It was impossible for me to curb the yearning that impelled me to them: I fell in love. I will not deny that when I did, I put all my faculties to work, that no dishonor might fall on either you or me, by my surrender to the temptation that lured me to a very natural sin. Love, pitiful of my plight, and kindly Fortune, both had found a secret way which they pointed out to me, and so I gained my desires, unknown to all the world. This I do not deny, whoever may have informed you of it, or by whatever means you came to the discovery.

"As for Guiscardo, I did not take him for my lover at random, as many women might have done. Only after deliberate consideration I chose him above all others, and won him to me, my mind fully conscious all the while, of what I was doing. Most prudently we persevered, he and I, and for a long time, I had full joy of my desires. Now, following common prejudice rather than truth, you would blame me all the more bitterly, it seems, not so much because I dared to sin by falling in love, but because I gave my heart to a man of lower station than myself. As though you would not have been every bit as wrathful had I chosen a nobleman to fall in love with! Don't you see it is not my fault you blame, but Fortune's? For all too often she elevates the undeserving, leaving the worthiest in the dust.

"But let us put this aside for the present, and briefly examine the first principles of things. You will observe that we are all made of one and the same flesh, and derive our souls, with all their equal forces, powers and virtues, from the one Maker. It was merit alone that first differentiated us, who were all created equal. Those who had a greater share of it, and took advantage of it, were called noble; the rest remained not noble. In spite of the fact that contrary usage has tended to thrust this law into the background, it has not yet disappeared from nature or innate good breeding. The man who acts righteously and well, proves himself a gentleman, and whoever calls him otherwise, is himself at fault.

"Look at all your courtiers! Examine their worth, their qualities and breeding, and then compare them with Guiscardo's. An unprejudiced judgment, free from hatred on your part, would call him the gentleman, and them the lackeys. I judged of Guiscardo's virtues, not from anything anyone had said of him, but from your own estimation of him, and the testimony of my eyes. Who was ever so lavish with praise of Guiscardo as yourself, when you lauded him for all the virtues becoming a gentleman? And you were perfectly justified. There was nothing for which you ever praised him, that I did not see him warrant by nobler deeds—unless my eyes deceived me—and more marvelously than your praise could have expressed. Even if I had been deceived, it would have been through you. Will you insist that I gave myself up to a lackey? You'll not be telling the truth. But if you were to say I gave myself to a poor man, it might be admitted to your dishonor, for not having better known how to reward your worthy servant as he deserved. Poverty does not make one less of a gentleman, though wealth often does. Many a king, many a mighty prince was once in poverty, and many a man who tills the soil and tends the flocks was once possessed of great riches.

"You wonder, finally, what you should do to me. Dispel that concern from your mind. If, in your hoary age, you are resolved to do what you never did in your youth—if, I say, you insist on acting with cruelty, vent it all on my head! I have no intention of pleading for your mercy, for you are the principal cause of my sin, if you will call it so. Furthermore, I want you to bear in mind that if you don't do to me what you have done, or intend doing to Guiscardo, my own hands shall accomplish it. Now go, go and weep with the women, and then, in the excess of your cruelty, slay both him and me with one and the same blow, if you think we have deserved death!"

The prince appreciated the greatness of his daughter's soul, but nevertheless, he did not believe her to be as determined as her words seemed to indicate. He left her, dispelling all thought of doing her any violence. However, he determined to cool her burning love at another's expense, and commanded the two guards who kept Guiscardo, to strangle him the following night without making a stir, and then bring him the dead youth's heart. They did as he told them.

The morning after, the prince called for a large, precious golden goblet, and placing Guiscardo's heart in it, sent it to his daughter by a trusted servant, instructing him to say, as he offered it to her: "Your father sends this, to give you as much cheer in the thing you most love, as you gave him in what he cherished above everything."

Meanwhile Ghismonda, her firm resolve unshaken, ordered all sorts of poisonous herbs and roots to be brought her as soon as Tancred had gone, and reduced them to a violent liquid poison, so that she might have it ready, if her fears were realized. When the lackey appeared, bearing the prince's gift and delivering his words, she took the goblet, her face set bravely, and removed the cover. At the sight, she recalled her father's message, and knew past all doubt it was Guiscardo's heart she held. Lifting her face to the messenger, she said: "Nothing but a golden casket could have been good enough for such a heart. My father has acted well indeed." Then, bringing the heart to her lips, she kissed it and added: "I have always found my father's love most tender to me in everything, even in this last hour of my life. But never has he shown more affection than now. Go to him, and for this great gift, bring him the last thanks I shall ever have to offer him."

Bending over the goblet, which she held tightly in her hands, she said, gazing on the heart: "O sweetest cradle of all my joys, cursed be the cruelty of him who made me behold you with my mortal eyes! I was content to muse on you forever, with those of my mind. You have now run your course, and fulfilled the destiny Fortune set aside for you. You have reached the end, to which all men must go. Now the tribulations and toils of the world are behind you, and your very enemy has given you the resting-place your virtue merited. Nothing remains to make your farewell complete—only the tears of her you loved so well, while you lived. That they might not be denied you, God himself inspired my relentless father to send you here to me. I shall shed them for you, though I had determined to die with tearless eyes and a face unmoved. Then I shall hasten, that my soul may be united with yours, which you ever strove to keep unsullied. With whom could I journey, more happily or more confidently, to those unknown shores, than with your soul, my heart? I know it is still hovering near, gazing on the places of its happiness and mine. It loves me still . . . it is now awaiting my soul, that it loves above everything!"

She bent over the goblet, letting no sigh or sob escape her, and as she kissed the lifeless heart over and over, the tears gushed in streams from the fountains of her eyes.

The maids who surrounded her had no idea whose heart it was she held, neither could they understand the meaning of her words. Moved by emotion, they wept and pleaded with her piteously to tell them why she mourned, doing all they could to comfort her, but in vain.

At last, when she had done weeping, after shedding the tears that were the heart's due, she raised her head and dried her eyes. "Dearest heart," she said, "all my offices are now over. Nothing remains for me but to come, with my soul, to join yours on its way."

She called for the small vial containing the poison she had distilled the previous day, and emptied it into the goblet where the heart was lying, bathed in her tears. Then, without a tremor of fear, she approached her lips to it, and drained it to the last drop. She went to her bed, the goblet still fast in her hands, and composing her body modestly, laid her dead lover's heart upon her own, resigning herself to the approach of death.

In the meantime, her ladies, who had witnessed her behavior and heard her words, not knowing what it was she had drunk, sent to inform Tancred of all that had happened. He descended to her chamber at once, full of foreboding of what indeed came about, and reached it in time to see her lie down on her bed. Too late, he came to her with his words of comfort. The end was near, and when he saw, he fell to bitter weeping.

"Spare your tears, father," said she. "Save them for a less wished-for fate than this, and don't waste them on me, for I do not want them. Who, but you, has ever been known to mourn for anything he himself desired? Still, if there is a spark of the love you once bore me in your heart, grant me but one request, as a last gift. Though you opposed my living with Guiscardo, openly or in secret, still let my body lie in the sight of all, united with his, wherever you may have flung him, dead."

Grief made Tancred dumb. Ghismonda saw her end was approaching, and pressing the dead heart to her breast, she murmured: "God be with you, for I am going." Her eyes were veiled; every sense fled her body, and she departed this vale of tears.

Thus tragically, as you have heard, ended the love of Guiscardo and Ghismonda. Too late, Tancred repented of his severity. After long mourning, he had the bodies of the two lovers laid in the same tomb, and buried in state amid the general lamentation of his subjects.

# THE SECOND STORY

*Brother Alberto gives a certain woman to understand that the Angel Gabriel is in love with her, and lies with her various times in his own shape. Later he jumps out of the window of her house for fear of her in-laws, and seeks refuge in the hut of a man who leads him to the square the following day, disguised as a wild-man. There he is recognized, rescued by his friars, and imprisoned.*

FIAMMETTA'S STORY HAD MORE THAN ONCE MADE TEARS WELL IN the eyes of her companions, but now that it was over, the king remarked with set features: "I'd consider it a small price to forfeit my life for half the happiness Ghismonda enjoyed with Guiscardo, and you ladies should not wonder at it, either, considering that with every hour I live, I die a thousand deaths, without the benefit of a fraction of delight. But let's not discuss my affairs for the present. Only let Pampinea continue our storytelling with some tale as hapless in its fortunes as my own, and perhaps if she keeps up Fiammetta's strain, some balm may fall upon my smarting wounds."

Pampinea, seeing her turn had come, judged by her own emotion, rather than the king's words, what must be the state of mind of her friends, and more anxious to divert them than to please him, except in the matter of resuming the thread of narrative, she decided to tell an amusing story without going beyond the limits of the theme.

There's a proverb current among the common people, she began, that says *a wicked man who bears good fame, may play the devil and get no blame.* It's a subject for ample expatiation, and offers material enough to illustrate how great is the hypocrisy of the religious orders, and what stuff they are made of. The friars' gowns are long and wide, it's true, their faces wan with artful pallor, and their voices humble and soft whenever they want to extract your money—but just listen to the violence of their ranting whenever they reproach others for the sins they're guilty of themselves! Or hear them, as they try to convince you that your salvation is assured only by your giving and their taking! And look at their attitude toward the after-life! They don't act as though, like the rest of us, they had to attain Paradise. Oh no! They're the possessors and lords of Heaven, and when a man dies, it is for them to give him a better place or a worse, according to the amount of money he has willed their brotherhood! And so they go on, deceiving themselves, if they believe their own words, and everybody else who has faith in their preachments. If it were proper for me to unmask them as completely as they deserve, I'd show many a credulous fool what it is these fine friars really hide under their tremendously wide gowns! Would to God they were all rewarded for their lies like a certain friar Minor, not so young, at that, who was considered quite a wonder in Venice. It will give me great pleasure to tell you about him, and perhaps his story will stir your spirits to fun and laughter, since you're all so downcast at the death of Ghismonda.

Well then, my friends, there was once at Imola a man called Berto della Massa, who led a life so corrupt and evil, and bore such a bad character among the townspeople who were aware of his monstrous deeds, that there wasn't a soul among them who had the least faith in anything he said, even when he spoke the truth. Considering, therefore, that Imola was quite aware of his tricks, he moved as a last resort to Venice, the harbor of all evil, planning there to find some other way of working out his mischiefs, than he had employed so far.

Once there, pretending his conscience bothered him for all his past misdeeds, he made a show of humility and sanctimoniousness, and joined the ranks of the brothers Minor, calling himself Friar Alberto of Imola. Under the protection of his holy gown, he embarked, seemingly, on a life of austerity, making much of penance and abstinence, eating no meat and drinking no wine, that is, whenever he had none to his taste. Indeed, hardly anyone could have recognized in the wonderful preacher, the thief, pander, forger and murderer he had once been. But for all that, he had not relinquished his vices, and still indulged in them whenever he could with impunity.

Once a priest, he never failed, while celebrating the mass before the altar, to weep at the passion of the Saviour, particularly when he had a large crowd to see him, for at his wish, tears came quite readily to his eyes. Indeed, he was so successful with his tears and preachments in cozening the Venetians, that no will was drawn up, but he was named trustee and executor. Moreover, most of the men and women of the town appointed him guardian of their savings, besides looking upon him as their father-confessor and spiritual adviser. Well, from a wolf he became a pastor, and indeed, his reputation for sanctity was so great in the district, that even Saint Francis of Assisi never enjoyed anything to equal it.

One day a foolish, conceited young woman called Lisetta da Ca Quirino, wife of an important merchant who had sailed to Flanders with his ships, came with some of her women-friends to confess to this most virtuous friar. While she was kneeling at his feet, telling him a lot of things about herself, like the true Venetian she was—nit-wits, all of them—Friar Alberto asked her whether she had a lover.

"Why, what do you think, Mr. Monk!" she said, looking quite

put out. "Where are your eyes? Do you imagine my beauty is as ordinary as my friends' here? I'd have lovers galore if I wanted them, but I'm not the sort to be loved by any one who comes along! How many women can you quote me, who can hold a candle to me? Why, I'd be considered good-looking even in Heaven!"

By and long, Lisetta chattered of her charms, until it was a bore to listen to her. Brother Alberto, however, knew immediately that she was a little cracked, and recognizing in her the proper soil for his tilling, instantly fell desperately in love with her. The time was not ripe for his wooing: he would leave that for later. He must show himself in his true sanctity, and therefore began admonishing her, saying she was guilty of the sin of vainglory, and many another thing besides. Promptly Lisetta rejoined that he was a fool, who couldn't tell the difference between one kind of beauty and another. Friar Alberto was not anxious to stir up her temper, and after listening to her confession, he sent her away with the rest.

For a few days, he bided his time. Then, taking a faithful companion, he went to see Lisetta at her house, and leading her away to an adjoining room, where no one could spy upon him, he threw himself on his knees before her. "For God's sake, good lady," he implored, "be merciful and forgive me for what I said to you Sunday, when I talked to you about your beauty. Lord knows I was so brutally beaten for it the following night, that I wasn't able to leave my bed until this morning."

"And who punished you that way?" asked Mistress Shallow-Pate.

"Listen and I'll tell you," answered Friar Alberto. "While I was kneeling at my prayers that night as usual—for I'm always at my prayers—I was blinded by a sudden heavenly brilliance in my cell, and I had hardly time to turn around and see what the matter was, when a very handsome youth fell upon me with a huge staff in his hand. He grabbed me by my gown, before I could say anything, and pulling me to my feet, beat me so unmercifully that he broke all my bones, I swear. When he was through, I asked him why he had done it, and he answered, 'Because to-day you dared to disparage the heavenly beauty of Mistress Lisetta, whom I love above everyone, excepting only God Almighty.' 'And who are you?' I asked. He replied he was the Angel Gabriel. 'O great Angel Gabriel,' I said to him, 'please forgive me for what I have done.' 'I will,' he replied, 'on condition that you go to her as fast as you can, and beg her pardon. If she refuses, I'll come back here and give you such a drubbing, that you'll bear the signs of it as long as you live.' I can't tell you what else he said—I dare not, unless you forgive me first."

Mistress Pumpkin-Head, who was rather lacking in the salt of mother-wit, basked in his words, believing every syllable of them. After some slight hesitation, she said: "Didn't I tell you, Brother Alberto, that mine was a heavenly beauty? God is my witness, I'm awfully sorry for you, and I'll forgive you on the spot, to spare you more beatings. But you must really tell me what else the angel said."

"Since you've forgiven me, Mistress Lisetta," said Friar Alberto, "I'll make no bones about telling you. But I must warn you about one thing! Whatever I may tell you, beware of repeating a single word of it to anyone, unless you want to spoil your luck—for you're the most fortunate woman alive! Well, the Angel Gabriel told me to tell you that he's so much in love with you, that he is often tempted to stay with you at night, except that he is afraid of frightening you. But now he wants you to know, by me, that he's anxious to come to you one of these nights, and spend a good long while by your side. Since he's an angel, you couldn't even touch him if he came in that form, so he says that for your pleasure, he'd like to come as a man, and begs you to let him know when you would have him, and in whose shape, for he'll visit you for sure. So there you are. Believe me, you ought to consider yourself blessed above every mortal woman!"

Mistress Impertinence said she was quite happy to hear that the Angel Gabriel was in love with her. For her part she was awfully fond of him, too, and never failed to light a good penny's worth of candles wherever she saw a painted image of him. If he really wanted to come to her, he would be welcome, and he'd be sure to find her all alone in her room, waiting. But he must swear to one condition—never to quit her for the Virgin Mary, because she had been told he loved her dearly, and one could see it too, for wherever she was painted, he was always sure to be seen, kneeling in front of her. As for the rest, he might come to her in whatever shape he pleased, provided he didn't scare her.

"You're talking like a sensible woman, Mistress Lisetta," said Friar Alberto, "and I'll do my best to have him do all you say. But you have it in your power to do me a great service, which will cost you nothing. It's simply that you let the angel come to you, in this body of mine. Now listen and hear how you'll be doing me a service. When he takes my spirit out of my body, and slips into it himself, he puts my soul in Paradise, and all the while he remains with you, it will be there in bliss."

Then said Mistress Scantwit: "Very well, then. I've no objection to letting you obtain this consolation, to soothe you for the whacks you received on my account."

"You must manage to let him find your door open," said Friar Alberto, "so he can get into the house tonight, for since he's coming in human shape, he can't enter except through the door."

She replied that she would see to it, and Brother Alberto went away, leaving her in such ecstasy, that she couldn't bear to let her smock touch her arse, while she counted the minutes before the angel should come to her.

Meanwhile, Friar Alberto reflected that he must be a galloping rider that night, not an angel, and braced himself with sweets and other dainties, that he might not easily come a cropper. He obtained his leave from his superior, and when darkness began to fall, repaired with a companion to the house of a lady friend, from whom he was accustomed to get a head start, whenever he was minded to go coursing the fillies. Then, when he thought it was time to leave, he changed his monk's gown, went to the house of Mistress Lisetta, and there masqueraded as an angel, by the aid of the trash he had brought. In this transformation, he ascended the stairs and entered her room.

On seeing the white presence before her, the woman flung herself on her knees, but the angel blessed her, raised her up, and motioned her to get into bed, which she did very promptly, in her anxiety to obey him. Soon the angel followed his faithful one, and lay down beside her.

Friar Alberto was a well-made man, vigorous and firm on his legs. On finding himself close to the fresh, plump, soft body of Lisetta, he treated her to quite a different sort of entertainment from her husband's, and many a time in the course of that night he soared without wings, to her extreme satisfaction. But that was not all, for he told her, in the bargain, ever so many wonders of the glories celestial! Soon day approached, however, so the Angel Gabriel got all his trumpery together and went out to rejoin his companion, whom the kindly house-keeper had graciously befriended, that he might not be frightened, sleeping all alone.

After breakfast, Mistress Lisetta, accompanied by her servant, hastened to Friar Alberto with news of the Angel Gabriel, reporting all that she had heard from him about the glory of life everlasting, and inventing many a wonderful tale of her own.

"I don't know how it was with you, Mistress Lisetta," said the friar, "I only know that when he came last night, and I delivered your message, he suddenly rapt my soul and transported it among so many roses and other wonderful flowers, that I have never seen the like or the abundance here on earth. There, in the most glorious place that ever was, I remained until dawn of this morning. As for my body, I haven't the least idea what happened to it."

"Am I not telling you?" cried she. "Your body was in my arms all night, with the Angel Gabriel. There—if you don't believe it, just look under your left breast, where I gave the angel such a long kiss, that you'll have the mark of it for a couple of days."

"Really!" said he. "Well, to-day I'll do something I haven't done in God knows how long. I'll undress myself, to find out if what you say is true."

She jabbered a good deal with him, and then went back home, where Friar Alberto visited her time and time again in his Angel Gabriel's costume, without meeting with any mishaps.

It happened one day, that Mistress Lisetta got into an argument with a neighbor of hers on the subject of beauty, and to advance her claims before those of any other living woman, she said, like the featherbrain she was: "If you only knew who's wild about my beauty, you'd shut up about other women's."

The neighbor knew with whom she was dealing, and was curious to hear. "You may be right, my dear," she said, "but since I don't know what man you're referring to, I can't very well guess."

Then said Lisetta, who had little ballast in her skull: "Don't breathe a word of it, but my sweetheart is none other than the Angel Gabriel, who's just crazy about me, because, he says, I'm the most beautiful woman in the whole world or of Maremma."

The woman could hardly refrain from laughing, but she controlled herself to give the other a chance to say something further, remarking: "Truly, my dear, if the Angel Gabriel who's your sweetheart, tells you that, it must certainly be so. But I had no idea angels were up to such tricks."

"You've been making a great mistake, then, friend," replied

Lisetta. "Lord, he beats my husband at it. And he says they do it up there where he comes from, too. It's because he thinks I'm better-looking than anybody else in Heaven, that he's fallen in love with me, and comes down so often to keep me company —do you see?"

The moment her neighbor left Lisetta, she was in such a hurry that she thought she'd never get to a place where she could spill her news, but meeting a crowd of women-friends at a party, she called them together and told them the whole story, word for word. They told it over to their husbands and other gossips, who in turn repeated it to their friends, until at this rate, in less than two days it was known all over Venice. Lisetta's brothers-in-law, among others, came to hear of it, and without giving her the least hint of their intentions, set their minds to finding this angel, and see whether he were indeed an expert at flying. For several nights they kept close watch about her house.

As it was, some inkling of the story reached Friar Alberto's ears, so one night he set out for her house to give her a sound rating. Scarcely had he taken off his clothes, when her brothers-in-law, who had seen him enter, came to the door and were about to force it open; but the friar heard the noise, and surmised what the trouble was. He got up, as quickly as he could, and seeing no other way of escape, opened a window fronting the Grand Canal, and dived headlong into the water. Fortunately, the canal was sufficiently deep at that point, and he was a good swimmer, so no harm came to him of it. Working his way to the opposite shore of the canal, he slunk hastily into a house whose door he found wide open, and implored the fellow he saw there to save his life, for God's sake, inventing at the same time, a plausible story to explain his being there, stark naked, at that hour. The man was touched. Moreover, he had to go out to attend to other matters, so letting him lie in his own bed, he told him to remain there until he got back. Then, locking him in, he went about his business.

Mistress Lisetta's brothers-in-law, in the interim, had found that the Angel Gabriel had flown away, leaving his wings behind, which provoked them at their defeat, and they vented their anger on the woman, calling her all kinds of unflattering names. Finally, they left her to her troubles and returned home, taking with them the angel's paraphernalia.

Next morning, in broad daylight, while the fellow who had come to the friar's help was walking along the Rialto, he heard

how a certain Angel Gabriel had gone that night to lie with
Mistress Lisetta, but that when her brothers-in-law had found
him out, he had pitched headlong into the canal, and no one
learned what had become of him. Immediately, he guessed that
the man at his house must be that very angel. He went home
without more ado, and recognizing the gentleman, gave him to
understand that if he didn't want to be turned over to Mistress
Lisetta's kin, he had better see to it that he secured fifty ducats.
That done, Friar Alberto was anxious to get away, but his host
said: "There's only one way out of it, if you consent. To-day,
we're holding a sort of celebration, in which it's customary for
us to bring either a fellow dressed in a bear-skin, or another
tricked up to look like a wild-man—all of us leading some
strange creature or other. Then we all get together in Saint
Mark's place, and hold a hunt, and when that's over the feast is
over, too, and we all go wherever we please with the sham
beasts we brought. If you're willing to let me lead you out,
dressed up somehow, I can manage to take you anywhere you
wish, before it's too late and folks come prying to see if you're
hiding here. I don't see any other way for you to get out and
not be known. Moreover, the woman's in-laws guess you must
be somewhere about, and they've posted guards all around to
catch you."

Though Friar Alberto considered it an indignity to escape in
that fashion, the thought of Lisetta's in-laws frightened him not
a little, and he consented, telling the man where he wanted to
go, and leaving the disguise to him. First his obliging host
anointed his body with honey, then plastered him with a coat of
down, and finally tied a chain around his neck, and covered his
face with a mask. In this guise, he gave him a huge club to
hold in one hand, and a brace of butcher's dogs in the other.
That done, he sent a fellow to proclaim that whoever was anxious for a sight of the Angel Gabriel, should go to Saint Mark's
square. So much for Venetian loyalty!

At the proper time he brought the wild-man out, making him
walk ahead, while he himself held him from behind by a chain,
amid the hubbub of the populace, who kept asking in their peculiar dialect: "Whaz zat? Whaz zat?" In this manner, he led
him to the square where, what with the crowd that had collected
behind them, and what with the people who had come from the
Rialto at the proclamation, there was a veritable sea of folk.

When he got there, he chained his wild-man to a column in a

conspicuous high place, and pretended to be waiting for the hunt to begin, unmindful of the friar, who was tormented by the flies and hornets attracted by the honey smeared on his body. Finally, when he saw the square could hold no more, he walked up to his wild-man as if to unchain him, but took off his mask instead.

"What ho, gentlemen!" he cried. "Since the pig hasn't been brought and there won't be any hunt, I don't want you to feel you have come in vain. I'll show you the Angel Gabriel instead, who descends from Heaven at night to comfort our Venetian ladies here on earth!"

The moment the mask was removed, Friar Alberto was recognized by all the people gathered there, who shouted and stormed, called him the vilest names and told him the worst things that were ever said to any living scoundrel. Not content with that, they slung all kinds of filth in his face, and kept up the sport for a long time, until by some chance the news reached the brothers of his order. No less than six of them ventured out, and appeared upon the scene. Throwing a gown over his naked body, they released him and took him back with them, followed by a boisterous mob. At the monastery they locked him up, and it is believed he gave up the ghost after a miserable existence.

So it was that this fine gentleman, who was reputed good and worked mischief without being suspected, went so far as to transform himself into the Angel Gabriel, only to be converted to a wild-man, until finally he was punished as he deserved, and repented of his sins too late. God bring all tricksters to a similar fate!

## THE THIRD STORY

*Three young men, in love with three sisters, elope to Crete, where the eldest girl slays her lover in a fit of jealousy. The second sister gives herself to the Duke of Crete, to save her from death, but is killed by her lover, who runs off with the rescued girl. As a result, the remaining pair are accused and put into prison, where they admit their guilt, for fear of punishment; bribing the guard they flee to Rhodes and die in poverty.*

FILOSTRATO SEEMED DEEP IN THOUGHT, WHEN PAMPINEA HAD FIN-ished her story, and after some hesitation, he said to her: "There was something worthwhile in the end of your story, but the beginning was too full of fun to please me." Then, turning to Lauretta, he added: "You try to tell a better one, if you can."

You're far too cruel to poor lovers, said she, laughing. Always wanting them to come to a bad end. But I'll obey, and tell you the story of three lovers who all came to disaster, after they had scarcely begun to enjoy their love. At that she began:

Young ladies, you know, doubtless, how detrimental a vice may prove to the individual who gives way to it, as well as to others, in many cases. Of them all, wrath seems to me the one most prone to rush us off to ruin. What is wrath? A sudden un-reflected emotion, incited by some insult. Reason is thrown over-board, the eyes of the mind are blinded with darkness, and the soul flares up in bitterest fury. Most often, men are guiltiest of wrath, some more than others; yet it has been known to bring about even greater disaster in women, as it is more easily kin-dled in them, burns at whiter heat and goads them on more rashly. It is not to be wondered at, however, for if we cared to look more closely into it, we'd find it is the property of fire to more easily kindle light and delicate textures, than things of grosser fiber. We women, it cannot be denied, are more deli-cate than men—let them not take it amiss—but of much more fickle temper. So then, considering that we're naturally disposed to fits of anger, and that on the other hand, our docility and mildness are of much more satisfaction and delight to the men we deal with, than wrath and fury, in themselves full of trouble and peril, I'd like us to guard ourselves against that vice more resolutely than ever. To drive the point home, I'll tell you the story of how three young men and their mistresses came to ruin, as I said before, through the jealous fury of one of the women.

The ancient and noble city of Marseilles, as you know, lies on the seacoast of Provence, and once boasted more rich men and mighty merchants, than you can find there in this generation.

Narnald Cluada, one of the city's foremost merchants, was a man of lowly birth but spotless honesty, and the possessor of tremendous wealth in money and property. He had a number of children by his wife, the three eldest of whom were daughters. The first two, twins, were fifteen years old, and the third girl fourteen, and nothing was wanting for them to be married but the return of Narnald, who had sailed to Spain with his cargo. Ninetta and Maddalena were the names of the two eldest; the third was called Bertella.

Now a young man called Restagnone, of good family, though poor, was passionately in love with Ninetta, who reciprocated his affection, and they had so ably managed that they enjoyed the delights of love, unknown of everyone. This state of affairs had been going on for a considerable while, when two friends, one named Folco and the other Ughetto, who had inherited great wealth by the death of their parents, fell in love, the first with Maddalena and the other with Bertella. Restagnone learned of the circumstances through Ninetta, and speculated that he could turn this love of theirs to his advantage. Soon he became friendly with the youths, accompanying them singly or together, on their visits to their respective ladies. One day, when he thought he was on a sufficiently familiar footing with them, he invited both to his house and said:

"Surely, dear friends, our intercourse must have proved to you by this time how much I love you, and that there's nothing I would not do for you, with the same diligence as for myself. It's because I am so fond of you, that I'd like to tell you what I've been thinking. Later we can decide on whatever course you prefer. If I'm not mistaken, your words and behavior, both day and night, incline me to believe you're as much in love with your mistresses, as I am with Ninetta. Well, I believe I have a sweet and pleasant balm for the smart of our passion, if only you'll consent to accept it.

"You're both rich, which alas, is not the case with me. Why not put your money together in a joint stock, and let me share it equally with you? Then think of some part of the world where we may go to live happily with our girls, and I assure you I'll succeed in persuading them to come along with us, wherever we please, bringing enough of their father's wealth. We'll live together like three brothers, each with his wife, and lead the life of princes. It's up to you now, to choose either to be happy or not."

A mighty hot furnace kept the two youths in torment and at the thought that they might obtain their mistresses, they were not at a loss for a decision. Without a moment's hesitation, they said they were at his disposal, provided they achieved their end.

A few days after obtaining this answer, Restagnone, not without much trouble, was able to see Ninetta. He remained with

her a while, and told her what he had proposed to her sisters'
lovers, giving her many a good reason to win her approval. It
was not a difficult task, for she was even more eager than he, to
enjoy their love without suspicion, and did not scruple to say
she was in favor of the plan. She assured him, in the bargain,
that her sisters would do anything she wished, particularly in
this instance. Yes, he might go about getting everything ready
for the elopement, as soon as he could possibly do so.

Returning to the two young sparks, who had given him no
peace since he had made his proposal, Restagnone told them that
the women's end of the matter was settled. Accordingly, they
decided to go to Crete, and sold several estates they owned,
claiming they were about to enter commerce with the proceeds.
All their other possessions they converted to cash, purchased a
ship, fitted it up in royal style with great circumspection, and
bided their time.

Ninetta, on her part, knew which way the wind blew, so far
as her sisters were concerned. She used so many wiles and honeyed words, and kindled them to such a pitch of desire for the
elopement, that they thought they would not be alive to see it
happen. The night they were to embark on the galley, the girls
forced open their father's strongbox, helping themselves to a
generous supply of money and jewels. Then the three of them
together slyly left the house, as they had agreed beforehand, and
joined their lovers, who were awaiting them. Instantly they got
on board, plied their oars, and away they sailed without making
a single stop, till they came to Genoa the following evening,
where the virgin lovers took the first joys and sweets of their
love. They remained a while longer to replenish their supplies,
and again got under weigh, sailing from port to port, until a
week later they arrived in Crete, after a prosperous voyage. They
purchased many splendid estates in the neighborhood of Can-
dia, which they turned into beautiful, comfortable homes, where
they settled down to a luxurious life with plenty of servants,
hounds, hawks and horses, living with their mistresses in the utmost bliss, following a round of pleasures, banquets and enter-
tainments.

Things went on gaily for some time. But alas, too much good
leads to surfeit, as we see happening every day, and so it was
with Restagnone. Though he had once loved Ninetta very dearly,
he began to be tired of her, now that he could have her at his
beck and call, without anyone to say him nay. Consequently his

love began to cool. What was worse, he had been smitten by a lovely Cretan lady, whom he had met at a reception. In the pursuit of this new flame, he employed all his blandishments, showering her with attentions and celebrating sumptuous feasts in her honor, until Ninetta flew into such a passion of jealousy that he couldn't take a step without her making his life and her own miserable with storms and scenes.

Still, just as too much of anything leads to boredom, denial, on the contrary, whets the edge of desire. So it was with Restagnone, the flames of whose new love Ninetta's storms only succeeded in fanning. Now whether Restagnone in the course of time came to enjoy the intimacy of his new mistress, or whether it was not so, Ninetta held it for an accomplished fact, however she came to learn of it. At first, she was sick with despondency, but then she fell into such a fit of wrath and uncontrollable fury, that her love for Restagnone was converted to ruthless hatred, and in the blindness of her rage, she swore that only his death could avenge the wrong she was certain she had suffered.

Somehow, she was able to get hold of an old Grecian woman, an expert at the art of concocting poisons, and by dint of promises and gifts, persuaded her to make her a deadly water. One evening, when Restagnone came home all overheated, she gave it to him without a moment's reflection, and he drained it all, unsuspecting. So powerful a poison was it, that before dawn of the next day, it had killed him. Great was the grief of Folco, Ughetto and the two sisters, who were far from suspecting he had been poisoned, and together with Ninetta, they wept over him and gave him honorable burial.

Not so long afterward, however, the hag who had compounded the poisoned water for Ninetta, was seized for some other mischief, and under torture made a clean breast of this crime as well, showing beyond a doubt what it had led to.

One night, the Duke of Crete, giving no indication of his intention, had Folco's palace surrounded and took Ninetta prisoner, without any outcry or resistance. It was not necessary to put her to the torture, and within a brief space, he learned from her all he wished to know of Restagnone's death.

As it was, Folco and Ughetto had been secretly acquainted by the duke with the reason for Ninetta's capture, and communicated the information to her sisters, which caused them no little concern. Surely, they judged, Ninetta would be condemned to the flames, as she certainly deserved to be. Nevertheless, they left no stone unturned to save her life. But it was all futile, for the duke seemed to have determined to carry out justice to the limit.

Now Maddalena, a very handsome girl, had long been importuned by the duke, but without yielding even an inch to his desires. Thinking, however, that she might save her sister from the flames if she showed herself obliging, she informed him by a discreet go-between, that she would comply with all his wishes, on condition that her sister be released and delivered to her, and that their affair be kept secret.

The duke was pleased with the proposal, and for some time deliberated whether to consent or not; at length he decided to yield, and said he was ready. One night, he had Folco and Ughetto confined in prison, with Maddalena's connivance, on the pretext that he wanted to learn what they knew, and himself went secretly to stay with her. First, however, he had Ninetta put into a sack, apparently to have her drowned that very night, but took her instead to Maddalena, to whom he delivered her next morning in compensation for the night he had spent with her. But before taking leave of her, he begged that their first night of love might not be their last, but urged her to send the guilty girl away, that blame might not fall upon him and compel him once more to deal mercilessly with her.

The following day, Folco and Ughetto learned that Ninetta had been put to death during the night, and believed it. When they were released, and returned home to comfort their mistresses for the loss of their sister, Folco discovered, however, that the girl was there, though Maddalena had done her best to keep her out of sight. He was thunderstruck, and instantly an evil suspicion entered his mind, for he had heard rumors of the duke's passion for his mistress.

"How is it Ninetta is here?" he asked.

Maddalena spun a long story in explanation, but it carried no conviction with Folco, who was a crafty fellow. He urged her again and again to tell the truth, and at last, after a lengthy struggle, she told him all. Grief and rage got the better of him. Seizing a sword, he slew her, as she vainly cried for mercy. But now he was afraid of the consequences, and the duke's justice; therefore, leaving her there dead, he went to Ninetta's hiding-place.

"Come with me," he said, with the cheerfullest face in the

world. "Soon we shall be where your sister told me to take you, so that you'll not fall again into the duke's hands."

Ninetta believed it really true, and the terror she felt made her anxious to leave. Without stopping to say good-bye to her sister, she hurried to the water-front with Folco, under cover of night, and with what little money he had been able to lay hands on, they found passage on a ship. Nobody ever learned what became of them.

When Maddalena was found dead the following day, some people, out of hatred and envy of Ughetto, lost no time in reporting it to the duke, who, because of his great love for the murdered woman, rushed in a frenzy of wrath to her house, arrested Ughetto and Bertella, and forced them, who were ignorant of the whole matter, as well as of Folco's flight with Ninetta, to confess themselves his accomplices in Maddalena's death. Rightly fearing that their confession would assuredly lead to death, they studiously contrived to bribe their keepers, giving them a sum of money, which they had secreted for emergencies. Then, together with them, the prisoners set sail on a ship, without taking time to stop for any of their belongings, and that night fled to Rhodes, where they did not long survive a life of poverty and squalor. Such was the disaster which Restagnone's rash love and Ninetta's fury brought upon themselves and others.

✳

# THE FOURTH STORY

*Gerbino attacks a ship belonging to the King of Tunis, despite the safe conduct given by his grandfather, King Guglielmo of Sicily, in order to abduct the King of Tunis' daughter, who is slain before his eyes by the ship's crew. Gerbino slaughters them, and is later beheaded.*

LAURETTA WAS SILENT AS HER STORY CAME TO AN END. EVERYONE in the party sympathized with the unfortunate fate of the lovers, some blaming Ninetta's temper, some expressing one opinion and some another, when the king rising suddenly from a brown study, lifted his head and motioned Elisa to continue.

Adorable ladies, she began, there are many people who are under the impression that Love only shoots his darts when kindled by the fire of the eyes, and laugh at those who maintain it possible to fall in love by hearsay. You'll clearly see by the story I intend to tell you, how very much mistaken they are, because in this instance, hearsay not only accomplished this, though the lovers had never laid eyes on each other, but also brought them to a tragic end.

King Guglielmo the Second of Sicily had two children, according to the Sicilians, one a son called Ruggieri, and the other a girl, Constance, the first of whom, dying before his father, left behind a boy by the name of Gerbino. The lad, brought up with great care by his grandfather, grew into a fine, stalwart youth, who was celebrated for his bravery and knightly virtues. Nor was his fame limited to the confines of Sicily, but it re-echoed through all parts of the world, where it was even more glorious in Barbary, then a state tributary to the crown of Sicily.

Among the hosts of people who had heard of the qualities and virtues of Gerbino, was one of the daughters of the King of Tunis, who, as all maintained that had ever looked on her, was one of the rarest creatures ever cast in the mold of Nature, and a well-mannered, noble, high-spirited lady. She used to take pleasure in hearing tales of heroic men, and whenever she listened to the valiant deeds of Gerbino, reported to her by this man and that, she listened to them so eagerly and with such delight, that constructing a mental image of the youth, she fell ardently in love with him. She would speak more readily about him, than about any other knight, and lent a more than willing ear to anyone who spoke of him.

Now, on the other hand, the renown of her beauty and virtue had spread in the same fashion to Sicily, as everywhere else, and come to the ears of Gerbino, not without keen pleasure, nor to no purpose. Indeed, he was stirred to as fiery a passion for her, as she had been for him, so that while waiting for some good excuse to obtain permission from his grandfather to go to Tunis, in his boundless desire to see her, he urged his every friend who traveled there, to declare his secret passion to her and bring him back news of her dear self. One of these friends succeeded, with extraordinary cunning. Pretending he was a merchant bringing all kinds of women's finery to display, he openly confessed Gerbino's love, and told her the prince and all he possessed were hers for the asking. Her face beamed as she received both the messenger and the message. She too was burning with a love as ardent, she answered, and sent the prince one of her most precious jewels, as proof of it. Gerbino accepted it with all the manifestations of joy one can express, on receiving a thing valued above all else in the world. Again and again, he communicated with her, through the same messenger, and sent her splendid gifts, making plans that would have enabled them to see each other face to face, if Fortune had only granted it.

While matters were progressing, but dragging more than they should, for the two lovers were consumed with passion, the King of Tunis married off his daughter to the King of Granada. She was grieved beyond words at the event, considering that she was not only being driven farther away from her lover, but taken from him altogether. Indeed, if she had seen any way of escape, she would unhesitatingly have fled from her father, and gone to Gerbino to prevent the marriage. He, too, was gnawed with agony upon learning of it, and made many desperate plans to abduct her by force, if she happened to go to her husband by sea.

Now the King of Tunis, hearing some rumors of Gerbino's love and intentions, was afraid of the prince's bravery and power, and when the time for his daughter's departure arrived, informed King Guglielmo of what he intended doing, asking at the same time some security that neither he, nor Gerbino, nor any other, should interfere with his purpose. King Guglielmo, who was an old man and had heard nothing of Gerbino's passion, had no suspicion that the security was asked on that account. He granted it, therefore, without hesitation, and as a pledge sent the King of Tunis a glove.

As soon as the King of Tunis received the assurance of safe conduct, he had a large, stately ship fitted up in the port of Carthage, and equipped with everything for the comfort of the travelers. It was handsomely adorned for his daughter's voyage to Granada, and nothing more was wanting, but favorable wind and weather.

The princess knew what was going on, and saw the preparations. Secretly, she sent one of her servants to Palermo, telling him to greet the comely Gerbino on her part, and say that in a few days she would be leaving for Granada: now was the time for him to show whether he was the valiant prince he was said to be, and prove his love as great as he had often professed to her. The man delivered his message to the letter, and then returned to Tunis.

Gerbino was in a quandary, for he knew that his grandfather had pledged his assurance of safe conduct to the King of Tunis. Nevertheless, spurred by love, he went to Messina upon receipt of his lady's word, and that he might not be accused of cowardice, he quickly armed two light galleys, manned them with brave soldiers, and sailed towards Sardinia, which, he calculated, the princess' ship must pass. Nor was he mistaken. He had scarcely lain in wait a few days, when the galley, barely moved by a sluggish wind, came in sight, not far from the place where he had awaited its appearance. As soon as Gerbino caught sight of it, "My friends," he said to his companions, "if you are the brave men I take you to be, there cannot be a single one of you who has not experienced love, without whose influence I believe no man can ever achieve anything of virtue and worth. If you have ever loved, if you are now feeling the sweetness of love, it will not be hard for you to understand my desire. I love, and it was love that impelled me to put you to this task. The lady I love is in the ship you see out there. It contains, besides my heart's desire, riches beyond number, which, if you are men, and fight like men, you can obtain with little effort. There's but one thing I want for my share of the conquest—only a woman, for whose sake I have taken up arms. Everything else is freely yours—I promise it this very moment. Let us go boldly then, to the attack. See, God is favorable to our undertaking, and holds the ship motionless for us, without a breath of wind."

The doughty Gerbino might have spared his words, for the men of Messina in his crew, eager for rapine, had already decided in their hearts to do the very thing to which he was exhorting them. They raised a shout of approval, at the conclusion of his speech. The trumpets sounded. Then, taking up their arms, they plied their oars and came to the princess' ship. The Saracen sailors had seen the galleys approaching from the distance, but as they could not flee in the dead calm, they made ready for defense.

Once alongside the ship, Gerbino issued a command that the captain surrender and come aboard the galleys, unless they were ready for battle. The Saracens, however, on discovering the identity of the newcomers and what it was they wanted, declared they were being attacked in defiance of King Guglielmo's pledge, and as evidence of their words held up the king's glove, staunchly refusing to yield or give up anything on the ship, except by force of arms.

Gerbino, who had seen the princess standing on the poop, fairer than he had ever beheld her in his imagination, was even more impassioned than before, and at the sight of the glove burst out: "There are no falcons I can see, for gloves to be needed!" Moreover, he declared that they had better prepare for battle, if they were not willing to give up the princess.

Then and there, they waged a ruthless battle, slinging darts and stones at one another and keeping up the fight for a long time, to their mutual damage. At last, when Gerbino saw he was accomplishing nothing, he took a little boat that had been brought from Sardinia, and setting it on fire, towed it alongside the ship with the help of both galleys. The Saracens realized that they had now come to the limit of their power; necessity obliged them either to yield or die. Summoning the king's daughter, who was weeping below, they brought her forward to the prow of the ship, and hailing Gerbino, put her to death before his horrified eyes, as she cried in vain for help and mercy.

"Take her," they said, throwing her body into the sea. "We give her to you the only way we can, and in such condition as your breach of faith warrants."

Gerbino, witnessing their cruelty, became desperate and reckless of life. Heedless of arrows and stones hurled at him, he had himself rowed to the side of the ship, and clambered into it despite the opposition of its crew. He was like a famished lion, that comes upon a herd of steers, massacres them ruthlessly with tooth and claw, gratifying his rage before his hunger. Whirling the sword in his hand, he struck blindly among the Saracens, slaughtering a vast number.

By this time, the flames were spreading in the burning ship. Ordering his sailors to save from it whatever they could for their own remuneration, he left the hulk, having won a most unhappy victory. He had the body of the princess rescued from the sea, and mourned over it long and bitterly. On his return to Sicily he buried it with pomp in the little island of Ustica, opposite Trapani, and then returned home again, a sad and heart-sick man.

The King of Tunis learned what had come to pass, and sending his ambassadors all dressed in black, to the court of

King Guglielmo, reproached him for the pledge he had so unworthily maintained. The old king, full of mighty wrath on learning how it had happened, saw no way of denying the retribution justice demanded, and ordering Gerbino to be seized, condemned him to death, though there was not one of his lords but exhorted him to clemency. There, in his own presence, he had the youth beheaded, preferring to die without male issue than be thought a dishonorable king.

And so, as I have told you, the two lovers died a miserable and tragic death, within a few days of each other, without having tasted the least fruit of their love.

# THE FIFTH STORY

*Isabetta's brothers slay her lover; he appears to her in a dream, and shows her where he is buried. She secretly unearths the head, and sets it in a pot of basil. As she weeps over it for a long time each day, the brothers take it away from her, and she dies for grief soon after.*

ELISA'S TALE ENDED AND RECEIVED THE KING'S APPROVAL; WHERE-upon Filomena was bidden to begin, who, full of pity for the unhappy Gerbino and his tale, commenced after a heart-rending sigh:

My story, gracious ladies, will not treat of people of such high station as were those of whom Elisa told her story, but perhaps it will not be the less moving. I was reminded of it a little while ago, by the mention of Messina, where the event came to pass.

There once lived in that city three young brothers, all of them merchants, who had been left in the possession of considerable wealth by their father, a man of San Gimignano. They had a sister called Isabetta, a young, very beautiful, sweet and modest girl, whom they had not yet given away in marriage, whatever the reason might be. In one of their shops, these three brothers employed a Pisan youth called Lorenzo, who used to manage all their affairs, and as he was very striking of face and person, he soon exerted a strange fascination over Isabetta, who allowed her eyes to fall upon him, time and time again. Lorenzo, likewise, grew conscious of her love, and abandoning his little flirtations, set his heart entirely upon her. Before very long, matters had progressed to such a degree, that in their passionate love of each other, they did that thing which each of them yearned for above everything.

They kept up their intimacy for a long time, deriving much joy and delight from their love. However, they did not go about it as prudently as they should have done, and one night, while Isabetta was tip-toeing to the place where Lorenzo slept, the eldest of her brothers caught sight of her without her being aware of it. Being a prudent youth, he was moved by a certain sense of honor, and in spite of the pain it gave him to know of it, he bided his time until the following morning, without sign or word, turning over in his mind the proper course to follow.

Then, at daybreak, he told his brothers what he had discovered the night before about Isabetta and Lorenzo, and after talking the matter over at great length with them, decided to let the affair pass over quietly, that no reproach might fall either upon themselves or on their sister; it was wiser to pretend complete ignorance, until such time as they might cast off this shame before it had progressed any farther, and with no harm or injury to themselves.

Abiding by this decision, and jesting and laughing with Lorenzo as they had always done, the three of them pretended to be going to the city for a merry time, and took Lorenzo along with them. They had no sooner reached a lonely and desolate place, than seizing the opportunity, they slew Lorenzo, who was off his guard, and buried him in such a way that no one was any the wiser. Later, on their return to Messina, they spread the rumor that they had sent him somewhere on business, which was readily believed, as they were often accustomed to send him on such trips.

However, when Lorenzo did not return, Isabetta often and insistently questioned her brothers about him, for the long absence was hard for her to bear. Once, while she was so urgently requesting news of him, one of them exclaimed: "What does this mean? What's there between you and Lorenzo, that you ask us about him so often? If you ask any more questions about him, we'll give you the answer you're looking for."

Mournful and sad, fearful and yet ignorant of the truth, the girl continued without asking further, and often in the night, she called upon him piteously and prayed that he might come back to her. Sometimes, with floods of tears, she complained of his long delay, and sadly she waited, expecting him always.

One night, after she had wept much over Lorenzo, who did not return, and had at last cried herself to sleep, he appeared to her in a dream, pale and disheveled, his clothes all torn and rotted with mold. And it seemed to her that he was saying: "O Isabetta, you do nothing but call upon me. You are saddened by my long absence, and with your tears you cruelly accuse me! Know then, that I can never return to earth again, for the last day you looked at me, your brothers murdered me."

Then, pointing out the place where they had buried him, he bade her call on him no more, or expect him; and he disappeared.

Awaking, the girl wept desolately, having faith in the vision. Rising in the morning, and not daring to tell her brothers anything, she determined to go to the place revealed to her, to see whether there were any truth in what had appeared to her in sleep. Asking her brothers' permission to go to the outskirts of the city for her diversion, she set out toward the place as soon as she could, in the company of a woman who had been with her and Lorenzo on other occasions, and knew all that concerned her. There, she cleared away the dead leaves from the earth, and where the mold seemed less hard, she began to dig. Scarcely had she begun, when she came upon the body of her unfortunate lover, still quite unspoiled or corrupted. She knew now for a certainty, that her vision had been true, and was the most wretched of women.

Realizing, however, that this was no place for weeping, she would willingly have carried away the whole body, if only she had been able, and given it more fitting burial; but seeing it could not be, she severed the head from the body, wrapped it in a napkin and laid it in her maid's lap. When the earth had been cast back over the body, she went away unobserved, and returned to her brothers' home.

Shutting herself in her room with the head of her lover, she wept over it long and bitterly, until it was bathed with her tears, kissing it all over a thousand times. Then she took a large and handsome pot, in which people usually plant marjoram and sweet basil, and in it she laid the head, wrapped in a precious cloth. Covering it with earth, she planted above it several sprigs of very beautiful sweet basil of Salerno. With no other water would she nourish it than her tears, or rose-water, or orange-blossom, and would sit always near this pot, brooding over it with her longing, and looking upon it as the treasure-box that hid her Lorenzo. Then after gazing at it a long, long time, she would lean over it and weep so persistently, that all the leaves of the basil were dripping with her tears.

What with her long continued care, and what with the richness of the soil, due to the rotting of the head, the basil became more and more beautiful and fragrant. It so happened that Isabetta, who was always behaving in this fashion, was several times surprised by her neighbors.

"We have noticed that every day she behaves in such and such a way," they told her brothers, who had indeed remarked with astonishment how her beauty was wasting away, and how her eyes had almost disappeared from her head with weeping. On hearing what the neighbors told them, and seeing it for themselves, they often scolded her, to no avail, whereupon they had the pot secretly stolen from her. Urgently, insistently she asked for it, but as it was not restored to her, she ceased neither her tears nor her lamenting, until she sickened, still calling for nothing but her pot of basil.

Her brothers wondered greatly at this constant request, and finally their curiosity was aroused to see what was in the pot. The earth emptied out, they came upon the cloth, and in it the head, not yet so wasted but that they could recognize it by the curling hair, to be that of Lorenzo. They marveled at their discovery, and dreaded that the deed might become known, so burying it without more ado, and arranging their affairs to enable their secret departure from Messina, they made off for Naples.

The girl did not cease mourning, still crying for her pot. And weeping, she died. So her unhappy love came to an end. But after a while the story became well-known to many, and one of them composed the song which is sung to this day:

> "Who can the heartless Christian be
> That took my pot away from me?"

❋

# THE SIXTH STORY

*Andreola, in love with Gabriotto, tells him a dream she has had, whereat he tells her another and then dies suddenly in her arms. While she is carrying him to his house, with the help of her maid, she is seized by the police, and she confesses how the death occurred. The provost, struck by her beauty, wishes to take her by force, but she struggles against him. The affair finally comes to her father's hearing, and when she is proved innocent, he has her set free, whereupon she takes leave of the world and becomes a nun.*

THE STORY FILOMENA HAD TOLD WAS RECEIVED VERY GRATEFULLY by the girls, who had heard that song countless times, without being able to discover, despite their inquiries, what had given rise to it. However, when the king had heard the narrative through, he requested Pamfilo to take his turn.

The dream mentioned in the preceding story, he began, makes me think of another in which two dreams occur, foreshadowing a future event, as the one in the last story told of what had already happened; and scarcely had they been spoken of, by those who had seen the visions, than the predictions of both came true.

You must know, dear ladies, that there's not a single person who hasn't had the common experience of seeing all kinds of things in sleep. They seem truth itself at the time, and even when the individual is awake, some still appear real, others bear some semblance of likelihood, while still others are proved to be utterly out of all probability. Nevertheless, it is a fact that many dreams have come true, so that you will find many people who place as much faith in a mere dream, as in the waking evidence of their senses, and are moody or joyful according as their dreams make them fear or hope. On the other hand, there are many who have no faith at all in any dream, and only realize its significance, when they find themselves in the midst of the danger prophesied. Personally, I favor neither the one nor the other belief, for dreams are no more unfailingly true, than they are always deceptive. That there is not always any truth in them, we have experienced often enough for ourselves. That they're not always deceptive, was shown in Filomena's story a little while ago, and I intend to prove it further in my story, as I said before. For my part, I think that if one is living a virtuous life and doing one's best, there's no necessity for swinging to the opposite extreme, for any dream whatsoever. Conversely, no matter how favorable dreams may be to the undertaking of perverse and wicked enterprises, or how encouraging their omens may seem to the one who beholds them, not one of them should be taken seriously. Indeed, one should incline rather to all that points to the contrary. But to proceed to the story. . . .

In the city of Brescia, there was once a gentleman called Negro da Ponte Carraro, who, among a number of other children, had a daughter called Andreola, a beautiful young girl, still unmarried. As it was, she had set her heart on Gabriotto, a neighbor of hers, a youth of humble birth, but rich in accomplishments and handsome and engaging of person. With the help and connivance of her maid, the girl so managed the affair that Gabriotto did not only learn of her love, but even gained access to a pleasant garden belonging to her father, where they met time and time again, to their mutual delight. However, that nothing might ever come between their beautiful love, but death the inevitable, they secretly became husband and wife. Time passed, and as they continued in their furtive bliss, Andreola saw one night in a dream that she was in her garden, holding Gabriotto tenderly in her arms. Suddenly, as they were thus embraced, it seemed to her she saw a black and fearful thing, of a form she could not distinguish, exuding from his body. Then it fell upon Gabriotto, tore him with preternatural force out of her clasp, despite her struggles, and carried him off underground. She saw him no more after that, nor the fearful thing which had made off with him.

The sorrow and excruciating agony of the vision woke her up, and when she saw it was not as her dream had shown her, she was consoled, although the omen filled her with a sense of dread. Consequently, when Gabriotto wished to come to her the following night, she did everything in her power to prevent him. But she saw he was eager with yearning, and as she had no wish to arouse unfounded suspicions in his breast, she met him that night in the garden, as usual. Many roses white and red she gathered, for their season was at its height, and she walked with him to the brink of a clear and lovely fountain, where for a long time they kissed and embraced each other most tenderly.

"Why did you ask me not to come tonight?" he asked.

Andreola recounted the vision she had had the night before as she slept, and told him of the apprehension it had aroused in her. Gabriotto laughed it off, and said it was the height of foolishness to place any faith in dreams, which usually proceed from overeating or fasting, and were daily found out for the vanities they were.

"If I had wanted to take stock in dreams," he added, "I shouldn't have come here, not so much because of your dream, as for one I myself had last night. It seemed I was hunting in a pleasant wood, and I had caught the most beautiful doe that was ever seen. Whiter than snow she was, and in a little while she had grown so attached to me, that she would follow me wherever I went. I, too, grew fond of her, and as I remember, I think I had put a golden collar about her neck, that she might not stray from me, and held her by a chain of gold in my hands. Later, I dreamed that while the doe was resting with her head snuggled against my breast, a famished bitch as black as coal and horrible to behold, dashed upon me out of nowhere. I was rooted to the spot, and offered no resistance. And I dreamed she thrust her muzzle into my bosom, here, on my left, and gnawed and gnawed until she had reached my heart. Then the cruel beast tore it out and carried it off. I felt such piercing pain, that I started up from my sleep, and the moment I awoke I put my hand to my breast, to see if anything had happened. Of course there was nothing the matter, and I had a good laugh at my own credulousness, for even feeling!

"What should this dream mean, more than any other? I've had many a one, every bit as awful, even more so, and nothing ever happened to me for all its ominousness. Come, then, love, let's forget about them, and think of having a good time."

Andreola, who had been frightened enough at her own dream, became even more terrified on hearing Gabriotto's; but she would not cause him needless worry, and concealed her apprehension as well as she could. Nevertheless, as she clasped him in her arms and kissed him, she would gaze searchingly into his face with a vague fear, sometimes peering into the garden to see if any evil thing were lurking there. All of a sudden, in the midst of their tenderness, Gabriotto drew a heavy sigh, clasped her to him and cried: "Ah, my love! Help me! I am dying!"

Without another word, he fell prone upon the grass of the garden. Andreola gathered him to her breast. "Darling! Darling!" she called, her voice quavering with tears. "What is it you feel?"

He made no answer. His breast heaved violently; a chill sweat covered him. In a moment he was dead.

You can imagine what a terrible blow it was to Andreola, who loved him more than her own life. Weeping bitterly, she called his name again and again, but in vain. At last, when she felt him and found that he was chill all over, she was convinced he was dead. What could she do or say? With tears streaming down her face, and her breast heavy with grief, she called her maid who knew of her secret love, and unburdened to her all her anguish and misery. Together they wept for some time over Gabriotto's lifeless face, when the young girl said to the maid: "Since the Lord has done this to me, I don't care to live any more. But before I die, I want to take measures to shield my honor, and the secret love that was between us, and bury that dear body whose gracious soul is departed."

"Don't say that, my child," said the maid, "don't speak of dying, for if you've lost your sweetheart here, you will also lose him in the other world, by laying hands upon yourself! Yes, you would be going to hell, where you know his soul has not gone—he was such a splendid man, God rest him! It would be far better if you plucked up courage, and thought of helping his soul with prayers and other good works, in case he has any need of it for some sin he may have committed. As for burying him, here's this garden all ready, and nobody will ever know a thing about it, just as nobody ever knew he came here. If you don't want to, we can take him there, out of the garden, and leave him. To-morrow people will find him and carry him to his house, and his people will bury him."

In spite of her overwhelming anguish and unceasing tears, Andreola listened to the maid's advice. The first part she would not hear of, and to the second she replied: "God forbid that I should ever consent to have so dear and beloved a man, and my husband, buried like a dog or left lying in the middle of the street! I have mourned for him, and I'll do my best to have him granted the last rites by his people. I know already how to go about it."

Then and there she sent the maid for a silken sheet, which she had in a chest, and spreading it on the ground, they laid Gabriotto's body upon it, his head upon a cushion. Tearfully, she closed his eyes and mouth, twined a wreath of roses, and strewed on his body all the flowers they had gathered together. Then, to the maid, she said: "It is not far from the garden to the door of his house. You and I will lift him as he is, with all the roses on him, and take him there, and leave him before his door. Soon day will be breaking, and someone will find him. It will give little consolation to his dear ones, but to me, in whose arms he breathed his last, it will afford some comfort."

Again, she fell to weeping upon his face, and allowed her tears to fall in a stream for a long time. At last, at the insistent urging of her maid, for day was dawning, she rose to her feet, drew from her finger the same ring with which Gabriotto had made her his wife, and slipped it on his own, saying: "Dearest love, if your soul is now witness to my tears, or if any sense or understanding still remain to the mortal frame once the spirit has flown, take this last gift in kindness from her you loved so dearly while you were of the living." At that, she fell swooning upon his body. She awoke from it some time later, and rising to her feet, with the help of her maid, she lifted the sheet on which the body was lying. Together, they carried it out of the garden in the direction of his house.

They had not gone very far, when they were discovered with the dead youth by the provost's officers, who happened to be going at that hour on another errand, and they were taken in custody. Andreola, who desired death more than life, knew who the officers were, and said openly: "I know who you are, and that it would do me no good to try to escape. I am ready to go before the judges with you, and tell all there is to be told. But because I am obedient to you, let no man dare lay a hand on me or remove anything from this body—unless he wants to run the risk of being accused by me."

She went to the court-house with Gabriotto's body, no one daring to touch her. The chief judge rose, hearing the commotion, and sending for her in his room, found out what had taken place. He had the body examined by physicians, to see whether the dead man had been killed by poison or other means; but they declared unanimously that it was not so, and that he had met his death by suffocation, when a vessel had burst near the region of his heart. On hearing their verdict, the judge saw that Andreola was not guilty, and making a pretense of offering her the freedom he could not sell, he said he would release her if she yielded to his wishes. His persuasions proving worse than useless, he tried against his better nature to do her violence; but Andreola, fired with indignant passion, defended herself tooth and nail, repelling his advances with words of noble scorn.

In the meantime, with the coming of day, Messer Negro was informed of the night's happenings, and stricken with sorrow, went to the court, attended by many of his friends. The judge told him everything, whereupon he asked sadly for his daughter to be restored to him. The judge, however, anxious to forestall any accusation Andreola might make against him, for his attempted violence, began by praising her and the constancy she possessed, saying he made his attempt simply to test her virtue. Then, because he had discovered in her such exemplary staunchness, he had fallen deeply in love with her, and declared that if he, her father, gave his sanction, and if she were willing, he would gladly make her his wife, in spite of the low-born husband she had had. While they were engaged in this conversation, Andreola came to her father, and throwing herself before him said, between her sobs:

"I know, dear father, that there is no need for me to tell you the story of my presumption and misfortune, as you surely have heard it, and must be acquainted with it by this time. Still, I humbly crave your forgiveness with all my heart for having, without your knowledge, married the man I loved above all other men. I am not asking you this mercy that my life may be spared, but to meet death as your daughter, and not your enemy."

Still weeping, she sank at his feet. At her prayer, Messer Negro, who was a man well-advanced in years and of a merciful and gentle nature, felt the tears starting to his eyes, and as they fell, raised his daughter tenderly to her feet, saying: "It is true, dear daughter, I should have wished you a husband whom I thought worthy of you, but even if you had chosen one to your own liking, I should have been content. It was the fact that you kept him from your old father, through your lack of confidence, that hurts, and more than that, to see you bereft of him, before I ever knew of it. But then, since this is how matters stand, the honor I would have shown him as my son-in-law, for your sake, while alive, I shall have him shown now that he is dead."

Turning to his sons and kin, he ordered them to prepare everything for a solemn and honorable funeral for Gabriotto.

In the interim, the dead man's relatives had thronged to the court on hearing the heavy news, and with them came all the men and women of the town. The body, lying on Andreola's silken sheet and all covered with the roses she had gathered, was laid in the middle of the court, where he was not only mourned by her and his womenfolk, but by all women generally and many men of the city. At length, he was removed from the public court, borne not like a plebeian, but a lord, on the shoulders of the most distinguished citizens, and taken with solemn pomp to his grave.

Some days later, the judge broached the subject of marriage once more, but when Messer Negro spoke of it to his daughter, she would not hear a word of it. Finally, wishing to solace her to some extent, he gave her permission to take the veil, and together with her servant, she entered a convent renowned for holiness, where they lived virtuously for many years.

✳

## THE SEVENTH STORY

*Simona loves Pasquino. Together, they are lying in a garden, when he rubs his teeth with a sage leaf and dies. Simona is arrested, and when she explains to the judge how Pasquino met his death, and rubs another sage leaf against her teeth, she also falls down dead.*

PAMFILO HAD JUST FINISHED HIS STORY, WHEN THE KING, SEEMing not all touched by Andreola's affliction, looked at Emilia and indicated his pleasure for her to resume the story-telling.

Pamfilo's story, dear friends, she began without hesitation, inspires me to tell you another which is like his in no other respect, except that the girl about whom I'm going to tell, lost her love in a garden, like Andreola, and when she was arrested, in the same manner, gained her freedom neither by constancy nor virtue, but by a most unexpected death.

Love, as we said before, though a willing guest in the homes of the wealthy, does not scorn to exert his dominion in the huts of the poor. On the contrary, he sometimes shows his powers among them so forcefully, that he is even feared by the mighty as a redoubtable lord—which will be demonstrated if not wholly, at least in part, by my story. I'm going to take the liberty of recalling you all to our own city, from which we strayed so far afield to-day, talking variously of different things and roaming all over the world.

Not so long ago, there lived in Florence a young girl called Simona, who was extremely pretty and charming for her walk in life. Her father was very poor, and although she had to earn her daily bread by the toil of her hands, and maintain herself decently by spinning wool, she was not so mean-spirited as to close her heart to Love, that had long sought admittance through the pleasant ways of a young man of the same condition as herself, who used to distribute wool to spin, for his employer, a wool-merchant. Well, Love proved the master, and she let him into her heart, in the handsome person of Pasquino, who was head over heels in love with her. All day long she would sit at her spinning, her mind filled with longing, but not daring to reveal it, and at every hank of worsted she wound about her spindle, a thousand scorching sighs escaped her, at the thought of him who had brought her the wool to spin.

The lad, on his part, had grown extremely solicitous that his master's wool be well-spun, and as though Simona's handiwork alone were to be used in weaving the cloth, he spent more time over her spinning, than over any other girl's. At this rate, while he went on supervising her work, and she delighted in his supervision, he gained in boldness as she lost in her usual timidity and shyness, and soon they yielded to mutual delights of so grateful a nature, that they did not wait for each other's invitation to indulge in them.

Time sped, and with every passing day their ardor grew all the more fiery, the more they surrendered to it. One day, Pasquino begged Simona to try to go with him to a certain park, where he wished to take her to enjoy their reciprocal pleasures with more freedom and less worry. She agreed. On Sunday afternoon, pretending to her father that she was going to attend the sale of indulgences at San Gallo, she set out for the garden Pasquino had told her of, together with Lagina, a friend of hers. There they found him, with a companion called Puccino, but nicknamed Stramba. A flirtation immediately got under weigh between Stramba and Lagina, so that Pasquino and Simona withdrew to one end of the park on their own business, and left the other couple at their ease elsewhere.

It so happened, that in the part of the garden to which Pasquino and Simona had gone, there grew a large, lush sage-bush, at the foot of which they sat down and dallied with each other a good long while, talking over the details of a picnic they intended having there some time, at their leisure. Turning to the sage-bush, Pasquino plucked a leaf and began rubbing his teeth and gums with it, saying it was very good for cleaning the teeth after meals. He kept it up for some time, and then returned to the subject of the picnic they had been discussing. He had hardly begun to speak, when his face underwent a strange transformation. Shortly after that, he lost both sight and speech, and in a little while he was dead.

Simona cried and screamed at the sight, and called for Stramba and Lagina, who ran to her as fast as their legs could carry them. But when Stramba saw Pasquino, not only lying still and dead, but all swollen, and his body and face covered with black blotches, he shouted: "Ah, wicked woman! You have poisoned him!"

Then and there, he raised a hue and cry which was soon heard by the people living in the vicinity of the park. Quickly, they turned out at the noise. When they saw the dead and swollen body, and listened to Stramba complaining and accusing Simona of treacherously poisoning his friend, while she stood by, like one bereft of her senses, unable to utter a word in her defense because of the anguish and shock that had deprived her of her lover, they were all convinced it was as Stramba said. Thereupon, they laid hold of her, as she wept and sobbed, and dragged her to the magistrate's palace, where at the instigation of Stramba, Atticciato and Malagevole, two other friends of Pasquino's who had come up in the meantime, a judge cross-examined her without delay. For all his questioning, he could not convince himself that Simona was guilty, or that she had employed any malice in her lover's death, whereupon he thought it advisable to see the body in her presence, the spot where Pasquino had died, and the way it had all come to pass, according to the story she told, which he could not very clearly understand.

Quietly, he had her escorted to the garden where Pasquino's body was still lying, swollen like a hogshead, and joined her there later. The sight of the corpse filled him with amazement. "How did it happen?" he asked her.

Again Simona told her story, and then to make it plainer, went to the sage-bush, plucked a leaf, and rubbed her teeth with it as Pasquino had done. Stramba, Atticciato, and other of the dead boy's friends, who were looking on mockingly at the scene, calling it vain and foolish in the judge's presence, condemned her wickedness more harshly still, deeming it deserving of no lesser punishment than the flames, when suddenly, the poor little wretch who was shrinking and cowering, what with grief at the loss of her lover and terror of the punishment Stramba demanded, fell down dead, like Pasquino before her at the taste of the sage-leaf, to the great wonder of everyone about her.

O happy lovers, who tasted the boon of love and death, on the selfsame day! O happier still, if you were reunited in the same blessed region! O happiest, if there you love as you loved below!

How much more blessed (at least to our way of thinking, who live on after her), was the soul of Simona, delivered by Fate, and whose innocence was not doomed to meet the judgment of such churls as Stramba, Atticciato and Malagevole! No, Fate found a worthier way for her, by a death like her lover's, and rescued her from her accusers' libel, to follow the soul of her dearly-beloved Pasquino.

The judge was as much aghast at the untoward event, as the rest of the people, and stood for a long time pondering, without knowing what to say. Coming to himself, at last, he pronounced: "This sage-bush is evidently poisonous, quite contrary to the nature of sage in general. To prevent its working similar mischief on other unfortunate mortals, let it be cut down to the roots and burned."

The park keeper did the judge's bidding in his presence, and scarcely had he hewn the enormous bush to the ground, when the cause of the two poor lovers' death was revealed. There, under it, they found a toad of monstrous proportions, whose venomous breath, they concluded, must have poisoned the whole bush. Not a man was bold enough to approach the creature. A tall hedge of brush was therefore built around it, and they set fire to it, together with the sage-bush, putting an end to the judge's inquest on poor Pasquino's death.

The two lovers themselves were borne, swollen as they were,

on the shoulders of Stramba, Atticciato, Guccio Imbratta and Malagevole, and buried in the churchyard of Saint Paul's, whose parishioners they happened to be.

✳

## THE EIGHTH STORY

*Girolamo, in love with Salvestra, goes to Paris at his mother's entreaties, and on his return finds the girl married. Secretly entering her house, he dies by her side, and when he is carried to the church for burial, Salvestra falls dead beside him.*

WHEN EMILIA'S STORY HAD COME TO AN END, NEIFILE BEGAN AT the king's request:

There are some people who imagine they know a lot more than everybody else, when in my opinion, they know very little. Still, for all that, they pit their small wisdom not only against the advice of those who know better, but against the very nature of things, causing all sorts of terrible misfortune by their presumption, and never a bit of good. Now love, of all natural emotions, is the very one that will not stand for opposition in word or deed, but will sooner burn itself out according to its kind, than be argued away. I'm thinking of telling you, therefore, the story of a woman who, when she tried to be cleverer than she thought, or had a right to be, or even than the matter required, imagined she was uprooting from her son's infatuated heart a love which heaven itself had perhaps decreed. She succeeded, but at the cost of the boy's life.

There once lived in our city, a very powerful and exceedingly wealthy merchant, from what our elders tell, by the name of Leonardo Sighieri, who had by his wife an only son, called Girolamo. After the child's birth the man died, leaving his affairs in excellent shape. The boy's guardians and mother took care of his inheritance, honestly and well, until he came of age, and as he grew up with the children of the neighborhood, he became very friendly with a little girl of his own age, a tailor's daughter. As time passed and he grew in years, that friendship was transformed into a love so passionate, that Girolamo was not happy unless he saw her; and as for her, she loved him with an equal love. The lad's mother discovered this infatuation of his, and frequently scolded him for it; but when she saw that he could not be cured of it, she complained to his guardians, thinking that because of his wealth, she could make an orange tree out of a thorn-bush.

"This young calf of ours," she said, "who's hardly turned fourteen, is already so crazy about the daughter of a neighboring tailor—Salvestra's her name—that if we don't get her out of his sight, he'll end by making her his wife one of these days, without our being any the wiser, and I'll eat my heart out as long as I live. On the other hand, he'll waste away to nothing, if he sees her married to somebody else. In either case, I think in order to avoid trouble, you ought to send him off somewhere far from here, on some business of the warehouse, so that when he's gone, it'll be out of sight out of mind with him. Then we can give him a girl of good family to wife."

The guardians said she was quite right, and promised to do everything in their power to bring this about. Sending for the boy, they had him led to the office, and one of them said very kindly: "My son, you are quite grown up now, and it's only proper that you should begin looking after the business yourself. We'd all be very happy if you were to go to Paris, and live there awhile, where you could see how a good deal of your wealth is invested. What's more, it would do you a world of good, as you would be gaining a liberal education, which you couldn't get here, rubbing elbows with all those fine gentlemen, lords and peers, and learning by their example. After that, you might come back home."

The boy listened attentively, and then answered explicitly that he would do nothing of the sort. What was there to prevent him from doing as well in Florence, as anywhere else?

At his refusal, the worthy men tried to convince him with further arguments; but when they could not get him to say anything else, they reported their failure to his mother. She was furious, not so much at his stubbornness in refusing to go to Paris, as at this infatuation of his, and she warmed his ears for him. Then, changing her tactics she coaxed and cajoled him, pleading with him gently to be good and do what his guardians told him. At last, she wrought upon him so with her words, that he said he would go to Paris and live there a year, but no longer.

Well, Girolamo left for Paris, as madly in love as ever, but what with delays and postponements, he was kept there two years. When he finally came back, even more in love than ever, he found his Salvestra married to a hardworking young tent-maker. The news nearly broke his heart. Nevertheless, when he saw there was nothing to be done, he resigned himself to make the best of it, strove to console himself, and inquiring where she lived, took to walking up and down in front of her house, like most young men in love, imagining she had no more torn him out of her heart than he had her. It was quite otherwise. She no more remembered him, than if she had never seen him in her life, or if she did have a vague stirring of memory, she pretended the contrary. It was not long before he found out how matters stood, to his great sorrow, but still he did everything he could to reawaken the old flame. Nothing seemed to be of any avail, whereupon he made up his mind to speak with her himself, even if he were to die in the attempt.

One night, after he had inquired of a neighbor how her house was arranged, he stole into it when she and her husband had gone to a gathering with some friends, and hid himself in her room behind some canvas sails that had been left to stretch on their frames. He waited breathless, until they returned and went to bed. When he felt that Salvestra's husband was fast asleep, he drew near the corner in which he had seen her lie down, and laying his hand on her bosom, murmured gently: "Dearest one, are you asleep?"

She was up and awake, and would have cried out, had he not added quickly: "Don't scream, for God's sake! It is your own Girolamo!"

"Go, then, go, for the love of God!" she pleaded, her body trembling at his voice. "The time is past when there was nothing wrong with our childish love. I'm now a married woman, as you see, and it wouldn't be right for me to have anything to do with any other man but my husband. I beg you, for the dear Lord's sake, go, please! If my husband should hear you, even if no other harm came of it, I'd never have a moment's peace and quiet with him any more, whereas he loves me now, and we're living a modest, peaceful life together."

He was stung with pain when he heard her, and called to her mind the days that had been, and his love, that even distance had not lessened. Many entreaties he whispered to her, mingled with ardent promises, but she would yield him nothing. Death itself seemed welcome to him. At last he implored her, for his great love's sake, to let him lie beside her until he could warm himself a little, for he had almost frozen waiting for her. He would neither speak to her nor lay a finger on her body, he swore, and as soon as he should be somewhat less numb, he would leave her and go his way.

Salvestra's heart was moved to pity, and she granted him his desire, on his own conditions. As he lay down beside her, therefore, without touching her, he was overwhelmed at once with his infinite love of her and her present cruelty. In the hopelessness of it all, he determined to live no more. Without another word, he held his breath, clenched his fists, and expired by her side.

Some time later, Salvestra, astonished at his stillness, whispered to him in her dread that her husband might wake up and discover him: "Girolamo! Girolamo! Why don't you go?"

At his silence, she thought he must have fallen asleep, so stretching out her hand, she touched him, in an attempt to rouse him. He was cold as ice. Filled with amazement, she shook him more violently, but as he made no stir, in spite of her repeated jogging, she knew that he was dead. For a long time, she did not know what to do in her affliction. Finally, she decided to test her husband, by telling him the story as though it were another person's case, and rousing him, she told him all that had just happened, asking him what advice he would offer if she had been the one involved.

The honest fellow replied that so far as he was concerned, he thought the man's body should be carried quietly to his home and left there, and the woman ought not be made to suffer, for from what he could gather, she had done no wrong.

"Well, then, that's just what we must do," said Salvestra, and taking his hand, made him feel the dead youth.

He got up in a haze. Lighting a candle, without saying anything more to his wife, he dressed the body in its own clothes; then laying it upon his shoulders, he bore it without delay to the door of the youth's house, Salvestra's innocence lending him aid, set it down, and left it there.

In the morning, when Girolamo was found dead before his door, there was a great to-do, especially on his mother's part. The doctors examined and searched his body all over, but when no wound or bruise was found, they pronounced generally that he had died of a broken heart, which was indeed the case.

The body was carried to a church. There, the grieving mother came with many other women, friends and neighbors of hers, and set up loud plaints and lamentations, according to our custom, shedding an abundance of tears.

While the mourning was in full swing, the man in whose house the youth had died, said to his wife: "Salvestra, cover your head with a veil and go to the church where Girolamo's body lies. Then get in among the women, and listen to what they have to say about it all. I'll do the same among the men, and so we'll find out if there's anything being said against us."

The young woman, too late aroused to pity, was comforted at the suggestion, in her anxiety to look on the dead Girolamo, whom she would not have favored with a single kiss while living. Accordingly, she went to the church.

Most wonderful it is, to realize how difficult of penetration are the ways of Love! That heart, which Girolamo's smiling fortune had not been able to open, misfortune unsealed; and the smouldering ardor bursting into flame at the sight of the dead face, moved her to such pity, that wrapping her veil more closely about her face, she made her way among the women, and did not stop till she had come to the body. A piercing shriek escaped her, and she flung herself face downward upon the dead youth. She did not have a chance to weep long over him; indeed, no sooner did she come in contact with him, than sorrow deprived her of life, as it had deprived him.

The women sought to comfort her and coaxed her to rise, not yet knowing who she was. She did not budge. They tried to lift her up; she was still motionless. At length they succeeded, and discovered she was Salvestra, dead.

Pity wrought doubly on the heartstrings of the mourning women, who broke into still louder wails. The news spread outside the church, where the men were gathered. Salvestra's husband, who was among them, heard it, and deaf to the attempts to comfort and console him, wept for a long time. Later, when he could find speech and told the many men around him what had taken place between the two lovers the night before, everyone knew the thing that had brought them to their death, and everyone pitied them. The lifeless girl was lifted up, dressed in the weeds of the dead, and laid beside the youth on the same bier, where the people long mourned over her. Afterwards, the two lovers were interred in the same grave; and thus they, whom love had not been able to unite in life, were joined by death in everlasting companionship.

✱

# THE NINTH STORY

*William of Roussillon gives his wife the heart of William Guardetang to eat, whom he had slain because she loved him; when she discovers it, she flings herself headlong from a high window to the ground, perishes, and is buried with her lover.*

NOW THAT NEIFILE HAD FINISHED HER STORY, NOT WITHOUT WRINGing the hearts of all her companions, no one else remained but Dioneo and the king who, not wishing to usurp the privilege of the former, began:

A story has just occurred to me, tender-hearted ladies, which, in your sympathetic response to the misfortunes of love, will rouse your pity no less than the previous one, both because the persons of my tale were of more consequence, and the accidents of their death more gruesome.

You must know that, as the story goes among the people of Provence, there once lived in that country two noble knights, lords in their own right over castles and serfs. One of them was called Sir William of Roussillon, and the other Sir William Guardetang. As they were both accomplished in knightly sports, a deep friendship took root between them, and at every tournament, joust or feat of arms, they would always go together, wearing the same device.

Now although they lived in their own castles, some ten miles away from each other, Sir William Guardetang, regardless of the friendship and brotherhood that was between him and Sir William of Roussillon, fell deeply in love with his comrade's wife, a beautiful, gracious lady, and what with gallantries and blandishments, made his passion known to her. She appreciated his worth as a brave and doughty knight, and was flattered. Little by little, she reciprocated his passion, until there was nothing in the world she loved or desired so much as his person, and waited only for him to take the initiative. He was not long in suing for her favor, and the two met again and again, enjoying together the wealth of their love.

As time went on, they were less prudent than they should have been, so that their secret passion came to the knowledge of the lady's husband. He was mad with rage. Indeed, the affection he had had for Guardetang turned to deadly hatred; but he kept himself from showing it, better than the two lovers had been able to conceal their love, and resolved to make an end of his rival.

While Roussillon was gnawing his hate, an important tournament was proclaimed in France, of which Roussillon immediately informed Guardetang, inviting him to come to his house, if he wished, and talk over the possibility of their going. Guardetang answered he would be glad to come to dinner the following day, without fail, whereupon Roussillon thought the opportunity had now come for him to kill him.

He armed himself next day, and taking along some of his servants, mounted his horse. About a mile from his castle grounds, he hid in a wood through which Guardetang had to pass, and lay in wait for him. A good long time he stood there concealed, when at last he saw him approach, unarmed, with two servants equally defenseless, like one who had nothing to fear from his friend. When he had him where he wanted him, Roussillon fell upon Guardetang, lance in hand, maddened with fury and rancor. "You are a dead man!" he roared. Before he had even uttered the words, his lance had pierced Guardetang's breast. The man fell backward at the thrust, powerless to defend himself or say a word, and soon breathed his last. His two servants turned their horses about without finding out who had done the foul deed, and fled to their lord's castle as fast as their beasts could carry them.

Roussillon got off his horse, ripped open Guardetang's breast with a knife, plucked out his heart with his own hands, and wrapping it in a lance pennant, ordered one of his men to carry it. Threatening them with violence if they dared breathe a word of the murder, he mounted his horse once more and returned to his castle, under the shadow of night.

His wife, who knew Guardetang was to have come that night and had awaited his arrival with impatient longing, marveled when he failed to make his appearance, and said to her husband: "How is it Guardetang has not come, my lord?"

"I've had word from him that he'll not be able to get here till to-morrow, my dear," he answered, leaving her uncertain and preoccupied. Then, dismounting, he had the cook hailed, and said to him: "Take that boar's heart there, and prepare as delicate and exquisite a dish of it as you can. When it's ready to be served, have it brought me at table in a silver platter."

The cook took the heart, and exerting all his art and care in preparing it, chopped it up, seasoned it with all kinds of spices, and converted it to a very tempting stew indeed.

Toward supper-time, Sir William sat down at table with his lady. The food was brought, but he ate little, his conscience troubling him for the evil he had committed. Presently, the cook sent up the stew, which he placed before his wife, praising its savouriness and pleading his own lack of appetite. She was not at all fastidious, and tasting a little liked it so well that she ate it all.

When the knight saw the empty plate, he asked: "How did you like the dish, madam?"

"Very much, indeed, my lord," she answered.

"I well believe it, by the Lord," said the knight, "and I don't wonder at all that you should like, dead, what you loved better than anything else, alive."

She was pensive a while, puzzled at his meaning, and then asked: "Why, what is this you have made me eat?"

"It is the heart of William Guardetang you have eaten," replied he, "whom you loved, like the faithless woman that you are! And don't think I am deceiving you, for with these very hands I tore it out of his breast before I came home!"

It is useless to inquire whether she was desolate on learning such news of the man she cherished beyond life. After a moment, she said: "You did all that is expected of a treacherous and villainous knight. He did not force me, ever, and if I made him master of my heart, wronging you by so doing, it was I and not he that should have borne the consequences. God forbid that anything else should pass my lips, after the noble heart of a knight so brave and courteous as Sir William Guardetang, who is now dead!"

Rising to her feet, she walked to a window behind her that was a dizzy height above the ground, and without a moment's reflection, allowed herself to sink backward, not only dying in her fall, but dashed almost to a thousand fragments.

Sir William, horrified at the sight, began to wonder whether he had not done wrong. Then, fearing the justice of the Count of Provence, and the people of the countryside, he had his horses saddled and galloped away.

The following morning the whole country knew how the tragedy had happened. The bodies of the lovers were recovered by the vassals of the murdered knight and the unfortunate lady, and buried amid tears and lamentation, in her castle-chapel—

both of them in one grave, over which verses were inscribed, telling who lay buried there, and what had brought them to their tragic death.

✳

## THE TENTH STORY

*A surgeon's wife, believing her unconscious lover dead, hides him in a chest, which is stolen, gallant and all, and taken home by two moneylenders. The lover regains his senses and is taken for a thief, whereupon the lady's maid tells the court she herself had hidden him in the chest that was stolen by the usurers. He escapes the gallows and the usurers are fined for having made away with the chest.*

DIONEO ALONE WAS LEFT TO SPEAK, NOW THAT THE KING HAD finished, and knowing it was his turn, began as soon as he was commanded:

The misfortunes of all these unhappy loves not only made you ladies miserable, but succeeded in wringing my heart as well, making me wish this day were over. Thank God those stories are at an end—unless, God forfend, I were minded to add my bitter drop to this ocean of miseries—but without lingering on such wretchedness any longer, I'll begin a merrier tale, setting a good example, I hope, for tomorrow's story-telling.

I'm sure you know, loveliest ladies, that not so long ago there lived in Salerno a celebrated surgeon, whose name was Dr. Mazzeo della Montagna. He entered matrimony at a great age, marrying a good-looking girl of a respectable family in his town, whom he kept better provided than any other woman in the city with expensive, stylish clothes, jewels, and all kinds of other toys dear to a fair one's heart. It's true she suffered with cold a great part of the time, being badly covered in bed by her doctor-husband. Indeed, like Judge Ricciardo di Chinzica, of whom we've already spoken, who used to keep his wife well versed in fast- and feast-days, Dr. Mazzeo taught his that a man paid a heavy penalty whenever he lay with a woman, causing him discomfort for many days before he could make up for it in energy—and suchlike stuff and nonsense. You may be sure, she had no rollicking time of it. But she was a clever woman and a bold one, and in order to spare the goods of her household, decided to look about her and lay waste to others' bounty. Many a young blade did she ogle and scrutinize before she came across one who struck her fancy. In him she placed all her hope, and was ready to yield herself up to him, body and soul. He became aware of her infatuation, and having quite a mind to it himself, fell in love with her likewise.

Now this gay buck, called Ruggieri da Jeroli, was a man of high birth, but of such low and disreputable a manner of living that he hadn't a single friend or relative left who cared a straw for him or wished to associate with him at all. Indeed, all of Salerno rang with robberies and other disgraceful crimes he had perpetrated, but the doctor's wife didn't worry her head about it, loving him, as she did, for quite other qualities. With the help of her maid, she contrived so skilfully that she was able to be alone with him. After they had indulged somewhat in sport, the lady gave him a lecture on his past life, urged him to abandon all such wickedness for her sake, and the better to work his salvation, replenished his waning finances again and again with goodly sums of money. So they got along, prudently and well.

At about this time, Dr. Mazzeo was charged with a patient whose leg was in bad shape. Upon examining it, he informed the sick man's family that unless the gangrenous bone were removed, either the whole leg might have to be amputated, or the man left to die. He added, however, that there was a chance of recovery, if the bone were operated upon, but that he could not consent to perform the operation, unless they ran the risk and gave the man up for dead. The patient's friends were willing to take the chance, and came to terms with the surgeon.

The morning of the day when the operation was to be performed, Dr. Mazzeo, knowing the patient would neither be able to stand the pain nor submit to the treatment, had a clear potion distilled from a prescription, of sufficient strength to drug him to sleep through the necessary period of agony; and when the drugged water was delivered to his home, he left it in his room without telling anyone what it was.

Toward dusk, however, when the surgeon was to have gone to his patient, he received a call from some dear friends to rush without fail to Malfi, where a furious quarrel had broken out, in which many of them had been wounded. Postponing the operation till the following morning, Dr. Mazzeo clambered into a little boat and set out for Malfi. His fair lady, knowing he would not be back that night, quietly sent for Ruggieri as usual, hid him in the doctor's room, and locked him in until the rest of the household had gone to bed.

While Ruggieri was waiting impatiently in the room for her to come, he was seized with a tremendous thirst, perhaps because of the strenuous labor he had performed that day, or the spiced food he had eaten, or just simply from force of habit. His eyes fell on the bowl upon the window-sill, containing the potion prepared by the surgeon for his patient. Ruggieri, thinking it only drinking water, brought it to his lips and gulped it down to the last drop. Before long, a mighty drowsiness took possession of him, and soon he was dead to the world.

His mistress slipped into the room at the first opportunity, and finding him asleep, prodded him and called to him softly to get up. She might have been talking to the wall: he neither replied nor budged an inch. Slightly vexed, she pushed him a little less gently. "Get up, sleepy-head!" she said. "If you were dying to sleep, you should have gone to your own house, instead of coming here."

Upon her violent thrusts, Ruggieri fell from the chest he was on, and lay in a heap upon the floor, giving no sign of life and looking, for all the world, not a whit different from a corpse. She was rather frightened, and doing her best to lift him up, gave him a sound shaking, tweaked his nose and pulled his beard. In vain. He had anchored his donkey to a pleasant post. By this time, she began to have fears that he was dead, but for all that, kept pinching him black and blue and scorching his skin with the flame of a candle. Nothing helped. She was no doctor, in spite of her husband's learning, and therefore was convinced her lover was dead. Need you ask if she was doleful, loving Ruggieri as she did, above all else?

Not daring to sob aloud, she wept over him silently, lamenting the dreadful calamity. After a while, however, in her fear that she might be adding insult to her injury, she thought it wiser to get the body out of the house, somehow, and very quickly, too; but as she could think of no way, she called her maid softly and displaying to her the disaster which had befallen her, she asked the girl's advice. The maid gaped with wonder, and in her turn fell to plucking and pinching him. Obtaining no response, she echoed her mistress' words, pronounced him dead as a stone, and said it were best to get him out of the house.

"But where can we put him?" asked the lady. "Where, without rousing suspicion, when he's discovered to-morrow morning, that he might have been carried out of here?"

"Late this evening, ma'am," replied the girl, "I saw a good-sized chest in front of the shop of our neighbor, the carpenter. If he hasn't taken it in yet, it'll be just the thing for us, because we could stuff this corpse into it, give him a couple slashes with a knife, and leave him there. Then, when he's found, I don't see why anybody should say he was carried out of here rather than out of any other place. On the other hand, people will more likely believe that he was murdered by some enemy of his, when he was up to some mischief, and then put into that chest. He was a pretty wicked spark, you know."

The lady approved the girl's advice, but wouldn't hear of any slashes, saying that nothing in the world would make her do anything of that sort. Then she sent her out to see whether the chest were still in its place. The girl came back and said it was. Now she was a young and sturdy wench, so taking Ruggieri on her back with the help of her mistress, she followed the lady, who walked ahead to see that the way was clear, and coming to the chest, they thrust him in. Then shutting the lid, they left him there.

As fate would have it, two young moneylenders had moved to a house in the neighborhood some days before. They were in need of house-furnishings, and noticing the chest during the day, decided in their eagerness to get something for nothing, that if it were still there at night, they would make off with it and carry it home. Finding the chest where they had expected, they did not stop to examine it further, but grasping it hurriedly, carried it to their house, for all that it seemed rather heavy. They laid it near the room where their wives were sleeping, without bothering to arrange it properly for the time being, and leaving it there, retired to sleep.

Meanwhile, Ruggieri, who had been in the deepest slumber for a considerable while, and had already digested the potion whose effects had worn off, woke up toward daybreak; but though he was awake and his senses had returned to normal, a certain stupor still lingered in his brain, which kept him dazed not only through that night, but for several days. He opened his eyes, and saw nothing. He felt about, and finding himself shut in the chest, his mind began to wander.

"What's this?" he said to himself. "Where am I? Am I asleep

or awake? Still, I remember I came to my mistress' room this evening—and now it looks as if I were shut up in a chest. What's the meaning of this? Could the doctor have perhaps come home unexpectedly? Did something unusual happen that made her hide me, while I slept? I suppose that's it. Surely, that's what it is."

He held his breath at that, and pricked up his ears to catch a possible rustle; and so he lay for a long time, more in discomfort than otherwise, for the chest was none too large. The side he had been lying on was numb and ached. He would have turned over on the other, but he did it so awkwardly, that bumping his buttocks against the side of the chest which had been placed in a precarious position to begin with, he first made it lean over, and then tumble down altogether. The thunder of its fall made the women who were sleeping close by start up, but they were so terrified that they couldn't utter a word. Ruggieri himself was scared to death. However, when he perceived that the chest had burst open in the crash, he thought it wiser, in case anything else should come up, to be out of it, rather than in.

What with the strangeness of the surroundings, and what with one and another, he went groping blindly about the house, in search of some staircase or door by which he might make his escape, so that the women, who were wide awake by this time, began to cry out at the noise: "Who's there? Who's there?"

Ruggieri, not recognizing the voices, was dumb as a post, which made them call aloud to their husbands, who, as a result of their unaccustomed vigil, were sleeping soundly and heard nothing of what was going on. More frightened than ever, the women got up, and going to the windows, set up a cry of "Stop thief! Stop thief!"

Immediately, a crowd of their neighbors appeared from all quarters, and rushed to the house, some over the roof-tops, some by one road, and some by another. In the midst of the tumult, the young men were also awakened, and got up. Laying hold of Ruggieri, who was almost out of his head with bewilderment on finding himself in an unfamiliar place, and with no way of escape, they turned him over to the town-police, who had hastened over at the sound of the hubbub, and led him before the provost. The poor wretch was immediately put to the rack, for he had always enjoyed an evil reputation, and surely enough confessed that he had broken into the moneylenders' house with intent to steal. The provost, therefore, thought it was only proper to condemn him to be hanged by the neck as soon as possible.

The following morning, all of Salerno buzzed with the news that Ruggieri had been caught robbing in the moneylenders' house, which so startled and amazed the lady and her maid, that they were convinced they must have dreamed the events of the past night. More than that, Ruggieri's mistress so grieved at his danger, that she went well nigh out of her mind.

Not long after, the surgeon, returning from Malfi, called for his drugged water to be brought, that he might attend to his patient, and finding the bowl empty, went into a frenzy, shouting and ranting that nothing in the house was ever left where he had put it. His wife, who was upset by quite another trouble, shouted back, impatiently: "What would you do about a very serious matter, if you make such a fuss over a mere bowl of water that's been spilled? Isn't there any more water left in the world?"

"I suppose you think it was just ordinary water, my dear," replied the doctor. "But it wasn't. It had something in it to drug one to sleep." He told her, besides, why he had prepared it. No sooner did she hear what he said, than she was certain Ruggieri had drunk it, and had therefore given them the impression he was dead. "We didn't know that, sir," she answered, "so you had better make yourself another dose of it." The surgeon saw there was nothing else to be done, and had more of it prepared.

Somewhat later, the maid who had gone out at the request of her mistress, to hear what was being said about Ruggieri, came back: "Everybody speaks ill of him, ma'am," she said, "and for all I could find out, he hasn't a single friend or relation who's come to help him, or seems likely to have any such desire. It's almost certain the judge is for hanging him to-morrow. There's something else besides, I want to tell you, a peculiar thing, that makes me think I know how he got into the brokers' house. You know the carpenter, in front of whose shop we found the chest we put him in. Well, he was just now having a grand argument with a man who, I think, owned the chest, because he was asking to be given the money for it, and the carpenter was saying he hadn't sold it, but that it had been spirited away in the night. 'No it wasn't,' says the owner. 'You sold it to the two moneylenders, you did, as they told me with their own lips when I saw it in their house last night, after Ruggieri was arrested.' 'They're liars,' says the carpenter, 'for I never sold it to them. Sure, they must have sneaked it away last night. Come along, let's go to them!' So they went off together to the brokers' house, and I came home again. You see for yourself that I've good reason to believe Ruggieri was carried away in that fashion, to the place where he was found. But how he managed to be a live-man again I can't see, for the life of me."

The woman now saw clearly through the whole matter, and in turn told the girl what she had gathered from her husband, begging her at the same time to help rescue Ruggieri, saying that if she wished, she had it in her power both to save him and preserve the reputation of her mistress.

"Show me the way, ma'am," said the maid, "and I'll gladly do anything you say."

Spurred on by the necessity of coming to her lover's rescue, the lady had a sudden inspiration of what course to follow, and imparted it carefully to her maid. First of all the girl presented herself before the doctor, and began, between sobs and tears: "Master, you . . . you must forgive me . . . forgive me for a terrible thing I did against you."

"Why, what is it?" asked Dr. Mazzeo.

With tears still freely flowing, the girl continued: "You know, sir, what kind of person Ruggieri da Jeroli is. He . . . he took a fancy to me, and between the fear and the love I had for him, I was forced to . . . to become his sweetheart. He knew you weren't going to be home last night, so he coaxed and coaxed and coaxed, until I took him into your home and brought him to bed in my room. Well, he was thirsty, and since I didn't want to be seen by your wife, who was in the parlor, and I couldn't think of where to go for water or wine quickly enough, I remembered seeing a bowl of water in your room, so I ran for it and gave it to him to drink, and then put the bowl back in its place. And now I hear you nearly tore down the roof because of it. I know I was wrong, but what person alive never makes a mistake? I'm awfully sorry I did it, really. Well, anyhow, because of it, and what happened afterwards, Ruggieri's on the point of losing his life. So please, please forgive me and let me go and see what I can do to help the unfortunate wretch!"

At her words, the doctor answered jestingly despite his anger: "You've given yourself your own punishment, my lass, for while you thought to be having a brisk cockerel to shake up your bacon for you, you had only a dummy for a partner. Go, go and save your lover's life, but take care you don't bring him into my house again, or I'll settle this score and that with you, I warn you."

Finding her first encounter successful, the girl ran as fast as she could to the prison where Ruggieri was confined, and so cajoled the keeper, that he allowed her to speak with the prisoner. After she had primed Ruggieri on what answers to give the chief of police, if he valued his neck, she turned half the world upside-down until she was admitted before that august personage. Seeing her so fresh and lusty, however, he would not hear of listening to her, until he had first grappled his hook just once onto the good little wench, which she didn't mind in the least, the better to be heard. Then, rising from her exercise: "Sir," said she, "you're holding Ruggieri da Jeroli here as a thief, when he's nothing of the kind." Whereupon, beginning at the beginning, she told him the whole story of how she, the prisoner's sweetheart, had taken him to the doctor's house, given him the narcotic water to drink without knowing what it was, and then had hidden him in the chest, believing him dead. She told him, besides, the argument she had overheard between the carpenter and the owner of the chest, and demonstrated how Ruggieri had come to be found in the brokers' house.

The chief saw that it was simple enough to discover the truth of the whole business. First of all, he asked the surgeon whether what the girl had said about the water were true, and found that it was. Then, summoning the carpenter, the owner of the chest and the moneylenders, he found, after a great deal of cross-questioning, that the brokers had indeed made off with the chest the night before, and carried it to their own house. Finally, he sent for Ruggieri, "Where did you sleep last night?" he asked. The youth replied he had no idea where he had slept, but that he remembered going to spend the night with Dr. Mazzeo's girl, in whose room he had drunk a bowlful of water, in his great thirst. What happened after that, he could not tell, except that when he woke up he had found himself in a chest in the house of the usurers.

The chief of police was very much amused by the whole story, and had the girl, Ruggieri, the carpenter and the moneylenders tell him their versions over and over again. At length, convinced of Ruggieri's innocence, he fined the moneylenders ten ounces for stealing the chest, and set him free.

Was Ruggieri glad? A question not to be asked! As for his mistress, she was the happiest woman alive! Later, the two lovers, together with the darling maid who had wanted to trim him with a knife, had many a good laugh and jest over it, as they persevered in their love and pleasure, bringing them to ever more perfect fruition—would that the like might happen to me, though not the episode of being shut up in the chest.

If the earlier stories had filled the hearts of the lovely ladies with sorrow, Dioneo's last tale soon roused them to laughter; particularly when he mentioned how the chief of police had grappled his hook onto the maid, they were brought out of their melancholy mood altogether. The king, however, observing that the sun was paling in the sky, and that the end of his rule had come, graciously begged the ladies' forgiveness for having made them tell stories about so doleful a subject as lovers' sorrows, and rising to his feet, removed the laurel wreath from his head. While the ladies waited to see upon whom he would confer it, he laid it gallantly on Fiammetta's golden tresses, saying: "I bestow this crown upon you, as the fittest spirit, best able to console our friends to-morrow for the melancholy of to-day."

Fiammetta's hair was curled and long and yellow as gold, flowing over her delicate ivory shoulders and her softly-rounded face, which gleamed with the mingled hues of whitest lilies and crimson roses. Two eyes, bright as the rarest falcon's, shone in her head, and her tiny mouth seemed twin-lipped of rubies. Smiling, she answered: "I take it from you gladly, Filostrato, and the better to impress you with what you have done, I want you all, from this moment on, to make up your minds to speak tomorrow *of the happiness that has finally come to lovers, after some cruel or unfortunate accident.*"

The subject pleased them all; therefore, sending for the steward and arranging all necessary details with him for the period of her reign, Fiammetta bade her small company rise, and with a smile gave them liberty to do as they wished until supper-time.

Scattering in groups, some wandered about the garden, whose beauty was not the sort to surfeit them too easily, others walked toward the mills, that turned beyond the grounds, and still others roved as they pleased, deriving their delight according to their tastes. So they indulged their whim until supper-hour, when they gathered as usual on the brink of the limpid fountain, and ate with great pleasure at the well-served tables. Then, rising, they indulged in their accustomed dances and songs.

"Filostrato," said the queen, as Filomena was about to lead the round, "I don't intend to make any innovations in the customs that have been established so far, and therefore I'd like a song to be sung at my request. I'm sure the songs you sing must be like the stories you tell, therefore entertain us with whatever you please now, so that no other day will ever be darkened by your lovelorn gloom."

"Willingly," replied Filostrato, and immediately plunged into the following:

> "Weeping I prove to all
>     What bitter reason has the heart to grieve
>     When Love itself does its own faith deceive!
> O Love, when first it was you wounded me
>     With love of her for whom I vainly sigh
>         Hoping no more for health,
>         So manifest you showed her virtues' wealth
>     That I thought light the very agony
>             Which to my heated brain,
>             With no surcease of pain
> Did lodge: but now, alas! my fault I know,
> For knowledge came, and with it, too, came woe.
>
> I only knew that I had been betrayed
>     When lorn and scorned I found myself of her
>         Who held my every thought.
>         For when at last I fancied I had wrought
>     Upon her grace, as humble servitor,
>             Without a care for me,
>             Or for my misery,
> A newer love she took for sport and play,
> And me, alas! and me she cast away.
>
> At last, when from her heart I found me banned,
>     A painful sobbing did my bosom tear,
>         Abiding there alway.
>         And oftentimes I curse the hour and day
>     When like a vision, amorous and fair
>             Her face before me came:
>             Still am I all aflame!
> But now my soul repeats its dying prayer,
> Cursing the faith, hope, love it cherished dear.

How void of hope and comfort is my pain,
   Love, you can hear, so dolorous the voice
      That calls upon you still.
       So great the torment's goad, so harsh, until
For lesser pain I'd make of Death the choice.
      Come, Death, and rend amain
      My life's harsh, bitter chain,
And make an end of it and of my woe.
Less hard will be my lot or e'er I go.

No other ease remains, no other way
    But Death to comfort my unhappiness.
      Then, Love, this solace send!
       Of all my miseries, ah, make an end!
Release my heart of its own life's distress!
      Grant it, for sport and play
      And joy are stol'n away!
Lord, make her happy with my death as you
Brought her new gladness with a lover new!

O ballad mine, if no one learn to sing
    And cherish you, I care not, for no man
      Could take you more to heart.
       One mission I would give you as we part:
That you find Love, and tell him if you can
      The drear and worthless thing
      I deem the life I fling
Away from me. And beg him, of his power
To grant a kinder port for my last hour.

Weeping I prove to all
    What bitter reason has the heart to grieve
    When Love itself does its own faith deceive!"

The words of Filostrato's song were explicit enough concerning his state of heart, and what lay at the bottom of it. Perhaps the embarrassment of one of the dancers would have made it even clearer, if the shadows of oncoming night had not veiled the blushes mounting to her face. However, other songs followed after he had finished his, until the hour approached for them to retire, when, at a sign from the queen, they all withdrew to their apartments.

# THE FIFTH DAY

✳

THE EAST HAD ALREADY WHITENED, AND THE BEAMS OF THE RISING
sun had scattered light abroad the land, when Fiammetta, inspired by the melodious caroling of the birds, that had lifted
their voices among the leafy arbors with the first peep of dawn,
arose, and had all the other girls and the three youths summoned. With an easy stride she wended her way down to the
fields with her company, across the wide-stretching plain and
dewy grasses; so, until the sun had fairly risen, she gloried in
the new day, conversing with her friends on everything that
struck her fancy. But when the sun's rays were beginning to
grow ardent, they went back to their apartments, where Fiammetta treated them to excellent wines and dainties, to refresh
them after their slight exertion. Then they wandered again
about the pleasant garden and played until dinnertime. They
sat down to dinner at the queen's invitation, but not until they
had sung a number of airs and ballads. Nor was their usual
dancing omitted, for no sooner was their cheerful and orderly
dinner over, than they indulged in various rounds, to the accompaniment of their songs and instruments, at the end of which
the queen gave them leave to do as they wished until their siesta was over. Some of them took a nap, others remained behind
to sport in the lovely garden, but all of them made sure to
gather at the fountain-side as was their wont, in the cooler hours
of noon, according to the queen's pleasure. Fiammetta took her

seat in the place of honor and, smiling at Pamfilo, requested him
to begin the day's blithe stories. He obeyed without demur, and
began:

✱

## THE FIRST STORY

*Cymon gains wisdom with the coming of love, and abducts his*
*lady Iphigenia, at sea. He is imprisoned in Rhodes, where he is*
*delivered by Lysimachus, and together both carry off Iphigenia*
*and Cassandra, on their wedding day. They go to Crete, where*
*they marry the ladies, and then are called back home.*

MANY STORIES, CHARMING LADIES, OCCUR TO ME, ALL OF THEM
fit to begin the happy day this is likely to be. But one of them in
particular is my favorite, for besides having the happy ending
we stipulated for to-day's narratives, it will make you understand how sacred and powerful and benevolent are the ways of
love, which so many wrongly slander and condemn, without
knowing what they say. It ought to be very comforting to you,
surely, since, if I am not mistaken, you are all the captives of
love.

Well then, as we learn from our history books, there once
lived in Cyprus a very noble man by the name of Aristippus,
who was richer in worldly goods than any other man in the
land, and if Fortune had not cursed him in one particular, he
might have been considered the happiest mortal living. His
misfortune lay in the fact that, among other offspring, he had a
son who far excelled all youths of his age, in stature and physical beauty, but seemed a hopeless dunce, almost an idiot. The
name he had been given was Galesus. However, since neither
the efforts of his teachers, nor his father's gentleness or violence,
nor the wisdom of anyone else, had been able to inculcate in
him the first rudiments of knowledge and breeding, but he still
went about with a rough, uncouth voice and manners more in
keeping with a beast than a man, he was called in mockery
Cymon, which in their language meant nothing less than donkey. Cymon's purposeless life weighed heavily upon his father,
who, having lost all hope of ever making anything of him, ordered him out of his house and sent him to the country to live
with his peasants, if only to have the source of his sorrow out of

sight. Cymon was very well pleased with this turn of events, for the ways and customs of rude country folk were much more agreeable to him, than the amenities of city life.

One day, a little past noon, Cymon, who had settled in the country and busied himself with the employments of rural life, was going from one plantation to another with his crook on his shoulder, when he entered a neighboring wood, all glorious with leaf and blossom, in the fair month of May. As he wandered about in it, he was led, as luck would have it, to a pleasant glade shut in by great, tall trees. A bright, cool spring glistened at one end of the enclosure, beside which he caught sight of a beautiful girl, lying on the green grass in gentle slumber. Her body was clothed in a gauzy veil, hardly concealing the snowy candor of the flesh beneath, and a light, milk-white coverlet was thrown over her, from the waist down. Two women and a man, her servants, were lying, also asleep, at her feet.

No sooner did Cymon set eyes on the girl, than he leaned upon his crook there, before her, and hardly daring to breathe, studied her with rapt wonder, as though he had never before beheld a woman's form. Then, in his uncouth breast, which for all the instruction he had received, no urbane delight had ever been able to penetrate, a spark of thought was kindled, which seemed to inform his gross and material spirit, that there before him lay the rarest beauty any man had ever seen. He dwelled upon her features, one by one, marveling at her hair, which he took for spun gold, at her forehead, nose and mouth, at the sweep of her throat, her arms, and most of all, her dainty, budding breast. Converted suddenly from a peasant to a judge of beauty, he was inwardly taken with a longing to see her eyes, which, heavy with sleep, she kept closed. More than once, he was impelled to rouse her, but seeing her so much more beautiful than other ladies he had ever looked upon, he was afraid she might be some goddess, for dull though he was, he knew enough to deem divine things to be more worthy of respect than the worldly. This alone restrained him, and he waited for her to awake by herself. The time seemed endless; still, captivated as he was by unaccustomed pleasure, he could not bear to tear himself away.

At last, after a long time, the young girl, whose name was Iphigenia, woke up before any of her companions. Raising her head, she opened her eyes, and seeing Cymon before her, leaning on his crook, she cried out in utter amazement: "What are you looking for, Cymon, in this wood, and at this hour?" Everyone knew him by his name, for he was a well-known figure in the country, both for his beauty and uncouthness, and for the wealth and dignity of his father.

He answered not a word, but seeing that her eyes were open, he fixed his own upon them, feeling a gentle sweetness communicating itself to him and filling him with a pleasure never before experienced. The girl, afraid that his steadfast gaze might arouse his rude nature, to her possible shame, called her women and arose, saying: "Good-bye, Cymon. Go in peace."

"I'm coming with you," he replied, and though Iphigenia would have none of him, afraid as she still was, she could not get rid of him until he had reached her doorstep.

Later, going to his father's home, he said he would not go back to the country for anything in the world. Now, although it was a hardship for his father and the rest of the family to have Cymon about, they allowed him to have his way, wondering what had got into his bonnet to cause this change in him. It was a fact, however, that from the moment that, because of Iphigenia's loveliness, the dart of love had pierced Cymon's breast, which no teaching had ever been able to penetrate, he began to astonish his father and everyone who knew him, by the radical change that came over him.

To begin with, he requested his father to provide him with clothes and all other appurtenances, like the rest of his brothers, which the old gentleman did very gladly. Then, mingling with exemplary youths, and learning how courtiers, especially lovers, were expected to behave, he not only began by acquiring the rudiments of literature in a surprisingly short time, to everyone's amazement, but he also became a philosopher of parts. Moreover, still inspired by the love he bore Iphigenia, he not only modulated his harsh, rough voice to the suave accents of the city, but became a distinguished singer and musician, and a brave knight and soldier, skilled in all kinds of warfare, both on land and sea. In short, not to expatiate on his virtues, suffice it to say that scarcely four years after he had fallen in love, he had become the most charming, most accomplished and valorous young gentleman that the whole island of Cyprus could boast of.

How can we explain Cymon's case, lovely ladies? Nowise, surely, than by the fact that the lofty qualities heaven had infused into his noble soul, had been imprisoned by strong bonds in a narrow region of his heart, by jealous Fortune; but Love, more powerful than Fortune, broke those bonds, and like the liberator of dormant instincts that it is, revealed his cruelly blighted virtues to the light of day, clearly showing from what depths it can raise spirits in its power, and to what splendor it may lead them, by its rays.

Now though the lovelorn Cymon sometimes overleapt himself in certain respects, which, after all, is the common failing of young men in his state of heart, Aristippus, considering Love had made a man of his son, from the donkey he had been, not only took his extravagance in good grace, but seconded his every wish. However, Cymon, who refused to be called by any other name, remembering that Iphigenia had first addressed him so, wished to bring his passion to an honorable conclusion, and more than once solicited her father, Cipseus, to give her to him in marriage. Invariably, Cipseus would answer that he had promised her to Pasimondas, a young gentleman of Rhodes, and that he had no intention of going back on his word. But when the time for Iphigenia's established wedding drew near, and her groom sent for her, Cymon reflected:

"Now the moment has arrived, O Iphigenia, to show you how dear you are to me. It was through you I became a man, and if I could only have you, what is there to prevent my becoming even more glorious than any god? One thing is certain: either I have you, or I die!"

After conferring with himself, he called together a number of young noblemen, his friends; then, causing a ship to be secretly armed with everything necessary for a naval battle, he lay in wait for the vessel which was to carry Iphigenia to her bridegroom, at Rhodes. Soon, after her father had entertained the groom's envoys with due honor and ceremony, the young lady embarked with them; they headed the ship for Rhodes, and got under weigh. Cymon, who had not had a wink of sleep, came upon them the following day with his own ship, and from the prow, shouted to the men on Iphigenia's galley: "Halt! Lower your rigging or you'll be overpowered and sunk to the bottom of the sea!"

Meanwhile, his adversaries had run to arms on deck, and were preparing to fight tooth and nail. Cymon, laying hold of a grappling iron, as soon as the words were out of his mouth, flung it onto the poop of the Rhodian galley, that was headed forward fullspeed, and brought it back, by main force, until it was against the prow of his ship. Fearless as a lion, he boarded it single-handed, considering the Rhodians less than his match, and urged on by Love, hewed powerfully among them, sword in hand, wounding many and cutting them down like sheep. The rest, seeing what sort of warrior they had to deal with, dropped their weapons, and almost to a man, declared themselves vanquished.

"Gentlemen," Cymon addressed them. "It was neither desire for booty nor any hatred against you that made me leave Cyprus and fall upon you, with violence, on the high seas. What impelled my attack was the desire for something whose possession means everything to me, and which it will cost you nothing to surrender peacefully to me. It is Iphigenia I want, whom I love above everything in the world. I could not have her from her father by peaceful means, when I approached him as a friend, therefore Love obliged me to wrest her from you by force of arms, as your enemy. It is my intention to be what Pasimondas would have been—her husband. Yield her to me, and then go your way in peace."

Compelled by force, rather than by any will of their own, the Rhodian youths delivered the weeping Iphigenia to Cymon, who, hearing her bitter lamentation, said: "Don't be disheartened, noble damsel. I am none other than your own Cymon, more deserving of you for the long love I've borne you, than Pasimondas could ever be, simply by virtue of your plighted troth."

Returning to his companions, after Iphigenia had been taken aboard, he left everything else that belonged to the Rhodians inviolate, and allowed them to go their way. He was blissfully happy at the acquisition of so dear a captive, and consoling her as much as possible, concluded with his companions that the time had not arrived to set sail for home. They agreed, instead, to go to Crete, where every one, particularly Cymon, had many relatives and friends, new and old, and where they were sure to be safe with Iphigenia. Accordingly, they headed their vessel's prow toward the island. But fickle Fortune, who had granted Cymon the conquest of his beloved all too easily, soon turned the lover's unbounded joy to sad and bitter tears.

They had scarcely left the Rhodian galley four hours behind, when, at the approach of the night that Cymon had been anticipating as the most blissful in his life, a raging, violent tempest rose as well, filling the sky with clouds and the sea with blustering winds. Not a thing could be discerned in the blackness. All sense of direction was lost. It was impossible for anyone either to keep the deck, or do the least service.

It is needless to inquire how disconcerted Cymon was at this state of affairs. Indeed, it seemed as if the gods had granted him his desire, so that death, which he would once have faced without a qualm, might be all the more terrible for the loss of it. His companions, too, lamented their fate, but Iphigenia was the most wretched of all, sobbing aloud and shrinking with terror from every beating wave, cursing Cymon's love with bitter words, in the midst of her weeping, and blaming his daring. The storm, she said, had broken out only because the gods would not brook that he, who wished to make her his wife against their will, should gain the enjoyment of his desire by sheer presumption. No, first he would see her die before his eyes, and then he himself would meet his doom miserably.

What with such lamentations and worse, and the howling wind, which was growing more tumultuous with every passing hour, the sailors gave up in despair. Driven every which way, the ship came to the vicinity of the island of Rhodes, and without knowing where they were, the sailors did all they could to bring the vessel to land, and, if possible, save the lives of those on board. Fortune was propitious, and led them to a small inlet, where, just a little ahead of them, the Rhodians whom Cymon had released, had arrived with their galley.

It was only when the first streak of dawn had cleared the horizon, that they discovered they had arrived at the island of Rhodes, and that they were only a bow-shot away from the galley they had released the previous day. Cymon's consternation knew no bounds, and fearful of what eventually happened, he commanded the sailors to put all their efforts to getting out of there, and to leave the rest to the whim of Fate, for surely they could not be worse off anywhere else, than in their present predicament. His men struggled to force the ship from harbor and direct it outward, but in vain. The blustering wind hove fiercely against them, so that not only were they prevented from leaving the inlet, but were pitched willy-nilly upon the shoals.

They had scarcely set foot on land, when they were recognized by the sailors of Rhodes, who had also left their galley. Instantly, one of them flew to a nearby hamlet, where the young Rhodian gentlemen had found shelter, and told them how luck, through the driving force of the storm, had brought Cymon and Iphigenia there upon their own ship.

The noble youths were rejoiced at the news, and recruiting a number of men from the village they hastened to the shore, fell upon Cymon, who had landed with his men in a desperate attempt to seek refuge in a neighboring forest, and led them all back to the hamlet, together with Iphigenia. There Lysimachus, who had been appointed chief-magistrate over Rhodes, arrived with a large, armed escort, and on the complaint of Pasimondas, who had learned all that had happened and brought suit before the senate, arrested Cymon and his friends and took them all to prison.

So it was that the unfortunate lover lost his Iphigenia, whom he had scarcely won before he had to surrender her without having taken from her anything but a kiss. As for her, she was cared for by many noble Rhodian dames, and comforted for all the suffering she had endured, both in her capture and the stress of the troubled sea; with them she remained until the day set for her wedding.

Meanwhile, Cymon and his companions escaped with their lives, for having given the Rhodian youths their freedom the day before (though it was much against the wishes of Pasimondas, who urged their death) and were sentenced to life imprisonment, where they pined in sorrow, as you can imagine, without the least hope of ever regaining their liberty.

Pasimondas, on the other hand, was expediting as much as possible, the preparations for his wedding, when Fortune, repenting of the unexpected wrong she had inflicted upon Cymon, wrought a new event for his happiness.

It so happened that Pasimondas had a brother called Osmisdas, who, though younger in years, was not inferior in worth. For many years this brother had been suing for the hand of Cassandra, a beautiful girl of quality who lived in town, and with whom Lysimachus was also passionately in love. Through one thing and another, the match had always come to nought. While Pasimondas was preparing to celebrate his wedding with the greatest possible magnificence, he considered it might be a good thing if Osmisdas married at the same time, and so avoid further expense and lavish festivities. Again he broached the subject to Cassandra's parents, and this time he succeeded. Accordingly, he and his brother decided that one and the same day would see Pasimondas married to Iphigenia, and Osmisdas to Cassandra.

When the information reached Lysimachus, he was exceedingly miserable, for now he saw that he had no further grounds for entertaining the hope that if Osmisdas did not succeed in winning Cassandra, he would surely have her for himself. He was wise enough to give no hint of his vexation, and began to wonder how he could prevent the nuptials from taking place. There seemed to be no other way but for him to abduct the bride. Outwardly, it was a simple enough task, considering the position he occupied; still, he knew it was all the more dishonorable because of his very position. However, after long deliberation, honor gave way to love, and he determined to carry off Cassandra, no matter what the consequences. While turning over in his mind the ways and means of going about his deed, and the people who could best serve him, he recollected Cymon, whom he still kept imprisoned with his friends, and reflected he could have no better or trustier accomplice. That night, he had him brought secretly to his room, and said:

"Cymon, as the gods are the best and most generous givers of bounties to mankind, they are also the wisest judges of their virtues: so when they find men who are strong and constant in all trials, they deem them most deserving of the highest rewards. It was their object to make a greater test of your worth, than you could have demonstrated in the confines of your father's house, whom I know to be a very wealthy man. First then, under the guiding influence of love, they made a man of the dumb brute you once were, as I have been told. Later, by misfortune, and now, by duress, they wish to put your spirit to the test, and discover whether it has suffered any change since your very brief happiness, with the prize you had won. If you are still constant, nothing you have ever enjoyed can equal the gift they are preparing for you. Listen, and I shall tell you about it, that you may regain your former fervor and resolve.

"As you know, Pasimondas, who took delight in your misfortune and did his best to procure your death, is expediting the preparations for his wedding with your Iphigenia as much as possible, so that he may then enjoy the gift that smiling Fortune had first given you, only to snatch away again in a moody fit. I know from personal experience what grief that must have caused you, for on the same day, Osmisdas, his brother, is preparing to wound me likewise, by marrying Cassandra, who is the

dearest thing I have. There is only one way fate has left open,
for us to escape her wrongs and trials. It lies only in the bravery
of our hearts and the trustiness of our right hands, which we
must arm with swords, and so hew our way to our ladies—you
to yours for the second time, and I to mine for the first. Now
then, if you are eager to regain what is dear to you—not only
your liberty, which surely is not worth a straw without your
mistress—but Iphigenia herself, the gods will put her into your
hands, provided you consent to follow me in my undertaking."

Cymon's lost hope reawakened in his breast at these words,
and he answered without delay: "Lysimachus, you could not have
a more resolute or faithful partner than myself in this enterprise, if what you promise really comes to pass. Command me
in everything you would have me do, and you will see how
scrupulously I shall obey you."

"Three days from now," Lysimachus explained, "the newly-
wedded brides will enter their grooms' house for the first time.
There, toward dusk, you and your friends, fully armed, and I, with
a few trusted men, will dash in, carry them off from among the
guests, and take them to a galley, which I've already secretly
equipped. If anyone should presume to stop us, death is the
word!"

Cymon was in favor of the plot, and waited quietly in prison
until the established time. The day of the double nuptials arrived, with pomp and magnificence, and not a corner of the
brothers' house but was loud with gaiety and rejoicing. At the
opportune moment, Lysimachus, who had prepared everything
for the event, made three groups of Cymon's companions and
his own, all bearing arms concealed beneath their clothing.
First inciting them to stand by him, heart and soul, by a fervent
speech, he sent one group quietly to the sea-port, so that no one
could prevent their embarkation, and with the other two, proceeded to the house of Pasimondas. One company he stationed
at the door, to ward against being locked in and having their
escape blocked, and with Cymon and the third section, he ascended the stairs into the house. Reaching the great hall, where
the newly-wedded brides were seated at table with many other
ladies, the lovers dashed in, overturned the boards, and each
one taking his lady, delivered her into the arms of his soldiers,
with the command to carry off the captives to the ship lying
ready in the harbor.

The brides began to sob and shriek, accompanied by the

women and servants, and soon wails, screams and tumult filled the house where joy had reigned.

Cymon and Lysimachus, however, with their companies, drew their swords, opening a way before them, without any violence, until they came to the stairs, where, just as they were descending, Pasimondas, having heard the stir, came upon them with a huge staff in his hand. Fiercely, Cymon struck him a blow on the head, that clove it in half and laid him dead at his feet. Osmisdas, too, who had run to aid his brother, was also laid low by another of Cymon's strokes; others who came forward, were likewise wounded and repulsed by the companions of both leaders. Then together they sallied forth unhindered with their captives, to the galley, leaving behind a house full of blood and confusion, mourning and sorrow. Embarking with the ladies and their comrades, they plied their oars and went their way rejoicing, as the shore was overrun by armed men, who had come too late to rescue the brides. At Crete, they were received with joy by numerous relatives and friends, and marrying their mistresses amid marvelous festivities, they enjoyed their prizes to the utmost.

Grave, and of long duration, were the troubles which ensued between Crete and Rhodes from these events. At length, through the intercession of their friends and kin in both states, they found a way to adjust the matter, so that after a brief period of exile, Cymon returned triumphant to Cyprus with Iphigenia, while Lysimachus went back to Rhodes with Cassandra. And so they lived long and happily in their own lands, each with his wife.

# THE SECOND STORY

*Costanza, who is in love with Martuccio Gomito, hears that he is dead, and getting into a little boat in her keen despair, is drifted by the wind to Susa. In Tunis, she finds her lover alive, and reveals herself to him. Then Martuccio, who has become a favorite courtier for the advice he had given the king, marries her and returns home with her in great state.*

WHEN THE QUEEN REALIZED PAMFILO'S STORY WAS OVER, SHE praised it highly, and turning to Emilia, requested her to resume the narrative thread with another tale.

It is only right, began Emilia, that one should rejoice on being rewarded according to one's desires. And since in the long run, love is more worthy of happiness than of misery, I shall obey the queen with much more zest by expatiating on that subject than I did the king, yesterday.

You must know, fair ladies, that very near the shores of Sicily, rises a tiny island called Lipari, where not so very long ago, there dwelt a lovely girl of distinguished family called Costanza. A young man of the island, by the name of Martuccio Gomito, handsome, well-mannered and skilled in his trade, fell in love with her, and she with him, so that she had not a moment's peace, except when she had him before her eyes.

Now Martuccio was eager to make her his wife, but when he asked her father for her hand, the old gentleman answered he would not consent, because of the youth's poverty. Martuccio flared up with scorn when he saw himself jilted because he was poor, and setting out with a group of friends and acquaintances, he swore never to set foot upon Lipari again, until he had money to burn.

He was as good as his word, and turning pirate, began sailing coastwise along the Barbary shores, plundering anyone who could not withstand him. Fortune smiled upon his enterprise, and everything would have gone well, had he known how to limit his desires. However, not content with the enormous wealth he and his company had accumulated in so short a time, he sought to gain even more, when he was suddenly attacked by a fleet of Saracen galleys. There was a long and bitter struggle, during which he was captured with his comrades, the ship sunk by the Saracens and the majority of the crew drowned. He himself was taken to Tunis, and kept in prison for long miserable years.

Many were the people who brought the tidings to Lipari that Martuccio had been drowned with the rest of the men on board. Costanza, who had been sufficiently heartbroken by her lover's departure, wept her eyes out on hearing he had met his doom with the others, and inwardly determined that she had had enough of life. She was not brave enough to lay violent hands on herself, and considered a way of meeting her death by other means.

One night, stealing quietly out of her father's house, she went to the seashore, where, as fate would have it, she came upon a fisherman's boat which was a little distance from the lest. Its owner must just have left it, for it was still furnished with mast, sail and oars. Getting into it, she rowed herself a distance out to sea, skilled as she was in seamanship, like most women of that island; then hoisting sail, and throwing away both oars and rudder, she committed herself to the mercy of the weather. Surely, she thought, the wind must overturn a boat without ballast or helmsman, or crash and split it against a rock; then, even if she had had any desire to live, she would be compelled to die. With this resolve, she swathed her head in a mantle and lay down sobbing in the bottom of the boat.

But things turned out quite differently from what she had expected. The wind, a mild, northerly breeze, wafted the sturdy boat over an almost placid sea, so that next day, toward nightfall, it was carried to the shores of a city called Susa, about a hundred miles from Tunis. Costanza, who had neither raised her head from her first position, nor had any intention of lifting it, no matter what happened, had no idea whether she was on land or sea. As it chanced, at the time the boat struck shore, a poor woman happened to be on the beach, taking in the nets of her fisherfolk from the sun. Seeing the little craft, she wondered who had been so careless as to make it land full sail, and thinking that perhaps the fishermen aboard were dozing, she went toward it and found nobody but the girl, sleeping soundly. Again and again she called her, until at last she woke her up. Recognizing her for a Christian, by the clothes she was wearing, the woman addressed her in Latin, and asked her how she had come there all alone in that little craft. Costanza, on hearing the woman speak Latin, was afraid a changing wind had carried her back to Lipari, and jumped quickly to her feet. When she looked about her, and saw herself on the strand of an unfamiliar country, "Where am I?" she said.

"You are near Susa in Barbary, my child," the good woman answered.

The girl, chagrined that the Lord had not willed her to die, was frightened and ashamed, and not knowing what to do, crouched at the bottom of her boat and burst into tears. The woman was filled with compassion seeing her weep, and pleaded with her until Costanza consented to accompany her to her hut. There, the woman coaxed her to tell her story, and seeing the girl had not eaten, she put a bit of fish and a crust and water before her, inviting her so insistently, that at last Costanza was persuaded to take a bite.

"Who are you, who speak the Latin tongue?" asked the girl; whereupon the kind woman told her she was from Trapani, that her name was Carapresa, and that she was employed there by Christian fishermen. On hearing the woman's name, Costanza, in spite of her deep woe, was prompted, for some inexplicable reason, to take it as a good omen, and began vaguely to hope and to yearn less for death. Accordingly, without revealing her own identity, or where she came from, she implored the good woman to have pity on her youth, and give her some advice which would serve to guard her from danger of insult.

Carapresa, like the kindly soul she was, left her in the little hut, gathered her nets as quickly as she could, and rejoined her. Then, wrapping her in her cloak, she took her to Susa.

"Costanza," she said, when they had arrived, "I'm going to take you to the house of a wonderful Saracen lady—a good old body and very kind, whom I sometimes help about the house. I'll speak highly of you and recommend you to her, and I'm sure she will gladly take you in and treat you like her own daughter. It's up to you, when you're there, to do your best in her service, and ingratiate yourself with her, until the Lord sends you something better."

She was as good as her word. The Saracen lady, who was quite advanced in years, was touched by the woman's story, and gazing into Costanza's face, wept with pity. Pressing her to her, she kissed her on the forehead, and taking her by the hand, led her to her house, where she lived with several other women, without any man among them, all of them variously occupied in doing handiwork in silk, palm-fibre and leather. In a few days, Costanza had mastered a few of the tasks, and set to work with the other women. Soon she had so won the heart of her old mistress and the rest of her companions, that it was marvelous to see, and before long she also acquired their language, through their teaching.

Now during the time Costanza was living in Susa, although given up for dead at home, a certain Mariabdela was king over Tunis. However, a young man of great family in Granada, and extremely powerful, claimed the throne of Tunis for himself, and gathering a tremendous army, he marched against the monarch, to drive him from his kingdom.

The report came to the ears of Martuccio Gomito, as he lay in prison. He was very proficient in the Barbary tongue, and learning that the king was turning the world upside down for his

defense, remarked to one of the keepers who watched over him
and his comrades: "If only I might obtain an audience with the
king, I've a feeling I could give him a bit of advice, which
would help him win the war."

The guard told his superior what he had heard, and he in turn
immediately reported it to the king, who commanded Martuccio to be brought before him.

"What advice have you to offer?" he asked.

"Your Majesty," replied Martuccio, "if I'm not mistaken, I
think I noticed on other occasions, when I visited your realm,
that whenever you wage battle you rely more on the strength of
your archers, than on anything else. Well, if Your Majesty
could find a way of keeping the enemy archers unprovided
with arrows, and your own well-supplied, I am confident you
would win your battle."

"If that could be," said the king, "I would assuredly deem
myself the victor."

"If Your Majesty wishes," continued Martuccio, "there is a way
of contriving it, and you shall hear how. You must have the
strings of the bows your archers use, made much thinner than
those commonly employed. Then you must have darts and
arrows made, whose notches are suitable only for these slim
thongs. All this you must endeavor to do with the utmost secrecy, so that your enemy may not know of it and find a way to
frustrate you. Now this is the reason I make these proposals.
After your enemy's archers and your own have exhausted their
supply of arrows, Your Majesty knows that your adversaries will
be obliged to gather what your men have shot, and yours to do
likewise with the enemy's while the battle lasts. Now your enemies will not be able to use your archers' darts again, because
the small notches will not receive the heavy cords, while the
contrary will be true of your archers and their adversaries' arrows, for the thin cords will be very well suited to take the
wide-notched shafts. This way your men will be copiously supplied with arrows, while your enemies will have a dearth of
them."

The king, who was a wise monarch, was pleased with Martuccio's advice, and following it to the minutest detail, found himself victorious in the war. As a result, he thought very highly of
Martuccio, and raised him to a position of great wealth and dignity.

These events were voiced about the country, and presently

Costanza heard that her lover, whom she had long thought
dead, was alive. Her love for him, which had slowly languished
in her heart, burst into sudden flame and grew more ardent
than ever; her dead hope broke into life. Accordingly, she unburdened her past sufferings and misfortunes to the good old
lady with whom she was living, and expressed her desire to
go to Tunis, that she might feast her eyes on what rumor
had made her long to see again. The lady approved her wish.
Like a mother, she took ship with the girl, and accompanied
her to Tunis, where they were both made welcome at the home
of one of her people. Carapresa also came along, and her they
sent ahead, to see what she could find out about Martuccio. On
discovering that he was alive and in enviable circumstances,
Carapresa reported it to the Saracen lady, who wished it to be
her privilege to inform Martuccio that his Costanza was there.

One day she sought him out in his home and said: "Martuccio, a servant of yours from Lipari happened to come to my
house, and would like to have a few words privately with you
there. I could not entrust the message to anyone else, and so, at
his wish, I came to inform you myself."

Martuccio was very grateful and followed her to her house,
where Costanza almost died with happiness on seeing him again.
Unable to repress her emotion, she ran to him impulsively
with open arms, and hung upon his neck, clasping him close.
The stress of the present joy was too great, and overpowered the memory of their past misfortunes. Unable to utter a
word, she wept tears of tenderness. Martuccio, on his part, marveled to see the girl, and for a while could not find his speech.
At last he said, sighing: "Are you really alive, dearest Costanza?
Is it really you? How long ago it was that I heard you had
been lost at sea! Even at home, no one knew a thing of what
had become of you."

With that, tears rose to his eyes, and he embraced and kissed
her lovingly. In due time, Costanza told him everything she had
gone through, and the hospitality she had enjoyed at the
home of the Saracen lady. After they had talked together and
reminisced a long time, Martuccio took leave of her, and going
to the king, narrated the adventures he and Costanza had experienced, adding that with the permission of his liege, he intended making her his wife, according to our law. The king
was astonished at the strange events. Sending for the girl, and
hearing from her own lips that things were as Martuccio had

told him, he said: "You have indeed earned him for a husband!"

He had a vast quantity of rich gifts brought, and divided them between Costanza and Martuccio, giving them leave, besides, to arrange their affairs as they thought best. Then the young man, expressing the deepest gratitude to the Saracen lady who had taken care of Costanza, thanked her for all she had done, gave her gifts in keeping with her state, and entrusted her to God's keeping. She went away, not without many tears on Costanza's part.

Some time later, he and Costanza, with the king's sanction, embarked on a small galley, taking Carapresa along with them, and reached Lipari on a prosperous wind. Who can describe the welcome they received? Suffice it to say, Martuccio married her in grand style, and they lived happily ever after in peace and contentment, and in the lasting enjoyment of their love.

## ✷

## THE THIRD STORY

*Pietro Boccamazza, eloping with Agnolella, falls in among thieves. The girl, fleeing through a wood, happens upon a castle, but Pietro is captured. He escapes from the thieves and eventually comes to the very castle where Agnolella found refuge. There he marries her, and returns with her to Rome.*

THERE WAS NOT ONE AMONG THEM BUT APPLAUDED EMILIA'S story, when the queen, knowing it had come to an end, turned to Elisa and called upon her to continue. Eager to obey, she began:

It occurs to me to describe the dreadful night two inexperienced young lovers underwent; but since it is succeeded by many happy days, I shall tell you the story, as it is quite in the spirit of to-day's theme.

In Rome, which was once in the fore, as it is now in the rear, of the world's cities, there lived a youth, not so long ago, called Pietro Boccamazza, scion of one of the noblest families of the town. He fell in love with a lovely, charming girl called Agnolella, the daughter of a common citizen who was nevertheless greatly esteemed by the Romans—a certain Gigliuzzo Saullo—and the lad was so skilful in his lovemaking, that in no time the young lady was as much in love with him, as he with her.

Suffering in the throes of his excessive passion, and unable to put up with the sting of desire he felt for her, the stripling asked for her hand in marriage; but no sooner did his relatives hear of it, than they attempted to squelch his intention. What's more, they warned Gigliuzzo Saullo not to pay heed to Pietro's words, no matter what he said, adding that if he gave his consent, they would never condescend to accept him, either as friend or kin.

Seeing the only way to his desire shut against him, Pietro nearly pined away in despair, and if Gigliuzzo had only given his consent, he would have sent the rest of his folks to the devil, and married the girl against their will. He did not give up hope, however, and resolved that if the girl were willing, he would seek to attain their mutual happiness, in spite of everything. Learning through a go-between, that she was not at all averse to his desire, he came to an understanding with her, to elope together from Rome. Accordingly, he got everything ready for the elopement, and one morning, rising at the break of day, he took horse with her and galloped toward Anagni, where he had a number of trusty friends. On and on they rode, and as they had no leisure to consummate their nuptials, through their dread of pursuit, they contented themselves with simply expressing their love in words and now and then snatching a quick kiss.

Pietro was not very familiar with the way, so that when they had left Rome eight miles behind, and come to a fork in the road, he turned to the left, instead of keeping to the right. Hardly had they ridden a couple of miles farther, when they found themselves approaching a little castle, from which they were perceived. Immediately, a dozen men came out. They were almost upon the two lovers, when the girl caught sight of them and cried: "Let's fly, Pietro! We are attacked."

Quickly, she turned her pony's head toward a deep forest, and guiding it as well as she could, pressed the spurs hard against its flanks, clutching on to the saddlebow. Feeling the prick of the spurs, the horse galloped madly on, and carried her to the depths of the wood.

Pietro, who had eyes only for her face, paying little heed to the road, had not been aware of the churls as quickly as she, and while he was still looking about for them, he was overtaken, captured and ordered off his horse.

"Who are you?" they asked. He told them, whereupon they

fell to discussing among themselves, saying: "This youth here is of our enemies' party. What better can we do than to take his clothes and horse and string him up one of those oaks, to spite the Orsini?"

They were all in favor of this procedure, and commanded him to strip. Pietro was about to obey them, well knowing what was in store for him, when suddenly, two dozen others who had been lying in ambush, fell upon his assailants shouting: "Death! Death! Kill them! Kill them!"

The ruffians, surprised by the attack, left Pietro and seized their arms for their defense. However, as their number was no match for the enemy, they took to their heels, the others following in hot pursuit. Pietro, seeing how the matter stood, gathered his clothes together in a hurry, and mounting his horse, fled until the sparks flew, in the direction he had seen Agnolella take.

No road nor path was in the forest, nor were any hoof marks to be seen, and the girl was nowhere to be found. When he saw himself safe from the clutches of the churls who had seized him, and from their assailants, he wept and went searching for her through the woods, sadder than any man alive, calling and hallooing. There was no answer. He dared not go back, and going forward was also a risk, for he could not tell what might happen to him. Moreover, terrified both for her sake and his, of the wild beasts that haunted the woods, he expected at every step to see his beloved slain by some bear or wolf.

All day long the hapless lover wandered shouting and calling through the forest, going about in circles in his bewilderment. By this time he was so exhausted, what with his shouting, weeping, his fear and long fasting, that he could scarcely go another step. Meanwhile, night had overtaken him. Not knowing what else to do, he dismounted when he came to a tall oak, fastened his horse to the trunk, and climbed and hid himself among its branches, that the wild beasts might not devour him in the night. Soon after, the moon rose. The air was clear and bright. Not daring to fall asleep for fear of falling from his perch (though his preoccupation and grief for Agnolella would have prevented him, even if he had wished to), he sighed and wept, and cursing his evil fortune, spent the night in wakefulness.

In the meantime, the girl, who had fled, as we said before, without knowing where she was going except that her pony was leading her as it pleased, was so deep in the woods that she could not find her way out again. Like Pietro she, too, went weeping and calling for him all day long, bemoaning her fate, and getting more and more inextricably lost in the wilds, as she wandered about, now pausing for rest and now proceeding farther. At last, when night was overshadowing her, and no Pietro was to be found, she came across a narrow footpath, which the pony followed for over two miles. Suddenly, she caught sight of a little cottage some distance away, and making for it as fast as she could, she came upon a very old man, who was living there with his wife, who was as old as himself.

"Poor child! What are you doing in these parts at this hour, and all alone?" they exclaimed when they saw her unattended. Between her sobs, Agnolella replied she had lost her companions in the woods, and asked how near they were to Anagni.

"Daughter," said the kindly old man, "this is not the way to Anagni. It's more than twelve miles from here."

"Is there any place near by, where I could lodge for the night?" asked the girl.

"Not so near, my child," said he, "that you could reach there by daylight."

"Then could you please keep me here for the night," asked she, "since I can't go anywhere else?"

"My poor girl," replied the honest fellow, "we'd love to have you stay with us to-night, but we must warn you that all kinds of wicked clans of friends and foes go prowling about this neighborhood day and night, causing us a lot of trouble and annoyance, day in, and out. If by some misfortune any such band should pass by and find you here, so pretty and so young, they might do you some terrible harm, and we could not be of any help to you. We want to have a clear conscience about it, and let you know about it beforehand, so that in case the worst should happen, you'll not be thinking ill of us."

Though the man's words struck terror in her heart, Agnolella, seeing how late it was, said, "If it is God's will, He will protect both you and me from this evil. Still, even if it should be, it is less terrible to be ill-used by men, than to be torn to pieces by wild beasts in the woods."

At that she dismounted, entered the cottage of the two good old people, and partook of the frugal supper they had to offer. Then she flung herself upon a bed with them, dressed as she was, and all through the night did not cease sighing and lamenting her fate and Pietro's, not knowing whether she could expect any but ill news of him.

It was nearing daybreak, when she heard a mighty stamping of people drawing nearer and nearer. Starting to her feet, she hurried to a wide yard behind the little cottage, and seeing a haystack on one side, hid herself in it. If those people came here, she thought, she could not be found so quickly. She had scarcely concealed herself, when they did come to the door of the cottage—a great company of desperadoes. Knocking loudly, to be admitted, they entered, and finding the girl's pony still bridled and saddled, asked who had arrived. The old man, seeing the girl nowhere about, replied: "There's nobody here but us two old souls. This pony—whomever it ran away from—got here last night, and we took it in so that the wolves wouldn't eat it up."

"Well," said the chief of the band, "since it lacks an owner, it will suit us perfectly."

Running amok in the cottage, some of them went out into the yard, and while they were putting aside their lances and targets, one of them, for lack of something better to do, flung his spear into the hayrick, nearly killing the girl, and almost making her reveal her hiding-place. The weapon, grazing her left breast, tore through her clothes; she would have shrieked in her terror of being wounded, but recalling where she was, did not dare breathe, but contained herself in an agony of dread.

After the men had roasted the kids and other meat they had brought, they ate and drank, and then breaking up into various parties went off in different directions about their business, taking the girl's pony along with them. They had left the house some distance behind, when the old man asked his wife: "What do you suppose has happened to the young lady who came here last night? I've seen nothing of her since we got up."

She said she had no idea, and looked for her everywhere. Meanwhile, Agnolella realizing the ruffians had left, came out of her hiding-place amidst the hay, to the relief of the old man, when he saw she had not fallen into their clutches. Day had dawned by this time, and he said: "Since it's morning now, we'll go with you, if you wish, as far as a castle, about five miles away from here. You'll be safe there. But I'm afraid you'll have to go the distance on foot, for those scoundrels who just left took your horse along with them."

Agnolella did not worry about the beast, but begged them to escort her to the castle, so they set out on their way and reached it about half-past nine.

This castle, as it happened, belonged to a gentleman of the Orsini family called Liello di Campo di Fiore, and at that time his wife, a very pious, charitable woman, was occupying it. On looking at Agnolella, she recognized her immediately, and making her comfortable, asked her how she had got there. The girl told her the whole story, at which the lady, who also knew Pietro as a friend of her husband's, grieved for their ill-fortune. Moreover, when she heard he had been attacked, she was almost certain he had been murdered. Turning to Agnolella, she said: "Since you don't know what has become of Pietro, you had better stay here with me, until I can find a way of sending you safely to Rome."

In the interim Pietro, huddled up in his oak-tree, was as miserable as could be, when, at about the time he should have fallen asleep, he saw a pack of about twenty wolves, which, at the sight of the horse, came crowding about it. The poor beast had pulled at its bridle at the scent of them, and broken loose in an attempt to escape; but they were already surrounding it. For a long time it defended itself with its teeth and hoofs, but at last it was laid low, strangled, and immediately disemboweled. The ravening beasts gorged themselves until they had devoured it completely, and then went away, leaving nothing but the skeleton. Pietro, who had looked upon the poor animal as a sort of companion and comfort in his misery, was aghast with horror, and gave up all hope of ever getting out of the forest alive. Toward sunrise, however, while he was shivering with cold up in the oak-tree, never ceasing to peer about him, he saw the glow of a great conflagration about a mile away. As soon as the sun shone more brightly, he climbed down the tree, not without some trepidation, and walked in that direction, until he came to a clearing, where he found a party of shepherds eating and making merry around the fire. They welcomed him among them, out of pity. Afterwards, when he was somewhat restored by food and comforted by the warmth, he told them what mishap had brought him there alone, and asked them whether there were any hamlet or castle in the vicinity, where he might find refuge. About three miles from there, they informed him, rose the castle of Liello di Campo di Fiore, where his lady was staying at present. Cheered by the information, Pietro begged to be accompanied by someone as far as the castle, and two men gladly volunteered.

Finally, when he reached the place and found some friends of his, he was about to get a party together, to scour the woods for Agnolella, when he was summoned by the lady. He went to her without losing time, and what was his delight when he found the girl there with her! He was dying to throw his arms about her and embrace her, but contained himself out of shyness in the lady's presence; still, if his happiness knew no bounds, Agnolella's was not to be exceeded.

The noble lady welcomed him with great rejoicing, and having heard from his lips what he had gone through, gave him a sound scolding for what he had sought to do, against his parents' wishes. Nevertheless, on seeing that he was unshaken in his resolve, and that the girl was in favor of it, she reflected: "Why am I wasting my breath? These two young people love each other; they've known each other a long time, and they're also friends of my husband. Moreover, their desire is legitimate enough, and I think God smiles upon it, for He rescued one from the noose, the other from a lance, and both from the wild beasts of the woods. Well, so be it, then!" Turning to them, she said aloud: "If you have made up your minds to marry each other, I have nothing against it. Marry, then, and let the nuptials be celebrated at Liello's expense. I'll see about setting things right with your people."

Then and there, the happy Pietro and the still happier Agnolella were married, and the wedding was celebrated by the noble lady, with all the pomp and ceremony possible in a mountain fortress. There they experienced the sweetness of love's first fruits, and a few days later, both of them and their benefactress, with a trusty following, took to horse and returned to Rome. They found Pietro's family in a rage at what he had done, but soon the lady made peace between him and them, and restored him to their good graces. So he lived happily with his Agnolella, in ease and pleasure, to a ripe old age.

\*

# THE FOURTH STORY

*Ricciardo Manardi, discovered by Lizio da Valbona with his daughter, makes her his wife and so lives in peace and harmony with his father-in-law.*

WHILE ELISA WAS SILENT, LISTENING TO THE PRAISE HER COMpanions bestowed upon her story, the queen bade Filostrato to tell one, and with a laugh, he began:

I've been lashed so often by your tongues for having made you relate tragic and pathetic tales, that I think I ought to make amends by telling you something to stir you to laughter. I shall narrate, then, a very short story of a love that at last ended happily, after no more serious disaster than a few sighs, and a little scare not unmingled with shame.

Well, then, not so very long ago, noblest of ladies, there lived in Romagna a considerable gentleman of excellent breeding, by the name of Lizio da Valbona. Upon the approach of old age, Fortune blessed him with a daughter by his wife, Mistress Giacomina; and as time went by, the lass developed more than any other girl in the countryside, both in beauty of feature and charm of manner. As she was the only child her mother and father had left, they loved her as the apple of their eye, and watched over her with all care and diligence, hoping through her marriage to make some fine connection.

As it was, a lusty young sprig of a lad called Ricciardo, scion of the Manardi da Brettinoro family, was a frequent visitor at the home of Master Lizio, and went about with him a great deal, neither the old gentleman nor his lady scrupling any more about him, than if he had been a son of their loins. Now as the stripling cast his eyes on the girl and saw how lovely and fair she was, full of pretty ways, and of the age when a young girl wants a husband, he fell passionately in love with her, though he was extremely careful to keep it hidden from everyone. The lass, however, was well aware of it, and showed no hesitation in falling in love with him, much to Ricciardo's delight. Many a time he had longed to speak to her, but had refrained, out of doubt concerning her feelings. Once, however, taking the bull by the horns, he said: "Catherine, have mercy on me! Don't let me die of love!"

Promptly she answered: "Would to God *you* had mercy on me, and not let *me* die!"

Her answer filled him with joy and made him bolder. "There's nothing I wouldn't do to give you pleasure," he said to her. "But it's up to you to find a way to save your life and mine."

Said Catherine: "You notice how strictly I'm kept, Ricciardo, so I can't possibly see how you could come to me. But if you can think of anything I could do, without ruining my reputation, why speak out, and I'll do it."

Ricciardo turned over various things in his mind, and said with celerity: "Sweetest Catherine, I don't see any other way, except for you to come down or manage to sleep out on the terrace that overhangs your father's garden. Then, if I were sure you'd be there at night, I'd manage to come to you by hook or crook, no matter how high it is."

"If your heart is set on coming," replied Catherine, "I think I'll know how to find a way of sleeping there, all right."

Ricciardo was pacified, and snatching a kiss on the sly, went away.

The month of May was coming to a close, and the following day Catherine began to complain to her mother of the terrible sleepless night she had spent, due to the dreadful heat. "What heat are you talking about, daughter?" asked her mother. "It wasn't hot at all."

"You should add *in my opinion,* mother dear, and then perhaps you'd be telling the truth," said Catherine. "Besides, you must bear in mind that young girls are much more warm-blooded than elderly ladies."

"You're right about that, my dear," said she, "but I haven't it in my power to make it hot or cold at will, as you'd like me to. We must put up with whatever weather the season gives us. Maybe it'll be cooler to-night, and you'll be able to sleep better."

"I hope so," said Catherine, "but it's not customary for the nights to get cooler as summer draws on!"

"What on earth would you have me do about it?" asked Mistress Giacomina. And Catherine answered: "If you and father have nothing against it, I'd like to have a bed put out near his room on the terrace, that overlooks the garden, and I'd sleep there. Then I could be much more comfortable, listening to the nightingale and lying in a cooler spot. It would be much better for me than in my room!"

"Very well, my dear," said her mother. "I'll tell your father about it, and we'll do as he says."

On hearing what his wife had to say, Master Lizio, who was old and consequently somewhat peppery, exclaimed: "A nightingale! What nightingale is this to whose tune she wants to sleep? I'll make her sleep to the chirping of crickets, I will!"

That night Catherine, who had learned his answer, not only remained wakeful, more out of petulance, than because of the heat, but also did not let her mother get a wink of sleep with her complaints of the insufferable weather. Next morning, therefore, good Mistress Giacomina went to her husband.

"You seem to have no feeling at all for our little girl," said she. "What is it to you if she wants to sleep on the porch? She hadn't a moment's rest all night long, for the heat. And what great wonder is it if she does want to listen to the nightingale, seeing she's such a young thing? All young people love everything that's as fresh and young as themselves."

"Very well, very well!" said Master Lizio. "Let her have a bed made there—as large as will fit. Curtain it around, and let her rest there, listening to the nightingale to her heart's content."

When Catherine heard her father's words, she immediately had a bed set up in the terrace. The night she was to sleep there, she waited until she caught Ricciardo's eye and gave him the signal they had agreed upon, which told him what he was to do. Then Master Lizio, noticing that the girl had gone to bed, bolted the door that led from his room to the terrace, and himself settled down to sleep.

Meanwhile Ricciardo, when everything was hushed, climbed upon a wall, with the help of a ladder, and grappling the palings of a neighboring wall, scrambled to the porch, at the risk of breaking his neck in a fall. Catherine welcomed him with suppressed delight, and made a great fuss over him, and after countless kisses, they lay down together. All through the night they took joy of each other, making the nightingale sing many a pretty song.

But the night was short, and their pleasure great, and already day was breaking, though they would never have thought it. However it was, whether they were exhausted because of the weather or their merry frolicking, they fell asleep without a stitch of covering on their backs, Catherine with her right arm under Ricciardo's neck and with her left hand clutching that affair which you ladies blush to call by its right name in the presence of men.

Well, as they were sleeping soundly in that position, day surprised them without rousing them. But Master Lizio got up. Recalling that his daughter was sleeping on the terrace, he pushed open the door very gently, and said to himself: "Let's see now how the nightingale charmed our little Catherine to sleep last night!"

Approaching nearer, he quietly raised the serge that curtained the bed, and saw the young man and his daughter sleeping embraced in that fashion, all uncovered and naked as the day they were born. Recognizing Ricciardo, he left the porch and going to his wife's room, woke her up, crying: "Up, up, wife! Quick, come and look at your little girl, who was so delighted with the nightingale that she has caught it and is holding it tight!"

"How is it possible?" she asked.

"You'll see, you'll see if you hurry," said Master Lizio.

Mistress Giacomina quickly put on her clothes, and quietly followed her husband. When they got to the bed and the curtain was lifted, Mistress Giacomina plainly saw how her daughter had caught and imprisoned the nightingale, whose song she had been so anxious to hear. She would have rebuked Ricciardo and given him a piece of her mind, for the guile he must surely have employed to seduce the girl, but Master Lizio stopped her, saying: "If you value my affection, wife, I warn you not to say a word about it, for indeed, if she's captured it, hers it will be. Ricciardo comes of a good family, and he is rich. We'd be getting only the best of connections through him. If he wants to remain a friend of mine, he must marry her first and realize he's put the nightingale in his own cage, not another's."

Mistress Giacomina was cheered to see that her husband had not flown into a fury at the event, and considering that her daughter had enjoyed a good night, rested well, and caught the nightingale in the bargain, she made no objection. They had scarcely exchanged a few words together, when Ricciardo woke up, and seeing that the sun was shining brightly, gave himself up for dead. "O my soul!" he called to Catherine. "How shall we get out of this scrape? It's broad daylight already, and here I am in this fix."

"We'll get out of it well enough," replied Master Lizio at his words, as he came forward and lifted the curtains. Ricciardo's heart was in his mouth, and starting up on the bed, "Mercy," he cried, "for the Lord's sake! I know I deserve death for the treacherous friend and wicked man I've been! Do with me as you please, only I beg you, let me get off with my life. Have mercy! Let me not die!"

Then Master Lizio addressed him: "Ricciardo, these are not the returns I had expected, for the love I bore you and the trust I placed in you. But since your impulsive youth led your better judgment to such a sin, you must make Catherine your lawful wife, to save your life and spare me shame. Thus, as she was yours to-night, she will continue to be yours as long as she lives. Only that way can you redeem your life, and be my friend again. But if you should not be willing, commend your soul to God!"

While her father was speaking, Catherine let the nightingale go, and pulling the bedclothes over herself, burst into tears, pleading with him to spare Ricciardo's life and urging her lover at the same time to do as Master Lizio wished, so that they might in all security enjoy together in the future, many more nights like the past. No great coaxing was necessary. For Ricciardo, impelled on the one hand by shame for his sin and anxiety to make amends, and on the other, by fear of death and a desire to live, was urged above all by his ardent love and the passion to possess the thing he loved; so that everything combined, made him declare he was willing to do whatever Master Lizio desired.

Accordingly, borrowing one of his wife's rings, Master Lizio had Ricciardo take Catherine to wife, then and there, and in their presence, without stirring an inch. That done, he and Mistress Giacomina took their leave, saying: "You'd better rest now, children, for I guess you need it more than anything else."

No sooner were they gone, than the lovers clasped each other again; and as they had gone only six stones that night, they went two more before they thought of rising, and making an end of the first day's mileage.

At length they arose and Ricciardo had a more adequate understanding with Master Lizio. A few days later he went through the wedding ceremony with Catherine once again, in the presence of friends and kin, as was proper, and took her home with him amid great rejoicing, celebrating his nuptials

with magnificence and splendor. Long and happily he lived
with his bride in peace and solace, catching nightingales aplenty
with her, both by day and night.

## ✳

## THE  FIFTH  STORY

*Guidotto da Cremona leaves his small daughter in charge of
Giacomin da Pavia, and dies. Both Giannole di Severino and
Minghino di Mingole fall in love with her at Faenza, and quarrel
because of her. At last, she is discovered to be Giannole's sister,
and is given in marriage to Minghino.*

THE LADIES HAD LAUGHED SO HEARTILY AT THE STORY OF THE
nightingale, that even though Filostrato had ceased speaking,
they still could not control their merriment.

"Really," said the queen, after a good laugh, "if you did give
us a bitter pill yesterday, you've certainly amused us so to-day,
that nobody can very well bear you a grudge." And turning to
Neifile, she asked her to continue with a story. Cheerfully smiling, Neifile began:

Filostrato carried us all to Romagna with his tale, and I shall
follow suit and wander there awhile in my narrative.

Once upon a time, then, two Lombards lived in the town of
Fano, one of whom was called Guidotto da Cremona, and the
other Giacomin da Pavia. Both of them, now fairly advanced in
years, had spent almost all their youth in warfare and feats
of arms. When Guidotto saw that death was at his elbow, he left
his little daughter, a child of about ten, to his friend Giacomin,
having no son, relative or comrade in whom he placed more
faith, and entrusted him besides with all his worldly goods. Then,
discussing at great length what his friend was to do, he breathed
his last.

At about that time, the city of Faenza, which had long been
racked by war and suffering, returned to a state of comparative
peace and the town gates were thrown open to any citizen who
wished to return. Giacomin had once lived at Faenza, and had
grown attached to the place, so gathering his effects together, he
removed there, taking along the girl Guidotto had left in his
care, and whom he loved and cherished as his own daughter.

As time went on, the girl, whose name was Agnesa, grew into as beautiful a young woman as any the city could boast of, and was as modest and virtuous as she was beautiful. Little by little, many a youth set his cap for her, but two young gentlemen, particularly, both handsome and of good family, fell so desperately in love with her, that they became mortal enemies out of jealousy. One of them was called Giannole di Severino and the other Minghino di Mingole. Neither of the two, now that the girl had reached the age of fifteen, would have hesitated a moment to rush her into marriage, had his family only allowed it; but since they were both denied their demands out of a certain sense of honor, they set about individually to gain possession of her, by fair means or foul.

As it was, Giacomin had an old maid-servant in his house, and a lackey, whose name was Crivello, who was a merry fellow and a good sport. Giannole struck up a friendship with him, and when he thought the proper moment had arrived, told him of the great love he bore Agnesa, and begged him to help him obtain his desire. There was nothing he hesitated to promise as reward.

"I'm afraid I can't be of very much service to you," answered Crivello, "except to admit you to the young miss' room sometime, when Giacomin is invited out to dine; for she'd never so much as listen to me if I ever said anything in your behalf to her. I can give you my word on this, if that satisfies you, and I'll keep it too. Once I've done what I said, it's up to you to act as you see fit."

Giannole told him he could wish for nothing better, and so the matter was settled.

Minghino, on his part, had got into the good graces of the maid-servant, and had succeeded so well, that she had delivered many an amorous message to Agnesa, stirring in her a responsive echo. Moreover, she had even promised to leave him alone with the girl the first evening Giacomin was called out of the house, for some reason or other.

Not very long after these agreements had been made, Giacomin was invited out to supper with a friend of his, through Crivello's machinations. The fellow, informing Giannole of it, arranged with him, that at a stipulated sign the lover should come to the door, which he would find open. The maid-servant, unaware of this, sent word on her part to Minghino, that her master was not supping at home, and directed him to be somewhere about the neighborhood, so that at her signal, he might come and slip into the house.

Toward nightfall, the two love-lorn youths, unaware of each other's purposes, and each suspecting the other of foul play, arrived on the spot with various armed companions, ready to claim their own. Minghino and his party stationed themselves in a friend's house, adjoining Agnesa's, waiting for the signal; Giannole, on the other hand, stood watch with his band not far from the door.

Meanwhile, now that Giacomin was away, Crivello and the servant did their best to get rid of each other.

"How is it you've not gone to bed yet?" Crivello asked the maid. "What are you prowling around the house for?"

"And why aren't you going out to fetch the master?" asked she. "What are you waiting for? You've had your dinner."

But neither could manage to get the other out of the house. Finally Crivello, seeing that the hour he had established with Giannole had come, reflected: "What the deuce do I care about her, anyway? If she doesn't keep quiet about it, she'll come in for a good drubbing, I swear." Thereupon, giving the stipulated signal, he opened the door. Accordingly, Giannole hurried there with two companions, entered, and finding the girl in the hall, seized her, to carry her away. She began to struggle and scream, the maid joining her, so that Minghino heard and rushed to her rescue with his troop. Agnesa was already being carried out of the house, when they drew their swords, shouting: "Ah, traitors! You'll die for this! Things won't turn out as you think. What do you mean by this violence?"

No sooner were the words out of their mouths, than they began a wholesale slashing and hewing, while the neighbors rushed out of their houses at the uproar with lights and weapons in their hands, taking sides with Minghino and condemning the whole affair. At length, after a weary struggle, Minghino wrested the girl from Giannole, and brought her back safely to the house of Giacomin. The skirmish was nowhere near ended, when the guards of the town-captain came upon the scene and arrested many of the rioters, among them Minghino, Giannole and Crivello, all of whom they led away to prison.

At last, when the tumult had subsided, and Giacomin came home, he was extremely grieved at the event. But when he looked into the matter, and found that Agnesa had not been in the least to blame, he calmed down somewhat and decided to marry her off at the first opportunity, in order to prevent further recurrences of such trouble.

The following morning, when the families of the two lovers learned the truth of the affair, they realized what a ticklish predicament the youths would be in, if Giacomin insisted on pressing charges to the full extent of the law, as he had good reason to do. Accordingly, they hastened to his house, and persuaded him, with temperate words, not to dwell upon the injury the lads had done him, but rather to follow the promptings of the affection they believed he had for them who pleaded with him. What is more, they were willing to place themselves and the fool-hardy young culprits under any obligation he required. Giacomin was a man of wide experience and sense, and had seen much in his day.

"Gentlemen," said he, without wasting words, "even if I were in my own city, as I am in yours, I couldn't consider myself a better friend to you all, and I would not think of doing anything in this matter, as in all else, unless it met with your approval. Moreover, in this case I am all the more obliged to yield to your demands, inasmuch as you inflicted the injury upon yourselves rather than upon me. Agnesa is neither from Cremona nor Pavia, as many believe. On the contrary, she is of Faenza, though neither she nor I, nor the man who entrusted her to my care, ever knew whose daughter she was. I can only act according to your dictates, in the question you have put before me."

The worthy citizens were astonished to hear the girl sprang of their own people, and thanking Giacomin for his broad-minded answer, begged him to relate how she had come to be left in his care, and how he knew she was of Faenza.

"Guidotto da Cremona was my brother-in-arms, and my friend," began Giacomin, "and on his death-bed he told me that when this city was captured by Emperor Frederick, and left to be sacked, he broke into a house with other soldiers of his troop. The house was full of goods, but had been entirely abandoned by its owners, except for a little girl of two or three, who called 'Papa' after him as he was going upstairs. The name softened his heart, and he took her along with him, together with everything in the house. Then, when he was about to die, he left her to me, with all his property, requesting me to find her a husband when the time came for her to marry, and give her as a marriage-portion all that had belonged to her. She is old enough to marry, but I have not been able to decide on a husband good enough for her, though I should be glad enough to do so, rather than have a recurrence of last night's mischief."

Among the emissaries, there happened to be one Guglielmino da Medicina, who had taken part with Guidotto in the pillaging, and knew very well whose house it was Guidotto had sacked. Seeing the man there with the rest, he drew up to him and said: "Do you hear what Giacomin is saying, Bernabuccio?"

"I certainly do," said Bernabuccio, "and I was just turning it over very seriously in my mind, for as I remember, during all that turmoil, I lost a little girl of about the age Giacomin mentioned."

Then said Guglielmino: "I'm sure this must be your daughter. I happened to be with Guidotto once, when he described the neighborhood of the house he had sacked, and I recognized it as yours. Try to remember if there's some mark by which you can identify her and let her be searched. I'm sure you'll discover that she's your own daughter."

Bernabuccio pondered awhile, and recalled that if the girl were his, she must have a scar in the form of a small cross above her left ear, caused by an abscess he had had lanced, a little while before the capture of the town. Immediately, he approached Giacomin, who was still among them, and begged him to take him home and let him see the girl. Giacomin readily complied, and taking him along, sent for Agnesa.

No sooner did Bernabuccio set eyes on her, than he seemed to see in her the image of her mother, who was still a very beautiful woman. However, he was not satisfied with the resemblance alone, and asked Giacomin's permission to raise her hair a little from above her left ear. Giacomin consented. Going up to Agnesa, who was standing there covered with blushes, Bernabuccio raised his right hand and lifted her curls. The cross-like scar was there, whereupon, convinced that she was indeed his daughter, he embraced her with tears in his eyes, though she resisted modestly, and turning to Giacomin said: "My friend, this is my daughter. It was my house Guidotto pillaged, where in the sudden panic the little one was left behind by my wife, her mother. To this day we've always believed her dead—burned in the house that was set on fire that same day."

On hearing Bernabuccio's words, and seeing him a man of middle-life, Agnesa, moved by some secret instinct, believed the truth of his words, and no longer struggling against his affectionate demonstrations, she mingled her tears of tenderness with his. Soon Bernabuccio sent for her mother, sisters and brothers and other kin, and showed her to them all, telling her strange story. They kissed and embraced her a thousand times, and made a great deal of her. Finally Bernabuccio took her home, to the great satisfaction of Giacomin.

The news reached the town-prefect, a good and worthy man, who, knowing this Giannole, whom he held in prison, to be a son of Bernabuccio and therefore the girl's brother, decided to show clemency and overlook the lad's offense. He conferred, besides, with Bernabuccio and Giacomin. With their aid, he patched up a truce between the two young men, whom he released together with Crivello and all the others who had been party to the mischief, and gave Agnesa to Minghino in marriage, to the satisfaction of all his family.

Amid gladness and rejoicing, the youth held a magnificent wedding-feast, and then, taking Agnesa home, lived in peace and prosperity with her for many, many years.

# THE SIXTH STORY

*Gianni of Procida, discovered with a young girl, with whom he had long been in love, but who had been given to King Frederick, is bound with her to a stake and condemned to be burned; he is recognized by Ruggieri dell' Oria, saved from death, and given the girl in marriage.*

NOW THAT NEIFILE HAD FINISHED HER STORY, WHICH HAD BEEN very agreeable to the ladies, the queen requested Pampinea to prepare to tell another. Lifting her beaming face, the girl began:

A mighty thing, sweet ladies, is the power of Love, and many are the struggles and woeful perils that it inflicts on hapless lovers, as you have seen from the stories we've heard to-day, and on previous occasions. But I wish to demonstrate it still further, by this story of mine about a love-lorn youth.

In the island of Ischia, close to Naples, there was once, among other young maids, a charming, vivacious girl by the name of Restituta, daughter of a gentleman of the place called Marin

Bolgaro. A youth of the neighboring islet of Procida, Gianni by name, loved her more than his life, and she as ardently returned his affection. So deep was the lad's love, that not content with sailing from Procida to Ischia by day for a glimpse of her, he would often swim by night, for lack of a boat, from his own island to hers, if only to gaze on the walls of her house. And so they continued in their youthful love.

One day, however, while the girl was all alone on the shore, leaping from rock to rock and plucking periwinkles from the stones with a knife, she came to a cave among the cliffs, where some young Sicilians, newly come from Naples with one of their small ships, were sheltered, partly for the shade the grotto afforded, and partly for the convenience of a cool spring which had its source there. They caught sight of her before she was aware of them, and finding her so lovely and unprotected, they decided to seize her and carry her off. No sooner said than done. They fell upon her, though she shrieked loudly for help, carried her aboard their vessel, and made off for Calabria. They had scarcely reached their destination, when a great clamor arose among them for possession of her. In short, each man wanted her for himself; but unable to come to any amicable agreement, and fearful of getting into a worse scrape and ruining their affairs because of her, they resolved to make a gift of her to Frederick, King of Sicily, who was a young man at the time, and took delight in amorous disport. Accordingly, they presented her to him upon their arrival at Palermo.

The young monarch was mightily pleased on seeing her so beautiful, but since he was somewhat run-down in health, he ordered her to be kept in one of his country-houses, called La Cuba, in the midst of gardens, and there carefully tended until he should be in better fettle. His wishes were carried out.

Meanwhile, Ischia was in an uproar at the young girl's abduction, and what made everything worse, was the failure of the people to discover who the men were that had carried her off. Gianni, however, whom Restituta's disappearance most affected, had no hope of finding out anything at Ischia, but learning in what direction the kidnapers' ship had sailed, he fitted up a small frigate and embarked. As fast as the wind would carry him, he scoured the coast from Minerva to Scalea along the shores of Calabria, inquiring everywhere for news of the girl, and there he was told that she had been carried away to Palermo by some Sicilian sailors. Thither he sailed without wasting time, and after long and assiduous search, found that Restituta had been given as a present to the king, and was being kept by him in La Cuba. Sorrow smote his heart, and he lost all hope that he should ever see her, much less have her for his own again.

Nevertheless, Love bade him stay. Sending away his frigate, he remained in Palermo, as nobody there knew him, and took to passing often before La Cuba. One day he happened to get a glimpse of Restituta at a window. At the same time she saw him, to their boundless joy. The place was lonely and unfrequented. Approaching as near as he could, Gianni spoke to her, and she in turn told him what to do, if he desired to have a more intimate talk with her. After examining the lay of the land, Gianni went away.

Waiting for a good part of the night to pass, he returned thither, and balancing himself on a ledge, where even a woodpecker would not have found foothold, he climbed into the garden. There he found a long pole, which he leaned against the window the girl had pointed out to him, and he clambered up to it with great ease.

Now Restituta, who considered her honor as good as lost, though in the past, she had shown herself most chary of it toward Gianni, pondered that she could not give herself to any man alive, more justifiably than to him. Moreover, considering that she might prevail upon him to take her away, she made up her mind to grant him his every desire, and had therefore left the window wide open for him to enter without any trouble. Things being as they were, Gianni slipped in quietly and lay down beside the girl, who had been watchfully waiting and lost no time in letting him know her wish, pleading earnestly with him to take her away from that place. Gianni replied that he desired nothing better, and promised he would set about arranging for her flight without fail. Indeed, he would take her away the next time he came to see her. That settled, they clasped each other with the keenest pleasure, and proved that rapture beyond which there is none greater that Love can give. Again and again they returned to it, and then, without being aware of it, sank into a deep sleep, twined in each other's arms.

The king, meanwhile, who had been struck from the first with Restituta's beauty, suddenly remembered her, and feeling quite fit, decided to while away some hours by her side, though dawn was near. With a few servants he made his way quietly to La Cuba, and entering, had the girl's chamber-door gently unlocked. Then, with a great lighted torch before him, he stepped into the room, when alas! as his eyes fell upon the bed, he saw her sleeping in Gianni's arms, both of them stark naked. A sudden access of wrath took possession of him, and blind with rage, he would have killed them with the dagger at his side, and without warning. But then, at the realization of how vile a thing it was for a man, much more so, for a king, to murder two naked creatures in their sleep, he restrained his impulse and resolved to burn them at the stake in a public place. Turning to the sole companion he had admitted, "What do you think of this lewd woman," he asked, "on whom I had placed all my hope?" Then, "Do you know the fellow," he added, "who has been so bold as to enter my house and commit such an outrage, and such an indignity against me?"

The man replied that he had never set eyes upon the lad before, whereupon the king left the chamber, seething with wrath. Then and there, he commanded the two lovers to be taken, naked as they were, and bound, and in broad daylight led to Palermo. There in the market-place they were to be chained to a stake, back to back, kept until the afternoon that all might have a chance to behold their shame, and then burned alive as they deserved. The order given, he returned to his palace in Palermo, mad with rage.

As soon as their sovereign had departed, a number of men fell upon the lovers without warning, and not only roughly awakened them, out of their sleep, but quickly seized them and bound them hand and foot. The poor wretches were stricken with terror when they saw what had happened, and you can well imagine how they wept and mourned and despaired of their lives. Later, in obedience to the sovereign's command, they were taken to Palermo, bound to a stake in the market-place, and before their eyes, the faggots of the pyre were stacked up, ready to consume them at the hour set by the king.

Crowds of men and women swarmed from all over the town to see the two lovers, the men trampling on one another to look at the girl. While they were engaged in praising her every perfection, the women, on the other hand, flocking to stare at the youth, outdid one another in heaping encomiums on his handsome and well-made body. The lovers, poor things, crushed with shame, hung their heads and mourned their fate, counting the hours that brought them nearer to the cruel pyre.

Now while they were being held there before the public eye, and the fatal hour approached, the report of their crime, voiced about everywhere, reached the ears of Ruggieri dell' Oria, a man of inestimable virtue and prowess, who was at the time admiral to the king. He, too, went to the place where the lovers were bound. At first he looked at the girl, admiring her for her beauty, but when his eyes fell on the youth, he recognized him without any difficulty.

"Are you not Gianni of Procida?" he asked him, drawing nearer. Gianni, raising his head, knew the admiral immediately and said: "I was once the man of whom you inquire, my lord, but I shall soon be no more."

"What brought you to this, my boy?" he asked.

"Love," replied Gianni, "and the king's wrath."

The admiral had him tell the story in detail. After he had heard how it all had happened, he would have left, but Gianni called him back and said: "Ah, my lord, obtain just one favor for me, of the man who has condemned me to this!"

"And what favor is that?" asked Ruggieri.

"I know I must soon die," said Gianni. "As a boon, I request that since I am bound here, back to back with this girl, whom I have held dearer than my life and who has loved me as dearly —let us be turned to face each other, so that when I die I may look upon her dear visage, and leave this life content."

"Gladly," said Ruggieri with a laugh. "I'll manage to have you look at her so much, that you'll be tired of having her before you."

Leaving Gianni, the admiral commanded the executioners in charge not to raise a finger until they received further orders from the king, and without waiting any longer, he presented himself before his monarch. Though he saw Frederick in a sullen mood, he did not deviate from his intention to speak out his mind, and said:

"Sire, how have those two young people offended you, that you have commanded them to be burned alive down there in the market-place?" The king told him, and Ruggieri continued: "Their crime is well worthy of such expiation, but not from you. Crimes, it is true, deserve their just punishment; but with equal justice, good deeds merit their rewards, not to speak of grace and mercy. Do you realize who those two are, whom you condemn to be burned?" Frederick answered he did not, whereupon Ruggieri resumed: "I want you to know who they are, so that you may appreciate how rashly you allow yourself to be carried away by your wrath. That lad is the son of Landolfo of Procida, brother of Gian di Procida, through whose offices you are king and lord of this island. The girl is the daughter of Marin Bolgaro, whose power makes it possible for your sovereignty to be recognized in Ischia. Above and beyond that, these two have long loved each other, and this sin—if what young people do out of love, can rightly be called a sin—they were constrained to, by the passion they feel for each other, and not out of any desire to set your authority at nought. Why, then, would you have them die, when you ought to be honoring them with the greatest courtesies and rewards?"

At that the king, after assuring himself that Ruggieri had spoken the truth, not only forbore to exercise his cruelty, but repenting of what he had already done, commanded the two lovers to be released at once, taken from the stake and brought before him. His command was carried out. Thereupon, learning all the circumstances of their case, he resolved to make amends for the wrong he had done them, by gifts and honors, and caused them to be dressed in magnificent clothes, and had Gianni marry Restituta, seeing that the two lovers were agreed upon that score. Then, loading them with splendid gifts, he sent them happily to their own land, where they were welcomed back with great rejoicing, and lived together in pleasure and joy to the end of their lives, rich in years.

✳

## THE SEVENTH STORY

*Teodoro, in love with Violante, the daughter of his master Amerigo, gets her with child and is condemned to the gallows. While he is being led to death and scourged on the way, he is recognized and delivered by his father, and later married to Violante.*

DURING THE STORY-TELLING, THE WOMEN HAD HUNG ON PAMpinea's words in their anxiety to learn whether the lovers would be burned, and hearing of their rescue, they thanked God and heaved a sigh of relief. The story over, the queen bade Lauretta continue, who cheerfully began:

Loveliest ladies, in the reign of the good King William of Sicily, there lived on the island, a gentleman called Amerigo Abate of Trapani, who was well provided with children, among other worldly goods. He was in need of servants, and as certain galleys belonging to Genoese corsairs arrived from the East, full of young boys who had been captured during coastwise raids on Armenia, Amerigo bought a number of them, believing them to be Turks. Among them was a child called Teodoro, remarkable for his gentle bearing and nobility in the midst of his companions, all of whom seemed to be only humble shepherd-boys. Although the child was treated in all ways like a slave, he grew up with Amerigo's children, in the palace, where, through his innate breeding, rather than out of any accident of Fortune, he developed into so fine and accomplished a youth, that Amerigo became attached to him and made him a free man. Still under the impression that the youth was a Turk, he had him baptized and renamed Pietro, and then, entrusting him with his most important affairs, reposed all his faith in him.

As time went on, and the children of Amerigo grew up, a daughter of his called Violante, a lovely, delicate girl, was reaching maiden-hood as rapidly. But Amerigo delayed so long in giving her away in marriage, that she fell in love with Pietro. Dearly though she loved him, and greatly though she admired his ways and the charm of his manner, she was too modest to make her passion known to him. Love, however, spared her the trouble, for Pietro, on his part, observing her again and again on the sly, had himself fallen so deeply in love with her, that no happiness was possible for him except when he could see her, though he was mortally afraid someone might discover his love, in his belief that he was not acting as he ought. Violante, who was only happy at the sight of him, was soon aware of his affection, and revealed herself, as indeed she was, more delighted than ever in his presence, the better to reassure him. So, for a long time they continued in their ardor, not venturing to address a word to each other despite their great yearning.

While they were both consuming in the flames of their love, Fate gave them the opportunity to banish the shyness that stood between them, as though what came to pass had been foreordained. About a mile away, in the environs of Trapani, Amerigo had a very pleasant country seat, whither his lady and Violante and other women and maids were wont to go for rest and recreation. On a very hot day, they set out toward it, as usual, taking Pietro along with them when, on their way, the sky was suddenly hidden by dark clouds, as often happens in the summer time, whereupon the lady and her companions turned back for Trapani, that the storm might not overtake them in the open road.

All of them ran as fast as they could, but Pietro and the girl, both young and fleet, far outdistanced her mother and the rest, Love, perhaps no less than fear of the weather, lending wings to their flight. Already they were so far ahead, that they were lost to view, when the storm broke, heralded by mighty claps of thunder, and followed by a sudden, thick down-pour of large hail. Hurriedly, the lady and her company took refuge in a peasant's cottage.

Pietro and Violante, for lack of nearer cover, crawled into a little old tumble-down hovel, deserted and almost in ruins, and under an overhanging patch of roof that still remained, pressed so close together for the meagerness of the shelter, that their bodies touched. The contact fired their minds with the boldness to express their passionate desire for each other.

"If only God would make this hail last forever," began Pietro, "that I might always remain as I am!"

"I wish so, too," said Violante.

The words led them to take each other's hands and clasp them; from that they proceeded to embrace and kiss, as the rain pattered above and about them. Well, to make a long story short, the storm had not abated, before they had tried the extreme delights of love, and arranged for secret meetings for their pleasure.

The hail ceased. Together the two lovers walked to the nearby town-gate, and waiting for the lady, returned to the castle with her. Here they met secretly, and with the utmost discretion, time and time again, to their mutual delight, and their love progressed so well, that Violante became pregnant. The lovers' consternation knew no bounds, and many were the arts Violante employed to bring about a miscarriage, contrary to the course of nature. Nothing availed. Pietro, fearing for his life at this turn of events, thought it safer for him to flee, and told her so, but she said: "If you go, I will kill myself, as sure as fate!"

Then Pietro, who loved her dearly, tried to make her understand. "How can you want me to remain here, dearest?" he said. "Your condition will soon betray my sin. You'll be forgiven without much difficulty, but, poor me, I'll have to pay the price for both your sin and mine."

"Pietro," replied Violante, "my sin will be obvious enough, but rest assured that no one will ever know of yours, unless you yourself confess it."

"Since you promise, I'll stay," said Pietro. "But do not fail me!"

Meanwhile, when Violante saw that her pregnancy, which she had sought to conceal as skilfully as possible, could no longer be hidden for the growing fruit in her womb, she told her mother about it with sobs and tears, begging her to save her life. The lady, grieved and shocked, minced no words in reproving her daughter's fault, and insisted on knowing how it had all happened. Violante was anxious to spare Pietro mischief, and invented a plausible story, veiling the truth. The good lady believed it, and to conceal Violante's condition, sent her away to one of their country places. There the time of her delivery approached.

While the girl was screaming with pain, like all women in child-bed, and her mother was far from suspecting that Amerigo, who hardly ever frequented the estate, would be there, he walked past the bed-room where Violante was lying, on his return from flying the hawks. Wondering at her shrieks and cries, he flung into the chamber without warning, crying: "What is the matter here?"

Quickly rising upon the sudden advent of her husband, the lady came to him in trepidation, and told him what had happened to their daughter. But he was not so credulous as she had been. It was impossible, he said, for the girl to have conceived without knowing who had fathered the child, and he clamored for the truth, adding that if Violante confessed, he would forgive her; otherwise she must prepare for death without hope of mercy. In vain, the good lady endeavored to persuade Amerigo to believe what she had said, and be satisfied with that. Flying into a fury, he brandished his naked sword, and rushing upon his daughter, who had been delivered of a boy during their argument, cried: "Either you tell me who fathered this child, or you die, this instant!"

Violante, in her terror of death, broke the promise she had made Pietro, and confessed all that had been between him and her. Amerigo, mad with rage, hardly forbore making an end of her on the spot. Nevertheless, after he had spent upon her the uncontrolled ire of his tongue, he mounted his horse once more, and returning to Trapani, complained to Messer Currado, the king's governor, of the indignity he had suffered at Pietro's hands. Immediately, the governor had the unsuspecting youth seized and put to the rack, where he confessed all he had done. Some days later, sentence was passed upon him. First, he was to be scourged through the streets, and then, hanged by the neck.

Amerigo's wrath was not assuaged by bringing Pietro to his doom. Indeed, that the self-same hour might see the earthly end of the two lovers and their child, he mixed poison in a bowl of wine, and calling a servant, gave it to him, together with an unsheathed dagger.

"Go, bring Violante these two things on my behalf," said he, "and command her to make an immediate choice of the death she prefers—poison or the knife. If she refuses, say I'll have her burned in the market-place before all the townspeople, as she has well deserved. When you have done this, take the new-born child and dash its brains out against the wall. Then give it to the dogs to eat."

That cruel sentence, pronounced by the merciless father against his daughter and little grandchild, the fellow, more disposed to wickedness than good, hastened to carry out.

Now while Pietro was being flogged through the streets by the men who were leading him to the gallows, he was made to pass at their pleasure before an inn, where three Armenian nobles were stopping. They had been sent as ambassadors by the King of Armenia, to discuss weighty matters with the Pope, regarding a crusade that was about to be initiated, and lodging at the hostelry for a few days' rest and recuperation, they had been greatly honored by the gentlemen of Trapani, and by Amerigo in particular. When these nobles heard the tumult of the crowd leading Pietro to the gallows, they came to the window to see what was going on.

Pietro was naked to the waist, with his hands tied behind him. One of the ambassadors, Fineo by name, a venerable gentleman of great authority, turned his eyes upon the youth, when he noticed on the lad's chest a large, crimson spot, a sort of birthmark which women commonly call a *rose*. At the sight of it, he thought instantly of a son of his, who had been kidnapped by pirates some fifteen years before, on the shores of Lazistan. He had never heard of the boy since. Taking into consideration the age of the unfortunate wretch who was being flogged, he reflected that if his son were alive he would be approximately as old as he. Thereupon, a vague emotion stirred him, and a feeling, all the more convincing because of the birthmark, that this might be his son. If it were really so, he mused, the youth must still remember his own name and his father's, and recognize his native language; therefore when the lad was close enough, he called: "Teodoro!"

At the voice, Pietro quickly raised his head, and Fineo, addressing him in Armenian, asked: "Where do you come from? Whose son are you?"

The officers leading the culprit came to a halt, out of reverence for the nobleman, and Pietro was able to reply: "I was born in Armenia. I am the son of a man called Fineo, and I was brought here as a child by whom I know not."

When Fineo heard, he knew beyond a doubt that this was the son he had lost, and going down into the street, accompanied by his friends, he ran to embrace him with tears in his eyes, there, in the midst of the sergeants. Taking a cloak of richest silk from his own shoulders, he threw it about his son, and besought the executioner who was leading him to his doom, to wait there until he should receive further orders. The officer made no objection, and said he would gladly do so.

As it was, Fineo already knew what fault it was that was bringing the youth to his death, for rumor had spread it abroad. Accordingly, he hastened with his friends and their following to Messer Currado, the governor, and said: "Sir, the lad you are sending to his death as a slave, is a free man and my son, and is ready to marry the woman whose virginity he took, according to report. I beg you, then, delay the execution, until we learn whether she is willing to accept him as her husband, so that in case she should be, you will not have acted against the law."

Messer Currado was astounded to hear that the prisoner was the son of Ambassador Fineo, and ashamed of the crime Fortune would have had them commit. He praised the justice of the gentleman's words, and had Pietro escorted home. Then, sending for Amerigo, he informed him of all that had happened.

Now Amerigo, who was almost certain his daughter and grandson had already been put to death, was the saddest man in the world at the thought of what he had done, realizing as he did, that if Violante were alive, everything might be satisfactorily adjusted. However, he still had hope, and sent a speedy messenger to prevent the execution of his command, if it were not too late.

The man found Amerigo's servant bitterly expostulating with the girl, for not choosing the knife or the poison he had placed before her quickly enough, and would have forced her to come to a decision. But when he heard his master's order, he left her in peace, and returning to him, recounted how matters stood. Amerigo was overjoyed. Hastening to Ambassador Fineo, he apologized as well as he knew how, with tears in his eyes, for all that had occurred, and begged his forgiveness, saying that if Teodoro was willing to take Violante, he would gladly have him marry her.

Fineo lent a willing ear to his apologies and said: "It is my intention to allow my son to marry your daughter, and if he should refuse, let the sentence against him be carried out."

Coming thus to an agreement, the two men betook themselves to Teodoro, who was still in mortal dread of his life, though happy on the other hand, at having found his father, and asked him what course he intended to follow in the matter. The youth, hearing that he was at liberty to marry Violante, was so delighted that he believed he had soared from hell to heaven with one bound, and replied that he would deem it the greatest privilege he could be offered, if they both were willing. At that, they sent to find out how the girl felt about it. On hearing how her lover had fared, and of how he was likely to fare, Violante, who had been on the verge of despair and had expected nothing but death, began to believe all was not lost. Plucking up hope, she replied that if she were to follow her desire, she could think of no dearer joy than to be Teodoro's wife, although she would consent to anything her father commanded. So Violante was married to Teodoro by common consent, and great was the splendor of the wedding and the rejoicing of the townspeople!

Before long, Violante, considerably cheered, gave her son into the care of a wet nurse, and became lovelier than ever. At last, when she rose from child-bed, she presented herself before Fineo, who had returned from his embassy to Rome, and greeted him with the respect due a father. Happy to have such a lovely daughter-in-law, he had the nuptials celebrated with splendor and rejoicing, and took her to himself as a daughter, cherishing her as such, as long as he lived.

Several days later, embarking on a galley with his son, Violante and his baby grandson, he took them all with him to Lazistan, where the bride and groom lived in peace and happiness to the end of their days.

✳

## THE EIGHTH STORY

*Nastagio degli Onesti loves a lady of the Traversari family, and squanders his riches for her sake without having his love requited. At his friends' insistence, he goes to Chiassi, where he has a vision of a knight giving chase to a lady, slaying her, and throwing her body to be devoured by two hounds. Thereupon, he invites his family and the people of his beloved to a banquet, where the hard-hearted damsel sees the phantom lady torn to pieces. Fearing a similar fate, she takes Nastagio for her husband.*

NOW THAT LAURETTA WAS SILENT, FILOMENA COMMENCED, AT the queen's bidding:

Adorable ladies, just as pity is always commended in us, our cruelty is also severely punished by divine justice. The better to prove it to you, and give you cause to banish it from your hearts, I shall be pleased to tell you a story, which is as moving as it is interesting.

In the very ancient city of Ravenna in Romagna, there once lived many noble gentlemen, among whom was a youth called Nastagio degli Onesti, who, through the inheritance he received upon the death of his father and an uncle, became phenomenally wealthy. As is always the case with young bachelors, he fell in love, with a daughter of Messer Paolo Traversari. Though the lady was of bluer blood than he could boast of, he hoped to prevail upon her to requite his love, through his noble deeds. Still, despite their greatness and splendor, they not only availed him nothing, but seemed rather to be counted against him, so cruel, harsh and relentless she revealed herself to him. Indeed, whether because of her extraordinary beauty, or the pride she felt in her family, she had grown so lofty and disdainful, that neither he nor anyone else seemed good enough for her. Her attitude was so painful to Nastagio, and so hard to bear, that often, weary of grieving, he would have laid violent hands upon himself; but he forbore. Then he made many a futile resolution to tear her out of his heart, or loathe her as she seemed to loathe him. In vain, for the more meager the hope his love fed upon, the greater it grew.

Now while he was going at a reckless pace, still persisting in his love and spending lavishly to impress her, his family and friends thought he would soon end by consuming both himself and his wealth, and often employed all their eloquence to persuade him to leave Ravenna and live elsewhere for a while, so that he might at least appease his love and spare his goods. Time and again, Nastagio laughed at their counsel or turned a deaf ear, but at last, unable to withstand their importunities, he consented to do as they wished. Marvelous were the preparations he made for his journey. One might have said he were setting out for France, Spain or some other distant country. But then, mounting his horse, and accompanied by his hosts of friends, he left Ravenna, and galloping to a little place called Chiassi, some three miles distant, declared: "Here I mean to stay. All of you may go back to Ravenna." With that, he ordered his tents and pavilions to be set up.

Once encamped at Chiassi, Nastagio began to lead the gayest and most luxurious life ever, and as usual, his tables were never empty of guests of all sorts and descriptions, whether at dinner or supper-time.

One very beautiful day, on the threshold of the May month, he fell to brooding over his cruel lady, and ordering his servants to leave him alone that he might have more leisure to indulge his melancholy revery, he walked on and on in a sort of haze, until he found himself in the midst of the surrounding pine-wood. It was well-nigh noon, and he had wandered about a half mile into the forest, without giving any thought to food or anything else, when suddenly the terrible shrieks and cries of a woman seemed to fall upon his ears. Startled out of his musing, he raised his head to see what could have happened, and to his astonishment found himself in the pine-forest. Even more, as he gazed before him, he saw a beautiful girl, all naked and disheveled, running through a thicket overgrown with brush and briars, toward the spot where he was standing, her body lacerated by thorns and brambles as she wept and shrieked aloud for mercy. Two huge, fierce mastiffs followed close upon her, and sank their cruel fangs into her flesh each time they overtook her; and behind them a dark knight came riding upon a black steed. His face was fiery with wrath, and brandishing the dagger in his hand, he threatened her with death, as he heaped harsh words of scorn upon her. At first, Nastagio was filled with wonder and terror at the sight, but then pity for the unfortunate lady moved him, and a desire to free her, if he could, from such anguish and death. As he was unarmed, he took the branch of a tree for a truncheon, and so went forward to face the hounds and the knight.

From a distance, the rider perceived his intent, and cried out: "Don't interfere with us, Nastagio. Let me and the dogs wreak upon this wicked woman the fate she deserves."

He had no sooner spoken, than the mastiffs seized the lady and held her by the flanks, unable to move. The knight, who had come up, dismounted, and Nastagio, accosting him, said: "I don't know who you are, who seem to know me so well. But I say it is villainy for an armed knight to want to murder a naked woman, and to set the hounds upon her, as though she were a wild beast! I warn you, I shall defend her, while I have the strength to do so."

"Nastagio," replied the knight, "I was of your own country, and you were still a little boy when I, Guido degli Anastagi, was more consumed with love for this woman, than you are now for her of the Traversari. Such was the misery to which she drove me, by her pride and relentlessness, that in my despair I slew myself with the dagger you see in my hand. Eternal punishment is now my lot. But not long after, this woman, whom my death rejoiced exceedingly, came to die. The sin of her cruelty and the joy she had had of my agony, doomed her also to the pangs of hell, for not a sign of repentance did she show at my suffering. Indeed, it was as though she had committed no sin, but rather expected to be rewarded for her deed! So when she came down to hell, both she and I were meted out our expiations: she, to flee before me, and I, who had so dearly loved her, to pursue her, not as a cherished mistress, but as my mortal enemy. Thus, as often as I overtake her, I slay her with this same dagger which I turned upon myself, tear open her loins, and pluck from her breast, as you will now see, that cold and stony heart, which neither love nor pity could ever move; and I cast it to these hounds, to devour, with her other entrails. But it does not end there! Not long after, as though she had not died, she rises again, and as God's righteousness and power decree, begins once more her dolorous flight, while I and the hounds renew the chase. Every Friday at his hour, I come upon her in this place, and here I put her through the torment you shall see. But do not think we rest on other days. Elsewhere, in other places where she was cruel to me in thought and deed, I come upon her; and thus from her lover I become her enemy. I am doomed to follow her, as you see, one year for every month she made me suffer by her harshness. Come, then, let me perform the dictates of divine justice, and do not pit yourself against what you could not prevent."

At the phantom's words, Nastagio recoiled in fear, every hair of his head standing on end. His eyes riveted on the hapless girl, he waited, terrified, to see what the man would do. No sooner had he finished speaking than, like a frenzied hound, the knight flew, dagger in hand, upon the girl, who, on her knees in the clutches of the fierce mastiffs, shrieked for mercy. With all his might he sank the blade into her breast, piercing her body through. The violence of the thrust flung her prone upon the ground, still shrieking and wailing, but the knight, taking a knife, slashed open her loins, and plucking out her heart with its surrounding organs, threw them to the two mastiffs, who devoured them instantly, in ravening hunger. Then, soon, as if nothing had taken place, the girl suddenly started to her feet, and ran off toward the sea, the hounds following close upon her heels, tearing and snapping at her flesh. Presently the knight, taking up his dagger, mounted his horse, and once more gave her chase; in a little while, all of them vanished from Nastagio's sight.

For a long time, after these visions, the youth remained there, plunged in fear and pity, but soon he reflected that they might stand him in good stead, since they occurred every Friday. Accordingly, he marked the spot and rejoined his servants. In due time, he sent for his friends and family and said:

"You've long been pleading with me to cease loving this enemy of mine, and put a stop to my lavish spending. I am willing to do as you say, provided you accomplish something for me. In short, manage to bring Paolo Traversari to dine with me here next Friday, together with his wife and daughter, all the ladies of his family, and whomever else you please. You'll find out then, why I am making this request."

This seemed a trifling enough thing for them to do, and on their return to Ravenna, they took the opportunity to extend an invitation to all the guests Nastagio had named. Moreover, though it was difficult to prevail upon the young lady with whom Nastagio was in love, to accept, she went anyhow, with the rest of the women.

In the meantime, Nastagio had ordered a sumptuous banquet, and had had the tables laid in the shadow of the pines, near the spot where he had beheld the murder of the stony-hearted beauty. At length, when the guests were assigned to their places, he contrived to have his beloved sit facing the spot where the spectacle would take place.

The final course had scarcely been served, when the desperate shrieks of the hunted girl rent the ears of all present. Wondering at the thing, questions flew among the guests, but no one knowing the cause, they rose in a body to see what it could mean. Presently, the wretched girl appeared, followed by the hounds and the knight. Not long after, they were among the guests. A tumult of protest arose against the knight and his hounds, and many advanced to rescue the lady; but the knight, addressing them as he had Nastagio before them, not only made them draw back aghast, but overwhelmed them with dread and wonder. Once more, he went through the gruesome spectacle, until all the ladies present, many of whom had been related by blood both to the girl and the knight, and still remembered his love and death, wailed as desperately at the sight, as though they themselves were being slaughtered.

The dreadful scene at an end, and the knight and lady vanished, the guests were thrown into many different arguments. Among those who had been most awed, however, was Nastagio's cruel beloved, who had plainly witnessed and heard everything, and realized that the spectacle touched her more keenly than anyone else for the rigorous behavior she had always affected toward Nastagio. Indeed, she already had a vision of herself fleeing before his wrathful countenance, with the mastiffs at her flanks. So great was the dread the sight inspired in her, that to avoid a like fate, she no sooner found an opportunity, which presented itself that very evening, than her cruelty suddenly turning to love, she sent a faithful maid of hers to Nastagio, requesting him to come to her, for she was ready to pleasure him in everything.

Nastagio sent back word that he was more than delighted, but that if she had nothing against it, he desired to enjoy the fruits of her love honorably, when she became his wife. The young lady, aware that she had been the only stumbling block between herself and her marriage to him, replied that she was ready, and broaching the matter herself to her father and mother, informed them, to their great joy, that she was willing to become Nastagio's wife. That very Sunday he married her, and the wedding-feast over, lived with her happily for many years.

His was not the only good come of the awful spectacle. All the ladies of Ravenna were so terrified, that from then on they became more docile toward their lovers' wishes than they had ever been known to be.

✳

## THE NINTH STORY

*Federigo degli Alberighi languishes in unrequited love for a lady. Wasting his goods in gallantry to win her favor, he is so reduced in circumstances that he has only a falcon left, which he serves her at dinner, for lack of other fare, when she comes to his house. Learning of his sacrifice, she suffers a change of heart, marries him, and makes him rich once more.*

FILOMENA HAD ALREADY CEASED SPEAKING, WHEN THE QUEEN, seeing there was no one else left to tell a story but herself and Dioneo, by virtue of his privilege, began, her face aglow with pleasure:

It is now my turn, and I shall acquit myself willingly, dearest ladies, with a story which somewhat resembles the preceding, so that you may not only know what power your beauty wields in noble hearts, but that you may learn to be the proper donors of your gifts, where gifts are due, without allowing the impulse always to come from Fortune, who, as most often happens, gives not moderately, but with an all too lavish hand.

I'm sure you must all have heard of Coppo di Borghese Domenichi, who was a worshipful man of great authority in our city, and will always be illustrious and worthy of lasting fame, much more for his accomplishments and merits, than for any pride of blood. Well, when he was old and hoary with years, he used to take great pleasure in talking over the past with his neighbors and other men, a thing which he could do better than anyone else, both because of his unfailing memory and the charm of his speech.

Among others of his lovely stories, he used to tell one of a young man, son of Messer Filippo Alberighi, called Federigo, famed above all other Tuscan cavaliers for his prowess in arms and deeds of gallantry. As is always the case with the majority of gentle spirits, he fell in love with a lady called Giovanna, deemed one of the loveliest and most gracious women in Florence; and to gain her favor he held jousts and tournaments, banquets and festivals, made lavish gifts, and spent his money without stint or measure. But Giovanna, whose virtue was a match for her beauty, did not give a thought to all that was done for her, or to the man who did it.

Now while Federigo continued spending his goods with a high hand, and getting nothing in return, his riches dwindled away, as most naturally happens, and soon he was so poor that he had only a little farm left, on the income of which he lived as modestly as possible, and an only falcon, the like of which was nowhere to be found. For all that, his love waxed greater than ever, but seeing that he could no longer maintain his usual elegance in the city, he removed to Campi, where his little estate was situated, and there, without being beholden to anyone, he flew his falcon whenever he could, and bore his poverty with patience.

Meanwhile, with Federigo at such a pass, Monna Giovanna's husband fell ill, and feeling the approach of death, drew up his will. He was a very wealthy man, and naming his son, already grown to boyhood, as his heir, he designated Giovanna, whom he dearly loved, to succeed the lad if he should die without lawful issue; and so he breathed his last.

Giovanna was now a widow. That summer, according to the custom of our women, she went away to the country with her son, settling in one of her cottages, near Federigo's farm. In a short time the boy became friendly with Federigo, and both had great sport together, hunting and flying the hawks. Many a time the lad had seen Federigo's falcon wing its flight upward, and had taken such a singular delight in it, that he wanted it for his own, though he never had courage enough to ask Federigo for it, seeing how much he loved it. At about this time the boy fell sick, much to his mother's grief, who had no other child and cherished him with every fiber of her being. All day long she was at his bedside, comforting him, and many a time she asked him if there was anything he wanted, pleading with him to tell her, and promising that if it could be had, she would surely obtain it for him.

Hearing her make her offer so often, the boy said: "Mother dear, if you can get Federigo's falcon for me, I'm sure I should get well."

The lady hesitated a little at his request, and wondered how to go about it. She was conscious that Federigo had long been in love with her, without having ever received so much as a glance from her, and pondered: "How can I send or go to Federigo and ask him for his falcon, which, from what I hear, is the finest that ever flew, and moreover, is the only thing which gives him a hold on life? And how can I be so selfish as to want to take it away from a poor fellow, who has no other delight left in the world?"

Troubled by her thoughts, and knowing that she had but to ask for the falcon to receive it, she did not know what to say, and without answering her son, remained silent. At last, allowing her love of him to get the upper hand, she determined inwardly to content him at any cost, and not to send for the falcon, but to fetch it herself.

"My son," she said, "be of good cheer and do your best to get well and strong again. I promise that the first thing in the morning I'll go for the falcon myself and bring it back to you."

Filled with happiness, the lad showed a marked improvement that very day.

The following morning, Monna Giovanna, taking another woman with her to keep her company, went to Federigo's house on a visit and sent for him. It was not the season for hawking, nor had he been out for some days past. As it was, he happened to be in his garden, looking after some small chores. On hearing that Monna Giovanna was at the door asking for him, he marveled greatly and hastened to her. With feminine grace she came to greet him, and upon his deep obeisance, she said: "Good day to you, Federigo." Then, "I've come to make up for all the harm you suffered through me," she added, "by placing more love in me than you should have, and I shall begin by dining with you in friendship, with this friend of mine."

Humbly Federigo replied: "Madam, I don't remember ever having suffered any harm through you. On the contrary, you did me such good that if I was ever worth anything, it was due entirely to your virtues and the love I've always borne you. Indeed, though you have come to a poor host, your generous visit is even more dear to me now than it would have been, had I had it in my power to spend my fortune over again."

With these words, he escorted her into his house with great embarrassment, and from there into his garden, where, as he had no one else to entertain her, he said: "Madam, since I have no one to do the honors, this good woman, the wife of that laborer there, will keep you company, while I see that the table is laid."

Not until then, despite his dire poverty, had he been so conscious of the want to which he had been reduced by the inordinate waste of his riches; but that morning when he saw that he had nothing with which to treat the lady for whose sake he had once been bountiful to hosts of men, he awoke with a shock. Up and down the house he wandered, bitterly grieving and almost out of his senses, ransacking the place and cursing himself and the fate which had brought him to such a pass. But no money did he find, nor anything to pawn. Besides, it was getting late. Anxious to do his lady honor, somehow or other, and loth to borrow from his own gardener, or anyone else for that matter, he looked about him perplexed. His eyes fell on his beloved falcon, sitting on its perch in the tiny parlor. It was his last resource. Taking the bird and finding it fat, he thought it would make a worthy dish for so fine a lady, so without another moment's thought, he wrung its neck, and giving it to his small servant girl to pluck and dress, had it put on the spit and promptly broiled.

The table was laid with the whitest of linens, of which he still possessed some; then, rejoining Monna Giovanna in the garden, his face beaming with happiness, he told her that what modest dinner he could furnish, was ready. The lady rose with her friend, and both took their places at table, where, without knowing what banquet was before them, they ate the good falcon in the company of Federigo, who served them with the utmost devotion.

The dinner over, they lingered a while, conversing pleasantly with their host, when Monna Giovanna, thinking the time had come for her to broach the subject of her visit, addressed him graciously: "I don't doubt in the least, Federigo, that you'll marvel at my boldness when I confess the chief reason that brought me here, as you look back upon your past life and my virtue, which perhaps you may have interpreted as cruelty and hardheartedness. Still, had it ever been your lot to have children of your own, to make you understand how great is the love one bears them, I am sure you would half condone my presumption. But though you have none, I, who have one, cannot escape the common laws of motherhood, and following their promptings, I must, despite myself, and contrary to all that is just and proper, ask something of you which I know is the dearest thing you have. And it is nothing to wonder at, for what other delight, what other pastime and consolation has been left you by your evil fortune? It is your falcon I would have, Federigo, your falcon, which my little boy wants so much, that if I don't bring it to him, I greatly fear his present malady will take a turn for the worse, and something terrible may happen. I might even lose him. I beseech you, then, Federigo, not for the love you bear me, for you owe it nothing, but for your own nobility, which you have proved above any other man's, by many worthy deeds—for the sake of that nobility, give me your falcon, that I may say I saved my son's life by your gift, and have him beholden to you for it, for as long as he lives."

When Federigo heard what Monna Giovanna was asking, and saw that it was beyond his power to oblige her, as he had served the bird to her at dinner, tears welled up in his eyes before he could utter a word. At first she believed his grief was caused by the thought of parting with his falcon, rather than by anything else, and was about to tell him that she did not want it; but she forbore, and waited to hear what he had to say.

"Dear lady," said he, drying his tears, "since God willed me to fall in love with you, I've had many an occasion to complain of Fortune, who opposed me in many things; but all were trivial in comparison with what she is making me suffer now! Nevermore can she and I be friends! To think that you came to see me in my poor little cot, where you never deigned to set foot when I was rich, and asked a little gift of me, only to have her make it impossible for me to grant it! Listen, and I shall tell you in a few words why it cannot be.

"When I heard that you, in your graciousness, wished to dine with me, I considered your rank and merit, and thought it would be only seemly and proper to serve you more precious fare, so far as I could afford it, than is generally offered to others. Therefore, thinking of the falcon which you now ask of me, and of its excellence, I deemed it a dish worthy of you, and today you had it, served roasted on a platter. Well-given I thought it, too! But alas! Now I see you wanted it otherwise, and I am so desolate because I cannot help you, that never may I have another moment's peace." To prove his words, he had her shown the poor bird's feathers, claws and beak.

At first the lady blamed him for having sacrificed so excellent a falcon to entertain a mere woman, but presently she began inwardly admiring the greatness of his spirit, which poverty had not succeeded, nor could ever succeed, in stifling. However, abandoning all hope of obtaining the falcon, and very much concerned about her son's recovery, she left Federigo and returned sadly to the lad's bedside. Whether he was disappointed because he could not have the falcon, or because the natural course of the disease destined him to die, he breathed his last before many days had passed, to his mother's extreme sorrow.

Long she remained in tears and grieving, but as she was still in the prime of youth and immensely wealthy, her brothers urged her again and again to remarry. Though she had no intention of taking another husband, at their insistence she began to dwell on Federigo's fine character, and his most recent proof of generosity by the killing of that marvelous falcon, to honor her, so she said to them: "I'd very gladly remain as I am, if you would let me. But since you insist on my marrying again, I'll have nobody but Federigo degli Alberighi."

They made fun of her, and taunting, said: "You foolish woman! What are you saying? What do you mean by choosing him, when he hasn't a florin to his name?"

"I know very well that it's as you say, my brothers," she said, "but I'd rather have a man in need of wealth, than wealth in need of a man."

Hearing her determination, the brothers, who knew Federigo to be a man of excellence, though poor, bestowed her upon him as she desired, together with her riches. As for Federigo, when he saw himself married to the woman he had so dearly loved, and possessed of so vast a fortune in the bargain, he learned to manage his affairs more wisely, and lived with her happily to the end of his days.

*

# THE   TENTH   STORY

*Pietro di Vinciolo goes out to dine, and his wife invites a young spark to be with her. Pietro unexpectedly returns, and she quickly hides her lover under a chicken-coop. When Pietro relates how, in the house of Ercolano, with whom he was dining, a gallant was found, whom his wife had concealed, Pietro's lady is loud in condemnation of her. Suddenly a donkey accidentally steps on the fingers of the fellow under the chicken-coop, causing him to cry out with pain. Pietro, finding him there, discovers his wife's trick, but he eventually comes to terms with her, for his own wicked ends.*

THE QUEEN'S NARRATIVE OVER, ALL OF THEM OFFERED UP THANKS to God for giving Federigo his just reward, when Dioneo, who never waited for a summons, plunged into his argument:

I don't know whether it is a chance fault, inculcated by evil practices, or simply a human weakness in us mortals, to be more easily amused at naughty things, rather than good, particularly when the misfortune is none of our own. Well then, since the trouble I've taken on other occasions, and which I'm about to take again, has no other aim than to draw you from your brooding and tickle you to mirth and laughter, I'm going to tell you the following story. Though the subject of it, loving ladies, is in spots not quite proper, I shall tell it to you anyway, that it may amuse you. As for you who listen to it, do as you would on entering a garden, when you stretch out your dainty hands to pluck the roses, but leave the thorns behind. Likewise, leave the wicked man to his lewdness—the devil take him!—and enjoy a good laugh at the amorous intrigues of his wife, sympathizing a little with the other fellow's troubles, where need be.

Not so long ago, there lived in Perugia a rich man called Pietro di Vinciolo, who, perhaps, more to throw dust into people's eyes and tone down the reputation his fellow citizens commonly gave him, than out of any desire for a wife, decided to enter the married state. Fortune was favorable to him in his desires, and to such an extent that the lady he married was a stocky, carrot-haired, fiery-humored hoyden, who stood in need of two husbands rather than one—whereas, poor lass, she struck upon a fellow who had quite other bees in his bonnet. It was not long before she learned of his peculiarity. When she realized how fresh and juicy she was, and felt the power of her lustiness surging in her, at first she flew into a fury and had many a scathing word with her husband because of his tastes, until their life together was a continual hell; but when she saw that this would sooner bring her to the grave, than turn her husband from his crooked ways, she said to herself:

"This sad dog scorns me, to go dry-shod on the path of his debaucheries, but I'll manage to take others aboard through the wet, I will! I took him for a husband, bringing him a mighty big dowry, in the belief that he was a man, and fond of those things which men are, or ought to be, fond of. If I'd not thought him a man in everything, I'd have had none of him. On his part, he was aware I was a woman. Why the devil did he have to marry me, if women were against the grain of him? No, this state of affairs can't be put up with! If I hadn't wanted to be of the world and things, I'd have renounced them all and taken the veil. But I preferred to be here, and here I am, as I wanted to be. Ah, but if I expect to get joy and pleasure out of this rake-hell, I can go on expecting and grow old in the expectation. Then when I realize my mistake, too late, I'll vainly be wailing for my lost youth! He's an apt teacher, all right, in showing me what to do with it, and sets a fine example of how I should take delight in the very things he enjoys, which, after all, would be excusable enough in me, though execrable in him. I'd only be offending moral law, whereas he sins against both law and nature."

Turning the matter over in her mind, perhaps on more than one occasion, she became friends with an old gammer, the better to carry out her plans in secrecy. The old crone seemed a veritable Saint Verdiana feeding her snakes. Her rosary forever in her hands, she attended every general pardon, and let no word cross her lips unless it concerned the lives of the church fathers, and the stigmata of the blessed Saint Francis. Indeed, she enjoyed an almost general repute for sanctity. When the lady saw the proper moment had come, she was not squeamish about telling the old woman what was on her mind.

"Daughter," replied the sainted hag, "God, who's informed about everything we do, knows how justified you are in doing what you intend—even if you or all other young women did it, for no other reason than to make hay while the sun shines; for there's no greater sorrow to a person of sense, than to have let the time of youth slip by. What the devil are we good for when we're old? Only to watch over the ashes on the hearth! I ought to know, if anyone ever should! Yes, now that I am old, I think in vain, but oh, with deep and bitter regret, of the time I allowed to slip through my fingers, though I did not lose it all! No, no, I don't want you to think I was such a fool! Still, I did not do all that I could have done!

"But from the time I became as you see me now, not a man was willing to set a spark to my kindling, and God knows how doleful I feel about it! In the case of men, it's not the same thing. They're born well-fitted for a thousand things, leaving alone this particular one, and a good many of them count for much more in old age than in youth. It's not so with us women. We're born only for this work, and to make children, and that's just why we're held so dear. You can prove it for yourself, if by nothing else, at least by the fact that we're always ready when there's anything of the sort to be done—which is hardly the case with men-folk. What's more, a single woman could wear out a dozen men, whereas it takes quite a number of them to wear out a single woman. Again, I want to impress upon your mind, that since we're made for this, you'd be perfectly justified in paying your husband in his own coin, so that when you're old, your conscience will have no cause to reprove your flesh. One has what one can get out of this world, especially in the case of women, who have to make the best of their youth while they have it, even more than men. For don't you see? When we get old, nobody will even look at us, neither our husbands nor anybody else. We're sent packing to the kitchen to tell tales to the cat, and count over the pots and pans. What's worse, we're put into doggerel, and they cry at us:

> 'For the young 'uns dainties good,
> But gags shall be the old crones' food.'

"And that's not the least of them! But I don't want to take up more of your time talking. I just want to assure you, that you couldn't have found a more useful confidante than myself, if you'd looked high and low. There's no man so conceited that I can't bring down a peg, and tell him what is what, not so stubborn and mulish that I can't bend him and lead him to what I want. Just show me the fellow you've a mind to, and leave the rest to me. But, daughter dear, let me only ask you to bear me in mind a little, as I'm a poor old woman. So come, have your due of the petitions and the paternosters I'll tell over for you, that the good Lord may shed lights and tapers on the souls of your dead."

At that, she finished her harangue, after which it was settled between them that when she came across a certain young sprig, who used to pass quite often through that neighborhood, and whose appearance the young woman described in detail, old Saint Verdiana was to know exactly what to do. Then, rewarding her with a slice of salt-meat, Pietro's wife sent her away in God's keeping.

Not long after, the old woman brought that particular young

man into the lady's bedchamber, and a little later supplied her with still another to keep up with her tastes, which she did not scruple to indulge to the best of her ability, despite the dread she felt of her husband.

Now it so happened that Pietro was invited out to supper one evening, at the home of a friend of his called Ercolano, and his wife, accordingly, commissioned the old hag to provide her with one of the charmingest, most delectable cockerels in all Perugia. The beldam did so with great expedition, but alas, no sooner had the lady and her young gallant sat down to their meal, than up comes Pietro to the door, clamoring to be let in. The poor woman thought her end had come, but still, anxious to find a hiding-place for the boy, and too nervous to think of a better shelter, she had him crouch under a chicken-coop in a shed adjoining the dining-room. Over it, she flung the ticking of a straw mattress which had been emptied that day, and the coop covered, she ran quickly to let her husband in.

"You gulped down that supper of yours in a mighty hurry," she remarked, the moment he had stepped into the house.

"Scarcely," he said. "We didn't even taste it."

"Why not?" she asked.

"Well, it was this way," began Pietro. "We had just sat down to the meal, Ercolano, his wife and I, when we heard the sound of a sneeze near by. The first time and the second we paid no attention to it, but when we heard it a third, a fourth and a fifth, and a lot of other times, we wondered what it was all about. So Ercolano, who was rather cross with his wife for having kept us outside a long time before she let us in, cried out, very angrily, 'What does this mean? Who's doing all this sneezing here?'

"Leaving the table, he went to a nearby staircase, toward the foot of which was a kind of shanty of boards—you know, that sort of thing in which people keep all manner of trash, after they have furnished their houses. Now Ercolano thought the sound of the sneezing came from there, so he opened a small door, and before you could say boo! out came the most suffocating stink of sulphur you can imagine. Just before, when we had a whiff of it and complained, the woman had said: 'You see, I was just in the midst of bleaching my veils with sulphur, and when you came, I put the pot over which I had spread them to catch the smoke, under the stairs. It must be smoking yet.'

"Well, after Ercolano had kept the door open so as to dissipate the fumes, he peeped in and saw who it was that had sneezed and was still sneezing, from the effects of the sulphur. To tell the truth, the vapors had already so clogged the wretch's chest, that if he'd remained there much longer, he'd never have sneezed or done anything else again. At the sight of him, Ercolano roared, 'Now I see, strumpet, why you kept us waiting outside so long, when we arrived! But may God never prosper me in my desires, if I don't pay you back for this!' When his wife heard what he said and saw she had been caught red-handed, she hadn't a word to say in her defense, but running off from the table, hid herself away, Lord knows where. Ercolano didn't notice her flight—he was too busy telling the sneezing fellow to get out of there; but the poor wretch couldn't move a finger, and for all Ercolano's ranting, he didn't budge an inch. Ercolano was furious. Dragging him by one foot, he pulled him out and was for running to get a knife and kill him, when I got up— I was afraid of the police myself, you see—and wouldn't let him do away with the fellow, or harm a hair of his head. No sir! I cried for help, and got between Ercolano and him, and carried on so that I brought some neighbors there, who took the unconscious man and carried him off. So you see, since the meal was interrupted by all this fuss, I was not only unable to gulp it down, but as I told you, I didn't even have a chance to taste it."

While listening to his story, the woman saw that there were others as clever as herself, though now and then one of them did get into a mess, and she would willingly have employed her eloquence to defend Ercolano's wife. However, considering that by blaming the errors of others, she would be giving further lee-way to her own, she held forth:

"Here's a pretty how-do-you-do! Here's a good holy woman for you! Here's an honest one! I swear I'd have gone to her for confession, she seemed such a saint! The awful thing about it is that an old hag like her should set such an example to young folks! God curse the hour she came to the world, and her, too, who disgraces the earth by going on living! Oh the harlot, the vile creature she must be! What a blot and disgrace to all the virtuous ladies of this town, flinging her honor and her plighted troth to the winds, and caring not a straw for the world's good fame! To think that her husband's such a fine man, and such an honored citizen! He treated her like a queen, he did, and here she wasn't even ashamed to bring dishonor on herself and him, for the sake of another man! God be my Saviour, I think one ought to have no pity for such as she! They ought to be put to death, yes, sir! They should be thrown alive into the flames, until there's nothing left of them but a heap of ashes!"

Then, calling to mind her lover, who was hiding under the coop quite close by, she fell to urging Pietro to go to bed, saying it was about time. However, he had more desire for food than for sleep, and asked whether there wasn't a bite of something for supper.

"Supper!" she cried. "Supper! A fine supper we're accustomed to, when you're not home! What! Do you think I'm Ercolano's wife? Go, go to bed and sleep off your hunger for to-night! You'll be doing a much better thing, I can assure you!"

That evening, as it happened, a number of Pietro's laborers had arrived, bringing some produce from the country, and had lodged their donkeys in a small stable adjoining the shed, without first watering them. One of the beasts, which was dying of thirst, wrenched its head out of its halter and wandered out of the stable, sniffing at everything in search of water, when suddenly it stumbled against the coop under which the youth was hiding. As luck, or rather ill-luck, would have it, the lad, who had to crouch on all fours, had allowed the fingers of one hand to slip out from under the coop, whereupon the donkey trampled them with its hoof. The gallant let out a terrible yell, at the awful pain. Pietro, wondering at the outcry, saw that it came from his own house, so leaving the room, and hearing the other still howling (for the donkey had not yet raised its hoof from his fingers, but bore upon them heavily), he called out: "What ho! Who's there!" At the same time, he ran to the chicken-coop, and lifting it, spied the youth, who over and above the pain he felt from having his fingers mangled, was quaking with fear lest Pietro do him violence. Pietro had no trouble in discovering who he was, as he had long besieged the youngster with his lecherous designs.

"What's your business here?" he asked. The youth did not answer his question, but pleaded with him, for the Love of God, not to do him any mischief.

"Get up," replied Pietro, "and don't worry about my hurting you. But tell me, how do you come to be here? And why?"

Presently the lad told him everything. Pietro, no less delighted that he had discovered him, than his wife was chagrined, took him by the hand and led him to the room where she was waiting in an agony of dread. Taking a chair, he sat down facing her.

"Hardly a moment ago," he began, "you were cursing Ercolano's wife, saying she ought to be burned alive, and that she was a reproach to all womankind. Why didn't you speak for yourself? And if you didn't choose to, how did you have the heart to speak against her, knowing you were guilty of the very thing she had done? Certainly nothing led you to it, except the fact that you women are all made of the same stuff, and try to cover your faults by blaming those of others—would to God you were all wiped out with the fire of heaven, perfidious brood that you are, without exception!"

Now when the lady saw that so far Pietro had hurled nothing but words, and seemed aquiver with delight, because he was holding such a handsome lad by the hand, she plucked up her courage and said: "Oh, I've no doubt you'd like the fire of heaven to burn up all of us poor women, seeing you're as fond of us as a dog is of a stick. But, by God, you'll not have the fulfilment of your wish! Still I shouldn't mind having a little talk with you, to see what you have to complain about! It's very good of you to compare me to Ercolano's wife, who's a sanctimonious old hag. She gets everything she wants from him, and he loves her as a wife ought to be loved, which is certainly not the case with me! What if I am well provided with clothes and shoes! You know what a lack I have of other things, and what an age it is since you slept with me! I'd sooner go barefoot, without a stitch to my back, and be well-handled by you in bed, than have all these luxuries, and be treated the way you treat me! Understand, Pietro, I'm a woman like the rest, and I'm anxious for the things they all desire. Therefore, if I go about supplying my needs when you don't give me my due, I'm not at all to be blamed. I'm at least considerate enough of you, not to have anything to do with muleteers and bald-pates!"

Pietro saw that her flow of speech showed no sign of diminishing, for the rest of the night, and caring not a fig for her concerns, he said: "Come, come, woman! Drop the subject for the present. I'll satisfy you well enough on that score! But have the kindness to fix us something for supper, for it seems to me this lad here has not had a bite, any more than I."

"Of course he hasn't," said she, "for we were just about to sit down to eat, when you popped in on us, ill-luck to you!"

"All right, but go and see that we have something to eat," said Pietro, "and then I'll manage this thing in such a way, that you'll have no reason to complain."

She got up when she saw her husband in a good mood, and setting the table, she called for the supper which had been prepared. Then, with her lecherous husband and the charming youth, she had her fill of it, in high spirits.

What Pietro devised afterwards for the satisfaction of the three of them, I can't recall. I only know that next morning, when the lad was escorted as far as the town-square, he was in a daze as to what part he had played most during the night—that of the wife or the husband.

So, then, dear ladies, take my advice: give tit for tat, and if you can't at the moment, bear it in mind till you can. You know, what's sauce for the goose is sauce for the gander.

Now that Dioneo had finished his story, which the ladies had greeted with less mirth than usual, more out of modesty than lack of enjoyment, the queen saw that the end of her rule had come, and rising to her feet, she raised the laurel-crown from her head and laid it gracefully on Elisa's, saying: "From now on it is your turn to command."

On assuming the honor, Elisa did as had been done before. Calling the steward, she arranged with him for all the needs of her period of regency, to the complete satisfaction of her band, and then she said:

"We have often heard how many folks, by means of some clever *mot*, retort, or quick flash of wit, have been able to dull the edge of another person's blade, and with their ready reply, have avoided imminent peril. Since the subject is a good one, and might prove useful, I want us to-morrow, God willing, to confine ourselves to that subject, that is, to tell *of people who extricated themselves from some predicament, by means of a witty retort, or prevented loss, peril or mockery, with some ready flash or quick prevision.*"

Later in the day, when the crickets had ceased their chirping, the queen summoned each and every one of her group, and all sat down to supper. That over, they devoted themselves to singing and dancing, and as Emilia had already taken the lead in a dance, at the queen's request, Dioneo was asked to furnish a song.

Promptly he pitched in with "Madam *Aldroda*, lift up your

*cod-a*, for the news that I bring you is good, tra la." Immediately all the women began to laugh, especially the queen.

"Leave that alone and sing us another!" said she.

"If I had a cembalo, my lady," he said, "I'd sing you 'Up with your petticoats, my Lady Lupa,' or 'The grass grows under the olive,' or perhaps you'd prefer to hear, 'The waves of the ocean cause me commotion.' But I have no cembalo, so tell me which others you'd prefer instead. Is it, 'Come out, come out and be cut down, like a harvest in the fields?' "

"No, sing something else," said the queen.

"All right," replied Dioneo, "then I'll give you, 'Mistress Simone, O, look to your tun, O. Is it or *ain't* it the month of October?' "

"No, no, plague take you!" said the queen, laughing. "Sing something nice, if you don't mind, for we'll have none of that!"

"All right, all right," said Dioneo, "but don't be angry, my lady. What do you like best? I know them by the thousands. Is it 'If this niche I do not prick,' or 'Not so fast, my little hub,' or 'I bought me a handsome cock, worth a hundred lire?' "

Then the queen, somewhat annoyed, though the other ladies were very much amused, reproved him: "Now stop, Dioneo! Enough of your nonsense, and sing us something lovely, otherwise you'll have a taste of my temper."

Seeing how the wind blew, Dioneo put a stop to his jesting and began to sing:

"O Love, the dreamy light
　　That shines within my lady's lovely eyes,
　　Has made me slave of her and you likewise.

It was the splendor of her eyes' own light
　　That kindled first your flame within my heart
　　　When through my own it sped;
How great your worth, it was her visage bright
　　That did the knowledge to my mind impart;
　　　And now my fancy fed
　　　With beauty, I am led
　　　　To lay all virtues at her feet I prize
　　　　Who is the new occasion for my sighs.

And so as follower I join the rest
　　Who serve you, dearest lord, and I implore

Humbly your power's grace.
Yet I know not if I make manifest
The high desire you set in my heart's core:
My faith I would not place
Save in the one whose face
So holds my mind enthralled, I would not prize
Nor cherish peace that came not from her eyes.

Therefore, my lord, I call upon your name
To show her how with love of her I burn
In your consuming fire.
Oh, let her feel some smart of that same flame
In my behalf, for see, at every turn
I melt within your pyre.
Reveal my sweet desire
And make it known to her in your own guise,
As I should plead for you, should need arise."

Dioneo ceased, his song ended. Praising it highly, in spite of everything, the queen had many more sung; but when a good part of the evening had passed, and she felt the heat of day superseded by the chill of night, she dismissed all her company and sent them to rest until the following morning.

# 6

# THE SIXTH DAY

✳

NOW THE MOON HAD PALED IN THE MIDST OF THE HEAVENS AND the radiance of the new-born day pervaded the world, when the queen, awakening from sleep, summoned her company. They took a leisurely walk over the dewy greensward, leaving the pleasant knoll some distance behind, and whiled away the time in discussing the merits of the stories that had been told. Again and again, their laughter rang out as they recalled the various incidents of the stories, until, with the ascending sun, the heat of the day began to make itself felt. Then they thought it better to wend their way homeward. Accordingly, they retraced their steps, and returned to the palace.

The tables had already been set, and everything had been strewn with fragrant herbs and gay flowers; there, at the queen's bidding, they sat down to their meal, before the heat of the day grew more intense. Heartily they ate and with delight and merriment, and when it was over they sang a number of charmingly gay ditties. Then they dispersed to take a nap, play chess or indulge in a party of tables, while Dioneo and Fiammetta sang of Troilus and Cressida.

The hour of their usual meeting arrived, and at the queen's summons they took their accustomed places about the fountain. The queen was about to request the first story, when something unexpected happened, and there was a frightful din, coming from the women and servants in the kitchen. Startled by the noise, they sent for the steward.

"Who is making all that noise, and what is the meaning of it?" they asked, whereupon he replied that Licisca and Tindaro were quarreling, but that he could not tell why, as he had been summoned in the midst of it, while attempting to quiet them.

The queen sent for the two culprits without delay, and when they were before her, "What is the reason of your boisterousness?" she asked.

Tindaro was about to offer an explanation, when Licisca, a matronly woman of rather overbearing disposition, turned upon him, still incensed by the heat of the argument, and cried: "Look at that fine example of manhood who dares to put in a word when I'm present! Let me have my say, if you don't mind, sir!" Then, addressing the queen, she said: "Madam, this fellow would like to teach me about Master John Thursday's wife, and as if I had never had dealings with her, he'd give me to understand that the first night John Thursday lay with her, Master Stock took possession of Black Hill by force and bloodshed. I said it wasn't so. He entered very quietly, on the contrary, and to the great delight of whoever was there. This fellow is such a donkey that he even thinks young wenches are silly enough to waste their precious years, awaiting the convenience of their fathers and brothers who, nine times out of ten, tarry from three to four years longer than they should, in marrying off the poor lasses! A jolly time they'd have if they really lingered so long on their maiden stems! Christ's faith—and I ought to know what I'm about, when I take such an oath—I haven't a single woman-friend who went to her husband with a whole maidenhead! Yes, and I could tell you, too, what pranks married women play on their husbands! And here this dunce wants to instruct me about women, as though I was born yesterday!"

During Licisca's speech, the women were shaken with laughter. More than a half-dozen times the queen had tried to silence her, but in vain. The women did not cease until she had blurted out all that she had to say. At last, when she had delivered herself, the queen turned with a laugh to Dioneo.

"This is a matter for your judgment, Dioneo," said she. "When our stories are over for the day, you'll give the final dictum."

"Why, no, my lady," he answered promptly. "The judgment's

passed without further hearing. Licisca is perfectly right. I believe things are as she describes them, and Tindaro's a dunce."

Licisca laughed with triumph at the decision, and said to Tindaro, "Didn't I tell you? Go in peace now. Why, did you imagine for a moment you knew more than Licisca? Why, you're hardly out of your diapers. Thank God, I've not wasted my life, no, not I!"

If the queen had not sternly silenced her and ordered her not to say another word, or stir up havoc under pain of a whipping, there would have been no time for anything but her chatter. But after the two culprits had been sent away, the queen asked Filomena to initiate the day's story-telling, whereupon she graciously began:

&ast;

## THE FIRST STORY

*A gentleman offers to take Mistress Oretta on horseback with a story, but he tells it so poorly, that she begs to be allowed to go on foot again.*

YOUNG DAMSELS, JUST AS ON CLEAR NIGHTS THE STARS ARE THE adornment of heaven, and in the spring, the flowers and blossoming bushes are the glory of mead and slope, so, too, are witty conceits the embroidery of courtly manners and pleasing speech, especially since because of their brevity, they are more becoming to women than to men. Abundant speech in women has always been prejudicial to them. Whatever the reason, whether our minds are inferior, or whether the heavens reveal a singularly unpropitious countenance to our times, the fact remains that there is hardly a woman alive who can make a clever reply when necessary, or, for that matter, grasp the meaning of one when it is made—to our common shame be it said! But why should I continue? Pampinea has already said enough on that score. I want you to see, however, how charming a clever sally can be, in its proper place and season, and I shall be glad to tell you of how a lady courteously bade a man be silent.

Many of you here, I'm sure, must either have seen or heard of a gracious, witty and well-spoken lady who used to live in our city, not so long ago. She was a wonderful woman, whose name deserves not to be left unspoken. She was none other than Mistress Oretta, the wife of Geri Spina.

Once, while in the country, she was going from one place to another, like us, for recreation, with a party of ladies and gentlemen, whom she had entertained that day at her home. The way was rather long, from the place they had left, to their destination which they had intended to reach on foot. So one of the gentlemen of her party said: "If you please, Mistress Oretta, I shall be happy to carry you a great part of the way on horseback, with one of the best stories in the world."

"By all means," she replied, "I beg you do so. I shall appreciate it very much."

The doughty knight, who was perhaps as poor a swordsman as a raconteur, plunged into his story, upon her encouragement. It was indeed a beautiful tale, but what with his repetition of the same word three or four times over, his recapitulations, his "No, no, that's not right," and his putting one name in place of another, he made a dreadful mess of it. Then, his diction was particularly bad, and entirely out of keeping with the circumstances, and the quality of his characters.

Mistress Oretta was impatient with the effort of listening, felt her heart sinking, and more than once she came near fainting away or dying on the spot. At last, when she saw him hopelessly entangled in a maze of his own making, she said kindly, unable as she was to put up with the torment any longer: "This steed of yours goes too hard a pace, sir, so please set me on my feet again."

Fortunately, he was much keener in drawing inferences than in telling a story, and taking the hint good-humoredly, he turned the conversation to other things, leaving unfinished the story he had begun and fared with so badly.

# THE SECOND STORY

*Cisti the baker brings an indiscreet request to the attention of Messer Geri Spina, by a clever retort.*

MISTRESS ORETTA'S WIT WAS BEING HIGHLY APPLAUDED BY EVERY-one in the party, and by the men, as well as the women, when the queen called upon Pampinea to continue.

Lovely ladies, she began, I find it hard to tell which is the sinner in this respect, Nature, in housing a noble soul in a wretched exterior, or Fortune, in subjecting a body endowed with a lofty soul to a mean trade, as we see in the case of Cisti, our fellow-citizen, and many others besides. Let us take Cisti. He is a man of noble loftiness of mind, but Fortune made him a baker! Really, I'd lay the blame on Nature as well as Fortune, were I not convinced that Nature is extraordinarily prudent, and that Fortune has a thousand eyes, though fools insist on representing her as blind. I presume that both of them, like wise managers, probably do what mortals are often known to do, when, in uncertainty of the future, they bury their most precious treasures against a time of need, in the humblest corners of their houses, as the places least likely of suspicion. Then, when necessity arises, they bring them forth again, the dark hole having proved a surer hiding-place than a beautiful room would have provided. So it is with these two rulers of the world, who often conceal their rarest treasures in the obscurity of trades that are deemed the humblest, so that when they are revealed by necessity, their light may gleam the brighter.

The matter in which Cisti the baker revealed the truth of this by opening Geri Spina's eyes is slight enough. The talk of Mistress Oretta, his wife, brought it to my mind, and it will give me pleasure to tell you about it, in a very brief story.

Well then, you must know that once upon a time Pope Boniface, at whose court Messer Geri Spina was held in high esteem, sent a number of his distinguished ambassadors to Florence, on a mission of great importance. They took up their lodging at the house of this Messer Spina, and as he proceeded to take charge of the pope's affairs with them, they somehow or other had occasion to pass in front of Santa Maria Ughi, almost every morning, where Cisti the baker had his ovens and personally supervised his business. Although Fortune had given him a very humble trade, she had so prospered him in it, that he had accumulated considerable wealth; indeed, he had no wish to change his calling for any other, for he derived such a splendid livelihood from it, that among other luxuries he had the best wines, light and dark, that Florence or the whole province could boast of.

Now, when he observed Messer Spina and the pope's ambassadors pass before his door every morning in the fiery heat, he thought he would be acting with great courtesy if he offered them some of his excellent white wine to drink. He reflected on his condition, however, and on Messer Geri's. It did not seem quite the proper thing for him to invite him; the invitation, he thought, must come from the gentleman himself, and he devised a way of leading him to it.

It was Cisti's custom always to dress in a white coat and spotless apron, which made him look more like a miller than a baker. Every morning, when he expected Messer Geri and the ambassadors to pass, he would have a brand new pail of sparkling, fresh water placed before his door, a little decanter of Bolognese pottery full of his best white wine, and two goblets so bright, they might have been made of silver. Then, sitting down comfortably, he waited for them to come by. No sooner did he catch sight of them, than, after gargling once or twice, he began tossing off this excellent wine of his, with such gusto that he would have made even a dead man yearn for it.

Once, Messer Spina observed this procedure, and then again, the next day. On the third, he could not refrain from calling out to him: "Well, well, Cisti! Is it good?"

Promptly Cisti jumped up and said: "Yes, indeed, sir! But I couldn't give you any idea of how good it is unless you drank some of it yourself!"

Whether the heat, or the unusual exertion, or perhaps the relish with which he had seen Cisti quaffing his wine had made Messer Spina thirsty, he turned to the ambassadors and said, smiling: "Gentlemen, I advise you all to taste some of this good man's wine. It may be so fine, that we'll surely be glad we did."

With the rest of the nobles, Messer Spina approached Cisti, who had a handsome bench brought out of his bakery, and begged them all to sit down. The gentlemen's servants then made ready to rinse the glasses, but Cisti stopped them. "No, my friends," said he. "Stand back and leave this business to me, for I'm as good at pouring wine as at baking. And don't expect to taste just a drop of it, either."

Rinsing out the four bright new beakers, he called for a pitcher of his best wine, and poured it out handsomely for Messer Spina and his companions. They thought it the most delicious they had tasted in a long time, and told him so; therefore during the rest of their stay in Florence, Messer Spina came almost every morning with the gentlemen to toss off a pot.

Finally, the ambassadors' mission was accomplished, and the

time came for them to take their departure. Accordingly, Messer Spina offered a magnificent farewell dinner in their honor, to which he invited a great number of the most important citizens of Florence. Among them he included Cisti, but on no condition could the baker be induced to accept, whereupon Messer Spina sent one of his servants to ask him for a flask of wine, sufficient to serve each guest a half-glassful with the first course. Somehow or other, the servant was full of spite, perhaps because he had never succeeded in tasting a drop of that wine, and he took along a huge flagon, the sight of which made Cisti exclaim, "Messer Spina is certainly not sending you to me, son."

The fellow insisted that such was the case, but when he could not get Cisti to give any other answer, he returned to his master and told him about it.

"Go back to Cisti and tell him I'm sending you to him, and to no one else," said Messer Spina, "and if he still gives you the same answer, then ask him to whom I'm sending you."

The servant did his errand, and again presented himself before the baker, saying: "Cisti, I assure you it's to you my master sends me."

"And I assure you, my son, it is not," insisted the baker.

"Well," said the other, "where is he sending me, then?"

"To the river Arno," replied Cisti.

The servant returned and repeated the new venture to Messer Spina, whose eyes were instantly opened.

"Show me the flask you took there," he said. "Cisti was quite right," he added, shocked at the sight of it, and giving the fellow a sound scolding, he had him take a flask of more seemly proportions.

"Now I know he sent you to me," said Cisti when he saw it, and he filled it ungrudgingly.

Later that day, he had a small barrel of the same sort of wine brought carefully to the house of Messer Spina, and followed close behind himself.

"Sir," said he, when he had found his host, "I don't want you to believe for a moment that I was daunted by the huge flagon this morning. I thought perhaps you had forgotten what I had meant to convey to you these last few days by my small decanters—mainly that this is no wine for servants—so I wished to bring it to your attention to-day. Now as I'm not going to be your cellarer any longer, I've had it all brought here to you. From now on, enjoy it or do with it as you wish."

Messer Spina was very grateful for Cisti's gift. Then and there, he thanked him for it as best he could, and ever afterwards esteemed him a wise man and a dear friend.

# THE THIRD STORY

*Nonna de' Pulci silences the Bishop of Florence by a ready retort to his indecent remark.*

AFTER PAMPINEA HAD FINISHED HER STORY, AND CISTI'S REPLY and generosity had received their share of everyone's praise, the queen was pleased to call on Lauretta to continue. Sweetly, she began:

Winsome ladies, first Filomena and now Pampinea struck the bull's eye, when they spoke of our meager talent and the beauty of ready replies. That there may be no further need for reiteration, I'd like to remind you, on that score, that such is the nature of repartée, that it should snap at the hearer, not like a dog, but rather like a sheep, for in the former instance, it would no longer be repartée, but insult. Now both Mistress Oretta's sally and Cisti's reply answer the proper requirements. In case a person snaps back like a cur, in reply to a remark of the same nature, I think he is not to be blamed as severely, as if he were to do so without provocation. It's a good thing, therefore, to bear in mind the proper occasion and person, as well as the time and place for playful banter. *À propos* of that, I'd like to tell you what happened to a churchman of ours who, through his carelessness, received as keen a thrust as he gave.

During the time Antonio D'Orso, a wise and virtuous prelate, was bishop of Florence, a Catalan worthy called Diego della Ratta, marshal of King Robert, emigrated here. Now this marshal, a remarkably handsome man and a gay blade with the fair sex, was taken with a beautiful Florentine lady, a niece of the bishop's brother, and upon hearing that her husband, although he came of a noble family, had all the instincts of avarice and miserliness, he arranged to give him five-hundred florins in gold for the privilege of lying one night with his wife. That settled, the marshal had certain silver coins then common currency gilded to look like gold, and after lying with the man's wife, though sorely against her will, he presented them to her husband. The affair later became a byword in the town, heaping shame and scorn upon the miserable wittol's head. However, the bishop's brother, like the wise man he was, pretended to be perfectly ignorant of the whole sordid business.

Now the bishop and the marshal used to go about a great deal together, and on Saint John's day, while they were riding side by side along the course where the race for the pallium was being run, looking at the fair ladies, the bishop caught sight of a young woman, Nonna de' Pulci, Alessio Rinucci's cousin. All of you must have known her, I'm sure—she was carried off by the present plague. Well, at that time she was a lovely, quick-tongued, fearless girl, who had been married, shortly before, in Porta San Piero. The bishop pointed her out to the marshal, and then, when they were nearer, he called to the young woman, laying his hand on his companion's shoulder. "Look here, Nonna, what do you think of this fine beau? Do you think you could resist him?"

In these words Nonna heard an echo of something impugning her virtue, and felt they might lower her in the esteem of the many people about who had also heard them. Accordingly, not only to justify herself, but to give blow for blow, she retorted, quick as a flash, "My lord, he might not succeed in winning me, but at any rate, I'd first want to make sure that the money was good."

No sooner did the two men hear her reply, than they found that the cap fit them alike, the marshal, because of the ignoble affront he had inflicted on the niece of the bishop's own brother, and the bishop, because he had swallowed the insult to his kin. Without daring to exchange a look, they went away in silence and in shame, and said nothing more to Nonna that day.

So it was, that since the young woman had been seriously affronted, it was permissible for her to bite as harshly as she had been bitten.

### ❊

## THE  FOURTH  STORY

*Chichibio, Currado Gianfigliazzi's cook, turns his master's wrath to laughter by a ready excuse, and avoids the punishment in store for him.*

NOW THAT LAURETTA WAS SILENT, AND NONNA HAD BEEN showered with praise, the queen called on Neifile to continue, who began:

Though one's own witty ingenuity, amorous ladies, often inspires one with ready words and useful answers apt for the occasion, Fortune has been known to come to the rescue of people in the stress of fear, by prompting their tongues to sudden flashes that in their calmer moments they would never have been able to think of—and that's what I'd like to demonstrate by my story.

Currado Gianfigliazzi, whom all of you must know, both by sight and hearsay, has always enjoyed the reputation of being a noble, generous and magnificent citizen, here in Florence. A follower of the knightly life, he is an assiduous sportsman. He is so fond of sports, in fact, that often his delight in hunting and hawking made him neglect his more important duties, for the immediate pleasure they afforded.

One day he brought down a crane near Peretola, with the help of one of his falcons, and finding the fowl fat and tender, he sent it to one of his competent cooks, Chichibio, a Venetian, with the injunction to roast it for supper, and prepare it as temptingly as possible.

Now Chichibio, who was as much of a greenhorn as he appeared, dressed the crane, and fixing it on the brazier, set to roasting it with all possible care. When it was nearly done to a delicious brown, and the smell of it as it turned upon the spit would have tempted the dead, a gossip of the neighborhood, called Brunetta, for whom Chichibio cherished a burning passion, came into the kitchen. The savor of the crane tickled her nostrils, and the moment she spied it, she coaxed and cajoled and begged Chichibio to give her a leg of it.

He answered with a song:

> "*I shall not give it to thee, Brunetta,*
> *I shall not give it to thee.*"

Annoyed at his flippancy, she said to him, angrily: "I swear, Chichibio, unless you give me one of the drumsticks, you'll never have any joy of me, as long as I live."

In short, she used so many arguments, that finally Chichibio, to keep his lady from flying into a temper, tore off a leg of the crane, and gave it to her.

Presently, when the one-legged crane was set before Currado and some foreign guests of his, he stared at it in astonishment, and sending for Chichibio, asked him what had become of the missing leg. Glibly, the sly-tongued Venetian answered, "Why, master, cranes have only one leg and one drumstick."

Wrathfully, Currado cried: "What the devil are you saying about one leg and one drumstick? Do you imagine I've never seen any other cranes in my life?"

Nothing daunted, Chichibio replied: "It's exactly as I say, master, and I can show you how it is with live cranes, any time you say."

To spare the strangers who were dining with him further annoyance, Currado forbore discussing the matter, but said simply: "Since you say you'll show me that it's true in live cranes—a strange thing, the like of which I've never seen or heard in my life—I want to prove it for myself to-morrow morning, and then I'll be satisfied. But I warn you, on my oath, if it's other than you say, you shall be taught such a lesson, that you'll bear me in mind to your sorrow, to your dying day!"

The matter was closed for the night. The following morning at daybreak, Currado, whose anger had not diminished with sleep, arose, ready to burst with rage, and sent for his horses. Motioning Chichibio to mount a nag, he led him to a river, on the banks of which cranes congregated in the early morning. "Now," said he to him, "we'll find out who was in the wrong last night, you or I."

Seeing that his master still persisted in his anger, and that he must somehow redeem his lie, Chichibio, not knowing how to get out of his scrape, rode beside Currado, quaking with fear. Had he been able, he would have run away without thinking twice, but flight was out of the question; so he kept a strict look-out, and stared now ahead and now behind, and now on either side, in his fancy seeing cranes everywhere; cranes, nothing but cranes, and standing on two legs.

However, on nearing the stream, he was the first to spy at least a dozen cranes on its banks, each teetering on one leg—a usual thing with them, when they sleep. Immediately, he pointed them out to Currado, saying: "Now there! You can see for yourself that I told you the truth about them last night, master. Cranes have only one leg and one drumstick. Look at 'em all standing there!"

"Wait," said Currado, when he saw them, "and I'll prove to you that they have two." Approaching nearer the birds, he shouted "Ho! Ho!" whereupon, startled at the sound, the cranes produced their other leg, and after strutting a few paces, took to flight.

"There, now, what do you think of that, numskull?" asked Currado, turning to Chichibio. "Are you convinced they have two legs?"

Chichibio, all in a fuddle, not knowing himself what prompted him, replied: "Yes, sir, I am. But you didn't shout *Ho! Ho!* to the crane last night, for if you had, it would have brought out the other leg and drumstick, like these fellows here!"

Currado was so delighted with the reply, that his rage turned to laughter and merriment. "You're quite right, Chichibio," he said. "I should have done that last night!"

And so it was that Chichibio got out of a bad scrape by a prompt and ludicrous reply, and patched up his difference with his master.

✳

# THE FIFTH STORY

*Forese da Rabatta and Giotto the painter come together from Mugello and tease each other on their disreputable appearance.*

THE WOMEN WERE QUITE TICKLED WITH CHICHIBIO'S REPLY, AND as Neifile was silent, Pamfilo continued, at the queen's pleasure:

Dearest ladies, just as Fortune has sometimes been known to conceal a wealth of fine qualities under some humble craft— a truth demonstrated a short time ago by Pampinea—so likewise, marvelous genius may be hidden by Nature under the wretchedest of human exteriors, a fact that held true in the case of two of our citizens, about whom I am going to tell you a very short story.

One of these men, called Forese da Rabatta, was a dwarfed, mis-shapen man, with a face so flat and doggish that it would have been a fright even had it graced the notoriously ugly family of the Baronci. Yet this ugly little creature was so well versed in law, that many a brilliant man looked upon him as a veritable storehouse of civil learning. The other, whose name was Giotto, was so extraordinary a genius, that there was nothing Nature, the mother of all things, displays to us by the eternal revolution of the heavens, that he could not recreate with pencil, pen or brush so faithfully, that it hardly seemed a copy, but rather the thing itself. Indeed, mortal sight was often puzzled, face to face with his creations, and took the painted thing for the actual object. Well, as he brought to light again that art, which had lain buried through the mistaken notions of those who painted more to flatter the eye of the ignorant, than to satisfy the intellect of the connoisseur, he might well be called one of the luminaries of Florence's glory. And all the more deservedly, because despite his mastery over others, he bore his honors humbly, and would never consent to be called 'master'. Yes—but that title which he would not adopt, reflected all the more resplendent glory upon him, the more invidiously it was usurped by his disciples, or others who could not compare with him. However, although his genius was phenomenal, he was no better off in personal attractiveness than Messer Forese. But to my story:

You must know that both Messer Forese and Giotto owned property at Mugello, and one day, during the season when lords hold open-court, while Messer Forese, mounted on a disreputable-looking nag, was on his way back to Florence from visiting his estates, he came upon Giotto, returning from a similar errand, and no better mounted or equipped than himself.

Both of them, at the time of my story, were fairly old men, so retarding the pace of their nags, they went their way together, when suddenly an unexpected summer shower overtook them. With all the haste they could muster, they fled to take shelter in the hut of a laborer whom both knew; but after a while, as the rain seemed to show no signs of abating, and as they were anxious to get to Florence before sunset, they borrowed two old fustian cloaks from the peasant for lack of anything better, and two hats, gnawed with age, and once more they proceeded toward the town.

Now when they had gone a while on their way, their clothes hanging limp with the wet, and all spattered and muddy from the continual splashing of their horses' hoofs (which certainly did not add distinction to their appearance) the sky began to clear, and the two, who had gone on in silence, struck up conversation anew.

Giotto was a very entertaining speaker, and as Messer Forese trotted on, listening to him, he could not help considering him from top to toe. The sight of him so disreputable, ill-dressed, and in that predicament, tickled his sense of humor, and without considering his own plight he laughed aloud, saying: "Ha! Ha! Giotto! If a stranger who had never cast eyes on you before, were suddenly to meet you in this condition, do you suppose he would take you to be the finest painter in the world, as indeed you are?"

"Perhaps he would," replied Giotto readily, "if when he saw you, he had the faintest suspicion that you had even learned your A B C."

Messer Forese no sooner heard Giotto's retort than he was aware of his mistake, and saw that he had been paid in his own coin.

✳

## THE SIXTH STORY

*Michele Scalza, by proving to certain young men that the Baronci family is the oldest and best in the whole world, or Maremma, wins himself a supper.*

THE WOMEN'S LAUGHTER WAS STILL RINGING, OVER GIOTTO'S ready answer, when the queen requested Fiammetta to resume the story-telling.

Young ladies, she began, Pamfilo's mention of the Baronci, whom I daresay you don't know as well as he, recalled to my mind a story in which their distinguished ancestry is demonstrated. It does not depart from our topic for to-day, and therefore I'll tell it to you with the greatest pleasure.

Not so very long ago, there lived in our city a young spark called Michele Scalza, who was the jolliest, merriest scamp in the world. He had all the newest stories at the tip of his tongue, and there wasn't a roistering crew of Florentine youths that wasn't anxious to have him of their party.

One day, while he was with a group of friends at Mount Ughi, a debate arose as to which were the oldest and most aristocratic gentlefolk of Florence. "The Uberti," said some. "The Lamberti," maintained others, all declaring themselves for this or that family, as their fancy swayed them. Scalza laughed at them all. "Nonsense, gulls that you are!" he cried. "You don't know what you're talking about! The oldest and the bluest-blooded men, not only of Florence but of the whole world with Maremma thrown in, are the Baronci, as any man of sense, or any other will say, who knows them as I do. I repeat it—make no mistake about it!—the Baronci, your neighbors of Santa Maria Maggiore!"

The youths expected him to explain himself further, but when they heard what he said, they jeered at him and said, "You're trying to make fools of us. As though we didn't know the Baronci as well as you!"

"On my word, I'm not making fun of you, really," said Scalza. "I'm telling you nothing but what is so. If any one of you is willing to stake the winner and half a dozen merry fellows of his pick, to a supper, I'll take the bet, and gladly. I'll go even further: I'll accept the judgment of any umpire you select."

Then spoke up one of them, Neri Mannini, by name. "Well, I'm ready to try my luck at this supper," he said.

They decided upon Piero di Fiorentino, in whose home they were, to act as judge, and approaching him, followed by the rest of the merry crew, who were looking forward to seeing Scalza lose his bet, so they might later plague him about it, they told him all there was to be told. Piero, a prudent young gentleman, first listened to what Neri had to say, and then, turning to Scalza asked, "How will you be able to prove what you affirm?"

"How? Easily enough," replied Scalza. "I'll give you such convincing proofs, that not only you, but Neri here, who denies it, will confess I'm right.

"You know that the older the ancestry of people, the nobler they are, as all of us here were saying a short while ago. Now the Baronci are older in ancestry than any other family extant. Hence, they are nobler. When I prove to you how they come to be the oldest, I've no doubt I'll surely win the bet.

"You must know that the Baronci were made by the good Lord when He had scarcely learned to draw, while the rest of us were manufactured later. You want to know how this is true? Simply compare the Baronci with other people. While all the rest have respectable-looking faces, properly proportioned, what is the case with the Baronci? There's one with a long, narrow mug, and another with a face as wide as a platter. Here's a fellow with a tremendously long nose, and one with a mere stump. Then again there is one with a chin that juts out and up, and a huge pair of jaws that would honor a donkey, and another with one eye larger than the other, or set farther down on his face—all of them looking like the caricatures children scrawl when they are just beginning to draw. You see, then, it's evident enough as I said before, that the good Lord made them when He was just learning, and therefore they're older than other people, and nobler."

Piero, the judge, Neri, who had staked the supper, and the rest of the gay youths, considered that things were really as Scalza claimed by his amusing argument, and amid peals of laughter, they declared him right. Yes, he had certainly won the supper, they agreed, and the Baronci were indeed the bluest-blooded and most anciently descended men extant, not only in Florence, but in the whole world, or even Maremma.

That's why Pamfilo was perfectly right when he said, describing the ugliness of Messer Forese's face, that it would have been a fright, even on a Baronci.

# THE SEVENTH STORY

*Filippa, called to judgment by her husband, on being found with a lover, avoids the penalty by a prompt and pleasing defense, and causes the law to be modified.*

FIAMMETTA WAS SILENT, IN THE MIDST OF THE GENERAL MERRI-
ment aroused by the droll argument Scalza had produced to elevate the Baronci above all others, when the queen charged Filostrato to continue.

Noble ladies, he began, it is an excellent thing to be well-spoken, but I think it is still more so, to have an apt tongue in the stress of necessity. Such was the case of a lady about whom I am going to tell you, who used hers so well, that she not only made her audience laugh with glee, but delivered herself from the toils of a shameful death.

Once upon a time, in the town of Prato, there used to be a law in force—as pernicious, indeed, as it was cruel, to the effect that any woman caught by her husband in the act of adultery with a lover, was to be burned alive, like any vulgar harlot who sold herself for money.

While this statute prevailed, a beautiful lady called Filippa, a devout worshiper of Cupid, was surprised in her bedroom one night by her husband, Rinaldo de' Pugliesi, in the arms of Lazzarino de' Guazzagliotri, a high-born Adonis of a youth of that city, whom she loved as the apple of her eye.

Burning with rage at the discovery, Rinaldo could scarcely forbear running upon them, and slaying them on the spot. Were it not for the misgivings he had for his own safety, if he gave vent to his wrath, he would have followed his impulse. However, he controlled his evil intent, but could not abandon his desire to demand of the town's statute, what it was unlawful for him to bring about—in other words, the death of his wife.

As he had no lack of evidence to prove Filippa's guilt, he brought charges against her, early in the morning, at daybreak, and without further deliberation, had her summoned before the court.

Now Filippa was a high-spirited woman, as all women are who truly love, and though many of her friends and relatives advised her against going, she resolved to appear before the magistrate, preferring a courageous death, by confessing the truth, to a shameful life of exile, by a cowardly flight that would have proved her unworthy of the lover in whose arms she had lain that night.

Accordingly, she presented herself before the provost, with a large following of men and women who urged her to deny the charges. She asked him firmly and without moving a muscle what he desired of her. The provost, seeing her so beautiful, courteous and so brave—as her words demonstrated—felt a certain pity stirring in his heart at the thought that she might confess a crime for which he would be obliged to sentence her to death to save his honor. But then, seeing he could not avoid cross-questioning her on the charge proffered against her, he said:

"Madam, here as you see, is Rinaldo, your husband, who is suing you on the grounds of finding you in the act of adultery with another man, and who therefore demands that I sentence you to death for it, as the law, which is in force, requires. I cannot pass sentence if you do not confess your guilt with your own lips. Be careful of your answers, then, and tell me if what your husband charges you with is true."

Filippa, not at all daunted, replied in a very agreeable voice: "Your honor, it is true that Rinaldo is my husband, and that last night he found me in the arms of Lazzarino, where I had lain many another time, out of the great and true love I bear him. Far be it from me ever to deny it.

"As you are doubtless aware, laws should be equal for all, and should be made with the consent of those whom they affect. Such is not the case with this particular statute, which is stringent only with us poor women, who, after all, have it in our power to give pleasure to many more people than men ever could. Moreover, when this law was drawn up, not a single woman gave her consent or was so much as invited to give it. For all these reasons, it surely deserves to be considered reprehensible. If you insist upon enforcing it, not at the risk of my body, but of your immortal soul, you are at liberty to do so; but before you proceed to pass judgment, I beg you to grant me a small request. Simply ask my husband whether I have ever failed to yield myself to him entirely, whenever he chose, and as often as he pleased."

Without waiting for the magistrate to question him, Rinaldo immediately answered that there was no doubt Filippa had always granted him the joy of her body, at each and every request of his.

"That being the case, your honor," she went on, directly, "I'd like to ask him, since he has always had all he wanted of me and to his heart's content, what was I to do with all that was left over? Indeed, what am I to do with it? Throw it to the dogs? Isn't it far better to let it give enjoyment to some gentleman who loves me more than his life, than to let it go to waste or ruin?"

As it happened, the whole town had turned out to attend the sensational trial that involved a lady of such beauty and fame, and when the people heard her roguish question, they burst into a roar of laughter, shouting to a man that she was right and had spoken well.

That day, before court was adjourned, that harsh statute was modified at the magistrate's suggestion to hold only for such women as made cuckolds of their husbands for love of money.

As for Rinaldo, he went away crest-fallen at his mad venture, while Filippa returned home victorious, feeling in her joy that she had, in a sense, been delivered from the flames.

✳

# THE  EIGHTH  STORY

*Fresco advises his niece not to look at her own image if, as she*
*said, she was annoyed by the sight of unpleasant people.*

AT FIRST, FILOSTRATO'S STORY PRICKED THE HEARTS OF THE AT-
tentive ladies with a sting of shame, which was betrayed by the
modest flush that rose to their cheeks, but as they listened further, exchanging furtive glances, they smiled archly and could
scarcely contain their laughter. The moment he had made an
end of it, however, the queen turned to Emilia, requesting her
to continue. With a sigh, as if awakening from a revery, she began:

Since an obstinate thought, sweet ladies, has kept me from
your midst for some time, I shall have to be satisfied with relating a much shorter story, in obedience to our queen's command, than I had intended. It concerns the inane haughtiness of
a young woman, which her uncle's humorous retort should have
corrected, had she had sense enough to understand it.

Well then, once upon a time there lived a certain Fresco da
Celatico, who had a niece called Ciesca for short. The lass was
comely enough of form and feature, though no angel-faced
beauty, like many we've seen; but she had so exalted a notion of
herself, and thought her lineage so distinguished, that she had
formed the habit of finding fault with her fellow-beings—in
short, with everything she happened to cast her eyes upon, regardless of her own shortcomings. She was more disagreeable, petulant and capricious than any woman alive, and never
satisfied with anything. Moreover, she was so overburdened
with pride, that it would have been unseemly, even had she
sprung of the blood of French kings. Whenever she walked
through the streets, she was so puffed up with the airs she assumed, that she did nothing but make wry faces, as if the
presence of those she saw or passed on the way, was offensive
to her nostrils. But let's not mention any more of her unpleasant and annoying faults.

One day, she returned home suddenly from a walk, and sitting down near Fresco, with all kinds of wearisome affectations,
she did nothing but snort and puff, until he could not help say-

ing, "What's the matter, Ciesca? To-day's a holiday, yet you've come back so early!"

"I've come back early, true enough," she replied, dripping with hypocrisy. "I verily believe there never were so many ugly and unpleasant men and women in this town as I saw to-day! I did not meet a solitary one whom I didn't loathe like the plague, and there's no mortal living who hates ugliness as much as I do. That's why I came home so soon, simply to avoid being afflicted by the sight of them!"

Fresco, who cordially hated his niece's snobbishness and affectation, thereupon replied, "Well, my dear, since you hate disagreeable things as much as you say, if you want to be happy, don't ever look at yourself in a mirror."

The girl, however, who was lighter-headed than a reed, although she held herself the peer of Solomon for wisdom, understood Fresco's real meaning no better than a dumb beast.

"But I do want to look at myself in a mirror, like other women," she said, foolishly.

Thus she remained in her stupidity, and may very well be no wiser to this day.

✳

## THE NINTH STORY

*Guido Cavalcanti civilly rebukes certain Florentine gentlemen who had come upon him in his meditations.*

THE QUEEN SAW THAT EMILIA HAD FINISHED HER STORY, AND AS she was the only one left to speak but for the privileged Dioneo, she began:

Although, charming ladies, you've appropriated at least two stories to-day, one of which I had intended telling, I have still another left, that closes with a retort of deeper meaning, perhaps, than any that has yet been told.

You must know that in olden times, many a good, praiseworthy custom prevailed, none of which survives to-day; for the avarice which sprang up with the influx of wealth, caused them all to perish. Now among these customs, there was one that required gentlemen from all over Florence to form clubs of limited membership, open only to those well able to keep up with the expense. They held their meetings in various quarters of the city. According to the rules, each member took turns, one to-day, another to-morrow, in treating the whole party to dinner, to which they sometimes invited distinguished guests, who came to Florence from other towns, as well as gentlemen of their own city. Following the same tradition, they provided themselves with uniforms at least once a year, and on the most notable days, they rode together through the town. Sometimes they held jousts and tournaments, which was usually the case on important holidays, or whenever news of victory or any other good fortune gladdened the city.

Among these various clubs, there was one to which Betto Brunelleschi belonged. Many a time, both he and the rest of his boon-companions had done their best, and not without reason, to lure into their midst Guido, the son of Cavalcante de' Cavalcanti, a youth who, besides being one of the world's keenest logicians, and a great natural-philosopher (for all of which the merry fellows did not care a rush), was a most gracious, accomplished, eloquent courtier, better versed in all that makes a gentleman than anyone of his day. Moreover, he was extremely wealthy, and for the asking, well knew how to feast and honor any man he thought worthy.

Messer Betto, however, had never succeeded in drawing him into his circle, whereupon he and his associates concluded that it was all because Guido was often too much taken up with philosophical speculation, and was aloof from the world of men. Indeed, since Guido was inclined to favor the tenets of the Epicureans, it was even whispered among the vulgar that all his speculation aimed to prove that there was no God.

One day, Guido left Orto San Michele and walked as far as San Giovanni along the Corso degli Adimari, a road which he was in the habit of frequenting. Great marble tombs, now in Santa Maria Reparata, were then sown about San Giovanni, and while Guido was standing between the porphyry columns of the church and those stones, with the door of San Giovanni shut fast behind him, Betto and his company came riding along the square. Catching sight of Guido among these gravestones, "Let's go and worry him," they said.

Spurring their horses, they went for him in play, like a charging squad, and before he was aware, they were upon him.

"Guido," they began, "why do you refuse to join our band? Tell us, what miracle will you have accomplished when you succeed in proving that there is no God?"

Seeing himself surrounded by them, Guido quietly replied, "Gentlemen, it is your privilege to tell me anything you wish in your own home." Then, resting his hand on one of those immense tombstones, he leapt over it nimbly, and landing on the other side, stole away and rid himself of them.

In the meantime, the men remained there quite aghast, looking at each other, calling him a crazy fellow and declaring that his answer was devoid of sense, as they were no more in their own homes in the cemetery than any other citizen, Guido included.

Betto, however, turned to them and said, "You are the crazy fellows if you fail to grasp his meaning. Civilly, and in a few words, he has made us swallow the worst reproof in the world. If you consider well, these tombs are the homes of the dead, for here they are laid to dwell. When he says we are in our homes, he wants to show us that all of us unlettered men and ignorant folk are worse than dead, compared with him and other learned doctors. That's why we're in our homes when we're here."

Then every man of them understood what Guido had meant to convey, and was ashamed. From that day on, they never worried him, and looked upon Betto as a gentleman and a scholar.

✳

## THE TENTH STORY

*Friar Onion promises to show some peasants a feather from the wings of Angel Gabriel. Finding coals in its place, he claims they are of the brazier on which Saint Lawrence was roasted.*

NOW THAT EACH OF THE COMPANY HAD TOLD A STORY, DIONEO knew his turn had come; so without waiting for a formal invitation, he began, when the rest, who were still praising Guido's pregnant answer, were silent:

Enchanting ladies, although it is my privilege to speak on whatever strikes my fancy, to-day however, I don't intend to depart from the subject all of you have so ably treated. No, I shall follow in your footsteps, and show you how skilfully one of the little brothers of Saint Anthony applied his nimble wit to avoid the trap two young rogues had set at his feet. You won't be bored, I hope, if I enlarge somewhat upon the story to do it justice, for see, the sun is still high in the heavens.

Now, then! Certaldo, as you must have heard, is a hamlet of Val d'Elsa in our own section of the country, and though a tiny place, it was once inhabited by noble and prosperous gentlemen. It was a field of plentiful harvest for a certain little monk of the order of Saint Anthony, and for a long time he had made it a practice to visit it once a year, and garner the fruits which the simple of soul gave to him and the rest of his brotherhood. He was called Friar Onion, and was a very welcome figure there, perhaps no less by virtue of his name as for more spiritual reasons; for, as you know, the soil of that part of the country yields onions that are famous all over Tuscany. He was a meager little person, was Friar Onion, carrot-haired and jolly-faced, and the merriest scamp in the world. Moreover, despite the gaps in his education, he was so eloquent and witty a talker, that anyone who did not know him well might have thought him not only an accomplished rhetorician, but a Tully —even Quintilian himself! In fine, there was not a soul in the whole district for whose children he had not acted as godfather, or to whom he was not bound by ties of friendship and sympathy.

One fine Sunday morning in the month of August, he visited the town as usual, and when all the good gossips and gaffers had gathered from the villages round about to hear mass, he stepped forward at the proper moment and addressed them:

"Sisters and brethren, you all know it's customary, every year, to send an offering of your grain and oats to the poor folks of our master Saint Anthony. Some of you send a great deal, and some a few handfuls, according to your means and devotion, in return for the protection the blessed Saint Anthony gives your oxen and your asses, your pigs and your sheep. Over and above this, all of you, especially those who are registered in our holy company, pay the little trifle you are scheduled to pay, once a year. It's for the collection of these dues that I've been sent among you by my chief, that is, by my master, the abbot, so— may the good Lord lay His blessing upon you!—when you hear the little bells tinkling this afternoon, come and meet me outside the church, where I'll preach to you as usual, and give you the Cross to kiss. There's one special attraction besides. Since I know you're all faithful followers of our master Saint Anthony, I'm going to reward you by a special favor, and show you a most wonderful holy relic, that I brought back myself from the Holy Land across the sea. It is a feather of the Angel Gabriel, my friends, one of those he dropped in the Virgin Mary's room, when he came to make the Annunciation to her in Nazareth."

Then, his message delivered, he was silent and continued with the mass.

While he was speaking, there happened to be among his numerous flock in the church two very clever rogues, one called Giovanni del Bragoniera and the other Biagio Pizzini. For some time they laughed together at this relic of Friar Onion's, but then, though they were his friends and boon-companions, they decided to play him a trick through this precious feather. That afternoon, they knew, the friar was to lunch with a friend of his at the hamlet. Accordingly, when they thought he must be at table, they slipped into the street and went to the hostelry where he had his lodgings, intending that while Biagio engaged Friar Onion's servant in conversation, Giovanni was to ransack the holy man's trappings in search of this feather, whatever it was, and take it away. The fun would come when the friar tried to explain the loss of his relic to the faithful.

Now Friar Onion had as servant, a fellow who had as many attributes as he had nicknames—Guccio the Whale was one, Guccio Greaser another, and some even called him Guccio the Pig. So mischievous and arrant a rascal was he, that even the notorious Lippo Topo couldn't have held a candle to him. Indeed, Friar Onion would sometimes expatiate upon his virtues, to his friends, and say, "I have a servant, my friends, who has nine such qualities, that if the least of them had been in Solomon, Aristotle or Seneca, it would have been enough to discount all their goodness, wisdom and piety. Think what a marvel my man must be, who possesses the whole nine of them, and not an ounce of goodness, wisdom or piety!"

Sometimes, when he was asked what these nine qualities were, he would answer, enumerating them in doggerel: "What are they, you ask? I'll tell you. He is lazy, dirty, thoughtless; ill-bred, foul-tongued, careless; lazy, crack-brained, heedless— not to mention other little flaws which I had better suppress. But the funniest thing about him is that wherever he may be, he's forever anxious to get himself a wife and go into housekeeping, thinking he's so handsome and irresistible with his thick, greasy beard, that all the women who clap eyes on him immediately fall victim to his charms. Really, if he were left to his own devices, he'd lose his belt-strap, chasing after them. He's useful enough to me, though, to be truthful, for no matter how confidentially anybody wants to speak to me, Guccio must be there to get an earful. If I should ever be asked a question, he's so afraid I won't know how to answer, that he immediately blurts out Yes, or No, as he sees fit."

This was the gentleman Friar Onion had left at the inn, with the explicit command to see that nobody tampered with his belongings, especially his saddle-bags, that contained his most sacred possessions. But Guccio Greaser hankered more after the kitchen than does the nightingale after the green arbor, especially when he scented some jolly slut about, and as it was, he had made a find in mine host's kitchen. A fat, dumpy, clumsy wench she was, with a brace of paps the size of two garbage cans, and a sweaty, oily, sooty mug that was a match for the Baronci's. Upon making his discovery, Guccio had swooped down upon her in the kitchen like a vulture on his carrion, leaving Friar Onion's room and baggage under the custody of heaven. Though it was August, he sat hugging the hearth, and struck up conversation with my lady Nuta, telling her he was a gentleman, he was, and had piles and piles of money, all belonging to him in his own right, plus what he had for other folks, which was even more than he owned himself. Yes, and he could do lots of things, and had as clever a tongue in his head as anyone, the Lord knows. Indeed, regardless of his hood, that was larded with more grease than would have served to baste Altopascio's caldron, despite his patched cloak, that hung in tatters and shone with sweat about the collar and armpits and was adorned, besides, with more spots and splashes than any plaid or India weave, unmindful of his shoes, all down at the heel and torn, and his yawning socks, he pursued her with a grandeur that would have done honor to a Sire de Chatillon. "I'll dress you up, and set you up fine, I will, girl," said he. "Indeed, I'll get you out of slavin' for others, and give you hopes of better fortune, even if you have no dowry or anything."

He made her many other grandiloquent promises: but for all his magnificent delivery, wind were his words, and wind they remained, like most of his undertakings.

Well, the two scamps found Guccio the Pig mighty busy courting Nuta, which gave them no little satisfaction, seeing that half their trouble was then over. No one stood in their way, so slipping into Friar Onion's room, the door of which was open, they made for his saddle-bags, which contained the precious feather. When they spread them open before them, they came upon a clumsy bundle of silk, inside of which they discovered a small box. They opened it quickly and found—a feather of a parrot's tail, the very feather, they were sure, that Friar Onion had promised to show his faithful at Certaldo.

In his day, it would have been easy for the friar to make the people believe his trumpery. The luxuries of the Orient had made but small headway into Tuscany, though since then, they have been introduced with a vengeance, to the ruin of all Italy. But if these eastern refinements were known anywhere in Italy, they were certainly unfamiliar to the people of that hamlet. Indeed, the primitive honesty of the ancients was still so much alive, that the inhabitants had never heard of parrots, much less set eyes on such creatures at all.

Now the youths, overjoyed at their find, spirited away the feather, and not to leave the case empty, filled it with a few coals, that lay in a corner of the room. Closing it again, and rearranging everything as before, they went away unperceived with their prize, all impatience to hear what Friar Onion would have to say, on finding the coals instead of the feather.

Meanwhile, the good folk on hearing that they were to be shown a feather of the Angel Gabriel in the afternoon, betook themselves to their homes after mass. By the time they had had their dinner, and the information had passed from goodman to goodman and gossip to gossip, so vast a crowd had flocked to the hamlet to be shown this marvelous feather, that there wasn't room enough left to admit a fly. Friar Onion, too, had had a good meal, after which he took a short nap. On rising in the afternoon, and hearing the hubbub of the multitude of peasants swarming for a sight of the feather, he sent Guccio Greaser to fetch the bells and saddle-bags. It was a great struggle for the amorous fellow to wrench himself away from Nuta and the kitchen, but he went with the necessary paraphernalia to the place his master had indicated, puffing and panting mightily, for the gallons of water he had drunk had swelled his bowels considerably. Once at the church, he stationed himself in front of the door and set up a vigorous jangling of the bells. The parish folk had gathered to a man, whereupon Friar Onion, unaware that anything had been tampered with, plunged into his sermon, with many a covert hint of his own personal needs. Soon the time came for the unveiling of Angel Gabriel's feather. With a solemn voice, he began by intoning the service; then, after two torches had been lighted, he uncovered his head, carefully undid the silken wrapper, and produced the box. Before thinking of opening it, however, he delivered himself of a few words in praise of the Angel Gabriel and his relic, and then pulled up the lid of the coffer. It was full of coals. At the revelation, he did not dream of suspecting Guccio the Whale—the fellow was not clever enough to have thought of it; nor did he curse him for not preventing others from playing the trick. No, he cursed himself inwardly for committing the scape-grace to the care of his belongings, knowing him as he did to be negligent, disobedient, crack-brained and heedless. Outwardly, he did not even change color, however, but raising his face and his hands to heaven, exclaimed loud enough for everyone to hear: "Almighty God, may Thy might be praised forever!" after which, closing the casket and turning to the populace, he said:

"Sisters and brothers, you must know that while I was still a mere youth, I was sent by my superior to those far lands where the sun rises, and was expressly commissioned to look for the dispensations for making porcelain, which, though they're cheap enough to seal, are more useful to others than to us. Well, setting out on this enterprise, I left Venice and journeyed through the Borgo de' Greci. From there, I rode through the Kingdom of Algarve and Baldacca, until I came to Parione, out of which, not without a dry gullet, I arrived in Sardinia. But why should I mention all the lands I traveled? After I had passed the Strait of Saint George, I landed in Truffle and Buffle, great regions, both of them teeming with folk; from there I came to the land of Trumpery, where I found many of our brethren and monks of other orders, all of them going about freely and easily, avoiding annoyance for the good Lord's sake, and caring not a whit for other people's woes, provided their own gains were assured. No coin did they spend, but what was unminted.

"From this territory, I passed into the district of Abruzzi, where men and women clatter about the mountains on wooden pattens, and dress the pigs in the pigs' own gut-skins. Still farther, I came across people who carried bread in staves and wine in bags. Then, from those regions, I reached the mountains of the Baschi, where all the streams run perpendicularly. In short, I got entangled so far inland, that I traveled as far as India Pastinaca, where—and I swear to the truth of this by the gown I'm wearing—I even saw feathered creatures fly, a wonder too strange to be believed by those who have not seen it! But Maso del Saggio will support my statement—Maso, whom I found established as a powerful merchant there, cracking nuts and carrying on a retail business in the shells.

"However, since I couldn't find what I was looking for, and as from that point on it is only possible to travel by water, I retraced my steps and came to those holy lands where, in the summer of the year, stale bread is worth four pence a loaf and the warm can be had for nothing. It's here that I met the venerable Father Blamenotme Ifyouplease, the most worshipful patriarch of Jerusalem, who, out of respect for the gown of my master Saint Anthony's order, which I have always worn, insisted on showing me all the precious relics he had collected. What a wealth of them! There were so many, that if I were to enumerate them, I'd have to talk for days before I reached the end of the tale! But I don't want to disappoint you, my friends, so I shall tell you about a few of them. First, he showed me the finger of the Holy Ghost, as perfect and solid as you please, a ringlet of the seraph who appeared to Saint Francis, and one of the fingernails of the cherubim. Yes, he also let me see a rib of the Verbum Caro Look-out-of-the-Window, and the clothes of the Holy Catholic Faith, a number of rays of the star that shone for the three Magi in the East, and a bottle containing the sweat shed by Saint Michael when he fought with the devil. Besides, he showed me the jawbone of Saint Lazarus' Death, and many, many other wonderful things. Well, after that, because I told him a lot of things gratuitously in our dialect, about the slopes of Mount Moretto, and recited to him a few chapters of the Caprezio, which he had long been seeking, high and low, he divided his holy relics with me. He gave me one of the teeth of the Holy Cross, an echo of the bells of Solomon's temple, shut up in a tiny bottle, the feather of the Angel Gabriel which I've already told you about, and one of the clods of Saint Gerard of Villa Magna. That relic, however, I presented to Gerard of Bonsi in Florence a little while ago, for his great devotion to that saint. Among other things, the patriarch also gave me some of the coals on which the blessed martyr Saint Lawrence was roasted, and all of these treasures I faithfully brought back with me. In fact, I have them, each and every one.

"Now, to tell the truth, I must inform you that my superior never allowed me to display them, until he had made sure whether they were the real article or not. Recently, because of certain miracles that have been performed by their virtue, and because of some certificates sent by the Patriarch of Jerusalem, he's been convinced of their authenticity, and has given me permission to exhibit them. However, in my nervousness over entrusting them to others, I always carry them about with me —the feather of the Angel Gabriel, in a box by itself, so that it won't be ruffled, and the coals that roasted Saint Lawrence in another. Now these two boxes are so much alike, that I've often mistaken one for the other, which is now the case, for thinking I had brought you the casket containing the feather, I find it's the one that holds the coals.

"I'm convinced it was no error that created the confusion. Indeed, I verily believe it was the manifest will of God, that guided my hand to the coals, for now that I think of it, the feast of Saint Lawrence will be around in two days. Yes, it was the Lord's will. He intended me to show you the coals on which the blessed martyr was roasted, that I might rekindle in your souls the devotion you ought to feel for that saint. Therefore, it was not the feather He let me take, as I had intended, but the blessed coals, quenched by the agonized sweat of that holiest of bodies. Take off your hats now, O my blessed children, as you approach to gaze upon these coals. But first, I'd like you to know that whoever has the sign of the cross marked on him by one of these coals, may rest easy all through the year that no fire will touch him, but he'll feel the sting of it."

His harangue over, he intoned a *laud* in honor of Saint Lawrence and opened the box, revealing the coals to the throng. Awed at the wonder of them, the sheepish multitude stared wide-eyed at the lumps, and flocked about Friar Onion, begging him, for a more generous consideration than usual, to mark them with the relics. Obligingly, the friar took the coals in his hand, and began scratching the biggest crosses he could on the men's white shirts and jerkins and the women's veils, reassuring them the while that though the lumps were used up in the marking, they always grew again in the box, as he had often had occasion to observe.

In this fashion, he decorated the good folks of Certaldo, much to his own advantage, and so with nimble cunning he played a prank on those who had sought to embarrass him by stealing his feather. As for the two rogues, they had been present at his sermon. So amused were they at his novel and far-fetched expedient, and at the style of his harangue, that they laughed almost to the point of lock-jaw. But later, when the crowd had dispersed, they hilariously confessed to him what they had done, and gave him back his feather, which profited him as much the following year, as the lumps of coal had done that day.

This last story had roused the whole band to irrepressible good spirits, and all of them were nearly in stitches laughing at Friar Onion, especially at his pilgrimage and the extraordinary relics he'd seen and brought back with him. Finally, the queen, seeing the story was over, and her rule as well, stood up, and taking the crown from her head laid it laughingly on Dioneo's, saying, "It's about time, Dioneo, you learned a little of the responsibility of having women in your charge, to rule and guide. Be king, then, and see that you rule us so well, that we'll have reason in the end to be glad of our choice!"

Accepting the crown, Dioneo replied laughing, "I'm sure you've seen many a king of the chess-board who was much more competent than I could ever be. But still, if you render me the obedience a king requires, I have it in me to give you some real pleasure, by a sport without which no merry-making can be called complete. But enough of this banter. I shall govern you as best I may."

He sent for the steward, according to precedent, ordered what was to be done while his rule lasted, and then said, "Virtuous ladies, we have told so many kinds of stories concerning human endeavor and the various shifts of fortune, that if Mistress Licisca had not a little while ago furnished me with the theme for to-morrow's narratives, by her chatter, I'm afraid I should have had a hard nut to crack in that respect. As you heard for yourselves, she said she hadn't a single neighbor who had gone to her husband with a whole maidenhead, and added that she knew all sorts of pranks married women play upon their mates. We'll set aside the first part, which after all belongs to adolescence, but I think the second should prove very entertaining matter for discussion. For to-morrow, then, since Mistress Licisca has started the ball rolling, I'd like you to tell *of the tricks women have played upon their husbands, either for love or in self-defense, with or without the poor fellows' knowledge.*"

Some of the ladies took exception to the theme as hardly proper for them to treat, and begged the king to change it, but he replied, "I know what I have asked you to do, dear ladies, as well as you do, and I'll not be swerved from it by what you would have me understand, for the times are such that, provided men and women take care not to tread on the toes of decency, all freedom is allowed. Don't you know that because of the evil days we've fallen upon, judges have left their benches, that divine as well as human laws are dumb, and that we are all given the maximum license to preserve our lives? Well, then, if you give your virtue a little more lee-way in speech—not for the purpose of following it up with immodest actions, but purely to afford innocent pleasure to yourselves and others—I don't see what grounds for blame could possibly be adduced against you in the future. What's more, our little band has been exemplary in behavior from the first day to this, and I don't see how anything we have said so far, could have cast a blot upon it—a record we'll maintain to the very end, with the help of God. Besides, what man is there who doesn't know your virtue? Why, neither our merry jests, nor even the terror of death, I am certain, could succeed in undermining it! To be frank, if anyone were to learn that you avoided speaking about such trifles, out of squeamishness, he would be inclined to think the cap fit you, and therefore you did not care to discuss the matter. Moreover, you would be paying me a fine compliment, if, after I obeyed you, you insisted on dictating to me, now that you've made me king, and refused to speak on the subject I've assigned! Come, away with this prudery, more appropriate to evil minds than to yours! Think of some fine story to tell, and good luck to you!"

Convinced by his arguments, the women agreed to comply, whereupon the king gave them all leave to do as they wished until supper-time. The sun was still high in the sky, for the story-telling had not taken up much time, and when Dioneo had settled down to a chess-game at the boards with the other youths, Elisa, calling all the women aside, said:

"From the first moment we came here, I've just been dying to take you to a lovely spot near by, where I don't suppose any of you has ever been—the Vale of the Ladies, it's called. I haven't had the opportunity to take you there until to-day, with the sun still high, so if you'd care to come, I haven't the least doubt you'll be glad you did so."

The girls replied they were ready; therefore, sending for one of their maid-servants, without letting the young men know of their escapade, they set out on their way. They had scarcely

walked a mile, when they came to the Vale of the Ladies, which
they reached through a narrow path bordered on one side by a
crystalline brook. It was so enchanting a spot, and so refreshing,
especially then, at the height of the hot season, that a more
beautiful locality could not have been imagined.

From what one of them later told me, the plain in the midst
of the valley was as round as though it had been drawn with a
compass, though it was obviously nature's handiwork, and not
art's, measuring perhaps a little more than half a mile in cir-
cumference, and circled by six not too lofty hills, on the crests
of which palaces built on the style of handsome manors could
be discerned. The hillsides sloped gently down to the plain,
much like the ordered descent of tiers in a theater, one after the
other, from the loftiest to the lowmost, in ever-narrowing circles. Of these slopes, the southern face was covered with vines,
olive, almond, cherry and fig-trees, and all kinds of fruit-bear-
ing growths, which left no patch of the fertile earth bare. The
sides that faced the constellation of the Plow, on the other hand,
were all overgrown with scrub-oak and ash-trees, and other
evergreens as flourishing and upright as could be. As for the
plain itself, it had no means of approach except by the way the
young women had entered it. Fir-trees, cypresses, laurels and
various species of pines grew there in great abundance, all of
them so well-formed and artistically arranged that one might
have thought expert landscape gardeners had planted them. Little or no sun, even at its highest, ever filtered through the thick
growth to the ground beneath—a meadow of the most delicate grass, dotted over with crimson flowers and blossoms of
many hues. But above these attractions, and affording as keen a
pleasure, was a streamlet flowing down the valley, between
two of the hills, rushing over the cliffs of living rock, and babbling, on its way, a song delightful to the ear. While it splashed
and bubbled, it looked, from the distance, as though jets of
quick-silver were leaping and bursting into misty spray at some
hidden pressure. Then, as it made its way to the little plain, it
became a handsome canal, through which it flowed with a rush
to the center, where it formed a miniature reservoir, like
the fish-pools we often see in the gardens of city-dwellers. The
water in the lake rose no higher than a man's breast, and it was
so sparklingly clear, that the fine gravel at the bottom could
have been counted, grain by grain, if one had had the leisure to
do it. But it was not only the sandy bottom that shone clearly

through the water, for many gleaming fish could be seen darting to and fro, with a liveliness that was not only a delight, but a wonder to behold. No embankment enclosed the lake, but the natural soil of the meadow, that thrived lush and more deeply green because of the moisture. Where the water overflowed its banks, it was received into another canal, through which it left the valley and wimpled downward to the low-lying plains.

It was to this spot that the young women came. Full of delight and appreciation, they drank in everything with their eyes, extolling the beauty that surrounded them. The heat was overpowering; the little lake was before them, beckoning. There was no fear of being spied upon. Why not bathe together?

Sending their maid to watch for a chance passerby, on the narrow path that led into the plain, and give the alarm in case of danger, all seven took off their clothes and dipped into the water, which concealed their snow-white bodies no more than thin glass could hide the flush of a vermeil rose. No cloud troubled the clearness of the lake while they were in it, chasing the fish hither and thither as best they could, seeking to catch them in their hands as the frightened creatures darted madly about for a place of shelter. A few were captured in the sport. After the girls had played in the water a while longer, they rose out of it and dressed once more. It would have been impossible for them to lavish more praise upon the glorious spot than they already had, and thinking it about time to return home, they started back at an easy pace, talking over its many attractions.

It was still early when they reached the palace, to find the youths engrossed in their game, as they had left them.

"We've outwitted you to-day," Pampinea called to them, laughing.

"What!" cried Dioneo. "Do you act first, and then tell?"

"Exactly so, sir!" she replied, and told him at greater length where they had come from, what the place was like, and how far off, omitting no detail of their exploits.

The king was most anxious to see the spot after the glorious description, and ordered supper to be served immediately. No sooner was it done away with, to their mutual relish, than the three youths and their valets left the women behind, and made for the plain. It was the most enchanting place they had ever seen, they agreed, as they examined its every aspect, for none of them had ever been there before. Then, after bathing in the lake, they dressed and returned home in the gradually approaching darkness, to find the women gayly dancing a round to a song Fiammetta was singing. In the silence that followed, the youths waxed eloquent in their praise of the Vale of the Ladies, each and every one agreeing on its beauties. Thereupon the king, sending for the steward, ordered the dinner to be prepared there the following day, and a few beds set up, in case any of them wished to rest in the noon-day heat, or take a nap, and then sent for lights, wine and sweets. When all had taken some refreshment, he requested them to make ready for the dancing. Pamfilo, at his wishes, took the lead. Then, turning to Elisa, the king said gallantly: "Lovely lady, to-day you honored me with the crown, and to-night it is my desire to let the honor of singing fall upon you. Sing, then, whatever is most to your liking!"

Smiling, Elisa replied, "At your command, my lord," and with a sweet, gentle voice began:

"O Love, if from your clutches I could gain
    My liberty, no more
Would other hook seize hold of me again!

I was a maiden, when I joined your fray,
    Thinking it sweetest joy and peace all-high;
And every weapon did I, trusting, lay
    Upon the ground, so confident was I
    Of glory. But, false tyrant, you did lie
        Cunning in wait, and tore
    Armored against me, with all might and main!

Then chained and fettered you delivered me
    To him who for my death was surely born;
With bitter tears I wailed my lot, yet he
    Received me, captive. With such mighty scorn
    And crude he wields his rod, that though I mourn
        And pine with weeping sore,
    Nothing can move him—tears, nor moans, nor pain!

All my entreaties the wind bears to him,
    But he heeds nothing, neither plaint nor sigh;
And every hour my torment grows more grim—
    Life is a burden, yet I cannot die.
    Ah, Love, have mercy on my agony.

Do what I can't—restore
Him to my power, fettered in your chain!

If this you will not do, I beg you tear
  The links that of my hope I welded fast!
Ah, I implore you, Love, fulfil my prayer,
  For if you do, I trust to be at last
  When all my rue behind me I have cast,
    Beautiful as of yore,
    And decked with flowers white and red again!"

A pitiful, deep-drawn sigh, and Elisa ended her song. Though they were all perplexed at the words, no one could guess what had given her cause to sing in that strain. The king, however, was in high spirits, and summoning Tindaro, had him bring his bag-pipes, to the tune of which they danced many a merry brawl, until a good part of the night had sped, when he ordered all his subjects to retire.

# 7

## THE SEVENTH DAY

✻

NOT A STAR WAS LEFT IN THE EASTERN SKY, EXCEPT THE SOLITARY
one we know as Lucifer, which still glimmered in the whitening
dawn, when the steward arose and started out with a plentiful
supply of provisions for the Vale of the Ladies, in order to get
everything ready, in obedience to his master's orders. Not long
after, the king, awakened by the noise and trampling of the
caravan and its beasts, also arose and ordered the rest of the
young men and women to be roused as well.

The sun's rays had already pierced the mists as they started
on their way, accompanied by the trilling of nightingales and
other feathered songsters. Never had they seemed to sing so
gayly, or so persistently, as on that morning. As far as the
Vale of the Ladies the birds caroled for them, and flocks of
others greeted them there with song, as though rejoicing at
their coming.

Once more, the little company wandered about the valley,
taking stock of everything, from one extremity to the other. If
anything, it seemed even more enchanting then than before,
with the light of early morning forming an even fitter setting
for its beauty. Presently, they breakfasted on dainties and wine,
and that the birds might not outdo them, they, too, raised their
voices in melody, which was re-echoed by the resounding vale,
song for song, while all the tree-musicians, unwilling to be
defeated, added sweet cadences and trills of their own.

Dinner-hour soon came. Along the lake's border the tables
were set, under flowery arbours and trees splendid with foliage.
There, at the king's pleasure, they took their places, watching
as they ate, the fish sporting in great number in the transparent

water, which afforded the company matter for conversation, as well as visual delight. The dinner over, and the tables and viands removed from sight, once again they burst into song, more heartily than before.

Beds had already been set up in various nooks about the valley. Indeed, the discreet steward had even had the foresight to screen them with French netting and canopies, behind which, if any chose, they might take their noon-day nap when the king dismissed them.

Finally, after they had all rested, and the hour came to gather again for their story-telling, the king had carpets spread upon the grass, not far from the spot where they had had their dinner, and there, by the lake's brink, they sat down.

"You begin," said the king to Emilia, who, smiling happily, said:

✱

## THE FIRST STORY

*Gianni Lotteringhi hears a knock at his door in the dead of night, and rouses his wife, who makes him believe it a ghost. They proceed to exorcise it, by a certain charm, and the knocking ceases.*

MY LORD, I SHOULD HAVE BEEN VERY MUCH OBLIGED HAD YOU seen fit to give someone else the privilege of starting the entertaining subject assigned us for to-day. But since you have laid upon me the responsibility of inspiring the other ladies with confidence, I shall willingly obey you. Indeed, dearest ladies, I shall even do my best to tell you something that may stand you in good stead in the future. For if you women are as great cowards as I, especially concerning ghosts—though the Lord knows, I've no idea what they are, or was ever able to find anyone to explain their nature, in spite of the fact that we're all equally in terror of them—you'd better pay attention to my story. You'll learn a potent and pious charm from it, which will be very useful to you, in case a ghost ever comes upon you and you wish to chase it away.

Once upon a time, there lived in the San Brancazio quarter of Florence, a wool-carder by the name of Gianni Lotteringhi, a man much more successful in his craft than his wisdom in other matters would indicate. However, despite his rather feeble intellect, amounting almost to simplicity, he was often elected president of the singers in Santa Maria Novella, with the power to dictate the laws of their society, and was also frequently entrusted with similar petty honors, which gave him quite a lofty opinion of himself. All this was due to the generous allowances which he, in his rôle of well-to-do citizen, made to the monks, who, in exchange for the gowns and socks and scapularies that were often obtained from him by one or another of them, taught him all kinds of useful prayers. The *Our Father,* in the vulgar tongue, was among them, and the canticle of Saint Alexis, the lament of Saint Bernard, the laud of Madam Matilda, and similar nonsense, by which he set great store, and which he chanted very religiously, for the good of his soul.

Now this simpleton had married a most handsome and charming wife, by the name of Tessa, a daughter of Mannuccio dalla Cuculia, and a canny, clever woman she was, too. As she was in love with Federigo di Neri Pegolotti, a fine young lusty spark who was as much taken with her as she with him, and as she knew what sort of numskull she had to deal with in her husband, she managed, with the help of one of her maids, to have her lover visit her at a pleasant country-cottage of Gianni's at Camerata, where she was wont to spend the entire summer-season. There Gianni would come of an evening to join her at supper and spend the night, and the morning after he would return to his shop, or perhaps to his choir-singers.

Federigo, who was dying to be with Tessa, took the first opportunity that offered itself, on a certain day which she had specified, and toward dusk he went up into the country. Gianni did not arrive that night. Very comfortably, therefore, and with exceeding pleasure, he supped and lodged with the lady, and as she lay in his arms that night, she taught him no less than half a dozen of her husband's lauds. Now since neither Tessa nor Federigo wished this first reunion of theirs to be their last, they struck upon a device, by which he might come to Camerata, without requiring the maid to come and fetch him. It was very simple. Every day, whenever he had to pass back and forth on his way to his summer-house, which was somewhat farther up-country, he was to keep a sharp watch for a certain pole in a vineyard beside her house. An ass' skull would be on that pole. Whenever Federigo saw its jawbones pointing toward Florence, he was to come to her after dark, without fail and in all confidence; if he did not find the door open, he was to knock softly three times, and she would let him in. But whenever he saw the snout of the skull turned toward Fiesole, he was to stay away, for it meant that Gianni would be there. Following this procedure, they came together on more than one enjoyable occasion.

Now it happened one night, that while Federigo was expected for supper at Mistress Tessa's, and she had had two juicy fat capons prepared for the meal, Gianni, who was the last person she was thinking of, surprised her, by coming at an unusually late hour. She was as disappointed as could be, but nevertheless, after she had partaken with him of a bit of salt-meat that she had cooked on the side, she had her maid wrap the two succulent capons in a table-cloth, together with a goodly number of new-laid eggs and a flask of the best wine, and carry them all to an adjoining garden, where she had often dined with Federigo, and where it was possible to go without passing through the house.

"Lay them at the foot of the peach-tree by the meadow," she enjoined her. But she was so cross, that she forgot to tell the girl to wait until Federigo came, warn him that Gianni was home, and ask him to take the food away from the garden.

Not long after, when she and Gianni had barely laid their heads on their pillows, and the maid had also gone to bed, up came Federigo and gave one cautious tap at the door. Immediately, Gianni heard it, for the door was very near the bedroom, and so did Tessa, but she pretended to be sound asleep, to afford her husband no grounds for suspicion. A little later, Federigo tapped a second time, whereupon Gianni was filled with amazement; and giving his wife a little pinch, he whispered: "Tessa, do you hear what I hear? I think there must be somebody knocking at our door."

The woman, who had heard the tap far better than he, made a pretense of starting up from sleep.

"What's that?" she cried. "What did you say?"

"I said," repeated Gianni, "that somebody must be knocking at the door."

"Knocking?" said Tessa. "God help us, Gianni, my dear, and don't you know what it is? It's a ghost that's been scaring me out of my wits these last few nights. And what a scare! I was so terrified, that the moment I heard it I thrust my head under the bedclothes, and didn't venture to poke it out again until broad-daylight."

Then spoke up Gianni, "Come, come, woman! Don't be frightened in that case, for I said the *Te Lucis* and the *Intemerata* just before, when we went to bed, and a lot of other holy prayers. I even made the sign of the cross on the bed, up and down, and from side to side, in the name of the Father, the Son, and the Holy Ghost, so we needn't be afraid, for it doesn't matter how powerful a ghost it is, it can't possibly do us any harm."

Now Tessa, worried that Federigo might perhaps suspect her of being up to a trick, and so be angry with her, made up her mind to get up at any cost, and let him know somehow that Gianni was there.

"That's all well and good, as far as you're concerned," she said to her husband. "You have your own prayers to save you. But as for me, I'll not feel safe or out of harm's way, until we've charmed the ghost away, now that you're here."

"So! And how is it charmed away?" he asked.

"I know how very well," said his wife. "The day before yesterday, when I went to Fiesole to attend the Pardon, one of those lady recluses—the holiest and most pious creature you could ever hope to lay eyes on, Gianni, my dear—taught me a most wonderful holy-prayer, when she saw me so scared. She told me that she had used it herself many times before she became a nun, and that it had always helped her. God knows, I'd never have had spunk enough to try it out myself, but since you're here, we may as well try to charm the ghost away."

Gianni said he was willing, whereupon both of them got up and tip-toed cautiously toward the door, behind which Federigo was still waiting, his mind already darkened with suspicion. Once there, Tessa said to Gianni, "Now you get ready to spit when I tell you to."

"All right," he said.

Accordingly, she commenced the charm, saying, "Ghost, O Ghost, that fly by night, Stiff-tailed you came, stiff-tailed take flight. Go to the garden, to the foot of the big peach-tree, and there you will find a basted, twice-basted one, and a hundred droppings of my setting-hen. Put your mouth to the flask and go away, and do no harm to me or my Gianni, I pray." So saying, she turned to her husband. "Spit, Gianni," she said; and Gianni spat.

Outside, Federigo, who heard everything that was going on, and whose jealousy had been dispelled, was almost dying with controlled laughter, despite his disappointment, and with every spitting of Gianni's, he said in an undertone, "If you'd only spit out your teeth!"

As for Tessa, after she had repeated the exorcism over the ghost three times, she returned to bed, and Gianni with her.

Now Federigo, who had expected to be supping with his mistress, had not had a bite to eat, and therefore he was not slow to understand the words of her spell. Going into the garden, he found the two capons, the wine and the eggs at the foot of the large peach-tree, and carrying them home with him, he supped comfortably and well. Later, when he visited his lady on other occasions, they had many a good laugh together over the charm.

Some people maintain that Mistress Tessa had really turned the ass' skull toward Fiesole, but that a laborer, who happened to be passing through the vineyard, had hit it a blow with his stick, making it whirl round and round until, as it stopped, it remained with its nose facing Florence. As a result, Federigo, believing he had been summoned, had come to visit his mistress, who had recited this version of the spell:

> "Ghostie, Ghostie, go away.
> I did not turn the skull to-day,
> Another did it, blast his hide—
> I'm here with Gianni by my side."

Then he had gone away, and remained with an empty stomach and no bed to lie on. A neighbor of mine, however, an ancient old soul, informs me that, from what she learned about it when she was a girl, both accounts are true, except that the second version did not happen to Gianni Lotteringhi, but to a man by the name of Gianni di Nello, who used to live at Porta San Piero, and was as much of a booby as Lotteringhi. Therefore, dear ladies, it's up to you to choose whichever incantation you prefer, unless you'd like to have both. They're most effective in such cases as the one you've just heard. Learn them, then, for they might still stand you in good stead.

✳

# THE SECOND STORY

*Peronella conceals her lover in a cask, when her husband returns home unexpectedly. On his telling her that he has sold the cask, she replies she had already struck a good bargain on it, with the man who had gone into it, to see whether it was sound. The lover promptly jumps out, makes Peronella's husband scrape the cask clean, and then has him deliver it to his house.*

EMILIA'S STORY WAS RECEIVED WITH PEALS OF LAUGHTER, AND the incantation pronounced by one and all, most efficient and pious. When the story came to an end, however, the king commanded Filostrato to continue.

Dearest ladies, he began, so numerous are the tricks which men, and especially husbands, play upon you, that whenever a woman succeeds in paying her mate back in his own coin, you should not only rejoice at the event, and be delighted when it comes to your notice, but you must make it your business to spread the news of it everywhere, so men may realize that though they're mighty clever, women are a pretty good match for them. After all, it could only be turned to your account, for when a man knows he's not dealing with a fool, he's not so ready to cheat and deceive. Who can doubt but that when all we say to-day comes to the knowledge of men, it may be quite instrumental in curbing their cozening propensity, when they realize that if you wish, you can give as good as you receive? It's my intention, therefore, to tell you the prank a clever, though low-born young woman played on her husband, through a sudden flash of inspiration in order to get herself out of a scrape.

Not so long ago, in the city of Naples, there lived a poor fellow who married a good-looking chit of a girl called Peronella. He was a mason by trade, and by dint of his work and the spinning she took in, they eked out a meager livelihood, and managed to keep the wolf from the door. It so happened that a gay young blade spied the jolly Peronella one day, and was so pleased with what he saw, that he fell in love with her, and contrived somehow or other to get sufficiently into her graces to become her friend. Accordingly, the better to manage their rendez-vous, they devised a plan.

It was the custom of Peronella's husband to rise early, either to work or to look for a job. It was agreed between the lovers, therefore, that the gallant should take his station somewhere in the neighborhood, whence he could see the husband take his leave, and the moment the mason was gone, he was to slip into Peronella's house, shielded by the solitude of the street, which was called Avorio. And so they met on many occasions.

On a certain morning, however, after the honest fellow had gone out and Giannello Stringario—for such was the lover's name—had entered his house to stay with Peronella, the husband unexpectedly returned, though he seldom came back until sundown. Finding the door locked from within, he knocked, and began saying to himself, "Your Name be praised forever, O Lord! Though You gave me poverty for my lot, at least You consoled me by giving me a virtuous young woman for my wife. Look You how quickly she bolted the door from within, the moment I stepped out of the house, so nobody could get in to bother her!"

Meanwhile Peronella, who knew from the knock that her husband was at the door, whispered, "Good heavens, Giannello! This is the end of me! Here's my husband—the devil take him!—popping in upon us, and I can't for the life of me understand it, for he never came back at this hour before! Perhaps he saw you coming in! Whatever it is, get into this cask, for God's sake, and I'll go open for him. Let's see what he means by coming home so early!"

Giannello quickly scrambled into the cask, while Peronella went to the door to let in her husband. Scowling angrily, she greeted him with, "What do you mean by coming home so early this morning? If I'm not mistaken, you're none too anxious to work to-day, coming back like that, with your tools in your hands! What do you expect we'll live on, if you keep this up? Where's our next loaf of bread coming from, eh? Do you think for a moment I'll let you pawn my petticoats, and my other miserable little rags? Here I wear my fingers to the bone, day and night, to keep our lamp provided with oil, and you—ah, husband! husband! There's not a housewife hereabouts, who doesn't wonder at my devotion and think me a fool for slaving as I do, and here you come home with your hands swinging gayly by your side, when you should be away at your work!"

At that, she burst into tears and continued, between her

sobs, "Woe! Woe! Poor, miserable wretch that I am! What dark star was I born under? What evil fortune brought me to this? I could have married the finest young man that ever lived, and I jilted him, and here I am, tied to this good-for-nothing lout, who doesn't care a whit for the woman he's married! Other wives enjoy themselves with their lovers—there's not a one of them, who hasn't two or three on the string! They enjoy life, and make their husbands see white for black! And look at me, poor fool that I am! Just because I am good, and have nothing to do with such trash, I get nothing but trouble and bad luck for it! I don't see what's keeping me from taking a couple of lovers myself, like the rest of them! I'll have you understand, beloved, that if I had any desire to be up to mischief, I'd have no trouble finding a willing partner, I assure you! There are lots of handsome young gentlemen who love me, and think a lot of me! Yes, sir, they've made me all kinds of propositions, offering me large sums of money, gowns and jewelry, anything I wished! But I could never lower myself to do such a thing. I'm not the daughter of that sort of mother! And here you are, shambling home idle, when you should be working!"

"For pity's sake, wife, don't be taking on so!" cried her husband. "You ought to know how much I appreciate your worth. Why, only this morning I had another proof of it! Sure enough, I did go out to work to-day, but I imagine you did not realize, any more than I, that it's Saint Galeon's day, and we laborers don't work. That's what brought me home so early. Still, I've managed to provide for us, and I found a way of keeping us in bread for more than a month. Yes, I've sold this good man you see with me, that great cask that's been cluttering up the house so long, as you know, and he's giving me five florins for it."

"All the more reason why I should complain," rejoined Peronella. "There you are, a man who goes in and out, and should know the ways of the world, and you sell a good cask for five florins, while I, a poor little woman who has scarcely ever set her nose out of the house, seeing what a bother it was to have around, struck a bargain over it and sold it for seven florins to an honest fellow, who had just crawled into it to see whether it was sound, the moment you came through the door!"

The husband was more than satisfied to hear what she had

to say, and to the man who had come for the cask, he said, "You'd better go your way, my good fellow. You see for yourself, my wife has sold it for seven florins, when you wanted to give me only a paltry five for it."

"It's all the same to me," said the man, and went away.

Then said Peronella to her husband, "Come and attend to our business with the man yourself, now that you're here!"

Now Giannello, who had listened with eager ears, in order to determine whether there was anything for him to fear or ward against, jumped nimbly out of the cask on hearing Peronella's words, and as though he were entirely ignorant of the husband's return, cried, "Where are you, good woman?"

"I'm at your service," said the husband, approaching him. "What can I do for you?"

"And who are you?" asked Giannello. "I'd like to speak to the woman with whom I bargained about this cask."

Said the mason, "Don't worry about that. You can deal with me. I'm her husband."

"Well," said Giannello, "the cask is in pretty good shape, but I think you must have kept wine lees in it, because it's all plastered over with the Lord knows what sort of crust, that's so dry that I can't even scrape it off with my finger-nails. I won't take it away unless I see it all cleaned out first."

"That's quite all right," said Peronella. "We'll not spoil a good bargain for such a trifle. My husband will scrape it all out for you."

"Surely," said the cuckold, and putting down his tools, he took off his coat and remained in his shirt-sleeves. Then, asking for a light and a scraper, he crawled into the cask and began to scrape merrily away. Peronella seemed very anxious to see how he got along, for sticking her head, and one of her arms up to the shoulder through the opening of the cask, which was none too wide, she directed him, saying, "Look, scrape here, and over there, too. See, here's a little spot you've overlooked!"

And so, while she was busy in that position, showing her husband where to scrape, and pointing out the places he had missed, Giannello, who had scarcely begun to appease his desire that morning when the good man arrived and cut everything short, realizing he could not have things as he wished, determined to do the best he could. Accordingly, drawing up to Peronella, who was completely blocking the mouth of the cask, he satisfied his lusty passion to the full in the same position as the untamed stallions, hot with desire, in the wide expanses of the fields, mount the fillies of Parthia. Almost at one and the same moment, his ardor was brought to a climax and the cask was completely scraped. He withdrew, Peronella drew her head out of the cask, and the mason came out.

"Here, good man," said Peronella to Giannello. "Take this light, and see if you're satisfied with the way it's been scraped."

Giannello peered in. "All right," said he. "It suits me perfectly," and giving the mason the seven florins, he had him carry the cask to his house.

✳

## THE THIRD STORY

*Friar Rinaldo goes to bed with his gossip, and when her husband surprises them in the bedroom, pretends he is performing a charm to rid his godson of worms.*

FILOSTRATO HAD NOT BEEN ABLE TO VEIL HIS REMARKS ABOUT the Parthian fillies so skilfully, but that the knowing ladies had laughed, pretending to be amused by something else. However, when the king was aware the story was over, he called on Elisa to speak, who began with ready compliance:

Agreeable ladies, the spell put on Emilia's ghost brought to my mind the story of another charm which, though not so interesting as hers, I shall tell you nonetheless, since, for the present, I can't think of anything else on our theme.

You must know that in Siena there once lived a very comely youth of an honorable family, whose name was Rinaldo. Having fallen deeply in love with a neighbor of his, a handsome woman married to a man of considerable fortune, Rinaldo was certain that if he could succeed in speaking his mind freely to her, he would obtain of her everything he desired. However, he could see no way of accomplishing it, until, seeing that the lady was about to become a mother, he thought he would stand godfather to her child, and hence make himself her gossip. Accordingly, he broached the subject to her husband in as seemly a way as possible, and his wish was granted.

Now that Rinaldo had become Mistress Agnesa's gossip, and had more feasible grounds for chatting with her intimately, he gained confidence, and expressed to her in words, what she had long surmised from his impassioned glances. It did him no good to speak, however, though Mistress Agnesa had not been at all averse to lending him a willing ear.

Not long after that, it so happened that, for some reason or other, Rinaldo became a friar, and however he found his new pasture, he pursued it diligently as his walk in life. At first, in the early days of his call, he set aside the love he bore his godchild's mother, and many other little vanities besides. Nevertheless, in the course of time, he resumed them again without relinquishing his monkish habit, and took delight in looking and dressing well, in observing neatness and elegance in everything, in composing canzonets, sonnets and ballads, in singing, and all kinds of similar pleasures.

But why am I harping on our Friar Rinaldo? Which of them does not act that way? Ah, blight that they are on this rotten world! They're not ashamed of their corpulence and florid cheeks. They do not blush at the effeminacy of their clothes, and all that belongs to them, and they strut about, not with the humility of doves, but with the arrogance of turkey-cocks, with crests triumphant and chests puffed out. We'll say nothing of the fact that their cells are full of crocks crammed with ointments and balms, of boxes full of all kinds of sweets, of bottles and flasks overflowing with liquors and oils, of casks running over with Malmsey and Cyprian wines and other generous vintages, so that the onlooker might easily take them for the shops of druggists or perfumers, rather than the cubicles of holy men. What is worse, they make no pretense about telling the world they suffer from the gout, believing that others are not well aware that frequent fasts, coarse rations and abstemious living make people lean, sinewy and generally healthy; and that when sickness does assail them, it is surely not the gout, for which medicine prescribes abstinence, and all other virtues that pertain to the life of a humble friar. Yes, they are certain that laymen haven't the least notion that besides meager living, long vigils, prayers and mortification should produce pale, ascetic men; and that both Saint Dominick and Saint Francis, far from boasting of four changes of tunics apiece, used to clothe their bodies neither in fine serges nor other luxurious stuffs, but in coarse, undyed wool, simply to keep out the cold, not to cut a fine figure. It's about time God looked after these evils, as well as the souls of the fools who encourage them.

Well, once Friar Rinaldo resumed his natural propensities, he began to pay frequent visits to his gossip, and as his boldness had developed apace, he grew more than ever insistent in urging her to grant him what he desired of her. Seeing herself besieged with such fervor, the good lady, perhaps finding Rinaldo handsomer than before, exclaimed when she was more hard pressed than ever, in the words to which all women resort when they are willing to comply, "Ah, what are you saying, Friar Rinaldo! Do you mean you holy men are up to such things?"

"My dear lady," answered Rinaldo, "once this gown is off my back—and I'm nimble enough about taking it off, I assure you—you'll find me no friar, but a man made like other men."

The lady looked coy. "Ah dear me!" said she. "You're the godfather of my little boy! How can we think of doing such a thing? It would be too terrible, and I've often heard say it is a very grave sin. If it weren't for that, I'd be happy to gratify your desire."

Then Friar Rinaldo said, "You would be foolish if you abstained because of such scruples. I'm not saying it isn't a sin, but God forgives even more serious sins to those who show repentance. Tell me, now, who's nearer your son, I who held him at the font, or your husband, who fathered him?"

"Why, my husband," she replied.

"Right!" said the friar. "Now tell me, doesn't your husband lie with you?"

"Of course," answered the woman.

"Well, then," said the friar, "since I am not so much akin to your son as your husband is, I am therefore privileged to lie with you, the way the good man does."

Mistress Agnesa, who was not versed in logic and needed little urging, believed, rather pretended to believe, that the friar was stating an obvious fact, and replied, "Who could find any reply to your wisdom?" And shortly after, in spite of the kinship that existed between them, she lent herself to his pleasure. Indeed, not content with that one embrace, they met for additional bouts, time and time again, under cover of that relation which allayed all suspicion.

Now one day Friar Rinaldo came to visit his mistress as usual, and seeing that she was alone, except for an agreeable little slip of a maid, he sent his companion to teach her the paternoster in the pigeonloft, and himself went to the bedroom with his lady, who held her child by the hand. Then they locked themselves in, and began their gay frolicking on a couch that was in the room. While they were thus engaged, the husband returned home unexpectedly, and he was already at the bedroom-door, knocking, and calling his wife, before anyone was aware of his arrival.

"This is the end of me!" exclaimed Mistress Agnesa, on hearing the knocks. "Here's my husband himself. Now he will certainly discover why we're so intimate."

At that moment, Friar Rinaldo was only in his nether tunic, having removed his gown and scapulary, and on hearing her words, he said: "You're right, there. If I were only dressed, we could find a way out, but if you open the door now and he finds me in this costume, there won't be any possible excuse to offer."

Then Agnesa, inspired by a sudden flash, said, "You hurry and put on your things. Once you're dressed, take your little godson in your arms, keep your ears open for what I tell my husband, and then see to it that your words agree with mine. Leave the rest to me." Then, to the poor fellow who hadn't stopped knocking for a moment, "I'm coming! I'm coming!" she called.

Rising, she composed her features, went to the door, admitted him and said, "Ah, dear husband! Believe me, Friar Rinaldo who came here to see us, must have been guided by God, I swear, for really, if he hadn't come to-day, we might have lost our son."

At these words, the gullible simpleton almost swooned. "How's that?" he cried.

"Oh, dear husband," said she, "the poor little one just threw such an awful fainting fit, unexpectedly, that I thought he was dead, and I didn't for the life of me know what to do or say. Just then Friar Rinaldo, his godfather, came, and taking him up in his arms, said: 'Friend, it's the worms he has in his body, that are affecting his heart and might easily be the death of him. But don't worry, I'll put a spell on them and kill them all, and before I leave this house you'll have the child as hale and hearty as ever you've seen him.' You were needed to tell over certain prayers, but because the girl couldn't find you anywhere, he had his companion offer them up in the pigeon-loft, while he and I came in here. Nobody can be present at such an office but the child's mother, so we shut ourselves in, so as not to be disturbed. There he is, still holding the baby in his arms, and I think he's only waiting for his companion to finish the prayers before he can call it accomplished, for the child has already come out of his fit."

The pious fool, crediting every word, was so worried over his son, that he was far from suspecting the least trickery on his wife's part. Heaving a deep sigh, "I must go in and see the little one," he said.

"No, no," she prevented him. "Don't go yet, or you'll ruin all the good that's been done. Wait, I'll see if you can go in, and then I'll call you."

Friar Rinaldo, who had kept his ears wide open for every word, and had put on his clothes in all comfort, took the child in his arms as soon as he was satisfied that all was well, and called, "Ho, there, gossip, isn't that my friend your husband I hear out there?"

"Yes, it's me," replied the simple fellow.

"Come here, then," said the friar, and the poor clown went. "Come, take your child, who's safe and sound by the mercy of God," he continued, "though there was a moment I feared you'd not see him alive any more, come vespers. See to it that you place a wax infant his size in thanksgiving to God, before the shrine of our patron, Saint Ambrose, through whose offices the Lord did you the grace of restoring your boy."

On seeing his father, the little lad ran to him crowing and shrilling in childish glee. With tears in his eyes, the poor wittol took him up in his arms, kissing him frantically, as though the child had been delivered from the grave, and thanking the godfather at the same time for having brought him back to health.

In the interim, Friar Rinaldo's companion had taught not one, but at least six paternosters to the little maid. Indeed, he had even presented her with a neat white knitted purse, which a nun had given him, and had converted her to his worship. On hearing the pious fool clamoring at his wife's bedroom door, he had glided down softly to a corner from which he could both see and hear what was going on unobserved, and noting that the matter had reached a harmonious juncture, he came out of his hiding.

"Friar Rinaldo," he said, coming into the room, "I've already performed the four orisons you set me to."

"Brother, you're in fine fettle," answered Friar Rinaldo, "and you've acquitted yourself nobly. As for me, I had only gone through two of them when my friend here, interrupted me. But what with your labors and mine, the good Lord has smiled upon our effort and healed the child."

Then and there, the foolish wittol ordered the best of wines and dainties to be served his dear friend and his companion—of which restoratives they were more in need than anything else—and later escorted them out of the house and commended them to God. You may be certain he lost no time in having the wax figure executed, and sent to hang with the rest in front of the image of Saint Ambrose—not the one at Milan, however.

\*

## THE FOURTH STORY

*Tofano locks his wife out one night. When she can not succeed in being let in, despite prayers and entreaties, she pretends to jump headlong into a well, but throws in a large stone instead. Tofano runs thither from the house, whereupon she steals in, locks him out and rails at him from the window.*

ON PERCEIVING THAT ELISA'S STORY HAD COME TO AN END, THE king lost no time in turning to Lauretta, and indicating that it was his pleasure for her to continue. Instantly, she began:

O Love, how great is your power, and how various! How many tricks and devices are you master of! What philosopher or cunning master is there, who has been able to teach, or will ever succeed in teaching all those arts, wiles and stratagems to which you suddenly prompt your devout followers! Truly, all other doctrines are mere child's play compared with yours, as may be easily gathered from the tricks that have already been told, and to which, loving ladies, I shall add still another, that was used by so simple a woman, that surely no master but Love could have taught it her.

Well, then, once upon a time there lived in Arezzo a well-to-do man by the name of Tofano, who acquired to wife a very comely lass called Ghita. Scarcely had he married her, than for some reason or other, he became insanely jealous. This jealousy coming to her notice, Ghita was filled with spite, and often demanded his reasons. He could offer her none but what were lame and commonplace, whereupon she made up her mind to be the death of him, by procuring him the very malady he was so unjustly in dread of.

Presently, she became aware that a young man of rare and fine accomplishments, according to her judgment, was rather taken with her, and before long she had made her pacts with him. Soon the affair had progressed so well, that nothing remained but for their vows to be converted to deeds, for which Ghita also resolved to find a way.

Among other bad habits of her husband's, she had discovered that he loved to drink, whereupon she not only spoke to him in praise of the bottle, but often wrought all her wiles upon him to get him drunk. He quickly became accustomed to it. Indeed, she would make him tipple at will, and when he was well-stewed, she would put him to bed.

The first time it happened, she joined her gallant, and from then on made a practice of it, staying with him in peace and security. She came to rely so much on her husband's drunken stupors, that she not only had the boldness to receive her lover in her own house, but sometimes went so far as to spend a good part of the night at his, which was no great distance away. Now while the amorous lady was up to these pranks, her sad sot of a husband perceived, little by little, that despite all her coaxings to make him drink, she herself never touched a drop. This made him suspect the true state of things—mainly that she got him drunk in order to be free to follow her own desires, while he slept off the fumes. In his anxiety to find out whether the case was indeed as he suspected, one night he made a pretense of talking and acting like the most besotted tippler in the world, though all day long he had not put his mouth to the bottle. Ghita was readily fooled, and believing he had had enough, she tucked him safely into bed at the first opportunity. That duty attended to, she left the house as she had done on other occasions, and made off for her lover's, where she remained until midnight.

Meanwhile, the moment Tofano was sure she was nowhere about the house, he jumped out of bed, rushed to the door and barred it from within. Then he stationed himself at the window, so that when he should spy her coming, he might show her that he had seen through her tricks, so he resigned himself to the rôle of sentinel until she returned. What was Ghita's chagrin on her return to find herself locked out! Knocking and pushing, she tried to force the door open, and after Tofano had stood it a time, he cried, "You're wasting your efforts, wife, for you'll not set foot within this house again. Go back where you came from, and be sure you'll never return here till I've paid you for this, as you deserve, before your people and the whole neighborhood."

Ghita pleaded with him and entreated, "Let me in, for God's sake," she cried. She did not come from where he suspected, she assured him. Ah no, for she had stayed up with a good neighbor-woman. The nights were long, you see, and she could not sleep them through, or stay up by herself all alone in the house. Her prayers availed her nothing, however, for her cuckold was anxious to shout his shame from the housetop to the whole world. Finally, when Ghita realized she was wasting her breath in prayers, she had recourse to threats. "If you don't let me in," she called, "I'll make you rue it to your dying day."

"Really! And what could you do to me?" he mocked.

Love had already sharpened the woman's wits, by its promptings, and she replied, "Rather than submit to the shame you want to inflict upon me so unjustly, I'll pitch myself headlong into this well, and after my dead body is found in it, there's nobody in the world who will not believe you threw me in, in a drunken fit. Then you'll either have to run away and forfeit all you have and lead the life of an exile and an outcast, or lose your head as my murderer, for that's what you'll be."

Tofano was not moved an inch from his foolish purpose, despite Ghita's eloquence, which made her say in exasperation, "Is that the way you feel about it? Very well, then. I can't stand your cruelty any longer—may God have mercy on you! See that you put away this distaff of mine, that I'm leaving by the well-side."

The night was so dark, that it would have been impossible even to discern a person meeting one on the road. Ghita, nevertheless, made her way to the well as soon as she had uttered her threat, took up a huge stone that lay at the foot of it, and crying, "God forgive me!" let it fall into the water. The stone sank with a tremendous splash, at the echo of which Tofano was convinced his wife had been as good as her word and jumped in. Seizing the bucket and the rope, he tore madly out of the house, and ran as fast as he could to the rescue.

Meanwhile, Ghita had slunk into hiding near the door of her house, and no sooner did she see Tofano rushing to the well than she slipped in, locked the door behind her, and then, going to the window, cried, "You should water your wine when you drink, and not at this hour of the night, after you've swilled!"

At the sound of her voice, Tofano knew he had been gulled, and went back to the door. He could not get in.

"Open! Open!" he shouted.

But Ghita, putting off the soft speech she had used until that moment, called down almost at the top of her lungs, "As God is my witness, you'll not set foot in this house to-night, you drunken pest. I'm through with your filthy habits! I must shame you before the whole world, and let everyone see what time of the night you see fit to come home!"

Tofano saw red, and in turn fell to bellowing and calling her names, until at the uproar the neighbors got up, goodmen and goodwives together, and all rushed to the windows to ask what the trouble was. Sobbing, Ghita told her story.

"Here's this fine specimen of manhood," said she, "who comes home to me drunk in the evening, unless he sleeps off his drunkenness in the taverns, to arrive here at this hour, as you see! I've put up with it long and patiently, but in vain! I can't stand it any longer. That's why I've shamed him before you, and locked him out. Maybe it will teach him a lesson, and make him turn over a new leaf."

The silly cuckold, on the other hand, told the true facts of the case, threatening to blister her back in the bargain; but turning to her neighbors, "Look at that fine sprig!" she cried. "What would you say if I were in the public-streets like him, and he were in the house as I am? God knows you'd believe readily enough that he was telling the truth! Just see how clever he is! He accuses me of the very thing I'd swear he himself is guilty of. He thought he'd scare me by pitching goodness knows what into the well! Would to God he had really jumped in head-long and drowned, that at least the wine he has swilled might know the taste of water!"

All the neighbors, men and women alike, took sides with Ghita against Tofano, blaming and rebuking him for what he said against his virtuous wife. In a little while the quarrel had been so noised about, that at last it reached the ears of the woman's kin, who hastened to the spot, and after hearing various versions of the story from the neighbors, fell upon Tofano and gave him such a beating that his bones rattled for many a day. Then, leaving him where he was, they entered the house, bundled all Ghita's belongings and took her back home with them, threatening Tofano with worse, if he moved a finger.

Now when Tofano saw what a mess he was in, because he had been led astray by his jealousy, he persuaded some of his friends to plead for him with his wife, whom he still loved with all his heart, and he finally succeeded in having her return in peace and harmony. He promised her solemnly nevermore to be jealous of her, and gave her leave besides, to do her sweet will, provided she went about it discreetly enough to keep her affairs from his knowledge. So, like a brainless fool, he learned his lesson, and then—to school. Hurrah for Love, then, and death to discord and the rest of its clan!

## ❋

## THE FIFTH STORY

*A jealous man, disguised as a priest, listens to his wife's confession, in which she pretends she is in love with a priest who comes to her every night. Then, while the jealous husband secretly guards the door, she admits a lover of hers through the roof and dallies with him.*

LAURETTA HAD FINISHED HER STORY, AND EVERYONE HAD EXpressed approval of the woman for having given her lout of a husband his just deserts, when the king turned to Fiammetta, and not to lose time, charged her pleasantly to continue with the story-telling.

Noble ladies, she began, this last story prompts me likewise, to tell you about a jealous man, for I'm of the opinion that whatever punishment is given such men by their wives, especially when their jealousy is unfounded, serves them right. Indeed, if our law-makers had looked into the matter thoroughly, they'd have assigned women who defend themselves the same sentence they pronounce upon individuals who attack others in self-defense. For what are jealous husbands if not menaces to the lives of their young brides, and diligent seekers after their deaths? All week long, women are pent up in their houses, attending to the duties of the household and the family and looking forward on the holidays to some pleasure, respite and diversion, like everybody else—farm laborers, city workers and law-givers—in observance of God's example, Who on the sev-

enth day rested from His labors, and in accordance with divine
and civil laws which, in worship of the Lord and in consideration of people's well-being, set days of rest apart from days of
toil. But will jealous men allow such a thing? Not at all! Days
that are full of joy for everybody else, they embitter and make
more miserable for their poor wives by keeping the unhappy
wretches shut in with double caution. Only those women who
have experienced such treatment, can tell you what a hell it is!
In fine, I maintain that whatever a woman does to a husband who
is jealous without reason, should not be condemned, but on
the contrary, commended.

Once upon a time, there lived in Rimini a merchant possessed
of vast wealth in goods and money, who had an extraordinarily
handsome wife, of whom he became insanely jealous, for no
other reason than that since he doted on her, thinking her the
most beautiful woman in the world, and saw that she did her
best to keep his love, he was certain that all other men were
also mad about her, and found her as beautiful, and that she, in
turn, used all her wiles to infatuate everyone else as she had
infatuated him—a doltish way of reasoning, worthy of a crack-
brained fool. Being thus a prey to his jealousy, he watched over
her so strictly, that I doubt not there are many prisoners sentenced to capital punishment, who are allowed more freedom
by their guards. Far from being permitted to go to weddings
and parties and to church, or even to set foot outside her house,
she did not dare to show her face at a window or look out into
the street, no matter what happened. Her life, as you can imagine, was no heaven of bliss, and she was all the more re-
bellious under the restraint, the less guilty she knew herself to
be of any fault. Well then, seeing herself so unjustly victimized
by her husband, she resolved, for her own pleasure, to find a
way, if she could, of providing him just grounds for his suspicion.

It was out of the question for her to post herself at the window, and thus impossible to encourage the courtship of some
gallant passing along the street. Knowing that in the house adjoining her own, there lived a youth who was both handsome
and charming, she determined that if she could find a hole in
the wall that separated the two buildings, she would keep peering through it long and often enough to catch sight of him, un-
bosom herself, and, if he wished it, grant him her love. Then, if
a way could be discovered, she would even manage a lit-

tle rendez-vous or so with him, and in this fashion, while away the boredom of her imprisonment until her husband was rid of his devil of jealousy.

While she was engaged in examining the walls of the house, now in one room and now in another, during her husband's absences, she found that in a hidden nook, the wall was broken by a crack. Putting her eye to the opening, she was able to discern, though with difficulty, that a bedroom lay on the other side of the wall, and she said to herself, "If only this were my neighbor Filippo's room, I'd already be half-way to my success."

With the utmost secrecy, she had one of her maids, who felt sorry for her miserable lot, make investigations, and surely enough, she found that Filippo, the young man, slept in that room by himself. Accordingly, whenever she sensed the youth to be at home, she often came to the cranny, and by throwing pebbles and other small trifles through it, at last roused the young man's curiosity, who drew near to see what could be the matter. Softly, she called him and he, knowing her by her voice, answered. Making good use of the opportunity, she quickly opened her heart to him, whereupon the delighted gallant made the fissure even larger on his side, but so skillfully that no one had the least suspicion of what was going on. Very often, they chatted through it and held each other's hands, but they could not go farther because of the strict surveillance the jealous husband maintained.

As Christmas-tide approached, the woman told her husband she wished to go to church on the morning of that day, if he had no objections, so she might make confession and take the sacrament, like all good Christians.

"What sins have you committed that you have to confess?" exploded the jealous man.

"What do you mean?" she exclaimed. "Do you perhaps imagine that because you keep me shut up in the house, I'm a saint? You know I have my own sins, like the rest of the world, but you're not the man I'll tell them to, for you're no priest, you!"

Suspicion got the better of him at these words. Immediately, he was itching to know what sins she could be guilty of, and revolving in his mind the means of satisfying his curiosity.

"Very well," said he. "But I don't want you to go anywhere but to our parish chapel," adding that she must see to it that she arrived there early enough, made her confession either to their chaplain or some other confessor recommended by him, and hurry back home as fast as she could. Some inkling of his true intention flashed across her mind. Nevertheless, she offered no objection, but agreed to do as he wished.

Bright and early Christmas morning, the lady rose, and donning her clothes, betook herself to the church her husband had indicated. But the jealous wretch forestalled her, for rising betimes, he hurried to the same chapel, and got there ahead of her. By the time she arrived, he had already won the priest over to his plan, dressed himself in one of his gowns, with a huge cowl that hung down on either side of his head—the sort of thing we are familiar with in the dress of confessors—and lowering it over his face, he sat waiting in the choir.

As soon as the lady arrived, she asked for the priest, who came before her, and on learning she wished to make her confession, regretted that he himself could not hear her, but offered to send her another of his brotherhood. At that, he went away and summoned the jealous man, to his misfortune. The day was by no means bright; still he came to her with great dignity, the cowl pulled low over his eyes. Despite all his precautions, he had not concealed himself so well but that he was recognized at once by his wife, who said inwardly, at her discovery, "God be praised for His miracles, Who made a priest out of a jealous brute! But let him enjoy himself, for I'll give him all he's looking for!"

Pretending not to know who he was, she sat down at his feet. Now our jealous friend had put some pebbles in his mouth to halt his tongue, so that she might not recognize him, believing he had been so clever about the rest of his disguise, that it was impossible for her to penetrate it. Well, when the time came for the confession, the lady told him she was married, and then informed him, among other things, that she was in love with a priest, who came to lie with her every night. The words went through the jealous husband's heart like a dagger-thrust, and had it not been for his craving to know more, he would have cut the confession short and left her then and there. He stood at his post staunchly, however, and asked her: "How is that? Doesn't your husband lie with you?"

"Why, yes, father," she said.

"Then how is it possible for this priest to lie with you too?" he asked.

"Father," she replied, "I don't know what charms that priest is master of, but I can tell you there's no door in the whole house, no matter how fast locked or barred, that doesn't open at his touch. He's also told me that when he comes to the door of my bedroom, he mutters certain words before he opens it, and thereupon my husband immediately falls asleep. Then, the moment the priest feels he's sleeping soundly, he opens the door, enters, and keeps me company. He doesn't miss a single, solitary night."

"Woman," admonished the green-eyed one, "you're doing great evil, and you must put a stop to it altogether."

"I'm afraid I'll never succeed in that, father," she said, "for I love him far too much."

"Then I can't give you absolution," he said curtly.

"I'm very sorry," she replied. "I didn't come here to tell you a pack of lies. If I felt I'd be strong enough to put a stop to it, I'd tell you so."

Then my Lord Jealousy replied, "Woman, I pity you from the bottom of my heart, seeing you imperil your immortal soul by this game. But for your sake, I will take the trouble to offer up some special prayers to God in your name. Perhaps they will help you. I'll also send you a little clerk of mine, now and then, to whom you'll report whether you've benefited by them or not. If you have, we'll keep up the good work."

"Oh, father, don't ever think of sending anybody to my house," exclaimed the lady, "for if my husband came to know of it, he'd be so jealous that all the arguments in the world could not convince him that the clerk didn't come for some evil purpose, and I'd not have a moment's peace in the house all this coming year!"

"Don't worry about that, madam," said the husband. "I promise to do it in such a way, that you'll never hear a word from him about it."

"Well, if you insist, I've no objection," she answered.

The confession over, and the penance assigned, the woman got up from sitting at his feet, and went to hear the mass through, while the hapless husband, panting with suppressed fury, threw off his priestly disguise and returned home, impatient for a way to surprise the priest and his wife together, and make them dance to a merry tune. On her return from church, the woman saw all too clearly by his looks, that she had spoiled his Christmas for him, though he did his best to hide what he had done, and feign ignorance of all he thought he had learned.

His mind made up to spend the night on guard, near the door leading to the street, he said to her:

"I'll be obliged to dine and sleep away from home to-night, so be sure to lock the street-door well, and the ones on the landing and the bedroom, and then go to sleep when you're ready."

"Very well," she answered, and at the first opportunity, she went to the chink in the wall to give the usual signal. Filippo heard it and drew near at once, whereupon the woman told him what she had done that morning, and what her husband had said to her after dinner, adding: "I'd wager my head that he's not going to leave the house at all, but will cool his heels keeping watch at the door. Now you come here to-night by the roof, and we'll have a jolly time together."

The young man was delighted at this joyous news, and said, "Just leave it to me, my dear."

With the first shades of night, the jealous husband slunk secretly down to the ground-floor room, taking his weapons with him, and lay in hiding, while his wife made all the doors fast, particularly the one on the landing, so that he could not come up. When she thought the time had come, she called her young gallant, who made his way to her from his side of the house by a secret passage, and so they went to bed, deriving pleasure and sport from each other until morning, when he went back to his own apartment.

In the meantime, the poor jealous brute stood guard with his weapons by the street-door, watching for the priest all through the night, supperless, chilled to the bone, and gnawed by mental torment. Only toward daybreak did he sink into a weary sleep there in the lower chamber, when his eyes refused to stay open any longer. Toward nine in the morning he awoke. The door of the house was already open. Pretending he came from somewhere else, he went upstairs and had breakfast. Not long after, he sent up a little boy to his wife, the supposed clerk of the priest who had heard her confession, to find out whether that certain party she knew of had again made his appearance.

She was keen to detect who had sent the messenger, and replied: "No, not last night. Tell the priest that if he keeps it up, perhaps I'll manage to tear the man out of my mind, though much against my will."

What more is there to say? The jealous cuckold cooled his heels many a night, in his zeal to fall upon the priest at the threshold, while his wife sported with her lover, until at last the dupe, unable to stand the suspense any longer, in a fit of rage insisted on knowing what she had told the priest the morning she had gone to confession.

"I won't tell you," she said. "It's neither right nor proper," whereupon he roared, "Vile slut that you are, I know very well what you told him. Yes, I know it, in spite of yourself! And mind you, I insist on knowing who this priest is with whom you're so madly in love and who lies with you every night by means of his spells! Out with it, or damn me, I'll slit your throat!"

She denied she was in love with any priest, which made him explode with rage. "How dare you!" he shouted. "Didn't you say this, and other things to the priest who heard your confession?"

"Yes, I did tell him so," she said, "and you couldn't have reported it better had he repeated it to you word for word, or had you been there yourself to take it all in!"

"Then out with it!" cried he. "Tell me who this priest is, and hurry about it!"

His wife smiled and began, "It gives me the utmost satisfaction to see how a clever man can be led by the nose by a mere woman, like a ram taken by the horns to the slaughterhouse. Though I can't really give you credit for being clever, as you haven't had an ounce of brains in your head from the moment you let the devil of jealousy enter your heart, God only knows why. The more of a fool and an ass you are, however, the less is the credit I take upon myself. Do you think, dear husband, I no more have eyes in my head than you have mental vision? Of course not. Well, having eyes, I saw who the priest was who received my confession, and I knew it was you. I made up my mind to give you what you were looking for, and I gave it to you good and proper. If you had been as clever as you think you are, you wouldn't have thought of choosing this way of discovering the secrets of your honest wife. Not at all! Without entertaining ridiculous suspicion, you would have immediately appreciated the truth of what she told you, though all the while she was guiltless of sin. I told you I was in love with a priest. Well, weren't you, the man I love—the more fool I!—weren't you a priest at the time? I told you that no door of my house could remain locked, whenever he wished to lie with me. What door of your house was ever shut against you, when you had a mind to join me? I told you the priest would lie with me every night. Can you mention a night you did not lie with me?"

"Each and every time you sent your little clerk to me, didn't I send word, after every night you know you were away from me, that the priest had not been with me? What other man, unless he were a brainless ninny like you, who let yourself be blinded by your jealousy, what other man, I say, couldn't have seen through it all? There you were, in this very house, standing sentinel all night long at the door, and you were stupid enough to think I believed the excuse you trumped up, that you had gone to sup and sleep elsewhere! Come, get your wits about you! Be a man again! Return as you were once, and don't make a laughing stock of yourself, to one who's as well acquainted with every one of your foibles as I! Enough of this silly watching, for believe me, if I had any desire to deck your head with horns, I'd go about doing my sweet will, and you'd be none the wiser, even if you had a hundred eyes, instead of two."

The sorry wittol, who had thought himself mighty ingenious in discovering his wife's secret, had to confess himself defeated on hearing her, and without offering a word in his defense, he esteemed her more than ever, as a good and prudent woman. Thus, when he had the greatest need of jealousy, he did without it, just as he had abused it when it was entirely unnecessary.

Accordingly, the clever woman, who was now in a sense privileged to follow her pleasures, no longer had her lover clamber over the roof-tops like a tom-cat, but admitted him through the door; and so, carrying on the affair with the utmost discretion, she had a gay and merry life with him for many a happy day.

✳

## THE SIXTH STORY

*While Mistress Isabella is entertaining Leonetto, she receives an unexpected call from a certain Messer Lambertuccio, who is in love with her. Suddenly her husband comes home, whereupon she sends Lambertuccio out of the house brandishing a knife; subsequently, her husband accompanies Leonetto as far as his door.*

FIAMMETTA'S STORY MET WITH TREMENDOUS FAVOR, AND ONE and all affirmed the lady had acted well in giving her brute of a husband the medicine he needed. As soon as it was over, how-ever, the king called on Pampinea to continue.

Many are those, she began, who foolishly maintain that Love robs people of their senses, and renders them well-nigh idiotic. It seems an absurd notion to me, especially in the face of the foregoing stories, and once again, I intend proving it.

In this city of ours, teeming with all good things, there once lived a very beautiful young lady, of good family, who became the wife of a brave and worthy knight. Now as it often happens that a person grows weary of the same fare, and longs for vari-ety, Isabella grew tired of her husband and took a fancy to a youth by the name of Leonetto, a handsome and well-bred lad, though he could boast of no high lineage. He fell in love with her, too; and since, as we all know, a thing most ardently desired by two individuals, is seldom without effect, their love was not long without fulfilment.

Well, it so happened that Isabella's beauty and attractive-ness turned the head of a certain knight, called Messer Lam-bertuccio, but as she thought him an unpleasant, disagreeable churl, she could not bring herself to reciprocate his affection, for anything in the world. He persisted in harassing her with messages of all kinds, and to no purpose, but at last, seeing they did him no good, he tried to frighten her with threats, saying that if she did not yield to his desire, he would blacken her character, for he was a man of vast influence. She knew what sort of customer she had to deal with, and frightened out of her wits, at last brought herself to the point of complying.

One day, when Isabella had gone to stay at a delightful country seat of hers, according to our custom in the summer months, and her husband had taken horse in the morning to spend some time away from home, she invited Leonetto to pay her a visit, which he did with great good will.

Now Messer Lambertuccio, hearing that Isabella's husband had gone away from home, mounted his horse, and riding off by himself, came and knocked at her door. A little maid went to open, and seeing the gentleman, hurried back to her mistress, who was in the bedroom with Leonetto. "Madam, madam!" she called. "There's Lambertuccio down below, all by himself!"

Isabella was woefully chagrined at the news, but terror of him got the upper hand, and she begged Leonetto to hide for a time behind the bed curtains, until Messer Lambertuccio had taken his departure. Leonetto was no less terrified than she, and con-

cealed himself while Isabella sent the girl to admit the unexpected guest. The maid opened the door. Lambertuccio
dismounted in the courtyard, fastened his palfrey to a cramp-
iron, and went upstairs. Isabella feigned delighted surprise,
and coming to the head of the stairs, greeted him as pleasantly
as she could, saying: "What brings you here, sir?"

He took her in his arms, and kissing her, said, "Soul of my
life, I heard your husband was away, so I came to keep you
company awhile."

Entering the bedroom, they locked themselves in, and Messer
Lambertuccio lost no time in taking delight of her. Suddenly,
far from Isabella's expectation, her husband returned, whom
the maid no sooner spied approaching the house, than she ran
to her lady's chamber. "Madam! Madam!" she called. "Here's
the master come back! He must be downstairs in the yard by
this time."

At this additional piece of news, Isabella, realizing she had
two men in the house, and that she could not conceal the presence of the knight, as his palfrey in the court provided evidence, gave herself up for lost. Nevertheless, she dashed
frantically out of bed, and with sudden decision said to Messer
Lambertuccio, "If you love me, and if you would rescue me
from certain death, you have only to do what I tell you. Take
your naked knife in your hand and rush downstairs, looking as
raging mad as you can, and shouting, 'I swear to God I'll
ferret him out elsewhere!' Should my husband stop and question you, say nothing but what I just told you. Then mount
your horse and don't stay with him a single moment, I beg
you!"

Messer Lambertuccio agreed, and drawing his knife, did as
Isabella bade him, his face red and glaring from the labor he
had just completed, and the anger he felt at the husband's
intrusion.

Meanwhile, the man had dismounted in the courtyard, and
marveled at the presence of the strange palfrey. He was about
to go upstairs, when down flew Messer Lambertuccio. Not
knowing what to make of the madman's words, or his fury,
"What's this, sir?" he asked.

Messer Lambertuccio steadied his foot on the stirrup,
mounted, and vouchsafing nothing but, "I swear to God I'll
ferret him out elsewhere!" galloped away.

The puzzled gentleman went upstairs, and found his wife on

the landing, bewildered and trembling with fear. "What does this mean?" he asked. "Whom is Lambertuccio chasing in such frenzy?"

Isabella, drawing near the bedroom, so that Leonetto might hear, replied, "O, my dear husband! I was never so terrified in all my life! Just now a young man I've never seen before, fled in here from Messer Lambertuccio, who was pursuing him with a knife in his hand. He happened to find this room open, and he pleaded, shaking like a leaf, 'Good lady, help me, for God's sake, if you don't want me to be butchered before your eyes!' I started up, and just as I was about to ask him who he was, and what had scared him so, up comes Messer Lambertuccio, crying, 'Traitor! Where are you?' I stationed myself at the threshold of the room, and kept him from coming further, and when he perceived I didn't want him to come in, he was decent enough to go down again, as you saw, saying all kinds of strange things!"

"You did well, wife," said he. "It would have been a great blot upon our honor had anyone been murdered in our house. But Lambertuccio did a dastardly thing, in following a man who had sought refuge here!" Then, "Where is the youth?" he asked.

"I don't know," she said, "I've no idea where he is hiding."

At that, the gentleman called out, "Ho, there, where are you? Come out and have no fear."

Leonetto, who had heard everything, left his hiding-place, quaking with fear, which, indeed, he had no need of feigning.

"What's this between you and Messer Lambertuccio?" asked Isabella's husband.

"Nothing that I know of, sir," he replied. "I'm convinced that either he's not in his right senses, or he must be mistaking me for somebody else, for the moment he caught sight of me in the street, just a little distance from your house, he immediately grasped his dagger, and cried, 'Traitor, you're a dead man!' I didn't lose time asking the why or the wherefore of the matter, but ran as fast as my legs could carry me and dashed in here, where thanks to God and this kind lady, I'm alive to tell the tale."

"Come, come now, courage!" said the gentleman. "Don't be afraid. I'll take you to your own house safe and sound, and then it's up to you to have it out with him."

After they supped together, Isabella's husband had the

youth mount a horse, and escorted him to Florence, where he left him at the door of his own house. That evening, Leonetto had a secret meeting with Messer Lambertuccio, according to Isabella's instructions, and came to an agreement with him, whereby in spite of all that was bruited about in after-days, the lady's husband never learned of the trick she had played upon him.

✳

## THE SEVENTH STORY

*Ludovico declares his love to Beatrice, his mistress, whereupon she sends Egano, her husband, into the garden disguised in her clothes, and lies with her lover, who later goes into the garden and gives Egano a good drubbing.*

ISABELLA'S QUICK-WITTEDNESS, DESCRIBED BY PAMPINEA, WAS pronounced most wonderful by every member of the party, when Filomena, who had been requested by the king to match the tale with another, said:

Unless I'm mistaken, loving ladies, I think I can cap that story with as good a one.

You must know, that in the city of Paris there once lived a Florentine gentleman, whom poverty had driven to engage in commerce, and his business had prospered so well that he had amassed a considerable fortune. He had by his wife an only son called Ludovico, and wishing the lad to grow up a gentleman and not a tradesman, he had never permitted him to work in any of his warehouses, but had sent him with other noble youths to serve the King of France, where the youth assimilated many excellent virtues and accomplishments.

Now while Ludovico was residing in France, a number of men returning from the Holy Land happened to overhear a discussion in which some youths, among whom was Ludovico, were engaged, concerning the respective merits of the beautiful ladies of France, England and other countries of the world. At that, one of the pilgrims broke in and said that of the many lovely women he had seen, in all the four corners of the earth, he had never met one to compare in loveliness with Beatrice, the wife of Egano de' Galluzzi of Bologna, whereupon all his fellows, who had been with him and seen her, granted that he was right.

Ludovico had never been in love, and on listening to the men, he was kindled with such longing to see Beatrice, that he could concentrate on nothing else. Accordingly, he determined to go to Bologna for a glimpse of her, and then, if she met with his expectations, remain there a while. Pretending to his father that he wished to make a pilgrimage to the Holy Sepulchre, he at last, though with great difficulty, obtained leave to go.

Changing his name to Anichino, he started out for Bologna, where, as luck would have it, he came face to face with Beatrice at a great entertainment. He found her beauty beyond all dreams, and fell so passionately in love with her, that he vowed never to leave Bologna until he had gained her favor. Many were the plans he devised to further his intent, but at last, putting everything else aside, he thought that perhaps if he became a retainer of her husband, who had a large household, he might attain what he so ardently desired. Thereupon, he sold all his horses, and placing his servants in comfortable quarters, with the injunction that they should pretend to be utter strangers to him, he struck up an acquaintance with his host, and told him that he was looking for a position, if possible with some well-to-do gentleman.

"You're just the lad for a nobleman of this city," said the host. "Egano's his name, and he keeps a lot of young retainers. All of them he insists must be good-looking, like yourself, for instance. If you wish, I'll broach the matter to him."

He was as good as his word, for before he took leave of Egano, he had already placed Anichino in the gentleman's service, to the youth's exceeding joy.

As time went on, and Anichino had no lack of opportunity to gaze upon the face of his lady, he took to serving his master so agreeably and so well, that Egano grew very fond of him and was helpless without him. Moreover, he not only made Anichino his personal servant, but also entrusted him with the care of all his affairs.

One day, when Egano had gone out to fly his hawks, and Anichino had remained behind, Beatrice, who had not as yet become aware of his love, though in studying his behavior she had often passed favorable judgment on him, and found him much to her liking, engaged him in a game of chess. In his anxiety to please her, he very cunningly managed to come out the loser, which made Beatrice laugh with glee. In the meantime, all of Beatrice's companions, tired of watching the game, had slipped away, one by one, leaving her alone with Anichino, who sighed deeply. She looked up at him. "What ails you, Anichino?" she asked. "Are you annoyed because I made you lose?"

"Ah, my lady," he replied. "It's a far more serious matter that made me sigh!"

"Come, tell me about it—for the love you bear me," she said.

On hearing himself implored, "for the love you bear me," by the woman he loved above all else in the world, he heaved an even deeper sigh and said nothing. Again she urged him, "Won't you tell me, Anichino? Won't you tell me what it is that makes you sigh so?"

"I'm afraid, my lady," said he. "You might be offended if I told you. Moreover, I'm afraid you might tell it to someone else."

"Nonsense, I won't be offended," she said, "and rest easy that no matter what you tell me, I'll not breathe a word of it to anybody, unless you yourself tell me to."

"I have your word," said Anichino, "and I will tell you."

With tears in his eyes, he unbosomed himself to her—told her who he was, how he had heard of her beauty, where and under what circumstances he had fallen in love with her, and why he had entered her husband's service. Then humbly, he begged her to soften her heart toward him, and if she could, grant him joy of his secret and ardent desire. "If not, let me only love you, unrequited, as your humble servant," he concluded.

O singular sweetness of Bologna's fair ones! How worthy of praise you have always been in matters of the heart! You were never fond of tears and sighs, but ever lent a willing ear to lovers' suits, and yielded yourself up to amorous desires! If only I had the eloquence to praise you, my voice would never weary!

During Anichino's speech, the gentle lady gazed steadfastly upon his face, believing him implicitly. Indeed, his pleading wrought such persuasion in her heart, that she was touched, and herself began to sigh.

"Gentle Anichino," she replied, "take heart. Many have been the men, courtiers and others, who have sought, and are still seeking my favor, but never, either by gifts, or promises or blandishments, has my heart been moved to feel love for any

one of them. But you, in the few minutes you spoke, caused
me to belong much more to you than to myself. You have well
earned my love, Anichino, and therefore I give it to you, with
the promise that before this night is over, I will have granted
you joy of it. But for that to be accomplished, you must come
to my room toward midnight: I shall leave the door open. You
know what side of the bed I lie on. Come to me there, and if I
should be asleep, nudge me awake, and I will then grant you
appeasement of your long desire. And that you may believe me,
I'll now give you a kiss as a pledge of my word."

Throwing her arms about his neck, she kissed him with great
love, and he in turn kissed her. Their pacts sealed, Anichino
took leave of her and went to look after his duties, waiting with
joyous anticipation for night to come.

Toward evening, Egano returned from flying his hawks, and
as he was exhausted from his sport, retired immediately after
supper. Soon Beatrice joined him, leaving the chamber-door
open, as she had promised Anichino.

At the appointed hour, the lover came, and stealing quietly
into the bedroom, shut the door softly behind him. Cautiously,
he walked toward the side of the bed where Beatrice lay. Placing his hand upon her breast, he found she was awake. Indeed,
the moment she heard him approach, she took his hand in both
of hers, and holding him fast, so twisted and turned about in
the bed, that she roused Egano, to whom she said:

"I didn't want to tell you anything this evening, because you
seemed quite tired, but pray, Egano, whom do you consider the
most faithful and devoted servant of all those in your household?"

"What's that you say, wife?" he asked. "As though you
didn't know! There's never been a man in my service whom
I've loved or trusted as I love and trust Anichino. But why the
question?"

On perceiving Egano to be awake, and further, on hearing
himself discussed, Anichino made several attempts to wrest his
hand from Beatrice and go, in his fear that she might be trying to play him false. She held it so fast, however, that he could
not extricate it, despite all his efforts.

"I'll tell you why," Beatrice replied to Egano. "I also thought
he was the sort of man you claim he is, and that he was more
faithful to you than anyone else in your service. But I find I
have been mistaken. This morning, after you had gone away to

fowl, he remained behind with me, and when he thought the moment was ripe, was shameless enough to urge me to yield to his desires. Now I didn't want to waste time and effort in convincing you, and make you see for yourself, so I replied I was willing, and that tonight, some time after twelve, I'd go down to the garden and wait for him at the foot of the pine-tree. Far be it from me to even dream of going! However, if you'd like to put your man's loyalty to the test, you could easily find out how wrong you are in trusting him. Put on one of my gowns, and cover your head with a veil, and then go down and wait and see if he'll turn up, as I've no doubt he will."

"I certainly will go," said Egano, after hearing what his wife had to say. Immediately, he arose, put on one of his wife's gowns as best he could in the dark, wrapped a veil about his head, and went to the garden, where, at the foot of the pine-tree, he waited for Anichino to make his appearance.

Meanwhile, as soon as Beatrice was sure her husband had risen and gone out of the room, she got out of bed and locked the door from within, to the delight of Anichino, who had never been so terrified in his life, as on that night. Indeed, while he was struggling to wrench himself free, he had sent both her and her favors and himself for trusting her, to the devil more than a hundred thousand times. Presently, she went to bed again, and at her wish Anichino undressed, got in beside her, and both had a joyous time of it, for a considerable while.

At length, when Beatrice thought he had stayed long enough, she urged him to get up and dress, and said, "Sweetest honey-mouth of mine, leave me now, and take a good stick and go down into the garden, making believe you had only tempted me, to put me to the test. Then give Egano a thorough scolding, as if you were talking to me, and drub him soundly, as I'm sure it will mean more days of wonderful pleasure and delight for us."

Accordingly, Anichino rose and went down into the garden, armed with a stout willow-rod. No sooner did Egano spy him, than he rose and walked forward to meet him, feigning joy at his coming, and pretending to welcome him with open arms.

But Anichino cried, "Ah, you foul baggage! So you did come, did you, thinking I really meant to play my master such a scoundrelly trick! You came at an evil hour, I can assure you!" and waving his stick in the air, he began playing a merry tune upon his shoulders.

At Anichino's greeting and at sight of the stick, Egano would have decamped, but Anichino followed after in hot pursuit, still crying, "Away! Away! God curse you, wicked slut that you are! I'll tell Egano in the morning, you may count on that!"

Egano, having already felt the smart of a good many blows, made off for the bedroom as fast as he could run.

"Did Anichino come into the garden?" asked Beatrice.

"He certainly did, though I wish to God he hadn't," replied Egano. "Evidently, he mistook me for you, trounced me almost to a pulp, and called me the worst names one could call a vile woman! I was quite astonished to think he had had the impudence to make you a proposal of that sort, to my dishonor, but I guess he simply wanted to put you to the test, seeing you're always so light and gay."

"Thank God, he's only put me to the test with words, and you with deeds," exclaimed Beatrice, "though he'd be right in saying I bear his words more patiently, than you his deeds! But, jesting aside, since he's so true to you, you ought to honor and cherish him as he deserves."

"You're quite right," Egano agreed, and judging by appearances, he was convinced he had the most virtuous wife, and the faithfullest servant any nobleman had ever had. Subsequently, although many a time, while Anichino was pleased to remain with Egano at Bologna, the three of them had a good laugh at the memory of this episode, the two lovers enjoyed plenty of opportunities to indulge in the thing that gave them most delight and pleasure, which might not have been the case, but for its timely occurrence.

# THE EIGHTH STORY

*The wife of a very jealous man ties a piece of string to her big toe and so knows when her lover comes to visit her. The husband discovers the ruse, and while he is busy chasing the lover, the wife puts another woman in bed to take her place. The husband beats the substitute, cuts off her hair, and runs to fetch his wife's brothers, who find his accusations apparently untrue, and revile him for his pains.*

ALL OF THEM, WITHOUT EXCEPTION, THOUGHT BEATRICE EX-
tremely crafty in making a dupe of her husband, and agreed
Anichino must have had quite a scare, when the lady clutched
him by the hand while she was accusing him of soliciting her
love. However, when the king saw that Filomena was silent, he
turned to Neifile. "You tell us a story now," he said.

Her face broke into a faint smile, and then she began:

Lovely ladies, I'd be hard put to it, if I wished to amuse you
with an interesting story as well as my friends have done, but
with God's help, I hope I'll acquit myself well enough.

You must know there formerly lived in our town, an extremely wealthy merchant called Arriguccio Berlinghieri. Like
most of his class, he was foolish enough to seek to improve his
social standing through marriage, and made a match with a
young woman of good family, called Sismonda, who was tem-
peramentally most ill-suited to him. Now as he was obliged to
travel a great deal, like all men engaged in commerce, and could
devote but little time to his wife, she fell in love with a young
man called Ruberto, who had long been suing for her favor,
and soon they became very intimate. Sismonda, being extremely desirous of his attentions, and perhaps, for that reason,
not so cautious as she should have been, her husband was
roused to insane jealousy, either through her carelessness, or
the fact that he got wind of the matter somehow or other.
Duties and business cares were thrown aside, and the poor
wretch spent most of his time spying on her actions. Indeed, he
would never fall asleep, until he had first made sure she had also
come to bed, which caused the woman tremendous annoyance,
preventing her, as it did, from dallying with her Ruberto.

She hatched many plots in her mind to enable her to be with
her lover who in turn spared no pains to importune her for
her favors. At last she thought of a ruse. She had remarked that
Arriguccio tossed about a long time, before he fell asleep, but
that when he did, he slept as soundly as a log. Accordingly,
she resolved to let Ruberto come to the door of the house at
about midnight, when she would let him in and stay with him,
while her husband slept. Her bedroom, as it happened, faced the
street, and so that she might know when her lover had arrived,
without arousing her husband, she hit upon the idea of hanging
a piece of string out of the window, so that one end of it almost
reached the ground, while the other trailed along the floor to

the bed. That end, she hid under the bedclothes, and then, when she went to bed, tied to her big toe.

Her plan laid, she communicated the details to Ruberto, with the injunction to pull the string. If her husband was asleep, she would let it go and open the door for him. If not, she would hold fast to it and pull it toward herself, which meant that he was not to wait. Ruberto was delighted with the invention, and came quite often to pull the string, sometimes succeeding in coming to her, and sometimes not. And so they kept up the pretty device.

One night, however, while Sismonda slept, Arriguccio, stretching his legs in bed, struck the string with his foot, and tracing the course of it with his hand, he found that it was fastened to his wife's big toe. "Aha! Some trick, I'll bet," he said to himself.

When he discovered, furthermore, that the twine trailed out of the window, he was firmly convinced of it. Cutting it stealthily from his wife's big toe, he twined it around his own, and kept watch to see what lay at the bottom of it. He had not long to wait, for Ruberto arrived and gave the string a good pull, as usual. Arriguccio started up. As it happened, he had not tied the knot securely enough, so that at Ruberto's yanking, the string gave way and fell into his hand, by which he understood he was to wait, and did so.

Arriguccio quickly got up, took his weapons and rushed to the door to see who the fellow was, and teach him a lesson, for though a mere tradesman, he was a brave and staunch fighter. When he got there, however, he did not open the door as gently as Sismonda would have done, so that Ruberto, who was waiting, noticed it, and suspecting which way the wind blew—in other words, that Arriguccio himself had opened for him, he took nimbly to his heels, the jealous husband following hot upon him. Finally, after Ruberto had run a long way with Arriguccio still at his heels, he pulled out his sword, for he, too, was armed, and turned upon him. The fight began in earnest, one attacking and the other defending himself.

Meanwhile, Sismonda had awakened at the sound of the bedroom door's opening, and Arriguccio's hasty exit, and finding the string cut from her toe, knew at once that her trick had been discovered, and that her husband had run out in pursuit of her Ruberto. She jumped out of bed in all haste, and suspecting the outcome, summoned her maid, who was privy to her

intrigue. She so implored and cajoled her, that she had the girl
go to bed in her stead, begging her to bear Arriguccio's blows
patiently, without letting him know who she was, and promising her such rewards that she would never have cause to
regret what she had done for her mistress. Then, extinguishing
the light that was burning in the bedroom, she went out, hiding
in another part of the house, to see what would happen.

In the meantime, the neighbors, who had been roused at the
noise of the quarrel between the two men, got out of bed and
began rebuking them in no sweet terms, whereupon Arriguccio,
fearful of being recognized, released Ruberto without having
succeeded in finding out who he was, or hurting him in the least,
and returned home, seething with fury.

"Where are you, vile slut?" he shouted in a rage, bursting
into the bedroom. "So, you've put out the light, so I can't find
you! But you've guessed wrong this time!"

Striding to the bed, he took hold of the maid, thinking it
was his wife, and rained kicks and blows upon her, as thick
and fast as his feet and hands would let him, until the poor
creature's face was all bruised. Not content with that, he cut off
her hair, without for a moment ceasing to heap upon her the
foulest abuse it was ever the lot of an evil woman to hear. The
girl shrieked and howled, as indeed she had good reason to do,
and though at times she could not help crying out, "Woe! Woe!
Mercy, for pity's sake," or, "Enough! Enough!" her voice was
so broken with sobs, and he so maddened with rage, that he
could not have recognized it as another woman's, and not his
wife's.

Well, after pummeling her to his heart's content, and cutting
off her hair, as we've told, he said, "That's enough for you
now, vile wretch that you are! But I'll go get your brothers,
and tell them about your fine accomplishments! Let them deal
with you as they see fit after that, and all honor to them! And
let them carry you home with them, for as sure as I'm alive,
you'll never set foot in this house again."

Having had his say, he flung out of the room, locked the door
behind him, and went off by himself. The moment Sismonda,
who had kept her ears on the alert, perceived that her husband
had gone out of the house, she opened the bedroom-door, made
a light again, and came to the help of her maid, whom she
found all battered and weeping bitterly. Comforting her as best
she could, she led her to her room, where she had her doctored

and taken care of, and so handsomely rewarded her with Arriguccio's own goods, that the maid had no reason to complain. These duties attended to, Sismonda then quickly remade the bed in her own room, fixed it all up and put everything in order, as though no one had lain there all night long, and rekindled the light. Later, she dressed and prepared herself to look as though she had not yet gone to bed, lighted a night-lamp, and collecting her clothes, settled down to some sewing at the head of the stairs, waiting to see what the outcome of the scrape would be.

In the meantime, Arriguccio had dashed post-haste to the house of Sismonda's brothers, knocking and clamoring at the gate until he was heard and admitted. On learning who it was, the three brothers and Sismonda's mother got out of bed, called for lights and came to him, asking what business brought him there alone, and at that hour of the night. He plunged into his story, beginning with the string he had found fastened to Sismonda's big toe, and giving them a complete description of all he had seen and done. To give them even more striking proof of what he had accomplished, he thrust into their hands the hank of hair which he thought he had cut from his wife's head, adding that they should hurry and fetch her, and treat her as they deemed consistent with their honor, for he would have no more of her in this house, no sir, not he!

The brothers were furious at what they heard, believing everything he said was true, and rankling with rage towards Sismonda, lighted their torches and followed Arriguccio to his home, murder in their hearts. At the sight of their wrath, their mother went after them in tears, going from one to the other, and pleading with them not to be so ready to believe, without first investigating and seeing for themselves, how the matter stood. Arriguccio might have had some other reason for being vexed with his wife, she argued, and so had beaten her, and was now trumping up this pretext to justify his behavior. "How could any such thing be possible?" she continued. "Don't I know my daughter, whom I raised and reared from a wee baby?" Such things she said, and many others like them.

At last they came to Arriguccio's house, and going in, made their way upstairs. Sismonda heard them. "Who's there?" she asked, from the head of the stairs.

"You'll find out soon enough, you shameless jade!" cried one of the youths.

Sismonda exclaimed, "God help us! What can this mean?" and starting to her feet, "You are welcome, dear brothers," she said. "But what can you be wanting this time of night, the three of you?"

Now when the brothers saw her sitting there, busy at her sewing, without the least trace of violence on her face, though Arriguccio had said he had beaten her to a pulp, they felt rather puzzled, and controlled the first impulse of their wrath.

"What's this Arriguccio complains of about you?" they demanded, threatening her with goodness knows what, if she did not make a clean breast of everything.

"I've no idea what stories you want me to tell you," she said, "or what Arriguccio could have found in me to complain about."

All the while, Arriguccio had been staring at his wife in a stupor, especially when he recalled he must have given her at least a thousand blows, and scratched and mauled her face, and done her all kinds of mischief. And there she was, as fresh and spry as though nothing of the sort had happened!

At Sismonda's apparent innocence, her brothers told her what Arriguccio had related about the string, and the beating and everything else.

"Lord help me, husband! What's this I hear?" she cried, turning to him. "What do you mean by blackening my character, to your own dishonor, and painting yourself worse than you really are? And pray, tell me, when did you come into this house to-night, not to speak of being with me? And when did you beat me? As for me, I have no recollection of any such thing!"

"What! Wicked woman!" he blurted out. "Didn't we go to bed together? And didn't I come home after chasing your lover through the streets? Didn't I beat you to an inch of your life, and cut off your hair?"

"No indeed! You did not sleep in this house to-night," she said. "But I'll not insist on that point, for, after all, I have nothing but my own statement to prove it. Let's come to what you say about beating me and cutting off my hair. You never laid a hand on me—and all of you here, you included, Arriguccio, can bear witness that there's not the least sign or trace of violence on my person. I'd advise you not to be so rash as to try it, either, for if you so much as lay a finger on me, I'll mar your face for you, true as fate! As for cutting off my hair, you did nothing of the sort, so far as I know. But perhaps you may have done so, and I didn't notice it. Let's see if it is cut or not."

So saying, she removed her veils from her head, and showed them all that her hair was as long as ever.

At the sight of all this, and on hearing what she had to say, her brothers and her mother began railing at her husband. "What are you up to, Arriguccio?" they asked. "So far, this hardly agrees with what you told us of your actions, and we don't see how you'll get yourself out of the rest of the mess."

Arriguccio was amazed, and wished to say something, but seeing that the very thing he wanted to prove was obviously untrue, he hadn't the courage to utter a word.

Then Sismonda, turning to her brothers, began, "Well, brothers, I can see he has chosen to gorge himself with the very dose I've never wanted to give him, that is, to let you into the secret of his debauchery and evil living. I'll tell you, then. It is my firm belief that he has really been up to all the adventures he's told you about, and that everything really did happen, and this is how. This fine spark, to whom you married me, to my bad luck, who claims to be a merchant, and wants to be respected as such, this fine specimen, I tell you, who to all appearances ought to be more abstemious than a holy friar, and more virtuous than a virgin, has been carousing for all he is worth in all the taverns roundabout, whoring with every lewd woman he meets and making me wait up for him, as you saw, until midnight, and sometimes until early in the morning. I have no doubt, that while he was good and drunk he must have gone to bed with some wench of his, and on waking up, found the string tied to her foot as he told you. Then I guess he accomplished all the wonderful feats he described, and finally went back, beat her and cut off her hair. I suppose the effects of his stupor hadn't worn off yet, so he thought, and I'm certain he still believes, he played all those pranks upon me. Take a good look at him! Can't you see from his ugly face that he's yet half-drunk? Still, despite everything of which he accused me, I don't want you to place any more stock in it than you would in the words of a drunken man, and so forgive him, as I forgive him."

Hearing her daughter's defense, the mother began ranting and said, "No, indeed, daughter! He'll not get off that easy. He ought to be killed outright, the troublesome, ungrateful cur that he is, who was never worthy of marrying a wonderful girl like you! Here's a fine kettle of fish! He couldn't have treated you worse, had he picked you up from the gutter! I'll see him dead, before you put up with the nonsense of a vulgar peddler of donkey's dung! Fine fellows they are, he and his kind! They march here to the city from the pigsties of their backwoods, dressed in cheap fustian, with falling trousers and a feather in their arse, and as soon as they have saved a paltry pile of money they're anxious to marry the virtuous daughters of gentlemen! They even learn fencing, like the best of men, and they'll tell you, 'My ancestors are So and So,' and 'The gentlemen of my family always did thus and so!' Ah, if my sons had only followed my advice! How well they might have done by you, my daughter, in the family of the Guidi—counts, all of them. And you needn't have brought them so much as a crust of bread as your dowry. But no! They had to give you to this shining light, who, although you're the best and most honest girl in all Florence, wasn't ashamed to proclaim you a whore to our very faces, and in the middle of the night at that, as though we didn't know you! Believe me, if they'd only listen to me, I'd see that he got such a drubbing for his pains, that he'd stink for it!"

Then, turning to her sons, she said, "What did I tell you, my children? Didn't I say this couldn't possibly be? Now do you see how your wonderful brother-in-law treats your sister? The lousy little peddler that he is! Why, if I were in your place and heard him say such things, after he'd been up to such scandalous doings himself, I'd never have a moment's rest or peace till I had cleansed the world of such vermin! Oh, if I were only a man, I'd not leave his punishment to other hands; the devil take him, the nasty, shameless sot that he is!"

Upon hearing all this exhortation, the young men fell upon Arriguccio, and gave him the worst preachment it was ever the lot of a ruffian to hear, ending with, "We'll let you off easy this time because of your drunken state, but if you value your life, have a care we don't hear of such nonsense again, for if anything of the sort ever comes to our ears again, we'll settle this score for you, sure as fate!"

With that threat they went away, leaving Arriguccio like one bereft of his senses, not quite sure whether what he had done had really happened or whether it had only been a dream. However, he did not say another word about it, and left his wife in peace. As for Sismonda, not only did she get herself out of this difficulty by her cunning, but paved the way for any future intrigue she might have wished to carry on, without being in any further dread of her husband.

✳

## THE NINTH STORY

*Lydia, the wife of Nicostratus, takes a fancy to Pyrrhus, who asks three things of her as proof of her true love. She accomplishes them all, sporting with him, as well, under her husband's nose, and making Nicostratus believe that what he saw was an illusion of the senses.*

NEIFILE'S STORY HAD SO TICKLED THE LADIES, THAT THEY COULD hardly stop laughing or talking about it, despite the fact that the king had already asked Pamfilo for his, and had more than once called them to order. At last they subsided, and Pamfilo began:

I hardly think a task exists, noble ladies, no matter how difficult or precarious, that a person who is ardently in love will not venture. The proof of it has been sufficiently demonstrated by a number of stories. Nevertheless, I think I can give you still more convincing evidence, by a story I intend telling, in which you will hear of a lady who had more luck on her side, than any prudence of wit. I shouldn't advise any of you to be so rash as to follow in her footsteps, for fortune is not always in a good mood, nor are men as easily duped the world over.

Once upon a time, there lived in the very ancient city of Argos in Achaia, renowned more for its vanished kings than its greatness, a gentleman by the name of Nicostratus. When he was approaching old age, fate saw fit to bless him with a wife of noble birth, called Lydia, a lady every bit as bold as she was beautiful. Now as Nicostratus was a man of both rank and substance, he kept a vast retinue of followers, and hounds and hawks aplenty, for he was passionately fond of hunting. Among his servants, he had a bright, good-looking youth called Pyrrhus, well-made of body, and skilful in everything his master set him to. Nicostratus was very much attached to the lad, loving him more than any one else in his service, and there was no one in whom he placed more trust.

It so happened, that Lydia became madly infatuated with the youth, so much so that she had no rest either day or night, thinking of him; but whether he was not aware of her love, or did not wish to be, he didn't seem to worry very much about it, which made the poor lady suffer intolerable agonies in the depths of her heart. However, she wanted him, willy-nilly, to know how the matter stood, so sending for one of her maids called Lusca, in whom she had great confidence, she said:

"Lusca, my dear, I'm sure all the gifts and favors I've showered upon you must have awakened in you both obedience and devotion toward me, your mistress, therefore take care to breathe no word of what I'm going to tell you, except to the man for whom it is intended. As you see, Lusca, I'm a young and healthy woman, and have no lack of all the good things anyone else in my position could desire. There's only one thing, in short, that I can really complain about, and that is, that my husband is very old compared to me, so that I'm very badly off for want of the pleasure in which lusty young women take most delight. I'm as eager for it as anybody else, and for quite some time I've been of the opinion, that since fortune was so little my friend as to give me such an old husband, I'll certainly not be my own enemy, by not knowing how to find a way to my pleasure and my well-being. Now I want them to be as perfect in this matter as in everything else, therefore I've decided to let Pyrrhus satisfy them with his embraces, since he's much worthier of my favor than anybody else. Indeed, I've given my heart so completely to him, that I'm never happy except when I see him or think of him, and unless I'm alone with him as soon as possible, I'm sure I'li simply pine away. If my life means anything to you, Lusca, bring my passion to his knowledge in whatever way you think best, and beg him, as you love me, to be so good as to come to me, whenever I send you to fetch him."

"Very well, my lady," said Lusca, and at the first opportunity she drew Pyrrhus aside and did her mistress' bidding, as well as she could. Pyrrhus was astonished to hear what she had to say, never having observed anything of the sort, and he suspected that the lady had made the proposal simply to test his fidelity. Therefore, he answered her harshly at once, "Lusca, I can't believe this message comes from my mistress, so take care how you let your tongue wag. Even if it did come from her, I can't imagine she meant you to take it so seriously. Still, suppose she did, my master treats me with more consideration than I deserve, and I wouldn't do him such an outrage for the world, so take care you don't broach such a subject to me again."

Lusca was not impressed by his sternness. "Pyrrhus," said she, "I'll broach this and any other subject my lady sees fit, as often as she commands, whether you like it or not. And you may take it from me, you're an ass!"

Then, flinging away from him with a little show of petulance, she carried his words back to her mistress. Lydia wished herself dead; but a few days later, she took up the subject again with her maid and said, "Well, Lusca, you know that the oak is not felled at the first stroke, so I think you had better go back to this strange fellow, who's so full of peculiar scruples, to my misfortune, and when you think the time is ripe, let him know the extent of my passion. Do everything in your power to let the thing bear fruit, for if it should fail, I'll surely die! What's worse, he will believe he was made a fool of, and we'll be rewarded with hate and not with the love we desire, for all our pains!"

Lusca consoled her lady and then went in search of Pyrrhus. She found him in a docile, receptive mood, and she said, "I told you a few days ago, Pyrrhus, that our mistress is burning for love of you, and now again I want to convince you that if you persist in the cruelty you showed the other day, she'll not have very long to live, you may be sure. Be good to her, please, and grant her her desire, for if you keep on being so hard-headed, I'll revise my opinion of you and think you an idiot, instead of the clever man I've always considered you. What more could you wish, than to have such a beautiful, kind lady dote on you above all else? Moreover, just think how grateful you should be to Fortune, for laying such a splendid opportunity at your feet. It's the very thing your youth requires, and what a resource for your needs! What man of your condition could you mention, who could boast of such delights as you'd be having, if only you'd be sensible? What other could you find, who would be better provided with arms and horses and clothes and money than you will be, if you give your love to my lady Lydia? Then take my words to heart, and come back to your right senses. Remember, fortune only comes to a fellow once with a smiling face and a lap full of bounty. The more fool he, who doesn't know how to take her then and there, and it's himself, and not she, who's to blame if he later finds himself a penniless beggar.

Moreover, who says there should be the same sort of loyalty between servants and masters, that ought to exist between friends and people of one's own flesh and blood? On the contrary, servants should deal with their masters, whenever they can, the way they themselves are dealt with. Do you suppose that if you had a good-looking wife, mother, daughter or sister, who struck Nicostratus' fancy, that he would give a straw for this same loyalty you're making such a fuss about concerning his wife? You're a fool if you believe it, for you may be sure that if promises and prayers were not enough, he'd make no bones about using force, no matter how you felt about it! Let's give them and theirs the same treatment they give us and all that is ours! Take the blessing Fortune is offering and don't chase her away. Go, run to meet her at once and make her welcome, for if you don't, not only will our mistress surely die, but you yourself will rue it and wish yourself dead a thousand times."

Now Pyrrhus had many times turned over in his mind what Lusca had told him, and he had come to the decision that if she were to broach the subject again, he would give her quite a different answer, and agree to satisfy his mistress in every respect. He wished to assure himself, however, that he was not being tricked, and therefore answered:

"Now listen, Lusca, granted that I know all you say is true; I also know, on the other hand, that my master is a wise and very clever man. Now as he has entrusted all his business to my care, I'm very much afraid Lydia may be doing this to put me to the test, at his own instigation, and with his connivance. Hence, if she will consent to do three things I'll ask, in order to convince me, there's nothing she can desire me to accomplish after that, which I won't do the moment she commands me. Here they are. First of all, I want her to kill Nicostratus' favorite hawk before his eyes; then, I want her to send me a lock of his beard, and finally, one of his teeth—a good, sound one."

Lusca thought the tasks pretty severe, and Lydia even more so. But still Love, a friend in need and past-master in all kinds of counsel, urged her to consent. Accordingly, she sent Lusca to tell him she would fully satisfy him in all his demands, very quickly, too, adding, moreover, that since he had such a lofty opinion of her husband's wisdom, she would frolic with him, Pyrrhus, under the nose of Nicostratus, and make the poor dupe believe it was not so. Pyrrhus agreed, and waited to see what his lady would do.

Some days later, when Nicostratus had invited a number of gentlemen to dinner, as he often did, Lydia, dressed in a green silk gown and decked with jewels, came out of her chamber as soon as the tables were cleared, and entered the room where the guests were gathered. While Pyrrhus and all the rest were looking on, she strode to the perch where her husband's favorite hawk was sitting, took it up as though she would have held it on her fist, and clutching it by the jesses at its feet, she dashed it against the wall, killing it. Then, when Nicostratus cried, "Alas, woman, what have you done?" she gave him no answer, but turning to the fine lords, his guests, said:

"Gentlemen, I'd hardly know how to wreak vengeance on a king who had done me wrong, if I hadn't the daring to wreak it on a mere hawk. You must know, this wretched bird has long been robbing me of the time which a gentleman ought to devote to pleasing his lady, for at the first peep of dawn Nicostratus rises, and mounting his horse with that hawk on his wrist, away he goes to the open fields, to see it fly, while I, poor woman, remain in bed, alone and dissatisfied. Many's the time I've had the desire to do what I just did, and I didn't do it sooner, for the simple reason that I wanted it to happen in the presence of men like you, who, I am confident, will be unprejudiced judges of my complaint."

The gentlemen who were listening to what she said, believed that her love for her husband was truly as deep as her words seemed to express, and turning to Nicostratus, who was still quite angry, twitted him, laughing. "Well, well, now! There's love for you, when a woman kills the offending hawk, to avenge her wrong!"

Lydia returned to her room, as the gentlemen, with many jesting remarks on the subject, turned Nicostratus' wrath to laughter. As for Pyrrhus, he said to himself, on observing the event, "It is truly a lofty beginning she has made for my happy love! Let us hope she keeps up the noble work!"

Not many days after Lydia had killed the hawk, and she was in her room with Nicostratus, fondling and caressing him, they began to play together, when he, pulling her by the hair in fun, gave her the opportunity to fulfil the second task set her by Pyrrhus. Quick as a flash, she grasped a little ringlet of his beard, and with a laugh, plucked at it so hard that she pulled it out of his chin by the roots. Nicostratus let out a howl of pain, but she said, "What's the trouble that you make such a face? Is it because I pulled out six little hairs of your beard? It couldn't have been half so bad as the pain I felt, when you took me by the hair just now."

So with one word and another, they continued their play, while Lydia made the best of the situation to hide the ringlet she had plucked from his beard. That very day, she sent it to her beloved.

The last of the three tasks gave her something to think about. She had no lack of wit, however, and what's more, Love sharpened it even further, so that she soon devised a way of executing it. As it was, Nicostratus had two lads of good family in his employ, who had been placed with him by their father that they might acquire some additional touch of polish. One of them used to carve before Nicostratus at table, while the other poured out his drink. Sending for them, Lydia convinced them both that their breath was foul, and therefore instructed them that whenever they served Nicostratus, they were to turn their heads away from him as far as they could. But they were not to tell a word of her injunctions to a living soul. The two boys, taking heed of her words, set about doing as she directed, and one day she said to Nicostratus, "Have you noticed how those two boys behave whenever they wait on you?"

"Indeed I have," he replied, "and I've been tempted to ask them why they do that."

"Oh, don't think of it, for I can tell you," she said. "For a long time I've kept quiet about it, so as not to embarrass you, but now I see that others are noticing it too, so there's no sense in keeping it from you any longer. This sort of thing is happening because your breath is terribly foul, and I don't know how that can be, for it was never so before. It's a very embarrassing predicament, especially since you have to deal with gentlemen. If I were you, I'd see about finding a way to cure it."

"What do you suppose causes it?" he asked. "Can I possibly have a bad tooth in my mouth?"

"That may be it," said Lydia.

Leading him to a window, she had him open his mouth wide, and after examining it closely, "Why, Nicostratus!" she exclaimed. "How could you have stood it so long? There's a tooth on this side of your mouth which, as far as I can see, is not only decayed, but entirely consumed, and if you leave it in your mouth much longer, it will surely ruin the sound teeth on either side of it. I'd have it pulled out, if I were you, before it gets a chance to do any more damage."

"Since you think so, I'd better have it done, then," said Nicostratus. "Send for a dentist immediately and let him pull it out for me."

"A dentist!" cried Lydia. "God forbid a dentist should be sent for to do this task! It's in such bad shape, that I'm sure I can pull it out for you myself, without the meddling of any dentist. Besides, they're a pretty merciless crew when anything of the kind has to be done, and I'd be heartbroken to see you in the clutches of any of them. I insist on doing you the service myself, for at least, if it hurts you too much I can let go right away, which would certainly not be the case if a dentist were doing it!"

Sending for the instruments appropriate to such an operation, Lydia showed everyone out of the room but her maid Lusca, and locking the door from the inside told Nicostratus to lie down on a table. Then, thrusting a pair of pincers into his mouth, she clutched one of his good molars, and while Lusca held on to him with might and main, Lydia pulled and pulled in spite of her husband's roars and bellowings of pain, until the tooth was extracted. Deftly she put it out of sight, and producing a frightfully rotted one, that she had concealed in her fist all the time, showed it to the poor wretch, who lay there more dead than alive from the pain.

"See?" she said. "That's what you've had in your mouth all this time!"

He could not but believe, for though the pain had been excessive, and he had howled and roared, he felt some relief once the tooth was out, and already imagined himself cured. Taking various stimulants to restore his spirits, he went out of the room, the pain almost gone. As for Lydia, she took the tooth and sent it to her lover with all possible expedition. Now he was firmly convinced of her love, and placed himself entirely at the disposal of her every pleasure.

However, Lydia was anxious to reassure him even more, and though every passing hour dragged like a thousand until she could be alone with him, still, she was resolved to keep the promise she had made him. One day, she pretended she was indisposed. After dinner, her husband came to pay her a visit, and when she saw that only Pyrrhus was with him, she begged him to help her into the garden, that she might at least feel it less of a bore to be ill. They took her up at her request, Nicostratus on one side and her gallant on the other, and set her down on a lawn at the foot of a handsome pear-tree. They had not been sitting there very long when Lydia, who had already given her lover instructions on the part he was to play, said, "I'm just dying to have a taste of one of those delicious pears! Won't you climb up, Pyrrhus, and throw us down a few?"

He climbed very nimbly into the tree, and threw down a few pears, but suddenly he cried, "Why, master! Master! What are you up to there? And you, madam, aren't you ashamed to let him do it before my very eyes? Do you think I'm blind, by any chance? You, madam, who were so ill a little while ago! How did you recover so suddenly that you can be up to such sport? If you're so anxious, you have lots of pleasant rooms to do it in. Why don't you go to one of them? It would be much more decent than to be doing it before me!"

"What's Pyrrhus saying there?" she asked, turning to her husband. "Is he crazy?"

"No, ma'am, I'm not at all crazy!" said Pyrrhus. "Do you suppose I can't see?"

Nicostratus did not know what to make of it, and said, "You're dreaming, Pyrrhus." But the youth replied:

"Oh no, sir! Indeed I'm not! And neither are you dreaming! You're carrying on such a merry shaking, that if this tree behaved the same way there wouldn't be a pear left on a branch!"

"What can this mean?" Lydia wondered aloud. "Is it possible he really can be seeing the things he describes? Oh dear, if I were only as well as I was, I'd be up there in a trice to see the strange wonders this fellow claims to be seeing!"

Meanwhile, Pyrrhus in his tree still talked his nonsense, until Nicostratus called, "Come down!" He obeyed. "Now tell us what you saw," said Nicostratus.

"You must be taking me either for a blockhead or a lunatic, master," said the other. "But if you insist—I saw you mount your wife, and then as I came down, I noticed that you got up and sat down where you are sitting now."

"You're certainly seeing things, if you say that," insisted Nicostratus, "for we haven't budged an inch from the time you climbed up the tree."

"What's the sense of arguing?" answered Pyrrhus. "I did see

you. But what of that? If I did, I only saw you on your own property."

Nicostratus was more and more amazed with every passing minute, until at last he said, "I must find out for myself if this pear-tree is really bewitched, to make any one on top of it see such wonders." And up he climbed. Hardly had he reached the top, when Lydia and Pyrrhus began to frolic with each other.

"How now, wicked jade!" thundered Nicostratus when he caught sight of them. "What are you doing there? And you, Pyrrhus, whom I trusted more than anyone else?"

So saying he dashed down the trunk, while Lydia and her lover replied innocently, as they resumed their original positions, "We are only sitting here!"

Once Nicostratus was on solid ground again, and saw them sitting as he had left them, he fell to heaping abuse upon their heads. Pyrrhus pacified him. "I must admit now, master, that I was seeing things, as you said before, when I was on top of that tree, and I am sure of it, simply because I saw for myself, and therefore know, that you were also deceived in what you must have seen. What greater proof could you have that I am speaking the truth, but for you to consider things as they are? Your wife is a model of virtue, and much more intelligent than most women. Do you suppose that if she had any desire to dishonor you in that fashion, she would be so foolish as to do it under your very nose—not to speak of myself, who'd sooner be drawn and quartered than think of, or much less perpetrate, such a thing before your eyes? Surely the tree itself must be to blame for this illusion, for nothing could have convinced me that you were not really in carnal conjunction with your lady, if I hadn't heard you exclaim at seeing me do the thing I most assuredly never thought of, or did in my life!"

No sooner had he spoken, than Lydia started to her feet, pretending to be mortally injured, and cried to her husband, "You can go to the devil, if you think so little of me as to imagine that if I had any desire for such lewd business as you claim to have seen, I'd come to do it before your eyes! Rest assured I wouldn't be coming out here in the open, if the longing ever seized me. I'd at least have sense enough, my dear, to hide in one of our rooms, and take such trouble about keeping it secret, that it would indeed be a miracle if you ever so much as suspected it!"

Nicostratus was convinced by this argument that they would

never have thought of doing him such an outrage under his nose, and laying aside blame and recrimination, he began to talk of the wonder of the thing, that so deceived the sight of all who climbed the pear-tree. But Lydia, who still seemed incensed at her husband's opinion of her, said, "This tree shall certainly play no more of its shameful pranks on me or any other woman—not if I have any say in the matter! Go, Pyrrhus, run and get an axe. Wreak your vengeance and mine upon it, by cutting it down, though you would be doing a better service if you smashed in your master's head with it, for being so quickly blinded in his wits without the least consideration! Yes, Nicostratus! For no matter how real the vision seemed to the eyes in your head, you shouldn't have allowed your mind's judgment to accept it, or even grant that such a thing were possible."

Meanwhile, Pyrrhus ran quickly for the axe and hewed down the pear-tree, and, when Lydia saw it laid low, she said to her husband:

"Now that I see the enemy of my virtue felled to the ground, my wrath has vanished." Benignly, she forgave Nicostratus, who had been pleading for her pardon. "But don't ever dare to think such a thing of me again, who love you more than my life," she admonished prettily.

And so the poor duped cuckold returned with his wife and her gallant to the palace, where the two took much joy of each other in later days with greater ease and comfort—may the Lord grant it us likewise!

## ✳

# THE TENTH STORY

*Two men of Siena are both in love with the same woman, who is related to one of them, through his being godfather to her child. This man dies, and keeping his promise to his friend, returns and tells him what sort of life is led in the other world.*

THE KING WAS THE ONLY ONE LEFT TO SPEAK, AND THEREFORE the moment he saw the ladies had ceased to bewail the felling of the pear-tree, for no fault of its own, he began:

It is a perfectly obvious fact, that a just king must be the first to obey the laws he makes, and if he does differently, he should be considered no king at all, but a culprit deserving of punishment like anybody else. I'm afraid I, your king, am almost obliged to fall into this transgression, this reprehensible offense. Yesterday, true enough, I suggested the subject of the stories we were to tell to-day, not intending to take advantage of my privilege on this occasion, but like you, to abide by the law I had laid down, and keep the theme which you have been elaborating. As it is, however, the story I had intended telling has not only been told, but so many other even more amusing ones have followed it, that I, for one, can't think of anything else on the theme, however I cudgel my brains. Nor can I summon up another story that will bear comparison with the foregoing. Well then, since I am compelled to violate the very law I myself laid down, I am ready even now to submit to any punishment you may administer, and for the present I shall avail myself once more of my usual privilege. But to come to my tale—Elisa's story of the friar and his godson's mother, and of the foolishness of the people of Siena was so compelling, that forgetting for the present the tricks which clever wives play on their silly husbands, I am tempted to tell you something else concerning them. Although, dearest ladies, there's a lot in the story that shouldn't be believed, still it will afford some diversion, at least in part.

In the city of Siena, there once lived two young men of the lower classes, one of whom was called Tingoccio Mini, and the other Meuccio di Tura. Both of them lived at Porta Salaia, and as they never went anywhere except together, they seemed to all intents and purposes to be very much attached to each other. Like the rest of the folk, they used to go to church regularly and listen to sermons from the pulpit, and more than once they had had occasion to hear of the blessedness or damnation, which was the lot of the souls of the departed in the other world, according to their merits. Since both were eager to have more definite information on these matters, and could see no other way of obtaining it, they sealed a pact to the effect that whichever of the two died first, would make it his business, if he could, to return to earth, and tell the other all he wished to know. This pact they solemnized with an oath.

Some time after they had sworn to the reciprocal promise, and were still as close friends as ever, Tingoccio became godfather to a son which Mistress Mita had borne her husband, Ambruogio Anselmini, who lived at Campo Reggi. From time to time, Tingoccio, accompanied by his inseparable friend, would visit this gossip of his, a fine, handsome woman, until despite the honorable relationship which was between them, he fell head over heels in love with her. Meuccio, on his part, who was pleased with her looks and had his brain fired by Tingoccio's praises of her, promptly followed suit; but each took care to keep this love secret from the other, though not for the same reason. Tingoccio guarded against revealing his passion to Meuccio, out of a scruple of conscience, feeling a certain guilt in loving his godson's mother; indeed, he would have died of mortification if anyone had discovered it. Meuccio had no such scruple to contend with, but forbore telling his friend because he had already noticed Tingoccio was fond of her. "If I were to tell him, he would grow jealous of me," he reflected. "He can speak to her any time he wishes because he's her son's godfather, and there's nothing to prevent him from turning her heart against me. If that were to happen, how could I persuade her to be nice to me?"

Well, as the two youths continued constant in their passion for Mistress Mita, it so happened that Tingoccio, who had greater opportunity to make his love known to her, acquitted himself so well, both in word and deed, that he obtained of her the pleasure he desired, which Meuccio was not slow to find out. However, although the knowledge vexed him, he still had hopes of gaining his end at some future time, and to give Tingoccio no cause for obstructing or hindering his purpose, he kept up the pretense of knowing nothing about it. As time went on, and the two companions persevered in their love, one with more success than the other, Tingoccio, finding his gossip's plot most sweet to till, so sweated and toiled, that he fell into a serious illness, which, within a few days, was aggravated to such an extent that he had no strength to fight it, and died.

Three days after his death (perhaps he had not been able to make it sooner), he appeared in Meuccio's chamber, true to the promise he had made, and called him out of a sound sleep.

"Who's that?" asked Meuccio, with a start.

"It's me, Tingoccio," said the apparition, "come back to keep the promise I made you, and give you news of the other world."

Meuccio was rather scared at the sight of him, but pulling himself together he managed to say, "I'm glad to see you, brother. And tell me, are you lost?"

"Lost?" said Tingoccio. "You lose only what you can't find. How do you suppose I could be here, if I were lost?"

"No, that's not what I mean," said Meuccio. "I'm simply asking you, if you're one of the damned, roasting in hell-fire."

"I should say not," answered Tingoccio. "But I can't say I'm not getting my share of pretty severe punishment for the sins I committed."

Meuccio asked him for further particulars of the punishments meted out for the various sins committed here below, and Tingoccio gave him complete details. Later, "Is there anything you'd like me to do here for you?" asked Meuccio.

"Yes," said Tingoccio, and instructed him to have some masses said for him, and a number of prayers, and to give alms in his behalf, adding that such things were extremely helpful to the souls of the dead, who had gone beyond.

"All right, I'll be glad to do that for you," said Meuccio.

Tingoccio was just about to leave, when Meuccio thought of their friend, Mistress Mita. Raising his head a little, he said, "Oh, it occurs to me, Tingoccio—what punishment did you get over there, because of your gossip, whom you used to lie with when you were here among us?"

"Brother," replied Tingoccio, "the moment I got there I came across a fellow who seemed to know all my sins by heart, down to the least peccadillo, and he ordered me to go immediately to a certain place, where I repented of my sins, in the midst of the worst torture you can imagine. I found a lot of other folks there, condemned to the same pains, and as I stood among them, thinking of all I'd been up to with Mita, expecting even worse punishment for it than I had already received, I began quaking with dread, though the awful flames I was roasting in were not too pleasant, I can tell you. A man who was near by, felt me shivering with fright, so he said, 'What's it you've done worse than the rest of us, that you're shivering even in this fire?' 'Ah, friend,' I said, 'I'm dreadfully afraid of the punishment I expect for a terrible sin I committed on earth!' He wanted to know what it was, so I said, 'I used to lie with the mother of my godson, and I did it so much and so often, that I gave up the ghost.' He laughed at that, and said, 'You silly fool! Don't carry on that way! In this place people don't bother their heads about mothers of godsons!' which made me rest easy after that."

Meanwhile, day was drawing near. "Good-bye, and God be

with you, for I can't stay any longer," he said, and immediately vanished.

Now when Meuccio heard that in the other world people didn't bother their heads about one's gossips, he laughed at his foolishness for having let so many fine opportunities slip by, and bidding farewell to his ignorance, from then on he learned wisdom.

Perhaps if Friar Rinaldo had heard it, too, he might not have had to use so many arguments in converting his good gossip to his desires.

A gentle breeze had risen as the sun declined towards the west, when the king, having come to the end of his story, and there remaining no one else to speak, took the crown off his head and laid it upon Lauretta's, saying, "My lady, I hereby crown you queen over yourself and our band. Henceforth, it is for you to order, as our ruler, whatever you consider meet for our pleasure and comfort." Then he resumed his seat.

Lauretta, now queen, sent for the steward and issued orders that the tables should be laid in the delightful valley a little earlier than usual, so that they might all have leisure to return to the palace in good time, giving him further details as well, of what he was to do during the period of her rule. Then, addressing her company, she said:

"Yesterday Dioneo requested us to speak of the tricks which wives play upon their husbands, and if it weren't for the fact that I don't want to be considered among the race of curs, who are quick to snap back vindictively, I'd suggest that, for to-morrow, we choose the theme of the pranks which husbands play upon their wives. But laying that aside, I'd prefer you rather, to think *of some story concerning the tricks, which are every day played by men on men, or by men on women, or by one man on the other,* a subject which I believe will make the story-telling no less diverting than it was to-day."

Then, rising to her feet, she gave them all liberty to do as they wished until supper-time. The rest followed her suggestions, some going to wade barefoot in the limpid waters, and others hastening to gambol among the noble upstanding trees of the green meadow. Dioneo and Fiammetta sang together for a long time, of Palamon and Arcite. In this fashion, and in various other amusements, they whiled away the hours enjoyably until supper-time.

They took their places at table along the water's brink, where, to the music of a thousand birds, and soothed by the gentle breeze rising from the surrounding hills, they had their meal in joy and leisure with not a fly to molest them.

After the tables were cleared, they took a stroll around the pleasant vale, for the sun was still not near its setting, when, at the queen's wish, they set out for their palace at an easy pace, chatting and laughing over a thousand things, the day's stories as well as other pleasant matter. So, toward nightfall, they reached the palace, where they refreshed themselves from the exertion of their brief walk with coolest wines and rare dainties, and then, to the fountain to dance, now to the tune of Tindaro's bagpipes, and now to other music. Presently, the queen requested a song of Filomena, who began:

> "Alas, my sorry life!
> And can it be I shall again return
> Whence I was taken by a hapless fate?
>
> I am in doubt (so burns within my breast
> The dearest wish I bear)
> If I shall find me in that place once more
> Where first I was. O my sweet rest,
> My lover, my heart's care!
> Ah, answer, for I dare it not implore
> Of other mortal more.
> Come, dearest lord, let me not vainly yearn,
> And let my poor soul's suffering abate!
>
> I cannot tell what was the sweet delight
> Which so did make me smart,
> That I can find no rest both night and day;
> For each the hearing and the touch and sight
> With an unwonted art
> Have fired a newer flame to my dismay,
> Wherein I melt away.
> No one but you can soothe me as I burn,
> Or summon back my senses sore distrait.
>
> Oh, tell me if it is in fate's control
> That you I shall yet find
> There, where to my own death, I kissed your eyes.

Oh, let me know, my dearest good, my soul!
　　Speak, and I pray, be kind.
　　　　Answering, 'Soon' to cheer my agonies.
　　　　Short be the time that flies
　　To bring you, and long bide, till you return.
　　　　So much I love, I care not what my fate!

If Fortune grant that I recapture you,
　　I shall not foolish be,
　　　　As once I was, to free you, dearest boy!
　　I'll hold you fast—I care not what ensue—
　　　　And then before you flee
　　　　　　From your sweet mouth I'll take my fill of joy.
　　　　　　But now I shall be coy.
　　　　Then come, and let us to embraces turn,
　　　　　　About whose every thought I grow elate!"

This song led them all to believe that a new and agreeable love held Filomena captive, for, as the words seemed to denote, she had gratified much more than her eyes with it. Considering her all the more fortunate for that, some of the ladies who were present could not but feel envious.

Filomena's song over, however, Lauretta recalled that the following day was Friday, so she turned to her company and said sweetly, "You must know, noble ladies, and you, gentlemen, that to-morrow is the day consecrated to the passion of Our Lord, which, if you recall, we honored with the proper devotion during the period of Neifile's rule, by laying aside story-telling for the day. The same held true for the subsequent day, Saturday. I'd like to follow the good example set by Neifile, so I think it would be commendable if we abstained from our pleasant pastime to-morrow and the day after, as we did on a previous occasion, and let our thoughts dwell on what took place on those days for the redemption of our souls."

All approved of the queen's suggestion, and as a considerable part of the night was already over, they retired at her wish.

# 8

# THE EIGHTH DAY

ON THE CRESTS OF THE TALLER HILLS, THE RAYS OF THE RISING sun were already shining, that Sunday morning; the shadows had fled and the shapes of things could be clearly distinguished, when the queen rose with her company, and walked a while on the dewy greensward. Later, though still in the early morning, they visited a nearby church and heard the divine service, and again sought their way homeward, where they breakfasted with pleasure and cheer. Nor did they forget to divert themselves a while with singing and dancing, until the queen dismissed them to take their noon-day nap, if they chose. But when the sun had passed its meridian, one and all met for their usual story-telling at the queen's pleasure, and took their places along the pleasant fountain's brink, where Neifile began, at her lady's bidding:

*

## THE FIRST STORY

*Gulfardo borrows a sum of money from Gasparruolo, in order to give it to the latter's wife, Ambrogia, for the privilege of lying with her; later, in the presence of Ambrogia, he tells her husband that he returned the money to her, which she cannot but admit.*

SINCE IT IS GOD'S WILL THAT I INAUGURATE TO-DAY'S STORY-telling, I am perfectly willing; therefore, loving ladies, as we've had no lack of instances of the trickery women have used on men, it will give me pleasure to tell you a story in which the tables are turned—not that I have any wish to condemn the man's deed, or say that it didn't serve the woman right. On the contrary, I want to show you that I have only praise for the man, and contempt for the woman, and that men can play clever tricks on their dupes every bit as well as those by whom they themselves are taken in. To be accurate, the instance I'm going to relate should scarcely be called a trick, but rather a salutary lesson. We all know that a woman should be a model of virtue, and as careful of her chastity as of her life, allowing no liberties with it under any condition. Though this purity is not always feasible, because of our characteristic frailty, still I maintain that a woman who sells her charms for money is fit to be burned alive, though she who yields them up for Love— whose powers are unconquerable—deserves to be pardoned by not too stern a judge, as in the case of Filippa da Prato, of whom Filostrato told us a few days ago.

Well, some time ago there lived in Milan a German by the name of Gulfardo, employed in the civil-service. He was a sturdy, well-made man, and a faithful servant of his employers—which can scarcely be said for most Germans—and so scrupulous in paying back the loans he secured, that he would have had no difficulty in finding scores of merchants quite ready to lend him any sum, at a small rate of interest.

During the time Gulfardo was living in Milan, he became enamored of a very handsome woman called Ambrogia, the wife of Gasparruolo Cagastraccio, a wealthy merchant and a good friend of his. He was very prudent in keeping his passion a secret from everyone, including her husband, and one day he sent her a go-between, begging her to grant him the favor of her love, in return for which he would be willing to do whatever she asked.

She had many objections to offer, but at last she declared herself ready to grant him everything he desired, on two conditions: first, that he should promise never to tell a living soul about it, and second, that he should give her two-hundred florins in gold for something she needed, he being such a rich man. After that, she would always be at his service.

When Gulfardo learned of the grasping propensities of Ambrogia, whom he had always believed a noble, great-hearted woman, he was disgusted with her vulgarity. His deep love almost turned to scorn, and he made up his mind to play a trick on her, and accordingly sent word to her that he would not only give her what she asked, but anything else her heart desired. Let her but tell him when he might come to her, and he would bring her the money personally, keeping the matter a secret from everyone but a dear, trusted friend of his who accompanied him wherever he went.

On hearing this message, the lady—the vile hussy, I should say—was filled with joy, and informed him that as her husband was expected to leave for Genoa on business in a few days, she would then let him know more definitely about an appointment, and send someone to his home to bring him to her.

Gulfardo, seizing the proper moment, went to Gasparruolo and said, "I'm just about to close a deal, for which I need two-hundred florins in gold. I'd appreciate it, if you'd lend them to me at the rate of interest you always charge me."

"Certainly," said Gasparruolo, and counted out the money for him then and there.

A few days later, Gasparruolo went to Genoa, as his wife had said, whereupon she sent for Gulfardo to come to her and bring the two-hundred florins. He set out for her house, taking his friend along with him, and the first thing he did, on finding her waiting, was to count the money into her hand in the presence of his companion, saying, "Take care of these florins, madam, and give them to your husband when he comes back."

Ambrogia took the money, never suspecting for a moment why he spoke as he did, thinking he was simply doing it so that his friend might not realize he was giving them to her, in payment for her favors.

"Gladly, sir," she said. "But first let me count them over again, to see how many there are."

Emptying the money-bag on a table, she made her count, and finding two-hundred florins as she had expected, was pleased with her bargain. She left for a moment to put them safely away, and returning to Gulfardo, led him to her chamber, where not only that night, but many a night thereafter, before her husband returned from Genoa, she surrendered her body for his gratification.

On Gasparruolo's return, Gulfardo, awaiting the chance to find him with his wife, paid him a visit with his friend, and said in her hearing, "Gasparruolo, after all I didn't need the two hundred florins you loaned me the other day, as I couldn't make the deal for which I borrowed them, so I gave them to your wife's keeping, for you. Don't forget to clear my account."

"Did you receive the money, wife?" asked Gasparruolo, turning to her. She saw the witness there before her eyes, and couldn't find a way of denying it, so she admitted it. "Yes, I did receive it—I hadn't had a chance to tell you."

"Very well, Gulfardo," said Gasparruolo. "Go with an easy mind, for I'll take care to straighten your account."

Gulfardo left the house, while the woman, shamed and foolish, gave her husband her dishonest gains. And so it was that the crafty lover enjoyed his mercenary mistress, without laying out a penny.

✳

## THE SECOND STORY

*The village-priest of Varlungo enjoys Mistress Belcolore, and leaves her his tabard as a surety; he then borrows her mortar, and on sending it back, demands his good tabard which he had left her in pledge, whereupon she returns it with pithy words.*

BOTH THE MEN AND THE LADIES WERE EXPRESSING THEIR APproval of the lesson Gulfardo had taught the grasping Ambrogia, when the queen turned to Pamfilo, and with a smile requested him to continue with a story.

Loveliest of ladies, he began, it occurs to me to tell you a little story aimed at a certain class of people who are continually taking advantage of us, without our being able to give them tit for tat. I'm referring to the priesthood, who have declared our wives under ban, though when they can manage to lay a woman under them, they imagine they've won a complete pardon for all their faults and sins, as if they had done no less a deed, than drag the Sultan in chains from Alexandria to Avignon. What vengeance can poor layfolk take on the culprits themselves, though they can vent their spleen on the priests' mothers, sisters, mistresses and daughters with no less zeal than the churchmen use on their own wives? I'm going to tell you, therefore, of a rustic love, more amusing in its conclusion than its length, one which you may still turn to your own purposes, by bearing in mind that priests are not always to be trusted. To my story, then.

In the village of Varlungo, not very far from here, as all of
you ladies must know either from hearsay or personal experience, there once lived a lusty priest, well-equipped physically
for the service of fair ladies. He was no great scholar, in fact, he
hardly knew how to read, but in spite of this deficiency, he
could still entrance the men-folk with a flow of homely and
pious eloquence of a Sunday morning, there at the foot of the
elm-tree. Whenever they happened to be away from home,
traveling anywhere, he would visit their wives more assiduously
than any other priest the parish had ever had before, bringing
them to their doorsteps, now a little church-loaf, with his blessing, now a vial of holy-water, and sometimes the heel of a
candle.

Now of all the ladies of his congregation whom he had eyed
from the very first with pleasure, one delighted him above the
rest—none other than Belcolore, the wife of a farmer known to
all as Bentivenga del Mazzo. A fresh, lusty, nut-brown, com-
pact lass she was, indeed, more apt for a good grinding than any
other wench he knew. What's more, she it was who played the
tambourine and sang: "The stream runs down the hillside,"
and led the brawl and the round-dance better than any woman
for miles around, holding a pretty little handkerchief in her
hand, just like a lady.

Everything conspired to turn the priest's head, so that he
didn't know whether he was coming or going, and all day long
he haunted her neighborhood, just for a look at her. On a
Sunday morning, if he caught sight of her during the service, he
would intone a *Kyrie* and a *Sanctus* of such lustiness, in his
anxiety to show her how accomplished he was in singing, that
he sounded like a braying donkey, while when she wasn't there,
he did very nicely without the music. In spite of the ardor of
his passion, however, he contrived very well to keep it a secret
from Bentivenga, and for that matter, from the rest of the
people. But with Belcolore, he was different. To render her
more accessible, he had taken to making her gifts, from time to
time, presenting her with a luscious bunch of fresh garlic, of
which he grew the best anywhere about, in a patch of garden
which he tilled with his own hands, or a wee basketful of peas,
and sometimes a few heads of onions or scallions. On these
occasions, he would slyly feast his eyes upon her, or tease her,
out of affection, while she, the rogue, playing the innocent
lassie, pretended she did not get the point of his jests, and

looked as guileless as you please. And so Master Longfrock could never succeed in mounting her.

Now one day, while the priest was wandering aimlessly about the village in mid-afternoon, he stumbled upon Bentivenga del Mazzo, who was driving a donkey loaded with a pack of goods, and greeting him, "Where are you going, Bentivenga?" he said.

"Why, sir, to tell the truth, sir, I'm agoing to town, sir, on a certain matter," Bentivenga informed him. "I'm ataking these goods to his worship Bonaccori da Ginestreto, sir. You see, it's like this. He's agoing to help me, sir, in something, I don't know what, for you see, sir, the judge of the court he sends for me and he says, says he, you must appear here—"

"You're perfectly right, my son," said the priest, tickled at the news. "Go with my blessing, and come back soon, and if you should come across Lapuccio or Naldino, don't forget to tell them to bring me the straps for my belts."

"Yes, sir, that I will, sir," said Betivenga, and drove on with his donkey toward Florence.

The priest watched him go, and thought that now was the time to go to Belcolore and try his luck. The ground flew under his feet, and he did not stop for breath until he came to the good wench's house. Gliding in through the door, "God bless us all," he said. "Is anybody home?"

Belcolore had just gone up to the loft, and on hearing his voice, she said, "Ah, father, it's you! Glad to see you. How can you be gallivanting about in this hot weather?"

"So help me, God" he said, "I came here on purpose, to stay with you a while, as I met your goodman going to town."

Belcolore came down from the loft, and taking a stool near him, settled down to pick the cabbage-seed which her husband had just finished threshing.

"Ah, Belcolore," sighed Sir Priest, "tell me, are you always going to let me pine away like this?"

"Why, what am I doing to you?" she said, laughing.

"Nothing," he replied. "But you won't let me do to you what I'd like, and what the Lord commands."

"Fie! Fie, father," cried she, "do you mean to say priests do such things?"

"That we do, and better than other men," he said. "And why not, pray? I'll tell you another thing. We're far more expert at it. Do you know why? Because we grind when the harvest is done. Come, be a nice girl and leave the rest to me. You'll have something to gain by it."

"What do you mean, I'll have something to gain by it?" asked Belcolore. "As if I didn't know you priest-folk are so close, you'd skin a flint."

The priest hastened to his own defense. "I'm not, though," said he. "Ask me for something, and you'll see. How about a pair of new shoes, or a kerchief, or a nice worsted girdle? Anything! Anything your little heart desires."

"Well-a-day, father," she said. "As though I didn't have any of these things! But if you're so crazy about me, how about doing me a favor, and I'll give you anything you wish?"

"Tell me what it is, and I'll be only too glad to do it," said the priest.

"Well," Belcolore began, "next Saturday I'll have to go to Florence, to take back some yarn I've spun and get my spinning-wheel fixed. If you'll lend me twenty lire, which I know you have with you, I'll get my silk gown out of pawn, and my best girdle, that I was married in, for you see, I can't go to church or any other respectable place because I've nothing to wear. Then, if you agree, I'll always do anything you say."

"God is my witness I have no money with me," he said. "But on my word, I'll do my best to let you have it by Saturday at the latest."

"Yes, I know," replied Belcolore. "You're all glib promise-makers, but you never keep your word to anybody. Do you think you'll make me do what Biliuzza did, who ran off with the fiddle-maker? Not if I can help it, my dear sir! She became a street-walker on account of it! If you haven't the money, turn right around and go home for it."

"Come, now," he complained, "don't let me make that long trip to my house! See, luck's been on my side so far, by letting me find you alone. How do I know that by the time I get back, there won't be somebody to interfere with us? Besides, I don't know when I'll have as good a stroke as now!"

"I don't care," she said. "If you want to go, well and good. If not, you can do without!"

When he realized she was in no mood to give in to his pleasure but *salvum me fac*, whereas he would have it *sine custodia*, he said, "So! You don't believe me when I tell you I'll get it for you! Well then, to convince you, I'll leave you this good serge tabard of mine."

"Your tabard?" said she, looking up. "Which, that thing? Why, what is it worth?"

"What do you mean, what is it worth?" he repeated. "I want you to understand it is two-ply, I might say three-ply, and there are some people in this town who insist it is four-ply. Why, only two weeks ago, I paid all of twenty-eight lire for it at Lotto's, the pawn-broker, and from what Buglietto tells me—and you know he's a mighty good judge of such materials—I got it for at least four lire less than it's worth."

"Is that so?" exclaimed Belcolore. "So help me God, I'd never have believed it! But hand it over to me first."

Master Longfrock, whose arbalest was already aimed to shoot, took off his tabard and gave it to Belcolore, who, after laying it away said, "All right, then, father. Let's go out to the shed, where no one will come to bother us." And off they went.

Once under shelter, the priest gave her the most luscious smacks in the world, and making her a kin to God the Father, frolicked with her a pleasant while. Later in the day, he went back to his church clad only in his tunic, looking as though he had just returned from performing a wedding.

In the quiet of his room, when he began to reflect that all the candles he received as offering during the year were not worth, all told, one half of twenty lire, he thought he had struck a bad bargain, and repented having left his good tabard behind. Little by little, he pondered ways and means of getting it back gratis, and being rather sly, he struck on a plan which could not have turned out better. Early next morning, which happened to be a holiday, he sent one of his neighbor's lads to the house of Mistress Belcolore, begging her to lend him her stone-mortar, as he wished to pound the ingredients of a sauce, since Biguccio dal Poggio and Nuto Buglietti were having dinner with him that day. Belcolore sent it to him by the boy, whereupon the foxy priest, biding the time Bentivenga and she would be at table together, summoned his clerk and said to him:

"Take this mortar and carry it back to Mistress Belcolore, and say, 'My master says thanks, and if you don't mind, will you please send him back his tabard, that the boy left with you as a pledge?' "

Away went the clerk to the house of Mistress Belcolore, whom he found at a deal board, having dinner with her husband. Putting down the mortar, the lad delivered the priest's message. At the request for the tabard, Belcolore would have made some response, but Bentivenga scowling angrily, interrupted her, saying, "So you take a pledge, do you, from the father? I swear by—by all that's holy, I've a good mind to give you a sound smack. Run, give it back to him right away, a murrain take you, and remember, if he ever wants anything else we have, even our donkey, you're not to say no, do you hear? You're not to say no!"

Grumbling, Belcolore got up, and going to the closet, took up the tabard and gave it to the clerk, saying, "Tell the father this for me: 'Belcolore says she takes a solemn oath, that you'll never make any more sauce in her mortar, since you played her such a nasty trick this first time!'"

The clerk returned to the priest with the tabard and told him what Belcolore had said, at which he remarked with a laugh, "You tell her for me, when you see her, that if she'll not lend me her mortar, neither will I let her have my pestle, so it's tit for tat."

Bentivenga, meanwhile, believed his wife had spoken as she did because he had rebuked her, and thought no more about it. But as for Belcolore, she became so angry with the priest, that she would have nothing more to do with him until the fall of the year, when the harvest was gathered in. However, when he threatened to send her headlong into the maw of Lucifer, the worst of the devils, she was so terrified that she patched up her quarrel with him over must and piping-hot chestnuts, and then made a regular habit of meeting him, to their mutual delight and fun. Moreover the priest, to make up for the twenty lire she did not get, had her tambourine rebottomed, and a lot of pretty jingling bells strung to it, which pleased her well enough.

✳

## THE THIRD STORY

*Calandrino, Bruno and Buffalmacco scour the banks of the Mugnone in search of a stone called heliotrope. Calandrino imagines he has found it, and returns home loaded down with all kinds of stones. His wife scolds him for coming home so late, where-*

*upon he gives her a beating and then tells his companions what*
*they knew better than he.*

PAMFILO FINISHED HIS STORY, AT WHICH THE WOMEN LAUGHED
so much that they must still be laughing remembering it. At
last the queen requested Elisa to continue, who began, still
bubbling over with mirth:

Not so long ago, in this city of ours which has always been
crammed with strange customs and peculiar people, there lived
a painter called Calandrino, a simple-minded fellow, who was
given to rather odd behavior. He had two boon companions,
also artists, with whom he used to spend a good part of his time,
the one called Bruno and the other Buffalmacco, both fond of a
practical joke, keen-witted and clever, who used to cultivate
Calandrino's friendship for no other reason than the enjoyment
they derived from his amusing ways and lack of wit. In those
days, there also lived in Florence a gay, young, venturesome
spark by the name of Maso del Saggio, remarkable for his
cleverness and the astounding way with which he brought all
his pranks to the desired end. Having heard a little of Calandrino's clownishness, he thought he would have some fun, by
playing one of his jokes on him, or by making him swallow
some unheard-of nonsense.

One day, he came upon him in the church of San Giovanni,
and seeing him study with keen interest the paintings and
carvings of the tabernacle, which had recently been installed
above the altar of that church, he saw the chance he had been
waiting for. Communicating his plan to a comrade who was
with him, they both drew up to the place where Calandrino
was sitting, and pretending to take no notice of him, entered
into a discussion on the virtues of various stones, on which
Maso spoke so glibly that one might have taken him for an
authority on the subject.

Calandrino pricked up his ears. Soon, feeling it was not gentlemanly of him to be eaves-dropping, he rose and approached
them, to Maso's great satisfaction, who carried on his disquisi-
tion even more enthusiastically, until Calandrino could not help
asking him where those remarkable stones he was talking about
were to be found. "Most of them in Berlinzone, a Basque
province," Maso informed him, "in a district called Bengodi,
where vines are fastened to the stakes with sausages, and a
goose can be had for a penny, with a duckling thrown in for

good measure." A wonderful mountain was also to be found in that country, he told him, all made of grated Parmesan cheese, and inhabited by folk who spent all their time making maccaroni and ravioli, which they boiled in capon-broth and then spilled out pell-mell, so that whoever was the nimblest, obtained the largest share. And last but not least, a stream of the most generous vintage flowed close by—the most delicious wine you'd ever hope to taste, with not the tiniest drop of water in it.

"Lord, what a country that must be!" exclaimed Calandrino. "But tell me, what happens to the capons they cook?"

"Why, the Basques eat them all up," replied Maso.

"Were you ever there?" asked Calandrino.

"Was I!" cried Maso. "I was there a thousand times, if I was there once."

"And how many miles is it from here?"

"Ten score miles and ten, there and back again," Maso jingled.

"It must be even farther off than Abruzzi, then!" gasped Calandrino.

"Indeed!" said Maso. "That and more!"

The poor fool of a Calandrino, observing Maso telling these fairy-tales with a somber face that never broke into a smile, believed them as he would have believed the most obvious facts, and taking everything for gospel-truth, remarked, "It's much farther away than I could afford with my means, though if it were a little nearer, you can bet your life I'd go with you, if only to see those maccaroni spilled down the hillside, and get me a bellyful! But tell me—bless your heart!—aren't there any of the wonderful stones you spoke of around here, in our part of the world?"

"Certainly!" said Maso. "At least two kinds, of most extraordinary virtues. Of one sort are the grey stones of Settignano and Montisci, by whose miraculous power wheat is converted into flour, when they're turned into mill-stones. That's why in those sections they have a saying, *God sends us boons, but Montisci mill-stones.* But the trouble is, there are so many of these stones in our country, that people think as little of them as the Basques of emeralds, of which they have whole mountains over there—Oh, much bigger than Mount Morello. And how they do shine in the darkness of midnight! You can imagine! Then there's another thing. If anyone troubled to take some fine grey stones, just as they are, before they're bored for the mills, and set them into rings, and present them to the Sultan, he could obtain any price he asked for them. As for the other sort that's to be found around here—it's what we lapidaries call the heliotrope, a stone of extraordinary virtue, for if anybody wears it on his person, he is invisible wherever he is, all the time he has it about him."

"That's quite a virtue!" said Calandrino. "But where can you get hold of that kind?"

"As a matter of fact, generally in the Mugnone," Maso informed him.

"Really! Just how big is this stone, and what color is it?" he asked.

"It comes in various sizes," answered Maso, "some of them bigger than others. All of them are dark, however, verging on black."

Calandrino stowed this precious knowledge away in his cranium, and pretending he had an urgent engagement, took leave of Maso, though as a matter of fact he had made up his mind to go in search of the stone. He decided, however, that it was wiser not to embark upon it until he had first informed Bruno and Buffalmacco, whom he especially cherished, and he went to look for them, so they might all set out immediately to discover these precious stones, before anyone else got there ahead of them. Up and down the streets he wandered, without coming upon his friends, though the whole morning was gone and a good part of the afternoon. Finally, he remembered they were engaged on a painting in the nuns' convent at Faenza, and despite the merciless heat he abandoned all the work he had to do and away he went, almost on the run. When he got there, he sent for them and blurted out:

"Listen, boys, if you'll only do as I say, we can be the richest men in Florence, for I've learned from a man who certainly knows what he's talking about, of a wonderful stone that's to be found in the Mugnone. Just think, if you carry it with you nobody can see you, nobody at all! We ought to make it our business to go after it right away, before anybody else gets a start on us! We'll surely find it, for I can tell it at a glance. Then, once we've found it, what's there to do, but to stuff it into our pockets and go to the exchange, where, as you know, the tables are always piled high with goldpieces? Then whisk! Away we'll go with as much as we can lay hands on, and nobody will be able to see us! In this way, we can get rich overnight, without having to daub our traces on the walls all day long, like so many snails!"

On hearing him rave, Bruno and Buffalmacco shook with contained laughter, and exchanged understanding glances from the corners of their eyes, pretending an exaggerated wonder, and approving of his advice.

"But what's this wonder-working stone called?" they asked.

Calandrino, whose head was full of sawdust, had already forgotten. "What do we care what the name of it is," he replied, "if we know what it's good for? Come, I think we'd better be hurrying, if we want to look for it."

"Wait a moment," said Bruno. "What's its description?"

"Description? It's all descriptions," said Calandrino. "But all of them are nearly black in color, so I guess we'd better pick up every black stone we can find, until we hit upon the one we're looking for. Come, move along, now. Let's not waste any more time."

"Just a minute," said Bruno, and addressing Buffalmacco, "I think Calandrino's proposal is a good one," he said, "but I doubt whether this is the best hour for the enterprise, for the sun is at its height and striking full on the banks of the Mugnone. Many a stone will therefore seem whitish which, in the morning, before the heat of the sun has dried up all the wet, appears black. Moreover, to-day's a workday, and a lot of people will be sure to be around for something or other, who, if they saw us looking about, might guess what we're after and follow our example, so that one of them might accidentally lay hands on the magic stone, making all our labor go for nothing. This sort of thing, in my opinion, and you will agree with me, should be undertaken early in the morning, when we can easily tell a black stone from a white, and on a holiday, so that none will be around to spy on us."

Buffalmacco said Bruno was perfectly right, and Calandrino agreed, whereupon they made arrangements to go in search of the stone together, the following Sunday morning. Calandrino especially swore them to secrecy, saying that he had been told of the stone in the strictest confidence. Then, after the warning, he launched upon the wonders he had heard of the land of Bengodi, swearing the most solemn oaths that it was all as he said. However, after Calandrino had gone, Bruno and Buffalmacco laid the plan which they were to follow.

Calandrino, meanwhile, waited with the utmost impatience for Sunday morning to dawn, and at the first streak of light got up, called for his comrades, and away they sauntered together through San Gallo and down the banks of the Mugnone, looking high and low for the wonderful stone. Far in advance of them raced Calandrino, being by far the most zealous of the three, skipping hither and thither. Whenever his eyes fell on a black stone, down he pounced upon it, picked it up, and thrust it into the bosom of his shirt. His two friends followed, gathering a stone here and a stone there, lackadaisically. Not so with Calandrino. He had scarcely gone any distance at all, before the bosom of his shirt was too full to contain any more. Picking up the skirts of his jacket, which was not skimpily cut, he made a capacious bag of them, by tucking the hems into his belt. Before long, that, too, was full. At last, converting his cloak into another sack, he also filled that to bursting with the stones.

Now when the two friends saw that Calandrino was loaded like a pack-mule, and that it was almost time for dinner, Bruno, according to their plan, asked Buffalmacco, "Why, where's Calandrino?"

Buffalmacco saw him clearly enough a few yards away, but turning about and scanning the distance from all angles, he replied, "I don't know, though just a few minutes ago he was right by us."

"A few minutes ago?" repeated Bruno. "I'll bet by this time he must be home, having a good dinner, and here he has left us like two idiots, looking for black stones on the sides of the Mugnone!"

"It serves us perfectly right if he did," said Buffalmacco, "since we were such fools as to believe the nonsense he told us. My word, who else would have been so shallow-pated as to believe we could find such a magic stone in the Mugnone?"

When Calandrino caught the drift of their conversation, he was certain the wonder-working stone had accidentally come into his hands, and that by virtue of its magic power, he was invisible to his friends, although he was almost under their noses. Overjoyed at this stroke of luck, he thought it best to make his way homeward without telling them a thing about it, and turning on his heels, retraced his steps.

"What are we going to do?" said Buffalmacco to Bruno on seeing Calandrino's move. "Why the devil don't we go?"

"That's right, let's go," agreed the other. "But I swear a solemn oath, Calandrino will play no more of his tricks on me. Believe me, if I had him within reach as I had him this morning, I'd give him such a rap on the heel with this stone, that he'd bear a souvenir of his prank for a month."

It took him longer to utter the threat than to fling the flint at Calandrino's shins; who jumped at the sting and hopped on one foot, but let out no sound, save a whistle of pain, and went on. Then Buffalmacco, taking and aiming one of the pebbles he had picked up, said to his friend, "Look at this magnificent stone. Oh, if I could only sling it at Calandrino's backside!"

Letting it go, he struck a good sharp blow with it on Calandrino's rump. To make a long story short, they kept up their pastime, accompanying each flying stone with some jest or other, from the banks of the Mugnone as far as Porta San Gallo, where they threw down their load, and stopped a while to chat with the guards at the toll-gate, who had previously been informed of their joke and accordingly had let Calandrino go by, pretending not to see him, to their huge amusement.

Meanwhile, Calandrino lost no time, but walked straight to his house near Canto alla Macina, luck conspiring so far that all the way from the stream up to the town, nobody had a word to say to him, though the passersby were infrequent enough, most of them, at that hour, enjoying a good dinner. At last he came to his house and went in, stones and all.

As it was, Mistress Tessa, his wife, a comely, good, home-loving woman, was standing at the head of the stairs, annoyed at his delay, and when she caught sight of him she said, crossly, "A fine fellow you are, the devil take you! Here everybody's done with dinner and you're just arriving!"

Calandrino, realizing from her speech that she had seen him, was torn with anguish and disappointment. "O woe, woe is me!" he groaned. "Is that you up there, vile wretch? Woe! Woe! You've ruined me, but by the Lord, I'll give it to you for that!"

Mounting first to a small room in the attic, he threw down the load of stones he had brought home. Then, rushing upon his wife in a frenzy, he seized her by the braids, flung her down at his feet, and belabored her with blows and kicks until he could hardly move his arms and legs, leaving her with scarcely a hair on her head, or a whole bone in her body. In vain the poor woman implored his mercy.

Buffalmacco and Bruno, in the meantime, had had a hearty

laugh with the guards at the toll-gate, and then had started out to follow Calandrino home at a leisurely pace. When they came to the door of his house, they heard the sounds of the merciless thrashing he was giving his wife, and called him, as though they had just arrived. Calandrino, red as a turkey-cock, and out of breath with exertion, looked out of the window, asking them to come up, which they did, pretending to be cross with him.

Upstairs, they came upon a room full of stones and pebbles, with Mistress Tessa in a corner, weeping pitifully, her hair disheveled, her clothes torn, and her face bruised and livid, while in another, Calandrino slumped dejected in a chair, untidy and panting with fatigue.

They stared about them a while in silence, and then remarked, "What's this, Calandrino? Are you thinking of becoming a stone-mason, with all this load of stones here? And what's the matter with Mistress Tessa?" they added. "It looks very much as if you'd given her a beating. Fie upon you! What sort of behavior is this?"

Calandrino, exhausted from the weight of the stones he had carried, the frenzy of the thrashing he had given his wife, and the irritation he felt at the loss of what he thought a stroke of luck, could scarcely gather sufficient wit to answer in anything but inarticulate grunts, so that after waiting for an answer, Buffalmacco continued:

"It seems to me, Calandrino, that if you had a grudge to vent, you shouldn't have taken it out on us as you did, first dragging us along with you to look for a magic stone in the Mugnone, and then leaving us there, like two fools, without so much as saying Good-bye, or By your leave, and coming back home by yourself! We're considerably offended at your behavior, I'll have you know, and I assure you this is the last time you'll ever fool us."

Calandrino struggled to speak, and at last managed to say, "Don't be angry, friends. The case is different from what you suppose. I had found the stone—ah, miserable wretch that I am! Do you want me to prove I'm telling the truth? Well, then, when you were asking each other about me, I was scarcely ten yards away from you, and seeing that you were about to go and didn't see me, I took the lead and walked on home ahead of you all the way."

Beginning from the beginning, he told them the whole tale of what they had said and done, showing them the bruises the pebbles had made on his back and shins. "I want to tell you further," he continued, "that as I came through the toll-gates with all these stones in the bosom of my shirt, nobody stopped me, not so much as with a word—and you know what pests those guards are, with their noses anxious to pry into everything! What's more, I met a number of friends and comrades in the street, who would ordinarily have stopped to invite me to a drink, but not a word did they say, not a syllable, as though they hadn't seen me! Finally, I reached the house, and who should pop up in front of me, but this damned devil of a woman, who saw me at once, for being a woman she has the power of making anything lose its virtue! But you know that as well as I. And so it was that I, who might have considered myself the luckiest man in Florence, am now the most unlucky! Oh, but I gave it to her for this! I beat her as long as I had the strength to do it, and I don't know what prevented me from slitting her throat—damn the moment I ever laid eyes on her, and the day she set foot in this house!"

His rage kindling to sudden flame, he would have got up to give her another drubbing.

During his account, the two friends made a great show of astonishment, although they nearly exploded in their effort to contain their laughter. However, when they saw him leave his chair in a fury to give poor Mistress Tessa another back-basting, they interposed and held him back, saying it had not been the woman's fault at all. Indeed, the blame was all his, since he was aware that women have the power of depriving things of their virtue, and had not warned her to keep out of his way all that day. Yes, they were sure God must have made him forget the precaution, either because that stroke of luck was not destined to be his, or because he had intended from the beginning to cheat his comrades, to whom he should have communicated his good fortune, the moment he had found the stone.

At last, after a great deal of parleying, they succeeded, though not without much trouble, in reconciling the doleful woman to her husband, whom they left vexed and gloomy amid a houseful of stones.

✳

# THE FOURTH STORY

*The rector of the church of Fiesole is in love with a woman who does not care for him, and thinking he is in bed with her, lies with a slattern of hers until the lady's brothers come in with the bishop, and expose him.*

WHEN ELISA HAD REACHED THE END OF HER STORY, WHICH SHE had told to the huge amusement of the entire party, the queen indicated that it was her pleasure for Emilia to continue.

Virtuous ladies, she began with alacrity, I know full well we've already had plenty of examples to show us how insidiously priests, friars and clergymen of all orders lay siege to our honor, but since, even if we continued from now until doomsday, there still would be enough left to tell on that score, I intend to add another instance to those already related. This time, it is about a rector who would have been willing to turn the world upside down to gain the love of a noble lady, whether she wished it or not. But she gave him all he was looking for, thanks to her wit.

As all of you know, I'm sure, Fiesole, the crest of whose hill we can see from here, was once a large and very important city, though there is little of its ancient splendor left now. Nevertheless, it remained a bishop's seat all through the years, and retains that honor to this day.

Once upon a time, a certain widow by the name of Piccarda used to live there in a very comfortable, though not too large house near the main cathedral, and as she had no great fortune, she spent the better part of the year in town with her two brothers, both of them genteel, respectable youths.

Now Madam Piccarda was still comparatively young, beautiful and charming. Almost every Sunday, she used to attend the services at the cathedral, the rector of which fell so passionately in love with her, that he had no mind for anything else. Indeed, he was so tormented by his passion that he lost no time in revealing his desire to her himself, pleading with her to return his affection and cherish him as he did her.

The rector was a man already well on in years, though poor in wit, bold and snobbish to boot, and with an exalted opinion of how much he could venture. His manners were well-nigh nonexistent, and the modicum he possessed was replete with arrogance and unpleasantness. He was, moreover, such a perverse, disagreeable curmudgeon, that scarcely anyone bore him any love. But if there was an individual who might have been said to love him least of all, it was Madam Piccarda, who not only loved him not a jot, but hated him more than a sick-headache.

On hearing his offer, she replied, like the prudent woman she was, "Father, I know I should be very grateful that you love me as you do, and I ought to return the same regard. I shall gladly endeavor to do so, but I want you to understand that nothing unworthy must ever come between your love and mine. You are a priest, and my spiritual father, and you are now on the brink of old age, all of which should tend to make you both virtuous and chaste. As for me, I'm no longer a child, and such amorous pastimes are not becoming to a woman of my years, and a widow, of whom, you ought to know, people expect the most exemplary behavior. Therefore, leave me out of your reckonings, please, for I'll never give you the kind of love you want, nor do I wish to receive the like from you."

That was as much as the rector could obtain from her at his first attempt. He did not give himself up for chastened or vanquished, however, but with his usual arrogance solicited her many other times by means of missives, messages, and whenever he saw her in church, even by broaching the subject himself.

The annoyance and vexation of the unpleasant suit were becoming more than the lady could bear, whereupon she determined to get rid of the nuisance by foul means, as he deserved, since he would not accept the good. Still, she did not care to undertake any measures before she had consulted her brothers, whom she informed of the rector's behavior and of what she intended to do to put an end to it. They gave her permission to carry out her plan to the full, whereupon in a few days she went to church again according to her custom.

The rector no sooner spied her, than he approached her with his usual mock-paternal solicitude, to harp upon the topic near his heart. On seeing him approach, she assumed a joviality which she was far from feeling, and then, drawing to a corner of the church, she said with a deep-drawn sigh, after listening to his customary blandishments:

"Father, I have often heard that no matter how strong the fortress, it is bound to fall before a daily attack. Such, as I can see, is my own case, for you besieged me so long and so persistently, what with honeyed words and courtesies and other gallantries, that you've at last succeeded in making me break my resolution. Now, since you will have me so, I confess myself ready to yield to you."

The rector beamed with joy. "Thank you, daughter, from the bottom of my heart," he said. "To be frank, I couldn't help wondering how you could have resisted so long—a thing quite without parallel in my experience. Indeed, I've often said to myself, 'If women were made of silver, they wouldn't be worth a brass farthing, for not a one of them could bear up under the hammer.' But enough of that for the present. Tell me, rather, when we can be together, and where?"

"Dear father," she replied, "as for when, it's for you to choose, since I've no husband to whom I'm accountable for the way I spend my nights. But as for the place, I've no idea."

"What, you've no idea!" said he. "And what about your house?"

She said, "You know, father, that I have two younger brothers living with me, who are always inviting parties of friends to make merry both day and night. The house is none too large, and we could not possibly be together there, unless you were willing to act like a dummy, without saying a word or making a sound, and stay in the dark, like the blind. If that suits you, I can manage it, as they never bother to come into my room. The only trouble is, that their bedroom is right next to mine, so that we couldn't even whisper the least little word without their hearing it."

"Well, we can put up with it for a night or two," rejoined the rector, "until I think of some other place, where we can be more at our ease."

"It's up to you, father," said she. "There's one thing I want to beg of you, though. Keep this thing secret, so that no one will ever hear a word of it."

Quoth the rector, "Never fear, my dear. And if you can, manage to let us meet to-night."

"Very well," she said, and giving him instructions about how to get there, and when, she said good-bye and returned home.

As it was, Madam Piccarda had a scullery-maid who was rather ripe in years, and had the ugliest, most villainous face anyone could ever hope to see. Her nose was squashed into her face, her mouth thick-lipped and twisted, her teeth huge and all askew, and she had, moreover, a marvelous squint. Furthermore, her eyes were always rheumy, and her complexion was sallow, verging on a yellow so tinged with green, that you would never have thought she spent the summers at Fiesole, but rather at Sinigaglia. As though that weren't enough, she was lame on one side, and crooked-hipped. Her real name was Ciuta, but because she was blessed with such a phenomenally bull-doggish face, she had been dubbed Ciutazza, Ugly Ciuta, by common accord. Though she was no rare beauty, she still had a touch of humorous shrewdness in her make-up.

When Madam Piccarda came home, she called her maid and said, "Listen, Ciutazza, if you'll do me a favor to-night, I'll give you a lovely new smock."

"A smock!" exclaimed Ciutazza to herself, and aloud, "Why, madam, if you were to give me a smock," she said, "I'd jump in the flames, to say the least."

"Good!" said Madam Piccarda. "Well, then, to-night I'd like you to lie in my bed with a man. Be nice to him, caress him, but be careful you don't say a word, so that my brothers won't hear you, for as you know, my brothers sleep right next door. When you've done that for me, I'll let you have the smock."

"I'll sleep with six of them, let alone one, if I have to," said the girl.

With the first shadows of night, our gay spark the rector came, as he had been told, while Madam Piccarda's two brothers posted themselves in their room, as she had directed, taking care they were not heard. The passionate lover glided stealthily into his lady's chamber, in pitch darkness, and groped his way to the bed as she had instructed him; Ciutazza, well-instructed by her mistress, came in and did likewise. Then our lusty rector, thinking he had his mistress by his side, clasped the wench in his arms and fell to kissing her passionately, without saying a word. Ciutazza returned his caresses, and soon the rector played a merry sport with her, as he took possession of what he believed to be the bounties he had so long coveted.

This part of her work done, Madam Piccarda sent her brothers to carry out the rest of the plan. Accordingly, they stole out of the room and went toward the square, where, much to their delight, luck favored their plot even beyond their expectation; for the bishop, whom they were seeking, coming to meet them as soon as he caught sight of them, invited himself of his own accord to go to their home, and there, as the heat was intense, to spend a few enjoyable hours over a friendly cup. Together, they returned to the house, sat down to rest in a pleasant, cool little courtyard gay with many lights, and drank one another's healths with great relish, in sparkling bowls of their excellent sack. After the bishop had been entertained with drink, the young men said to him:

"Your worship, since you were so gracious as to honor us by your visit to this modest little house of ours, as we were coming to invite you, we should like you to do us the courtesy of looking at something we wish to show you."

"Gladly," said the bishop.

Taking a lighted torch in his hand, one of the youths led the way to the room where our jolly rector was lying with Ciutazza. The bishop and his company followed close behind. Now the lusty gallant had made the best of his gallop, so eager had be been to reach his destination, so that by the time the unexpected guests arrived, he had gone more than three stones, which had exhausted him not a little, and plunged him into sound slumber, with Ciuta still tight in his embrace, despite the heat. Thus it was, when the youth entered the room with the light in his hand, that the rector was revealed to the bishop, and the others who had followed close behind. Suddenly, he woke up, and at the sight of the bishop and all his company, he was so mortified, that he pulled his head in under the covers.

Grave were the reproaches the bishop heaped upon him, which culminated with his asking the culprit to come out of hiding, and look full on the creature with whom he had been lying. Then the lady's trick dawned clear upon the rector's mind. What with the realization and the dishonor he had cast upon himself, he was the most miserable man alive. Trembling, he dressed at the bishop's command, and he was marched away under close guard to the rectory, to expiate his grievous sin.

Later, the bishop wishing to know how the rector had come to be lying with Ciutazza in their house, the two brothers related the story from the beginning, which made him praise Madam Piccarda's virtue and their forbearance alike, in not wishing to stain their hands with the blood of a priest, but preferring to deal with the wretch as he deserved.

The rector was made to suffer a forty-day penance for his sin; but frustrated passion and rancor made him repine more than forty days and nine, all the more because, for a long time, he could scarcely set foot in the streets without being pointed at by the urchins, who cried, "Look! Look! There's the man who went to bed with Ciutazza," which so galled him that he nearly went mad. So it was that the honest laymen put an end to the importunate rector's unpleasant suit, while Ciutazza gained a brand new smock and a jolly night in the bargain.

✳

# THE FIFTH STORY

*Three merry scalawags pull down a judge's pantaloons, while he is on the bench hearing his cases.*

SO EMILIA TOLD HER STORY, AFTER WHICH, THE WIDOW HAVING received unanimous applause, the queen looked at Filostrato, saying: "Now it is your turn to speak."

"Your servant," he replied promptly, and began:

Winsome ladies, the merry fellow mentioned by Elisa a little while ago, that is, Maso del Saggio, made me lay aside the story I had intended telling, in favor of another about him and several cronies of his. There's nothing in it, I assure you, that is scandalous, even though it does contain certain words you blush to use. It is such an amusing tale, however, that I shall tell it, in spite of everything.

You've all heard of the provosts from the Marches, who often come to our city. They are mean-spirited creatures as a rule, and so petty and narrow in their way of living, that whatever they undertake seems degraded to a petty, worthless little business. Such is their innate meanness and avarice, that even the judges and notaries who trail at their heels look more like clodhoppers dragged from their plows or cobblers' benches, than products of the law-schools.

On a certain occasion, one of these gentlemen from the Marches came to act as provost here, and among the hosts of judges he brought along with him was a certain Messer Nicola da San Lepidio—for so he called himself—a man who looked more like a tinker than anything else. Nevertheless, he was raised to the bench, and like the rest of the judges, heard criminal cases.

Though our honest citizens have nothing to do in the courtroom, still they sometimes go there, and as it happened, Maso del Saggio shambled in one morning, looking for one of his friends. While looking about, he chanced to glance in the direction of Messer Nicola. "A strange-looking bird," thought he, and examined him narrowly. The fellow's cap was black with soot; a sorry-looking quill and horn hung at his side; the tunic he wore was longer than his cloak—in short, he offered many peculiarities foreign to the nature of a well-bred gentleman. But what was most astonishing, in Maso's opinion, was the pair of breeches that graced him which, as he sat, and his clothes spread open back and front because of the stinginess of their cut, revealed a baggy seat, that hung at least half-way down his thighs.

Maso didn't waste much time idly staring, but forgetting the purpose of his search, he went a-hunting newer sport, and sought out two of his comrades, Ribi and Matteuzzo, both of them scalawags, no less merry than himself.

"As you love me," said Maso to them, "come with me to the court-room, where I'll show you the most peculiar scare-crow you've ever laid eyes on."

Together, they hied to the palace of justice, where he showed them the stylish judge and his breeches which, even at a distance, made them roar with laughter. Drawing nearer the bench where our venerable judge was sitting, they perceived it would not be difficult for one to slip under it. What's more, they also observed that the boards on which he rested his feet were broken, so that it would be no great matter for a hand to be slid through, and the whole arm as well.

Maso said to his friends, "Let's pull these precious breeches off, altogether. It's so easy!"

The other two had already perceived how readily it could be accomplished, whereupon conferring on the way to go about it, they made off and returned the following morning. The court-room was crowded. Matteuzzo, taking advantage of it, slipped unobserved under the bench, and crawled right under the spot where the judge's feet were dangling.

Meanwhile, Maso approached the venerable gentleman, and clutching him on one side by the tail of his gown, as Ribi followed suit on the other, he began, "Your honor, O your honor! Please, for God's sake, grasp that insignificant little thief on the other side of you, before he has a chance to fly the coop, and let him give me back the pair of boots he stole from me. He denies it, but I tell you I saw him having new soles put on them, scarcely a month ago!"

On the other hand, Ribi was shouting at the top of his lungs, "Don't you believe him, your honor, for he's a notorious rapscallion. He knows I came here to reclaim the pack-saddles he stole from me, that's why he's telling you that story about the boots, which I've always had in my house—as a matter of fact until yesterday. Trecca, my next-door neighbor, will be my witness, and Grassa, who sells lungs and tripes and lights, and the man who sweeps up the garbage at Santa Maria Verzaia, who saw him as he was coming from the country."

Here Maso interrupted Ribi, shouting to drown him out, and Ribi, not to be daunted, shouted even louder. Meanwhile, as the judge stood up and came closer to them, the better to grasp what they were haranguing about, Matteuzzo saw his chance, and thrusting his hand through the broken plank, got hold of the seat of the venerable pantaloons, and tugged for all he was worth. Down came the breeches in a trice, for the judge was skinny, and had no flesh on his buttocks. When he felt what was happening, though he could not tell exactly what it was, the judge tried to pull his gown together, to cover his nakedness and sit down, but Maso on the one hand, and Ribi on the other still clutched him, shouting with all their might, "Your honor, you are behaving outrageously, not to listen to my case, and trying to get out of giving me justice by stealing out of here. You know I can't be given a warrant in this city for such a small case as this!"

They cried for justice so long, and held on to the judge's coat until everyone in the courtroom was at last aware that the venerable's breeches had been pulled down. Then Matteuzzo, who, from under the plank, had held them by the seat a considerable time, let them go, and stole out of the palace without being seen, at which Ribi, satisfied with his own share in the work, cried, "I swear to God I'll bring my case before the Mayor," and released the judge's coat. Maso, too, released his hold, crying, "Not I, though! I'll keep on coming here day in and day out, until I find you less distracted than you seem to be this morning, your honor!" Then, having spoken, both of them scampered away in opposite directions, out of the court, as fast as their heels could carry them.

As for the venerable judge, he hoisted up his breeches before the whole assembly, as though he were just rising from a nap, and then, seeing how matters stood, asked where the two plaintiffs had gone, who had been quarreling about the boots and pack-saddles. However, as the two rogues were nowhere in sight, he fell to ranting and vowing by God's bowels that he would determine, for his own information, whether it was the custom of the Florentines to pull down their magistrates' breeches while they sat on the bench, hearing law-cases. The provost, too, on learning what had happened, raised the devil. But when his friends made him understand that the trick had been played only to show him that the Florentines knew full well that he had brought tatterdemalions with him, instead of judges, in order to cut down expenses, he thought it best to curb his tongue and, for the moment, no more was said about it.

# THE SIXTH STORY

*Bruno and Buffalmacco steal Calandrino's porker, and then persuade him to try to get it back by means of an ordeal of ginger cakes and wine. One after the other, they give him two dog-biscuits prepared with aloes, by means of which Calandrino apparently stands accused. Thereupon, they compel him to pay them a bribe, by the threat of telling everything to his wife.*

HARDLY HAD FILOSTRATO MADE AN END OF HIS STORY, WHICH HAD roused them to resounding mirth, than the queen requested Filomena to continue.

Gracious ladies, she began, just as Filostrato was drawn by mention of Maso's name, to tell the story you've been hearing, I've likewise been inspired by the jest of Calandrino and his comrades, to relate another story about them, which I believe you will enjoy.

I needn't tell you who Calandrino, Bruno and Buffalmacco were, for you've already heard enough about them, so I shall proceed without further prelude. You must know that not very far from Florence itself, Calandrino had a bit of property which his wife had brought him with her marriage-portion, and among the various benefits he derived from it, year by year, was a fine porker. Accordingly, it was his custom to go to the country every December, and there slaughter the hog and have it salted.

One year, it happened that Mistress Tessa was not feeling well, whereupon Calandrino went by himself to kill the porker.

The circumstance reached the ears of Bruno and Buffalmacco who, on learning that his wife was not going with him, betook themselves to an intimate friend of theirs, a priest who lived near Calandrino's farm, and there settled down for a few days. The morning of their arrival, Calandrino had just killed the pig, and seeing his friends with the priest, hailed them and said, "Welcome, welcome! Come over and I'll show you what a good husbandman I am!"

Taking them to his house, he showed them the porker. They perceived that it was a fine, fat, succulent fellow which, according to Calandrino, was destined to be salted for him and his family.

"What an idiot you are!" exclaimed Bruno. "Sell it, why don't you, and let's make merry with the proceeds! Then you can tell your wife it was stolen from you."

"I think not," said Calandrino. "She wouldn't believe me, in the first place, and she'd chase me out of the house. Don't trouble yourselves about it, for I'll never do any such thing."

They employed many methods of persuasion, but without success. At last, he invited them to dinner, but so half-heartedly that they did not accept, and went their way.

Said Bruno to Buffalmacco, "What do you say, shall we carry off that porker to-night?"

"But how can we do it?" asked Buffalmacco.

"I've seen to the how of it, already," said his friend, "provided he doesn't move it from where it is now."

"Good! I'm with you. Let's do it," said Buffalmacco. "And why shouldn't we? Then we can enjoy it with our host, the domine."

The parson, too, said he would relish the sport, whereupon Bruno said, "We have to be crafty in this business. You know, Buffalmacco, how stingy Calandrino is, and how eagerly he drinks when someone else pays the bill. Let's call for him and take him to the tavern, where the parson will make believe he's treating us as his friends, and will not allow him to spend a penny. Calandrino will then drink himself senseless, and everything will be simple enough, since he's all alone in the house."

Bruno's suggestion was put into effect. Accordingly, when Calandrino saw that the priest would not permit anyone to pay, he drank with a will, and though he had no need of such ballast, soon loaded himself excellently well. It was well on into the night, when they left the tavern. Calandrino set off without worrying about supper, and going straight home, flung himself upon the bed for the night, confident that he had bolted the door.

The two friends went out to supper with the domine, and as soon as it was over, provided themselves with certain instruments for breaking into Calandrino's house, and stole thither quietly. On finding the door open, they walked in. Then, taking the pig off its hook, they made off with it to the parson's house, where they set it down and then retired to sleep.

The following morning, when Calandrino's brains were clear of the fumes of wine, he got up and went downstairs. Alas, on looking around, he saw no pig and the door wide-open. He ran, hither and thither, asking all and sundry if anyone knew who had made off with the pig, but when he could learn nothing, he set up a howl, "Alas! Alack! Poor me! Miserable me! My pig has been stolen!"

As for Bruno and Buffalmacco, the moment they got up, off they went to Calandrino's house, to hear what he had to say about the pig. "Alas! my friends! Alas!" he cried, almost in tears on catching sight of them, "my precious porker has been spirited away!"

But Bruno drew close to him and whispered, "Well, it is a wonder you were sensible once in your life!"

"Alas! I'm telling the truth!" said Calandrino.

"That's right," Bruno advised him, "shout at the top of your lungs, so that people will think it's really as you say."

Calandrino howled all the louder, "I swear to you, it's really and truly been stolen from me. On my word! I swear!"

"Excellent! Wonderful," applauded Bruno. "That's the way you should go about it. Shout! Shout! Let them all hear, so that it'll seem true!"

"You're driving me to damnation!" bawled Calandrino. "I'm telling you what's what, and still you don't believe me! I swear to you—may I be hanged by the neck, if the pig hasn't been stolen!"

Then cried Bruno, "Heavens! How is it possible? Why, I saw it only yesterday with my own eyes! Would you have me believe it flew away of its own accord?"

"It's just as I say!" insisted Calandrino.

"My Lord!" gasped Bruno. "Can it really be?"

"I should think so!" said Calandrino. "That's just how it is, and I'm so desperate about it, that I don't know how I'll ever have the nerve to go home again. My wife will not believe it—I take that for granted—and even if she should, I'd not have a moment's peace with her the whole year!"

"It's a pretty serious predicament, God help me—if it's true," replied Bruno. "But only yesterday, Calandrino, I prompted you to say this, and I'd hate to think you're deceiving us, as well as your wife."

Calandrino flew into a fury and railed, "Hell! Why will you exasperate me, and make me curse God and the saints and all that's holy? I tell you my porker was spirited away last night!"

At that, Buffalmacco interposed, "If it is really so, we must see what we can do to get it back again, if there's any chance."

"How can we go about it?" asked Calandrino.

"Surely nobody took the trouble to come all the way from India, to steal your pig," replied Buffalmacco. "It must have been some neighbor of yours. If you could manage to get the folks hereabout together, I know how to put them through the ordeal of bread and cheese, and we'd immediately find out who did the taking."

"A fine suggestion!" mocked Bruno. "Much you'd find out that way, from the crafty fellows of this neighborhood! I'd lay down my head that some one of them has it, but the moment you suggest bread and cheese, he'd see through the ruse and decline to put in an appearance."

"What's to be done, then?" asked Buffalmacco.

"I have a suggestion," replied Bruno. "Perform the ordeal with delicious ginger-cakes and good white wine, and invite them all to drink. They'll never suspect it, and so they'll all come. As for the ginger-cakes, they could be blessed as easily as the bread and cheese."

"That's a great idea," said Buffalmacco. "What do you say, Calandrino? Shall we do it?"

"By all means, do, for God's sake," he said. "If I only knew who had the pig, I'd be half resigned to the loss."

"So be it, then," said Bruno. "I'm even willing to go as far as Florence, to buy those things for you, if you give me the money."

Calandrino had perhaps some forty shillings on his person, and these he gave Bruno. Immediately, Bruno betook himself to a friend of his, a spice-dealer in Florence, and bought a pound of dainty ginger-cakes, ordering him to prepare for him two dog-biscuits, mixed with a compound of fresh hepatic aloes. He had them covered with a sugar-icing like the rest, and in order not to confuse or mistake them, had them marked with a little secret sign, by which he could distinguish which was which. Then buying a flask of good white wine, he returned to Calandrino in the country and said:

"It's up to you now to invite all the people you suspect, to have a drink with you to-morrow morning. It's a holiday, and folks will gladly come. As for me, I'll perform the spell on the cakes to-night, with the help of Buffalmacco, and bring them back to your house in the morning. For your sake, I'll even distribute them, and do and say all that's required to be said and done."

Calandrino followed his suggestion, and the next morning he collected about the elm, in front of the village-church, a considerable group of country-folks, and whatever young Florentines happened to be there. Bruno and Buffalmacco presently made their appearance with the box of ginger-cakes and the flagon of wine, and arranging the men in a circle, the former addressed them:

"Gentlemen, it is my duty to inform you why you are assembled here, so that if anything should happen to rouse displeasure, you'll have nothing to blame me for. Last night, Calandrino, here present, was robbed of an excellent fat porker, and he has not been able to find out who took it. Since only someone present could have stolen it, he is giving each of you one of these cakes to eat and some wine to drink, in order to discover the guilty party. I warn you in advance, that whoever has the pig in his possession, will not be able to swallow the cake. Indeed, it will be bitterer than gall in his mouth, and he'll be compelled to spit it out. Therefore, I suggest that in order to avoid the mortification of being found out in this crowd, he had better confess his deed to the domine, and I'll drop the matter right here."

All the men present manifested their willingness to eat the cakes, whereupon Bruno, placing them on line and putting Calandrino with the rest, began at one end, and distributed a cake to each one. On coming to Calandrino, he took one of the dog-biscuits and handed it to him. Immediately, Calandrino put it into his mouth and began to chew; but scarcely had his tongue tasted the bitterness of the aloes, than he spewed out the cake because of its unbearable taste. The men, meanwhile, were watching one another narrowly, to see who would spit out his cake, and as Bruno still went on distributing them, pretending to know nothing of what was going on, he heard someone ask behind him, "Why, what's the meaning of this, Calandrino?"

He quickly turned around, and seeing that Calandrino had spat out his cake, said, "Wait a minute! Maybe he spat it out for some other reason. Come, here's another for you, Calandrino." Taking the second biscuit, he thrust it into Calandrino's mouth, and finished distributing the remaining cakes.

Now if Calandrino had found the first cake bitter, the second was even more so. Still, he was ashamed to spit it out, and kept on chewing it for a while, shedding tears the size of hazel-nuts, so enormous were they! Finally, unable to bear the bitterness any longer, he got rid of the second cake, as he had done the first.

Buffalmacco, meanwhile, was busy pouring out the wine for Bruno and the company, and when all of them saw what was happening, they said with one accord, that Calandrino must have stolen his own porker. Some even went so far as to give him a good piece of their minds. At last, when they had gone and only Bruno and Buffalmacco remained, the latter began:

"I was certain all along that you had stolen your own pig, Calandrino, and wanted to make us believe someone else had taken it, so that you would not have had to treat us to a miserable little drink, out of the profits."

Calandrino, who had not yet got rid of the bitter taste of the aloes, swore again and again that he had not taken the pig; but Buffalmacco still persisted. "Tell us, friend, all joking aside," he said, "how much did you get for it? Six florins, eh?"

Calandrino almost went mad with exasperation, whereupon Bruno took up the strain, "Listen, Calandrino, I want you to know that a certain fellow who ate and drank with us just now, told me you're keeping a young girl here as your mistress, and giving her whatever you can manage to put away, yes, and that he was sure you had sent her that pig. You've been learning some peculiar tricks, these days. Some time ago you took us gathering black stones, down the banks of the Mugnone, leaving us flat after you had led us on a wild goose-chase, and then trying to make us believe you had found the magic one. Now, by swearing yourself black and blue you think you can convince us that the pig you must have given away or sold, was spirited away from you. But we're used to your tricks, and well aware of them, so you won't be fooling us any more. Well then, to be frank, since we've gone through a world of trouble getting the charm ready for the ordeal, we want you to treat us to a couple pairs of capons, otherwise we'll tell Mistress Tessa the whole story."

Calandrino saw he was wasting his pains, without being believed; therefore, thinking he had had misery enough, and not over-anxious to suffer his wife's temper in the bargain, he gave two braces of capons to the rogues who, after having salted the pork for themselves, went off to Florence with their booty, leaving Calandrino gulled and the poorer for his losses.

# THE SEVENTH STORY

*A scholar falls in love with a widow, who has another gallant. She makes the new lover spend a whole winter's night waiting for her in the snow; but he succeeds, by his cunning, in having her remain naked on a tower all during a hot July day, at the mercy of the sun, mosquitoes and hornets.*

MUCH AMUSED, THE WOMEN LAUGHED AT THE MISHAPS OF POOR Calandrino, and they would have been even more amused, had they not felt sorry to see him deprived of his capons, by the same rascals who had stolen his pig; but when the story was over, the queen commanded Pampinea to tell hers, and she began without delay:

Dearest ladies, it often happens that cunning is outwitted by cunning, so that it is foolish to take pleasure in laughing at another's expense. We've had much fun, listening to the pranks which people have played upon one another in many of the foregoing stories, none of which seems to have been indulged in as a sort of retribution. In my story, however, I wish to rouse you to pity, of a just punishment that a woman of our city brought down upon her own head, as a result of a practical joke she played. Indeed, she nearly lost her life in consequence. Perhaps this tale of mine will not be entirely unprofitable to you, as it may teach you the salutary lesson of being careful of the way you make sport of others.

Not so many years ago, there lived in Florence a young woman called Helen, possessed of a beautiful body, but a snobbish disposition. She came of an excellent family, and had a fair amount of fortune's blessings, so that when her husband died she did not wish to marry again, having set her heart on a handsome, pleasant youth after her own desires. As she had freed herself of all responsibilities, she managed, through the help of a maid in whom she had the utmost confidence, to meet her lover and live with him in wondrous pleasure and delight.

Now at about that time, a young nobleman of our city, called Rinieri, returned to Florence from Paris, where he had studied for many years, not for the purpose of marketing his knowledge at retail, like many others, but for the pure pleasure of learning the first principles and the nature of things—a virtue becoming a gentleman. Here, in his native town, he was held in high esteem, both for his noble blood and his learning, and so lived contented, in the enjoyment of civic pursuits.

However, as we have often observed that the wisest of men fall soonest into the snares of love, so likewise did Rinieri. One day, when he had gone to an entertainment in search of distraction, Helen, in her black widow's weeds, appeared before him, looking so alluring, and, in his opinion, also so rarely beautiful and fascinating, that he could not think of anyone who had ever seemed so marvelous a creature to him. Soon he found himself reflecting that the man to whom God granted the grace of holding her naked in his arms could well consider himself blessed.

Stealing repeated glances at her from the corner of his eye, while bearing in mind that great and precious things are not lightly to be won, he resolved, on the spur of the moment, to spare no pains in gaining her favor, that he might eventually attain her love and finally the unstinted possession of herself.

Meanwhile, the young woman, who did not keep her eyes fixed on a prayer-book, but darted them furtively about out of an exalted opinion of her charms, was quick to mark what men enjoyed looking at her, and perceiving Rinieri, said to herself with a laugh, "I didn't waste my time by coming here to-day, for if I'm not mistaken, I've hooked a fish by the nose."

At that, she flashed her eyes time and again in his direction, trying, to the best of her ability, to make him understand that she was aware of his attention, imagining that the more men she captivated and lured by her beauty, the greater its worth, especially to the man upon whom she had bestowed it, together with her love.

All thoughts of philosophical speculation flew from the

learned scholar's mind. Thinking to gain her grace, he set his heart upon her, and learning where she lived, proceeded to walk back and forth past her house, justifying his promenades with flimsy excuses. Helen, for the reason already told, was puffed up with vanity, and pretended to take great pleasure in seeing him about, whereupon the scholar found a way to approach her maid and declare his love, pleading with her to exert all her influence upon her lady, that he might at last win her. The maid was liberal with her promises, and reported everything to her mistress, who listened amid bursts of laughter, and then said:

"Do you want to see this scholar lose all the brains he brought back from Paris? Heigh-ho, let's give him what he's looking for. If he should broach the subject to you again, tell him I'm more ardently in love with him than he is with me, but that I must be very scrupulous of my virtue, so that I may look my peers squarely in the face. That should make him love me all the more, if he's as clever as he pretends to be!"

Ah, poor, foolish little woman! She didn't know, dear ladies, what it means to meddle with scholars!

Well, the maid sought him out and delivered her lady's message, which, for the joy it gave him, made him press his suit even more warmly. He sent many letters and gifts, all of which were accepted, but received no replies except indefinite promises. In this fashion, Helen kept him for a long while in suspense.

In the long run, she confessed the whole affair to her lover, which angered him not a little, and pricked him to fits of jealousy; therefore, to prove that he was suspecting her unjustly, she sent her maid to the impassioned Rinieri, with the message that so far, since he had assured her of his love, she had not been able to give him any token of her affection, but that during the approaching Christmas holidays, she hoped to have the opportunity of being with him. Indeed, if he wished, the night after Christmas he might wait for her in her courtyard, where she would call for him, as soon as she could manage. Rinieri was as happy as could be, and at the appointed hour, hastened to Helen's house. The maid led him to the court and shut him in, and there he began to wait for his lady.

That evening Helen had sent for her lover, and after they had enjoyed their supper in jollity together she disclosed to him what she intended doing that night, adding, "Now you'll be able to see for yourself how much I loved, and still love the fellow you're so ridiculously jealous of." The lover listened to her with joy in his heart, eager to see the performance of what her words implied.

As it happened, there had been a heavy snowstorm that day, and everything was covered with a blanket of white, so that the scholar had scarcely begun waiting in the courtyard, before he felt colder than he would have cared to. Nevertheless, he bore it patiently, looking forward to the comfort that would follow.

Soon Helen said to her lover, "Let's go to the bedroom and peep out of the window, to see what your rival is doing, and what he has to say to the maid, whom I sent to speak to him."

They went to a lattice, from which they could look out without being seen, and heard the maid calling down to the scholar from another window, "Rinieri, my mistress is as sorry as can be, for tonight one of her brothers arrived unexpectedly, and kept her talking and talking. Later he invited himself to supper, and he hasn't gone yet, though I think he'll soon be leaving. That's what's been keeping her from coming down to you, but I guess she'll soon manage it. In the meantime, she begs you not to be angry with her for keeping you waiting."

Rinieri believed every word she said was true, and answered, "Tell my lady not to worry about me, until it is convenient for her to come down, but please tell her to do so as soon as she can."

The maid left the window and went to bed, when Helen said to her lover, "Well, what have you to say? Do you suppose if I loved him as much as you fear, I'd let him remain down there and freeze?"

So saying, she retired with her lover, who was reassured to a certain extent, and for a considerable while they sported and made merry together, laughing and joking at the unhappy scholar's expense.

Meanwhile, the poor fellow was performing all kinds of gymnastics in order to keep himself warm in the open courtyard, with no shelter where he might sit down, or seek refuge from the chill of night. Cursing the brother for delaying the woman so long, he started at every sound, thinking perhaps a door was opening to let him in to her; but he hoped in vain.

Toward midnight, after having frolicked all that time with her lover, Helen said to him, "What do you think of our scholar, sweetheart? And which do you consider greater, his wisdom, or my love for him? Will the cold I'm making him suffer drive out the silly jealousy that entered your heart the other day, because of the words I said of him?"

"O my heart of hearts," replied her lover, "I am convinced that as you are my happiness, my peace, my delight and all my hope, so too, am I yours."

"Well, then, give me a thousand kisses to prove it," she said. Clasping her close in his arms, he gave her not only a thousand, but more than a hundred thousand of them, when, after they had so dallied for some time, she said, "Come, let's get up awhile and see if those ardent flames are spent, in which this new beau of mine declared he burned the live-long day."

Getting up, they posted themselves at their window, and peering down into the courtyard, caught sight of the scholar who, goaded by the cold, was dancing a jig of so rapid and brisk a tempo, to the tune of his chattering teeth, that never had they seen anything to equal it before.

"What have you to say now, sweetest hope of mine?" Helen then asked her lover. "Don't you think I can make men jig, without the need of horns or bagpipes?"

"O my dearest joy, indeed you can," he said, laughing.

"Let's go down as far as the door," she suggested. "You keep quiet, while I talk to him, and we'll hear what he has to say. Perhaps we'll have just as much fun listening to him, as we had watching his antics."

Opening the door very quietly, they padded down to the threshold, whence, without opening the leaves a crack, Helen softly called to the scholar through the keyhole. Rinieri thanked the Lord, thinking all too hastily that he would be admitted, and drew up to the door.

"Here I am, Helen," said he. "Open, for God's sake. I'm nearly dead with cold."

"Really!" she said. "You must be a coldblooded fellow. Can it be so frightfully cold, just because we've had a miserable little snowfall? As if I didn't know there are far worse ones in Paris! I'm sorry I can't let you in yet, as that plague of a brother of mine, who came to have supper with me to-night, hasn't left yet. But he'll be going soon, and I'll make it my business to let you in right away. You don't know what trouble I had, to slip away from him and come down to beg you not to mind waiting a little longer."

"For the love of God, madam," he pleaded, "please open the door and let me in, that I may at least get out of the cold in there. It's begun to snow very heavily, these last few minutes, and it's still coming down. I'll wait as long as you wish, if you'll only let me in."

"Alas, dear one, that I cannot do," she said. "This door makes a tremendous racket every time it's opened, and my brother would surely hear, if I let you in. I just want to go and tell him it's time for him to leave, so that I may return and open the door for you."

"Go quickly, please," entreated the scholar, "and I beg you let them make a good fire, so I may thaw out a little. I'm so numb with cold, that I can scarcely feel my own touch."

"How can that be?" said Helen. "How, if what you wrote to me so many times is true, about your burning for love of me? Of course you're jesting! Bye-bye, I must go now, but you wait, and be of good cheer."

The lover, who heard every word of their conversation, enjoyed the joke immensely. Presently, he returned to bed with her, but they slept little all of that night, spending it all in frolic and pleasure, and in laughing at the hapless scholar.

Finally Rinieri, who looked almost like a stork, so violently did his teeth chatter, realized he had been the dupe of a trick. Several times, he tried to force the door open, and looked about for a means of leaving the courtyard, but seeing it could not be done, he paced about like a lion in his cage, cursing the foul weather, the woman's heartlessness and the interminable night, together with his own stupidity. Contempt for her took possession of him, and converted the fervent love he had long borne her, to cruel and bitter hate. He considered all kinds of complex plans to gain revenge, which he now desired more than he had formerly desired to be alone with her.

At great length, the night drew to a close; dawn began to glimmer in the east, and with the new day, down came Helen's maid, well instructed for her office. Opening the door to the court, she said, pretending exaggerated compassion for his plight, "Damn that person who came here last evening! All night long he kept us on pins and needles, and nearly made you freeze to death. But take my advice, bear this disappointment with patience, for what couldn't be done last night will be so much sweeter some other night. I, for one, know nothing in the world that could have vexed my mistress as much as this."

The indignant scholar, grown wise through all the insults he had suffered, knew only too well that threats are the defensive weapons of the threatened, therefore, swallowing the rage his uncontrollable temper would have vented, he replied gently, without the least show of anger in his voice, "I must confess I've spent the most terrible night in my life, but I knew very well your mistress was not at all to blame, as she came down herself out of pity for me, to apologize and cheer my spirits. As you say, what did not happen to-night will be for another night, so give her my best wishes and God be with you."

Then, almost crippled with cold, he made his way to his house as best he could, where, nearly dead with fatigue and lack of sleep, he flung himself upon his bed to snatch a little rest, only to rise a few hours later, with arms and legs well-nigh paralyzed. Immediately, he sent for several doctors, and informing them of the cold to which he had been exposed, placed himself entirely in their care. Still, in spite of their efficient and very powerful remedies, it was some time before they could manage to relieve the numbness of his muscles and sinews, and bring them back to their normal flexibility. Had it not been for the resistance of his youth, and the coming of more temperate weather, he might have had a most unpleasant time of it. At length, when he regained his health and vigor, he concealed the hatred he nursed in his heart, and pretended he was more passionately in love than ever with his fair widow.

Not long after, fate proved propitious to the scholar, and presented him with the opportunity to satisfy his craving for vengeance; for the youth whom Helen loved, caring little for all her affection, set his heart on another woman, and would have nothing to do or say to his first love, keeping her languishing in tears and vexation. Helen's maid, however, who was devoted to her, seeing no way of rousing her from the despair into which she had sunk at the loss of her lover, conceived a peculiar notion of a way to cure her. Observing Rinieri promenading back and forth as usual about the neighborhood, she thought, since he was a scholar and therefore an expert in black magic, that he might perform some spell, by means of which he could restore the old lover to her lady. Accordingly, she communicated the brilliant idea she had. Helen, by no means clever, without stopping to think that had the scholar known anything of black magic, he would have employed it in his own case, took heed of the maid's words, and sent her immediately, to find out whether Rinieri would be willing to work a charm, assuring him of the coveted reward, if he succeeded. The maid acquitted

herself diligently and well of her charge, much to the delight
of the scholar, who said to himself on hearing the message, "O
God, all praise to Thee. The time has come when with Thy
help, I shall be able to make the foul woman pay for the indignity she inflicted upon me, as a reward for the great love I
bore her!" But to the maid he said, "Tell my lady not to worry
about it, for even if her lover were in India, I could promptly
bring him to her feet and make him apologize for whatever he
had done contrary to her desires. As for the means she must
employ, I will have to communicate them to her myself, whenever and wherever she pleases. Tell her this, and urge her, for
me, to bear up and be of good cheer."

The maid carried back his answer, and arranged an appointment for them at Santa Maria del Prato. Thither they went,
the lady and the scholar, and spoke a while alone together. Forgetting that she had once nearly brought him to an untimely
end, Helen frankly disclosed her predicament to him, explained
what she desired of him, and implored him to do his best for
her.

"Madam," said Rinieri, "I must confess that among the things
I learned in Paris was the art of necromancy, of which I know
all there is to know, backwards and forwards. But since the
practice of it is sinful in the sight of the Lord, I had sworn an
oath never to use it, either for my sake or for anybody else's.
Still, frankly, the love I bear you is so great, that I don't know
how I could find it in me to refuse you anything you asked.
Therefore, even if I should be damned to hell for this very
thing, I am ready, since it is your pleasure. I must warn you,
however, that it is a much more difficult thing to perform than
you perhaps imagine, especially in cases where a woman wishes
to recall a man to her affection, or a man a woman, for this
particular spell must be practiced by the individual concerned.
Moreover, great courage is necessary, for the person who performs the spell must do it in the depth of night, alone, and in
desolate places, all of which I don't imagine you would be willing to consent to."

At that Helen, more infatuated than wise, replied, "Love
urges me on so powerfully, that there's nothing I would stop at
to recover the man who so unjustly abandoned me. If you
please, then, explain to me why I must have courage."

The scholar, who had a bad streak in his nature, accordingly
answered, "Madam, I shall have to make you a leaden puppet,

in the name of the man whose affection you wish to regain.
When you have received it from me, you must go by palest
moonlight to a stream of living waters, about the hour when
you would ordinarily be falling asleep, and there, all alone, you
must bathe yourself seven times in the water, stark-naked, with
the leaden image. After that, naked as you are, you must climb
up to the top of a tree, or to the roof of some deserted house,
and turning toward the north with the puppet in your hand,
you must repeat, seven times, a certain incantation, which I'll
write out for you. After you've said it over, two of the most
beautiful maidens you have ever seen will appear before you,
and bow, asking you your wish. Then it is for you to tell them
clearly and explicitly what you desire, and take care you don't
mention one man for another. After you've expressed your wish,
they'll disappear, and you may go down to the place where you
have left your clothes, put them on again and return home. I
can safely promise you that before the twelfth hour of the following night your lover will come to you, contrite and weeping,
to beg your forgiveness and mercy. And rest assured that from
then on, he will never forsake you again for any other woman."

Helen listened intently to what he said, and placed the utmost confidence in his words. Already, she imagined herself
clasping her lover in her arms, and half-regaining her spirits, she
said, "Don't you worry! I'll carry it all out to perfection, for I
have the most convenient spot you can imagine for the purpose.
Along the upper border of Val d'Arno, I have a country-place,
very close to the river's brink. We're now in the month of July,
and bathing will be delightful. Now that I think of it, not very
far from the stream, there's a little old deserted tower, which
only the shepherds sometimes climb by a ladder of chestnut
rungs, to see, from a little platform on the roof, whether they
can locate their lost sheep. It's quite a lonely, out-of-the-way
place, you see. That's where I'll go, and there, on top of the
tower, I hope to carry out perfectly whatever you give me to do."

Rinieri was very well acquainted with the lady's country-home
and the abandoned tower she described, and glad of the assurance she had given him of her intention, he said, "Madam, I've
never been around that part of the country, so I'm not
acquainted with your house or the little tower you speak of; but
if everything is as you say, you couldn't find a more adequate
spot. Well then, as soon as I can, I shall send you the leaden
puppet and the written charm, but I implore you, after you

have your wish, and realize that I have done my best for you, think of me just a little, and keep the promise you made me."

"Indeed I will," she said, and taking leave of him, she returned home.

Rinieri, overjoyed at the favorable prospect of carrying his plan into effect, manufactured an image out of various preparations he had, and composed some meaningless twaddle for a charm. At the first opportunity he sent them to Helen with the injunction that she do what he had told her that very night, without delay, and himself went secretly with his servant, to the house of a friend close by the tower, that he might more successfully execute his scheme.

Helen, on the other hand, set out for her farm with her maid, and at nightfall, pretending she was going to retire, sent the girl to bed. About the hour she usually went to sleep, however, stealing cautiously out of the house, she walked to the brink of the river Arno, at the foot of the little tower, and after reassuring herself by scanning the vicinity that no one was about, she took off her clothes and hid them under a bush. Seven times, she bathed with the leaden puppet, and then, still holding it in her hand, went on toward the tower.

Rinieri, meanwhile, with the first shades of night, had concealed himself with his servant, among the willows and other trees growing near the tower, and had seen everything she did. As he perceived her passing by, almost brushing against him, her gleaming white nakedness dominating the darkness of night, and as he gazed at her breasts and the other parts of her body, well-formed and beautiful, he felt a twinge of pity for her, to think of what would become of them before long. As though that were not enough, the desire of the flesh pricked him instantly, making a certain person start up who had been quiescent, and spur him to leave his ambush, seize her and have his will of her. What with this urge and that, he was on the point of surrendering; but then, remembering who he was, and what the insult he had suffered for no reason at her hands, his ire kindled anew. Pity and passion were flung overboard; he remained staunch to his resolution, and let her pass.

Accordingly, Helen climbed to the tower, and turning to the north began repeating the charm Rinieri had given her. Presently, he glided softly into the tower after her, and stealthily took away the ladder which led up to the platform where she stood. Then, with bated breath, he waited to see what she would say and do.

Seven times, Helen repeated the incantation and waited for the beautiful maidens to come. However, so long did she have to wait in the dampness of the night air, which was more chilly than she would have desired, that at last she saw dawn lighting up the east. Chagrined and disappointed that the affair had not turned out as the scholar had said, she pondered:

"I'm afraid our fine gentleman may have wanted to give me a dose of my own medicine, in return for the night I had him spend. But if that's the way he meant to do it, he's accomplished a weak revenge, for this night was not a third the length of his; besides, the cold was of another sort entirely."

Not over-anxious to have the dawn surprise her on the tower, she tried to descend, but found the ladder was gone. Then, as if the world had slipped from under her feet, she lost courage and fainted on the platform, only to weep and wail and complain bitterly when she regained her senses. She knew too well that this had been the scholar's doing, and compunction seized her, first, for having offended him, and then, for having placed too much confidence in a man whom she should have deemed her enemy, for cogent reasons; so she continued for a long time. Later, examining the tower to see if there might be any other way of going down, and finding none, she began lamenting afresh and plunged into bitter thoughts, musing:

"O unfortunate wretch! What will your brothers say, and your relatives, and your neighbors and everybody in Florence, when they learn you were found here stark-naked? The wonderful reputation you have heretofore enjoyed will be discovered to have been a sham, and even if you tried to gloss over the whole affair with plausible excuses—that is, if you can trump up any— that damned scholar who knows all your business, will give you the lie! Ah, unhappy wretch, fated to lose the youth you loved unwisely, and your honor, at one blow!"

After her soliloquy, she was overcome by so deep a paroxysm of despair, that she would have flung herself headlong from the tower. The sun had already risen, however, and as she crawled nearer to the wall on one side of the tower, to see if some shepherd-lad were passing with his flocks, that she might send him to her maid, she spied the scholar who had just awak- ened from a desultory nap at the foot of a bush. He caught sight of her at the same moment, and said: "Good-day, madam. Have the maidens arrived yet?"

On seeing him and hearing his words, Helen burst into sobs once more, entreating him to come into the tower, so that she might speak to him. He complied courteously; therefore the woman, lying flat on her stomach upon the floor of the tower, and allowing only her head to appear through the trapdoor, addressed him between her sobs:

"Ah, Rinieri, surely, if I had you spend a wretched night, you have been sufficiently avenged, for even though it is the month of July, all night long I thought I should freeze, naked as I was. What's more, I've cried so long over the trick I played you, and over my stupidity in placing my faith in you, that it's a wonder to me I have any eyes left. I beg you, therefore, not for my sake, whom you've no reason to love, but for your own, as an honorable gentleman, that you consider this sufficient retaliation for my insult to you. Send someone for my clothes, that I may come down from here, and don't insist on robbing me of that which you could not give me back, even if you wished—my honor, Rinieri. Even if I did deprive you of the pleasure of being with me that night, I can compensate you with many more nights for that one, any time you choose. Let this punishment suffice you, then, and like the courteous gentleman you are, be satisfied with the triumph of having avenged your honor, and making me admit it. Don't strive to use your power against a mere woman. It's no glory for an eagle to have triumphed over a dove. For the love of God, then, Rinieri, and for your honor's sake, have mercy on me."

Rinieri still bore the indignity he had received in his proud mind, and when he saw Helen weeping and entreating, he at once felt pleasure and vexation—pleasure in his revenge, which he had wanted more than anything else, and vexation for the pity his humanity awakened in his breast, at the plight of the hapless woman. Still, humanity could not conquer his fierce desire for revenge, and he replied:

"Helen, if my prayers, which, indeed, I had not the heart to bathe in tears or coat with sweetness like yours—if my prayers, I say, had been able to move you to grant me a sheltered corner, the night I was dying of cold in your snow-filled courtyard, I might perhaps find it easy to grant you your own. But now, if you are so much more tender of your honor than you were in the past, and find it so mortifying to remain up there naked, address your prayers to the one in whose arms you did not blush to lie naked, that particular night you remember, though you knew me to be wearing a path in your courtyard, my teeth chattering as I stamped down the snow. Let him help you now. Let him fetch you your clothes. Let him set up the ladder for you to come down. Inspire him now with some regard for your honor—the man with whom you did not worry about sullying it, on that occasion and a thousand others! Why aren't you calling upon him to come and help you? Whose concern is it, if not his? You belong to him. Whom can he protect and help, if he does not protect and help you? Call him, foolish woman! Find out if the love you bear him, if his wisdom and yours combined can deliver you from my stupidity, of which, as you played with him, you asked, 'Which do you think greater, his wisdom, or the love I bear you?' Nor need you be generous now with what I don't desire, and which you could not refuse me, if I did. Keep your nights for your lover, if you should manage to get out of here alive. Let them be yours and his to enjoy. I had too much of one, and it's enough for me to have been duped once.

"Moreover, employing all your guile in your speech, you strive to worm your way to my benevolence by flattery, calling me courteous, and a gentleman, thinking that thus you will succeed in making me take refuge in my generosity of soul, and so refrain from punishing you for your wickedness. But your arts will not blind the eyes of my mind, as your lying promises did in the past. I know myself now, and truly, in all my stay in Paris, I did not learn so much about myself, as you taught me in the one night you gave me. Still, granting I were indeed generous of soul, you're not the sort toward whom magnanimity should be exercised. The aim of punishment and vengeance toward a wild beast like you, should be death; the generosity you mentioned, ought to be reserved for human-beings alone. Hence, as I am no eagle nor are you a dove, but the venomous serpent I know you to be, it is my purpose to carry out my revenge against you, my ancient enemy, with all the hate and power in me, though properly speaking, what I am doing to you can hardly be called revenge, but a just retribution. Revenge should overstep the indignity, whereas this punishment hardly compares with it. Indeed, if it were revenge I sought, your life would scarcely suffice, considering the depths to which you plunged my soul. No, nor a hundred lives like yours, for in killing you I'd only be ridding the world of a foul, wicked, jaded, insignificant slut. Besides, omitting your merely pretty face, which a few years will ruin with their harvest of wrinkles, what the devil are you, more than any other miserable little slattern? Whereas, it was not through any fault of yours that you failed to murder an honorable gentleman, as you called me a moment ago, whose life may still prove to be of more value to the world in a single day, than a hundred-thousand of your lives, as long as the world is destined to last. I'll teach you, through the suffering and humiliation you are now enduring, what it means to ridicule men of feeling, and scholars in particular. I'll give you food for thought, which will keep you from ever being so foolish again, if you live to tell the tale.

"Then, again, if you're so anxious to come down, why don't you pitch yourself headlong to earth? Perhaps by breaking your neck, God willing, you would be getting out of the torment in which you think you find yourself, and at the same time, you would be making me the happiest man in the world. That's all, for the present. I contrived to the best of my ability to get you up there; it's up to you to use the same ingenuity in coming down that you expended in making a fool of me."

While the scholar was delivering his harangue, the miserable woman did not cease weeping. Time sped by and the sun kept climbing higher in the heavens. When she saw Rinieri had come to a halt, she said:

"Ah, cruel man, if you found that accursed night so hard to bear, and my sin so grievous that neither the beauty of my youth, nor my humble prayers can move you to pity, at least let one thing touch you and soften your unrelenting harshness —the confidence I bore you. Yes, my faith in you, that made me bare my heart to you of its every inmost secret, and paved a way for your vengeance to make me conscious of my error. Had I not unbosomed myself to you, nothing in the world would have given you the occasion to vent your revenge upon me, which you seem to have yearned for so ardently! Come, away with your grudge and forgive me, and I promise that if you do, and allow me to come down from here, I am willing to give up my faithless youth completely, and take you alone for my lord and lover—yes, in spite of your apparent scorn for the beauty which you claim is so transient and worthless. Still, whatever its worth in comparison with other women's charms, one thing I know: it has at least the merit, if nothing else, of being the delight and joy and rapture of man's youth, and you are by no means old. Besides, even though I am so cruelly maltreated at your hands, I can't believe you would want to see me die the unbecoming death you suggest. No, you would not have me fling myself down from here, like a miserable wretch before your eyes which, if you were not the liar you've recently become, you would admit once took great joy in me. For pity's sake, and for the sake of God above, have mercy on me! The sun is beginning to burn fiercely, and causes me as great suffering as the cold I bore through the night."

Rinieri enjoyed the sport of the conversation, and replied, "It was not through any love you had for me, Helen, that you trusted me with your confidence, but only to win back what you had lost—a thing which, at best, deserves still harsher punishment. You are sorely mistaken if you think that was the only way that offered itself to the execution of my revenge. There were a thousand others—a thousand snares I had wound about your feet, through my pretense of love for you, and sooner or later, if this opportunity had not come, you would have been caught in one or another of them. Indeed, you couldn't have been caught in any other that wouldn't have caused you even more suffering and humiliation than this—which I seized, not out of any regard for you, but to be sooner appeased. Nevertheless, even if all ways had failed me, my pen would not, with which I would have written so many, and such terrible attacks against you, that when you learned of them, as you doubtless would have, you would have cursed a thousand times a day the hour you were born.

"The pen is far mightier than is imagined, by people who have not discovered its power from personal experience. I swear by God—may He rejoice to the end in this revenge on you, as He did in the beginning!—I swear by Him, that I would have penned such things of you that in your shame not only before others, but before yourself, you would have plucked out your eyes with your own hands, rather than look at yourself again! So don't rebuke the sea for having been increased by a tiny brook.

"As for your love and your favors, I don't care a straw for them, as I told you before. Give yourself, if you can, to the man who once possessed you, the rival whom I once hated, as I now love him for the way he behaved toward you recently.

"It is usual with you women to give your hearts to lusty

youths, and hanker after their passion, because you see them
rosier of complexion, darker of beard, and with more zest for
dancing and sporting. All these virtues once also graced men
of maturer years, who are, besides, past-masters in what those
striplings have yet to learn. Again, you consider them better
gallopers and adepts in making more miles in a day than
older men. I admit they're more brisk in shaking up your hide
for you; but elderly men, rich in experience, know far better
where the flea bites. Therefore, it is far more preferable to
choose the little and sweet, rather than the much and tasteless.
Besides, rough-riding will tire and get anybody out of wind,
no matter how young, whereas slow and sure pacing will lead
one to the shelter in good form, though perhaps a little late.
You don't realize, brainless animals that you are, how much
harm is hidden under that trifle of fine exterior. Young men are
never satisfied with one woman. Not at all! They will lust
after every female they set eyes on, and think the world owes
everything to them. Under such conditions, their love could
not possibly be constant, as you can convincingly testify from
your own case. They esteem themselves worthy of their
women's respect and adoration, and there's no greater glory for
them than to boast of the conquests they have made—a bad
trait, which has caused many a woman to seek refuge under
the gown of the friars, who know how to keep their mouths
shut.

"Although you declare nobody ever knew of your intrigues,
except your maid and me, you are under sore misapprehension
and guilty of false assurance if you believe it. Why, his neighborhood and yours talk of nothing else! But then, as often
happens, the one concerned is the last to hear what's said of
him! Disregarding this, youths take from you, whereas mature
men give. You, who have chosen so badly, then, stick to the
fellow to whom you gave yourself, and leave me, the object of
your jibes, to others—for I have found a lady much nobler
than you, who recognized my worth better than you ever did!

"You didn't seem to understand my words aright, when I
spoke of what I'd like to see you do. If you want to bear
convincing proof to the other world of my desire, just fling
yourself down, and then your soul, which I am sure will fall
directly into the devil's arms, may see for itself whether I
winked a lash seeing you tumble to your death. But I know
you do not want to do me this pleasant favor, therefore accept

this bit of advice. When the sun begins to scorch you too fiercely, think of the cold you made me bear, and I'm sure that if you mingle it with your smart, you will find the sun's heat to be much assuaged."

The woeful Helen wept anew to hear the scholar's words end in cruel sarcasm, and said, "Hear me, then! Since nothing I can do stirs you to compassion, be moved by the love you bear this lady who, you say, is so much better than myself, and who loves you. For her sake, forgive me and bring my clothes, that I may dress. And oh, let me come down from here!"

Rinieri laughed at that, but seeing that it was already long past nine, answered, "I can't very well refuse you now, since you have made your appeal by so beloved a lady. Tell me where your clothes are, and I will fetch them and help you come down from there."

Helen was somewhat cheered, believing he meant what he said, and showed him where she had hidden her clothes. Rinieri, however, on leaving the tower, cautioned his servant not to quit the spot, but to keep as close to it as he could, and to do his best to prevent anyone from entering the tower, until he himself had returned. Shortly after that, he went to his friend's house, dined in ease and comfort, and then, at the proper hour, took his siesta.

Meanwhile, Helen remained upon her tower. Though somewhat comforted by ill-founded hope, she drew near the section of the battlement where a patch of shade fell, and there, sad beyond measure and the prey of bitterest thoughts, she crouched upon her haunches, and resigned herself to wait. Thought followed thought in quick succession. Then, thinking gave way to hope and hope to despair of his returning with her clothes, until at last, overcome by her sorrow and the fatigue of a wakeful night, she sank into a profound sleep.

By this time, the intensely hot sun had risen to its noon. Glaring and merciless, it beat down upon her tender body, upon her head, unprotected by any covering, and with such violence, that not only did it scorch her flesh wherever it was exposed to its beams, but little by little blistered and split it. The agonizing smart awoke her, though she was sleeping soundly, and feeling the heat of the sun, she tried to move farther away. Then it was as though all the skin of her body were cracking and bursting with the motion, like scorched parchment when someone pulls it. As if that were not enough, her head ached so that she thought it would burst, which was indeed no wonder. The platform of the tower, too, was so scorching hot, that she could scarcely bear to find foothold or rest, so that unable to sit or to stand still, she was compelled to move about as she wept. No breeze stirred the torrid air. Flies and hornets, lured by her raw flesh, came there in swarms, and gathering on her bruised body, bit her so cruelly, that each sting was like a stab. In despair, she flapped her hands to chase the insects away, cursing herself, her life, her lover and the scholar every moment of her agony.

Finally, what with the indescribable heat of the sun, the mosquitoes, the hornets, hunger, and worst of all, a suffocating thirst, not to mention myriad maddening thoughts that stung and goaded and tormented her, Helen jumped to her feet to scan the horizon and listen for any human sound, determined to call for help, no matter what the outcome. But alas! even this unfriendly fate denied her! Hardly any of the peasants had gone to work that day, most of them being occupied with threshing their grain near their cottages, while the few who had ventured out had all returned home because of the merciless heat. Therefore, only the chirping of the cicadas reached Helen's ears, and the river Arno was the only moving thing she saw, whose inviting waters did not allay, but rather intensified her thirst. Here and there, too, she made out patches of forest, and green shady nooks, and houses, all of which were an added sting to tantalize her.

What more shall we say of the hapless woman? The sun above her, and the fire of the tower-floor beneath her feet, together with the stings of flies and hornets from all quarters, had so disfigured her, that though the previous night the candor of her body had dominated the surrounding gloom, she had now become so red and inflamed and flecked with blood, that to look at her, one would have thought her the ugliest creature in creation.

As time crawled by and Helen continued in her misery, without hope or a friendly word, and awaiting certain death, the scholar awoke from his nap toward mid-afternoon, and calling his lady to mind, went back to the tower to see what had become of her, and, at the same time, relieve his servant, who was still fasting. Helen heard him. Weak and aching from the agony she had suffered, she dragged herself to the edge of the trapdoor and crouching over it, spoke to him, in the midst of her wailing:

"O Rinieri, you have had your revenge, and more, for if I made you freeze in my courtyard at night, you've caused me to roast on this tower today—broil, I might say, besides making me die of hunger and thirst. I beseech you, for the sake of the One true God, come up here to me. I am not brave enough to take my life. Kill me, out of mercy, for there's nothing I desire more than the relief of death, so awful is the anguish I feel! If you will not grant this boon, send me at least a bowl of water to moisten my parched mouth, for my tears are not enough to assuage the drought and the fire I feel in it!"

The scholar heard from her voice how weak she was, and also caught a glimpse of her body, all scorched and burned by the sun. A twinge of compassion softened him toward her at the sight and at the humble prayers she addressed to him. Nevertheless, he replied:

"You'll never die by my hands, vile woman that you are! You're welcome to take your own life, if you're so anxious to die! As for water to relieve your heat, you'll have as much of it from me, as I had fire from you to soothe the cold I suffered. There's only one thing I regret. While I had to doctor the sickness resulting from my chill with the warmth of stinking dung, your smarts will be treated with cooling applications of rosewater; and whereas I was on the verge of losing the use of my limbs, my life itself, you will come out of this flaying even more beautiful, like a serpent that has sloughed off its old skin."

"Alas, unhappy me!" cried Helen. "To my enemies may God give beauty purchased at such a price! But you, Rinieri, crueller than a wild beast—how can you bear to torture me like this? Even if I had put to death everyone near and dear to you, under the most atrocious tortures, what greater cruelty could I have expected from you, or any other man? I can't conceive what worse punishment could be inflicted on a traitor who had caused the slaughter of a townful of people, than the pain to which you are subjecting me, by having the sun broil my body and the flies devour it. Not even a bowl of water will you grant me, when murderers sentenced by law are often given wine, if they wish, as they are led to their death!

"Well then, since I see there's no swerving you from your ruthless cruelty, since my woes cannot touch the least fiber of your heart, I shall resign myself patiently to accept death. So may the Lord have mercy on my soul! And may He look with unprejudiced eyes upon this deed of yours!"

With these words, she crawled painfully to the middle of the roof, despairing of ever escaping with her life from the raging heat. In the stress of her many afflictions, not once, but a thousand times, she thought she would faint for very thirst, as she wept aloud and bewailed her misfortune.

It was already dusk by now. Rinieri, thinking he had punished her enough, had his servant wrap her clothes in his cloak, and he himself went to her house. There he found Helen's maid sitting upon the doorstep, sad and forlorn, not knowing what on earth to do.

"What's happened to your mistress, girl?" he asked.

"I don't know at all, sir," she replied. "This morning I expected to find her in bed, where I thought I saw her go last night, but I found her neither there nor anywhere else. I haven't any idea what's become of her. You can't imagine how miserable I am! Perhaps you could tell me something about her, sir?"

"Ah," exclaimed the scholar, "if I had only had you, with your mistress, where I've been keeping her, so I might have punished you for your part in the game, as I punished her for hers! But you won't escape my clutches, I swear, until I've given you all you deserve! Ah, no! You won't be playing any more pranks on men, I assure you, without first thinking of me!"

So saying, he turned to his servant. "Give her those clothes," he said, "and tell her to fetch her mistress if she wants to."

The man did as he was told. When the girl recognized whose clothes they were, and heard what the scholar had said, she was so terrified at the thought that they might have murdered her mistress, that she could scarcely contain a shriek. The moment Rinieri had gone, she ran with the bundle to the tower, weeping and moaning.

It so happened that one of Helen's gardeners had lost two of his pigs that day, and as he was going hither and thither looking for them, he came upon the tower, shortly after the scholar's departure. As he looked through every nook and cranny to see if he could discover his pigs, he heard the wailing of the hapless woman, and climbing aloft as far as he could, called out, "Who's that crying up there?"

Helen recognized her gardener's voice, and calling him by his name pleaded, "For heaven's sake, please run for my maid, and see that you manage to have her come up here to me!"

The man knew her to be his mistress. "Goodness, madam!" he cried. "What the devil brought you all the way up there? Your girl's been looking high and low for you all day long, but who would ever have thought you'd be way up there?"

Taking the side-beams of the ladder, he set them up in place, and got to work fastening the rungs across with ropes. At this point, the maid came into the tower, and unable to repress her anxiety any longer, began striking and tearing at herself with her hands, shrieking, "O, my mistress! My darling mistress! Where are you?"

No sooner did Helen hear her, than she answered as loudly as she could, "Here, I'm up here, sister! Don't cry, but bring up my clothes to me as soon as you can."

The girl was relieved to hear her lady's voice, and climbing the ladder, which the laborer had almost entirely fixed up again, she came to the platform with his aid. But on seeing her mistress lying there on the roof naked, exhausted and haggard, looking more like a charred stump than a human creature, she fell to tearing her face with her nails, and mourned over her as though she were dead.

"For God's sake keep quiet and help me dress," said Helen, who, learning from her that nobody knew where she had been except the men who had delivered her clothes, and the gardener, was somewhat consoled. She begged them not to breathe a word of the event to a living soul. Finally, after a good deal of talk, the gardener took Helen, who was unable to move, and carried her safely out of the tower; but the poor maid, who had remained behind, coming down with less caution, missed her footing and fell from the ladder to the ground, breaking her leg, the pain of which set her roaring like a lion. Laying his mistress on a patch of grass, the gardener ran to see what ailed the maid, and on finding her with a broken leg, took her likewise to the patch of grass and set her down beside the lady. When Helen saw this new misfortune added to the sum of her woes, and realized that the one from whom she expected most help had broken her leg, she wept still more in sheer desperation, so that the gardener was not only powerless to comfort her, but himself joined in the lamentation.

The sun was already low on the horizon. That darkness

might not overtake them in that desert place, he went to his cot at Helen's suggestion, whence, recruiting two of his brothers and his wife, he returned to the grass-patch with a board, on which they laid the maid and so carried her home with them. They refreshed Helen with a cool draught, and comforted her with cheery words; then the gardener took her on his back, and carried her to his wife's room, where a woman fed her gruel, undressed her and put her to bed. That night they managed to carry her and the girl back to Florence.

Once there, Helen, who had fables and wiles galore at her beck and call, fabricated a plausible tale which had nothing in common with what had really occurred, and gave her brothers to understand, as well as her sisters and everyone else, that both she and her maid had suffered what they did through devilish witchcraft.

Doctors were sent for at once, and finally, not without excruciating pain and torment on the part of Helen, who more than once left her skin piece-meal on the bedsheets, they cured her of a fierce fever and other ailments, and likewise the maid of her broken leg.

The lesson drove all thoughts of her lover out of Helen's mind, and from then on she took judicious care not to trifle with people and love. As for the scholar, on hearing that the maid had broken her leg, he was satisfied with what he thought a complete, well-rounded vengeance, and went his way without another word.

These, then, are the returns the ill-advised young woman received for her folly, when she thought she could jest with a scholar as with any ordinary man, little knowing that scholars —I don't say all, but the majority of them—know where the devil's tail springs from. Take care of playing foolish pranks, then, ladies, especially on scholar-folk.

# THE EIGHTH STORY

*Spinelloccio and Zeppa are close friends. The former lies with the wife of the latter, who discovers it and contrives to shut the offender in a chest. There, while Spinelloccio is imprisoned, he dallies over his head with the former's wife.*

THE NARRATIVE OF HELEN'S WOES HAD BEEN HARD AND DISTRESS-
ing for the women to hear, still, when they considered that to a
great extent she had brought her punishment on her own head,
they glided over it with milder pity, though they looked upon
the scholar as a fearfully harsh, stubborn, yes, even cruel man.
However, when Pampinea had brought her story to a close, the
queen called on Fiammetta to continue, who, eager to obey,
began:

Adorable ladies, since, as I believe, the indignant scholar's
harshness seems to have crushed you somewhat, I think it might
be wise to cheer your downcast spirits with something in a
lighter vein; so I shall tell you a short tale, of a young man who
took an affront with more docility and avenged it with greater
temperance—all of which should serve to show that in cases of
revenge, the injured party should be content to give as good as
he receives, without seeking to overstep the proper bounds of
just requital.

As I heard some time ago, there once lived in Siena two
young men of good urban origin, both fairly comfortably situated, one of whom was called Spinelloccio Tanena and the other
Zeppa di Mino. They were neighbors in Camollia, and went
about together a great deal, so that to all intents and purposes
they were as devoted to each other as though they had been
brothers—even more so. Besides, each of them had a very
comely wife.

Now Spinelloccio was a frequent visitor at his friend's house
at all times of the day, whether Zeppa was at home or not,
and in the course of time, he struck up such a close intimacy
with his wife, that he even lay with her, keeping up the amorous
relation a long time before anyone became aware of it. But at
length, one day, while Zeppa happened to be at home, unbe-
known to his wife, Spinelloccio came to call for him.

"He's not in," Zeppa's wife called to him from the parlor,
whereupon Spinelloccio, joining her there and seeing she was
alone, threw his arms about her and kissed her heartily, receiving a kiss in return for every one he gave. Zeppa, who saw
what was going on before his eyes, did not dare to breathe, but
remaining in his unintentional hiding-place, waited to see what
would follow this sport. Soon, he saw his wife and Spinelloccio,
still in each other's arms, make for the bedroom and lock themselves in. He was mad with rage, but then, reflecting that
whether he stamped or fumed or carried on in any other fash-

lon, the scandal would not be mitigated, but on the other hand might become even more shameful, he wondered what revenge he could take which would soothe his wounded spirits, and still be a secret from gossiping neighbors. After long reflection, he thought he had hit upon what promised to be the best way, and remained in his hiding-place as long as Spinelloccio stayed with his wife. As soon as the lover was out of the house, however, Zeppa went into the bedroom and found his wife had not yet readjusted her coif, which Spinelloccio had torn off in the sport.

"What's that you're doing, wife?" he asked.

"Can't you see?" she replied.

"Yes, indeed I can," he said, "and I saw much more besides than I could wish!" Then and there, he confronted her with what he had seen, until in her great dread, the woman confessed what she could not easily have denied, concerning her intimacy with Spinelloccio. Weeping and wailing, she begged his forgiveness, and Zeppa said:

"You must realize you've done a wicked thing, wife, and if you want my forgiveness, you must carry out in every detail what I am going to have you do. Listen, you must tell Spinelloccio that tomorrow, at about nine o'clock, he must find some excuse to leave me, and come here to you. When I'm sure he's here, I shall come back, and the moment you hear me, have him hide in this chest and lock him in. After that, I'll tell you what else to do. And don't be afraid to carry out what I say, for I give you my word I'll not hurt a hair of his head."

To satisfy him, the woman said she would execute his orders, which she did. The following day, when Zeppa and Spinelloccio were together about nine o'clock, the latter, who had promised his mistress a visit at that hour, said to his friend, "I'm sorry, Zeppa, but to-day I'm to have dinner with a friend, and I don't want to keep him waiting, so good-bye."

"It won't be dinner-time for quite a while yet," said Zeppa.

"Oh, that's all right," the other assured him. "I've a certain business to talk over with him, so I'd better get there early."

He left him, therefore, and taking a stroll around the square, went to his mistress, both of them retiring to the bedroom. They had hardly gone in when Zeppa returned, whereupon the woman, feigning the utmost terror, had her lover scramble into the chest her husband had designated, locked him in, and went out of the room.

"Is it time to eat yet, wife?" asked Zeppa, coming upstairs.

"Right away," she said.

"Spinelloccio had a dinner engagement with a friend to-day," he continued, "and has left his wife all alone. Go to the window and call her, and invite her to have dinner with us."

Fear for herself had rendered the woman a model of obedience, and without question, she did as he told her, coaxing Spinelloccio's wife, and urging her so well, that on learning her husband was dining out, she accepted the invitation. The moment she arrived, Zeppa greeted her effusively, took her familiarly by the hand, and softly ordering his wife into the kitchen, led her to the bedroom, where they had no sooner entered than turning about, he locked the door from within.

"Gracious, Zeppa! What does this mean?" she cried on observing his tactics. "Is that why you had me come here? And is this the great love and true friendship you bear my husband?"

Zeppa did not let her go, but approaching the chest in which her husband was concealed, said to her, "Before you protest, my friend, listen to what I have to tell you. I have always cherished Spinelloccio as a brother, and I still do. But yesterday, unknown to him, I discovered that the faith I placed in him bore such fruit that I found him lying with my wife, as he does with you. Now since he is very dear to me, I don't intend to punish him more than his offense deserves. He's had my wife, and I intend to have you. If you're not willing, I'm afraid I'll have to catch him red-handed, and as I've no mind to leave my revenge unfulfilled, I'll give him such a taste of his own medicine, that neither you nor he will ever have a moment's joy again."

On learning the state of affairs, and after being reassured of the truth again and again, she believed Zeppa and said, "Well, friend, since this vengeance will have to fall on me, I'm willing, provided you manage to keep your wife on friendly terms with me, despite what we're about to do, as I intend to be with her, in spite of the injury she has done me."

"Of course I'll do that," he said, "and in the bargain I'll give you a finer and more precious jewel than any you may have."

With these words, he embraced and kissed her, and throwing her upon her back on the chest wherein her husband was imprisoned, he enjoyed her to his heart's content, and she him.

Spinelloccio, in the meantime, had heard from within the chest all that Zeppa had told his wife, and her answer as well; but later, when he was aware of the antic hay carried on over his head, and for so long a time, at that, he was so angry, that he thought he would die on the spot. Indeed, had he not been afraid of Zeppa, he would have hurled the vilest imprecations upon his slut of a wife, chest or no chest. But when he realized that he had been the first to give offense, and that Zeppa was perfectly justified in doing what he was doing, in truth, that he had behaved toward him like a merciful man and loyal comrade, he made up his mind to be greater friends with him than ever, provided he wished it.

After Zeppa had been with his friend's wife as long as he desired, he got off the chest, and upon her asking him for the promised jewel, he merely opened the bedroom-door to admit his wife, who had nothing to say but, "Well, dear neighbor, you've turned the tables on me," and that, with a laugh.

"Open the chest," Zeppa bade her, which she did, whereupon he showed the woman her precious Spinelloccio.

It would be difficult to say which of the two was the more mortified, Spinelloccio on confronting Zeppa, and conscious that his friend was aware of his guilt, or his wife, on seeing her husband, and knowing that he had heard and felt how she had served him, over his head.

"Here's the jewel I give you," said Zeppa to her.

Spinelloccio climbed out of the chest, and without wasting words said, "We're even now, Zeppa, and as you just said to my wife, I think we should continue being as good friends as ever. Our wives are the only things we have that we don't share. Well, let's do so, from now on, and be done with it."

Zeppa was satisfied, and so the four had a good dinner together to seal the pact. From that day forward, each of the two women had two husbands, and each man two wives, with never a word or quarrel among them to mar their common joy.

✻

# THE NINTH STORY

*Master Simon, the doctor, inveigled by Bruno and Buffalmacco to go to a certain place one night, on a pretense of being initiated*

*into a secret band of rangers, is thrown by Buffalmacco into a*
*cess-pool, and left to get out of it as best he can.*

AFTER THE WOMEN HAD CARRIED ON A LITTLE DISCUSSION ON
the joint ownership of wives instituted by the two young men of
Siena, the queen, who was the only one left to speak, began, so
that she would not be infringing on Dioneo's privilege:

In my opinion, loving ladies, Spinelloccio certainly deserved
the lesson Zeppa taught him, and therefore I don't believe
Zeppa is to be harshly judged, since, as Pampinea demonstrated
a little while ago, a man is not to be blamed if he punishes people who deserve, or seek out trouble. Spinelloccio deserved
what he got, and I am going to tell you the story of a man who
brought his punishment upon himself. I firmly believe the men
who gave him what he sought are rather to be praised than
blamed. The gull himself was a doctor, who went to the schools
of Bologna an ass, and returned all befurred with dignity.

We've had occasion to observe every day, how the people
of our city come back from Bologna in the long, wide gowns of
judges, doctors, lawyers, all bedecked with scarlet and murrey,
and tricked out with other pompous pretensions. We've also
had a chance to notice from our daily experience, how the appearance belies what is actually behind it.

Now among these birds of fine feather, a certain Master Simon da Villa, richer in worldly inheritances than native mother
wit, came back not so long ago, a full-fledged doctor of medicine—at least, so he styled himself, as he displayed a great
scarlet gown and a huge, furred doctor's cap—and took up his
residence in a street which nowadays we call Cucumber Row.
This newly-returned doctor had many odd habits, among them
a peculiar way of asking anyone who was with him all kinds
of questions about chance passersby, and storing the details in
his memory, as though the medicines he gave his patients were
to be compounded of these odd scraps of information.

Of the many individuals he saw, two neighbors of his particularly struck his notice, the inseparable companions, Bruno and
Buffalmacco, the painters whom we've already mentioned twice
to-day. As he studied them, and observed that they seemed to
have no cares in the world, and to live as gayly as could be,
which was indeed the case, he asked various informants concerning their circumstances. On learning from all sources they
were both poor artists, a strange notion entered his mind. It was

impossible, he thought, for them to be leading such merry lives on their meager earnings. They were clever, crafty fellows, as everyone told him. Surely they must have some secret source of income, unknown to the world at large, from which they must derive tremendous profits. The thought made him itch to strike up an acquaintance with them both, if he could, or at least with one of them. As it happened, he became friendly with Bruno.

It did not take the painter more than a few interviews to discover that this doctor was a veritable donkey, and soon he derived the finest sport in the world from observing his peculiar antics. The doctor, too, greatly enjoyed his new friend's company, and thinking that because he had invited the artist to dinner several times, he could therefore pry into his business and discuss his private affairs, he confessed to him his wonder at the gay life he and Buffalmacco led, though so poor, ending by begging him to let him into their secret.

Bruno listened to the doctor, and thinking the request was none other than a bit of his usual impertinent nonsense, laughed and decided to give him the answer his stupidity deserved.

"Doctor," he said, "there aren't many people to whom I'd confess how we manage to live as we do. But I'll make no pretense about telling you, since you're a friend of mine and wouldn't think of betraying my confidence. It's true Buffalmacco and I live as gayly as you see—more so, in fact, though if we depended on our art, or the income of any of our bits of property, we wouldn't even be able to afford the water we use. But I don't want you to think for a moment that we go breaking into people's houses. We simply go bush-ranging, and without doing anybody harm, we take whatever we like or need. That explains why we live as merrily as you see, without a care in the world!"

The doctor did not quite grasp what he meant. Nevertheless, he swallowed the story whole, marveling at the wonder of it. Immediately, he was burning with an intense desire to know what this bush-ranging was, and pleaded earnestly with Bruno to tell him, assuring him that he would never whisper a word of it to a living soul.

"Heavens, doctor! What are you asking me?" he cried. "It's a tremendous secret, this thing that you want me to tell you, and enough to ruin me and banish me from the world. Indeed, it would be enough to throw me into the jaws of the Lucifer of San Gallo, if anybody else got wind of it! But so great is the love I bear your honorable doltishness, and the faith I have in you, that I can't find it in me to deny any of your requests. So I shall tell you my secret, but on one condition. You must swear by the cross of Montesone never to breathe a word of it to a living soul, as you promised."

"On my word, and by the cross of Montesone," swore the doctor.

"Well, doctor honey," began Bruno, "you must know that not so long ago there lived in this town a great wizard, known as Michael Scott, because he came from Scotland, and he was held in great honor and esteem by many noblemen, very few of whom are still alive to-day. He was anxious to leave this city, so at the earnest prayers of his hosts, he left behind him two expert and well-trained pupils of his, with the express command that they should always be ready to carry out the wishes of the gentlemen who had offered him hospitality. Accordingly, the disciples put their art very generously at the disposal of these lords, in matters of love and other little things. But then, developing a certain fondness for the city and the ways of its folks, they decided to make it their permanent home, and grew very friendly with some of the citizens, irrespective of who they were, gentlefolk or not, rich or poor. Only one thing they demanded, and that was, that these people be men of their own tastes, and congenial folk. Well, in order to please these new friends of theirs, they got together a society of about twenty-five members, which met at least twice a month at a place they decided on in advance. Then, once they were gathered there, each man expressed his wish, and quick as a flash, the wizards granted it for the night.

"Now my friend Buffalmacco and I became quite intimate with these two, so that we were admitted to the society and are still members of it. Believe me, whenever we hold our meetings, you ought to see how marvelous it is to behold all those gorgeous tapestries hung around the banquet-hall, and the tables set fit for a king, and the hosts of noble, beautiful servants, men and women, all at the beck and call of each guest! And oh, the bowls and beakers, and the flasks, and all the gold and silver goblets, and the dinner-service out of which we eat and drink! And most of all, the huge quantities and varieties of delicacies to please every taste, that are served to us, course after course, all in good time! I could never describe the sounds of sweet music produced by countless instruments, and the

melodious carols that soothe the ear! No, nor could I do justice
to the quantities of wax burned up to light those banquets, or
the delicacies that are consumed, or the rare, costly wines
drunk! Don't fancy we sit there in the suits of clothes you see
us in, O worthy simpleton! There's not a man of us, however
insignificant, who doesn't look like an emperor, so richly are we
dressed and decked with gorgeous ornaments!

"But beyond all these pleasures offered us, there's that of
beautiful women. You have only to wish, and they are brought
before you from the four corners of the earth. There, you may
come face to face with the Lady of the Bearded Niche, and the
Queen of the Basques, the wife of the Sultan, the Empress of
Osbech, the Blabalot of Nornland, the Halfthere of Berlinzone,
and the Lackwit of Zanyton. But what am I telling you? We
have all the queens in the world, even the Redpoll of Prester
John, who has his horns planted in the middle of his arse—can
you imagine such a thing? Well, after these ladies have quaffed
a bowl, eaten a tid-bit or so, and taken a couple of turns around
the dance-floor, each one retires to her bedroom, with the man
at whose wish she was summoned there. Ah, those bedrooms!
Believe me, they look like a glimpse of Paradise, so beautiful
are they, and no less fragrant than the spice-jars of your shop,
when you have your cummin pounded. There are beds that
you'd swear were more magnificent than the Doge's of Venice,
and it's in those beds they go to rest. Heavens, what a to-do with
the pedals, what a pulling of cleats these fair weavers carry on,
to get a close weave! I leave it to your imagination!

"The luckiest of them all, though, in my opinion, are Buffalmacco and myself, for he sends for the Queen of France most of
the time, and I for the Queen of England, two of the handsomest
women in the world. We know so well how to handle them, that
they have no eyes for anybody else. You can see for yourself,
whether we have good reason to live more happily than other
men, and have a jollier time, considering the fact that we possess the love of two such glorious queens—not to mention that
whenever we want a thousand florins or so from them, we're
ever accommodated.

"Well then, this is the thing we call bush-ranging in the
vernacular—for just as rangers despoil men of their possessions, so do we, with the simple difference that they never give
it back, whereas we always do, after we've made use of it. You
understand, then, worshipful doctor, what we mean when we

say we go bush-ranging, and you see how important it is to keep the matter secret. I needn't say any more about it, or urge you further to keep it to yourself."

Well, our worthy doctor, whose science went no farther, perhaps, than to cure babies of milk-rash, believed Bruno's words as though they had been gospel truth, and was kindled to as great a pitch of desire to be admitted to the society, as any man might feel for the most desirable thing imaginable.

"It's no great wonder both of you are so happy," he remarked to Bruno in all seriousness. It was with great difficulty he put off for another time his request to be made a member of the band, thinking that after he had shown Bruno further kindnesses, he could more confidently voice his prayers. Therefore, reserving his plea for a more propitious occasion, he developed still more friendly relations with Bruno, inviting him to meals night and day, and showering upon him the most extravagant affection. So close indeed was this friendship, that it looked as if the doctor no longer knew how to live without him, or could, for that matter.

Bruno, on his part, seeing he had fallen on soft ground, had no wish to seem ungrateful in the face of the doctor's favors, and painted a whole Lent on the walls of his parlor, an Agnus Dei in the foyer of his bedroom, and above the street-door a handsome chamber-pot, so that patients in need of his services might be able to distinguish him from others of his profession. Moreover, in a little gallery of the doctor's house, Bruno painted the battle of the rats and the cats, over whose beauties his host went into raptures.

Sometimes, the artist would say to the doctor, when he had not been invited to supper, "Last night I went to a meeting, and as I was a little tired of the Queen of England, I had them summon for me the Prettybitch of the Grand Cham of Tartary."

"What's this Prettybitch?" asked the doctor. "I'm not well up in those names."

"I don't wonder at all, doctor honey," replied Bruno, "for I've heard Porcograsso and Vannacena make no mention of them."

"You mean Ipocrasso and Avicenna," corrected the doctor.

"My word, I suppose so!" replied Bruno. "I know as little of your names as you do of mine. Well, Prettybitch, in the vernacular of the Grand Cham, means the same thing as quean in ours.

What a damn fine wench you'd find her, though. She'd make you forget your medicines, I swear, and all your pots and plasters!"

Again, and again, he set fuel to the doctor's fire in this fashion. At last, one night, as the doctor was holding up the light while Bruno was busy on his fresco of the battle between the rats and the cats, he thought he had now won him over with his many kindnesses, and decided to open his heart to him. As they were alone, he said:

"God knows, Bruno, there's no man alive for whom I'd sacrifice everything as I would for you, and even if you were to ask me to walk from here to Peretola, I'd do it, believe me! So I don't want you to be surprised, if I ask you to do something for me in all friendship and confidence.

"As you recall, not so long ago you told me of the good times you have in your jolly society, and I wanted so to become a member, that I don't remember ever yearning as much for anything in all my life. And not without reason, as you will discover, if I should ever be admitted to it. Yes, you may even call me a fool and an idiot, if I don't summon the most wonderful and beautiful servant-girl you've ever laid eyes on! It was at Cacavincigli I met her last year, and I'm just wild about her. Christ's body, I offered her ten round shillings, if she'd give in to me, and the wench wouldn't! So I pray you, with all my heart and soul, tell me what I must do to become a member. And you, do all you can, exert all your influence to get me in. I promise, you'll have a trusty comrade in me, and one of considerable standing, too, I'll have you know! First and foremost, look at me! You see what a good-looking chap I am—and I have a leg! My face is as fresh as a rose, and what's more, I'm a doctor of medicine, which your company has none of, I'm sure. Yes, and I know a lot of jolly stories and ballads, too. Listen, I'll sing you one." Immediately he burst into song.

Bruno was dying to laugh, and nearly exploded into a roar, but still he contained himself. The ballad sung, "What do you think of it?" asked the doctor.

Bruno said, "Marvelous! On my word, cheap reed whistles are nothing to you, so gloriously did you sing off-key!"

"Yes, indeed," said the doctor. "You'd never have believed it, if you hadn't heard it with your own ears."

"Right you are, no doubt about it," agreed Bruno.

The doctor resumed, "I know plenty more, but we won't

speak of them now. You see me here before you, the son of a gentleman, even though my father did live in the country. Moreover, I'm sprung of a mother who boasts of Vallecchio blood. Then, as you've been able to see for yourself, I have the finest books and the best clothes of any doctor in Florence. Faith, I've a suit that cost me over four hundred lire, all told, and that was more than ten years ago, mind you! So please, I urge you with all my heart, do your best to get me admitted to your society. If you'll only manage it, I swear you can be as sick as you please, and I'll never charge you a penny for my cures."

Bruno took heed of the doctor's words, and was more than ever convinced he was a blockhead.

"Pardon me, doctor," he said, "hold the light a trifle more this way, and don't be impatient while I put tails on these rats. Then I'll answer you." The tails duly provided, Bruno turned to the doctor, pretending his request weighed heavily upon his mind, and said, "Yes, doctor, I admit there are no lengths to which you wouldn't go for my sake. Still, though what you ask me to do for you may be little enough for a man of your intellect, it's a serious problem so far as I am concerned. There's no man for whom I'd do it more willingly than yourself, if it lay in my power; first of all because I love you as you deserve, and then for your words, which are so rich in sense that they'd move a stone, not to speak of shaking my resolve. Truly, the longer I know you, the wiser you seem to be. But even if there were no other reason, I could not help loving you, considering you are so crazy about a creature as lovely as you described. I can tell you this, though. I haven't as much to say over matters of initiation as you seem to imagine, and so I could not do for you all that is required. However, if you swear to me your solemnest and most inviolable oath, that you'll keep it to yourself, I'll tell you the way to go about it. I'm almost sure that in view of the fine books and clothes you mentioned just now, you'll have no trouble in getting what you want."

"Speak, speak in all security," urged the doctor. "Ah, I see you still don't know me intimately, and have no notion of how well I can keep a secret. Why, when Master Gasparruolo da Saliceto was judge at Forlimpopoli, he never did a thing without telling me about it, he had such faith in my secrecy. Do you want proof? Well, I'm the first man he ever told he was going to marry Bergamina. Just fancy that!"

"That's settled, then," replied Bruno, "for if this worthy

trusted you, I can do likewise. Well, here's what you have to do. In this society of ours, it is our custom to have a president and two counselors, who are elected every six months. There's no doubt Buffalmacco will be chosen president the beginning of the month, and I shall be counselor—that's already arranged. Now you must know that the president can be very influential in having any man he wishes admitted to the society, so I think you should do your best to make friends with Buffalmacco, and get in his good graces by treating him royally. He's the sort of man who would like you immediately on discovering what a scholar you are. After you've overwhelmed him into friendship with your wit, and the good things you have aplenty, you can broach your request. He couldn't possibly refuse you. As it is, I've already told him about you, and he's very fond of you. So, then, after you've done as I say, let me deal with him."

"That's fine advice," said the doctor, "and I like it. If he's really the kind of man who enjoys the company of scholars, let him exchange a few words with me, and you'll see how I'll make him seek me out after that. Why, as for wisdom, I've enough to furnish a town and still remain a sage!"

After Bruno had come to an agreement with the doctor, he told the whole story to Buffalmacco, who could scarcely control his impatient desire to give this extraordinary numskull all he was looking for; while Dr. Simon, equally anxious to go bush-ranging, did not have a moment's rest till he succeeded in striking up an acquaintance with him. Then began a round of tempting dinners, banquets and feasts in honor of Buffalmacco and Bruno, who, sampling the generous wines, fatted capons and goodies worth a fabulous amount, furnished by their host, stuck close at his heels. At last, like the obliging good fellows they were, they ended by becoming the doctor's permanent guests, without much coaxing, though they never failed to assure him they would not have done any other man the honor.

Finally, when Dr. Simon thought the moment ripe, he bearded Buffalmacco on the subject of membership to the society, as he had already done Bruno. The cunning rogue simulated dreadful fury and rated Bruno soundly, saying, "By the Lord of Pasignano, I don't know what's keeping me from bashing you on the head till your nose falls to your heels, you stool-pigeon! You're the only one who could have given the doctor this information."

Dr. Simon took the other's part, staunchly denying Bruno

had told him anything, and swearing he had learned of it from other sources, until, by dint of his moving eloquence, overflowing with its usual wisdom, he succeeded in pacifying Buffalmacco.

"One can well see you've studied at Bologna, my dear doctor," he said, "and that you've brought back a sealed mouth to this town. It's also obvious that you did not learn your ABC on the apple, like most numskulls, but on the squash, which is so long. And again, if I'm not mistaken, you must have been baptized on a Sunday. Bruno, here, told me you went to Bologna to study medicine, but it seems to me you studied to persuade men, a thing you can do better than anybody else I know, with your great wisdom and eloquence."

The doctor let him go no further, and said, turning to Bruno, "See what it means to have to do with wise men! Who could have grasped every particular of my mental make-up as readily as this estimable gentleman? Why, you weren't half so quick to appreciate my good points as he was! But confess, don't you think I lived up to what I said, when you told me Buffalmacco liked to rub elbows with scholars?"

"You certainly did, and more!" assented Bruno.

Dr. Simon then addressed Buffalmacco. "You'd have had plenty to talk about, if you had seen me in Bologna. There wasn't a soul in that town, great or small, master or pupil, who didn't go wild over me, so much did I delight them with my talk and cleverness. I never said a word, I tell you, that I didn't have every man of them rocking with laughter—that's how much they liked to hear me speak. Yes, when I left they mourned and cried and begged me to remain, and they went to such limits that, if I had only stayed, they would have had me alone deliver the lectures on medicine to the body of students. I didn't want to, though, as I was anxious to take possession of some very valuable property that's always been in the family, and so I came back."

"What do you say now?" Bruno asked his friend. "You wouldn't believe me when I told you! I swear, there's not a doctor in these regions who can hold a candle to him, when it comes to understanding ass' piss, and I'll bet you could not come across another like him if you were to go from here to the gates of Paris. Now try to keep from doing what he asks you!"

"Bruno's right," said Dr. Simon. "But I'm not appreciated in these parts. You're all rather stupid people here on the whole.

But you ought to see me among my kind, the scholars, where I belong!"

Said Buffalmacco, "Indeed, doctor, I must admit you know our folks better than I should have thought. But speaking as one ought, to men of learning like yourself, I tell you right now, that I will most assuredly manage to have you elected a member of our society."

After this promise, the doctor's liberality towards the two rogues knew no bounds. They, for their part, lived like princes while they could, and led him a merry dance, palming off the most arrant nonsense on him, to the extent of saying they would procure for his mistress the Countess of the Latrine, the most beautiful thing to be found in all the outskirts of the human generation.

"And pray, who is this countess?" asked our precious pumpkinhead.

"Ah, my friend," Buffalmacco informed him, "she is a mighty great lady, and there are very few homes the world over where she hasn't some control, not to mention the friars Minor, among other folks, who kow-tow to her, to the clatter of castanets. I must say, whenever she goes out, she lets the world know about it, even though a good part of the time she's very much shut up. Only the other night, nevertheless, she passed by your door, as she was going to the Arno to wash her feet and take a breath of air, but most often she remains in the country of the Latrine. You can see many of her sergeants about very often, all of them carrying the staff and the sphere, as a sign of her authority. As for her knights, they're everywhere to be found—for instance, His worshipful Highness of the Door, Master Shyte, Lord Broomhandle, Spattersplash and many others besides, who must all be friends of yours, though you can't recall them just now. Forget the wench of Cacavincigli, for it's to the arms of this great lady we'll bring you, unless we're mistaken."

The doctor, a Bolognese by birth and training, did not understand their slang, and was therefore mighty well pleased at the prospect of such a mistress. Not long after this conversation, the two rogues came and brought him the welcome news that he had been accepted as a member of their confraternity, whereupon the doctor invited them to dinner the day preceding the night of the society's meeting.

"What am I to do to get there?" he asked, when the dinner was over.

"You see, doctor," began Buffalmacco, "to begin with, you must have steady nerves, for unless you have, you might meet with some obstacle, and at the same time bring us to serious harm. Now I'll tell you why you need courage. To-night, at about the time when you would ordinarily be falling asleep, you must make it your business to be on one of those raised tombs that were erected some time ago beyond the walls of Santa Maria Novella. Be sure to wear one of your most gorgeous suits, so that you'll create a fine impression on your introduction to the society, and also because, from what we were able to gather from report, the countess intends to knight you with the Order of the Bath at her own expense, seeing you are a gentleman of good family.

"Well, when you get to the tombs, wait until the guide comes, whom we'll send for you. I want to prepare you beforehand for all this, so pay attention. This thing that will come for you, is a black beast, not too large, with horns on its pate. Now, the moment it appears, it will try to scare you by prancing and leaping about, and raising the devil with its bellowing and roaring. But when it sees you're not afraid, it will come near you as gently as a lamb. Then you are to jump down fearlessly from the monument, without calling on God or the saints, and mount upon its back. Don't touch it any more after that, but just fold your hands across your breast as a sign of submission, and it will gently go its way and carry you to our meeting-place.

"But I must warn you, if you call on God or the saints, or show the least sign of fear, it may throw you off its back and pitch you into some hole, where you'd surely stink for it. So I repeat, if you think you haven't the courage to go through with it, for goodness' sake don't come, for you'll only bring yourself to harm and do us no worldly good."

"You evidently don't know me yet," answered the doctor. "Perhaps you imagine I'm a ninny, because of my gloves and my long gown. If you knew the mischief I used to be up to in Bologna, when I went whoring with my chums, you'd be surprised! My word, I remember a certain night when a girl refused to come along with us—a sorry little slut she was, no higher than my knee! Ha-ha! First I gave her a sound drubbing, and then, lifting her off her feet, I think without exaggeration, I must have carried her at least a good bow-shot, until finally, by hook or crook, she had to give in and come along. And that other night, when I was all alone with my servant, and walked past the burial ground of the friars Minor! Think of it, a woman had been buried that very day, and I wasn't even frightened! So don't you give yourselves any concern about me. I'm a brave fellow, I am, and mighty strong, too. As for my clothes, I want you to know I'll have you proud of me! I'm going to wear the scarlet gown in which I got my degree, and we'll see how glad your society will be to have me. I'll bet they'll make me president then and there! Imagine the stir I'll make when I'm present in person, if, even before clapping eyes on me, this countess is so mad about me that she's willing to knight me with the Order of the Bath! What, as if I can't wear the honor as well as any, or fail to carry it off with as good a grace. Just leave it to me!"

"That's splendid," said Buffalmacco, "but don't play us a trick by not appearing at the appointed place when we send for you. I'm merely mentioning this, because it's pretty cold these nights, and you doctors are awfully finicky about such things."

"The Lord be thanked, I'm none of your frozen turnips," said Dr. Simon. "I never worry about the cold. Indeed, whenever I have to get up at night to obey a call of nature, as a man sometimes has to, I hardly ever put anything over my nightshirt but my fur-coat—so I'll be on the spot, without fail."

The two friends went away. Accordingly, as the coming darkness heralded the night, the doctor gave some plausible excuses to his wife, and cautiously drew his best gown out of the closet. Then, when he thought the moment had come, he slipped it on and sallied forth to Santa Maria Novella. Climbing upon a raised tomb, he drew his clothes about him because of the bitter cold, and hugging himself tight, resigned himself to await the coming of the beast.

In the meantime, Buffalmacco, who was a great, strapping hulk of a man, arranged to get hold of one of those masks much used in certain games now out of fashion, and putting on a black fur coat, with the hairy side outward, dressed himself to look very much like a bear, except that the mask was made to resemble a devil's face, with great big horns. So disguised, he went to the square of Santa Maria Novella, Bruno walking a little behind, to see how the joke would turn out. No sooner did Buffalmacco catch sight of the doctor huddled upon the tomb, than he set up a gay dance of his own, jumping and leaping and tumbling and capering about the square, accompanying the frolic with such fearful roaring, shrieking, whistling and howling, that one might have thought him a thing possessed.

The doctor's hair stood on end when he caught sight of the beast and heard its unearthly clamor, and being more timid than a woman, he quaked and shivered and wished himself safe at home, rather than where he was. Since he had gone so far, he plucked up his spirits and resolved to see it through, pricked as he was by his impatience to witness the wonders the two friends had described.

Buffalmacco, after playing the devil a while, made a feint of calming down, and approaching the tomb where the doctor was crouching, stood still and waited. Dr. Simon, trembling with dread, was in a quandary, not knowing whether to mount the beast or to stay where he was. At last, fearing the creature might hurt him if he refused, he chose the lesser of the two evils, and coming down the gravestone, clambered on the beast's back, ejaculating a whispered, "God help me!" Although he did not cease shivering for a moment, he still made himself as comfortable as he could on the back of his mount, and folded his hands across his breast in an attitude of submission, as he had been told. Then Buffalmacco took the road toward Santa Maria della Scala, going slowly on all fours, until he approached the cloister of the nuns of Ripole.

Now at that time, there were a number of ditches in that district, into which the farmers of the surrounding fields used to drop the Countess of the Latrine, in order to fertilize the soil. Up walked Buffalmacco to the edge of one, and seizing the opportunity, took the doctor by the leg, pulled him suddenly off his back, and threw him headfirst into the hole, accompanying the gesture with grunts and howls, prancings and stampings and playing the very devil. Finally, he retraced his steps along Santa Maria della Scala, toward the field of Ognisanti, where he rejoined Bruno, who had disappeared from the scene, finding it impossible to contain his peals of laughter. Together, they rejoiced over the success of the joke, and then posted themselves at a distance from the ditch, to see what the bemerded doctor would do.

Now when our Dr. Simon found himself in that loathsome place, he struggled to get to his feet and climb out, but with every step he lost his foothold and slipped, until he was a foul, filthy mess from the crown of his head to the soles of his feet, even swallowing a taste of the abomination. Nevertheless, he finally managed to scramble out at the expense of his doctor's cap, which he had to leave behind, and cleared himself of as much ordure as he could scrape off with his hands. Then not knowing what else to do, he returned home and clattered at the gate until someone let him in.

Scarcely had the door closed upon the poor, foul, stinking devil, when the two rascals popped up to witness the reception he got from his wife, whom they could hear from outside, giving him a lecture in round terms. "Good, good!" she was saying. "It serves you right! You had gone whoring, eh? And you had put on your fine scarlet gown to show the wench how handsome and wonderful you are! What, am I not enough for you? Believe me, I'd be plenty for a whole nation, let alone your paltry self! Would to heaven they had twisted your throat while they were at it, instead of simply throwing you where you deserved to be thrown! Here's a fine specimen! Here's a respectable doctor for you, who has a wife of his own, and goes prowling about at night hunting other men's!"

With such words, and others in the same key, she stood by while the doctor was being washed, and did not cease tormenting him until well-nigh midnight.

The following morning, the two rogues presented themselves at the doctor's house, taking care beforehand to bedaub themselves, under their clothes, with black and blue streaks resembling the contusions left by a beating. They found the doctor already risen, and were admitted. As they walked toward his room, their nostrils were everywhere assailed by a lingering stench, for it had been impossible to remove it from his clothes, in spite of many washings. Upon hearing the sound of their steps, Dr. Simon got up to meet them and wished them good morning, but the two rascals, who had arranged beforehand how they were to proceed, replied, feigning great anger:

"We wish you no such thing! On the contrary, would to God He would send you afflictions enough to make you die like a beast, traitorous wretch that you are! It's no fault of yours we weren't killed like two dogs, after we went through all that trouble to pleasure you and show you honor! Last night we were so belabored with blows, that half of them would take an ass to Rome! And all because you played us false! Do you think that's all? We even run the danger of being expelled from the society, to which we had arranged to admit you. If you don't believe us, look at our bodies and see what they're like!"

In the dim light of the room, they opened their smocks and gave him a glimpse of their chests all adorned with painted bruises, then quickly covered them up again. Dr. Simon would have apologized, and recounted his own tale of woe with complete details of how he had been thrown from the beast, and into what foul a place, but Buffalmacco interrupted him.

"I wish it had thrown you plumb off the bridge into the river," he cried. "Why the devil did you have to call on God and the saints? Didn't we give you sufficient warning in advance?"

"I didn't, I swear," said the doctor.

"What do you mean you didn't!" cried Buffalmacco. "You certainly did. Over and over, too! Our guide told us you trembled like a reed, and didn't know what you were about. You've played us a mean trick, all right, but nobody will ever catch us again! We'll get you yet for it, though, mark my words!"

"For God's sake, forgive me," pleaded the doctor. "Don't shame me before my neighbors," and with all the eloquence at his command he strove to win them over.

His fear of their telling the story abroad and shaming him publicly, had a salutary effect for Bruno and Buffalmacco, for if in the past the doctor had overwhelmed them with his generosity, from that time on he waxed even more generous, showering them with honors, dinners, banquets and other good things.

So it was that wisdom was taught to the scholar who had learned so little of it at Bologna.

*

## THE TENTH STORY

*A Sicilian woman cunningly cheats a merchant out of the profits he made in Palermo; but the man, pretending to have returned with more valuable merchandise than before, borrows money from her and leaves her nothing but water and oakum in exchange.*

YOU NEED NOT ASK HOW HEARTILY THE QUEEN'S STORY HAD MADE them all laugh by its various details. It is enough to say that every woman there had laughed to the point of tears, at least a dozen times. However, when it drew to a close, Dioneo, knowing his turn had come, plunged into his own.

Gracious ladies, he began, it is a well-known fact that the more cunning the person befooled, the more gratifying we find the tricks that do it. Although all of you have told very good stories, I am going to tell you one on the same theme, that you should appreciate more than the others, for the simple reason that the trickster who was fooled in the end, was a subtler mistress of the art than any of the men or women you've told about.

Well, there was once a custom, which I believe may survive to this day, in all countries having ports on the open sea, that whenever merchants arrived with a ship-load of merchandise, they unloaded the cargo and had it transported to a storehouse commonly known as the customs-house, which was generally maintained by the town or the prince of the country. There, the merchants presented an invoice of their cargo to the proper functionaries, together with a declaration of its value, and upon being assigned a warehouse, stored their goods under lock and key. Then the customs officers noted in their records the value of the goods to the merchant's credit, and as the merchandise was disposed of, entirely or in part, they deducted their commission from the profits. It is this customs record or directory from which brokers derive their information, concerning the quality and quantity of the goods and standing of the merchants to whom it belongs. Then, depending on what they need, they enter into business relations with the merchants, and carry on their exchanges, barters, sales and other affairs.

Now this custom was in force, as everywhere else, in Palermo, Sicily, where there were likewise to be found, as you may find to this day, many women beautiful of body, but at loggerheads with virtue,—though anyone not acquainted with them might mistake them for well-born, modest ladies. As soon as a foreign merchant comes to town, these women, given over heart and soul, as they are, not simply to shave men, but to skin them alive, consult the customs directory to see what goods he has, and how much he is worth, and then with their pleasant ways, soft speech and artful, amorous wiles, do their utmost to catch him in their net, under pretense of love. Many a man has been caught in this fashion, from whom they have filched a large share of his merchandise. And many a one has been robbed of everything, yes, to the extent of making the poor devil leave both goods and ship, and sometimes his skin and bones behind, so cunningly did the lady-barber know how to wield her razor.

Well, not so long ago, one of our young Florentine merchants arrived in Palermo, commissioned by his employers to dispose of a quantity of woolen cloth, which had been left over from a fair at Salerno, and was perhaps worth five hundred florins in gold. Declaring its value to the customs officers, he stored it in a warehouse, and caring little about getting rid of it in a hurry, he wandered about the city, to see the sights and have a good time.

Now Salabaetto, for so he was called, though his name was Nicolo da Cignano, was a fair, golden-haired, attractive youth with a body straight and lithe as an arrow, and as he went about, it chanced that Iancofiore, one of these lady-barbers, having learned of his circumstances, fell to ogling him. He became aware of her attentions, and thinking she must be a great lady, attracted to him by his physical charms, decided to carry on the love-affair with discretion, and therefore, without making anyone privy to his intentions, he began walking up and down in front of her house. Iancofiore was not slow to notice it, and for a few days kept him in a flame of passion by the glances of her eyes, pretending she was pining away for love of him. Then secretly she sent a maid-servant of hers, an accomplished mistress in the procurer's art, to speak to him. The woman first talked of things in general, but then, almost with tears in her eyes, she informed him that his good looks and graciousness had so bewitched her mistress, that the poor lady could find no peace, either day or night.

"So, at your convenience," she added, "she would like more than anything imaginable to meet you secretly at a bath." And taking a ring out of her purse, she made him a gift of it, on behalf of her mistress.

Salabaetto was the happiest man alive at the news, and taking the ring, held it to his eyes. Then, kissing it, he slipped it on his finger and said to the good woman, "If Iancofiore loves me, tell her her love is requited a thousandfold, for I love her more than life itself," adding that he would go anywhere she wished, any time she commanded.

The go-between, returning to her mistress, reported Salabaetto's answer, whereupon the youth was soon informed at what bath he was to await her the following day, after vespers.

Accordingly, Salabaetto was punctual to keep the rendezvous at the appointed hour, and without saying a word about it to anyone, found the bath Iancofiore had engaged. He had scarcely been waiting a minute or so when two slave-girls appeared, loaded down with all kinds of things, one carrying on her head a fine mattress stuffed with cotton wool, and her companion a basket of provisions.

Laying the mattress on a bed in a private room of the bath, they spread over it a pair of dainty sheets, decorated with silk embroidery, and over them, a coverlet of Cyprian buckram, white as driven snow, with two pillows wrought in open lace that was a wonder to see. That done, they doffed their clothes, and climbing into the bath, scoured it until it gleamed.

Iancofiore herself was not long in coming, and arrived escorted by two other slave-girls. At the first opportunity, she greeted him effusively, and heaving the deepest sighs, said, after a shower of kisses and embraces, "I don't know who but you could ever have brought me to this! You've kept me in a furnace of love, O my precious Tuscan darling!"

Then, when she was ready, they entered the bath together stark-naked, and with them, two of the slave-girls. But she wouldn't hear of their laying a hand on him. Oh, no! She herself washed him all over with soap, scented with musk and cloves, and later rinsed him in a way that was wonderful to see. Then she had her own body soaped and massaged by the slave-girls. When the bath was over, the attendants brought two snow-white sheets, so redolent of roses that the surrounding air seemed a cloud of attar, in one of which they wrapped Salabaetto, and in the other, the lady, and then, lifting them up bodily, carried them to the bed made ready for them.

For a while, they were left there to perspire, when the slave-girls relieved them of their wet sheets, and they remained naked on the others. At this stage, the attendants produced graceful silver perfume-bottles, some full of rose-water, and some of orange-blossom lotion, jessamine and extract of citron blooms, with which they sprinkled the bathers' bodies. Later came boxes of sweets and flasks of precious wines, and for some time the lovers partook of the refreshments.

Salabaetto believed himself in heaven, and cast a thousand languishing glances at Iancofiore, who was indeed a beautiful woman. The time seemed never to pass before the slave-girls would leave them and he would find himself in her embrace. At last the attendants took their leave at Iancofiore's request, after lighting a torch in the chamber, and the lovers fell to embracing each other, dallying for a long time, to the youth's delight, who believed she was consumed with love of him.

At length, Iancofiore thought it time to go home, and summoning the attendants, the two lovers dressed and regained their dissipated forces with another sip of wine and a taste of the sweets. Then, washing their hands and faces in the scented toilet-waters, they were ready to go, when Iancofiore said, "If you've no objection, Salabaetto, I'd consider it a great privilege for you to sup with me this evening, at my home, and spend the night with me."

Salabaetto had already been entirely seduced by her beauty and artful wiles, and was certain she loved him as her immortal soul. Therefore he replied, "Iancofiore, every wish of yours is most agreeable to me, hence to-night and all other nights, I will do whatever is your wish and pleasure."

Iancofiore returned home, had her bedroom adorned with all her dresses and knick-knacks, and ordering a delicious supper, waited for Salabaetto to come. The night had hardly fallen when he set out for his mistress' house, where he was welcomed with joy and cheer and royally entertained.

After supper, Iancofiore and he retired to the bedroom, full of a heady fragrance of burning lign-aloes. The bed was richly embroidered with Cyprian singing-birds; costly gowns hung from the racks. "Truly," thought Salabaetto, "she must be a grand lady, and a rich one, too." It is true he had heard gossip to the contrary about her way of living, but he would not believe it for anything in the world. Indeed, if he had a slight suspicion that she might have taken advantage of other men, he was certain that such a thing could never happen to him.

All night long he lay with her in a heaven of bliss, adding fuel to the flame of his passion. In the morning Iancofiore, girding about him a handsome silver belt with a purse, said, "Dearest love, I commend myself to your pleasure, and as my body is at your command, so is everything I possess. Speak, and I will do for you all that is in my power."

Salabaetto took her in his arms and kissed her happily; then leaving her house, he went to the meeting-place of merchants like myself.

Time passed, and the youth was a frequent visitor at Iancofiore's house. His amusement cost him nothing, but he became more and more embroiled with her. Now during this state of affairs, he struck a bargain over his cargo of stuffs, and cleared a goodly profit, which soon came to Iancofiore's knowledge, though not through Salabaetto. One night, therefore, when he went to see her, she began to chat and play with him, giving him a thousand kisses and embracing him, indeed, feigning such ardent passion that she looked ready to expire in his arms for very love. She would even have given him two beautiful silver plates, but Salabaetto would not accept them, scrupling at the thought that with one gift and another, he had already accepted some thirty florins' worth of bounties from her, and still he had not succeeded in making her take as much as a penny's worth from him. Finally, when she had roused him to the highest pitch of desire by her passionate and wanton behavior, one of her slave-girls came in as she had arranged, and called her.

Iancofiore left the room, and a little later returned all in tears. Then, flinging herself face downward on the bed, she wept in despair and wailed as no woman had ever done before. Sala-baetto did not know what to make of it, and gathering her in his arms, said, as he wept in sympathy, "Tell me, beloved, what has come over you so suddenly? What makes you despair so? Come, tell me, darling!"

She allowed herself to be coaxed and begged for a suffi-ciently long time, and then replied, "Alas, my love, I don't know what to do or say! I've just received some letters from my brother in Messina, bidding me sell or pawn everything I have here, as I must send him a thousand florins within a week without fail, otherwise he'll forfeit his head. I'm at my wits' end. How can I raise that amount at such short notice? If I had only two weeks' time, I'd find a way of obtaining it, from certain sources from which even more money is owing me. I could even sell a bit of our property. But I can't! I can't! O God, would I had died before such dreadful news ever reached me!"

Her despair knew no bounds, and not for a moment did she cease lamenting. Now Salabaetto, whom the flames of love had robbed of his usual common sense, believed that her tears were genuine and her words even more so.

"Dearest one," he said, "I cannot accommodate you with a thousand florins, but I can let you have five hundred, if you think you can return the money to me in two weeks. It's very fortunate for you that I was able to dispose of my stuffs yester-day, for if I hadn't, I couldn't have let you have even a penny."

"Oh, poor darling!" cried Iancofiore. "Do you mean to say

you've ever been in financial straits? Why didn't you ask me for money? Though I may not have a thousand florins at my disposal, I could always have spared you one hundred, even two hundred, if necessary. Really, you've made me feel uncomfortable about accepting the kindness you offer."

Salabaetto was more than ever deceived by her words and answered, "Please don't let that prevent you! Believe me, if I had ever needed money as you do at present, I wouldn't have hesitated a moment about asking you for it."

"Ah, my own, dear Salabaetto!" sighed Iancofiore. "Now I know how true and wholehearted is the love you bear me! To think that without even waiting to be asked, you're so ready to help me out of my difficulty, and with such a large sum of money! Darling, you know that even without this, I belonged to you, body and soul. But now I shall be all the more yours, and I shall never fail to remember that I owe my brother's life to you! God knows I'm unwilling enough to accept the money from you, knowing you are a merchant, and that merchants carry on all their business by means of it. But since necessity obliges me, I'll take it. Besides, I'm certain I'll be able to give it back to you soon. As for the balance, well, if I can't find a way of scraping it together, I'll pawn all my belongings."

With that touching speech, and tears still streaming from her eyes, she let herself sink upon the youth's breast. He was ready with words of comfort, and spent the night with her. The following morning, the better to prove his generous devotion, he brought her the five hundred florins, without waiting for her to remind him. She took it with tears in her eyes, but with a heart leaping for joy in her breast, Salabaetto taking no surety but her simple promise.

Once Iancofiore had the money in her clutches, she played her lover quite a different tune. Whereas formerly, he had been free to come and go as he pleased, now all sorts of excuses began to crop up, so that he was lucky if he could see her once out of seven times. Nor was he showered with kisses and caresses and beaming looks, as in former days. The two weeks during which he should have received his money had come and gone. A month had passed, and another, and whenever he asked for it, he received only vague words in payment. At last, the scales fell from his eyes; he saw clearly through the crafty woman's wiles, and appreciated his own folly.

Realizing that he could make no demands upon her, since he

had neither a written statement nor any other testimony to prove he had given her the money, and ashamed to confide in anyone, because he had been warned against her in advance, and was therefore afraid of the ridicule he might naturally expect for his foolhardiness, he swallowed his misery, and in silence bewailed his stupidity.

His employers meanwhile had been plying him with letters, asking him to change the money and send it to them. Finally, fearing that if he did not, his error might be discovered and made public, he resolved to go away, and taking ship he went —not to Pisa, his rightful destination, but to Naples.

Now at that time, our friend Pietro dello Canigiano happened to be holding office in that city, as treasurer to the Empress of Constantinople. He was a learned man, of great wit and subtle understanding, and as it was, closely related to Salabaetto and his family. As Master Pietro was the sort of man who could keep a secret, Salabaetto, some days after his arrival, confided all his troubles to him and asked his help and advice about obtaining something to enable him to earn his livelihood, as he never intended to show his face in Florence.

"That was an evil thing you did," said Canigiano, distressed at what he heard. "You have behaved unworthily. It was a shabby kind of obedience you showed your masters, throwing away such a sum of money at once, and all for lechery! But what's done can't be undone, and we must cast about for some solution."

However, like the quick-witted man he was, he soon thought of a course to follow and told Salabaetto about it, who was delighted with the plan, and immediately prepared to carry it out. He still had a little money, and with the help of an equal sum, loaned him by his friend, he purchased a number of bales of cargo, which he had securely rolled and bound with cords. Then, buying twenty oil-casks and filling them, he loaded his merchandise on a ship and returned to Palermo. At the dock, he declared the value of his goods and casks to the customs officials, had the whole credited to him in the records, and depositing them in the warehouses, informed the men he was not going to dispose of them until the arrival of a new shipment of cargo which he expected.

Iancofiore was soon apprised of the event. Upon learning that the merchandise her former lover had brought on this occasion, was worth a thousand florins or more, without taking the shipment he expected into account, which was easily computed at three thousand more, she thought she had fleeced him of entirely too little. Accordingly, planning to bait him by returning the five hundred florins in order to obtain a goodly part of the five thousand, she sent for Salabaetto.

The youth's wits by this time had been sharpened, and he went to her. Marvelous was the effusiveness of her welcome as, pretending to be wholly ignorant of the cargo he had brought, she said, "Are you angry with me, dear, because I didn't pay back your loan when I should have?"

Salabaetto burst out laughing and said, "Well, to be frank, I was a little hurt, considering that I would tear out my heart for your sake, if I thought it would give you any pleasure. But I'll show you how angry I am. I'm so much in love with you, that I've disposed of most of my property, and bought up merchandise that is worth over two thousand florins. It's here with me now, and I'm waiting for another shipload from the West, to the value of three thousand florins more. Well, I've decided to set up a warehouse of my own in this town, and live here the rest of my life, just to be near you, for truly, I obtain more happiness from your love, than any man ever enjoyed with his mistress."

"Salabaetto," answered Iancofiore, "you see how happy I am at everything you do, for you're my darling, whom I love more than my life. Oh, what a joy it is to think you have come back with the intention of settling down in this city! Think of the good times we're going to have together—at least, I hope so. But I have some apologies to make, dear. You remember, when you were about to leave the city, you were sometimes anxious to come here, but you couldn't see me, and when you did, you weren't given the happy reception you were used to. Moreover, I didn't return your loan when I promised. You must realize, dear, that at that time I was in the depths of despair and affliction, and when one is in that state, she can't be expected to look cheerful and make a fuss over anybody, no matter how much she loves him, or how much he expects attention. Then, you must know it is no simple matter for a woman to get together a thousand florins. We get nothing but lies the live-long day, broken promises, and disappointments, and as a result we must lie to others. That's the reason, and the only reason, I didn't give you back your money. I did manage to get it, though, a little after you sailed away, and if I had known where to reach you, I'd have sent it to you, on my word. But I didn't know, you see, so I kept it for you."

Thereupon, she sent for a purse containing the very money he had brought her, and handing it to him she said, "Count it over, and see if it's five hundred florins."

Salabaetto was never so overjoyed in his life; counting the money, he found it to be the correct amount, and said, as he put it into the purse once more, "Iancofiore, I am convinced of your love, for you have given me sufficient demonstration of it. Both for that, and for the affection I bear you, there's no sum at my disposal which you could ask of me, that I wouldn't be glad to let you have for your needs. Wait until I am settled, and you can put me to the test."

Thus, with many words, their love was patched up. Once more, Salabaetto resumed his intimate relations with her, while she pampered and spoiled him with the greatest kindnesses, and pretended to be dying with love. However, he was resolved to pay back her deceit with deception, and one day, when he had been invited to sup and spend the night with her, he arrived so melancholy and woebegone, that he looked as though he were about to give up the ghost. Iancofiore put her arms around his neck and kissed him, and then plied him with questions as to the cause of his sorrow. For a long time, he allowed himself to be entreated, and then answered, "Iancofiore, this is the end of me! I'm ruined! The ship that was to bring me the merchandise I've been expecting, has been seized by pirates from Monaco, and they're holding it at a ransom of ten thousand florins in gold. I'm to pay a thousand as my share, and I haven't a penny, as I immediately sent your five hundred to Naples for a consignment of stuff to be sent me here. If I should be so foolish as to sell the merchandise I have here in storage, I'd hardly realize half of what it's worth, for this is the off-season. What's still worse, nobody here knows me well enough to want to help me, and I'm at my wits' end, because unless I send the money right away, the goods will be shipped off to Monaco, and I'll never be able to claim any of them again."

Iancofiore was deeply concerned by her fear of losing all she had been bargaining for. Therefore, thinking quickly of what she should do to keep him from going to Monaco, she said, "God knows it is a dreadful blow to me, for your sake. But what's the sense of making oneself miserable? If I had the sum at my disposal, God is my witness I'd let you have it without more ado. But I haven't. Of course there's a certain moneylender, who let me have five hundred florins the other day when I needed it, but he charges an enormous rate of interest—thirty per cent at least, and if you should want to borrow from him, you have to provide him with a good guarantee. I, for one, am perfectly willing to pawn everything I own—myself, if need be, for whatever he's disposed to let me have. But what security will you give him for the rest?"

Salabaetto knew too well what motives prompted her to do him this service, as he also suspected that she herself was the moneylender in question. He had no objections to make, however, and thanking her, said, "My need is too great for me to be daunted by such exorbitant interest. As for security, I'll pledge my goods lying in dock, in favor of the person who lends me the money. But I must keep the key of the warehouse, for you see, I may have to show the things to prospective buyers. Besides, I want to be sure nobody molests the stuff, or tampers with it, putting in one thing for another."

"You're quite right," said Iancofiore, adding that the security was all one could wish it to be.

Early the following morning, she sent for a broker strictly in her confidence, and telling him how the matter stood, gave him a thousand florins. This he gave to Salabaetto, and in return, the merchant signed over to him all the goods that were lying in the warehouse. The documents were duly signed and sealed to their mutual satisfaction, and parting friends, each went his way to look after his own affairs.

Salabaetto did not wait for the grass to grow under his feet, but boarding a galley with his fifteen hundred florins, he returned to Pietro dello Canigiano in Naples, and thence sent to his employers in Florence a full and scrupulous remittance for the stuff they had commissioned him to sell. Furthermore, he reimbursed Pietro and everyone else from whom he had accepted any loans, and for many days had a good time with his friend over the trick he had played the fair Sicilian. Thence he went to Florence, cured of all desire to be a merchant.

Meanwhile Iancofiore, seeing no trace of Salabaetto at Palermo, began to wonder at his strange disappearance and to feel suspicious. For more than two months she waited for him, but then, seeing that he did not come, she had the broker force open the warehouse. First of all they tested the casks that were believed to contain olive-oil, but alas, found they were filled with sea water, with perhaps a gallon or so of oil floating on the surface, near the bunghole. Then, unpacking the bales, they discovered that all of them but two, which held cloth, were stuffed with common oakum. In short, all the merchandise put together, was not worth more than two hundred florins.

Long and bitterly did the outwitted woman bewail the five hundred florins she had returned, and still more bitterly, the thousand she had lent Salabaetto, often saying to herself,

> "Who with a Tuscan would sell or buy,
>   Sharp must be of wit and eye."

And so she was left to swallow her loss, and the scorn of defeat, realizing too late that some people can be as clever as others.

As soon as Dioneo had finished his story, Lauretta knew the period of her reign was over, and commending Pietro Canigiano for his advice which had borne good fruit, and Salabaetto's wisdom, no less praiseworthy for carrying it out, she took her laurel-crown from her head and laid it on Emilia's, saying, with feminine charm, "I don't know whether you'll make a good queen, but at least we're certain to have a lovely one in you. Strive, then, to make your deeds conform with your beauty."

With that, she resumed her seat, as Emilia full of embarrassment, not so much at the honor bestowed upon her, as at being complimented for the gift which most women desire, blushed until her cheeks looked like roses filled with the flush of dawn. Then, keeping her eyes lowered until the blush was faded from her face, she made arrangements with the steward for everything necessary to their entertainment, and then addressed her company.

"My friends, we've often observed that, after the oxen have toiled under the yoke a good part of the day, they are released of their burden and allowed to roam through the pastures at their sweet will. Again, we have seen that gardens adorned with a variety of leafy blooms are no less beautiful, but indeed, more so, than woods flourishing with nothing but oak trees. I believe, then, considering how many days we have told our stories in accordance with a set theme, that we, no less than others toiling under restraint, will find it not only beneficial, but necessary to romp at will, the better to regain our strength for the yoke once more. Accordingly, I have no intention of setting restrictions on the sort of theme you choose in your usual pleasant story-telling. No, I'd like each and every one of you to regale us with whatever he likes, firmly believing, as I do, that the variety thus afforded will be no less charming than the result we would get by following a specified subject. After this, whoever succeeds to the kingship, will feel stronger for the task, and will therefore be able to keep us within the bounds of our usual laws with greater assurance."

With that she gave them leave to follow their inclinations until supper-time.

They all praised the queen for the wisdom of her suggestion, and then, rising to their feet, gave themselves over to various pastimes, the ladies to twining chaplets and romping about, and the youths to games and dancing. Thus, they passed the time before supper, when they gathered about the pleasant fountain and partook of their meal with cheer and goodwill. Afterwards, they enjoyed themselves singing and dancing, as they always did. At last the queen, following the precedent set by the rulers before her, requested Pamfilo to sing a song, in spite of the many which various members of the group had already sung of their own accord. But he began without waiting to be urged:

> "So great, O Love, the good,
>      The sweetness and delight you make me feel,
>      That I am glad to burn in your ordeal.
>
> The bounteous pleasures that fill up my heart
>      For the great joy and dear
>           To which you led me late,
> All overflowing from their vessel start
>      And on my visage clear
>           Reveal my happy state;
>           For of a high estate
>      My true love is, and of much worth and real.
>      Therefore I lightly bear the smart I feel.
>
> Neither with music nor with colors fair,
>      O Love, can I express
>           The joyousness I know.
> Yet if I could, I'd not my feelings bare;

> For were I to confess,
>     My joy would turn to woe.
>     With such content I glow,
> That did I vent a little of my weal,
> All words were halt that sought it to reveal.
>
> Beyond all dreams it was that ever I
>     Should in my arms enfold
>     That most desired place,
> Or to the sweetest of all spots so nigh
>     My burning visage hold,
>     For my soul's health and grace.
>         So fortunate a case
> Is mine, none would believe. Therefore I burn and reel,
> And what rejoices me from all conceal."

And so Pamfilo's song came to an end. In the course of it, all, without exception, had taken up the refrain, nor had they failed to note the words with more careful attention than was usually accorded the singer, striving to guess what he had to conceal from them. Nevertheless, though there were as many different conjectures as there were people conjecturing, not one of them was able to arrive at the truth.

But when the queen heard the song come to its close, and perceived that both the young men and women were anxious to rest, she dismissed them and sent them to bed.

# 9

## THE NINTH DAY

*

LIGHT, FROM WHOSE SPLENDOR THE SHADOWS FLEE, HAD ALREADY transmuted the deep azure of the eighth heaven to a rich blue, and the flowerets had begun to lift their heads in the meadows, when Emilia arose and had her fair companions summoned, as well as the youths. They came at her summons, and regulating their steps by the queen's easy pace, followed her to a greenwood not far from the palace. They went through the leafy alleys, and there found many animals, goats and deer, waiting for them like tame or friendly beasts, as though they were conscious of the existing plague and no longer had terror of the hunter.

The youths and maidens played with them awhile, chasing this one and that about, as though they wanted to catch them, and deriving the keenest delight from seeing them leap and scamper. But when the sun rose higher in the heavens, they thought it wise to retrace their steps. All of them were crowned with wreaths of oak-leaves, their hands full of flowers and fragrant herbs, so that anyone meeting them on the way, might with justice have said, "These are not meant for death, but if it does take them, it will find them in the height of joy."

So, step by step, they sought their way homeward, enlivening their walk with songs and jests and carefree chatter, until at last they came to the palace, where they found everything set for them, and the servants waiting, blithe and merry. They rested for a while, but they would not hear of going to dinner until they had sung together at least half a dozen songs, each jollier than the other. That pleasant duty done, they washed, and the steward assigned them their places at table, according to the queen's wish, when the courses were served and they fell to with cheer and relish.

After dinner they gave themselves up to dancing and playing for a time, when, at the queen's pleasure, all who wished retired to take their siesta. However, when the accustomed hour drew nigh, they all gathered at their usual meeting-place for the story-telling, and the queen, turning to Filomena, requested her to inaugurate the business of the day. Smiling, Filomena began:

❋

## THE FIRST STORY

*Francesca is besieged by the attentions of two gallants, Rinuccio and Alessandro; but as she loves neither, she gets rid of both by imposing on one the task of getting into a tomb, and on the other, of carrying him out. They cannot follow her command to the full, and so she is freed of their importunities.*

MY LADY, SINCE IT IS YOUR WISH FOR ME TO RUN THE FIRST course in the free and open expanse you were so generous to allow us for our story-telling, I shall be glad to obey, for I am sure that if I acquit myself well, those who follow will do equally, if not better.

We have often had proof before, from our stories, charming ladies, of how great and various are the powers of love, though even if we were to treat no other theme for a year on end, I fear we couldn't do full justice to it. We know that not only does love bring the lovelorn to the brink of death, but sometimes it may even persuade them to violate the abiding-places of the dead. On that subject, there's a story I'd like to tell you, in spite of the many already told, whereby you will not only appreciate the might of love, but also the cunning used by a noble lady in getting rid of two gallants who insisted on forcing their attentions upon her.

Well then, once upon a time, in the city of Pistoia, there lived a comely widow with whom two banished Florentines, one called Rinuccio Palermini and the other Alessandro Chiarmontesi were head over ears in love. Neither knew of his rival's suit, and therefore each did his best, on his own account, to gain her love. Now Francesca de' Lazzari, a lady of good family, had for a long time put up with the attentions of the two men, who pestered her with messages and entreaties, which at first she had unwisely encouraged, so that now that she wished to escape the predicament with some show of discretion, she found it quite a task. At last, after pondering how best to be rid of the nuisance, she hit upon the plan of imposing a duty upon them, which, though in the realm of possibility, she was certain neither of the two would be willing to accomplish. That being the case, she would then have a plausible and reasonable pretext for turning a deaf ear to all their pleas. Her plan was as follows.

That very day, there had died at Pistoia a man who, in spite of the nobility of his ancestry, had been considered the worst example of mankind who ever lived, not only in that town, but in the world at large. Moreover, he had been an ugly monster, so fierce and horrible to look at, that a man seeing him for the first time would have been terrified out of his wits. This horror, nicknamed the Ripper, had been laid in a sepulcher outside the walls of the church belonging to the friars Minor, and it was this man Francesca thought most suitable for her design. Calling her maid, she said:

"You know what a source of annoyance and vexation are the messages I'm forever pestered with by those two Florentines, Rinuccio and Alessandro. Now I've not the least intention of favoring them with my love, and in order to get rid of them, I've made up my mind to put their elaborate promises to the test, by asking them to do something which I'm sure they'll never manage to accomplish. And thus I'll be free of a nuisance. Now listen to my plan.

"This morning, as you know, a man was buried in the cemetery of the friars—I mean none other than the Ripper, the sight of whom, alive, used to terrify the bravest men in town. You can imagine how much more terrible he must be, dead. Well, first of all, I want you to go secretly to Alessandro and say to him, 'My mistress Francesca says the time has come when you may have the love which you've been yearning for. You may even be alone with her, if you desire, but this is how. To-night, for a reason you'll discover later, the body of the Ripper, who was buried this morning, will be brought to her house by one of her relatives. She's in mortal terror of the monster, dead though he is, and she would be very happy not to have him there. So she begs you, if you love her, to do her a special favor. To-night, when you would ordinarily be going to bed, betake yourself to the tomb where the Ripper is buried, put on the dead man's clothes and lie down in his place until they come for you. You mustn't venture to say a word, or even breathe, but simply let yourself be taken out of the tomb and carried to Francesca's house, where she'll receive you. Then you may stay with her and go when you will, and leave the rest for her to worry about.'

"If he agrees to do this, well and good. If not, tell him for me never to show his face to me again, and if he values his life, to refrain from plaguing me with any more of his letters and gobetweens. When you have settled with him, go to Rinuccio Palermini and say, 'My mistress Francesca says she is ready to grant your every pleasure, provided you do her a great service—simply this. To-night, toward twelve, go to the tomb where the Ripper was laid this morning, and without breathing a word of what you may hear or see, take him out as quietly as you can, and carry him to her house. You'll find out there why she wanted him, and you will be rewarded by having your desire of her. If you don't care to do this, don't ever dare to send her any letters or messengers again.' "

The maid went to the respective gallants and delivered her messages, as she had been commissioned, whereupon each answered that if it was his lady's pleasure, he would not only be willing to go into a tomb, but into the very mouth of hell.

The maid went back with their answer to her mistress, who waited to see if they would be mad enough to be as good as their word.

When night had fallen, at about the hour when good folks go to bed, Alessandro Chiarmontesi, stripping to his waistcoat, set out of his house to take the Ripper's place in the sepulcher. While on his way, a terrifying thought entered his head, and he pondered, "Good Lord, what an ass I am! Where the deuce am I going? How do I know if the woman's folks, realizing that I love her, and perhaps believing the worst, may not be up to this mischief in order to do away with me in the tomb? In that case, I'd be the one to get the worst of it, and not a word would be whispered against them in the outside world. And how do I know whether some enemy of mine may not have brought this upon me—some gentleman she may be in love with, and for whose sake she may be playing me this shabby trick?" And again he argued, "Granted none of these suppositions is true, and that her folks will really be carrying me to her house, I can't be so foolish as to think they wish to have the Ripper's body to dandle in their arms, or to deposit in hers. Indeed, it is more reasonable to suppose they intend to do it some violence, as the husk of the man who may have done something contrary to their pleasure in the past. She says I mustn't breathe a word, no matter what I see or hear. Well and good! But supposing they gouge my eyes out, or draw my teeth, or cut off my hands, or do me some other dreadful injury? How could I keep quiet? On the other hand, if I should make a sound, they'd either know me, and perhaps give me the devil, or, if they did not harm me, they surely would not leave me alone with her. So all my trouble would be for nothing. Again, the woman might say I didn't abide by her injunctions, and she'll never consent to do anything to oblige me."

Reasoning in this fashion, he almost decided to go home, but still, the great love he bore her urged him on, with counter arguments of such persuasiveness that they brought him to the Ripper's tomb. Forcing it open, he entered; then, undressing the corpse, he put its clothes on his own back, shut the tomb upon himself, and stretched out in the dead man's place. Little by little, rumors of what the man had been swarmed through his mind. Moreover, as he thought of the many stories he had heard, telling of dreadful accidents which had happened in the darkness of night, not only in the tombs of the dead, but in less frightful places, the hair of his body stood on end, and with every passing moment he saw the Ripper starting up and pouncing upon him, to slash him then and there. However, bolstered by his passionate love, he conquered these and other nightmares, and lying stiff and straight like a corpse, he resigned himself to await his adventure.

Toward midnight, Rinuccio left his house to execute the commands of his lady, and as he went his way, many and various were the fears that beset him, of the various things that might happen to him. He might fall into the clutches of the police, with the evidence of the Ripper's body upon his back, and be sentenced to the flames as a warlock. Or, if the thing leaked out, he might get into a bitter feud with the dead man's kin. Such, and similar considerations almost kept him from his purpose, but then, thinking the matter over, he said, "Well, well! Am I going to refuse the woman I've loved so much, and for whom I'm still consumed with passion—am I going to refuse her the first favor she has ever asked of me? And when I'm on the point of gaining her grace, at that? My word, even if I were sure to die in the attempt, it's up to me to do what I promised!"

Going bravely forward, he came to the sepulcher and had no difficulty in pushing it open. Alessandro, from within, hearing it open, was seized with mortal terror, but still he did not utter a sound. Rinuccio entered, and believing he was taking the Ripper's body, grasped Alessandro by the feet, and dragged him out of the tomb. Then, heaving him upon his shoulders, he started for Francesca's house.

On he walked, having no thought for anything but his destination, knocking his load now against a corner and now against a pile of benches lying on the street, for the night was so dark and murky that he could scarcely see where he was going. Finally, he had nearly reached the street-door of his lady, who had been watching with her maid from the windows, to see if Rinuccio would bring Alessandro, and was ready with a pretext at her tongue's end, to send them both about their business, when a party of police, who had been quietly lying in wait in that neighborhood to fall upon a certain outlaw, heard the shuffling of Rinuccio's feet. Suddenly flashing a light, to see what was happening and what course to follow, they shook their targets and halberds, shouting, "Who goes there?"

Rinuccio knew them on the instant. There was little time for deliberation so, dropping his burden, he took to his heels as fast as his legs could carry him. Alessandro quickly jumped to his feet, and in spite of the encumbrance of the dead man's shroud, which was very long, skipped away in his turn.

Meanwhile, in the circle of light thrown by the officers' lantern, Francesca had plainly distinguished Rinuccio, with Alessandro close at his heels. She had also noted that the latter was dressed in the Ripper's grave-clothes, and wondered greatly at the two men's daring. In spite of her amazement, however, she could not help bursting into a peal of laughter at seeing Alessandro thrown off like a dead-weight, and then watching both men scamper nimbly away.

The untoward chance rejoiced her exceedingly, and thanking the Lord for having delivered her of their importunities, she turned into the house and retired to her room, both she and her maid agreeing that the two men must indeed have loved her greatly to accomplish, as it seemed, the tasks she had imposed upon them.

In the meantime, Rinuccio, chagrined and cursing his ill-luck, did not return home in spite of it all; but waiting until the police had left the neighborhood, returned to the place where he had dropped his burden, groping in the dark to see if he might find him and so finish his business. He did not find him, however, and thinking the police had carried the body away, returned home in the worst of humors. As for Alessandro, not knowing what else to do, he too went home, annoyed at the mishap, and without having the least notion of who the man might be who had carried him out of the tomb.

Next morning, when the sepulcher was found open and no trace of the Ripper's corpse visible, for Alessandro had thrown it into the bottom of the pit, all of Pistoia was in a hum of conjecture, many fools believing that the devils had come and carried the body away. But the lovers told Francesca in turn what each of them had done, and what had interfered with the complete execution of her command; then, apologizing for not carrying it through as they should have wished, they demanded her love and favor. The canny woman, however, pretended she believed neither the one nor the other, and got rid of them both by telling them outright that she would never consent to pleasure them in any way, since they had not carried out what she had requested them to do.

# THE SECOND STORY

*A lady-abbess gets up hurriedly in the dark, to catch one of her nuns in bed with a lover, according to the accusations made to her. She herself had been in bed with a priest, and thinking to throw her wimple about her head, put on her lover's breeches instead. The accused nun sees the pantaloons and brings them to her attention, whereupon she is absolved, and is free to lie with her lover.*

FILOMENA WAS NOW SILENT. THE WOMAN'S WIT IN DISPOSING of her unwelcome lovers received general commendation, while on the other hand, the daring presumption of the two gallants was deemed not love, but madness. Then the queen, turning blithely to Elisa, said, "You follow now." The girl began readily:

Dearest ladies, as we have heard, Francesca was truly skilful in ridding herself of the nuisance of her lovers. But a young nun was even more so, in getting out of approaching danger by the help of fortune and a timely remark. As you know, there are many in the world who are arrant fools, and still set themselves up as preceptors and judges over others. However, as you will be able to gather from my story, fate sometimes shames them rightfully, as in the case of the abbess under whose rule the nun lived, of whom I am to tell.

Well, as you must all know, there is in Lombardy a certain convent famous for holiness and piety, in which, among other nuns, there once lived a noble damsel by the name of Isabetta, endowed with extraordinary beauty. One day, when a relative of hers came to see her at the grate, she fell in love with a handsome youth who happened to be with him. He, on his part, seeing her so beautiful, and grasping her desire with his eyes, was likewise inflamed with love of her. Nevertheless, they bore this passion of theirs a long time without fruit, though not without great torment. Both were eager for some approach, and finally the young man discovered a way of visiting his nun in all secrecy. She was pleased with his plan, and so not once, but many times he came to her, much to their mutual delight.

While this state of affairs was going on, one night he was discovered by one of the nuns, unknown to Isabetta or himself, as he was taking leave of her and going on his way. The woman communicated her find to a number of the sisters. At first, they decided with one accord to bring charges against Isabetta, before the lady abbess, Madam Usimbalda, a good and holy woman, according to the opinion of the nuns and everyone who knew her. Then, to leave no room for denials on the young nun's part, they thought it best to have the abbess catch her *in flagrante* with her lover. They kept the matter hushed, therefore, and secretly posted themselves to spy upon her, each taking turns at playing sentinel.

Now Isabetta knew nothing of these trammels, nor took any precautions, and one night she had her lover come to her as usual. It soon came to the attention of the nuns spying upon her, who, choosing the proper moment, broke up into two bands, when a goodly part of the night had passed, one group stationing itself at the door of Isabetta's cell, while the other hastened to the abbess' room. Knocking repeatedly at the door until she answered, they cried, "Hurry, mother! Get up right away! We've discovered that Sister Isabetta has a young man in her cell!"

As it happened, that night the abbess was enjoying the company of a priest, whom she often had carried to her in a chest. When she heard the nuns' excitement, she was afraid that in their eagerness they might burst the door open, so jumping out of bed in all haste, she dressed herself in the dark as best she could. Such was her hurry, that thinking she had laid hold of certain plaited veils which nuns wear on their heads and call a wimple, she seized, instead, the good priest's breeches, and without noticing what she was about, threw them over her head instead of the headdress and went out, shutting the door quickly behind her.

"Where's this creature accursed of God?" she cried. Then, with the rest of the nuns, who were too anxiously bent on catching Isabetta in error to notice what the abbess was wearing on her head, she came to the door of the girl's cell. With the help of the other nuns she broke it open, and entering the room, found the two lovers in bed, locked in each other's arms, so taken aback at their sudden discovery that they remained stock still, not knowing what to do.

Immediately, the girl was taken by the nuns, and at the lady abbess' orders carried off to the chapter-house for judgment. The young man, left behind in the room, dressed himself and remained to see the outcome of the case, determined at the least harm to Isabetta to take vengeance on all and sundry who came within his reach, and carry his mistress away with him.

In the chapter-house, meanwhile, the abbess sat in judgment, surrounded by the sisters, intent, all of them, on staring only at the culprit, and she began to heap the vilest opprobrium upon the girl's head. If the scandal were known to the outside world, she said, the holiness and virtue and good repute of the convent would be sullied, and all because of her foul and shameless practices. And as though the reproach were not enough, she added threat to injury.

Isabetta, timid and shamed by the consciousness of guilt, did not know what to answer, and her silence aroused pity in the breasts of the other nuns. Still, as the abbess redoubled the eloquence of her preachment, Isabetta raised her head, and her eyes fell on the lady's headdress, the trouser-legs of which were draped on either side of her face. Guessing what it meant, she plucked up courage and said, "Mother—the Lord have mercy on you!—tie up your wimple and then scold me to your heart's content."

The abbess, not knowing what she meant, "What wimple are you talking about, vile jade?" she asked. "Have you the face to joke at such a time? I suppose you think you can laugh at what you've done!"

Again the girl insisted, "Mother, please tie up your wimple, and then you may revile me as you wish."

At her words, many of the nuns looked up at the abbess' head, and the moment she raised her hand to it, she realized, with the rest, why Isabetta spoke as she did. Immediately, the abbess knew her own guilt. She saw, moreover, that it had been apparent to them all beyond any excuse she might trump up, and changed the tone of her sermon. Proceeding therefore, in quite a different strain, she concluded that it was impossible for frail human nature to defend itself against the stings of the flesh, and advised each and everyone of them to gather rosebuds while they might, as discreetly as they had been doing until that day. Furthermore, releasing Isabetta from all punishment, she went back to sleep with her priest, while the girl repaired to her lover, whom she invited to her bed many and many a time, in spite of those who looked upon her with envy. As for the nuns who had no lovers, they tried their luck in secret as best they could.

✳

## THE THIRD STORY

*At the suggestion of Bruno, Buffalmacco and Nello, Dr. Simon makes Calandrino believe he is pregnant, as a result of which the patient gives them capons and money for medicines, recovering in the end without being delivered.*

AFTER ELISA HAD FINISHED HER STORY, AND ALL THE LADIES HAD rendered thanks to God for so felicitous a rescue of the young nun from the fangs of her envious sisters, the queen requested Filostrato to continue, who began without awaiting further orders:

Loveliest of ladies, the ill-bred clodhopper of a judge, of

whom I told you yesterday, took out of my very mouth a story about Calandrino, that I wanted to tell you. Even though we have had a great deal about him and his cronies, I shall tell you the one I had in mind yesterday, knowing as I do that whatever we say of him can only add to our fun.

We're already sufficiently well-acquainted with Calandrino and the rest mentioned in this story, so without wasting words, I shall plunge right into it. You must know that an aunt of Calandrino's happened to die and bequeathed him eight hundred lire. On receiving his inheritance, he began to talk about wanting to buy a farm, and consulted the real-estate agents of Florence, as though he had had ten thousand florins in gold at his command. As it was, the deal always came to naught when they arrived at the price of the property.

Bruno and Buffalmacco, aware of what was going on, had told him many a time that he would be doing a much more sensible thing if he spent the money on a good time with them, instead of bothering to buy land, as though he wanted to play with mud-pies. But far from convincing him to follow their suggestion, they had never even succeeded in getting him to treat them to a dinner.

One day, as the two companions were complaining of his stinginess, a friend of theirs, an artist by the name of Nello, joined them, and the three deliberated on a way to ease their dry throats at Calandrino's expense. They soon decided upon a course to follow, and without allowing time to slip by, the following morning they watched for him to leave his house. Scarcely had he walked a few steps, when Nello drew up to him, saying, "Good morning, Calandrino."

"God give you good morning and a good year," replied Calandrino. Nello seemed to hesitate to speak, and then riveted his eyes upon his friend's face.

"What are you staring at?" asked Calandrino.

"Was there anything wrong with you last night?" said Nello. "It seems to me you're not quite yourself to-day."

Calandrino at once began worrying about his health. "God help me! What do you mean?" he cried. "What do you suppose is the matter with me?"

"Goodness only knows," said Nello. "But you look strangely altered to me. Perhaps I'm only imagining it, though." And with that he let him go his way.

Calandrino walked on, full of concern, though he felt per-

fectly well. Buffalmacco, however, was not far away, and on seeing him leave Nello, approached him with the greeting, "Is
there anything the matter with you?"

"I don't know," replied Calandrino. "Just now Nello was
saying he found me quite changed. Is it possible I may be
ill?"

"I should think something must be wrong with you," said
Buffalmacco. "You look half dead!"

Calandrino felt the fever rising in him. Suddenly, up popped
Bruno, who, before saying anything else, cried, "Why, Calandrino! What sort of face is that? You look like a corpse! What
ails you, friend?"

Calandrino, hearing what each of them had to say, was convinced he must be seriously ill, and showing his trepidation on
his face, asked, "What should I do?"

"In my opinion," Bruno suggested, "you had better go home
and get straight into bed under a lot of blankets, to keep you
warm. Then send a specimen of your urine to Dr. Simon, who's
much beholden to us, and he'll tell you immediately what you
have to do. We'll come along with you, and if there's anything to be done, we'll do it."

Nello joined the party, and all of them returned home with
Calandrino, who hastened in a funk to his bedroom, saying to
his wife, "Come and cover me up warm! I feel awfully sick."

He was quickly put to bed, and a specimen of his urine sent
by a little servant-wench to Dr. Simon, who then had his office
in Oldcheap at the sign of the Pumpkin. Said Bruno to his
cronies:

"You stay here with Calandrino, while I hurry to the doctor
and find out what he has to say. If there's any urgent need, I'll
have him come here with me."

"Go, go by all means, dear friend," Calandrino urged. "Hurry,
and let me know what the matter is, for I feel the devil
only knows what's inside of me!"

Bruno hurried away to the doctor's, and got there before the
little servant-girl with the urine. He told Dr. Simon how the
case stood, so that when the wench arrived and the doctor examined the specimen, he said to her, "Go and tell Calandrino
to keep himself covered up warm. I'll be over right away and
let him know what's wrong with him and how to take care of
himself."

The girl delivered his message to her master, and it was not long before Bruno arrived with the doctor, who sat down beside the patient and felt his pulse. After a few moments' reflection, he said to Calandrino, while his wife was in the room, "Listen to me, Calandrino, as friend to friend, there's nothing in the world the matter with you, except that you're pregnant."

The moment Calandrino heard the doctor's pronouncement, he howled and shrieked in despair, saying, "Woe! Woe! Poor, unhappy me! It's all your fault, Tessa, for always wanting to lie on top. I told you so! I warned you!"

Mistress Tessa, a most virtuous woman, flushed scarlet with shame at the remark, and bowing her head, slunk out of the room without saying a word, as Calandrino went on moaning, "Alas! Woe is me! What shall I do? How can I give birth to this child? Where is it going to come from? I see clearly that this is the end of me, and all because of the crazy itch of this wife of mine, may the Lord give her as much sorrow as I want joy in life! Oh, if only I were as well as I should be! I'd get up and give her the beating of her life, until she hadn't a whole bone left in her body! Though it serves me right! I should never have consented to let her ride on top. But I swear, if ever I get out of this alive, she can die of desire, before I let her do it again!"

Bruno, Buffalmacco and Nello were almost bursting with repressed laughter, hearing him carry on in that fashion. Still, they kept a straight face, though Dr. Addlepate broke into such uproarious guffaws, that you might have pulled every tooth out of his mouth. When at last Calandrino placed himself at the doctor's mercy, begging him to give him help and counsel in his predicament, "Don't be discouraged, Calandrino," he said, "for God be praised, we have discovered the cause of your sickness early enough for me to rid you of it in a few days, without much trouble. But you must be prepared to spend a little money."

"For God's sake, doctor dear," cried Calandrino. "Rid me of it, by all means. I've eight hundred lire, with which I meant to buy a farm. If you need it all, take every cent of it, only don't let me bear a child! God knows how I'd ever be able to go through with it, considering the way women behave when they're about to be delivered, though they're well provided with the means of doing it. Upon my word, if I had to bear that pain, I'd die before I succeeded in giving birth!"

"Don't worry your head about such things," said Dr. Simon. "I'll have them prepare a certain draught of distilled waters for you, that's pleasant to the taste, indeed, very delicious. In three days it will rid you of everything, and leave you healthier than a fish. But you must be sensible in the future, and not get into any more of these silly scrapes. As for that medicinal water, we must have three pairs of good, fat capons. For other necessary minor items, give one of your friends here twenty lire to buy them with, and let everything be delivered to my office. To-morrow morning I'll send you that distilled beverage without fail, and you'll begin the cure at once, by drinking a tumblerful of it at a time."

"Doctor dear," said Calandrino, "I'm entirely at your mercy." Then giving Bruno twenty lire in change and money besides for three pairs of capons, he begged him to look after the purchases for his sake.

The doctor went away, and ordering a clear beverage to be prepared for Calandrino, sent it to him. Bruno, in the meantime, bought the capons and other delicacies required for the feast; and the three friends and the doctor made short work of them.

Three mornings in succession Calandrino drank the clear draught, at the end of which period the doctor and his three friends came to pay him a visit. Dr. Simon felt his pulse.

"You're perfectly well now, Calandrino, no doubt about it," he said. "You needn't stay home any more on this account, but go safely about your affairs from now on."

Calandrino got out of bed, rejoicing, and took care of his business, praising Dr. Simon's marvelous cure in no mean terms to every one he chanced to meet. It had rid him of his pregnancy in three days, without the least discomfort, he exclaimed. Bruno, Buffalmacco and Nello were pleased with themselves for having known how to get the better of Calandrino's stinginess through their trickery, though Mistress Tessa, discovering it, gave her husband many an earful for his credulity.

## ✳

### THE FOURTH STORY

*Cecco Fortarrigo gambles at Buonconvento and loses all his goods as well as the money of his master, Cecco Angiolieri, whom he pursues in his shirt. Then, accusing Angiolieri of having robbed him, he has him captured by some peasants, and putting*

*on his clothes, rides away on his horse, leaving the poor fellow*
*almost naked.*

CALANDRINO'S ACCUSATION OF HIS WIFE HAD ROUSED THE WHOLE
company to peals of mirth, but when Filostrato was silent,
Neifile began at the queen's bidding:

Noblest ladies, if it weren't a greater task for men to demonstrate their virtue and wisdom to others, than it is for them to
make a show of their foolishness and vice, many a man would
strive in vain to curb his tongue. This has been clearly shown
you by Calandrino's perversity. What need was there for him to
drag his wife's secret pleasures into the open, if he wished to be
cured of the illness his stupidity caused him to believe he had?
This story calls up an entirely different one to my mind—in
short, of how one man's craftiness got the better of another's
prudence, to the harm and shame of the one who was imposed
upon, as I shall tell you.

Not so many years ago, there lived in Siena two youths
who had already reached man's estate. Both of them were called
Cecco, though one was the son of Angiolieri, and the other of
Fortarrigo. Despite their dissimilarity in most instances, they
agreed in one respect, namely in the hatred they bore their
fathers. That one point so linked them together, that they had
become fast friends and were very often to be found together.
Soon, however, Angiolieri, who was a personable and courteous youth, seeing he could scarcely make both ends meet in Siena on the allowance his father gave him, decided to go to the
Marches of Ancona, where he had heard a great patron of his,
a cardinal, had been sent as papal-legate. There, thought Angiolieri, he might perhaps succeed in improving his financial condition. He communicated his intention to his father, and arranged with him to receive his six months' allowance in a lump
sum, so that he might furnish himself with a horse and the
necessary trappings befitting a gentleman. The only thing lacking was a servant for his journey, and when Fortarrigo heard
what he desired, he immediately presented himself to his
friend, begging him as earnestly as he could, to employ him.
"I shall be your valet and bodyguard and everything else," he
said, "and I'll take no salary if my expenses are paid."

Angiolieri demurred, saying he had no objection to make
to his ability, for he knew he could do anything required of

him. But he was fond of gambling, and what's more, he some-times got himself all befuddled with drink.

"I'll keep myself from gambling and drinking, I promise," said Fortarrigo, and swore so many solemn oaths, backed by touching entreaties, that Angiolieri at last yielded and said he was willing.

Accordingly, they set out together on their journey, and stopped off for dinner at Buonconvento. The weather was un-bearably sultry, therefore after dinner Angiolieri had his bed prepared at the hostelry, and undressing, with Fortarrigo's as-sistance, lay down for a nap.

"Call me punctually at three," he said to his friend.

The moment Angiolieri had fallen asleep, Fortarrigo hastened to the tavern. Drink flowed free, and presently he began gam-bling with a group of men, who soon relieved him of what little money he had and of his clothes in the bargain. Anxious to retrieve his fortune, he mounted to Angiolieri's room, just as he was, in his shirt, and seeing he was fast asleep, took every cent out of his purse. Again he returned to the gaming-table, losing his master's money as he had lost his own.

Meanwhile, Angiolieri awoke, got up, and called for Fortar-rigo. He was nowhere in sight. Thinking he must be sleeping off the effects of drink in some corner, as he often did, Angio-lieri resolved to leave him behind and provide himself with another valet at Corsignano. He had his horse bridled, and the pack-saddles put on its back; but when he tried to discharge his debt to the host and so take his leave, he found himself penni-less.

Great was the uproar that ensued. The whole inn was turned upside down, as Angiolieri insisted he had been robbed there and threatened to have everyone, host and all, arrested and taken to Siena.

Suddenly, along came Fortarrigo in his shirt, on his way to despoil his master of his clothes, as he had robbed him of his money. Seeing Angiolieri about to take horse, "What's this, friend?" he cried. "Are we going already? Wait a minute! Hold your horse! There's a fellow coming here in a little while, who's taken my waistcoat in pawn for thirty-eight francs. If you re-deem it right away, I'm sure he'll let me have it for thirty-five."

He was still speaking when a man joined them, who con-vinced Angiolieri that Fortarrigo had stolen his money, by show-ing him the sum the scapegrace had gambled away.

His anger was great, and many were the rebukes he heaped upon his head. Indeed, if he had not been more in fear of the people about him than of God himself, he would have made him pay dearly for his fault. But threatening to have the culprit hanged by the neck or run out of Siena, he mounted his horse. Fortarrigo, however, taking no more heed of Angiolieri's words than if they had been addressed to someone else, resumed:

"For heaven's sake, friend, enough of this foolish talk that doesn't lead us anywhere and let's get down to business. Listen, if we redeem the waistcoat right away, we can have it for thirty-five francs, whereas if we let it go till to-morrow, he won't take a cent less than the thirty-eight he advanced me on it. He's doing it as a special favor, too, as I pawned it on his advice. Come, now, be a good fellow! Why shouldn't we have the benefit of the three francs?"

Angiolieri was well nigh driven frantic by this nonsense, especially when he saw the bystanders looking at him suspiciously, as if they thought that Fortarrigo had not robbed *him,* but that he himself was withholding the rogue's money.

"What the devil have I to do with your waistcoat?" he was saying. "Would to heaven you were dancing a jig at the end of a rope! First you steal my money, then you gamble it away, and now you keep me from going on my way, and make a fool of me in the bargain!"

Fortarrigo still held his ground, as though Angiolieri's words were not meant for him. "Hell," he exclaimed. "Why don't you want to save me these three francs? Don't you think I'll be able to let you have them some other time? Come, be a sport, if you care for me. Why are you in such a hurry? We'll get to Torrenieri before sundown. Come, find the purse. Why, if I were to turn all Siena upside down, I wouldn't be able to find another waistcoat to fit me so trim! And to think I surrendered it to that fellow for thirty-eight francs! It's worth forty francs, or even more, so I'll be the loser both ways if you don't help me."

Angiolieri was at the end of his patience, first, at being robbed, and then made a laughing-stock by the scamp's words. Without deigning to answer, he turned his horse's head and entered the road leading to Torrenieri.

Fortarrigo suddenly thought of a cunning expedient, and set off as he was behind his master, at a run, and in his shirt, clamoring for his waistcoat. For two miles he followed him, and while Angiolieri spurred on his horse, to be out of earshot of the nuisance, the scoundrel caught sight of some peasants a little farther up the road, who were working in a field. "Stop thief! Stop thief!" he cried to them, at the top of his lungs.

Immediately, they barred the way before Angiolieri, some of them wielding spades, others mattocks, and inferring that he must have robbed the man who was shouting after him in his shirt, took him prisoner. In vain he struggled to make them understand who he was and explain the true facts of the case.

Fortarrigo came up, and mad with rage, cried, "I don't know what's keeping me from butchering you on the spot, thieving knave, running off with my belongings!" And turning to the peasants, he said, "See what a pickle he left me in, after he squandered all his money gambling! I can say with justice that I owe the little that I'm recovering to God and you, gentlemen, and you may be sure I'll always remember you kindly for your service."

Angiolieri, on his part, gave his version of the story, but his words fell on empty air. He was forced from his horse, and there, on the ground, Fortarrigo undressed him with the help of the peasants, and then donned the clothes himself. Getting to horse, he left Angiolieri barefoot and in his shirt, and returned to Siena, declaring to all that he had won his master's horse and finery through gambling.

And so the poor wretch, who had intended going like a gentleman to the cardinal in the Marches, made the best of his way to Buonconvento, penniless and almost naked, not venturing to go back to Siena for very shame. Some clothes were procured for him, however, and mounting Fortarrigo's nag, he repaired to his folks at Corsignano, with whom he stayed until his father again came to his rescue.

And so Fortarrigo's craftiness got the better of Angiolieri's good intentions, though you may be sure the rogue's knavery was not left unpunished by the victim, when the occasion offered.

✳

# THE FIFTH STORY

*Calandrino becomes infatuated with a young woman, whereupon Bruno writes him a charm, at the touch of which she is bound to follow him. Mistress Tessa surprises him, and he is made to pay the piper.*

WHEN NEIFILE'S SHORT STORY WAS ENDED AND THE COMPANY
had let it pass without too much laughter or discussion, the
queen turned to Fiammetta, requesting her to continue.

"Willingly, my lady," she replied, and began:

Most gracious friends, you know, I'm sure, there is nothing,
however hackneyed, that will fail to give pleasure, if only the
person who speaks of it knows how to choose the proper moment and place for it. Now when I consider why we are here—
chiefly, I believe, to amuse ourselves and have a good time—I
think that anything that tends to give us occasion for mirth and
joy, has both its due time and place. Indeed, even though we
may have recurred to the subject a thousand times, it should be
every bit as enjoyable if we recur to it again. Many a time
we've talked of Calandrino's antics and funny sayings, but still,
believing with Filostrato that they're all very amusing, I'll take
the liberty of telling you another story about him, although, if I
had wished to avoid the issue, I could easily have managed to
conceal the source, and given it to you under other names. Still,
as the listener's pleasure is greatly diminished if one departs
from the actual facts, I shall for that reason present the story as
it is.

Nicolo Cornacchini, one of our fellow-citizens and a rich
man, owned, among other property, a handsome plot of land at
Camerata, where he had a fine, noble villa built, which he arranged with Bruno and Buffalmacco to decorate for him. There
was much work to be done, therefore the friends recruited
Nello and Calandrino, and all settled down to the task in good
earnest.

Now although several rooms of the villa were provided with
beds and other necessary pieces of furniture, and an old woman
lived there as a sort of guardian, none of the owners ever came
to the villa, except a son of Nicolo's, by the name of Filippo.
He was a young, lusty sprig, and as he had no wife, he sometimes invited a woman there for his pleasure, entertained her
for a day or two, and then bid her good-bye.

As it happened, he once took with him a certain Niccolosa,
who was kept in a house at Camaldoli by a pimp who used her
both for his own ends and loaned her to others for money. This
Niccolosa was a fine figure of a woman, well-dressed, and for
one of her calling, courteous and soft-spoken. One day, toward
noon, she chanced to come out of her apartment in a white
petticoat, with her hair twined about her head, and just as she

was busy washing her hands and face at a well in the middle of the court, Calandrino came out to draw water. He greeted her familiarly, and she returned his greeting, staring at him the while, more because he struck her as a peculiar bird, than for any pleasure she got out of it. Encouraged, he too cast sheep's eyes at her, and finding her a personable woman, thought of all kinds of excuses for lingering there with her, unmindful of his companions, who were waiting for him to return with the water. Niccolosa observing the way he ogled her, threw him a tempting glance now and then, with a little sigh thrown in, simply to tease him. That was all Calandrino needed to lose his heart completely to her, and he did not budge from the wellside until the woman was called in by Filippo.

Back at his task, Calandrino did nothing but heave heartrending sighs, which Bruno could not fail to perceive, interested as he still was in his friend's antics, for the sport they afforded him.

"What the devil ails you, partner?" he asked. "You do nothing but sigh and sigh."

"Partner," replied Calandrino, "if only I had someone to help me, I'd get along first rate."

"How's that?" asked Bruno.

"You mustn't tell a soul," Calandrino informed him, "but there's a girl up here lovelier than a fairy princess. She's so mad with love for me, that you'd be surprised! I noticed it just now, when I went to fetch water."

"Good heavens!" cried Bruno. "Be careful you're not getting mixed up with Filippo's wife!"

"I guess that's who she must be," said Calandrino, "for he called her and she went into his room. But what of it? I'd snatch her from Christ himself, to say nothing of Filippo. But to tell you the truth, comrade, I love her so much that I can hardly express myself."

Bruno said, "Comrade, I'll find out for you who she is, and if she is Filippo's wife, I'll pave the way for you with a word, for she's a great friend of mine. The question is, how can we keep the thing from Buffalmacco? I can never exchange so much as a word with her, without his prowling around."

"He's the least of my worries," said Calandrino. "We'd better watch out for Nello, though. He's Tessa's cousin, and he would upset everything."

"You're quite right about that," agreed Bruno.

Now Bruno knew perfectly well who the woman was, as he himself had seen her come. Furthermore, Filippo had told him about her. Well, no sooner did Calandrino quit work and go out for a glimpse of his flame, than Bruno informed Nello and Buffalmacco of the whole affair, and together they arranged what they were to do about this infatuation of his. As soon as Calandrino returned, Bruno said in a whisper, "Did you see her?"

"Alas, yes!" he sighed. "She has slain me with her eyes!"

"I want to go and see if she's the one I mean," said Bruno, "and if she is, well—leave the rest to me."

Bruno went down, and finding Filippo and Niccolosa, he told them what sort of bird Calandrino was, and all that he had confessed about his love. Then, arranging with them what they were to do and say, to have a good time at the expense of the lovelorn Calandrino, he returned to him and said, "That's she, all right, so you had better carry on your affair with the greatest discretion, because if Filippo ever came to know of it, all the water in the Arno could not wash you clean again. But what is it you'd like me to tell her for you, if I get a chance to speak to her?"

"My word," said Calandrino, "tell her first of all that I wish her a thousand quarts of that wonderful bounty that makes the belly grow, and that I'm her humble slave, and that if she wants anything—you understand, don't you?"

"Indeed I do," said Bruno, "so leave everything to me."

When supper-time drew nigh, the artists left their work and went down to the court, and as Filippo and Niccolosa were there, they remained awhile for the sake of Calandrino, who began rolling his eyes at her and going through such antics that even a blind man would have noticed them. Niccolosa, on her part, did everything she could to add fuel to his fire, while Filippo, following Bruno's instructions, had a good time of it, though he pretended to be engaged in conversation with Buffalmacco and Nello, and unaware of all that was going on. Finally the painters went away, to Calandrino's great disappointment. As they were nearing Florence, "Ah, Calandrino," said Bruno, "I can assure you you've made her melt like ice in the sun. By heaven, if you brought your rebec and sang her a couple of love-songs to its accompaniment, I warrant she'd throw herself out of the window to get to you."

"Do you think so, partner?" he asked. "Do you think I'd win her?"

"No doubt about it," Bruno assured him, and Calandrino continued, "You wouldn't believe me this morning when I told you about it. But my word, partner, I see I'm a better hand than anybody else in carrying out what I want to do. Who, if not I, could have succeeded in making a grand lady like that fall madly in love with me, and in such a short time? Certainly, none of your boastful young cockerels, who go gadding about the live-long day and couldn't manage to pick three handfuls of nuts in a thousand years! Just wait till you see me with my instrument. That's a sight for sore eyes! Besides, I want you to understand that I'm not as old as I look, as she could see for herself, the dear wench! But I'll convince her even more when I get my hands on her. By the true body, I'll hand her such good sport, that she'll follow me like crazy Meg after her child."

"Yes, sir, you'll handle her good and proper," Bruno humored him, "I can just see you, with those buck-teeth of yours, biting that pretty little red mouth, and her cheeks fresh as twin roses, and then eating her all up!"

Listening to Bruno, Calandrino imagined himself in the act, and went warbling and capering so merrily, that he could scarcely stay in his breeches. The following day he brought along his instrument, and to the huge amusement of the whole party, sang a number of songs to its accompaniment. In short, he was so pricked with longing for the merest glimpse of his lady, that he no longer paid any heed to his work, and at least a thousand times a day he would rush to the window, or the door, or into the court, though truth to tell, Niccolosa, cleverly following Bruno's precepts, gave the love-sick loon reason enough to keep him hopping. To make matters worse, Bruno fabricated his own answers to the messages Calandrino sent her, and even brought him others which purported to come from her. Whenever she was not there, which was a good part of the time, he delivered him letters, in which Bruno had her encourage his desire, as she pretended she was spending some time at home with her relatives, where he could not possibly come to see her.

And so Bruno kept up the deception with the help of Buffalmacco. They had huge sport at the witlessness of Calandrino, from whom, ostensibly at his lady's instance, they first extracted an ivory comb, then a purse, and again a penknife or some such trifle, giving him in exchange all kinds of imitation gold rings of no value, with which he seemed tickled to death. But that was not all, for the better to further his assiduous courtship,

Calandrino gave the two rogues many dinners and countless tokens of gratitude.

After they had kept him on tenter hooks for about two months, without allowing him to advance a step farther in his suit, Calandrino, considering that the painting was nearly finished, and that if he did not bring his love to fulfilment before then, he might never have another chance to do so, redoubled the fervor of his prayers and solicitations to Bruno. Accordingly, on Niccolosa's next visit to the villa, Bruno first came to an understanding with her and Filippo on the course they were to follow, and then said to Calandrino, "Listen, comrade! This lady has assured me at least a thousand times that she's willing to do anything you wish, and then she does nothing at all. It strikes me that she's leading you by the nose, so since she won't stick to her promise, we'll bring her to it willy-nilly. How do you feel about it?"

"Do it, by all means!" said Calandrino. "And for God's sake, do it soon!"

"Well," said Bruno, "do you feel equal to touching her with a charm I'll give you?"

"Most assuredly," he replied.

"Very well, then," said Bruno. "See to it that you get me a bit of parchment from an unborn sheep, a live bat, three grains of incense, and a candle that's been blessed, and leave the rest to me."

All that night Calandrino was busy with snares of his own invention to catch a bat, and when at last he captured one, he hurried off to take it to Bruno, together with the other items. Withdrawing to an adjoining room, Bruno daubed some stuff and nonsense on the parchment, with certain preparations he had, and then, handing the script to him, said, "Calandrino, you must know that the moment you touch her with this charm, she'll come after you right away and do anything you wish. Now if Filippo should happen to go anywhere to-day, get near her, somehow or other, touch her with this, and then go to the hayloft near by. It's the best place here for your purposes, and nobody ever goes in there. You'll see, she'll follow you, and once you have her, you know mighty well what to do."

Calandrino was beside himself with joy, and taking the parchment, said, "Partner, leave that to me!"

Meanwhile Nello, of whom Calandrino was very wary, was having as much fun out of this love-affair as the rest, and played his part in befooling him. At Bruno's suggestion, he went to the gallant's wife in Florence.

"Tessa," he said, "you remember how mercilessly Calandrino beat you for no reason at all, the day he came back from the Mugnone loaded with stones. I want you to give him tit for tat, and if you don't, never look upon me as your cousin and friend again. He's infatuated with a woman up there, a slut shameless enough to shut herself up in a room with him. A little while ago, they made an appointment to meet again this very day, so I'd like you to come along and surprise him, and give him a good piece of your mind."

On hearing what Nello had to say, Mistress Tessa thought it no matter for sport, and starting to her feet, shrilled, "What, filthy scoundrel that you are! Is that the way you treat me? By God's own cross, things won't turn out as you think! I'll pay you for it, all right!"

Seizing a mantle, she took along a servant-girl to bear her company, and away she went at a good speed to the villa, as Nello led the way.

The moment Bruno caught sight of him from a distance, he said to Filippo, "Here comes our friend," whereupon Filippo hastened to the room where Calandrino and the rest were at work. "Friends," he said, "I shall be obliged to leave for Florence very soon, so keep busy."

With that, he left them and went to hide in a secret place, from where he could see all that Calandrino might do, without being seen himself.

Now the moment the amorous lout thought Filippo well on his way, he descended into the court, and finding Niccolosa all alone, chatted gaily with her, as she, well-informed of the rôle she was to play, toyed with him more familiarly than usual. Emboldened, Calandrino touched her with the charm, and then, without another word, made for the barn, Niccolosa following close at his heels. No sooner was she there, than shutting the door, she threw her arms about Calandrino, and flinging him back upon the hay on the ground, she sat astride him, her hands pinning him down by the shoulders, so that he could not draw near her face. Gazing into his eyes, as though he were her heart's delight, "Ah, Calandrino," she sighed, "my sweetest heart of hearts, soul of my body, my treasure, my blissful peace! How long have I yearned to hold you and embrace you! Your seductiveness has drawn every thread out of my smock! You've charmed my heart with your instrument. Ah, can it be true I hold you in my arms?"

Calandrino, scarcely able to budge, pleaded, "O my sweet soul, let me plant a kiss upon your lips!"

"You're in an awful hurry," said Niccolosa. "Let me first satiate my eyes with the sight of you! Ah, let me feast them on your beauteous face!"

In the meantime, Bruno and Buffalmacco joined Filippo in his hiding-place, and the three heard and saw what was going on. At last, as Calandrino tried to force his kisses on Niccolosa, in came Nello with Mistress Tessa. "I'll bet you they're together," he said, upon arriving. They had come to the door of the barn, when Mistress Tessa, in a frenzy of rage, gave it such a violent push with her hands, that she burst it open. And behold, as she entered, there was Niccolosa, mounted on Calandrino!

At the sight of the irate wife, up started Niccolosa, and away she fled, taking refuge in Filippo's hiding-place—and none too soon, for Mistress Tessa had pounced upon Calandrino, who had not yet got up, and clawing at his face, had left it a mass of scratches. Taking him by a tuft of his hair, she raved, pulling his head to and fro, "You filthy, shameful cur! Is that the way you treat me? Mad old wretch that you are! God curse the day I ever came to love you! So! You haven't enough to do at home, I suppose, and you think you can be loving other people's wenches! Look at that fine figure of a lover, if you please! Don't you know yourself, villain? Don't you know what you are, you miserable dotard? Why, if you were squeezed dry, all the juice that's in you wouldn't make an ounce of sauce! By heaven, it wasn't your wife Tessa just now who was getting you pregnant! —God curse her, whoever she is!—a filthy trollop, surely, to find pleasure in such a gem as yourself!"

Now when Calandrino saw his wife coming upon him, he did not know whether he was dead or alive, and hadn't the courage to raise even a finger in his defense; but, picking himself up all scratched, peeled and confounded as he was, he took his cap and pleaded humbly with her not to scream so much, unless she wanted to see him made into mince-meat, as the woman who had been with him was the wife of the master of the house.

"All right," she said, "may the Lord give her a year of bad luck!"

Presently Bruno and Buffalmacco, who had enjoyed a hearty

laugh at the scene, together with Filippo and Niccolosa, came in as though brought there by the noise. It took them no little persuasion to quiet Mistress Tessa. They advised Calandrino in all friendship to go back to Florence, as Filippo might play him a nasty trick if he ever learned what had happened.

And so Calandrino, mournful and crestfallen, with his body all peeled and scratched, returned to Florence, and never dared set foot at the villa again. But that was not all. By dint of the nagging and scolding which Mistress Tessa dealt him day and night, he was cured of his grand passion, after he had afforded Filippo, his mistress and his own friends a world of amusement.

# THE SIXTH STORY

*Two young men spend a night at an inn, where one lies with the daughter of the host, while the host's wife inadvertently goes to bed with the other. But the one who had slept with the girl, gets into bed with her father, and tells him everything, believing him to be his companion. They quarrel, whereupon the host's wife, seeing what it is all about, slips into bed with her daughter, and restores harmony by explaining away the misunderstanding.*

ONCE MORE CALANDRINO, WHO HAD AMUSED THE COMPANY MANY times before, gave them cause for laughter, and when the women had ceased talking over his antics, the queen commanded Pamfilo to continue.

Commendable ladies, he began, Niccolosa, the name of Calandrino's beloved, called to my mind the story of another Niccolosa. It will give me pleasure to relate it to you, as you will learn from it how a prudent woman's resourcefulness prevented a serious scandal.

Not so long ago, in a village of the Mugnone, there lived a goodman who used to lodge wayfarers overnight and give them food and drink as well, for money. Though he was poor, and had only a tiny house, he was sometimes of necessity obliged to accept not only strangers who passed by, but even various acquaintances.

Now this goodman had a fine, goodlooking wife, who had borne him two children—a handsome, sprightly lass, some fifteen or sixteen years old, as yet unmarried, and a baby-boy, not quite a year old, still nursing at his mother's breast.

As it was, a handsome debonair youth of our town, who used to go about in the country a great deal, happened to catch sight of the girl and fell madly in love with her; while she, mighty proud to have won the love of a young man of his class, used all her wiles to retain his affection and thereby lost her own heart to him. Many and many a time this love of theirs would have come to its desired fruition by common accord, had not Pinuccio (for such was the youth's name), scorned to bring shame upon himself and her.

But alas, his passion grew more and more urgent with every passing day, until he could no longer control his yearning to be with her. At last he decided to find a way of lodging at her father's house, confident, from his knowledge of the interior, that he could then spend the night with the girl, unknown to a living soul. No sooner did the plan enter his head, than he lost no time in putting it into execution.

Late one evening he hired two horses, which he fitted out with a pair of saddle-bags, perhaps filled with straw, and with Adriano, a friend of his, who was acquainted with his amour, left Florence and rode about a while until he came to the vale of Mugnone rather late at night. Once there, the two youths turned their horses' heads, as though they were returning from Romagna, and setting out for the goodman's house, knocked at the door. The man knew both of them quite well, and opened to them without delay.

"Friend," Pinuccio said to him, "I'm afraid you'll have to put us up for the night. We thought we'd be able to get to Florence early, but we miscalculated, so here we are at this time of night, as you see."

"Pinuccio," said the innkeeper, "you know how ill-equipped I am to lodge two young gentlemen like you. But since you're here and it's so late, and there's no time for you to go anywhere else, I'll gladly put you up for the night as best I can."

The two youths dismounted and went into the inn, where, after making their horses comfortable, they supped with their host on the provisions they had taken care to take along with them.

Now you must know that the man had only one very small bedroom, in which three little beds were set up, as the host thought best—two at the broad end of the room, and one along the width of them, at the narrower end, leaving only enough space for passing back and forth, though not without great difficulty. Of these three beds, the host had the least uncomfortable made ready for the two friends and saw to it that they retired. Then, when he thought they were fast asleep—which they made a great show of being, though neither of them slept—he had his daughter lie down on one of the remaining two, while he himself got into the third with his wife, who put her baby's crib along the side of the bed where she was lying.

When the accommodations had been so disposed, Pinuccio, who had observed the lay of the land, waited a while, and when he thought everyone was sleeping soundly, got up very cautiously and slipped into his beloved's bed. Joyfully he was welcomed, though very timidly, and no sooner had he lain down beside her, than they began taking that delight which both of them most desired.

Now while Pinuccio was in bed with the girl, the house cat threw some things down, the clatter of which awakened the innkeeper's wife. Not knowing what it might be, she jumped out of bed, and naked as she was, groped in the dark toward the place whence she had heard the noise. In the interim Adriano, without any thought of mischief, arose to obey a call of nature, and as he was on his way, found the crib where the woman had placed it, blocking the path. As he could not go a step farther without moving it, he lifted it from its place and set it beside his own bed. Then, after expediting what he had got up to do, he went back and lay down in his bed, without any thought of the cradle.

Meanwhile, the woman had investigated the noise. Finding that what it had thrown down was not what she thought, she did not bother to make a light, but scolding the cat, returned to the bedroom, groping her way to the bed where her husband was sleeping. However, when she did not find the crib, "Lord help me!" she exclaimed to herself. "Imagine what I was about to do. Heavens, if I wasn't about to get into our young gentlemen's bed!"

She groped her way onward a little farther, and coming to the cradle, she got into the bed alongside of which it stood, and lay down with Adriano, believing herself to be lying with her goodman. The youth had not yet fallen asleep. Perceiving what had happened, he greeted her with cheer and joy, and without breathing a word, boarded her and heaved ho amain to her infinite relish.

When things had reached this pass, Pinuccio, afraid that sleep might surprise him in the arms of Niccolosa, rose from her side, having enjoyed her to his heart's content, and would have retired for a wink of sleep to his own bed. He found the cradle in the way, and thinking he had struck the host's bed, advanced a little farther and lay down in the other bed. The goodman, who was occupying it, awoke at the youth's touch, whereupon the lad, thinking it was his friend, said, "Believe me, there was never a girl as sweet as Niccolosa. I've enjoyed the greatest pleasure with her that ever any man had with a woman. I can swear! I tell you, I've gone into the woods more than six times since I left your side."

The host heard, and was by no means pleased. "What the devil is this fellow doing here?" he said to himself. Then aloud, more incensed than prudent, he said, "You did a wicked, villainous deed, Pinuccio. I can't understand why you should have done me this dishonor, but by the Lord, I'll make you pay dear for it!"

Pinuccio was no paragon of wisdom. Realizing his error, he did not try to retrieve it as best he could, but said, "What'll you make me pay for? What could you do to me?"

At the noise of their quarrel, the goodwife, thinking she was with her husband, whispered to Adriano, "Mercy on us! Listen to the way the two lodgers are quarreling together!"

"Let them quarrel and the devil take them," said Adriano, laughing. "They drank too much last night."

Now from the beginning, the woman thought she had heard her husband's angry voice, and at Adriano's words she knew at once where she had slept, and with whom. Like the discreet woman she was, she started up without a word, and taking the infant's crib, groped with it in the unlighted room, to the bed where she guessed Niccolosa was sleeping. There she laid it down and got in beside her daughter. Presently, as if her husband's wrath had awakened her, she called him.

"What are you quarreling about there with Pinuccio?" she asked.

"Don't you hear?" he cried. "Don't you hear what he says he did to-night with Niccolosa?"

"He lies in his throat," she said. "He certainly wasn't with

Niccolosa, for I've been lying here with her all night long and I haven't been able to get a moment's sleep. You're a fool for believing him. You men-folk drink entirely too much at night, and then, troubled by your drunken dreams, you go gadding about in your sleep, imagining you're doing Lord knows what! It's a pity you don't break your necks. Pray, what's Pinuccio doing there, and why doesn't he stay in his own bed?"

When Adriano saw how cleverly the woman was cloaking her daughter's shame and her own, he said in turn, "I told you a thousand times, Pinuccio, not to go roaming around. This sleep-walking of yours and your way of relating the nonsense you dream for gospel will get you into a nasty mess some day. Come back here to bed, damn your hide!"

At his wife's words and Adriano's corroboration, the goodman was firmly convinced Pinuccio had been dreaming, and taking him by the shoulders he shook him, and called him, saying, "Wake up! Wake up, Pinuccio! Go back to your own bed!"

The young man by this time had gathered all that had been said, and like one in a trance uttered more stuff and nonsense, making the host roar with laughter. At last, pretending he had been roused by all the shaking, he called Adriano, saying, "Is it day already that you call me?"

"Yes, yes, come here!" said his friend.

Pinuccio then rose from beside his host, counterfeiting a doze and looking as sleepy-eyed as could be, and returned to bed with Adriano. The following day they arose and the goodman had a merry time laughing at Pinuccio and twitting him about his dreams. Thus, with one pleasantry and another, the young men attended to their horses, set the pack-saddles on their backs, and after drinking with the host, mounted their beasts and returned to Florence, no less delighted with the adventure than with the outcome.

In after-days, Pinuccio found other ways of being with Niccolosa, who still insisted to her mother that the lad had been dreaming, while the good wife, recalling Adriano's embraces, inwardly imagined that she alone must have been awake.

\*

# THE SEVENTH STORY

*Talano di Molese dreams that a wolf tears his wife's throat and face. He warns her, but she does not heed him, and the vision comes to pass.*

WHEN PAMFILO'S STORY WAS OVER AND THE GOOD HOSTESS' RE-sourcefulness rewarded with general commendation, the queen called upon Pampinea, who obediently began:

We've had occasion before, adorable ladies, to speak of realities revealed in dreams, which, alas, many women are inclined to laugh at. In spite of what we have already said on that score, I'll not hesitate to tell you, in a very brief story, what happened to a neighbor of mine not so long ago, for not believing a vision that was revealed to her husband in sleep.

I don't know whether you are acquainted with Talano di Molese, a gentleman of great worth. Well, he married a young woman called Margarita, who surpassed all others in beauty, but was so capricious, disagreeable and self-willed that she would never condescend to follow anyone's advice or offer to be pleased with anything people ever did. Her evil disposition was quite a trial to Talano, but since he was powerless against it, he suffered it in silence.

One night, while Talano was staying with Margarita in one of his country-homes, in his sleep it seemed to him that he saw his wife walking through a beautiful greenwood, not very far from their house. And as he gazed at her wandering through it, he thought he saw a huge, fierce wolf spring out of a thicket and rush straight for her throat, forcing her to the ground, and struggling to drag her off to its lair, as she screamed for help. At last, it seemed to him that she tore herself free of its fangs, but her throat and face had been disfigured.

He was very much concerned by the vision, and when he arose the following morning, he said to his wife, "Margarita, though your perversity has never suffered me to enjoy a day's bliss with you, I should still be most unhappy if anything ever happened to you, so take my advice and don't leave the house to-day."

"Why not?" she asked, whereupon he told her all that he had dreamed. Margarita only bowed her head and said, "He who wishes you ill, will dream ill dreams of you. You seem to be terribly concerned about me, but you dream the very things you'd like to see happening to me. Rest assured I'll take care to-day and forever not to give you joy of this misfortune, or any other you may wish me."

"I knew exactly that's the answer you would give me," answered Talano, "for that's what a fool must expect for his pains. Believe whatever you please, but I'm telling you this for your own good. I warn you again, stay home to-day, or at least beware of going into the woods."

"Very well, I'll take care," replied Margarita, but inwardly she said, "Just see how cunningly that fellow thinks he's frightened me from going into the woods to-day! I'll wager he must be planning to have a love-tryst in that very wood with some whore, and he doesn't want me to spy upon him! Oho, he's reckoning without his host! What an idiot I'd be if I didn't see through him and believed what he said! Ah, but it will fall through, that pretty plan of his! I'll catch him, even if I have to stay there all day. I'll see what sort of deal it is he wants to make to-day."

Accordingly, no sooner did her husband go out at one door, than she stole out at the other, and as stealthily as possible, made straight for the wood. Hiding in the densest part of it, she stood on guard, spying in all directions to see if anyone were coming.

Suddenly, as she lay there in hiding, thoughts of danger being farthest from her mind, a huge, terrible wolf sprang out of a thicket, and before she could even say, "God help me," it was already at her throat. Fiercely and fast it clutched her in its fangs, and made off with her as though she were a lamb.

She could not scream, so tight did it sink its fangs into her throat, nor could she help herself in any way. The brute would surely have strangled her as it dragged her off, had not a party of shepherds met it. Shouting and threatening, they made it release its grip, when the shepherds recognized Margarita and carried her home, a sad and wretched woman.

After many months under the doctor's care, the wounds were at last healed, but not without leaving the woman's throat and part of her face so terribly ravaged, that whereas she had once been beautiful, she was from then on ugly and disfigured. She was ashamed to appear in public places, and all too often she bewailed her stubbornness in refusing to believe her husband's veracious dream, when it would have cost her nothing.

✳

## THE EIGHTH STORY

*Biondello plays Ciacco a trick which the latter adroitly returns, by having him soundly beaten.*

EVERY MEMBER OF THE GAY BRIGADE SWORE THAT WHAT TALANO had beheld in his sleep was no dream but sheer clairvoyance, so scrupulously had it been verified in all its details. When all were silent, however, the queen requested Lauretta to resume the story-telling, who began:

Wisest of ladies, just as everyone who has spoken before me to-day has been inspired by something already told, so too am I. In this case, it's the cruel vengeance of the scholar which Pampinea told us about yesterday that moves me to tell you of another which was certainly unpleasant for the victim, though not half so ruthless as Rinieri's.

Once upon a time, there lived in Florence a man whom everyone commonly knew as Ciacco, the greatest glutton and guzzler that ever was, though otherwise a courteous gentleman and a wit. As his circumstances were not sufficient for him to meet the expenses his extravagant tastes incurred, he gave himself wholly to the calling, not altogether of a court-jester, but of a hanger-on in the society of rich folk who furnished and enjoyed a good table. Day and night he might be seen in their company, at dinner and at supper as the case might be, although he had not always been invited.

At that time, there also lived in Florence a man called Biondello. He was a wee little fellow, spry as a fly and trimmer than a pin, with a cap upon his head and flowing yellow locks, not a hair of which was out of curl. He too followed the same profession as Ciacco.

One Lenten morning, while Biondello had gone to the fish-market to buy a pair of handsome lampreys for Master Vieri de' Cerchi, he met Ciacco, who approached him, saying, "What's all this?"

Biondello said, "Oh, last night Master Corso Donati was sent three lampreys much finer than these, and a sturgeon besides, but as they were not enough for the entertainment of certain gentlemen, his guests, he had me buy these other two. Aren't you going to be at the dinner?"

"Of course you know I'll be there," said Ciacco.

When he thought it time for him to visit Master Corso, he started for the gentleman's house and found him with a party of neighbors. Dinner had not yet been served.

"What brings you to these parts, Ciacco?" asked Master Corso.

"I've come to dine with you and your guests, sir," he said.

"You're welcome," said Master Corso, "and since it's time, let's go to dinner."

Accordingly, they took their places at table. First of all, they had chick-peas and salted tunny. The next course was fried fish from the Arno, and then there was nothing more.

Ciacco was soon aware that Biondello had played him a trick. He was not a little angered, though he did not show it, and swore to make him pay for it.

Not many days had passed, before he again encountered Biondello, who had already made many a man laugh at his prank. "Good day to you," Biondello greeted him with a laugh, "and how did you enjoy Master Corso's lampreys?"

"Before the week is past you'll know much better than I," replied Ciacco.

Taking leave of Biondello, he lost no time in seeking out a certain crafty porter, with whom he came to terms. Giving him a large glass flagon, he took him to the arcade of the Cavicciuoli, pointed out to him a gentleman called Filippo Argenti, a strapping, burly, sinewy hulk of a man, as scornful, irascible and eccentric as could be, and said, "You go up to that man with this bottle in your hand and say to him, 'Sir, Biondello sends me to you, and begs me to ask you to please encarnadine this flask with your good red wine, as he wants to have a little pleasure with his pets.' Be careful he doesn't get hold of you, or he'll make you remember it and you'll be ruining my plans."

"Is there anything else I have to say?" inquired the porter.

"No," said Ciacco. "Go now, and after you've said what I told you, come back here to me with the bottle and I'll pay you."

The porter went in and did as he was told. Now Filippo was no great wit, and believing that Biondello, whom he knew, was playing a joke on him, he turned crimson with rage.

"What *encarnadine* and what *pets* are you talking about?" he roared. "The devil take you and him together!"

Jumping up, he tried to seize the porter. The fellow, however, had been on his guard, and making off in double quick time, he rejoined Ciacco by another route. Then to him, who had seen everything, he reported what Filippo had said. Ciacco was satisfied and paid the porter for his trouble, but from then on, he had no rest until he again met Biondello, to whom he said, "Have you been going to the Cavicciuoli arcade these days?"

"Why, no," said Biondello. "Why do you ask?"

"Because Master Filippo has been looking for you, I don't know why," replied Ciacco.

"That's fine," said the other. "I'm passing that way now, and I'll speak to him."

Thereupon he went on, with Ciacco following close behind to see how the matter would turn out.

Now when Filippo had failed to catch the porter, he had been maddened by a rage that still gnawed within him, all the more because he had not been able to make head or tail of the message, except that perhaps Biondello, at some man's instigation, was having a joke at his expense. He was still seething with fury, when along came Biondello, whom he no sooner saw than he pounced upon him with a resounding cuff.

"Mercy, sir!" cried Biondello. "What does this mean?"

But Filippo seized him by his yellow hair, ripped off his cap, and flinging it on the ground, thundered to the accompaniment of great blows, "You scoundrel! What does this mean, you say? You'll find out soon enough! *Encarnadine* and *pets* indeed! What's all this nonsense that you put people up to tell me? Do you take me for a child, that can be fooled?"

So saying, he fell on the poor wretch with his fists, that were like iron, bashed in his face, and left no hair on his head that was not at odds with the other. Then he rolled him in the mud, ripping his clothes off his back, and all in such a rage that Biondello could not put in a word, or ask him why he was treating him that way. True, he had heard Filippo say something about *encarnadine* and *pets,* but he had no idea in the world what he meant by the words.

Finally, after Filippo had pummeled him soundly, the people who by this time had collected about them in great number managed, with great difficulty, to deliver the poor wretch from his assailant, ruffled and disordered as he was, and told him why he had been served in that fashion.

"You ought to know him, by this time," they said. "He's not the kind of man to be trifled with, and you had no business to send him such messages."

Biondello denied everything, moaning and wailing. "I never sent to him for any wine," he protested.

However, after he had somewhat recovered from his misadventure, he returned home, aching and dismayed, firmly convinced that the trick had been of Ciacco's doing.

At last, after many days, when the bruises on his face had healed and he took to going out again, Ciacco met him and said with a laugh:

"Ho, there, Biondello! How did you like Filippo's wine?"

"As much as you did Master Corso's lampreys," he answered.

"It's all up to you from now on," said Ciacco. "If you ever treat me again to the sort of dinner you gave me, I'll requite you with the kind of drink you had."

Biondello had to admit that any ill-will he bore Ciacco would always far exceed any actual mischief he could do him, so he patched up the quarrel with him, and from then on took care not to trifle with him.

\*

## THE NINTH STORY

*Two youths go to Solomon for advice—one seeking to know how to gain the love of his fellow-men, and the other how to cure his wife of her perversity. To the first he answered, "Love!" and to the other, "Go to Goose-Bridge!"*

THERE WAS NO ONE ELSE LEFT TO SPEAK NOW BUT THE QUEEN, if Dioneo's privilege were to be observed, and therefore, after the ladies had enjoyed a laugh at the hapless Biondello, she cheerfully began:

Lovable ladies, if we take the trouble to consider with an open mind, the way things are arranged in the world we'll soon discover that women, as a class, are subject to men by the laws of nature, custom, and tradition, and are obliged to govern themselves accordingly. Hence, if a woman is anxious to enjoy peace, comfort and harmony with the men to whom she is related, she must be humble, forbearing and obedient, besides being virtuous—a quality which every discreet woman holds as her chief treasure. Indeed, even if human laws, which first and foremost consider common good, and custom, or tradition, whose power is both far-reaching and praiseworthy—I say, even if these did not teach us the lesson, nature alone makes it manifest. For has she not made us tender and delicate of body, timid and faint of heart? The physical strength she has given us is puny. Furthermore, she has endowed us with soft, gentle voices and easy, harmonious movements—all testifying to our need of man's protection.

Whoever wishes to be protected and taken care of, must necessarily be obedient, submissive and respectful toward his protector. And whom have we to help and protect us if not man? It is to man, therefore, that we owe our submission, which is to him a supreme honor, and any woman who departs from this rule I consider not only worthy of severe blame, but also of rigorous punishment.

I was led to these reflections—though not for the first time, I must confess—by the story Pampinea told a little while ago of Talano's wayward wife, upon whom God visited the punishment her husband had not expected to give her. I maintain, as I said before, that all women who depart from being the pleasant, gentle, compliant creatures that nature, custom and tradition would have them, are each and every one deserving of ruthless and rigorous punishment.

*À propos* of what I have just said, I'd like to tell you a story about a certain bit of advice Solomon offered as effective medicine for curing women suffering from such ills. Let no one who is in no need of that sort of cure take it personally, though men have a certain proverb that says, 'Good horse and bad horse with spur you prick; good wife and bad wife both need the stick.' Interpreted in jest, the words, we must confess, hold a grain of truth. Even if we understood them as a moral precept, we must again admit their verity. Women are naturally giddy and inclined to waywardness, therefore the stick is necessary to punish the wickedness of those who overstep their bounds. Again, to maintain the virtue of the others who do not permit themselves to go astray, the stick is also needful, both to encourage and intimidate them. But enough of my sermon and let's proceed to the story.

The lofty fame of Solomon's marvelous wisdom, as you know, had been spread well-nigh throughout the world, and as he was also renowned for his generosity in offering proofs of it to whoever cared to experience it at first hand, many flocked to him from everywhere for advice in their direst and most pressing needs.

Now among the numbers who came to him on this errand, there was a youth of rank and substance by the name of Melisso, who left Lajazzo, his home and birthplace. Beyond the gates of Antioch, on his way to Jerusalem, he met a young man called Josepho, and as he too was going to the same city, they traveled together a while, striking up a conversation, as travelers usually do. Melisso had already learned from Josepho who he was and where he came from, and accordingly he asked him where he was going, and on what errand.

"I'm on my way to see Solomon," said Josepho, "for advice about my wife," and told him further what a wayward woman she was, more so than anyone else in the world, and so perverse that neither his prayers, cajolings or anything else could move her from her frowardness. "And where do you come from?" he inquired in turn, "and why have you undertaken your journey?"

"I'm of Lajazzo," answered Melisso. "And as you have your affliction, so have I mine. I am rich, and I use my wealth in keeping open-house and honoring my fellow-citizens at table. But it's a strange and very puzzling thing, that for all this, I cannot find a man who loves me. Hence, I am going where you are going, to obtain some word on how I may succeed in winning the love of my fellow-men."

The two continued together until they arrived in Jerusalem, where an introduction was effected by one of Solomon's knights and they were admitted to his presence. Briefly, Melisso explained his need to the king.

"Love!" Solomon answered him.

The advice uttered, Melisso was ushered out of the audience-chamber as Josepho told the wise-man what had brought him there.

"Go to Goose-Bridge!" Solomon advised him, and said no more. Then similarly, Josepho was ushered out of his presence.

Outside, he rejoined Melisso, who was waiting for him, and informed him of the answer he had received. For a long time the youths pondered over the wise-man's words, but unable to make anything out of them or deduce some benefit for their needs, they set out on their journey homeward, feeling not a little foolish.

They had been traveling a few days when they came upon a stream spanned by a handsome bridge. A long caravan of mules and pack-horses was crossing at the time, so the two were obliged to await their turn, until all the beasts had crossed to the other side. Soon nearly all had filed past, but suddenly one of the mules took fright, a fairly common occurrence with those beasts, and would not go ahead under any circumstances. Seeing how the case stood, the muleteer seized a stick and began giving the beast a moderate dose of it to urge it forward. But the mule, pitching now to one side of the path and now the other, and sometimes even dashing backwards altogether, would not consider going across. The muleteer was at the end of his patience, and fuming with rage lay on mercilessly with the stick, now on the creature's head, now on its flanks and again on its rump. Still it was of no avail.

Melisso and Josepho were witnesses to this beating, and again and again exclaimed to the man, "Stop, wicked lout! What are you doing? Do you want to kill the beast outright? Why don't you try to be kind to it and coax it across? It will obey you more readily than if you thwack it the way you do."

But the muleteer answered, "You know your horses and I know my mule. Leave me to handle it."

The words were scarcely out of his mouth when he fell to beating the beast once again, dealing so lustily right and left, that the mule at last was persuaded to go across and the muleteer came out of the contest victorious.

The two youths were about to resume their journey, when Josepho asked a poor fellow who was sunning himself at the bridge-gate, "Tell me, good man, what bridge is this?"

"Sir, it is called Goose-Bridge," replied the other.

Instantly, the name recalled Solomon's counsel to the youth's mind, and turning to Melisso, he said, "I tell you, friend, after all, the advice Solomon gave me may turn out to be wholesome and true, for I'm now convinced that I didn't know how to beat my wife. This muleteer has certainly taught me what I have to do."

Some days later they came to Antioch, where Josepho invited Melisso to stay with him a day or so, to rest from the fatigue of the journey. It was no joyous welcome the wife gave the guest. Nevertheless, Josepho requested her kindly to prepare a dinner according to Melisso's wish. The latter, seeing it was his friend's desire, told her in a few words what he would have, whereupon the woman, true to her perverse habits, followed none of his instructions but did the contrary, in almost every detail. Josepho grew wroth.

"Weren't you told what sort of meal you were to prepare?" he asked.

She turned upon him insolently. "Indeed!" she said. "What may you be driving at? Come and eat if you wish. Did you tell me to do otherwise? Well, I preferred to do it this way. If you like it, very well. If you don't, leave it."

Melisso was aghast at the woman's impudence, and condemned her. Josepho, on the other hand, simply remarked, "You're still your old self. But, believe me, I'll make you mend your ways." Turning to Melisso, he said, "Friend, we'll soon test the efficacy of Solomon's advice. But please don't be hurt at what you're going to witness. Look upon it as a sort of game. Then, if you should feel moved to stop me, think of the answer the muleteer gave us when we felt sorry for his beast."

"I am in your house," answered Melisso, "and while I am in it, I don't intend to hinder anything you may wish to do."

Thereupon Josepho, providing himself with a good, stout, round stick of young oak, went into the bedroom where the woman had gone grumbling on rising vexed from the table, and clutching her by the braids, flung her down at his feet, putting his cudgel to use. At first the woman began to shriek and then to threaten, but when she saw that nothing could stop Josepho, although she was already bruised all over, she pleaded with him. "Mercy, for God's sake!" she cried. "Don't kill me, and I promise always to do as you say!"

Still Josepho did not desist. Indeed, he continued basting her more zealously than before, overlooking neither ribs, thighs, nor shoulders in his search for every seam. Not until he was compelled by weariness, and there was no bone or inch of flesh left unhurt on his wife's body, did he give up the sport.

The beating administered, he joined Melisso and said, "Tomorrow we'll see what fruits the advice about going to Goose-Bridge will bear."

Then, after he had washed his hands and rested a while, he had supper with his friend and in due time went to bed.

The poor woman, meanwhile, dragged herself with great difficulty to her bed, and snatched what rest she could until the day dawned, when, rising with the lark, she sent to find out what Josepho desired for dinner. He laughed at this, and so did his friend, and he gave his order.

At dinner-time, when they returned to the dining-room, they found everything beautifully prepared, according to their instructions, upon which they highly praised the advice they had once so little understood.

Some days later, Melisso bade his friend good-bye, and returning to his own home confided to some wise-man the advice Solomon had given him.

"He could not have offered you truer or better counsel," said the man. "You know you love nobody. All the honors and favors you heap upon people are prompted not by the love you bear your fellow-men, but by a love of pomp and show. Learn to love, as Solomon told you, and you will be loved."

So, then, was the wayward woman chastened by Solomon's advice, and the youth beloved, by loving.

# THE TENTH STORY

*Brother John, at the request of his friend Pietro, performs a charm to transform his wife into a mare; but when the priest is about to attach the mare's tail, Peter says he will have none of it, and so ruins the spell.*

THE QUEEN'S STORY EVOKED MURMURS OF DISAPPROVAL FROM the ladies and laughter from the men, and when all of them had calmed down, Dioneo began:

A black crow among a bevy of fairest doves, charming ladies, does more to enhance their beauty than would a snow-white swan. Similarly, a person of none too lofty intellect among wisemen, not only adds to the radiance and worth of their understanding, but affords amusement and sport. You ladies are all exceedingly wise and modest, therefore I, the black sheep of this party, should be all the more appreciated for enhancing the light of your virtue by my own shortcomings, than if I obscured it by showing greater worth. For this reason, I deserve more latitude to reveal myself as I am, and you must bear with me more patiently in what I say or do, than if I had sounder wits in my head. Well, then, I'm going to tell you a fairly short story, from which you will gather how necessary it is to observe all the rules laid down by those who perform wonders by means of magic charms, and how easy it can be to ruin the good work by sinning in the least detail.

About a year ago, a priest called Brother John of Barolo came to Barletta. He had a miserable little parish at best, and so to keep body and soul together, he took to peddling goods by going about the fairs at Apulia with a mare of his, engaging in a small way in buying and selling. As he pursued this calling, he became quite friendly with a goodman by the name of Pietro di Tresanti, who carried on the same business with the help of his ass, and like the good Apulian that he was, he called him Friend Pietro as a token of love and fellowship. Indeed, whenever he stopped at his parish in Barletta, he would always take him to his house and put him up for the night in his own room, showing him all the courtesy his small means could afford. Friend Pietro, on his part, returned the compliment. Although he was as poor as a churchmouse, and only had a wretched little hut at Tresanti scarcely big enough to hold him, his young and comely wife and his ass, he would always take the priest home with him, whenever the holy man chanced to pass that way, and there he feasted and entertained him as best he could, out of gratitude for the hospitality he received from him at Barletta. However, it was always difficult for Friend Pietro to put up the priest as he would have wished. The house contained but one little bed, in which Friend Pietro slept with his luscious wife, hence he was obliged to house Brother John's mare with the donkey in a wee stable, and there the good priest had to share with his beast the mound of hay that was their pallet.

More than once, during the priest's visits, Friend Pietro's wife, knowing the courtesy the holy man showed him at Barletta, suggested sleeping with a neighbor by the name of Zita Carapresa, the daughter of Giudice Leo, so that Brother John might share the bed with her husband. She had made the proposal again and again, but he would never agree to it.

"Don't worry your head about me, Gemmata, my dear," he said on one occasion, "I'm perfectly well-satisfied with things as they are, for whenever the whim takes me, I change this mare into a jolly lass and lie with her. Then, at my wish, I change her to a mare again. I wouldn't part with her for anything."

The young woman believed him and gaped with amazement. Presently, she communicated the wonder to her goodman, adding, "If he's such a friend of yours as you say, why don't you ask him to teach you that charm? Then you could change me to a mare and carry on your business with both a donkey and me. We'd be earning twice as much together, and when we got home you could turn me back to my womanly shape."

Friend Pietro had no great wit in his noddle. He lent a credulous ear to what Gemmata said and concurred with her plan, plaguing Brother John to teach him this wonderful charm. The good priest did his utmost to drive this nonsense out of the fellow's cranium, but since he could not, "Well," he said, "as you insist, to-morrow we'll get up before dawn, as usual, and I'll show you how the trick is done. I must confess, though, it is a mighty hard thing to attach the tail, as you'll see for yourself."

All night long, Friend Pietro and goodwife Gemmata scarcely slept a wink, so impatient were they for the deed to be done. With the first peep of dawn they rose and called Brother John, who came in his nightshirt to his friend's bedroom, saying, "There's no other man alive for whom I would do this, and as you insist, I'll go ahead with it. But I must stress one point. If you want the charm to succeed, you must do exactly as I say."

Both the goodman and his wife nodded assent, whereupon Brother John, taking a light and thrusting it into Friend Pietro's hand, counseled him, "Watch closely what I am going to do and try to remember all I say. But first and foremost, be careful you don't let out a single word, no matter what you hear or see, or the whole thing will be ruined. Only pray to God that the tail will be well stuck."

Friend Pietro held the lamp tight. "I'll be careful to do as you say," he promised.

Then Brother John, turning to Gemmata, had her strip to the skin and crouch on all fours, like a mare. "Beware, and don't utter a word, no matter what happens," he cautioned her likewise.

So saying, he began passing his hands over her face and head, mumbling, "Let this be a fine mare's head." Sliding his fingers through her hair, "Let this be a fine mare's mane," he said, and feeling her arms, added, "and these a fine mare's sturdy legs and pretty feet." When he felt of her breasts and found them firm and round, a certain one awoke who had not been summoned, and popped right up. "Let this be a fine mare's chest," continued Brother John, and kept up the incantation until he had gone over her back and belly, buttocks, thighs and legs. At last, when nothing further remained for him to do but to attach the tail, he raised his shirt and taking the peg with which he planted men, slipped it nimbly into the hole already made for it, saying, "And let this be a fine mare's tail."

Friend Pietro had so far watched everything with the closest attention, but this last twist did not seem quite right to his eyes. "Ho, there, Brother John," he cried suddenly, "I don't want any tail there! I won't have it there!"

Just then, that primal moisture had come, by whose aid all plants sprout, whereupon Brother John, withdrawing his dibber, exclaimed, "Good heavens, Friend Pietro! What have you done? Didn't I warn you not to breathe a word, no matter what you saw? The mare was almost finished, and you had to ruin everything by crying out! The worst of it is, there's no way of working the spell again as long as we live!"

"So much the better then," said Friend Pietro. "I didn't want that tail there, no, not I. Why didn't you say to me, 'Stick it on yourself?' Moreover, you were putting it on too far down."

"I didn't ask you to attach it, because you wouldn't have done such a good job of it as I, myself, the first time," said Brother John.

Meanwhile, Gemmata rose to her feet, and hearing their words turned to her husband in all seriousness, saying, "You blockhead! Why did you have to ruin your chances and mine? Where did you ever see a mare without a tail? Faith, you're a starving wretch, but it would serve you right if you were even poorer than you are!"

Convinced that she could no longer be turned to a mare because of the disenchanting words her husband had uttered, Gemmata donned her clothes again, vexed and disconsolate, while Friend Pietro set out for the Bitonto fair with his donkey, to pursue his usual calling, accompanied by Brother John, whom he never again importuned for such a task.

The laughter evoked by Dioneo's story, which the ladies had understood better than he had intended, let her imagine, who is laughing at it this very moment.

Now that the stories for the day had been told and the sun was beginning to wane in strength, the queen, knowing that the end of her rule had come, stood up and, taking the laurel-crown from her head, laid it on Pamfilo, who was the only one left to receive the honor.

"My lord," she said, smiling, "you, as the last one to hold the honor that devolves upon you, assume an added burden with it, for it is up to you to remedy my shortcomings and those of the queens and kings who wore the crown before you. But the Lord give you grace, as He has granted it to me to crown you king."

Pamfilo accepted the honor gracefully and said, "Your excellent qualities and the merits of the rest of my subjects will, I trust, make it possible for me to be adjudged as worthy a monarch as the others were before me."

Following the custom of his predecessors, he arranged with the steward all that was necessary to their general comfort, and turning to the women waiting for him to address them, began:

"Dear ladies, it was the wish of Emilia, our recent queen, to give you freedom to treat whatever subject you desired, that you might relax your powers. Now that we are all rested, I think it advisable for us all to return to our usual procedure. Hence, for to-morrow, I'd like you to be ready with a story on the theme *of such as have distinguished themselves in the accomplishment of generous or magnificent deeds, in love or other fields*. I am sure the stories themselves and the deeds described will inspire your minds to noble endeavor; and so our life, which can have but too brief a span in its mortal husk, will endure immortal in glory—a consummation which all who do not live to serve the belly alone, like mere beasts, should not only desire, but strive earnestly to achieve."

The theme was agreeable to the whole company. One and all, they rose to their feet by the new king's leave, and betaking themselves each and severally to the amusement that most delighted them, they played and romped until supper-time, when they gathered cheerfully at table and were served with order and diligence. Afterwards they danced, as usual, and sang perhaps a thousand ditties, all more humorous of content than excellent of music. At last the king, turning to Neifile, said, "Sing us a ballad in your own name, I pray you."

Without waiting to be coaxed, she graciously began in a clear, joyous voice:

"I am in girlhood bloom and with glad heart
  I joy and carol in the budded spring,
    All thanks to love and its vagaries sweet.

In meadows green I seek the multitude
  Of flowers white and gold and crimson dight,

The roses crowning thorns, and lilies white—
In each of them I find similitude
Of my beloved's face, all am'rous-hued.
   He holds me fast, and as his treasured thing
     All my desires turn his love to meet.

When 'mid the blooms I find a flower that vies
   To my own seeming, with my lover dear,
   I cull and kiss it, and I bid it hear
The burden of my soul, confessor-wise,
And of my heart bespeak the yearning sighs.
   Then on my hair with flowers blossoming,
     I interweave it in a garland meet.

Beyond the pleasure and ah, far above
   A flower grants the sight, one more is mine—
   To find within its core the youth divine
Who has inflamed me with his gentle love.
But ah! the raptures that my senses prove
   From the sweet scents that from its petals spring,
     Only my sighs could witness or repeat!

For all my sighs come not from out my breast
   Harshly nor doleful, as when others sigh,
   But warm they rise, and soft, and gently fly
Toward my beloved, who, when thus addressed
Moves of himself to grant my own love's quest.
   And still he comes, the sweet delight to bring,
     When 'Come, or I shall languish,' I entreat."

The king and the ladies praised Neifile's song lavishly. A good part of the night had sped, however, so shortly after this last ballad, the king dismissed his little company to rest until the following morning.

# 10

## THE TENTH DAY

✳

A GROUP OF LITTLE CLOUDS WAS STILL ROSY IN THE WEST, WHILE in the east others were edged with the brightest gold by the sun's rays, when Pamfilo, arising, summoned all the ladies and his companions to him.

When they were assembled, he consulted with them about where they might go for their amusement, and with slow steps he led the party, accompanied by Filomena and Fiammetta. They discussed many things about their future life together, making suggestions, asking and answering questions, and for a long time they took their recreation.

Meanwhile, during their long walk, the sun's rays had begun to beat down upon them with burning heat, so they retraced their steps to the palace. The cups were rinsed at the clear fountain, and those who were thirsty, drank; then, in the grateful shade of the garden, they disported themselves until dinnertime. A nap followed the meal, according to their custom, and later, all refreshed, they gathered again at the place the king designated. He called upon Neifile to tell the first story, and sweetly she began:

✳

## THE FIRST STORY

*A knight in the service of the King of Spain thinks himself ill-rewarded for his pains, whereupon the king gives him certain proof that Fortune, and not he, is to blame, and rewards him with royal munificence.*

I OUGHT TO CONSIDER MYSELF GREATLY COMPLIMENTED, NOBLE ladies, that our king has favored me so greatly by asking me to begin upon the theme of generosity, which as much constitutes the light and brilliance of every other quality as the sun is the glory and ornament of heaven. I'll tell a little story *à propos* of it, a very nice little story, I think, which it certainly would do you no harm to remember.

Well then, you must know that of all the valiant knights our city has ever produced, perhaps the most remarkable was Messer Ruggieri de' Figiovanni, a wealthy and high-spirited man, who, seeing that the life and customs of Tuscany afforded him little or no opportunity to show his prowess to the best advantage, resolved to stay a while at the court of Alfonso, King of Spain, whose reputation for valor far transcended that of any contemporary ruler. Furnishing himself with arms, horses and soldiers as became his honorable rank, he betook himself to Spain, where the king graciously received him.

Messer Ruggieri settled there, living in splendor, and performing such marvelous feats of arms that he was soon renowned as a man of prowess. When he had been living in Spain a considerable time, keeping close watch over the king's behavior, it seemed to him that the monarch was overly imprudent in bestowing his castles, towns and feudal titles indiscriminately, on people who did not deserve them. Nothing, on the other hand, was ever given to him. Now he knew his own worth, and thinking his renown would suffer in consequence of the king's neglect he decided to leave and asked the monarch's permission. The king granted it, and gave him besides one of the best and most beautiful mules that had ever been mounted. Messer Ruggieri gladly accepted it, especially when he considered the long journey that was ahead of him.

This accomplished, Alfonso charged one of his trustworthy servants to contrive as best he could to ride with Messer Ruggieri, but in such a way as not to appear in league with himself, and to listen to everything Messer Ruggieri said of him, so as to be able to carry it back, and then, the morning after, he was to order the knight to present himself before him at court.

The servant stood watch, and as soon as Messer Ruggieri left the country, he shrewdly contrived to join him, pretending that he too was on his way to Italy. As they traveled pleasantly together, talking of one thing and another, Messer Ruggieri, who was riding the mule the king had given him, said toward night-fall:

"Perhaps it might be wise to give our beasts a rest," and entering a stable, all the animals were relieved, except the mule, which would not rest. As they rode on, and the squire kept his ears pricked to catch everything the knight said, they came to a stream where they stopped to water their beasts. Immediately, the mule balked.

"May the devil take you, beast!" cried Messer Ruggieri. "You're just like your master who gave you to me."

The king's servant buried these words in his memory as well as many others he had gathered as they traveled all day long, but not another did he hear him utter, that was not in the highest degree flattering to the king.

The following day, when they had mounted their horses and Messer Ruggieri was about to pursue his way to Tuscany, the squire made the king's command known and the knight turned back at once.

The king was already informed of what Ruggieri had said about the mule, and sending for him, received him with a smiling face.

"Why did you liken me to my mule," he asked, "or rather, why did you liken her to me?"

"My lord," replied Messer Ruggieri with candor, "I likened her to you simply because you bestow your gifts where they are not deserved and give nothing where gifts are due, just as your mule refused to rest where she should have, and balked where she shouldn't."

"Well, Ruggieri," said the king, "if I did not reward you as I did others, who are of no account compared to you, it was not because I failed to appreciate your worth as a most courageous, highly deserving knight. It was your own luck that wouldn't permit me, and I'll give you sufficient proof that I am right."

"My lord," replied Messer Ruggieri, "it was not because I desired greater riches that I was troubled when I received no reward from you, but simply because you did not immediately testify to my merit. Anyhow, I accept your excuse as valid and honest, and I am ready to see whatever you please to show me, though I believe you, even without that."

The king then led him to a vast hall, where, as he had arranged beforehand, they were confronted by two massive sealed chests. There, in the presence of many courtiers, he said, "Ruggieri, one of these chests contains my crown, the royal scepter and the sphere, and many handsome girdles, brooches, rings and precious gems belonging to me. The other is full of earth. Choose one, and whichever it is you select, accept. Thus you'll be able to judge who has been unappreciative of your merit—I or Fortune."

Ruggieri saw that it was the king's pleasure and selected one of the chests, which the king commanded to be opened. It was the one that was full of earth.

"You can see for yourself, Ruggieri," said the king, laughing, "that I was right in what I said about luck. But your deserts merit my opposition to its power. I know you have no desire to become a Spaniard, therefore I shall give you neither castle nor town, but the very chest of which your luck deprived you. In spite of its decree, I want that chest to be yours to take with you to your own land, that you may glory in your merits among your neighbors, through the testimony of my gifts."

Messer Ruggieri accepted the chest, and thanking the king as befitted him for so splendid a gift, he went back to Tuscany with it, eminently satisfied.

✳

## THE SECOND STORY

*Ghino da Tacco captures the Abbot of Cluny, cures him of stomach-trouble and then lets him go. Back at the court of Rome, the abbot reconciles Ghino to Pope Boniface who makes him a Prior of the Hospitalers.*

THE MUNIFICENCE OF KING ALFONSO TO THE FLORENTINE KNIGHT was duly appreciated and succeeded in pleasing Pamfilo tremendously. Turning to Elisa, he asked her to continue, and very readily she began:

Exquisite ladies, no one can deny that it is a fine and laudable thing for a king to be munificent and bestow his generosity upon a man who had served him. But what shall we say when we hear of a prelate who was admirably magnanimous to one he would have been justified in treating as an enemy? Surely, that the king's deed was virtue and the prelate's a pure and simple miracle, for it is well-known that churchmen are even stingier than women, and the sworn enemies of generosity in every manner, shape or form. It is true that everybody naturally hungers after vengeance for insults suffered; but holy men, as we can see for ourselves, in spite of their vaunted patience, and above all, their much extolled virtue of forgiveness, seek it even more hotly than other mortals. But now you will have manifest proof, from the story I am about to tell you, just how generous a prelate could be.

Ghino da Tacco, notorious for his cruelties and daring robberies, was banished from Siena. As he was at odds with the Counts of Santa Fiore, he incited Radicofani to rebel against the church of Rome, and settled there to live, setting his marauders to rob any man bold enough to pass that way.

At that time, while Boniface the Eighth was pontiff at Rome, the Abbot of Cluny, believed to be one of the wealthiest prelates of the church, came to his court, and there, falling sick of stomach-trouble, was advised by the doctors to take the baths at Siena in order to be cured. The pope readily gave him leave to go, and so, without being at all concerned about Ghino's notoriety, the abbot set out with pomp and ceremony to Siena, taking horses and retainers without number.

Ghino da Tacco was soon apprised of his coming. Accordingly, he spread his nets, and without letting even a single pageboy slip through, he hedged the abbot, his followers and all his appurtenances into a narrow enclosure. This accomplished, he commissioned one of his most capable men to go with an honorable escort to the abbot and courteously request him, in his name, to come and stay at his castle. The abbot raged at the invitation. "I'll do nothing of the kind!" he cried. "What have I to do with this Ghino? I'll go right ahead, and I'd like to see the man who dares to stop me!"

Humbly, the emissary spoke again, "Your worship, you find yourself in a part of the world where we have no fear baiting the Lord's might. Here interdicts and excommunications are themselves excommunicated, therefore be so good as to favor Ghino by accepting."

In the course of the conversation, the whole place had been surrounded by Ghino's men, and the abbot suddenly found that he and his followers had been taken prisoner. There was nothing for him to do but to go to the castle, though much against his will, and away he went, escorted by the emissary and followed by his men and his trappings. In the court he dismounted, but at Ghino's command he was confined alone in a dark, uncomfortable hole of a room in one of the galleries, while the rest of the men were most handsomely lodged in various quarters of the castle, each according to his rank. Not a hand was laid on the horses and provisions, which were all placed in safety.

This accomplished, Ghino himself went to the abbot.

"Your worship," he said, "Ghino, whose guest you are, charges you in all courtesy to tell him where you were going, and on what business."

The abbot, a wise man, knowing how to make pride bow before necessity, told him where he was going and why. Ghino then took leave of him and made up his mind to cure him without the help of any baths. Ordering a large, cheerful fire to be kept burning in the abbot's room, and setting a watch outside the door to guard it well, he went away and did not return until morning, when he brought him two slices of toast on a snow-white napkin, and a tumblerful of the abbot's own Corniglia vintage.

"Your worship," he said, "when Ghino was a young man he took up the study of medicine, and he learned there was no better treatment for stomach-complaints than the one he intends to apply to your case. These things I bring you are only the beginning of the cure, so take them, sir, and be of good cheer."

The abbot, who was more anxious for food than jests, ate the toast, though he swallowed his indignation with it, and drank the wine, and then gave vent to his indignation in arrogant speeches, demanding information, dispensing advice, and finally ending with a request to see Ghino. Patiently, Ghino listened to his torrent of speech, turning a deaf ear to some of it, answering the rest in all politeness, and assuring him that Ghino would come to see him as soon as he was able. So saying, he left the abbot and did not make his appearance until the following day, when again he brought two slices of toast and another glass of wine. This treatment he continued for a number of days, until he discovered that the abbot had eaten some dry beans, which he had secretly and ingeniously brought there for the purpose.

"Your worship," he said, on making this discovery, "Ghino would be pleased to know how your stomach feels."

"I'd feel excellently well if I were out of his hands," replied the abbot. "Besides that I'd like nothing so much as a good dinner—so well has his treatment cured me."

Accordingly, Ghino had a handsome room fitted out for the abbot by his own retainers and decked with his own furnishings, and then prepared a splendid banquet, to which he invited many notables of the town and the abbot's whole following. Next morning he went to his guest.

"Your worship," he said, "since you feel well again, it is time you were out of the hospital."

Taking him courteously by the hand, he led him into the room arranged for him, and there he left him in the midst of his retainers, while he himself went his way to see that the banquet should not be lacking in magnificence.

Meanwhile, the abbot chatted with his men and described his vicissitudes. They attested to quite the contrary concerning the treatment they had enjoyed, saying they had been shown all the courtesies of hospitality by Ghino. Dinner-hour came, however, and they betook themselves to the tables where they were courteously regaled with great store of delicacies and rare wines, Ghino all the while keeping his identity from the abbot. At last, after the prelate had been entertained in this fashion for a number of days, Ghino had all his provisions brought into one large room and his horses, down to the meanest nag, collected in a court directly beneath the windows, and presented himself before him.

"How does your worship feel?" he asked. "Are you strong enough to ride?"

"Indeed I am," said the abbot, "and I'm cured of my stomach-trouble. I assure you I'd feel excellently well if I were out of Ghino's clutches."

Ghino escorted him into the hall where all his provisions and his attendants were collected, and leading him to a window whence he could look down on all his horses, "Sir Abbot," he said, "you must know that no innate evil, but the fact that I was a gentleman, banished from my home, and impoverished, and that I had so many powerful enemies, brought me, Ghino da Tacco, to be a highway-robber for the defense of life and honor, and to become estranged from the court of Rome. You seem to me a brave gentleman, therefore, now that I have cured you of your stomach-complaint, I have no intention of dealing with you as with any other man in your place, from whom, under like circumstances, I should help myself to as many of his possessions as I pleased. On the contrary, I propose to let you give me whatever you choose, of your own free will, considering my need. All your goods are before you. From this window you can see all your horses gathered in the court. Take part of your belongings, or all of them, as you wish, and henceforth go or stay according to your will."

The abbot wondered greatly that a highway-robber should speak with such generosity of spirit. He was so gratified, that he immediately forgot his wrath and spite. Indeed, his former feelings were converted to one of benevolence and, his heart filled with friendship, he ran to embrace Ghino, saying:

"I swear to the Lord that I'd gladly receive greater injuries than those I thought to be suffering at your hands, to gain the friendship of a man such as I deem you to be. May Fortune be cursed for compelling you to pursue such a wicked calling!"

A little later he set out for Rome, taking with him only a few horses and such provisions as were necessary for the journey, leaving everything else to Ghino.

Meanwhile, in Rome the pope had heard of the abbot's capture, which had caused him no little alarm. Nevertheless, when he saw him, "How did you find the baths?" he asked in jest.

"Holy Father," replied the abbot, smiling, "I found an excellent physician closer at hand than the baths, who cured me perfectly."

He told him the whole story, to the pope's amusement, whereupon the abbot, continuing his speech and moved by a generous impulse, said, "Holy Father, I have a favor to ask of you."

The pope, thinking it concerned quite another matter, freely offered to do whatever he might ask.

"Holy Father, the boon I would ask of you, is that you take my doctor Ghino da Tacco once more into your favor, for of all noble and worshipful men he is certainly of the best. Whatever the mischief he's done, I think Fortune is much more to be blamed than he. I have not the least doubt that if you change it, by granting him some benefice, by means of which he might live in a way more befitting his station, in a little while you too will esteem him as much as I do."

The pope was a generous man, and an admirer of worthy people. On hearing what the abbot had to say, he replied he would gladly grant him his wish, if Ghino were indeed as worthy as he described. "Let him come here with all confidence," he said.

At the abbot's invitation and assurance, Ghino accordingly came to the papal court, where he was not long the pope's attendant, for the pontiff, discovering him to be a truly admirable man, took him once more into his favor and gave him a grand priory of the Hospitalers, after having knighted him to the order. Ghino enjoyed this office to the end of his days, establishing himself as a friend and servant of Holy Church and the Abbot of Cluny.

✳

# THE THIRD STORY

*Mithridanes, envying Nathan his reputation for courtesy and generosity, sets out to kill him. Unknown to him, he meets Nathan, to whom he reveals his intention. Nathan then tells him how to accomplish his end, and goes to a wood to meet his murderer. Mithridanes recognizes him, and ashamed of his fault, becomes his friend.*

THEY ALL THOUGHT IT WELL-NIGH MIRACULOUS THAT A PRELATE should have done anything out of so generous a spirit, and when the ladies had ceased commenting on the wonder, the king called upon Filostrato to continue.

Noble ladies, he began without delay, the generosity of the King of Spain was great, but the abbot's almost unheard of. Still, I think you will find it no less wonderful to learn how a man sought to show his great-heartedness to another, who desired nothing less than his blood and the very breath of his life, by planning secretly to let him have his wish. Indeed, he would have willingly surrendered his life, had the other still wished to take it, as I intend to show you by a short story of mine.

It is definitely known, if we can believe the reports of certain Genoese sailors and other travelers who have been in those parts, that in the region of Cattajo there once lived a man of noble lineage, who was rich beyond compare. His name was Nathan. He owned a tract of land close to a public-road which was necessarily traveled by all wayfarers going from east to west and vice versa, and as he was great and magnanimous by nature, and anxious to reveal these facts by good works, he called together a multitude of builders and craftsmen, and in a very short time had erected on the spot one of the vastest, richest and handsomest palaces that had ever been seen, furnished with everything necessary to welcome and accommodate guests in the

best style. Moreover, he had a numerous retinue of skilled servants, and thus he kept open-house and offered cheerful hospitality to all who came and went, pursuing this noble custom
until not only the East but also the West resounded with his
goodness.

He was already great in years, though not at all weary of
dispensing largesse, when his fame reached the ears of a young
man called Mithridanes, of a province not far from his own.
The youth realized that he himself possessed no less wealth than
the renowned Nathan, and, overcome by envy of his fame and
goodness, determined in his heart either to darken or entirely
obliterate his rival's virtues, by a show of even greater liberality on his own account. Putting his intention into effect, he
had a magnificent palace built, a peer of Nathan's, and plunged
into the most extravagant prodigality towards all those who
came and went his way, until in a short time everyone knew of
his fame.

One day, while the youth was seeking solitude in the atrium
of his palace, a little old woman came through one of the gates,
begging for alms. He gave her what she sought. Then she came
through the second gate, besought him once more, and again received what she asked, continuing through all the gates, one
after the other, until she had begged twelve times in succession.
When she returned for the thirteenth time, Mithridanes said to
her, "My good woman, you're certainly most assiduous in this
begging of yours." Nevertheless, he gave her alms this time as
well, but at his words the old woman cried, "Ah, Nathan's generosity, how wonderful you are! Through the thirty-two gates his
palace possesses, like this one, I came to him, asking for alms.
Not once did he show he knew me, and each and every time I
was rewarded. How different from this place! Here I've only
come through thirteen gates and I've been discovered, and lec-
tured, too!" And so she went away and never showed her face
there again.

Mithridanes blazed into a fury at the old woman's words,
construing the praise of Nathan's fame as belittling his own.
"Ah, miserable me!" he groaned. "When shall I ever attain to
the generosity of Nathan in his great deeds, not to speak of
surpassing it, as I struggle to do, when even in the meanest of
his actions I cannot approach him? Truly, all my efforts will be
wasted if I don't remove him from the earth. If old age doesn't

carry him off, then I'll have to do it with my own hands, and that, soon."

Rising impulsively to his feet, he mounted his horse, followed by a small retinue, and without revealing his purpose to a living being, he set out for Nathan's country. Three days later, toward evening, he had arrived there. Commanding his companions to pretend they were not of his party, indeed, that they did not know him, and advising them to seek lodgings until further notice, he went off by himself to a place not far from the great man's palace, where he met Nathan taking a walk for his pleasure, without escort of pomp or raiment. The youth did not know him, and therefore asked him if he could direct him to Nathan's house.

Graciously, the venerable man answered, "My son, there is no one here who could show you it better than I, so whenever you're ready, I'll be glad to lead you there."

"I shall be very much obliged to you, sir," said Mithridanes, "but if you can manage it, try not to let Nathan see me or know me."

"I'll also do that for you, since you desire it," replied Nathan.

Alighting from his horse, Mithridanes walked toward the splendid palace, led by Nathan, who engaged him in edifying conversation before very long. At the palace, he had one of his servants take care of the youth's horse. "Tell everyone of the household not to reveal to this young gentleman that I am Nathan," he whispered in the man's ear; and his wish was respected. Then he assigned to his guest a handsome suite, where nobody came to intrude upon him but the attendants he had deputed to his service, and treated him royally, he himself often coming to keep him company.

Mithridanes lived thus with him a while, and though he revered the old man as a father, one day he could not help saying, "Who are you?"

"I?" replied Nathan. "I am a humble servant of Nathan's, grown old and hoary with him since my boyhood. Never has he raised me a step from the position in which you find me, so that even though the rest of the world may be well content with him, I have little cause to be grateful."

These few words inspired Mithridanes with greater hope of achieving his wicked purpose more safely and surely. Accordingly, when Nathan courteously asked him who he was and what had brought him to those parts, offering aid and counsel in everything that lay within his power, the youth at first hesitated, and then, exacting his promise of secrecy, revealed his intention after long circumlocution, and asked his help and advice about putting it into effect.

Nathan was shocked to his heart's core on hearing Mithridanes' fatal purpose, but without much hesitation, he answered with untroubled face and courageous mind, "Mithridanes, your father was a noble man, and you have shown that you do not care to depart from his virtue, by embarking upon your lofty enterprise of becoming a model of generosity. I can find it in me to admire the envy you feel of Nathan's worth, for if there were many more like you, this most miserable world would soon become a heaven. You may rest assured that I shall keep the purpose you revealed to me a strict secret. As for your execution of it, I am afraid I can more easily offer you advice than help. Look, from here you can see a certain little grove, about half a mile away, where almost daily Nathan goes walking for his pleasure, for quite a time. There you will have no trouble finding him and carrying out your desire. Now should you kill him, don't go back by the path you took going there, if you want to return home safe, but follow another which you will see leading out of the wood on the left-hand side. True, it is a little wilder than the first, but it's nearer your house, and safer for you."

As soon as Mithridanes had received these instructions and Nathan had gone, he secretly informed his followers, who were also living in the palace, to wait for him at a certain place the following morning. Day dawned; Nathan's spirit had not swerved in the least from the counsel he had given Mithridanes. At the customary hour of his walk, therefore, he set out resolutely for the grove to meet his death.

Mithridanes also rose, took his bow and sword, as he had no other weapons, and rode toward the wood. From a distance, he spied his victim walking alone. Before falling upon him, the youth resolved first to meet him face to face and hear him speak. Accordingly, he rode toward him, and seizing him by the turban about his head, cried, "Old man, your end has come!"

Nathan offered no resistance, but said simply, "Then I must have deserved it."

On hearing the man's voice, and peering into his face, Mithridanes recognized him at once as the man who had so affec-

tionately received him, so intimately befriended him, and so
faithfully advised him. Immediately, his fury vanished and gave
way to a feeling of shame. Flinging away the sword he had
unsheathed to strike him, he leaped down from his horse and
cast himself weeping at the old man's feet.

"Dearest father," he said, "now I know how truly great is your
generosity, when I see what precautions you took to come here
secretly, and surrender to me the life which, for no reason at
all, I thirsted for, even in your presence! But God, more careful
of my duty than I myself, in the hour when I needed to see
most clearly, opened the eyes of my understanding, which unworthy envy had sealed. Thus, O father, the more unselfishly
ready you were to comply with my evil wish, the more I recognize what need I have to repent of my crime. Take, then, oh,
take whatever vengeance you deem sufficient to expiate my
sin!"

Nathan lifted the youth to his feet and tenderly kissed and
embraced him. "My son," he said, "there is no need at all for
you to ask forgiveness, or for me to forgive you for your intent,
or whatever you wish to call it, good or ill, for it was not hate
that spurred you on to follow it, but a desire to be considered
the better man. Live, and have no fear of me, for be confident
that there is no man who loves you as I love you, considering
the loftiness of your soul, which inclined not to amassing fortunes, like meaner spirits, but towards spending what you have
in largesse. Do not be mortified that you sought to kill me for
your renown, nor think that I wonder at it. The mightiest emperors and the greatest kings have extended their realms and
so gained vaster glory by employing no other art than that of
murder—not of one man, as you would have done, but of infinite numbers—yes, and by burning whole countries and dev-
astating cities. Hence, if to gain fame you had killed only one
man, myself, you would have done nothing new or unusual, but
only a common, very common thing."

Mithridanes would not consider himself justified in his evil
purpose. He was all admiration and respect for Nathan's magnanimity of soul in seeking to find an excuse for him, and as
he spoke to the old man he could not help saying, "How could
you bring yourself to come to your death? How could you have
been so great of heart as to advise and show me the way to do
it?"

"Ah, Mithridanes," said Nathan, "do not be astonished at my

courage or at my telling you how to kill me, for ever since I
came into my own rights and devoted myself to the sort of life
you have undertaken, not a man ever came to my house whom I
did not seek to gratify to the best of my ability, in any wish he
expressed. You came here thirsting for my life. I heard you demanding it with my own ears. Immediately, I resolved to grant
it to you, that you might not be the only man to go forth from
my house without his desire. Then, in order that you might accomplish it, I offered you what advice I thought best-suited to
give you my life without your losing yours. Again, I implore
you, if you would have my life, take it, and gain your heart's desire. I know of no other way of yielding it more worthily. I have
already made the best of it for eighty years, spending it in my
pleasure and comfort, and I know that, as is the case of all men
and things, it can be left me but a short time longer, according
to the laws of nature. Hence I think it far better to bestow it
as a gift, as I have always bestowed my boons and treasures,
than to cherish it until it is wrested from me against my will, by
nature. It is little enough to give away a hundred years. How
much less is it to give the six or eight years that I may still have
to spend on earth? Take my life then, I beg you, if it will afford
you pleasure, for in the course of it I have never found a man
who wanted it. When could I ever find another if you, who require it, do not take it? Again, even if I should chance to come
across such another, don't you think I know that the longer I
keep it, the less will be its worth? So take it, then, I pray you, before it becomes more paltry still."

Shamed to the very heart, Mithridanes replied, "God forfend
I should sever the thread of so precious a life, or that I should
even wish to, as I did a little while ago! Ah, rather than take
from it a moment of its span, how willingly would I add to
it the years of my own!"

Promptly, Nathan replied, "Tell me, if it were really in your
power to add years of your life to mine, would you do so?
Would you really allow me to do to you, what I've never done
to any man alive—to *take?*"

"Indeed I would," replied Mithridanes instantly.

"Well, then," said Nathan, "you must do as I say. Remain here
in my house, in the glory of your youth, and call yourself Nathan, while I go to your palace and be called Mithridanes."

"Ah, my father," replied the youth, "if I knew how to act as
wisely and as well as you have always known, and as you are

now acting, I would not hesitate an instant to accept your offer. But alas! I know too well that my actions would tarnish Nathan's fame, and therefore, as I have no intention of ruining in another what I cannot remedy in myself, I must refuse."

After having engaged in these and many other courtly conceits of a similar nature, the two, at Nathan's request, returned to the palace, where the youth was shown the highest honors for many days, while Nathan encouraged him in his noble and lofty resolve with all the persuasions of his understanding. At last, when Mithridanes expressed the desire to return to his own country with his followers, Nathan gave him leave to depart.

And so the youth left him, convinced that he could never outdo his host in generosity of heart or hand.

✳

# THE FOURTH STORY

*Messer Gentile de' Carisendi, on his return from Modona, delivers his beloved from the tomb where she had been laid for dead. Under his ministrations, she revives and is brought to bed of a boy, and Messer Gentile restores her and the infant to Nicoluccio Caccianimico, her husband.*

IT STRUCK THEM AS INDEED MARVELOUS THAT A MAN SHOULD have been generous with his own life's blood, and all declared that beyond a doubt Nathan's magnanimity of soul far surpassed that of the King of Spain and the Abbot of Cluny. After they had exhausted the argument, the king turned his eyes toward Lauretta, indicating his pleasure for her to continue, whereupon she began, without losing time:

Young ladies, beautiful and truly marvelous are the things that have been told to-day, but the subject of generosity and greatness has been so thoroughly treated, that I'm afraid there's little choice left for us who still have to speak, except to resort to matters of love, always a fertile field for the story-teller. Both for this reason and because our youth naturally inclines in that direction, I shall be pleased to tell you of an act of generosity indulged in by a lover. Perhaps, everything considered, it may not seem less important than the examples we've already had, if there's any truth in the saying that treasures are given, enmities forgotten, and life, indeed, honor and glory imperiled a thousand times, for the acquisition of the beloved object.

In Bologna, a famous city in Lombardy, there once lived a young gentleman by the name of Gentile de' Carisendi, renowned both for his virtue and the nobility of his blood. He fell passionately in love with Catalina, a distinguished lady, the wife of a certain Nicoluccio Caccianimico, and as she did not requite his love, in sheer desperation he accepted the post of governor at Modona, to which he had been appointed, and took his departure.

At that time, Nicoluccio was away from home, and the lady, being great with child, had taken up her residence perhaps three miles from the city, in one of her country-homes. Unexpectedly, she fell ill. So deadly was the disease and so violent, that all signs of life were soon spent in her, and she was pronounced dead by the physicians. Now since the women of her family declared that according to her she had not been pregnant long enough for the child to be fully developed, they did not trouble themselves further about her, and placing her just as she was in a vault of the neighboring church, they left her there, after many manifestations of sorrow.

The event was soon made known to Gentile by a friend, and though he had not received the slightest gift of her favor, he was stricken with grief. "Ah, Catalina, you are dead," he mourned, on waking from the shock. "While you lived, I never enjoyed so much as the boon of a glance from your eyes. But now that you cannot deny me, I will take from your sweet mouth one only kiss, even though you are dead!"

Night had already fallen; still Gentile, taking care that his departure should remain secret, mounted his horse and rode away with a single servant for escort, until he came to the church where the lady was entombed. Pushing open the door of the vault, he went in quickly and lay down beside her, his face pressed close against hers. Again and again he kissed her, as tears streamed from his eyes. Now it is well known that men's desires, especially lovers', are not content to be gratified with little, but will be ever seeking more, and though Gentile had inwardly decided not to remain there any longer, he pondered, "Come, now, why shouldn't I lay my hand on her breast a little while since I am here? I'll never touch her sweet body again, as I've never laid a hand on it before."

Dominated by his appetite, he slipped his hand in her breast, when suddenly, after he had left it there a while, he felt a light flutter, as though the heart were still beating. Casting off the dread that had seized him, he listened more intently and found that she was not dead, though there seemed but little life remaining in her. Nevertheless, with the help of his servant he drew her gently out of the sepulcher, and placing her before him on his horse, took her secretly to his house in Florence.

Now his mother, a virtuous and capable woman who was living there at the time, upon listening from beginning to end to what her son told her, was moved to pity, and without more ado, attended quietly to the fire and the bath, until what with the warmth and her ministrations, she succeeded in calling back the poor lady's wandering senses. Catalina stirred, and a deep sigh escaped her.

"Where am I?" she said.

"Be of good cheer, my daughter," said the kindly soul. "You are among friends."

Catalina upon coming to, and looking about her without knowing where she was, became even more astonished, especially when she saw Messer Gentile standing before her.

"Tell me, I beg you, where I am!" she pleaded, turning to his mother. "How did I come here?"

Gentile told her the whole story from the beginning, which grieved her not a little. She hesitated a while, and then thanked him as best she could, but, "For the sake of the love you bore me," she besought him, "and for your honor's sake, let me not, while I am in your house, suffer anything at your hands that might reflect upon my virtue or the honor of my husband. And to-morrow please let me return to my own house."

"Catalina," replied Gentile, "whatever my desire may have been in the past, I intend neither now nor ever, to treat you otherwise than as a dear sister, whether here or anywhere else, since the Lord has vouchsafed me the grace of recalling you from death to life, by virtue of the love I bore you. Still, I think the good turn I did you to-night is deserving of some reward, and I trust you will not deny me the favor I shall ask of you."

"I shall be happy to grant it," she graciously replied, "if it is in my power and in keeping with my virtue."

"You know," said Gentile, "that all your friends and kinsfolk, in fact all the people in Bologna are certain you are dead. There is no one waiting for you at home. Promise me, then, as a special favor, to live here quietly with my mother until I return from Modona, which will be soon. The reason for my request? Simply that I would like to bestow you as a dear and precious gift upon your husband, in the presence of Bologna's foremost citizens."

Catalina, realizing her obligation to the young gentleman, and knowing that his request was honorable, consented to do as he said despite her impatience to rejoice the hearts of her dear ones by her resuscitation.

"I promise, on my word," she said.

Scarcely had the words escaped her lips, when she felt the throes of labor upon her. Tenderly, Gentile's mother ministered to her, and before long she was delivered of a handsome boy, to the infinite joy of them all. After the gentleman had taken care that she was provided with everything necessary for her comfort, and that she was assured of the attention she would have had if she had been his own wife, he returned secretly to Modona.

In due time, as his term of office drew to a close, he arranged for a magnificent reception to be held at his home on the morning of his arrival, to which he invited the most distinguished gentlemen of the town, among whom was Nicoluccio Caccianimico. Upon his return, he dismounted and found his guests already gathered. Catalina was home, too, lovelier and fresher than ever, with her baby-boy, radiant with health. His joy knew no bounds as he led his guests to their places at table, and had them served royally with various courses.

The dinner was nearly at an end when, after informing Catalina of his intention and instructing her concerning her behavior through it all, he addressed his guests.

"Gentlemen," he said, "I remember having heard of a certain Persian custom, in my estimation a gracious one. When a man would like to show his friend the greatest possible honor, he invites him to his home, and there shows him the thing he holds most dear, whether wife, mistress, daughter or anyone else, signifying that just as he sets before him his dearest treasure, so, too, even more willingly, would he show him his heart, if he could. It is this custom I would like to observe in Bologna. All of you have courteously honored my banquet, and I therefore would like to honor you, Persian style, by showing you the dearest thing I have in the world, or ever hope to have. But first and foremost, I'd like your opinion on a question I wish to set before you.

"Let us suppose a man has in his house a good and faithful servant, who suddenly falls mortally ill. The master, without even waiting for the servant to draw his last breath, has him thrown to the gutter and washes his hands of him. Then let us suppose a stranger comes along, who, out of pity for the sick man, carries him to his house, and with all tenderness and no care for expense, nurses him back to health. Now the question is, were this new master to keep him and avail himself of his services, would his former lord be justified in complaining of the second, or blaming him, if he, upon being asked to return the servant, should refuse?"

Many and various were the arguments advanced by the guests, but when they arrived at a common opinion, they chose Nicoluccio Caccianimico, a fine, accomplished orator, as their spokesman.

First of all, he commended the Persian custom, and then he declared that both himself and the rest of the men concurred in the opinion that the first master had no further right to his servant, since he had not only forsaken him in his need, but cast him out into the street. Again, because of the second man's kindnesses, the servant had rightfully become his, for by keeping him, he did no harm, violence or injustice to the original master.

At that, all the other gentlemen seated about the tables—and many a worthy there was, too—declared themselves unanimously in favor of the view Nicoluccio had expressed.

Gentile, gladdened at the answer, and at the coincidence that Nicoluccio had been chosen to voice it, said he, too, was of their mind and then added, "It is now time for me to honor you as I promised."

Calling two of his servants, he sent them to Catalina, who was magnificently arrayed and adorned, according to his bidding, with the request that she do his guests the honor of gladdening them with her presence. She obeyed, and taking her lovely baby son in her arms, she entered the banquet-hall between the two attendants. Gentile then escorted her to the right of a noble lord, and said, "Gentlemen, this is the thing I hold most dear in the world, and which I shall ever most dearly cherish. Behold her, and see whether I am not justified!"

The guests showed her great honor, and their praise of her was lavish, as they declared to Gentile that he ought assuredly to hold her dear. Upon looking at her closely, there were many who would have taken her for Catalina, had they not thought her dead. Nicoluccio, most of all, gazed at her raptly, burning to know who she was. At last, unable to control his curiosity any longer, he waited until Gentile had drawn aside, and said, "I pray you, tell me, madam, are you from Bologna or are you a stranger?"

It was difficult for Catalina to refrain from answering her husband, still, in obedience to her promise to Gentile, she was silent. Another asked if the child were hers, and still another whether she were married to Gentile, or related to him by ties of blood. But to all of them she answered not a word.

When Gentile returned, one of his guests remarked, "Truly, sir, this lady of yours is a lovely creature, but she seems to be dumb. Is she so, indeed?"

Then he said, "Gentlemen, the fact that she has not spoken is no small argument for her virtue."

"Tell us then yourself who she is," said the man who had first spoken.

"Willingly," Gentile answered, "but you must all promise solemnly that no matter what I say, you will not leave your seats until I have finished my story."

They promised, one and all; therefore, when the tables had been cleared, Gentile, taking a seat beside Catalina, began, "Gentlemen, this lady is that good and faithful servant concerning whom I raised the question a little while ago. Like him, she too, was ill-cared for by her people, and like a worthless thing that had outlived its usefulness, she, too, was flung into the middle of the street. But I raised her up. With my solicitude and the toil of my hands, I wrested her from death itself, while God, considerate of my unselfishness, made her flourish under my care, from a horrible corpse to the beautiful creature you now see. But the better to make you understand how all this came about, I shall tell you everything in a few words."

Accordingly, beginning his story from the time he fell in love with Catalina, he related to his hearers all that had happened up until that moment, much to their astonishment. "For these reasons," he added, "this lady justly belongs to me, if you, and Nicoluccio particularly, have not changed the opinion you expressed a short time ago. Yes, she belongs to me, nor could anyone rightfully claim her back from me."

No one dared reply; all were tensely waiting to hear what more he had to say, while Nicoluccio, Catalina and many of the guests wept silently for the pity of it. At last, Gentile rose to his feet. Taking the infant in his arms and the lady by the hand, he walked toward Nicoluccio.

"Come, rise, my friend," he said. "I am not returning to you the wife whom your kin and hers cast away. Rather, it is my intention to give to you this lady, my godson's mother, and this child, who I know is the fruit of your loins and whom I held at the font and named Gentile. Though she has lived in my house nearly three months, I beg you, do not hold her the less dear. For, by that God Who perhaps made me fall in love with her, that my love might be the cause of her salvation, as it has indeed proved to be—by that God I swear to you that never has she lived more honorably, either with her father or mother, or with you yourself, than she has here, under my mother's care, in my own house."

Then, turning to Catalina, he said, "Dear lady, henceforth I release you from all pledges made to me, and leave you free to return to your husband." With that, he placed the mother and child in Nicoluccio's keeping and resumed his seat. Passionately, Nicoluccio gathered his wife and son in his arms, his joy all the more intense for the meager hope he had had of fulfilling it, and offered thanks to Gentile as best he knew how. The guests, still weeping for pity of the strange case, commended Gentile for his nobility, as did everyone who ever heard of it. Amid great rejoicing, Catalina was welcomed to her own house, and for a long time the people of Bologna could not help looking upon her with wonder, as one risen from the dead.

As for Messer Gentile, as long as he lived, he remained a dear friend of Nicoluccio and of his people, and of his beloved lady's kin.

What have you to say to this story, kind ladies? Do you think that the fact that a king gave away his crown and scepter, that an abbot brought back a lost sheep to the pope's fold, and that an old man surrendered his throat to the knife of his enemy—do you think all these can compare with Gentile's sacrifice? He was young and passionate. He felt himself entitled to possess what the indifference of others had cast away, but which he, with the aid of his own good fortune, had gathered up. And still, even though he had in his power the being he desired with every thought of his brain, even though he was master of the dear object he yearned to seize, he not only tempered his passion like a man of honor, but generously restored his treasure to its owner.

Truly, I think none of the deeds already described can equal this for magnanimity.

✳

## THE FIFTH STORY

*Dianora requires Ansaldo to give her a garden that in the month of January would be as beautiful as in May. With the help of a magician, to whom he pledges himself for a large sum, Ansaldo grants his lady's wish. Dianora's husband, learning what has happened, gives her permission to grant herself to her lover, who, hearing of the man's generosity, releases her from her word. At that the magician, too, relieves Ansaldo of his pledge and refuses to accept any reward for his pains.*

EVERYONE OF THE HAPPY BAND HAD ALREADY EXTOLLED MESSER Gentile to the skies, when the king called upon Emilia to continue, and she plunged boldly into the argument, as though she had been waiting for a chance to speak.

Tender ladies, she began, no one can justly deny that Gentile acted most magnanimously. But if you say it is impossible for anyone to do more—well, it will not be so hard to show it can be done, as I intend proving by a short story of mine.

In the country of Friuli, which, though cold, is enlivened with noble mountains and a wealth of running streams and clear springs, there is a city called Udine, where once upon a time Dianora, a lovely lady, lived. She was married to a distinguished lord of great wealth called Gilberto, a charming man of amiable grace, but such was the lady's beauty that it obtained her the passionate love of Messer Ansaldo Gradense, a mighty baron of lofty rank, famed high and low for his prowess in arms and his feats of chivalry. He was so deeply enamored of her, that he left nothing undone to gain her favor. Again and again he pressed his suit by means of messages and letters, but to no avail. Now Dianora had become weary of the baron's solicitations, but seeing that although she denied him everything he sought he did not abandon his suit, she resolved to get rid of him by setting him a strange, and to her mind, impossible task.

Summoning the woman whom he often sent to her with his messages, she said to her one day, "Good woman, you've often assured me that Ansaldo loves me above everything in the world. Indeed, the gifts he's offered me through you are marvelous. But let him keep them, for as far as I am concerned, they'll never induce me to love him or yield myself to his pleasure. However, if I could have definite proof that he loves me as much as you say, I should certainly give him my love and grant his every wish. So listen! If he promises to put his love to the test by performing the task I shall set him, I'll then place myself entirely at his disposal."

"What task would you have him do, my lady?" asked the woman.

"Only this," replied Dianora. "This coming month of January, I should like a garden on the outskirts of this city, full of verdant lawns, flowers and leafy shrubs, all as beautiful as in the month of May. If he does not give me this park, don't let him dare send you or anyone else to me again, for I swear if he troubles me again, just as surely as I have concealed his suit from my husband and family, I'll complain to them in such a strain, that I'll succeed in ridding myself of him."

When the baron heard the task the lady had set him, he thought it arduous indeed, and beyond the reach of possibility. Still, in spite of that, and in spite of the realization that she had imposed it for no other reason than to deprive him of all hope, he inwardly resolved to determine if it could be done, and sent messengers into various countries to find out whether there were anyone who could help or advise him in the matter.

At last, a certain individual presented himself, who offered to create the garden by magic, provided he were well rewarded for it. Messer Ansaldo came to terms with the wizard by offering him a fabulous sum of money, and joyfully awaited the appointed time.

Finally the first of January came, and bitter cold it was, with snow and ice covering the face of the earth. Nevertheless, in an open field on the outskirts of the city, the magician wrought his necromancy so skilfully all night long, that the following morning, according to the testimony of eye-witnesses, there sprang up one of the most exquisite gardens ever seen, glorious with grass, flowers and fruits of all kinds.

No sooner did Messer Ansaldo set eyes on it, to his great joy, than he had the most beautiful fruits and flowers growing there gathered and quietly brought to his lady, with the invitation that she should go and behold the garden she had asked of him, and be convinced of his great love. Furthermore, he urged her to remember the promise she had made him and sealed with her oath, which, as a woman of her word, she should do her utmost to keep.

Dianora, however, upon seeing the flowers and fruits of the marvelous park, news of which had already reached her ears, began to regret her promise. Still, regret or no regret, she was curious to see the novelty, and set out to visit it with a group of other ladies of the city. It was a glorious sight indeed, and she praised the wonder of it, not without a feeling of awe, even though, on her return home, she was sadder than any woman alive at the thought of it and what it was going to cost her.

All day long she brooded and brooded upon it, until she could no longer conceal her despair. Her husband at last noticing that there was something preying on her mind, insisted on knowing what it was. For a long time, she could not utter a word for shame, but at last, compelled to speak, she told him everything as it had happened.

Anger at first flamed in Gilberto's breast, but then, considering the purity of Dianora's intention, he banished his wrath and said, with better judgment:

"Dianora, it is not proper for a discreet and modest woman to pay attention to such messages, or to make any kind of bargain involving her chastity, no matter what the conditions. Words that arrive at the heart through the ear's flattery, have much more power than many would believe, and almost anything is possible to men in love. You were wrong, Dianora, first to lend an ear to the suit, and then to make a bargain. But since I know you acted in the innocence of your heart, I shall grant you what perhaps no other man would, to enable you to fulfil your promise, influenced, too, as I am by fear of the wizard, who might be persuaded to work us some dreadful mischief by Ansaldo, if you played him false. I want you to go to Ansaldo. If you can, manage to make him release you from your pledge, while preserving your virtue at the same time. If not—this once only, yield your body to him, but not your soul."

In tears, Dianora listened to her husband and shook her head, refusing to accept such a favor from him. But Gilberto insisted in spite of her protests, and would not hear of being gainsaid.

Well, toward daybreak the following morning, Dianora, simply dressed, made her way to Messer Ansaldo's house with two of her lackeys before her, and her maid following in the rear. Ansaldo was amazed to hear that she had come, so rising, he sent for the magician and said, "I want you to see what loveliness your art has gained for me."

Respectfully, he went to meet her, accompanied by the magician, and received her honorably in a luxurious room where a cheery fire was burning, the lover, all the while, permitting no disorderly urge to rise in him. Then, after she was comfortably seated, he said:

"My lady, if the love I have cherished for you so long deserves to be rewarded, I beg you, do not be offended if I ask you to tell me candidly what brings you here at this hour, and in such company."

Flushed with shame, and with tears welling in her eyes, Dianora answered, "Sir, it is not any love I bear you, nor is it my promised word that brings me here, but the command of my husband who, more considerate of the labors of your ungoverned passion than of his honor and mine, obliged me to come. At his request, then, I am ready to do your will, for this once only."

If Messer Ansaldo wondered at the opening of Dianora's speech, his amazement grew apace as she went on. Touched by Gilberto's liberality, his passion gave way to tenderness.

"My lady," he said, "since things are as you say, far be it from me to wreck the honor of one who is considerate of my love. Hence, while you are pleased to stay here in my house, you will be treated with as much respect as though you were my sister. Then, when you are ready, you may go home in peace, render my thanks to your husband for such supreme courtesy, and assure him that henceforth he has in me a brother and a faithful servant."

Dianora was beside herself with joy at his assurance. "Ansaldo," she said, "knowing you as I did, nothing could have made me believe my coming here could have had any other outcome than this, and from the bottom of my heart I shall always be grateful to you for it."

Bidding him good-bye, she returned to her husband, followed by an honorable escort, and told him what had happened, which, from then on, bound him and Ansaldo in a close tie of friendship.

Meanwhile, when the magician, to whom Ansaldo was preparing to give the promised reward, saw Gilberto's magnificent gesture toward Ansaldo, and then Ansaldo's toward the lady,

"God forbid," he cried, "that after seeing Gilberto generous with his honor, and you with your love, I should not also be generous with my reward. Keep your money then, I beg you, for you can use it to good advantage."

Ansaldo was embarrassed by such liberality and did his utmost to persuade the magician to accept his payment, or at least part of it, but his coaxing was of no avail. On the third day the magician, removing his wonderful garden, decided to return to his own land. Accordingly, Ansaldo took leave of him and commended him to God, and quenching in his heart his lustful passion for Dianora, kindled in its place the pure flame of friendship.

What shall we say of this, tender ladies? Are we to place a lover's relinquishment of a lady well-nigh dead to him, and a love grown tepid with hope deferred, above the generosity of Ansaldo, who was much more ardently enamored than ever and, in a way, stirred to new hope by the possession of the dear object he had so long pursued? It is foolish to think that such a sacrifice could even be compared with the other!

✳

## THE SIXTH STORY

*King Charles the First, called the Victorious, falls in love with a young girl but, ashamed of his folly, gives her and her twin-sister away in honorable marriage.*

IT WOULD BE A LONG STORY INDEED TO RECOUNT THE MANY arguments the ladies advanced in their effort to prove whether Gilberto, Ansaldo or the magician had behaved with the greatest magnanimity concerning Dianora. But after the king had given sufficient lee-way to the discussion, he looked at Fiammetta. "Tell us another story," he said, "and put an end to the dispute."

Without hesitating a moment, Fiammetta began:

Radiant ladies, I always thought that in merry gatherings like ours people usually spoke fully enough not to leave room for further dispute about the matter under discussion, for after all, arguments and debates are more in keeping with scholars in universities than with us women, who have all we can do to handle the distaff and spindle. I had in mind to tell you something a little puzzling, but as what's already been told has raised such a storm among you, I'll lay that aside and tell you another story—not of any common mortal, but of a mighty king, who, as you shall hear, behaved most admirably, and much to his credit.

Every one of you, I'm sure, must often have heard of Charles the Old, or more properly, the First, through whose splendid undertaking, as well as through his glorious victory over King Manfred, the Ghibellines were banished from Florence and the Guelphs restored. As a result of this change, a certain gentleman called Neri degli Uberti left the city with his whole family and a considerable fortune, and resolving not to settle anywhere except under the protection of King Charles, in some quiet, solitary spot where he might end his days in peace, withdrew to Castellamare di Stabia, where, perhaps a bowshot from other dwellings, he bought a tract of land among the olive and walnut and chestnut trees that abound in that section of the country. There he had a fine spacious house built with a pleasant garden adjoining, in the midst of which, for the abundance of living water found therein, he had a sparkling fish-pond constructed in our fashion, and stocked generously with all kinds of fish.

After he had established himself in his comfortable house, with no other care in mind than to improve his land more and more each day, King Charles happened to come to Castellamare, seeking relief from the heat, and hearing of the beauty of the gentleman's garden, was most anxious to see it. However, upon discovering to whom the garden belonged, and that Neri was of the opposing faction, he thought it wiser to treat him like a friend, and therefore sent him word that he and four of his companions would be pleased to sup with him incognito the following evening, in his garden. Messer Neri appreciated the compliment immensely, and the preparations he made for the king's reception were splendid. After consulting with his family on what was to be done, he went into the garden and welcomed the king with all the tokens of joy he could manifest.

The king wandered all through the garden, and through the house, praising the beauty and comfort he saw. Then, after the tables had been laid beside the fish-pond, he performed his ablutions and took his seat, requesting Count Guy of Montfort, who had come with him, to sit on one side of him, and Messer Neri on the other. The rest of the companions he had brought with him, he commissioned to serve at table, according to their host's instructions.

The viands served were exquisite; the wines rare and excellent. Nor was there anything lacking in the courteous service, with its exactness and silence, which the king highly praised.

While he was relishing the good cheer and enjoying the seclusion of the place, two young girls of some fifteen years of age came into the garden. They were lovely and fair, with hair of spun gold curling about their shoulders and lightly clasped with a dainty wreath of myrtle blossoms. From the delicacy of their faces they seemed to be angels; so beautiful were they. Both were clad alike in gowns of soft, snow-white linen over their bare bodies, molding their forms tightly from the waist up, and falling in wide folds tent-wise to their feet. The first of the two carried a pair of small casting-nets over her shoulders, the ends of which she grasped in her left hand, and in her right she held a long rod. The other had a skillet slung over her left shoulder, a small bundle of kindling under the same arm, and in her left hand a tripod, while in the right she held a cruse of oil, and a light.

The king marveled at the sight of them, and waited in suspense to see what their coming meant. First, the girls came modestly before him, and blushing rosily, curtsied to him respectfully. Then they went to the entrance leading into the fish-pond, where the one who carried the skillet laid it down, together with the rest of her burdens, and took the rod the other carried. Both then stepped into the pond, the water of which covered them to the breast. As they did this, one of Messer Neri's attendants quickly kindled a fire under the tripod, placed the skillet above it, poured into it a quantity of oil and waited for the girls to throw him some fish.

Meanwhile, one of the damsels was busy prodding with the rod in the crannies where she knew the fish loved to hide, and the other cast the nets, to the great delight of the king who had eyes for nothing but for their sport. Soon they had netted a great number of fish, part of which they threw to the attendant, who placed them in the skillet almost alive, as he had been instructed, and some, the finest, they flung upon the table before the king, Count Guy and Messer Neri. The creatures flopped about the table, to the huge delight of the king, who took them likewise in his hand and cast them back playfully to the fair fishermaids. So they played awhile, until the attendant had cooked the fish he had been given, which he set before the king as Messer Neri had instructed him, not so much for the daintiness of the fare as for the sport it had afforded them all.

When the girls saw that the fish was ready and that their duty was done, they came out of the water, their thin white gowns that clung to their flesh scarcely concealing anything of their delicate bodies, and gathering up their implements, they passed before the king on their way to the house. Now the monarch, the count and the rest of his companions who were serving at table, had gazed their fill at the girls, each inwardly extolling them for their beauty of form and feature and for their modesty and charming manners. But the king had been smitten most deeply of all. Indeed, as they had come out of the pond, he had been so rapt in admiration of every detail of their bodies, that had anyone pricked him, he would not have been conscious of the pain.

The more he dwelt on them in his mind, the more zealously was his heart wakened to pleasure them, even though he had no inkling of who or what they were. He clearly saw that he would be in danger of falling in love if he didn't take care, but the strange thing was that he himself did not know which of the two damsels pleased him more, so wonderfully did they resemble each other. After he had let his thoughts range at their sweet will a while, he turned to his host.

"Who were those two young damsels?" he asked.

"Sire," replied Messer Neri, "those are my twin-daughters, one of whom is called Ginevra the Lovely and the other Isolde the Fair."

The king was expansive in his praise of them to his host, and advised him to give them away in marriage, but Messer Neri excused himself, saying his means did not allow of his doing it with the honor he desired. Supper had by this time been served, and only the fruit remained to be brought, when the two girls reappeared clad in exquisite silks, and bearing in their hands two large silver bowls full of the season's wealth of fruit, which they set upon the table before the king. Then, drawing a little aside, they began to sing a ballad, which opened with the words:

> "O Love, 'twere long to sing
>  How deep my heart is wounded by thy sting."

They sang so sweetly, and with such winsome grace, that the king, who was all eyes for them, and listened with delight, felt as though the angelic choirs of heaven had come down to sing for him. Their song ended, the two sisters kneeled reverently before him, begging his leave to go, which he graciously gave them, though he was loth to have them leave.

Supper was soon over. The king and his companions took horse, and leaving Messer Neri, returned to the royal palace, talking and chatting of one thing and another.

Although the king kept his love a secret, he could not drive out of his mind the grace and charm of Ginevra the Lovely, no matter what grave duties he had to attend to; and for her sake he also loved her sister, for the resemblance she bore his beloved. As time went on, he became even more inextricably enmeshed in the snares of love, so that he could not bear to think of anything else. Thus, under pretense of other business, he struck up a close friendship with Messer Neri, whom he often visited in his delightful garden, merely for a glimpse of the lovely Ginevra.

Finally, he could put up with the torment no longer. Seeing no way of attaining his desire unless he took not only the one, but both girls from their father, he confided his passion and his resolution to Count Guy. The count, however, was a noble soul and a man of honor.

"Sire," he said, "I am aghast at what you tell me, and more so than any other man could be, for I was convinced, through my close contact with you since your childhood, that I knew your ways better than anyone else.

"In your early years, when love more readily lays hold of one, I never seemed to discover any such passion in you, and the thought that now, when old age is almost upon you, you should be seized with such love, is so strange and new to me, that I think it almost a miracle. Truly, if it were becoming in me to cast any reproaches upon you for it, I know what I should say. Here you are, scarcely with your armor off, in the kingdom you've newly acquired, in the midst of people unknown to you and full of stratagems and treasons—here you are, I repeat, burdened with serious cares and the business of state, and not yet quite assured of your throne, and with all that, you have found room for a beguiling love. That is not the way for a great king to behave, but rather for a callow youth. What's more, and worse, you say you have decided to take the two girls from the innocent gentleman who entertained you in his own house with hospitality far beyond his means, who, the better to honor you, showed you his two daughters almost naked, proving to you thereby how great is the faith he reposes in you, whom he firmly believed to be a monarch and not a ravening wolf. What! Have you so soon forgotten that it was Manfred's dishonorable violences to women that opened you a way into this realm? What perfidy was there ever more deserving of eternal damnation than this you would be guilty of, by stealing from the man who generously received you his honor, his hope and comfort? What would people say if you did such a thing? Perhaps you think you could lightly exculpate yourself by saying, 'I did this to him because he was a Ghibelline.' Is it the habit of kingly justice to deal in this fashion with those who place themselves under its protection—no matter who they are? Bear in mind, O king, that if it was a great glory for you to have conquered Manfred, it is a still greater one to conquer yourself. You, then, whose duty it is to chasten others, triumph over yourself! Curb this appetite, and don't let such a blemish sully what you have so gloriously gained!"

These reproaches touched the king vitally, and stung him the more cruelly for his consciousness of their truth. After an ardent sigh or two, "Count," he said, "I assure you that no matter how strong the enemy the well-tried warrior has to conquer, he will find him far weaker and easier to overcome than his own appetite. Still, great though the effort and inestimable the will required, your words have so goaded me, that before many days have passed, I'll prove to you that just as I can conquer others, I can also be a victor over myself!"

Not long after this conversation the king returned to Naples, where, perhaps as much to rid himself of the temptation to behave unlike a man of honor, as to reward his host for the hospitality he had enjoyed, he resolved to give the two girls away in marriage, bitter though he found it to enrich others with what he desired for himself. Dowering them magnificently, not as Messer Neri's daughters, but as his own, he bestowed Ginevra upon Messer Mazzeo da Palizzi, with her father's consent, and Isolde the Fair upon Messer Guglielmo della Magna, high-born gentlemen both, and barons in their own right.

Thus, after giving the two damsels into their husbands' keeping, he returned, bitterly frustrated, to Apulia, putting his fiery appetite under such merciless discipline, that bursting at last through the sundered chain of love, he lived free of such passion to the end of his allotted days.

There are some, perhaps, who will say it was really no great matter for a king to give two girls away in marriage. Granted. But I call it great, very great, for a king to give the girl he loved to another, without having tasted so much as a leaf, a flower, or fruit of his love.

Well, so it was that this great-hearted king behaved, rewarding the noble knight magnificently, honoring the girls he loved by a praiseworthy deed, and courageously uprooting his passion from his heart.

✳

## THE  SEVENTH  STORY

*King Pedro, upon hearing how fervently he is beloved by the pining Lisa, comes to comfort her in her sick bed; then, marrying her to a noble youth, he kisses her on the brow, and declares himself from then on her knight.*

WHEN FIAMMETTA HAD CONCLUDED HER STORY AND THE MANLY generosity of King Charles had been much extolled, though a certain lady present was chary of her praise because of her Ghibelline sentiments, Pampinea began at the king's command:

No one of unprejudiced mind, worthy ladies, would deny good King Charles the praise you give him, unless, of course, she had other reasons for bearing him a grudge. Something no less praiseworthy, which one of his political opponents did for one of our Florentine ladies, has just occurred to me, and so I shall be glad to tell it to you.

During the time the French were being driven from Sicily, a Florentine apothecary of excellent means called Bernardo Puccini, was living in Palermo with the only offspring with which his wife had blessed him, a rarely beautiful girl, ripe enough for marriage.

One day, while King Pedro of Arragon, who had recently become ruler of the island, was holding a magnificent festival in that city with all his knights and lords, and tilted in the style of the Catalans, Bernardo's daughter, whose name was Lisa, happened to see him racing in the ring, from a balcony where she was standing with other women, and was so marvelously smitten with him that as she gazed and gazed, she fell desperately in love. When the tournament was over, and she remained in her father's house, she could think of nothing but this splendid high-flung love of hers, and only one thing made her misera-

ble—the knowledge of her own lowly station, which gave her
no hope at all of any happy outcome. Nevertheless, she could
not persuade herself to relinquish her love, though for fear of
great trouble she dared not reveal it. The king, on his part,
knew nothing of this infatuation, nor did he care, which caused
Lisa more intolerable suffering than anyone can imagine.

Now while Lisa's love grew stronger and stronger within her,
and hopeless melancholy settled on melancholy, she could not
bear up under the strain and fell sick, visibly languishing
more and more each day, like snow in the heat of the sun. The
girl's parents, in despair at this misfortune, did their utmost
to recall her to health, getting her the best of physicians and
medicines. But nothing availed, for hopeless and sick at heart,
she had elected to live no more.

One day, when her father offered to grant her every wish if
only to rejoice her, she was suddenly inspired to make her love
and resolution known to the king before she died, if possible,
and therefore she begged him to bring before her Minuccio
d'Arezzo, renowned in those days as a skilled singer and musician, and a favorite of the monarch's. Bernardo thought Lisa
simply wished to hear him sing and play for her a while, and
sent a messenger to the bard, who, being a kindly and pleasant
man, came to her immediately.

At first he sought to comfort her with loving words, then,
on his viol, he softly played her a sweet melody and sang a song
or two which, instead of soothing the love-sick maiden as he
intended, only intensified her ardor. Finally, she said she wished
to have a word alone with him, and when the others had with-
drawn, she said,

"Minuccio, I have chosen you as the trusty confidant of my
secret, first, in the hope that you'll never disclose it to anyone
but the man I mention, and then, that you may help me as much
as it is in your power to do so. That is my prayer. You must
know, dear Minuccio, that the day our King Pedro celebrated
the high festival of his rise to power, it was my fortune to see
him at his feats of arms to such advantage, that my soul was
kindled to flame for love of him—and you now see how that
flame has consumed me! I knew of how little value my love
was to the greatness of a king, but as I could not cool my ardor,
much less quench it altogether, it became so hard for me to
bear that, as the lesser suffering, I chose to die, as indeed I
shall. I am aware, however, that I would depart this world in

misery if my king did not know of it. Thus, not knowing by whom I could better communicate my resolution to him, I wish to commit the charge to you. Do not deny me, Minuccio, I beg of you. Then, when you have told him of my love and grief, let me know, that I may die comforted and escape my suffering."

Weeping, she said no more.

Minuccio marveled at the nobility of her soul and at her ruthless resolution. Pity plucked at his heart, and in a flash he saw how he could honorably serve her.

"Lisa," he said, "I pledge you my solemn faith, by which you may rest assured you'll never suffer betrayal. You have my admiration for having set your heart to love so great a king, and I offer you my aid, which, if you'll be of good cheer, I shall so well employ, that before three days have passed I hope to bring you news to rejoice your soul. I shall go instantly, that I may begin at once."

Again, before he left, the pining girl entreated him to do his best, promised to be of good cheer, and wished him the best success. Minuccio then took leave of her, and went in search of a certain Mico de Siena, an accomplished rhymer of his day.

"Make me a poem on such and such a theme," he said, and had him compose the following canzonet:

"Make haste, O Love, and to my master go,
　　And tell him one by one the pains I bear;
　　　Say how my death I near,
　Hiding through fear what I would have him know.

With folded hands your mercy, Love, I cry,
　　Begging you go there where my sweet lord stays;
Say how for yearning oft he makes me sigh,
　　And with his gentle art my heart waylays.
So great his scorching flame, I fear to die
　　Burning therein, and yet I count the days
　　Before relief my woeful pain allays,
　　　Which yet for longing of him I must bear
　　　In modesty and fear.
　　　　For God's sweet sake, let him my torment know!

Since first, O love, my heart to him I gave,
　　You did not grant me courage to reveal

A single spark of my dear wish, or brave
  To manifest the yearning that I feel
For him who holds me in such torment grave.
  Alas, this death to die were anguish real!
  Still, it might please him were I to reveal
    And not withhold the agony I bear!
      If only Love would dare
        Him but a little of my flame to show!

And yet, O Love, since you would not inspire
  Me with assurance such to open wide
My weary heart to my sweet lord and sire—
  For sign or message ever was denied!—
  I beg you of your mercy, Love, require
    Him to remember how I saw him ride
      That day with shield and lance, full panoplied
        Among the knights, and gaze so debonair
          That I could not forbear
            To look and love, to my heart's bitter woe!"

These words Minuccio then set to the soft, sad music they required, and on the third day presented himself at court. The king, as it chanced, was still at table, and when he saw the bard, "Sing me a song to the music of your viol!" he said.

Accordingly, Minuccio sang this new song, and so sweetly did he chant and play, that everyone in the royal hall seemed spell-bound listening, so hushed were they, and rapt, the king if possible even more so than his men. At last, when Minuccio had let the echoes of his voice die away, the king said, "Where did you get this new song, for it seems to me I've never heard it before?"

"Sire," replied Minuccio, "scarcely three days have passed since the words were made, and the melody," and when the king wished to know for whom, "I can disclose it only to you, sire," he said.

The king, curious to hear what the troubadour had to say, called him to his chamber as soon as the tables were cleared, and there Minuccio told him everything meticulously. The king was glad to hear the story, and he praised the maiden highly, saying it behooved one to be considerate of so brave a girl. "Go to her," he said, "and comfort her on my part, and tell her that to-night at eventide I shall come to visit her."

Minuccio, happy to be bearing such glad tidings to Lisa, hastened to her with his viol, and when he was alone with her first told her all that had happened, and then sang for her the song of her love, to the music of his instrument. So joyful was the girl, and so comforted, that in a very short time she showed remarkable signs of returning health, to the wonder of her people, who did not know to what it was due. Anxiously, she waited for evening to fall, when she would behold her love.

After Minuccio's departure, the king, who was a good and magnanimous lord, had thought again and again of the things the bard had told him. He knew Lisa, and her great beauty, and became more than ever compassionate of her lot. Toward vespertime he mounted his horse, and pretending he was going riding for his pleasure, came to the apothecary's house. He had the gate leading to Bernardo's handsome garden opened for him, and dismounting, said to his host after a while, "How is your daughter Lisa? Is she married yet?"

"Ah no, sire," replied Bernardo. "She is not married. On the contrary, she has been very ill, and is still in great danger, though strangely enough, since early this afternoon, she seems to have improved wonderfully."

The king instantly understood what lay beneath this improvement and said, "In faith, it would be a great shame for so lovely a creature to be taken from the earth. We should like to go in to see her."

Unattended except by two companions, he soon followed Bernardo into Lisa's room, and going to the bed where the girl had awaited his coming with longing and impatience, he took her hand in his, as she lay upon a mound of pillows, and said, "What is this, dear child? You are young. You should be a comfort to others, and here you allow yourself to pine away! Pluck up your spirits, I beg of you, for love of us, and return to health again."

When Lisa felt upon her the touch of the man's hands whom she loved above everything in the world, she experienced such joy, mingled with shyness, that she felt as though she had been in heaven. "My lord," she said to him with an effort, "it was the strain to subject my feeble strength to great burdens that caused my illness, from which you will soon see me delivered, thanks to your kindness."

The king alone could understand the girl's veiled speech. His admiration for her grew apace, and more than once he inwardly cursed Fortune for having made her the daughter of so humble a man. Then, after staying with her a little longer and encouraging her to bear up, he went away.

This consideration on the part of the king was highly extolled by the people, and interpreted greatly to the credit of the apothecary and his daughter, who was as happy over the event as ever any woman was over her lover. Buoyed by more hope, Lisa recovered her health in a few days, and became even more beautiful than ever before.

Meanwhile, the king had consulted his queen about what reward to bestow upon the maiden for such adoration. When Lisa was well again, he took horse with a large following of his lords, and going into the apothecary's garden, he sent for him and his daughter. The queen presently made her appearance with many ladies in waiting, who received the young girl in their midst with welcome and acclaim. The sovereigns then called her to them, and the king spoke.

"Noble child," he began, "the love you bear us has won you a great honor with which, for our sake, we hope you will be content. Since you are of an age to enter the state of matrimony, we would have you marry the youth we have chosen for you; but we shall still consider ourselves your knight, and claim, of your exceeding love, one single kiss."

Lisa, flushing scarlet with embarrassment, subjected her will to the king's pleasure, and in a soft voice she said, "My lord, I am aware that if it were known I had dared to fall in love with your highness, I should be considered insane by most people, who might perhaps suppose that I had failed to take into consideration your lofty estate and my mean condition. But God, Who alone penetrates into the hearts of us mortals, God, I say, knows that from the first moment I fell in love, I was well aware you were a king, and I only the daughter of Bernardo the druggist, unworthy of setting my fervent love so high. Your highness knows better than I, however, that nobody here on earth falls in love according to fitness, but only according to the dictates of desire and pleasure. More than once, my feeble strength pitted itself against that law. I was powerless against it. Thus I loved you, I still love you, and will continue loving you as long as I live. From that first moment, I resolved always to make your will my law. Therefore, I shall not only gladly accept the husband your highness sees fit to bestow upon me, and cherish him in the state and honor of matrimony, but even if you were to command me to stand in the midst of flames, I would consider the pain a joy, if I thought it gave you pleasure. As for having your highness, a king, as my knight—what can I answer? Your highness knows how such an honor befits a poor girl like me. Nor can I grant you the only kiss you would claim of my love, without the leave of my lady, the queen. Nevertheless, for the great goodness your highness has shown me, and also her ladyship the queen here beside you, may the Lord give you thanks and the reward you deserve, for I could never be rich enough to repay you fittingly."

Then she was silent.

The queen was mightily pleased with the girl's answer, and found her to be indeed as wise as her husband had described her. Then the king, summoning Lisa's father and mother, and finding them quite content with what he intended doing, sent for a highborn but indigent youth by the name of Perdicone, and putting some rings into his willing hand, married the happy youth to Lisa. Then and there, besides the many rare jewels which he and the queen gave the bride, he bestowed upon the youth the thriving and fruitful lands of Ceffalu and Calatebellotta, saying, "We are merely giving you these as the bride's portion. What more we intend doing for you, the future will display." Then, turning to Lisa, "Now we shall claim the fruit owing us from your love," he said, and taking her head between his hands, he kissed her on the brow.

The groom and Lisa's parents and the bride herself were as happy as could be. The bridal-feast was magnificent, and the wedding joyous. According to what many asserted, the king kept his promise faithfully to the lady, for as long as he lived he always called himself her knight and never engaged in any feat of arms unless he wore only the favor she had sent him.

It is by such behavior that a king gains the love of his subjects, inspires others to do well, and acquires undying fame, toward which, alas, few princes nowadays bend the bow of their intellects, fallen as they are into ruthlessness and tyranny.

# THE  EIGHTH  STORY

*Sophronia, believing herself married to Gisippus, discovers she is the wife of Titus Quintius Fulvus, and goes with him to Rome*

*where Gisippus later arrives in dire poverty. He is under the im-*
*pression Titus has scorned him, and accuses himself of having*
*murdered a man, so that he may be put to death. Titus recognizes*
*him, and to save his friend, takes the guilt upon himself. The true*
*murderer, however, on beholding Titus' noble action, gives him-*
*self up, whereupon they are all set free by Octavianus. Later Titus*
*gives his sister in marriage to Gisippus, and shares all his goods*
*with him.*

NOW THAT PAMPINEA HAD CEASED SPEAKING AND KING PEDRO
had been highly commended by the ladies, particularly by the
Ghibelline, Filomena began, at the king's request:

Who doesn't know, noble ladies, that if only kings desire,
they have it in their power to accomplish any deed, however
great—in fact, that magnificent endeavor is especially required of them? The man who has the power, and does what is
expected of him, does well. But people should not wonder at it,
or exalt him to such heights with their praise as they should another of humbler means, of whom less is demanded. Now if you
appreciate the deeds of kings to such extent, and lavish such
praise upon them, I've no doubt you'll admire and extol those of
our equals even more, particularly when they compare favorably, or even surpass a monarch's in splendor. Accordingly, I
intend to illustrate my idea by telling you the story of the noble
and generous behavior of two citizens and friends toward each
other.

In the days when Octavianus Caesar was not yet Augustus, but
governed the Roman empire in the Triumvirate, there lived a
patrician called Publius Quintius Fulvus, who, because his son
Titus showed remarkable mental prowess, sent him to Athens
to learn philosophy and earnestly commended him to the care
of an old friend of his, an Athenian gentleman called Chremes.
Titus was adopted as a member of the family, and shared the
apartment of Gisippus, Chremes' son. Then, when the time
came, the two youths were sent to study together under the
tutelage of Aristippus, the philosopher.

As the young men associated with each other, they discovered
that they were so similar in their tastes, that a great bond of
friendship sprang up between them, never to be severed by any
hazard but death, nor could they enjoy a moment's comfort
and peace unless they shared it. They commenced their studies

together, and since each was equally endowed with a fine intellect, they rose to the glorious heights of philosophy with equal speed, receiving wondrous praise. Thus for three years they pursued their studies, to the extreme gratification of Chremes, who scarcely knew which was the more his son. But alas, as is the way of all things mortal, Chremes, already stricken in years, departed this life, causing the youths such grief by his loss, who was almost their common father, that the friends and kinsfolk of the departed scarcely knew which of the two young men required more consolation.

After the friends and kin of Gisippus had been with him some months, both they and Titus advised him to marry, and found him a wondrously beautiful Athenian girl of noble rank called Sophronia, who was then about fifteen years old. One day Gisippus, as the time of his marriage to her approached, begged his friend to accompany him on a visit, as Titus had not yet seen her, and he consented. When they arrived at her house and Sophronia sat between them, Titus began to look at her closely, perhaps to judge the beauty of his friend's future wife, but as he gazed and gazed, and every lovely feature of her filled him with pleasant admiration, he fell as madly in love with her as ever man did with woman, though outwardly he evinced no sign of change. For a while they sat and chatted with her, and then took leave of her and returned home, Titus going directly to his room, where, in solitude, he thought of Sophronia, falling the more hopelessly in love, the more he dwelt upon her. He could not but recognize what had happened to him, and sighing like a furnace, he reflected:

"Ah, woe to your wretched life, Titus! Where, and upon whom do you set your heart, your love and all your hope? Don't you realize that for all the consideration you've received from Chremes and his people, for the friendship that binds you and Gisippus whose bride Sophronia will be, you must hold her in such esteem as you would a sister of your own flesh and blood? Do you know whom you love? To what lengths will you let yourself be carried by your treacherous love and your deceptive hope? Open the eyes of your mind, and know yourself, poor wretch! Let reason hold sway! Curb your lustful passion, temper your unholy desires, and address your thoughts to other pursuits! Come, nip your lust in the bud and triumph over yourself while you can. What you desire is not becoming to you! It is not honorable! Even if you were certain of gaining it—which you are not!—it would be the better part of valor for you to flee from it, if you had any regard for the claims you owe true friendship. What are you going to do, then, Titus? If you care to do what you ought, abandon this unbecoming love of yours."

But then, as he called to mind the beautiful Sophronia, his reason turned tail and denounced all his good resolutions, saying, "The laws of Love are stronger than all others. They not only render those of friendship null and void, but even the laws of God. How often have we heard of a father falling in love with his daughter? Of a brother with his sister? Of a stepmother with her foster son?—all of them far more monstrous than for a youth to love his friend's wife, which has been known to happen a thousand times at least! Over and above this, I am young, and youth is entirely subject to the laws of Love. If Love ordains, it is for me to submit! Honor and such things are for older folks: I am acting only according to Love's bidding. Sophronia's beauty deserves the adoration of every man alive, and if I, a youth, love her, who can with any justice condemn me for it? I don't love her because she belongs to Gisippus: I would love her no matter whose she was! In this case, Fortune alone is to blame for giving her to Gisippus instead of to someone else. Moreover, if it is Sophronia's lot to be loved—and such beauty as hers certainly deserves love! —Gisippus should be grateful to learn that I'm the one who does the loving and not an utter stranger."

This new argument sent him back to the first in contempt of himself, but only to return again to where he had begun, carrying on the bootless debate until he had not only wasted all that day but also the following night and many others besides, until for loss of sleep and appetite, he was obliged to take to his bed.

For several days, Gisippus had noticed his friend brooding and aloof, and now that he saw him quite ill, he was deeply affected. He would not leave his side for a moment, but tried every possible wile and tenderness to cheer him, pleading with him repeatedly to tell him the cause of his melancholy and his sickness. Many a time Titus had put him off with some transparent lie, which Gisippus had discovered, but at last, feeling it incumbent upon himself to confess, he answered him with sighs and tears:

"Gisippus, dear friend, if it had only pleased the gods, I assure you death would have been far more preferable to me than life. To think that fate gave me the opportunity of putting my virtue to the test and—to my shame be it said, virtue failed! But I expect from it only the reward I deserve—death, Gisippus, and a speedy death, for I assure you it will be far more acceptable to me than life with the memory of my dastardliness! Yes, I will confess it to you, dear friend, for I cannot, I must not hide anything from you. But oh, the shame for me!"

Thereupon, beginning from the beginning, Titus confessed the cause of his brooding to his friend, told him of his mortal struggles, confessed which side had triumphed, and finally avowed that he was dying for love of Sophronia. "I knew how unbecoming it was of my friendship," he declared, "and to atone for it I am resolved to die, which I trust will be soon."

Upon hearing his friend's words and witnessing the tears that accompanied them, Gisippus reflected a while before answering, for he, too, had been captivated by Sophronia's charms, though in a lesser degree; but it was not long before he concluded that Titus' life should be dearer to him than the girl. Tears welled in his eyes, stimulated by those of Titus, and weeping he answered him:

"Dear friend, if you were not in such need of comfort, I should bring a case against you for violating our plighted friendship, by keeping your ardent passion hidden from me so long. Though your love does not seem an honorable thing to you, still, what is dishonorable should no more be concealed from one's friend than what is honorable, because just as a man shares his friend's joy in honorable deeds, he also shares the task of freeing his mind from what is dishonorable. Enough of this now, and let me come to what I know is more important. It is no great wonder to me that you should love Sophronia, my betrothed. Indeed, I'd wonder if you did not love her, cognizant as I am of her beauty and the nobility of your mind, which is the more readily moved to love the greater the excellence of the adored object. Now the more justified you are in loving Sophronia, the more unjustly you condemn fate (though you do not say so), for having given her to me, thinking as you do that your love would have the sanction of honor, had she belonged to someone else.

"But pray, tell me, if you are still as wise as you used to be, to whom could fate have better given her than to me—for which you should be mighty thankful! If Sophronia had fallen to the lot of any other man, no matter how chaste your passion, he would have preferred to keep her for himself than to give her to you—which you may rest assured you need not fear from me, if you consider me as much your friend as I am. When, since we first knew each other, can I remember ever having had anything that was not as much yours as mine? Even if my relations with Sophronia had become such that nothing else were possible, I would still do with her as I have done with everything I've ever had. As it is, however, the affair is still in a stage where I can make her entirely yours, as I will. For why should you hold my friendship so dear, if when I found it possible to do something honorably, I failed to make your will my own? True enough, Sophronia is my betrothed, whom I dearly loved, and whose marriage to me I anticipated with great joy. But since you, more appreciative than myself, yearn for so precious a thing much more ardently, rest assured that when she enters the bridal-chamber she will not come as my wife, but as yours. Dispel your gloomy thoughts, then! Chase away melancholy and summon back your lost health, your cheer and gladness! Come, and from this very moment, look forward happily to the reward of your love, which is more deserving than mine."

As Titus listened, the more his friend's roseate hopes filled him with pleasure, the more his reason moved him to shame at the consciousness that, the greater Gisippus' generosity, the more unseemly it was of him to take advantage of it. Hence, without ceasing his weeping, he answered him with difficulty, "Ah, Gisippus, your true and loyal friendship shows me all too clearly what it behooves mine to do. God forbid I should ever deprive you of the woman He gave you, who are the more deserving of her! If He had thought her more fitting for me to have, neither you nor anyone else could believe He would have given her to you! Rejoice in your election, then, and use your prudent counsel and His gift! Leave me to waste away in the tears He has adjudged my lot, as one unworthy of such a treasure! Either I triumph over them, which will gladden your heart, or they master me, in which case I shall be free of suffering!"

"Titus," said Gisippus, "if our friendship permits of my compelling you to acquiesce to my desire, and if it can succeed in persuading you to do so, I will certainly take advantage of it to the utmost in this instance. And if you should not submit docilely to my prayers, I will bring you to do so with the compulsion permissible for the good of one's friend, and manage things in such a way that Sophronia will be yours. I know how much Love's powers can encompass, and that not in a single instance, but in many cases, it has brought lovers to an unhappy death. Indeed, I can see you are so near the verge of it, that you can neither turn back, nor even control your tears. You'll perish, surely, at this rate, and I know beyond a doubt that I should soon follow you. Even if I loved you for nothing else, Titus, I must cherish your life for the sake of my own. Sophronia will be yours, then, my friend. You could not easily find any other woman to love so dearly, whereas I, on the contrary, could lightly bend my heart to another. Thus, you see, I'll be satisfying you and myself at the same time. Doubtless I'd not be so magnanimous if wives were as scarce and as hard to find as friends. So, then, since I can very easily find myself another wife but not another friend, I had rather—I shall not say lose her, for I should not be losing her by giving her to you, but simply turning her over to another and better self—I had rather, as I said, offer her to you, than lose you. Now then, if my entreaties have any power to move you, I pray you, pull yourself out of this dejection and make us both happy at the same time. Rejoice! Think hopefully of taking that happiness which your ardent love desires of your loved one!"

Although Titus was ashamed to consent to his friend's wish and stood his ground a while longer by refusing to take Sophronia as his wife, nevertheless, urged on the one hand by his passion and on the other by the pleas of Gisippus, he said, "I must confess, dear friend, I don't know which I'd be doing more, your pleasure, or mine, if I did what you so earnestly urge me to do. But since your generosity is so great that it dominates my just shame, I will do as you say. But be sure of one thing: I am not going into this like a man who does not realize that he owes you not only the woman he loves, but with her, his life. The gods grant it may be possible that some day I may still prove to your honor and credit how grateful I am for what you, more merciful of me than I myself, are doing for me."

When he had done, "Titus," said Gisippus, "if we want to be successful in this undertaking of ours, this, I think, is the way to go about it. As you know, after much parleying between my kin and Sophronia's, she has at last become my betrothed, so that if I were now to say I no longer wished to have her for my wife, a great scandal would be raked up, to the sorrow of my family and hers. That's the last thing that would trouble me, however, if through it all I could see my way to make her yours. I'm afraid, though, that if I gave her up at this point, her people would immediately marry her off to someone else who perhaps would not be yourself, and so you would be losing what I had not obtained. With your consent, therefore, I think I shall proceed with what I have begun, bring her home as my bride, and celebrate the wedding. Later we'll know how to arrange to have you lie with her as with your wife. Then, at the proper time and place, we'll reveal the true state of affairs. If her folks are content with them, well and good. If not, we cannot undo what has been done, and they'll have to be satisfied, willy-nilly."

Titus found the proposal satisfactory and soon recovered his pristine vigor. Accordingly, Gisippus welcomed Sophronia home as his bride, and after the joyous festivities were over and night had fallen, the women left the newly-married girl in her husband's bed and went away.

Now Titus' bedroom adjoined his friend's, so that it was easy for one to go from one room to the other. Thus, when Gisippus was in his chamber and all the lights were extinguished, he went softly to his friend and told him to go and lie with his lady. Shame took hold of Titus at this point, and he would willingly have given up everything and refused to go; but Gisippus was as wholeheartedly bent upon his friend's pleasure as his words had indicated, and finally, after a long struggle, he persuaded the youth.

In the bridal bed, Titus clasped Sophronia in his arms, and then, as if in jest, asked her softly, "Do you consent to be my wife?" "I do," she said, thinking he was Gisippus, whereupon the youth, slipping a fine and precious ring upon her finger, said, "And I want to be your husband."

The marriage performed, he took long and amorous joy of her body, and neither she nor anyone else ever suspected that any man but Gisippus had lain with her.

Now while Sophronia and Titus were living in this manner as man and wife, Publius, his father, died, and word was sent him to return at once to Rome to look after his affairs. He deliberated with Gisippus about taking Sophronia along with him, which could not easily be contrived without disclosing to her how the matter stood. One day, therefore, they called her into the room and revealed the whole situation to her, which Titus further clarified by pointing out various little incidents that had happened between them.

At first she looked from one to the other somewhat indignantly, and then, condemning Gisippus' deceit, she burst into a flood of angry tears. Before even venturing to discuss the matter in the house of Gisippus, she took refuge in her father's, and informed her parents of the treachery the youth had practiced both upon her and them. "I am not his wife, as you believe, but Titus'," she cried.

It was most unwelcome news to Sophronia's father, and many and bitter were the complaints he made to his people and those of Gisippus, stirring up endless tale-bearing and to-do about the whole affair. Not only the family of Sophronia, but Gisippus' own flesh and blood turned against the youth for his deed, saying he deserved not only censure but dire punishment. On his part, he staunchly maintained that he had done an honorable deed, for which Sophronia's kin should have been grateful, in that he had given her in marriage to a better man than himself.

Titus, on the other hand, listened to all the recriminations with exceeding annoyance, knowing as he did that the Greeks were bold with threats and noise until they came upon the person to bring them to their senses, when they became not only meek, but craven. "They need someone to put a check on their nonsense," he thought, and having himself the spirit of Rome and the wisdom of Athens, he skilfully managed to assemble Sophronia's and Gisippus' relatives in a temple, where, entering with his friend as his sole companion, he addressed them.

"It is believed by many philosophers," he began, "that whatever mortals do has been decreed and preordained by the immortal gods, making all that has either been or has ever to be, the fruit of necessity, though there are some who maintain that this necessity applies only to what has been. Now if these opinions are shrewdly looked into, it will be clear as daylight that to resent an event that cannot be altered, is tantamount to declaring one's wisdom greater than the gods', who, we must believe, ordain and regulate us, and all that concerns us, with infinite judgment and no possibility of error. Hence you can see at once how foolish and presumptuous it would be to take exception to their divine operations, and how much in need of restraint are those who let themselves be carried away by their boldness in this respect. To my judgment, you are all as I describe, if there's any truth in what I believe you said and are still saying about the fact that Sophronia became my wife, though you had bestowed her upon Gisippus, failing to realize that *ab eterno* she was destined not to be his, but mine, as is manifest from the actual result.

"However, since it is difficult and beyond the reach of many to understand this talk of the secret providences and intentions of the gods, I shall be pleased to descend to the ways of mankind, supposing for the nonce that the gods care nothing for our concerns. But speaking in terms of understandable humanity, I shall be obliged to do two things contrary to my nature—first, to speak somewhat in praise of myself, and then, to blame or belittle someone else. Still, as I've no intention of straying from the truth, either in the one or the other of these things, and as the present subject demands it, I will do it.

"All your complaints, incited more by wrath than reason, your continual protests, indeed, your vulgar recriminations, blame, attack and condemn Gisippus for having given me as my wife, of his own judgment, the woman you had given him of yours. For this deed of his I hold him to be worthy of the highest praise. Why? First, because he did his duty as a friend, and second, because he acted with greater wisdom than you did. It is not my present purpose to expatiate on what the sacred laws of friendship dictate that one friend should do for another. It suffices me to have reminded you solely that the ties of friendship are more binding than those of blood or kin, since we choose our friends, while Fortune thrusts our kin upon us. Hence, if Gisippus esteemed my life dearer than your goodwill, it is not to be wondered at, as I am, and hold myself to be, his friend.

"But now for the second reason, whereby it will be necessary to prove more clearly to you that he was wiser than you, seeing that you apparently care nothing for the decrees of the gods, and know less of the duties of friendship. Granted that your wisdom, your counsel and your deliberation gave Sophronia to Gisippus, a youth and a philosopher. His wisdom bestowed her upon a youth and a philosopher. Your counsel gave her to an Athenian; his, to a Roman. Again, yours gave her to a man of high rank; his, to a man of still higher degree. Yours gave her to a rich youth; his, to a very rich. Yours, to a youth who not only did not love her, but hardly knew her; and his, to one who loved her above every happiness, more than his very life.

"Would you care to know that what I say is true, and that Gisippus was wiser in his deed than you? Let us examine the matter in detail. That I am young and a philosopher like Gisippus, both my face and the studies I have pursued will clearly show, without dwelling longer on that score. We are both of the same age, and together we progressed in our studies with an equal pace. True, he is an Athenian and I am a Roman. But shall we argue about the glory of our respective cities? Well then, I am of a free city; he is of a tributary. I am of a city that is mistress of the world; he is of one obedient to mine. I am of a city flourishing in arms, in power and in learning, whereas he is of one that can boast only of the last. Again, though you see me here, a very humble scholar, don't imagine I have sprung from the dregs of the Roman people. My houses and the public squares of Rome are full of the ancient statues of my forebears, and Roman annals abound in countless triumphs led by the Quintii to the very capitol. Nor has the glory of our name decayed with age, for to-day more than ever it flourishes triumphant.

"Modesty bids me say nothing of my wealth, bearing in mind as I do that honest poverty has since time immemorial been the vastest patrimony of Rome's noble citizens. Still, since poverty is despised in the opinion of the vulgar and wealth glorified, I may say, not as a grasping man, but as one whom Fortune favored, that I am well-provided with riches.

"It is easy to understand that you should have been glad to have Gisippus here in Athens as your relative. But there is no reason why I, in Rome, should be less appreciated, when you take into account the fact that there you would have in me an excellent host, and a useful, zealous, influential patron in all your needs, both public and private. Who is there, then, who judging this with reason and not with his own peculiar prejudice, would commend your wisdom above that of Gisippus? Nobody, surely. Accordingly, Sophronia is well-bestowed as the wife of Titus Quintius Fulvus, a noble, wealthy Roman citizen of ancient lineage and the friend of Gisippus. Anyone, therefore, finding anything to blame or bewail in this, does not behave as he should, nor does he know what he is doing.

"Some of you may object that Sophronia does not complain because she is the wife of Titus, but because of the way she became his wife—secretly and by stealth, neither kith nor kin knowing anything about it. It is no miracle, neither is it anything unheard of. I say nothing of girls who marry against their fathers' will, of others who elope with their lovers and are their mistresses before they become their wives, and again, of those who disclose their marriages to the world by the fruits of pregnancy and childbirth, before they confess them with a word—all of which necessity has rendered acceptable to their relatives. None of these was the case with Sophronia. On the contrary, she was given in marriage by Gisippus to Titus, in due form and in all propriety and honor.

"Others will say that it was not the place of Gisippus to bestow her on a husband, a foolish objection, and a womanish, arising from little reflection. It is nothing new for fate to bring matters to their predestined course by devious ways and means. What do I care if a cobbler, rather than a philosopher, had handled some concern of mine according to his lights, secretly or otherwise, if the result is good? Should the cobbler prove indiscreet, I have only to take care that he'll not have a chance to meddle with my affairs again, and give him my thanks for what he has done. The fact is, if Gisippus bestowed Sophronia well, it is unnecessary puerility to complain about him and the way he went about it. Have you no confidence in his wisdom? Take care that he'll not have a chance to marry off any other of your daughters, and thank him for this once.

"There's one thing I want you to know, however. Never, either by cunning or fraud did I seek to defile the honor and purity of your blood, in the person of Sophronia. True, I married her in secret. But I did not come as a ravisher to rob her of her virginity, nor as an enemy, scorning to ally my blood with yours or seeking to have her in any but an honorable way. Her radiant beauty and her virtue inflamed me to passionate love. However, realizing that if I had asked for her hand according to the procedure you think I should have used, she would have been denied me because of the great love you bear her, in your fear that I would have taken her to Rome, I employed the secret stratagem which may now be revealed to you, and entreated Gisippus to do that which he did not desire—consent in my name. Again, though I loved her passionately, never did I seek her embraces as a lover, but only as a husband. I did not even approach her, as she herself can truly bear witness, until I had duly made her my wife with the proper ceremony and the ring, and asked her whether she would accept me as her husband, to which she answered, yes. If now she considers herself sinned against, it is not I who should be blamed, but herself for not asking me who I was.

"This, then, is the dreadful wickedness, the heinous sin, the atrocious crime that was committed by Gisippus as my friend, and by me as her lover; that Sophronia secretly became the wife of Titus Quintius! And for this reason you rend and tear him, for this you are loud with threats and hatch plots against him. What more could you indulge in, had he turned her over to a boor, a good-for-nothing, or a lackey? What chains, what dungeons, what scaffolds would have seemed adequate punishment? But enough now, of all this.

"The thing which I had not yet expected has happened. My father is dead, and I must return to Rome. Thus, in my anxiety to take Sophronia with me, I have disclosed to you what I perhaps should still have concealed. If you are wise, you will gladly bear this parting, for had I intended to cheat and make a mock of you, I could have left her behind, dishonored. God forbid that such infamy should ever harbor in a Roman breast! Sophronia is mine. By the will of the gods, by the might of human laws, by the praiseworthy wisdom of my dear Gisippus and, ay, by my own lovers' cunning—she is my own! It is this very thing you seem foolishly to decry, perhaps deeming yourselves wiser than the gods and mankind in general, by showing your disfavor in two ways exceedingly odious to me: first, in wishing to hold Sophronia, over whom you have no right except insofar as I allow it, and second, by treating Gisippus as an enemy, to whom you ought justly be grateful. I'll not waste time now showing you how ridiculously you are behaving in both instances, but as a friend I say to you, away with your prejudices. Forget your rancors and the grudges you bear me, and give me back Sophronia, that I may peacefully depart as your friend and live as such. For I assure you, if you do otherwise, whether you are content or not with what I have done, I will take Gisippus from you. Then, if I should reach Rome, I will certainly recover the woman who is rightfully mine, no matter how you resent it, and as your relentless enemy I'll give you a taste of what the indignation of a Roman is capable!"

No sooner had Titus had his say, than rising to his feet, his face flaming with wrath, he took Gisippus by the hand, and showing how little he cared for all the people in the temple, walked out shaking his head and fuming with threats.

Those who remained behind, partly won over to countenance his alliance and friendship for the reasons he had given, and partly intimidated by his closing words, finally concurred that it was better to have Titus as a kinsman, since Gisippus had not wished the honor for himself, than to lose Gisippus as a friend and acquire the Roman as an enemy. Accordingly, they went out in search of Titus and told him they were willing that Sophronia should be his, yes, and to have him as a dear kinsman and Gisippus as a good friend. Thus they exchanged friendly courtesies and made good cheer, and after they had gone away, they sent Sophronia back to him. Like the discreet woman she was, she made a virtue of necessity, and quickly transferring to Titus the love she had borne Gisippus, accompanied him to Rome, where she was welcomed with exceeding honor.

Gisippus, in the meantime, remaining behind in Athens, was looked on with disfavor by nearly everyone, and not long after, being implicated in some civic broils, he was banished from town with those of his household and condemned, poor and wretched, to perpetual exile. Things went from bad to worse. Well-nigh a beggar, he made the best of his way to Rome, to see if Titus still bore any remembrance of him, and there he learned that his former friend was alive and held in high esteem by his fellow-citizens. Gisippus, therefore, discovering where he lived, posted himself before his door and waited until Titus came home. When he saw him, however, he did not dare to make himself known by a single word, so wretched was his state, but simply strove to catch his eye, that Titus, recognizing him, might have him sent for. But Titus passed on. Gisippus, thinking his friend had ignored him, went away, wounded and desperate, especially when he recalled what he had done for him.

Night had already fallen. Gisippus had not eaten anything, and furthermore had no money at all. Without knowing where he was going, and yearning above everything for death, he happened upon a desolate quarter of the city, where, seeing a vast cave, he went in to seek shelter for the night. Upon the naked ground, in his ragged clothes, he sank to sleep, overcome by the stress of long weeping.

Now two rogues, who had gone out on a robbing expedition that night, came to that cave toward daybreak with their plunder, and while they were quarreling about it, the stronger slew the other and made his escape. Gisippus had witnessed the whole scene, and thought, "Here is a way of achieving the death I seek without having to lay hands upon myself." Accordingly, he did not move from the spot until the sergeants of the court, who had heard rumors of the murder, arrived, put Gisippus under arrest and led him none too gently away with them.

Upon being brought to trial Gisippus confessed the murder, saying he had not been able to get out of the cave in time, whereupon Marcus Varro, the praetor, ordered him to be crucified, according to the custom of those days.

By some chance, Titus happened to come into the courtroom at that moment, and as he looked into the face of the wretched man, and learned for what reason he had been sentenced to death, he instantly recognized Gisippus. Aghast at the evil days that had fallen upon his former friend, and wondering how he had come to Rome, he was desperately eager to come to his aid. But seeing no other way of saving his life except to accuse himself and so clear Gisippus of guilt, he quickly stepped forward and cried, "Marcus Varro, call back the poor man you have sentenced to death, for he is innocent. I sinned enough against the gods in one crime, when I murdered the wretch your guards found this morning, without offending them further with the death of another guiltless man."

Varro was astounded and grieved that all the praetors had heard him. Still, as he could not honorably refuse to carry out what the laws decreed, he had Gisippus summoned back, and in the presence of Titus asked him, "How could you have been so mad as to confess yourself guilty of a crime you never committed, even without having been put to torture, and knowing that you would be placing your life at stake? You declared you were the culprit who killed a man last night, and now here is one who says you did not kill him, but that he did."

Gisippus looked up at the self-accuser and recognized Titus who, he had no doubt, was doing this to save his life out of gratitude for the boon he had once received from him. Weeping with pity, "Varro," he said, "I am the true murderer, and Titus' compassion for my welfare comes too late."

Titus insisted, "Praetor, you see this man is a stranger in our town. He was found unarmed beside the slain man, and it is obvious that his miserable state makes him in love with death. Set him free, then, and inflict the punishment upon me, who have deserved it."

Varro wondered at the determination of the two men. The truth that neither of them was guilty was already dawning upon him, and as he was revolving in his mind some way of releasing them, a notorious scapegrace called Publius Ambustus, a youth known to all the Romans as a scoundrel and a thief, presented himself. He had committed the murder, and therefore knowing that neither of the two men had perpetrated the crime of which each accused himself, he felt such grief softening his heart at their innocence, that moved to exceeding pity, he came before Varro and said:

"Praetor, my fates urge me to solve the difficult argument between these two men, and I don't know what spirit within me goads and pricks me on to confess my crime to you. Know, then, that neither of these men is guilty of what each stands self-accused. I, and none other, killed that man toward dawn this morning, and I saw this poor fellow who is here now, lying there asleep as I was dividing the ill-gotten gains with my accomplice. It is not necessary for me to plead on behalf of Titus. His blameless conduct is too well known for him to be thought capable of such a crime. Set them free, therefore, and give me the punishment which the laws demand."

By this time Octavianus had heard of the strange event. Calling for the three to appear before him, he questioned them individually upon the reasons that impelled each to take the blame upon himself. One by one, they told him. The first two he acquitted for their innocence, and the third, too, he forgave for their sake.

Titus, after rebuking Gisippus for his lack of faith and his diffidence, welcomed him with joy and happiness and took him to his home, where Sophronia received him like a brother, weeping over his lot for pity. Nursing him tenderly and furnishing him with clothes, they brought him back to a state befitting his worth and rank, when Titus shared everything he had in treasures and estates with him, and gave him in marriage a young sister of his called Fulvia. Then, "Gisippus," he said, "it is for you now to choose whether you will stay here with me, or go back to Achaia with my gifts."

Exile and banishment from his native land on the one hand, and the love he bore the grateful friendship of Titus on the other, pleaded with Gisippus, and he agreed to become a Roman. And so he settled down in Rome, where he with his Fulvia and Titus with his Sophronia lived happily for many years, all in the same house, their friendship becoming deeper and closer, if that were possible, with every passing day.

Most holy is the virtue of friendship. Not only is it deserving of special esteem, but it should be praised forever as the prudent mother of generosity and honesty, the sister of gratitude and charity, and the enemy of hatred and avarice. It never waits to be solicited, but is always ready to do virtuously to others what it would have done unto itself. These days its divine manifestations are seldom to be met with in two individuals at once —be it said to the shame of human greed, which, in its own self-seeking, has relegated it in eternal banishment to the furthest corners of the earth.

What love, what wealth, what ties of blood could have caused Gisippus to feel in his own heart the passion, tears and sighs of Titus to such an extent as to make him surrender to him the beautiful, charming bride he himself loved? What, I say, if not friendship? What laws, what threats, what terrors could have kept the lusty arms of Gisippus from encircling the lovely girl in secluded places, in the dark, yes, in his very bed, she herself, perhaps, inviting him—what, if not friendship? What glories, what merits, what advancements could have made Gisippus indifferent to the loss of his own kith and kin and Sophronia's people, to the indecent murmurs of the populace, to their mockery and insults—all to gratify his friend—tell me, what, if not friendship?

Then again, what, if not friendship could have made Titus so ready to procure his own death, to deliver Gisippus from the crucifixion he sought, when without any dishonor to himself he could have closed his eyes to the other's peril? What could have impelled Titus to share his vast patrimony unhesitatingly with Gisippus, from whom fate had filched all—what, if not friendship? And last, but not least, what if not friendship could have made Titus so ready to grant his own sister to Gisippus, when he saw him so miserable and in such dire need?

Let mortals desire multitudes of friends, hosts of brothers and countless children; let them increase the number of their servants by purchasing their services. They do not consider that every one of these, no matter what his condition, is sure to be more concerned with the least little danger threatening his own safety, than solicitous to protect his father, or his brother or his master from a mighty peril. Could this be said of friendship? Never!

*

# THE NINTH STORY

*Saladin, traveling incognito, enjoys the hospitality of Torello. Soon a crusade is undertaken and Torello sets out upon it, en-*

*joining his wife not to marry again until a year is past. He is cap-*
*tured by the Saracens, and because of his excellence in training*
*hawks, comes to the notice of Saladin who recognizes him, makes*
*himself known, and loads him with honors. Torello suddenly falls*
*sick, and by virtue of magic arts is transported overnight to Pavia,*
*where during the ceremony of his wife's remarriage she knows*
*him and they both go home together.*

FILOMENA WAS SILENT. WHEN THE MAGNIFICENT GRATITUDE OF
Titus had been extolled by the whole company, the king, leaving Dioneo his privilege of telling the last story, began:

Charming ladies, Filomena's discourse of friendship contains a
world of truth, and it was with good reason she complained of
how little it is appreciated by mankind nowadays. Indeed, if we
were here to correct the shortcomings of the world, or even to
censure them, I'd second her words by a lengthy sermon. But
since our purpose is quite a different one, I'd like very much to
tell you a rather long but interesting story concerning an act of
generosity on the part of Saladin. Thus, if we cannot gain
friends because of our errors, we can at least, as you will see by
my story, take pleasure in serving, so that perhaps at some future time that service may receive the reward that is its due.

According to what some people maintain, during the reign of
Emperor Frederick the First, the Christians proposed to undertake another crusade to regain the Holy Land. News of it
reached the ears of Saladin, a brave and noble monarch who was
at the time Sultan of Babylon, and the better to make provisions
against the incursion, he resolved to see for himself what preparations the Christians were making. Thereupon, after settling
his administration in Egypt, he gave his people to understand
that he was going on a pilgrimage, but instead, set out on his
journey disguised as a merchant, accompanied by only two of
his foremost and wisest counselors and three lackeys. So they
traveled through many Christian countries.

Toward dusk one evening, as they were riding through Lombardy on the road between Milan and Pavia, to get across the
mountains before night overtook them, they met a gentleman
called Torello d'Istria, of the latter town, who was traveling with
his servants, hounds and falcons toward a handsome country-
home he possessed, above the Tesino. The moment he caught
sight of Saladin and his attendants, he knew they were gentle-

men and strangers in those parts, so that when the Sultan asked one of his servants how far they still were from Pavia and whether he and his men were still in time to reach it before the gates were closed, Torello did not give the fellow time to reply but answered, "Gentlemen, you'll not get to Pavia to-night in time to enter it."

"Can you please tell us, then, where we may put up for the night," asked Saladin, "for as you see, we are strangers here?"

"With pleasure, sir," replied Torello. "I was just thinking of sending one of my men on an errand to the neighborhood of Pavia. I'll have him accompany you and he will conduct you to a place where you will be comfortably lodged."

Accordingly, drawing near the most discreet of his attendants, he instructed him what to do and sent him to keep the strangers company, while he himself hastened to his house, arranged for the best possible supper that was to be procured, and ordered the tables to be set in one of his gardens. This accomplished, he stood at the door to await his guests' arrival.

In the meantime, the servant, engaging the gentlemen in conversation, led them, without their knowing it, through various roundabout ways to his master's house, where Torello himself came to greet them, smiling, "Gentlemen, you are heartily welcome!"

Saladin, a shrewd reader of men, knew instantly that their host had feared that they might not have accepted his invitation if he had proffered it at their first meeting, and had thus conducted them skilfully to his house, where they could not refuse to spend the night with him. Greeting him in turn he said, "Sir, if one could complain of gentlemanly behavior, we should have good reason to complain of you. I am not speaking of your taking us somewhat out of our way; but here, without your being beholden to us except for a mere greeting, you have placed us in a position to accept, willy-nilly, the exemplary hospitality you are showing us."

At that Torello, an intelligent, well-spoken man, replied, "Gentlemen, what you are receiving from us is but poor accommodation, if we were to take into consideration what you really deserve, to judge by your appearances. But you must believe me when I say that it would not have been possible for you to find any suitable lodging-place outside of Pavia. Don't be annoyed, then, if you've been taken a little out of your way to gain less discomfort."

While he was speaking his servants came to help the strangers dismount, and then took care of their horses. Then Torello, leading the three gentlemen to the suite he had prepared for them, had them remove their riding-boots and refresh themselves with draughts of coolest wines, as he engaged them in pleasant talk until the hour for supper.

Now Saladin, as well as his two attendants and the lackeys were acquainted with Latin, and they could easily understand what was said to them while making themselves understood. Conversing with Torello, they thought him the most pleasant, courteous and agreeable speaker of any man they had ever met, while on his part he was sure they must be magnificent gentlemen of far greater rank than he had at first suspected. He was embarrassed at the thought, and inwardly regretted that he had not been able to honor them that night with a more sumptuous feast and other guests to keep them company. "But I'll make up for it to-morrow," he comforted himself.

After sending one of his servants with instructions to his wife, a most prudent and noble-hearted woman who was then at Pavia, hard by, where no gates were ever shut or barred, he took the gentlemen to his garden and courteously asked them who they were.

"We are Cyprian merchants," Saladin answered him, "on our way to Paris for some business matters of ours."

"If only our country could boast of such gentlemen as Cyprus does of merchants!" Torello exclaimed.

Such conversation, and more in the same strain engaged them until supper-time, when Torello led them to the tables and left them to their own devices. It was an excellent and well-served supper, for one prepared without notice. When it was over and the tables were cleared, Torello, knowing his guests must be fatigued from their journey, put them up in fine, comfortable beds and himself retired.

The attendant who had been despatched to Pavia accomplished his errand with Torello's wife, who, with a spirit not merely womanly but queenly, collected as many of her husband's friends and servants as she could muster and arranged everything for a sumptuous feast. Then, sending retainers with torches to invite the town's noblest citizens to the banquet, she brought out her best cloths and tapestries and vairs, and followed her husband's orders to the letter.

The following day, when the stranger gentlemen had risen,

Torello, mounting his horse in their company, sent for his falcons, and leading his guests to a nearby ford, showed them how
his birds flew. Later, when Saladin asked him for someone to
conduct him and his party to the best hostelry in Pavia, Torello
answered, "I shall escort you myself, as I have to go there anyway."

They believed him, and were pleased, and together they set
out on their way, the strangers thinking they were bound for
Pavia's best inn. Toward nine o'clock they came into the town.
Torello conducted them to his house, and at least fifty of the
city's most notable citizens were already there to welcome the
strangers and came forward to assist them from their horses.
Saladin and his attendants knew in a trice how matters stood,
and said, "Torello! Torello! This is not what we had asked you
for. You went through enough trouble for us last night—much
more than we should have wished—and you could easily have
let us go our way to-day."

"Gentlemen," replied Torello, "for all I did last night I am
beholden to luck more than to you, for it was luck that brought
you upon that road at an hour when you had no choice but to
come to my humble house. But for to-day's visit I shall be your
debtor, as well as all these gentlemen you see about you. If you
think you can justly deny them the honor of being their guests,
you are at liberty to do so, if you wish."

Saladin and his companions were persuaded by the argument
and dismounted. Thereupon, the gentlemen of the town gave
them a glad welcome, escorted them to the chambers that had
been richly adorned to receive them, and after having had
then remove their traveling-clothes, refreshed them with cooling
drinks and brought them into the banquet-hall, which was magnificently decked in their honor. Water was passed around for
the ablutions and the guests took their places at the tables,
where, in grand and noble order, they were served with such
bounty and largesse, that if the emperor himself had come, he
could not have been shown greater honor. Even Saladin and his
companions, in spite of their being noble lords and accustomed
to splendor, could not but marvel at the lavishness, all the more
astonishing when they considered Torello was no great lord but
a citizen.

At last when the dinner was over and the tables cleared, they
passed the time talking of sundry things; but as the heat of the
afternoon was intense, the gentlemen of Pavia, at Torello's sug-

gestion went to take their siesta, and he remained alone with his three guests.

There was no cherished thing in his possession that he did not wish them to see, therefore, leading them into a room apart, Torello sent for his wife to come to him.

She was a beautiful woman, tall and stately of figure, clothed in a rich and splendid gown. Courteously she entered with her two little sons, fair as angels, on either side of her, and came before the guests with a gracious greeting. They rose at her appearance, and received her with respect, and showing her to a seat among them, complimented her on her lovely children. They conversed pleasantly for some time, when, at her husband's withdrawal, she asked them civilly, "May I ask where you come from and where you are going?"

They gave her the answer they had given Torello, at which the lady said with charming grace, "I can see that my womanly forethought will prove useful. I beseech you, as a special favor, do not reject or scorn the modest gift I shall send for. Accept it, I pray you, with the understanding that women, in the simpleness of their hearts, make only simple gifts; therefore, do not consider the gift, but the spirit in which it is given."

At that she called for two robes of honor for each man—one lined with silk, and the other with vair. No mere townsman's clothes were they, nor merchants' either, but fit for great lords. Besides these robes, she also presented them with three shirts of sendal and breeches of fine linen.

"Take them," she said, "for I have also provided my husband with similar garments. As for the other things, trifling though they are, you may still find them welcome, considering the fact that you are traveling and far from your women, and have still a long way to go. Moreover, merchants are neat men, and careful of their appearance."

The three men were filled with wonder, and saw clearly that Torello did not wish to leave a single gracious gesture unaccomplished. When they perceived the magnificence of the robes, however, which were not at all for simple merchants, they were afraid he had perhaps penetrated their disguise, and one of them said to the lady:

"Madam, these are very rich gifts, not to be lightly taken. Truly, we should scarcely have dared accept them, if your prayers, which we cannot find it in ourselves to deny, had not compelled us."

, By this time Torello had returned, whereupon the lady, commending the strangers to God, took leave of them and set about providing their servants with such changes of raiment as suited their station. After many prayers, Torello succeeded in having the strangers remain his guests the rest of the day. They took their siesta, and then dressing themselves in their robes, they rode about the town until suppertime. They were magnificently served, amid a host of honorable companions, and then, at the proper time, they retired to rest.

At daybreak the following morning they arose, to find three sturdy, powerful steeds awaiting them in place of their tired horses, as well as fresh, robust mounts for their servants. Saladin, at this new token of generosity, turned to his companions and said, "By heaven, there never was a more accomplished, courteous or noble gentleman than this! Truly, if Christian kings are as kingly as this man is a gentleman, I'm afraid the Sultan of Babylon is no match for a single one of them, not to speak of all those who are getting ready to fall upon him!"

Knowing full well that it would have been bootless for them to refuse Torello's new kindness, they thanked him very graciously and took to horse. For many miles beyond the town, Torello and a number of his companions escorted them. At last Saladin, who had taken a great fancy to his host and was loth to part from him, though his need impelled him to journey on, urged him to turn back. Much against his will, Torello, who found the parting difficult, said,

"Gentlemen, I shall obey you, since it is your wish. But I'll tell you one thing; I don't know who you are, and I shall not insist on knowing any more than it is your pleasure to tell me. But whoever you may be, you will never make me believe you are only merchants. Farewell, then, and the Lord keep you."

Saladin had already said good-bye to all of Torello's friends and now turned to him. "Torello," he said, "perhaps it may happen that some day we'll be in a position to show you some of our merchandise, so that we may make you believe us. But now, God be with you."

So he went away with his attendants, swearing a solemn oath that if death spared him and the expected war did not wreck his kingdom, he would show Torello no less honor than he had received. He spoke much of him with his companions, and of his charming lady, and of the many kindnesses and courtesies the gentleman had shown them, finding no words to praise him sufficiently.

Finally, after he had visited all the western countries, not without stress and fatigue, he took ship and returned to Alexandria where, fully cognizant of the Christians' plans, he prepared his kingdom for defense.

Torello, on his part, went back to Pavia, where for a long time he racked his brains wondering who the three strangers could have been, without ever attaining, or even approaching the truth.

Meanwhile, the time for the crusade drew near, and great were the preparations made for it throughout the Christian world. Torello, too, in spite of his wife's prayers and tears was firmly determined to go on it. Indeed, he arranged all his affairs for the departure, and when he was about to mount his horse, he said to his wife, whom he loved with a high and noble love:

"As you see, my dear, I am going on this crusade for the honor of my body and the welfare of my soul. I leave all we have, our goods and our honor in your keeping. As I am sure of going, but not so sure of coming back, because of a thousand hazards that may come between, I have one favor to ask of you. No matter what happens, whether or not you have definite word that I'm alive or dead, wait for me a year, a month and a day from this of my departure, before you marry again."

The good lady was choked with sobs and answered, "O Torello, I don't know how I can ever bear the sorrow you leave me with your going! But if I should survive it and anything should happen to you, rest assured that I shall live and die the wife of Torello and his beloved memory."

"I know, dear wife, that if it rested with you, all that you promise would surely be," said Torello. "But you are young and beautiful and of good family, and your great virtues are everywhere recognized. I have no doubt, therefore, that if there were the least suspicion of my death, many gentlemen of rank would ask your brothers and your family for your hand. Then, no matter how you wished to rid yourself of their suits, you could not do so, and you would be obliged to give in to their demands. That is why I am asking you to wait for me just so long and no longer."

"I shall endeavor to do my best in what I said, Torello," she answered, "and should I be obliged to act otherwise, I shall obey your request without fail—pray God He may never bring you or me to such a pass!"

Weeping, she threw her arms about his neck; then, drawing a ring from her finger, she gave it to him, saying, "If I should die before I see you again, let this remind you of me whenever you look at it."

He took it from her, and mounting his horse, bade all his friends farewell. So he set out on his journey. At Genoa, where he arrived with his contingent, he embarked on a galley. In a short time he was at Acre to join another army of crusaders, among whom, almost immediately, great sickness trailed disastrous mortality in its wake. At this juncture, whether through Saladin's tactics or his good luck, almost all the surviving Christians were made captive, scattered throughout his towns and confined in the prisons. Among them, Torello was seized and brought a prisoner to Alexandria. Nobody knew him there, nor did he wish to make himself known, and as his great need constrained him, he devoted his time to training falcons, an art at which he was a master. His skill was brought to the attention of Saladin; presently the monarch ordered him to be released and appointed him his falconer.

As it was, neither of the two recognized the other, and Saladin knew him by no other name than *the Christian*. Torello, on his part, had no mind but for Pavia, and many times had sought, without success, to make his escape. One day, when a party of Genoese gentlemen had come as envoys to Saladin to broach the ransoming of some fellow-citizens who were being held captive, Torello thought of letting his wife know of his condition and that he was alive, and hence that she should wait for him, as he would fly to her as soon as he could. He did as he planned, and approaching one of the ambassadors whom he knew, he earnestly entreated him before his departure, to deliver the letter he had written into the hands of his uncle, the abbot of the church of San Pietro in Ciel d'Oro.

Once, during this state of affairs, while Saladin was talking about his birds with Torello, the falconer smiled in a way peculiar to him, which the Sultan had remarked in his house at Pavia. Immediately, he thought of his courteous host, and looking at Torello narrowly, seemed to recognize him. Forgetting about his falcons, he said, "Tell me, Christian, what country do you come from in the West?"

"My lord, I am a Lombard," he replied, "and I come from a city called Pavia. I am a poor man, of low degree."

At his words Saladin, certain that his supposition was well-founded, said happily to himself, "God has been good and granted me an opportunity to show this man how much I appreciated his courtesy."

He did not say a word to Torello himself, but ordering all his robes and gowns to be spread in a room of the palace, led him there.

"Look, Christian," he said, "tell me if there is any robe here that you've seen before."

Torello looked about, and saw those which his wife had given Saladin. He thought it out of the question for them to be the very gowns; nevertheless, he said, "My lord, I don't know any of these garments, though I admit that those two over there look like certain robes with which I was fitted long ago, together with three merchants who happened to come to my house."

Saladin could no longer contain his joy, and embracing him tenderly, "You are Torello d'Istria," he said, "and I am one of those three merchants to whom your wife gave these robes. The time has come for me to show you my merchandise, as I predicted when I took leave of you."

Joy and embarrassment took possession of Torello at the revelation—joy at the thought that he had entertained such a guest, and embarrassment because it seemed to him he had shown him but meager hospitality. But Saladin broke into his meditation saying, "Since God has sent you here to me, Torello, you are master henceforth and not I."

Great was their joy at having found each other. Saladin soon dressed him in a robe of honor, and presenting him to his greatest lords, said to them, praising his excellence, "All of you, who cherish my favor, honor my friend as you would honor me."

His wishes were scrupulously carried out, especially by the two nobles whom Torello had entertained with the Sultan at his house.

This sudden glorious good fortune drove all preoccupations about Pavia out of Torello's mind, all the more since he firmly believed that his letters had by this time reached his uncle.

Now on the day the Christians had been captured by Saladin, there had perished in the camp, rather in the crusading army, a Provencal knight of little note called Torello de Dignes, and he had been buried. As Torello d'Istria had gained renown throughout the army for his nobility of character, it so happened that when a crusader heard, "Torello is dead," he immediately thought the Italian had met his doom and not the knight of Dignes. The eventual disaster of their capture did not allow them to learn the truth, so that many Italians returned with the news, two of them even going so far as to declare that they had seen his corpse and been present at the burial.

How great and infinite was the grief into which this news plunged Torello's friends and kin, indeed, all who knew him, would be a long task to describe—especially the sorrow and grief and tears of his lady, who mourned and lamented his loss continually. When, after some months, her grief had somewhat abated, she began to be wooed by the noblest gentlemen of Lombardy, and her brothers, with the rest of her family, gave her no peace as they urged her to marry again. She had repeatedly refused them, bursting into uncontrollable weeping, but at last she was compelled to give in to their pleas, though on condition that she would not be wedded until the time stipulated by Torello had expired.

While, in Pavia, the good lady was in this plight and the day set for her remarriage was perhaps some eight days removed, Torello met a man in Alexandria whom he had seen going aboard the galley that was taking the envoys to Genoa. Sending for him, he asked him what sort of passage they had had, and when they had reached Genoa.

"It was a mighty bad trip, sir, as I learned in Crete where I got off," he said, "for as the ship was neighboring Sicily, there arose a violent north wind that dashed her on the Barbary shoals. Not a man escaped alive, sir, and two of my brothers among others were drowned."

Torello, crediting the man's words, which were alas! too true, and remembering that in a few days the period of time he had set his wife would expire, was well-nigh certain that since nobody in Pavia could have known anything of his circumstances, she must by this time have remarried. The thought drove him to such despair that he could neither eat nor sleep, and taking to his bed resolved to have done with life.

On learning of this, Saladin, who dearly loved him, came to his bedside. When, after many fervent entreaties, he discovered the cause of his friend's despair and illness, he reproached him for not having told him of it sooner.

"Come, cheer up," he encouraged him, for "if you do as I say,

I'll get you to Pavia in time, upon my word." Then he told him how he would contrive it.

Torello had faith in what Saladin told him. Moreover, he had often heard it said that what he suggested was possible and had been done many times before. He plucked up his spirits, therefore, and besought Saladin to do what he intended as soon as possible.

The Sultan, calling one of his magicians, whose art he had already had occasion to put to the test, commanded him to devise a way by means of which Torello might be transported from Alexandria to Pavia in a single night, as he lay in bed.

"That I shall do, sire," answered the magician, "but for his comfort, I must first put him to sleep."

After this had been arranged, the Sultan rejoined Torello, and on discovering that he had made up his mind either to be in Pavia at the stated time if there were any possibility of doing so, or, if not, to give up the ghost, he said to him:

"Torello, far be it from me, God knows, to blame you in the least for loving your wife as dearly as you do, and for not wanting to lose her to another man. Of all women I've ever seen, she is the one whose sweetness and charm and behavior—not to speak of beauty, which, after all, is a transient bloom—seem to me most worthy of being commended and cherished. I should have considered it a great privilege, since Fortune was so good as to bring you here, for us both to have lived the span of our mortal lives as joint rulers of my kingdom; or, if this divine boon was not intended for me, and you were resolved either to return to Pavia in time, or else to pine away, I could have wished with all my heart that you had at least told me about it early enough, so that I might have sent you home with all the pomp and grandeur and equipage that your worth demands. But since that has not been vouchsafed me and you are determined to go back as soon as may be, I shall send you there as best I can, in the way I described."

Then said Torello, "My lord, even without verbal assurances, your deeds have given me sufficient proof of your goodwill, which I never deserved to such a supreme degree, and though you had not expressed your feelings in the matter, I should have lived and died fully cognizant of what they are. But I am firm in the decision I have taken, therefore I beg you do what you suggest as soon as you can, for to-morrow is the last day that I am to be expected."

"That I will do, and without fail," Saladin assured him.

That day (for he expected to have him transported the coming night), Saladin had a rich, handsome bed of mattresses made according to their fashion, of velvet and cloth-of-gold, set up in a hall of the palace, and decked with a coverlet embroidered in geometric designs, strewn with large pearls and costly gems—which were later kept as a priceless treasure here in Italy. Two pillows, suitable for such a bed, added the final touch.

When the couch was ready, Saladin had Torello, who had recovered his health and spirits, clothed like a Saracen in a most gorgeous robe, the richest and most magnificent imaginable, and his head swathed in a long turban. As it was already late, Saladin, with many of his lords, came to Torello's room, and sitting beside him said, the tears welling in his eyes:

"Torello, the hour approaches when we must part. As I may not come with you nor send anyone to keep you company, since the nature of your voyage will not allow it, I must bid you farewell here in this room, and that is why I have come. But before I wish you godspeed, I beseech you, by that tie of love and friendship that binds us, think of me. Perhaps some day, before we have done with life and you have taken care of your duties in Lombardy, you may come to visit me, once only, so that when my eyes are again rejoiced at the sight of you, I may make up for the deficiencies that are now made necessary by your haste. Until that time, however, I trust it will not be too much trouble for you to write to me and ask of me whatever you care to have, for beyond a doubt there is no man alive for whom I would more willingly do my best."

Torello could not restrain his tears. Emotion choked his voice, and very briefly he answered, "Never, my lord, can I forget your many kindnesses and your nobility," adding that he would not fail to do his every wish at the earliest opportunity. Affectionately, Saladin embraced and kissed him. "God be with you," he murmured through his tears, and withdrew from the chamber. One by one the other lords bade Torello farewell and then entered the great hall with Saladin, where the couch had been made ready.

It was already quite late, and the magician was impatient for them to make haste. At that point, a physician came into Torello's room with a beverage which, he said, would strengthen him for the journey. "Drink it," he said. Torello obeyed him, and before long he had sunk into a deep sleep, when, at Saladin's orders, he was borne into the great hall and laid upon the couch. A large, beautiful crown of great price was placed there, too, inscribed with such sentiments as made it manifest that it had been sent as a gift to Torello's wife. Furthermore, Saladin slipped on the sleeping man's finger a ring of inestimable value, set with a carbuncle of such luster that it glowed like a flaming torch, and girt him with a sword whose chasing alone could not easily have been appraised. Then he had a brooch set on his breast, of pearls the like of which were never seen, and other precious stones of rarest varieties. On either side of him, two massive basins of gold were placed, heaped with gold coins, and all about him were strewn nets of pearls, and rings, and girdles and other treasures that were too many to enumerate.

When everything was ready Saladin kissed his friend once more, and turning to the magician, "Proceed," he said. Before his very eyes the couch, with Torello and everything upon it, was whisked away, and the Sultan remained behind, talking about the worthy man with his lords.

At last, Torello was transported to Pavia and set down, couch, jewels and all in the church of San Pietro in Ciel d'Oro, as he had requested. He was still sound asleep when the matin-bells began to ring and the sacristan came into the church with a light in his hand. Upon suddenly seeing before him the magnificent couch, he was not only astounded but terrified, and took to his heels as fast as he could. The abbot and the monks with him, who saw the sacristan's strange behavior, wondered, and said, "What's the matter? Why are you running?" He told them what he had seen. "Fie, you're no child," said the abbot, "and you're not such a novice in the church as to be so easily terrified. Come, let's go and see who has tried to scare you."

Torches were kindled, by the light of which the abbot and his monks went into the church, where they beheld the rich and splendid couch, with the man lying there asleep. As they stood by, marveling and frightened, gaping at the wonderful jewels and not daring to draw a step nearer the bed, Torello suddenly awoke, as the effect of the drug had been dissipated, and sighed deeply. That was all the monks needed. Abbot and all, they dashed away in terror, crying, "God help us! God help us!"

Torello opened his eyes, and as he looked about him, saw to his great joy that he was indeed where he had requested Saladin to have him brought. He sat up and examined more closely the treasures that were scattered about him; if he had known Sala-

din's magnificence before, the greatness of it was now redoubled
in his estimation.

When he saw the monks fleeing from him, he guessed
the cause of their fright, and without budging from his place, he
called the abbot by his name. "Don't be afraid, uncle," he said,
encouraging him, "it's I, Torello, your nephew."

The abbot was even more frightened at this, since for many
months he had believed him dead. Still, on hearing himself called,
and being further reassured by sound arguments, he crossed himself and drew near the couch.

"How are you, good father?" Torello greeted him. "And
what's there to be afraid of? I'm hale and hearty, thank the
Lord, and I've just returned from across the seas."

The abbot, after looking at him a while, recognized him in
spite of his long beard and Saracen garb. Confidence returned to
him, and taking Torello by the hand, "My son," he said, "you are
indeed welcome home. But you must not wonder at our terror,"
he continued, "for there's not a soul here who doesn't firmly believe you to be dead. Indeed, I must tell you that Adalieta, your
wife, is to be married again, much against her will, to be sure,
intimidated by the threats and importunities of her people. This
very day she is to go to her new husband, and the feast is already set, with everything else that pertains to a wedding."

Torello rose from his couch. He greeted the abbot and the
monks with exceeding joy. "But do not tell anyone I have come
back," he enjoined them, "until I have taken care of a certain
matter."

After the precious jewels had been hidden in a safe place, he
told his uncle the story of his adventures up to that point, which
made the good man rejoice with him at his stroke of fortune.
Together they offered prayers of thanksgiving to the Lord, after
which Torello said, "Who is to be my wife's new husband?"

The abbot gave him the name.

"Before anybody learns I have come back," said Torello, "I'd
like to see how my wife feels about this new marriage. I know
it is not the usual thing for men of your dignity to go to such
banquets, but for my sake, uncle, I'd like you to manage to have
us both invited."

"Very well, my son," replied the abbot, and early in the morning he sent a messenger to the bridegroom-to-be with the request that he be invited to the wedding with a friend of his.
The groom replied that he would be delighted to receive them.

Well, toward dinner-time, Torello, still dressed in his foreign costume, went with his uncle to the bridegroom's house. Great was the wonderment of all who saw him, but no one knew him for Torello; moreover, the abbot informed everyone that he was a Saracen noble on a mission for the Sultan to the King of France.

When the seats were assigned at table, he was placed opposite his wife, upon whom he gazed with the greatest joy in the world; so far as he could discern, she looked unwilling and sad at the prospect of this marriage. Adalieta, too, sometimes looked in his direction, not that she knew him, for his long beard and foreign costume and the assurance that her husband was dead, drove all such notions from her head.

At last, when Torello thought the opportune moment had come for him to discover whether she still bore him in mind, he called to him the page who served her, and taking the ring she had given him at their parting, said, "Tell the bride this for me. It is the custom of the land I come from, that when a stranger like me is a guest at the table of a newly-married bride like herself, she sends him the bowl out of which she drinks, brimful of wine, as a sign that she is glad of his presence. Then, after the stranger has drunk as much as he wishes, he covers the bowl again, and the bride drinks the rest of the wine."

The boy did as he was told. Adalieta, like the virtuous and prudent woman she was, thinking the stranger some great lord, ordered the massive golden bowl before her to be washed and filled with wine, and to show him that he was welcome at her feast, had it brought to him. In the meantime Torello held the ring in his mouth, and as he drank, skilfully let it fall into the cup unobserved, leaving very little wine at the bottom. He then covered the bowl again and sent it back to Adalieta.

Upon uncovering it and bringing it to her lips in order to drink the remaining wine and so fulfil the rest of the ceremony, she saw the ring and examined it a moment without saying a word. At last she recognized it as the one she had given her husband on his departure. Taking it out, she gazed intently upon the man she had thought a stranger, and knew him at once. Then, as if she had lost control of her senses, she flung down the table before her, crying, "It is my husband! It is indeed my Torello!"

Dashing toward the board at which he was seated, she leaned

forward as far as she could, unmindful of her gown or anything that lay upon the table, and clasped him close in her embrace. Nothing, neither the words nor the efforts of the guests could tear her away, until Torello himself told her to refrain for a while, as she would have plenty of time to embrace him to her heart's content.

She loosed her clasp and rose. By this time, the wedding-feast was in turmoil, though in a way merrier than ever for the return of so worthy a gentleman. At Torello's request, the guests subsided to silence, whereupon he related to them his adventures from the day of his departure up to that moment, saying in conclusion to the gentleman who was to have married Adalieta, "I trust, my friend, since I've come back alive, that you will not take it ill if I reclaim my wife whom you would have married, believing me dead."

Although the groom felt rather humiliated, he answered freely and amicably, "Torello, you are the master of what is yours, and free to do with it what you think best."

Adalieta, taking off the bridal-wreath and the wedding-ring that had been given her by her new groom, put on her finger the ring she had taken from the cup and set upon her head the crown the Sultan had sent her. Together she and Torello left the house, and followed by the wedding-procession went to their own, where with a long and happy feast they rejoiced the friends and kin, indeed, all the townsfolk who had mourned Torello for dead, and now looked upon his return as nothing short of miraculous.

Torello gave some of his precious gems to the disappointed groom who had defrayed the expenses of the wedding-feast, some to the abbot, and many others to his friends. To Saladin, whose friend and humble servitor he always deemed himself, he sent many messages, telling him of his happy return to his native land, where he lived for ever afterwards with his lady, exercising his magnificent generosity more than ever.

So ended the troubles of Torello and his dear Adalieta, and such was the reward of their cheerful and ready courtesy. There are many who, having the means, exert themselves to generosity, but they do it with such ill-grace that they make their favors cost more than they're worth. Hence, if no honor reverts to them, it is not for them or anyone else to wonder at it.

# THE TENTH STORY

*The Marquis of Saluzzo, urged into matrimony by the importuni-*
*ties of his subjects, but resolved to choose his wife for himself,*
*marries Griselda, a peasant's daughter, and has two children by*
*her, both of whom he pretends to have put to death. Then, giving*
*Griselda to understand that he has tired of her and married again,*
*he brings his daughter home as though she were his new wife, and*
*turns Griselda out in her shift. But when he finds that she has*
*been constant in the stress of all her suffering, he takes her home*
*again, shows her their children already grown, and loves her more*
*than ever, he and his subjects honoring her from then on as*
*their lady.*

WHEN THE KING'S LONG STORY, WHICH APPARENTLY HAD BEEN
well liked by everyone, had reached its close, Dioneo said with
a laugh, "The simple fellow who tried to hoist down the ghost's
stiff tail that night wouldn't have given a farthing for all the
praise you shower on Torello." Then, knowing that he was the
only one left to tell his story, he began:

Well, my dear gentle ladies, from what I've been able to
gather, all this day has been devoted to kings and sultans and
such grand people. Now I don't care to stray too far from your
topic, so I shall tell you about a marquis. It is no magnificent
deed I am going to relate, but a mad piece of stupidity, which,
though resulting in much good so far as he was concerned, I'd
warn you against imitating, for it was indeed a great shame
that he should have derived any benefit from it.

A long time ago, the heir to the house of the lords of Saluzzo
was a young man by the name of Gualtieri, who, since he had
neither wife nor children, used to devote his time to nothing
but hawking and hunting, without a care in the world about
marrying or raising heirs—which, by the way, showed him to
have been a mighty clever fellow. His subjects, however, were
not at all pleased with this state of affairs, and many times
they importuned him to marry so that he wouldn't remain without an heir to succeed him, or they without a ruler. Indeed,
they even offered to find him a damsel of such exalted rank and

noble parentage, that he could not but be eminently satisfied and entertain the highest expectations of her.

"My friends," Gualtieri answered, "you are forcing me into a thing I had made up my mind never to undertake, considering what a task it is to find a woman entirely suited to one's temperament. Just see how many examples there are of domestic infelicity, and how hard is the lot of the man who has stumbled upon an uncongenial mate! When you argue that from the ways of the parents you can know the daughters, and thence deduce that you can give me a wife with whom I shall be pleased, it is arrant nonsense. By what art can you know their fathers, or learn the secrets of their mothers? Even if you did avail to know them, daughters are often quite different from their fathers and mothers. Still, since you are pleased to bind me in these fetters, I am willing to satisfy you. But as I wish to have no one to blame but myself if things should go wrong, I will be the chooser of my wife, warning you that if you do not respect the woman of my choice as your lady, no matter who she may be, you will experience, to your great disadvantage, how unpleasant it was for me to have married at your insistence but against my will."

"We'll agree to anything provided you marry," the worthy men replied.

Now for a long time Gualtieri had been favorably impressed by the ways of a poor country-girl who lived in a hamlet close to his estate. Moreover, he found her to be very beautiful, and so thought to himself that with a girl like her, he could live a fairly peaceable life. Accordingly, without searching any farther, he resolved to have her as his wife, and calling her father, a very poor, humble fellow, arranged with him about the marriage. That settled, Gualtieri, collecting his friends from the whole countryside, thus addressed them:

"Friends, for a long time you have desired me to marry, and I am disposed to consent, more to gratify you than for any wish I have to take a wife. You recall the promise you made me—that you would be satisfied with any woman I chose, whoever she might be, and that you would show her the respect due your lady. The time has come for me to abide by my promise, and I expect you to do likewise. In a hamlet near by, I found a young girl after my own heart. It is this girl I intend to marry in a few days and bring to my house as my lady. It is for you now to make the wedding-feast as splendid as possible, and to welcome your mistress with due honor, so that I may have as much reason to be satisfied with your side of the bargain, as you have to be pleased with mine."

The honest people joyfully declared themselves well content, and assured him that whoever the wife of his choice might be, they would look upon her as their liege-lady and respect her as such in everything. Thereupon, they began to make preparations for a splendid feast and a joyous celebration, Gualtieri with the rest of them. Magnificent was the banquet he planned, and many were the friends and kin, as well as guests from the country round about, whom he invited, gentlefolk and others. More than that, he had a number of rich and elegant gowns cut to the measure of a young woman who seemed to have the same proportions as the girl he was to marry, and prepared girdles, rings, a beautiful bridal-wreath and everything else that a bride required.

On the morning set for the wedding, Gualtieri mounted his horse, together with the gentlemen who had come there to attend him, and after seeing that everything was as should be, he said, "Gentlemen, it is time to bring the bride home."

Accordingly, he rode with his company to the village, where, as he came to the house of the girl's father, he met her hastening with the water she had fetched from the fountain, so that she might go with the other women to see Gualtieri's bride as she passed by.

"Griselda," he called her by name. "Griselda, where is your father?"

Shyly she answered, "He is in the house, sir."

Gualtieri dismounted. "Wait for me," he said to his retinue, and entered the little hovel alone, where he found Giannucolo, the girl's father.

"I have come to marry Griselda," he said to him, "but first I would like to know something from her lips in your presence."

Then turning to her, he asked whether, if he took her to wife, she would do her utmost to please him, and not be angry with anything he said or did, and whether she would always be obedient to him, and many another thing to the same purport. To each one Griselda answered, "Yes."

Thereupon Gualtieri, taking her by the hand, led her out of the house, and before his retainers and many onlookers, bade her strip naked. "Bring hither the clothes I had made," he said to his attendants. In these new garments he had her quickly clothed, and shoes put on her feet, and upon her hair, rumpled as it was, the bridal crown was laid. Then, while everyone was gazing upon everything in awe, "Gentlemen," he said, "this is the wife I have chosen for myself, if she will have me."

Turning to her, standing there blushing and bewildered, "Griselda," he said, "will you take me to your lawful husband?"

"Yes, my lord," she said.

"And I will take you to my lawful wife," he added. And so, in the presence of all, he married her.

The ceremony over, he lifted her upon a palfrey and with an honorable following brought her home, where the wedding was celebrated with as much splendor and magnificence as if he had married the daughter of the king of France.

As time went on, the young bride seemed to have changed her ways and temperament together with her clothes. She was, as we have said, lovely of body, and with her beauty she became so charming, so pleasant and gracious, that rather than the daughter of Giannucolo, rather than the little shepherd-lass, one might have thought her the offspring of some great lord, which was a wonder to everyone who had known her in her former state. She was moreover so obedient to her husband, and so willing to serve, that he considered himself the happiest and the most fortunate of mortals. Toward his subjects, too, Griselda was so kind and gracious, that there was not a man of them who did not love and respect her with profoundest feeling, or failed to pray for her welfare and glory. Indeed, though once they had said that Gualtieri showed little wisdom in marrying her, they were now unanimous in declaring that he had been a most shrewd and wise man, as none but he could have seen what a gem was hidden under those poor peasant rags. In short, such was Griselda's conduct, that before many months had elapsed, not only in her husband's domain, but everywhere, people spoke of her virtue and good management, turning to Gualtieri's favor everything that had been said when he had taken her to wife.

Not long after she had been with Gualtieri, she conceived, and in due process of time, gave birth to a baby-girl, to her husband's delight. But alas! shortly thereafter a strange whim seized him, to try her patience by long suffering and unbearable cruelties. In the beginning he stung her with words, and pretending grave concern, told her that his subjects were poorly satisfied with her because of her humble origin. They were even less pleased, he continued, that she was bringing children into the world, and were so discontented at the birth of her daughter that they did nothing but complain.

Griselda did not wink a lash at his words, or waver in her meekness. "My lord," she said, "do with me what you deem most becoming your honor and comfort and I shall be content, for I know I am less than the least of them, and that I was not worthy of this estate to which you raised me out of the generosity of your heart."

Gualtieri was exceedingly gratified by her reply, knowing thereby that she had not become puffed up with pride because of the honor she had received from him or others. But not long after he had spoken generally to her of his subjects' resentment at the birth of her daughter, he sent her one of his servants, whom he had previously instructed. The man came to her with a doleful countenance.

"My lady," he said, "if I value my life, I must do what my lord commands. He has ordered me to take this daughter of yours and—." He said no more.

Griselda, seeing the grief on the man's face and hearing his words, and recalling moreover what her husband had told her, understood that the man had been commanded to put the little girl to death. But instantly she took the infant from the cradle, kissed her and said a blessing over her, and then, without revealing on her face the grief that wrung her heart, she laid her in the man's arms.

"Take her," she said, "and do faithfully what has been commanded you by your lord and mine. But do not leave her to be devoured by wild beasts and birds of prey, unless he bade you do that too."

The servant took the child and went to his master to tell him what Griselda had said. Gualtieri, marveling at his wife's constancy of purpose, sent the man to a relative of his at Bologna with the child, praying the good lady to rear her in goodness and modesty, without ever divulging whose daughter she was.

As time went on, Griselda again conceived, and in due time gave birth to a baby-boy, which rejoiced Gualtieri tremendously. Nevertheless, not content with what he had already done, he tortured her more than ever, and coming to her one day looking sorely troubled, "Griselda," he said, "since you brought this son of yours into the world, there's been no living with my subjects, who do nothing but murmur at the thought that a grandson of Giannucolo's will be lord over them after my death.

Therefore, I'm afraid that unless I want to be chased out of my realm, I had better do what I did before, and finally put you aside and take another wife."

Griselda listened to him, her soul bowed to patience, and said nothing but, "My lord, think only of contenting yourself and gratifying your pleasure. Have no care for me, for there's nothing gives me joy but what I see pleases you."

A few days later Gualtieri sent for the boy, as he had sent for the girl, and this child he likewise sent to Bologna to be reared, pretending he had had him slain. Again Griselda neither looked nor spoke other than when her daughter had been taken away.

Gualtieri was astonished, and avowed to himself that no other woman in the world could have done what she did. Indeed, had he not witnessed with his own eyes how devoted she had been to the babes during the short time he had been pleased to let her have them, he might have been led to believe she bore up so well out of indifference, though he was convinced she did so out of prudence and constancy.

Meanwhile his subjects, believing he had had his children murdered, were loud in condemnation, thinking him a cruel monster. They pitied Griselda, for never did she make any other answer to the women who sympathized with her over the loss of her infants in this barbarous fashion, but, "Whatever seems good to him who fathered them must please me too."

Years passed since the birth of the girl, and Gualtieri thought now the time had come for him to put his wife's patience to the extreme test. One day, while many of his people were assembled, he told them that he could no longer bear to have Griselda as his wife. "It was a foolish mistake of my youth," he said, "and therefore I shall try my utmost to obtain a dispensation from His Holiness, so that I may put her away and take another wife."

Bitterly, the worthy men reproached him, but he cut the matter short by saying, "It must be so."

When Griselda heard what was going on, and thought that she would have to go back to her father's hut, perhaps to tend sheep again as in the olden days, while another woman enjoyed the embraces of the man she loved most in the world, she grieved and suffered in the depths of her heart; but as she had suffered the other strokes of fortune, she strengthened herself to suffer this.

Not long after, Gualtieri had some forged documents sent to him from Rome, whereby he pretended to his subjects that the pope had granted him a dispensation to put away Griselda and remarry. Sending for her, he said before a number of his vassals, "Griselda, by a special grant from the pope I am now at liberty to cast you aside and take another wife. My ancestors have always been great nobles and lords of this country; yours have only been peasants. Therefore, I want you to be my wife no longer and to go back to Giannucolo's house, taking with you the marriage portion you brought me, so that I may bring hither the other bride I have found, who is more suited to my rank and station."

Courageously, and with more than feminine strength, Griselda contained the tears rising to her eyes. "My lord," she said, "I have always known my poverty to have been ill-matched to your great station. What I have been to you I have always regarded as a boon from you and Almighty God—a boon that I never claimed entirely for my own as a gift bestowed upon me, but only as a loan. You are pleased to take it back; I must find it good to return it, as I do. Here is the ring with which you took me to wife: take it. You tell me to carry away with me the marriage-portion I brought you. My lord, you will need no treasurer to pay it, and no sumpter to bear it away, for I have not forgotten you took me naked. If you think it worthy that this body which carried the children engendered by you should be stared at by all, then, my lord, naked I shall go. But I beg you, as the claim of my virginity, which I brought but do not carry away, grant me to take only a shift over my dowry."

Gualtieri, though moved to weeping, steeled himself to look stern and ruthless. "You shall have that shift, then," he said.

Everyone pleaded with him to give her at least a gown, that the woman who had been his wife for more than thirteen years should not be seen to leave his house in poverty and shame. But their prayers were vain. Griselda, however, commended them all to God, and left his house barefoot, with her head uncovered, and only a shift over her body. And so she returned to her father, amid the tears and weeping of all who saw her.

Now Giannucolo, who had never been able to believe that the mighty lord would always keep his daughter as his wife, had been living in daily expectation of this event, and had kept for her the clothes which she had cast off the day Gualtieri took her to wife. He gave them back to Griselda, therefore, and she put them on, devoting herself once more to the humble duties of her father's home, as she had once done, bearing with unbowed spirit the cruel strokes of unfriendly fortune.

After Gualtieri had sent his wife away, he gave his subjects to understand that he had chosen as his new bride one of the daughters of the lords of Panago, and accordingly entered into elaborate preparations for the wedding. Then, sending for Griselda, he said to her:

"The new bride I have chosen will soon be brought home to me, and I'd like to welcome her with due honor on this first visit of hers. You know, Griselda, that I have no women here who are handy at arranging the rooms and doing any of those little things which such a reception requires. You, best of all, know how to add all those gracious touches. Therefore do everything that is to be done, invite whatever ladies you think should come, and welcome them as though you were mistress here. After the wedding, you may go home again."

No knife-thrust could have hurt Griselda more, for she had not succeeded in laying aside her love for him as she had her good fortune. Nevertheless she replied, "My lord, I am ready to do your service."

In her poor peasant clothes she entered the house which she had left in her shift not long since, and swept and cleaned and arranged the rooms, directing where tapestries were to be hung on the walls and benches placed. With her own hands, she prepared the meats and saw after everything as though she had been the merest scullery-maid. She had no respite until everything had been done to her satisfaction. The work accomplished, she invited all the ladies of the country round, and then awaited the coming of the day appointed for the wedding when, although the clothes she wore were poor and humble, she welcomed the guests with all the courtesy, cheer and graciousness of a lady.

By this time Gualtieri's children, who had been brought up in Bologna by a lady of his family, wife of one of the lords of Panago, had grown, his daughter into a most beautiful girl of twelve, and his son to a lad of some six years. Now Gualtieri had sent a message to the lady's husband, begging him to come to Saluzzo with his son and daughter, and to bring a large and honorable escort with him. "But let no one know who the girl is," he told him. "Say simply you are escorting my new bride."

The Count of Panago did as Gualtieri told him and set out on his journey. Some days later, toward noon, he had arrived with the girl, her brother and a noble company at Saluzzo, where peasant-folk and people from the neighboring hamlets were everywhere gathered to await the coming of their lord's new bride. The ladies who had been invited by Gualtieri came forward to receive her and led her to the great hall, where the tables were spread for the banquet. Then Griselda, in her poor garment, came forward with a happy face to greet her. In vain, the ladies had pleaded with Gualtieri either to allow the poor woman to remain in one of the rooms, or to let her wear one of the gowns that had been hers, so that she would not have to appear so wretched before his guests. Therefore, just as she was, she said to the new bride, "My lady, you are heartily welcome."

Presently, the guests were shown their places at the board and the meats were served. Everyone had eyes for no one but the girl, and avowed Gualtieri had made a change for the better; but most of all, Griselda admired her and the little lad.

When Gualtieri saw that the unheard of situation in no way changed Griselda, of whose keen understanding he had had too many proofs to believe it was stupidity that rendered her so patient, he thought it high time to deliver her from the suffering which he guessed lay hidden beneath her brave reserve.

Summoning her before him, he asked her with a smile in the presence of all his guests, "What do you think of our bride, Griselda?"

"My lord," she answered, "I think very highly of her, and if, as I believe, she is as wise as she is beautiful, I have no doubt you will be the happiest man in the world to have her as a wife. One only prayer I have to ask of you from the bottom of my heart: Do not torment her with the agonies you inflicted upon that other woman who was once yours, for I scarcely think she can bear up under them; for she is young, my lord, and has been tenderly reared, whereas the other had borne continual hardships from her very childhood."

Gualtieri, seeing she was convinced that the girl was to be his wife, and had therefore spoken worthily in every way, bade her sit on his right hand and said, "Griselda, it is now time your long-suffering patience were rewarded, and that all those who have looked upon me as a cruel, iniquitous monster should know that all I did was done with an end in view—namely to teach you to be a wife, and them to know how to choose and keep one. At the same time I strove to procure myself enduring peace while I lived with you—a thing I was afraid I should never have, if I married. It was to this end that I tortured and tormented you in all the ways you have borne. I am convinced now that you can give me the bliss I sought, for never, either by word or deed, have you deviated from my desires. Therefore, Griselda, it is my intention soon to restore to you all at once the joys I took from you at various times, and to reward you with supreme happiness for the many torments I have made you suffer. Take, then, Griselda, take with a joyful soul this girl whom you think my bride, and this little lad, her brother—take them, your children and mine! Ay, for they are those whom you and many others believed I had cruelly murdered. Take me, your husband, who loves you above everything in the world, for truly, I can well boast there is no man alive who has better reason to be satisfied with his wife!"

With these words, he took her in his arms and kissed her, and rising to his feet, led her, weeping for joy, to where their daughter sat bewildered. They folded the girl tenderly in their arms, and her little brother, too, and relieved her and all the guests of any doubts they may have had.

Presently, the women left their places at table and retired with Griselda to a room apart. More auspiciously than on her marriage, they tore off her miserable frock, dressed her in one of her own rich gowns and escorted her again into the reception hall, splendid as a lady, which, even in her rags, she had never failed to be. Marvelous was her happiness in her children, and great was the joy of the guests at this unexpected turn of events. The festivities waxed more and more joyous, and continued for many days, all men reputing Gualtieri a very wise man, though they condemned as cruel and intolerable the trials he had made his lady endure. But the admiration was all for Griselda, the model of wisdom and patience.

Some days later, the Count of Panago went back to Bologna, and Gualtieri, taking Giannucolo from his toil, elevated him to a rank more becoming his father-in-law; and so the poor fellow ended his remaining years in honor and comfort. Then he bestowed his daughter nobly in marriage, and lived long and happily with Griselda, whom he ever afterwards cherished and held in high esteem.

What more can we say, except that divine spirits may sometimes descend from heaven, even to wretched hovels, just as in kingly palaces others may be born who are fitter to keep swine than to rule over men? What other than Griselda could have suffered dry-eyed, even cheerfully, the harsh, unheard of trials imposed upon her by Gualtieri? In my opinion, it wouldn't have been a bad thing for him if he had come across the sort of woman who, on being turned out of doors in her shift, would have had some jolly spark so rummage her hide for her that perhaps some good thing might have resulted.

Dioneo's story over, the women fell to discussing it. For a long time, some took one side and some the other, one blaming this and another praising it, until the king, looking up at the sky and seeing that the sun had already sunk to twilight, addressed them without rising from his seat:

"Accomplished ladies, as I believe all of you must know, human understanding does not simply consist of bearing in mind what is past, or in taking thought of the present; but the ability of employing both to foresee the future has always been deemed the rarest wisdom by men of intellect. To-morrow, as you know, will mark fifteen days since we left Florence. Our purpose in coming here was to have some little relaxation for the sake of our health and lives, and to forget the gloom and woe and misery that have taken possession of our city since this dreadful plague broke out.

"In my estimation, we have come out of it with flying colors, for even if we have told gay tales, perhaps conducive to lasciviousness, even if we have dined and drunk well, even if we have danced and sung, in short, done things that might lead weak minds to unbecoming deeds, I could detect nothing either in you or in us men to reprehend. Everywhere I saw and perceived nothing but continual seemliness, harmony and innocent friendship, which both for your sakes and mine is most gratifying to me.

"Now since each one of us has already had his day in which to enjoy a share of the honor still vested in me, to avoid our continued relations from resulting in boredom, and also to keep anyone from casting a shadow of suspicion on our remaining here so long, I think it would be wise for us to go back where we came from, that is, if it is agreeable to you. There is also something else. Our little group has already come to the attention of several people hereabout, and soon it may become so large that we shall no longer be able to derive any joy of it.

"So then, if you approve of my advice, I'll hold the crown

of office until our departure, to-morrow morning, but if you should decide otherwise, I've already chosen my successor."

A lengthy discussion ensued between the ladies and the youths. Finally, they accepted the king's suggestion as sound and all for the best, and decided to act upon it. He summoned the steward, therefore, instructed him in what was to be prepared for the following morning, and then, rising to his feet, gave them all leave to do as they wished until suppertime. They all rose, following his example, and betook themselves to their various pastimes as usual. When supper-hour came, they fell to, and ate with cheer and relish, and afterwards they danced and played and sang. While Lauretta led the round, the king bade Fiammetta sing a song, which she began in a most pleasing voice:

"If only without jealousy love came
　　There were no other maid
Would more rejoice than I, whate'er her fame.

If happy youth's first flower
　　Might please a maiden in her lover, each
　　　　Of valor's worth and pride,
Daring and courage, power,
　　Wisdom and courtesy and gentle speech—
　　　　All virtues undenied—
　　　　I am the one for whom they are allied
　　　　　　In my sweet lover, made
　　　　To be my health and hope and my heart's flame.

But oh, when I'm aware
　　That other women are indeed as wise
　　　　As I, then much I fear
To think they, too, desiderate and prize
　　My spirit's pain and cheer.
　　Then that which of all good I hold most dear
　　　　　Causes me be dismayed
　　　And sigh and pine and live in grief and grame.

If but my love I knew
　　As rich in constancy as in his worth,
　　　　I should not jealous be.
But then, before one's view

Such great allurements tempt a man on earth,
    That trust is misery.
  I grieve and weep, and gladly I would flee
      This life; for never maid
    Can see him, but I give her bitter blame.

I pray each lady fair,
  For God's sweet sake, most kindly to refrain
    From playing such a turn.
For oh, should any dare
  With words, or arts, or blandishments to gain
    My harm, or should I learn
    Her ill intent, I swear I'd reck and burn
      Until I sorely made
    Her rue the day she ever brought me shame."

Fiammetta's song at an end, Dioneo, who was beside her, said with a laugh, "Fiammetta, you would be doing the ladies a favor if you told them who he is, so that they mightn't steal him from you inadvertently, if you're going to fly into such fury as that!"

Other songs followed this one, and as by this time the night was well-nigh half spent, they all went to rest at the king's pleasure.

With the first streak of dawn they arose, and guided by their wise king, they made their way toward Florence, whither the steward had already despatched all their bags and baggage. At the church of Santa Maria Novella, from which they had all set out together, the three youths took leave of the seven ladies and then saw after their other pleasures; then, when they were ready, the ladies, too, returned to their homes.

# THE AUTHOR'S
# CONCLUSION

\*

MOST NOBLE LADIES, FOR WHOSE DELECTATION I APPLIED MYSELF
to this lengthy task, at last with the help of that divine grace
which was granted me more by virtue of your prayers than
any merit of mine, I believe I have entirely fulfilled the promise I set out with, when this work was first begun. The Lord
be praised, therefore, and you too, dear ladies—and then to
give my pen and weary hand a needed rest! But before that,
there are some trifling matters which you or others might say,
that I should like to dispose of very briefly, taking it for
granted that such questions have been raised, although I am cognizant of the fact that a work of this nature should enjoy no
more special privileges than any other, as I remember pointing
out at the beginning of the fourth day.

There may be some of you who will say that I took too great
a liberty in writing these stories, and that I sometimes had ladies
tell, and often listen to, things that are not very proper for virtuous women either to relate or hear. I deny this outright.
There is nothing so gross that people may not talk about it, provided it is expressed decently, which, I think, I have managed
to do. But supposing it were as you say (I wouldn't argue with
you for the world, as I'm no match for you), I have plenty of
reasons at hand to justify myself. To begin with, if there is anything of the sort in any of the stories, their very character demands it; indeed, if they are examined with an open mind

by any reasonable individual, it will be obvious that I couldn't have told them in any other way, unless I had wished to make something entirely different out of them. Even if there should be some little passage or word a little too strong to be stomached by your virtuous, sainted spinsters who place more stock in words than in deeds, and strive more to create the impression of goodness than to practice it themselves, I should no more be condemned for using them than one would condemn people in general for bandying all day long such words as *hole* and *peg, mortar* and *pestle, sausage* and *bologna,* and all kinds of things of the same import. Besides, why should my pen be given less freedom than is allowed the brush of the painter, who has no qualms at any rate, no just ones—about making Saint Michael strike the serpent with a sword or spear, and Saint George hew at the dragon at whatever part of its anatomy he pleases? But laying that aside, he paints Adam male and Eve female, and even nails to the Cross with one nail or two as he sees fit, the feet of Christ Himself, Who elected to be crucified for the salvation of mankind.

Again, it is quite apparent that these stories are not told in a church, for churchly things should be treated with a pure mind, and spoken of in most reverent terms (although in the history-books of the church itself there are plenty of tales in quite a different strain from those I have written). Nor were they told in schools of philosophy, where propriety is expected of one, as anywhere else. No, they were not told by clerics or philosophers in any church or school, but in gardens and places of recreation, and among youths and maidens who, though young, were sufficiently mature not to be led into wrong courses by such things as stories. Moreover, they were told at a time when it was not thought amiss if even paragons of decency walked about with their drawers over their heads to save their lives. But whatever their nature, these stories, like everything else, can be turned to good or evil ends, depending upon who the listeners are.

Who doesn't know what a boon wine is to the healthy, according to Cinciglione, Scolaio and other authorities, and how dangerous to the sick? Are we to say, then, that wine is bad simply because it is injurious to the fevered? Who doesn't know how useful, indeed, how essential fire is to man? Are we to say that because it burns down houses and wipes out whole hamlets and cities, that it is a curse? Weapons safeguard the welfare of those who desire to live in peace; nevertheless, they often shed blood, not through any evil inherent in them, but through the wickedness of the men who use them to unworthy ends.

Never has a corrupt mind given any word a pure meaning. Just as virtuous words can do an evil mind no good, others, not so decent, can no more avail to corrupt the well-intentioned than mire can stain the rays of the sun or earth's ugliness obscure the beauties of heaven. What books, what words, what scriptures are holier, worthier, more to be revered than the Holy Bible? But how many have there been who have damned themselves and others through perverse interpretation of it?

Everything is in itself good toward some end, but when used toward evil, it may be in many ways ruinous. So with my stories. Should anyone wish to use them to bad intent or wicked deed, nothing will prevent him, if there is anything in the stories that will permit of being twisted and turned to that purpose. If, on the other hand, any wishes to derive use or benefit from them, they will not prevent him. Furthermore, they will never be thought otherwise than profitable and proper, if they are read at the proper time and to those for whom they were intended. If there is any woman too busy telling paternosters or making black-pudding and tarts for her pastor, let her leave my stories alone; they don't chase after anyone to be read—although your precious holy ladies often say many a little naughtiness, ay, even practice it.

There may be others of you, dear ladies, who will say there are some stories that would have been better for being omitted. Well and good. However, I could not, indeed, I ought not have written anything but what was told. It was up to the ladies who did the telling; if they had told beautiful tales, I would have written them so. Still, even if, as some people claim, I had been both the writer and the inventor of these stories—which I am not—I tell you point-blank that I should not be at all mortified if they were not all beautiful, as there's no one aside from God, who can create anything well and without flaws. Even Charlemagne, who was the maker of the Paladins, could not create so many of their perfection, that he could muster an army of them alone. Among a multitude of things, the quality varies. There never was a field so well-tended that some burdock, nettle or other rank weed could not be found mingled with the finest growths. Besides, it would have been foolish for me to have exhausted myself searching out over-exquisite matter and polishing my style, when I was addressing such unschooled young women as most of you are. At any rate, whoever browses among these tales of mine need only leave those that prick and read just those that give pleasure. All of them, to avoid mistakes, have on their brow what they conceal in their bosoms.

Again, there may be some of you who will say a number of them are too long. To these I answer that it is foolish for anyone who has something else to do, to bother reading stories, even short ones. Although a long time has elapsed from the time I began writing to the present moment, which marks the end of my labors, I have not forgotten that I offered this effort of mine to women with plenty of time on their hands and not to others. To one who reads in order to while away the hours, nothing can be long if it does what is expected of it. Succinctness is far better suited to students, who do not labor to pass the time but to use it to good advantage, than to you, dear ladies, who have as much of it left over as you do not spend in the pleasures of love. Then again, as none of you goes to Athens, Bologna, or Paris to study, it is necessary to expound things at greater length to you than to men who have had their understanding sharpened by learning.

I have no doubt there are still others who may say these stories are overladen with jests and nonsense, and that it is hardly becoming a serious, weighty person like myself to have written in this strain. To them I am much beholden, and I thank them for the solicitude which, in their honest zeal, they are moved to display toward my good fame. My answer to their criticism is this. I confess I am weighty and have been weighed many a time; therefore, for the benefit of those women who have not felt my weight, I insist I am not too heavy; indeed, I am so light that I float on the surface of the water.

Again, considering the fact that the sermons our good friars preach nowadays to admonish us for our sins are in the majority of cases full of jests, jibes and jokes, I thought these trifles would not have been inappropriate in my stories, written as they were to rid women of melancholy. Still, if for that reason they are made to laugh too much, Jeremiah's Lament, the Passion of the Saviour and the Complaint of the Magdalen would cure them of merriment quickly enough.

Who can doubt in the least that some women will be found to say I have an evil-speaking, venomous tongue, because here and there I've written the truth about the friars? We must condone with women who speak in this fashion, since we cannot but believe they are motivated by some just reason. Friars, you know, are good men. They flee from discomfort for the Lord's sake, they thresh when the harvest is done, and they tell no tales. If only they didn't have a hint of a goatish smell, they would be far pleasanter to deal with.

I admit, however, that all things in this world are not fixed and stable, but are always in a state of change. That may also be true of my tongue which (I have had it not on my own judgment which I never trust in personal matters) a lady of my acquaintance assured me not so long ago was the best and the sweetest in the world. To tell the truth, when she said it there were only a few of the above stories still to be written. I believe then, that these critics are simply talking out of personal animus, so let them be content with what I have said as an answer.

But enough. Let everyone say what she pleases from now on. It is time to have done with words, and to proffer my humble thanks to Him whose aid has guided me to the desired end, after such long toil. And you, fair ladies, remain peacefully in His grace, and think of me if any should find herself at all benefited for having read these tales of mine.